# THE PUZZLE HORSE

# THE PUZZLE HORSE

Robert Lee Engel

Copyright © 2011 by Robert Lee Engel

*All rights reserved*

ISBN  978-0-9836918-2-2

Library of Congress Control Number: 2011910845

Printed in the United States of America

*For Gere*

# PART ONE – THE KEY

# 1 *THURSDAY - SAN FRANCISCO*

The Garden Court is not a place I would have expected be targeted. With its immense colored marble columns and the great expanse of its Victorian glass roof, it has drawn the aloof and bumpkin gawkers since 1875. For me, it is a quiet and dignified breakfast respite from the raucous clamor of modern San Francisco. I stretched my feet under the starched tablecloth as I returned my coffee cup to its saucer next to my newspaper. The small clink attracts the attention of my waiter, who flashes up with his silver pot from the old Sheraton service, to pour me a refill. Just as he leans over the table, he is bumped by a passing diner and a dribble of the brown liquid splashes on my shirt cuff. The Maitre d' rushes over. "Oh, Mr. Chess, please accept my apology. We will, of course, take care of the dry cleaning."

"Thanks, Foster, I'm sure it was an accident." Reluctantly, I climb the few steps to the Men's Room. Inside, I hang my blue blazer on a chrome hook next to the marble sinks, and rinse my cuff. At the next sink, a man in dark slacks and a hooded pullover is drying his hands. It seems a bit ridiculous to have his hood up indoors, but I suppose fashions change and people do whatever they think is 'cool'. We certainly are an opposite pair, my lavatory buddy and I. I am taller – about 6'-2" while he is just under 6'. My eyes are dark and my hair is still mostly black, although since crossing my 40th birthday last year, a few white hairs are sprouting. I am also a little stockier, although 185 isn't exactly running to fat. Fortunately, I still keep in shape with regular sessions on the dojo mat. My friend here looks like he spends most of the time doing computer games, although with the hooded sweatshirt, it is hard to tell. I think that if I could see his face, I would guess that it has that vacant stare so common among younger people today, like they don't care about anything. My face is like a map of my life, harder and with a ghost of recent pain. I think that before my wife was murdered, my face was softer. I still draw a second glance from women, but frankly, I don't care much these days. Maybe that's what some find appealing.

The young man dries his hands, and turns to leave, averting his face as he passes behind me and brushes his shoulder against my hanging coat on his way out. I wonder where he is going in such a hurry. But enough speculation, I need to get outside. I can't stand here and let memories take over.

As I leave the hotel and walk along Montgomery Street, a subtle feeling sneaks up on me, one that I remembered from my days undercover – someone was tailing. To test my instinct, I tried Kim's Game with the crowd. I slowed a bit less than the typical stroller, recording the faces of those around me, Once these become fixed in my mind, I picked up my speed just enough to pass two dozen people, then slow down to take another snapshot. I still remembered the lessons from years ago. One across the street and one ahead were the same.

I decide to grab the cable car up California Street. As it passes, I turn and jump on the car's rear platform at the last second. No one else runs to follow, so maybe my imagination is working overtime. Up at the top of the hill where Powell St. crosses, I step off and wait for a car heading down towards Union Square. As I stand in small group of tourists, the feeling returns, sending prickles down my back.

No one seems to be paying special attention to me as we clatter and sway, bell clanging and pine brakes smoking down the Powell St. hill. But my awareness is still heightened or else the others are very good. I step off at the St. Francis Hotel, cross the street to Union Square and take a seat on a convenient bench.

The brightness and sharp shadows reminds me of Rome. It was just after we had decided to get married. Jean and I planned to meet in the Piazza de Spagna, at the foot of the Spanish Steps, by Bernini's La Barcaccia Fountain. I had just made an Embassy drop up at Via Veneto and didn't have to be back before the morning pickup. Jean had opted out of a meeting with the Banca Intesa Group, so we had almost a whole day free. As I stood in the piazza, next to the oversized marble rowboat with water pouring over the sides, there was the same gnawing feeling like today. I remember that I had seen Jean look down at me from the top, wave wildly and start descending the broad stairs. Apprehension seized me. I held up my hand to signal her to stand still. But she misread it for a sign to hurry and started running down towards me. The piazza is shaped like an X, with the rowboat sculpture at the crossing. A car driving around the north end of the Piazza sped towards me, the window on the passenger side opening as it accelerated. I was weaponless, so I just started waving at the car as it closed on me, to draw attention away from Jean. It sped by, three kids inside laughing insanely at my discomfiture. When Jean reached me, I was

4

still breathless from excess adrenaline. It had been nothing then, but I have the same the crawly feeling today.

It is impossible to pick out a minder in the crowd. Finally, I shake off the hypersensitivity, get up and cross through the park to Gump's Department Store. In the back of the first floor a large display of carved wood puzzle boxes attracts my attention. One in the form of a T'ang Dynasty horse seems particularly well articulated. As I hold it up to examine it more closely, looking for the disguised latch, I also keep an eye out for anyone that might be interested in my focus. No one stands out so I berate myself again for slipping into an old habit.

The horse is just the perfect thing for a private detective like me. When I go to pay for it, I discover a velvet drawstring bag in my jacket pocket that certainly wasn't there earlier this morning. Opening the bag, I find a strange ornate yellow key. It has a very intricate and unusual filigree design which seems to be woven around some odd scratchings. It is a fairly large key, but instead of teeth, has holes of different sizes bored partially through the shaft. It looks very old. I have no idea where it came from, or what it could possibly fit.

The puzzle horse again draws my attention and finding the latch plate, I push it in, rotate the square mortise on the other side so that the teeth match the slot below it. When they align, I pull the pin further, which releases a spring in the horse's tail. The tail on the horse drops down, revealing a metal ring. I pull the ring, which causes the saddle to flip up, opening a shallow compartment underneath. I return the key to its soft bag and stuff it into the compartment, where it fills the available space. I push back the saddle, reversing my actions to close it up. With a shiny black Gump's bag holding my tissue-wrapped horse, I turn to leave the store on Post Street when I notice a man in a Raiders jacket and matching sweatpants watching me across the rows of merchandise. When I glance at him, he drops his eyes back to the counter. He looks familiar, like one of the pair on Montgomery St. So now I have a choice. I decide to walk across the floor and stand in his face.

"Was there something you wanted from me?" I asked.

"Excuse me?"

"You are following me. Why don't you just tell me what this is about?"

I could see hesitation in his eyes, which then shifts to a decision. "Come with me and they'll be no trouble." He leans forward and pulls his jacket open slightly. Protruding from his waist is the distinctive angled butt of a Walther PPK. "Just walk out the front door ahead of me."

I don't see his partner anywhere, but I assume he is waiting outside. It seems like a good time to slip the pincer. Grabbing a stack of wooden trays from the display, I throw them past him to the floor. The crash distracts him as I move the other way. Behind the service counter is a doorway marked "Associates Only." I duck inside to find myself in a storage room ceiling high in merchandise shelves. Recessed on one side is a small toilet room with a high vent window covered in grimy translucent wire glass. I push out the lower sash as far as it will go. From the curtained doorway, I can hear someone speaking loudly. "You can't go in there, sir."

I hoist myself up by the window frame and stick my legs outside. Hooking my feet on the projected sash, I lean back inside to retrieve my parcel from the toilet tank. Then I slide out the window and drop about 5' to the street. When I reach upwards to swing the window closed, the latch falls back into place.

The alley leads to Post Street and I emerge just next to the store entrance. The other one must have run into the store, because I don't see anyone familiar. Seeing a taxi stand across the street, I wave and a Yellow Cab leaves its spot at the back of the taxi line. I jump in, slamming the door and telling the driver to head towards Fisherman's Wharf. The car jolts forward, making an immediate right turn on Stockton, away from my destination. The security window is closed, and I rap on it but the driver ignores me, I rap again, but there's still no response as he turns north on Kearney and then west on Pine. When the cab stops for the light at Van Ness, I try the doors, but they are locked and the handles are inoperative. I tried banging on the side windows, but they are secured. So I sit back and try to stay calm to see where my ride will take me. When we turn into Golden Gate Park, I gather myself for a stop and rob somewhere along the way – but we weave through the twisted cypresses to the beach where the shore road leads north to Seal Rocks and Point Lobos.

The taxi driver parks in front of the Cliff House overlooking the Point, unlocks the rear door and holds it open for me. I follow him through the main entrance to the dining room, which does not seem to be open for business yet. The room is completely empty except for a corner table by the windows, where a tall man in his 70s or 80s sits reading some papers with a partially empty coffee cup at his elbow. As the driver pulls out a chair, I sit opposite my apparent host. The man ignores me and continues scanning his documents. He is elegant, fitted out in a dove grey suit, white shirt and maroon tie. The man's skin is almost exactly the same color as his suit and is paper-thin. I can see delicate veins in the hollows under his light eyes. The hands that protrude from his cuffs are also lightly veined and though he is certainly quite old, there is an aura of vitality about him.

His white hair is exceedingly fine and moves with every slight shift in the air currents. He is not smiling. Finally, he lifts his glance from the papers, fixes me with his sharp blue eyes and speaks to me very quietly, with only a tinge of Eastern European accent.

"Good morning Mr. Chess. I appreciate your taking time out of your busy day to see me. You have in your possession, something of mine. It is not very valuable, but it is a keepsake that has been in my family for quite some time. Might you please return it?"

His formality speaks to his elegant appearance and age. Perhaps English is not his first language. I keep my face blank and stare at him. After a moment he continues, "The key" as he holds out his hand with the palm up.

"You seem to know who I am, but who are you?" I ask.

"I am not important, but please indulge me and you shall have my gratitude. The key, if you please."

"I am sorry, but I have no idea what you are talking about."

"I will ask only once more. As I said, you will earn my gratitude with your acknowledgement of my request, but the depth of my displeasure will astonish you if you continue to act ignorantly."

I continue to be mute. The key that I believe he was requesting rests beneath our feet in the Gump's shopping bag. If he takes the horse, so be it. But my curiosity is now aroused.

Gesturing to the windowed kitchen door, two very large men in dark suits come out; haul me out of the chair, and rifle through my pockets. They open the Gump's bag and discover the tissue package which they tear open revealing my sculpture. My host looks at it, turning it over in his hands to see all sides, but apparently doesn't recognize it as a puzzle box, so he dismissively drops it back into the bag. The two thugs stand by, their arms hanging loosely out from their sides, like construction cranes.

"I know that you were contacted at breakfast. As I said, the key is not valuable, but let us say $5,000 for its return? It's far more than you would earn for a brief morning's detective work."

"What makes this key worth so much?"

"The value is entirely an issue of family history. Mr. Chess, please accept my offer. Let us say that it is a consulting fee for recovering an object that had been stolen and let's be done with this between us."

"Why it is so important to you?"

"Mr. Chess, I know something of your history. You lived in Woods Hole on Cape Cod as a boy, attended Boston University on a Navy scholarship, and then volunteered for Special Warfare. Although you completed your SEAL training in Coronado, you were tapped by Naval Intelligence and served in that department until 3 years ago, when you abruptly resigned. You were married until your wife was murdered while on assignment with the NSA in Israel. Currently, you are working as a Private Investigator here in San Francisco. I understand that you are still quite angry over the cavalier treatment you received from our government over their suppression of any investigation into your wife's murder. I empathize with your pain, as I too have been treated badly by our government. But even though we share these unfortunate circumstances, I must insist that you cooperate with me in the return of this key. It is very important to me and to my family, although I cannot explain precisely why. Please do not ignore this old man's plea."

He had pulled at scars that I would rather not tear away. Although I was drawn to help, I felt that there was something beneath his attitude that was not innocent. I thought I would give it another round to test my gut. "I'm sorry, but I really cannot return something I do not have."

"I am sorry too, young man. Good day, sir," he says with some resignation. "Remember the lesson you are about to receive."

The grey man returns to his cappuccino and dismisses me. His offhand threat is almost casual, but with an undercurrent of certitude that made a far deeper impression than if he shouted. The two men take one arm each and lock-step me out of the empty dining room to the stair leading down to the open plaza overlooking the ocean. As we start down, I try to bluff them by simulating a trip, dropping one knee to follow with a leg sweep, but they both drop with me and still maintain their inexorable hold. Past the gift shop we go, around the telescopes and the IMAX Theater to the stone breakwater at the edge of the old Sutro Baths foundations. As we stand by the narrow stone wall, the waves surge over the foundations to crash against the breakwater just below us. One of the men reaches into his pants pocket and withdraws a black switchblade which he flicks open. The other man transfers his grip on one arm to hold both while he turns me to face the water. I feel the point enter through my shirt and lightly prick the skin in the small of my back. I have little choice but to lean forward. I am held off balance for a moment and then shoved forward. I start to fall, and try to catch myself, but grab only air as I fall outward. As I go over, I tuck and grab for a ledge projecting from the wall just below my feet. My fingers

8

slide into a groove and I grab hard as my legs cartwheel out over the water. Fortunately, my hold does not break when my body slams against the wall below the ledge and I hang on while the spray from the waves below soaks my pants and my hand is bent back almost to the breaking point. It will be only a matter of moments before a particularly large wave knocks me off my precarious perch. I grab the ledge with my other hand; pull my aching fingers from the cleft and push off, turning to face the wall. I recapture the groove with my free hand and pull hard, levering up until my knees touch the ledge. Then I slide them over until my knee can hold some of my weight and search for another grip higher up. I can just reach the top of the wall, so I am finally able to pull myself upright and swing my legs to rest on the breakwater. I look around, but both men are gone.

After a few deep breaths, I brush gravel from my knees and make my way back up the steps and around to the front of the Cliff House. The taxi is gone. My instincts about the old man were right. While I stand there deciding what to do, behind me, the restaurant opens for lunch business. "How many for lunch?" the green sheathed receptionist asks - all angles, elbows and coiffed hair.

"Just one," I reply as I am led to the small table recently occupied by my departed host. Against the window under the table is my shopping bag. I rummage inside and find that the horse is still there.

While I am contemplating the proffered menu, hearing the threat again in my ear, a voice appears at my arm, "I hope you don't mind; I am alone and feel a bit uncomfortable sitting by myself." The lilting voice belongs to a 30s leggy blonde. "My name is Lauren," she breathes as she sits opposite, while tastefully arranging her short cream silk skirt. "Normally, I wouldn't be so forward, but I just had to share the sea lions with someone. What could go awry on such a perfect sparkle of a day?" Her aqua eyes flirt past me to the menu as she becomes absorbed by the choices.

"What indeed" I muse. Was it such a short time ago that I was sitting at breakfast? I tuck the shopping bag into the third chair between us and return to the menu. "Have you eaten here before?" I asked, changing the subject.

"Oh no," she fluttered, "But I heard that it was a very special San Francisco landmark."

"Well, the restaurant is new, but with great reviews, it has become popular." In a moment, a waiter stops to take our order. "If I may suggest," he recites, "Try the Dungeness Crab Roll, followed by Beef Culottes, or for a lighter dish, have the local swordfish; both are outstanding." She

9

glances out the window for a moment, then returns to the menu. The hovering waiter looks inquiringly at my companion. Lauren asks for the crab and fish.

I added my selections. "I'll join the young lady with the crab, but I'll follow with bouillabaisse and we'll take a bottle of San Suprey Sauvignon Blanc as well."

As we waited for the appetizers, minions bustled about with crusty sourdough bread, still warm from the oven and unsalted butter in a tub. Lauren reaches over the table to the third chair and lifted the shopping bag.

"Is this something special?" she asked.

"No, it's just something I picked up for my desk. Do you like it?"

She ruffled through the tissue and lifted the wooden horse. "Oh my; it's Chinese, isn't it?"

"Yes; T'ang Dynasty." I wondered if this was the Grey Man's follow-up. "Do you like Asian art?"

"I adore it."

She seemed to be charming and innocent, but one can never tell. Not so many years ago, a 12-year old Bosnian girl nearly ran me through with an ice pick while she continued licking a lollipop that I had shared with her. I won't forget the innocence in her eyes when she folded from a reverse elbow to her throat as I spun from the pick.

I snapped back to the present. "Then let's go to the museum this afternoon, if you don't have any plans."

"I would love to."

As we chatted during lunch, the only undercurrent I could tell was a mutual visceral attraction between us. While she sits in her chair very decorously, she has a habit of punctuating her comments by leaning forward so her hair floats from behind her ears and swishes across her cheeks. Then she would sit back and tuck it back behind her ear, only to have it launch forward with another verbal point. The color of her hair appears to be blonde, but not a shade from a bottle; darker with an undertone of umber except where the sun has lightened it. Her blouse is of very fine silk, and there is a very thin amethyst necklace that peeks out of its high scoop neckline when she leans forward. She wears no rings, and her watch has an elongated rectangular face with a gold filigree band. Her nails are just barely colored, but shiny and perfectly tapered.

We listen to just a hint of Mozart surrounding us, while just outside on the rocks, dozens of barking, growling and fin flapping California sea lions were making a wild ruckus. I am intrigued. As much as I pry, she says very little about herself, but keeps deftly turning it back to me. I do learn that her last name is Sylfern, but not much more. The only hint that I get about her objectives are her questions about my work. But aside from telling her that I am a P.I., I give her nothing else.

As we stood and move to the door, I could see she was tall, about 5'-8," and slim, though her breasts push against the cream silk blouse, and her walk has a definite sinuous grace. Lauren invites me to ride with her – she had brought her car. I slid into the cream Porsche convertible, which matches her outfit and idles in a throaty whisper as she turns on the engine. I wonder for a moment about her "visiting" San Francisco. Lauren confidently holds the leather wheel in two hands while she sits back in her seat, her arms extended almost straight in front of her, smoothly guiding the machine into banked curves as we match the road contours. Her face is almost that of a teenager; completely unlined and innocent like a waif who needs rescuing. It is a stark contrast to her confident driving style. Her nose is aquiline thin, but her lips are full and wide. I would guess she has a tartar ancestor somewhere since her eyes have an appealing tilt, and her skin has a warm buttery complexion. When she turns into the Asian Art Museum parking lot, I realize that she had never once asked for directions. Also, she never asked how I got to the Cliff House in the first place without a car. Along the route, I took opportunities to check for a tail, but there did not seem to be one.

So here I am, in a museum with a rather attractive woman who tells me that she is totally unfamiliar with the Cliff House, yet apparently knows San Francisco as a native. I am not particularly sought after by beautiful, seemingly well-to-do young ladies with an interest in art. It would be very flattering if the two encounters were not related, but somehow, I doubt it.

When we leave the car to enter the museum, an afterthought prods me to lift my shopping bag and check it. The receipt makes me chuckle, since it is a unique ivory Netsuke figure of a crouching tiger with its mate tied to my bag. During our walk though dimly lit galleries filled with delicate scrolls and fierce warriors, Lauren impresses me that she really knows Asian art, and has an educated palate.

The museum seems to put her at ease, since she begins talking about herself. She tells me that she lives in Albuquerque, but works in Washington for the State Department. She went to private school in New Mexico, and then on to Stanford. The opening moves in a courtship dance follow a set series of rules. She gives out so few clues that I find it very difficult to assess what her real motives are. I guess this is part of the "off balance" scenario that is designed to keep the other at a distance, yet still interested. In response, I tell her nothing about my years with the Navy. Instead, I mention briefly my current work. I also say nothing about this morning's incident.

I can tell that something is troubling her behind the cultured language and coquettishness. Abruptly, she stops and turns to me with a glance at her watch. "I am so sorry, but I have to run. I have an important appointment. Can you get home by yourself? Call me, I am sorry. Thanks, enjoyed lunch, let's have dinner. Wine was fabulous, talk to you." And off she runs, her jacket waving farewell as the heels chattered on the marble floor.

'Oh well, so much for debonair Simon.' I say to myself. I walk out to the checkroom and fish the netsuke out of my pocket and hand it to the attendant. She brings me the Gump's bag but when I look into it, of course the horse is gone. Instead, all I find is a silver picture frame, empty. 'Thanks, Lauren' I continue to myself.

"Are you sure there isn't another bag here?" I asked as I lift open the counter gate and walk into the storage room.

"I'm sorry, sir, but you may not come back here. Please, sir. This is the only bag of its kind. Could you be mistaken as to the contents?"

"No I just bought it. There should be a receipt inside." But of course that was gone as well.

"You'll have to go to the office and fill out a claim." She suggests.

"Thanks anyway. Perhaps there is someone that noticed the lady leaving?"

"Check with the Security Guard."

The security guard, an ex-city-cop type with a pugilist's jaw in a uniform about one size too small for his fireplug body, walks me out towards the front door. "Yeah, I seen her" he growled. "And no, she weren't carrying nuttin'. There was a guy with her, who were in a big hurry, he half-drug her out."

"Can you tell me about the man?"

"He was almost as tall as you, but a lot younger. It looked like she knew the wiseguy, so I didn't step in. He looked maybe 30 with a marine brush cut."

"Suit?"

"Nah, black Raiders sweatshirt, you know, the one with a hood."

"What about the car?"

"Listen buddy, I ain't no answer man."

"I would really appreciate your help. I think that the lady switched the contents of my bag and it is really important to track her down."

"OK, one last answer; then make a report. The car was an older model black Mercedes with a local plate. No, I did not get the number."

"Thanks for your help. Can I get a taxi here? She took my ride."

The guard grumbled to himself as he waddled away. "I ain't paid enough …" as he returned to his post by the ticket counter.

Outside, of course the Porsche is gone as well. When the taxi I called shows up, I give him my address. Along the way, I pull out the picture frame and looked closely at it. The photo in the frame is type that you see in a store displaying frames for sale; a group of nondescript people, printed on cheap photo stock. The frame was quite attractive though, a clean modern rectangle of polished silver with a Greek-key design etched around the edge. There's nothing else in the bag but torn tissue paper.

My home and office share a three story Victorian style frame house on Vallejo Street in the Union District. The previous owners had restored the detailing and painted it a unique shade of light blue, with sparkling white moldings and trim. Inside, the original wide plank pine floors had been stained dark and glowed in the soft light which filtered through the stained glass transom over the substantial front door. The walls in most of the interior rooms were ochre, and there wasn't a hint of drywall anywhere. One of the first things I did when I took occupancy three years ago was to pull down the heavy velvet drapes and replace the fussy colonial furniture with wood and leather.

The office is on the first floor, with a reception area that Stephanie, my girl-everything, keeps watch over. Behind the Reception Room is a short hall with a bathroom on one side and a closet kitchen on the other. Behind that is a large office, whose windows open to a courtyard garden with a fountain, wind-chimes, and bamboo that I have let grow wild. Peeking through the bamboo are clumps of colored fuchsia and an occasional mouse. A brick walk circles the fountain stone and disappears in the Lilliputian forest. Above the office is my living space, accessed with a stair alongside the reception room, and which consists of a large living room, a small formal dining room with a corner fireplace, and the large brick floored kitchen which projects over my office. The only room that I substantially changed was the kitchen. I really enjoy cooking, and the space was large, but poorly arranged. So even though my budget was tight, I put in a large Farmers' sink, double door refrigerator with a separate freezer, and a commercial stove with a downdraft hood. I keep a small informal office across from the kitchen there as well so that if I need to, I can listen to a client's most private secrets. One more stair leads to my sleeping lair, a large granite open shower room which the previous owners installed, paneled closet, and a smaller guest bedroom with its own bath and sitting area in the front of the building covering the entry. Although there is an attic above this level, it is a mean space except for a raised skylight area that houses my telescope which gets dustier each year through non-use. This attic also houses my small laboratory and armory.

When I enter the darkened house and disarm the alarm system, I notice that the message light is blinking on the telephone. Checking the caller-ID, I see only an "Unidentified Caller Missed Call" on the screen. In hopes that it is possibly Lauren calling to explain, I hear the now familiar voice of the grey man. "Mr. Chess, by now you should understand the precarious nature of your condition. I expect you to telephone me before tomorrow morning at 9, after which you may expect a personal visit from some of my associates. The responsibility is yours. Please respect my wishes and your own good judgment." Following the warning is a telephone number with a "505" area code.

I climb up to my private office and sit at my desk. The computer is on, but the screen is dark. I start my browser and find a reverse telephone directory on the Internet. The number comes back as a New Mexico prefix, but the 7-digit number has no name or address associated with it.

In my absent minded way, I had carried up the shopping bag which I now open. The picture frame again stares back at me. The stock photo shows a group of people sitting at a table in a restaurant. The walls behind the people have old fishing photos on them; nothing more. I open the back of the frame; just cardboard. I see someone has written something on the cardboard in pencil but with the waxed surface, the pencil didn't leave much of a mark.

I get an idea – and call the Cliff House. The Lunch Manager has since gone home, and the Evening Manager tells me nothing was left for me. I tell him I had accidentally switched bags with a lady that I met casually at the restaurant, who the other manager seems to have known. The bag, I told him, has a valuable item in it and I wanted to return it to her. He offered to call his counterpart for me, but then gave me the number since he was so busy with diners.

14

Back to my computer, it is listed to Mr. Wayne Hudson at 5340 Fulton Street. I start to punch in the number, but then hang up, thinking that it would be better if I dropped in to see him during dinner to catch him in and off guard.

So with an hour to wait, I again study the photo. It was a little too dark in my office to see more detail, so I go up to the lab and pull out a binocular microscope. With a low power lens, the grain on the picture stands out sharply. The resolution is higher than expected for a stock photo. The people are not smiling the way you would expect. Also, the dining table in the picture has menus on it, like it was a candid shot. Two have their backs to the camera: a man and a woman. One man facing the camera is pointing out something to a companion. Nothing seems out of the ordinary, except that the restaurant definitely is not the Cliff House. I can't imagine what the photo has to do with my puzzle horse, Lauren, or the grey man.

I turn the photo over and examine the cardboard backing. To enhance the pencil line depression, I reach for my fingerprint dusting kit. Touching the soft badger brush to the powder, I gently swirl it across the pencil mark. Tiny flecks of dust cling to the slight ridges. Now when I hold it back under the light, it reads "Dinner – 8:30," but there was no signature or even any indication that it was addressed to me. I drop the photo and go back to the frame, scanning it and turning it under the scope. Again, nothing appears except that it is quite heavy for its size. It looks to be made of silver – not something that would be picked up at a Woolworth's. The cardboard backing had been taken out and replaced several times – I could see quite a few indentations along the edge. I take down my jacket from its lab hook, shrug into it and drop the photo in my pocket.

Descending back through the house to my office on the first floor, I enter the garage just next to the garden. My black Saab sits in its space facing towards me. Inside, I touched the control to open the garage door, and back into the alley. Alongside the driveway, trash cans are awaiting pickup the following morning and a frizzled cat watches me as I pass.

Out of the garage, it's up the hill to cross over and down the other side towards Golden Gate Park. Along Fulton Street, the houses which face the park look like so many rows of false teeth, with their white stone steps, spaced basements and recessed entries. Hudson's house is indistinguishable from the rest. There's not a soul is in sight. It's beginning to get dark and the sunset fog has not come in this warm evening. Lights were on behind the translucent curtains, like the ones my grandmother used to keep: filmy but starched. Tonight, the image behind the curtains shows only faint shifting glimmers of pale walls and a sturdy floor lamp.

Hudson himself answers the doorbell: a pale, earnest man of middle age with gold-rimmed reading glasses perched on his brow. Noticeably small ears balanced his squinty eyes as he inquisitively looks at me, leaning back to look up at my face. He is in shirtsleeves, with a vest buttoned all the way to the bottom and the shirt cuffs tightly closed. His pants still hold a knife-edge crease which descends to highly polished brogans. In spite of his coloring, his skin has the thickened look of someone who spent a lot of time in the sun.

Before I could speak, he suddenly leaned forward, his glasses dropping to his nose. "You were at the restaurant this morning. What do you want?" His voice was startlingly deep and gravely, for all his prissy manner and appearance.

"Good evening Mr. Hudson," I said kindly, "I am sorry that I did not telephone, but I was very concerned about the young lady that came to my table. You see, I took something of hers and have no idea as to where to return it."

"Why ask me?." Hudson turns back toward the hall and gestures for me to follow. "Until this morning, I never saw her before," he says over his shoulder. "She came into the restaurant and announced that you were waiting for her."

"Are you sure she wasn't waiting for me?" I asked.

"No, no." he replied quickly. "You see, we had just opened for lunch and you came in, and a lot of other people came in and I was keeping things going and it was noisy and then she was there and I didn't know who you were but she just walked past me to your table." He said it all in one breath like some kind of confession. People who give out too much information like this are often hiding something. I was about to ask another question, when he says "I'm sorry, but I was just about to have dinner" and started ushering me towards the front door.

The front hall is slightly seedy with sea prints on the walls in plastic frames. The air is musty and two of the three bulbs in the ceiling fixture are out. He takes off his glasses, rubbing them on the sleeve of his shirt, and then turning towards the front room, says, "Please excuse me, I was expecting someone and they're late. I have to call."

Hudson rushes into a dilapidated parlor and picks up the telephone. Turning back to look at me he curls the telephone next to his cheek, punches the numbers and speaks quietly into the receiver. I cannot make out anything as I strain to hear while gazing innocently at a fishing boat model on the hall table.

Replacing the telephone, he again repeats that dinner is waiting and he is sorry that he can't help me find the young lady. As he ushers me towards the front door, I sidestep and turn back. "Would you mind if call myself a taxi. I came in one but didn't ask him to wait. Thanks." Before he could reply, I stroll into the parlor and pick up his telephone. It was slightly slick with perspiration. With the receiver against my ear, I locate the Redial button. The screen lights up with the number that Hudson most recently called. It is the same 505 number that I had on my message machine. Before the telephone starts ringing at the other end, I disconnect; speaking into the dead telephone to ask for a taxi. I then give the address, hang up and tell Hudson that I will not bother him again.

After he shuts the door behind me, I look up and down the street, then descend the short flight of stairs, pass just out of sight of the front windows, and cross the street to the park. By now, the darkness is fuller, and the streetlights are spaced far enough apart so that it is quite gloomy between them. There is a stone wall along the street just above head height, with large twisted cedars leaning out over the wall. I duck under them and press myself against the rough stones.

Periodically, when the light turns green at the end of the street, there is a brief rush of cars. There are no walkers and no dogs. Waiting is a normal part of my P.I. work, so I am used to it. Most often, I learn more by being quiet and waiting than I do by flapping my lips. Tonight is no exception. Hudson gave himself away by his rush to get out his story. I wonder what such a milquetoast of a man would have to do with old keys and stolen puzzles. But we'll see.

It doesn't take long. In about 20 minutes a large dark car comes around the corner and slows to a stop by the front door of Hudson's house. With the streetlight shadows, there are no silhouettes against the side windows. Two men get out of the rear seat and go up the steps. Both are wearing dark clothes. When the door opens, Hudson is hustled into the car, which immediately takes off.

I can just make out the illuminated plate. I walk to my car and start the engine. There is enough light to see by and virtually no traffic, so the headlights stay off. After about a dozen blocks, the car turns right on Park Presidio Boulevard which goes directly to the Golden Gate Bridge. There is much more traffic here, so I turn on my lights and stay about 5 cars back. Once through the Presidio, the car ahead enters the 101 Freeway and leads me over the bridge. I overtake a few cars, trying to stay focused on the shape and color of the taillights. Past the bridge, the road goes through a short tunnel, and I catch a glimpse of it again in the overhead lighting, but then lose it almost immediately after we emerge. The next two miles I spend searching for the car, but it has disappeared. It must have taken one of the first Sausalito exits. I give up for the time being. When I get back to Golden Gate Park, Hudson's lights are still on, but there is no sign of movement. On a chance, I go up to the door, but my ring is unanswered. Inside, a ship's bell clock toll 8 bells.

The evening sounds of tree frogs sweep in from the park. Funny, it's April and the frogs usually stop in February when the winter rains end. They sing and make me remember the Low County, where I trained in swamp assault. In Charleston, the frogs announce evening and chattered all night, covering most sounds, except for the occasional grunt of an alligator or the almost soundless swoop of a hunting night heron. How long could I stay under the mud, while fleas and leeches nibbled at my skin, as I waited for my target to move first? Then quietly with no splash or sudden move to trigger peripheral vision, I would rise to a squat and slowly duck walk, freeing my boots from the muck clasping my SOG S-37 2000 knife with only four fingers, in case I had to throw it. As I neared my target, I would stay low and shifting the grip on my knife, strike upwards, squeezing his throat to stifle any sound, so my target would collapse into me, slide down my chest, and slip under the black water.

This evening, I have more questions and no action plan. At Richmond Street Police Station, I am directed to a desk piled in disorder, hiding the bulk of the wart hog with three stripes on his arm. After introducing myself, I explain that a car sideswiped me nearby but I was able to get the license number as they drove away. The Sergeant reaches for an Incident Report Form from his lower desk drawer, grunting loudly as his belly obscures his hand. Placing it precariously on top of the pile, he turns to his computer terminal and logs on, keying in the license number I recite to him. There is a bowl of hard candies at the desk's corner and I reach over to take one, pushing aside a large mound of spent wrappers in the process. As the Sergeant bends over the, I see that the car is registered to Daniel Towson of 1050 Vallejo – just down the block from my home.

"Ok, Mr. Chess, you gotta sign the report."

"Never mind, Sergeant, I've changed my mind, it really is a small ding, and I know that you have lots more to do than to worry about trivialities."

The Sergeant tears the form in half and waves me away with a "Thanks for coming in." like he was thanking me for my dog pooping on his lawn.

The end of Vallejo where Towson's house is located is up a dead-end street on Russian Hill. Over the crest of the hill, high-rises terrace down to look over Coit Tower and the Oakland Bay Bridge. The anti-collision lights wink on the top of the Tower and the bridge, while across the bay, Berkeley's sparkling carpet is mostly obscured by the evening haze. At this end of Vallejo, there is a short row of stately homes behind sturdy fences, framed by old spreading California Oaks. Towson's house is finished in white stucco with large square granite blocks set at the corners. The roof is covered with blue Spanish tile, and corkscrew cypresses march down a curving gravel driveway leading to the porticoed entrance. I park the car in the driveway, backing into an extended arm that smells of cedar and camphor. The gravel crunches lightly as I walk up to the door and pull the old-fashioned bell handle. A low double octave note sounds inside. Steps announced a woman's approach.

"May I help you?" A spare woman holds the door open to her question. Her rimless glasses and untouched hair frame someone who boasted, rather than hid her age. She stands squarely in the doorway and looks at me in almost a challenge.

"I wonder if you would be so kind as to let Mr. Towson know that he has a visitor." I asked politely.

The lady loses her balance for a moment. Then she recovers and a fleeting angry expression crosses her face as she replies in a cultured, though thin voice, "Mr. Towson died about a year ago; please excuse me." She backs up a step and starts to close the door.

"Please wait. Is it Mrs. Towson?"

"Yes," she replied. "But I am sorry; I can't see anyone just now."

"Mrs. Towson" may I show you something?" An idea had just caught my mind. Reaching into my jacket pocket, I pull out the photo, now with a crumpled corner.

She lets go of the door to hold out her hand for the photo. Then she backs into the hall where a lamp is illuminating a side table with a leather basket in the center. The lampshade lets very little light through it, so she bends down to peer at the photo. Then she utters a brief cry and retreats into a library, letting the photo drop to the floor. Her face fills with grief and tears begin to roll down her high cheekbones.

Spotting a bar table near the couch, I ask her if I can get her anything.

"Bourbon, please. Neat."

On the table there are several decanters of cut glass, reflecting in multi-colored disarray as I reach out, sniff one and put about 2 inches in the bottom of a faceted glass. She takes half in a single swallow, and then sips at the remainder. I pour myself a draught of very smoky single-malt and watch her across a heavily patterned oriental carpet. The photo lies on the floor between us. She takes a lace handkerchief from the pocket of her gabardine slacks and dries her tears, while sharply eying me while I could see the wheels churning with questions.

"My name is Simon Chess. This morning, a young lady that I had just met by the name of Lauren Sylfern accidentally switched shopping bags with me and I ended up with that photo instead of my parcel. I followed a lead to the house of Wayne Hudson. Do you happen to recognize either of these names?"

She shook her head.

"Hudson seemed to be upset with my questions, so after I left him I waited, only to see him drive away with three men in a car that was identified as belonging to Mr. Towson. I got your address from the police, and came here with the idea that perhaps you could clear up my confusion and help me recover my package."

"Well, you must be mistaken about the car. My husband was killed last year. The car was totally destroyed so I don't understand how you could see it today. You must be mistaken about the plate number."

"Mrs. Towson, I was threatened this morning by a man who I never met before, but I have a theory that he may be your husband."

"Ridiculous! I told you, Daniel was killed almost exactly one year ago." She sits back on the couch and looks miserable.

"Why did the picture shock you?" I pointed to the floor where it lay.

"Not that it is any business of yours."

"Mrs. Towson..."

"You've had your drink. I think that you should leave now." Her cheeks have red spots as she works herself up into a snit.

Quickly, I say, "Please, I have no wish to bring you any grief, I only want to recover my parcel."

"I know nothing about your parcel or any of the people you named. Please go."

"I am really sorry to barge in and upset you, but the item I lost was quite important to me. Please forgive my prying, but do you have any idea about when the photo might have been taken?"

"Well, yes." She knelt down and picked up the picture, looking at it very closely. "It appears to have been taken at dinner, on the night that he died."

"What happened, if you wouldn't mind telling me?"

"I really do mind, but I suppose you will not go away until I answer your questions. When my husband left our house for dinner that evening, he told me that he was meeting the daughter of an old friend of his, that she needed something from him, or his help with something. Later that night, the police came here and told me that his car had gone into the Bay, and that he drowned. They presumed he had been drinking. That was the last information I ever received."

"Did he usually have a few drinks during dinner?"

"Mr. Chess, my husband rarely drank because alcohol upset his stomach. But the police wanted a simple answer, so drunk was the official word."

"What about the woman?"

"The police said that there had been someone else in the car – a purse or shoe or something had been found in the car, I really don't remember exactly. The police asked me if I knew who it might be, but Daniel was always helping someone. They told me that they would keep me informed of their progress, but that was the last I heard from the police and the women never turned up. Of course, there was a Coroner's Inquest, but it was ruled an accidental death, contributed by alcohol. I told them that Daniel was a careful driver and never took any chances behind the wheel. The car was always serviced and in good condition."

"What about enemies? Did your husband have any?"

"What is your interest besides your package? You sound like an interrogator. Are you a lawyer?"

"No Ma'am. I happen to be a Private Detective, so I suppose I have an affinity for prying. Please don't take offense. I just find it odd that your husband's car turns up again after a year, and a young lady is again involved in something. Your story interests me."

"As to enemies, he was a successful businessman and didn't get to his position without creating enemies along the way. But I can't think of one that would be motivated to kill him. After all, it wasn't like he was a monster or anything; just a tough businessman."

Thinking that she had more to say I waited.

"And the answer to your unasked question is No; he was not having an affair. I never had a clue to the girl's identity.

"Forgive me, Mrs. Towson, but what about the photo?"

"She held it up to the light again. "The picture is of my husband Daniel, with several other people, including a young girl, presumably the one he met for dinner. I can't see the woman very well with her back turned, but I am sure it must be her."

She hands me the photo and I look at it again carefully.

"Is there a chance that you might know which restaurant the photo was taken in?"

"Of course; Daniel was particularly fond of Scoma's, down on the Wharf. He used to eat there almost every time he had guests."

'Scoma's', I thought to myself. I wonder. "Thank you for your patience, but I forgot that I have a dinner date. May I call you if I discover any additional information?"

"If you must; but I would rather you simply left me alone."

I apologize, thank her again and go out to my car. As I pull away from the house, the door opens slightly and I can see her staring out at my taillights.

Scoma's is located down an alley out on a pier near Fisherman's Wharf, but away from the rest of the restaurants and honky-tonks. Between the fish processing buildings, the alley opens to a valet parking lot and a building that looks more like a diner than a fine restaurant. I give my car to an attendant and climb the four steps. Glancing at my watch, it is 9:15. Inside the main entrance, the noise assaults me. The bar stretches out to the left and is five deep with young executives and wanna-bee's. I elbow my way up to the desk. Just then, a voice calls out to me from a table against the wall. "I see you finally made it."

Flipping open the menu, she burrows into it. I thought that it was definitely time for a stiff one, so I snag a passing waiter and order a double single-malt. With a dozen questions in my mind, I decide to wait her out. While waiting, I look out through the windows where I see an occasional crab boat or shrimper come in with today's catch.

"Has madam made a decision?" The hovering voice in my ear calls.

Lauren slaps the menu down on the table, "Yes, I will have the halibut, broiled, plain with no sauce, and a salad, and bring the gentleman a dead fish wrapped in newspaper."

22

"I beg your pardon, madam?"

I break in. "Madam is expecting an apology for my lateness."

"Yes of course," the waiter replies without batting an eye "And for you, sir?"

"Squash and crab soup followed by steamed mussels and a small plate of sautéed spinach with lots of extra garlic to keep the lady vampire at bay."

"Yes, of course." He goes away shaking his head.

"I've been here since 8:30. What took you so long?" asked Lauren.

"After you left me at the museum, I had a few errands to run, and your message was so cryptic that it took me until just now to figure it out."

"I really don't think you are that dense, but then again," she tossed back to me. "You must know that my coming to the Cliff House wasn't entirely accidental."

"Yes, I gathered that."

"When I left home, I was looking for some help with a problem."

"Go on."

"First you must agree that anything I tell you has to be kept strictly confidential."

"That's what I do."

"I need to tell you a story. It takes place during World War II."

"Don't you want to eat first?"

"Don't patronize me; this is important."

"Sorry. Go on."

"During that time, near the Polish border, a German Patrol was escorting two young scientists on their way to a secret laboratory when their car broke down. While they were fixing the engine, a small group of Polish Resistance Fighters came upon them. The German patrol was killed and the two scientists were captured. On their way back to Poland, someone betrayed the group to a German garrison. All the Poles were killed. The two scientists were escorted back across the river to Germany, where they joined others at the Peenemunde weapons labs developing the atom bomb and rockets. After the war, the scientists were recruited by the Americans and were accepted as immigrants; one continuing his weapons and other work at Los Alamos National Laboratories in New Mexico, while the other was assigned to Oak Ridge, Tennessee. My father was one of the scientists. His name is Ernst Zilbern. When he died, his attorney gave me a letter relating the old story and asking my help in finally apprehending the other scientist who had betrayed the Polish Resistance group."

"The remaining scientist though now almost 80, is extremely well respected among both the scientific elite as well as in government circles, is a member of the National Security Council as well as a confidant of the President's National Security Advisor. Since leaving Oak Ridge, he patented a small piece of software connected to generating large prime numbers that are used in making keys for high-security codes. He made several versions that were good for corporate and institutional use as well, and in the process earned him a substantial fortune. He was the one who betrayed my father to the Germans. I tried to bring the matter before authorities, but could never get a hearing. In the process, however; I attracted the ire of this scientist, and almost lost my job as a result."

"But this incident was forever ago. Why now?"

"If it were only this one issue, I think that I could let it go. But it's more than that. My father believed that his former associate went out of his way to make life tough for us. In fact, my father told me that if he ever was to die suddenly, that he would be certain that his former friend would be behind it, and hoped I would avenge it. The problem is that there is no proof of anything."

"So how does that affect you?"

"My father told me that his old associate stole his inventions. I think that he also had my father killed."

Before I could comment, our dinner arrives, and I shift subjects to have time to decide if I want to know more, or just to put her off. I don't want to ruin a perfectly good meal with challenges so I wait until the dishes are cleared and the check is paid.

"Let's walk", I suggested, as I rise to help her out of her seat.

By this time in the evening, many of the tourists were off the streets, except for a few sailors on liberty, some kids sitting and smoking in art gallery doorways, and an occasional cruising police car. The concrete pier is cold as the night breeze comes in across the moored fishing boats. Alcatraz Island warning lights reflect rills in the Bay. A large Navy ship on its way towards the Golden Gate is identifiable by a floodlight on the hull number painted on its deckhouse. We walk up the alley on Pier 47 to Jefferson Street, where we stroll along the water. We get as far as

Ghirardelli Square. Although it is late, the chocolate shop in the upper plaza is still open for a few customers. Lauren eyes the goodies, so we order coffee and share a small dish of toasted almond ice cream, sitting at one of the little marble tables. Suddenly, Lauren stands, picks up her coffee and runs out of the store to perch on the edge of the Bird Fountain. There, she waits for me to join her. Looking up at me with those aqua eyes, she recaptures her composure, blinks once to gain my attention and then continues speaking.

"My father was the brightest man I ever knew", she murmurs, the steam from the coffee framing her compressed lips. "When he died, I lost my hero. He always took time while I tested my wings. He was my safety net and never shirked from catching me if I failed at something. He was the quietest man I ever knew, yet with a single gesture or inflection, would tell me that I was OK."

There was nothing I could say. I decide to change the subject. "Tell me about the Cliff House."

Lauren pulls out a folded newspaper page from her purse, showing it to me. The article is about a special meeting of the National Security Council that is to be held in San Francisco this week, which will be attended by 6 Silicon Valley software companies, to review current computer security standards. One of the presenters at this conference is Dr. Johann Froehlich, a noted expert in this field. "Froehlich is the man my father knew during the war. He is the one that betrayed them to the Germans, and then later was expatriated along with the rest."

"What does it matter now?"

"My father carried this secret most of his adult life. When his estate was being settled, his attorney told me that my father believed that Froehlich would not have betrayed the Poles simply because he had loyalty to the Third Reich. He must have had another reason, something far more personal. What matters to me is that my father thought it was important, or he wouldn't have left me a note about it. My father felt he couldn't do anything about this so long as he was alive. But now, I want the truth to come out."

"So what do you want from me?"

She fussed with her coffee, which had certainly turned cold. Then she looked up at the darkened building and around the square. "I tried to find out what plane Froehlich would be on this morning. I flew in from Albuquerque last night and early today I went out to the airport to wait for him. When he arrived, I followed him to The Huntington and learned that he had reserved a suite for the week. While I was waiting in the lobby, trying to decide if I should confront him, he suddenly appeared and got in the back of waiting limo. As they drove off, I ran to the concierge and said that Dr. Froehlich has forgotten his files which I needed to give to him before his meeting. The concierge told me to try the Cliff House since he made a lunch reservation there. So I drove out, arriving when you were being dragged out of the dining room."

"I didn't know what had happened, but after the others left, when you returned alone, I asked the manager if he knew your name. When he told me, I recognized it from a suggestion that my father made to me before he died. I decided to go inside, and try to figure out where you fit and if I could trust you."

"So what was the Horse swap all about?"

She looked blankly at me. "What?"

"Don't play the innocent," I chided, "the only reason I came here was because of the obtuse note you left on the picture."

She said "I left you a note, but there was no picture." Annoyed, she stood, gathering her purse and was about to walk off.

"Lauren, maybe you usually get men to help you by crying and playing victim, but your story doesn't ring true. You said you left a note, but it was far from clear."

Red spots showed on Lauren's cheeks as she retorted "Did you even bother to look at my note carefully?"

I dig into my pocket and come up with the picture. "The note was on the cardboard backing in the frame,"

"But that wasn't the note I left you. Mine was on an ad for Scoma's that I tore out of the newspaper. That's why I thought you dense not to figure out where to meet me."

"And where did you put this note?"

"In your shopping bag. There was a copy of The Chronicle on the desk at the museum and I opened it to the restaurant listings, tore out the ad and wrote my invitation on it. Then I tipped the attendant to put it your bag at the museum."

"Look at the picture," I said, gently.

She looked at the picture again. "But that's a picture of my father and me." Looking at it in greater detail, she says "At Scoma's, but when?"

26

"Lauren, maybe you answered my question about the Cliff House, and Scoma's, but you still need to tell me what you want aside from some vague retribution for something that happened before you were born. Also, you need to tell me how your father happened to tell you about me."

She was too absorbed in memory to answer. Instead she mused "It was last year, I came here with my father when he was teaching a seminar at the University. We ate here and then left for the airport. If only my father hadn't taken the detour up to Twin Peaks. He always loved the view of the city from there, and tried to re-visit it each time he got the chance. The road there is very narrow and winding. That's where the accident happened."

"Let's leave that for a minute. Who are the others in the photo? I asked.

"I don't remember. Where did you get this?"

"Tell me about the horse."

"What do you mean: What about the horse?'

"Did you take it?"

"I will say that it is a very nice horse, but…now wait a minute. You think that I took your horse? Did someone steal it?"

"OK I will play along with you. Yes, Lauren, it was gone. I went to pick up the bag, and the horse was missing. In its place was this picture in a silver frame. The note was on the back."

I look at her. Whichever her role: distressed innocent or accomplished actress, I am starting to lose my patience. "OK, if you don't want to tell me about the horse, then what about the man who was at the restaurant this morning, Was that Froehlich?"

"No, I thought that you knew. That was Daniel Towson."

'Towson! But he's…not around anymore." I finish lamely.

"But you met with him," she accused. "And now you say that you don't know him?"

"My meeting with him was anything but planned, at least on my part – tell me about him."

"I really don't know much. My father knew him and I don't think he liked him very much, although I really don't know why. I think he knew Towson from the War. Anyway, shortly after my father died, I received a visit from him. He just appeared one morning at my door and told me that he was friends with my father. I wasn't in the mood to receive visitors. But he was insistent that he wanted to be sure that I was getting on all right. I told Towson that I was not feeling well. He gave me his card and told me to call if I should ever feel the need to talk to someone."

"And this was..."

"Almost a month after my father died."

"In Albuquerque."

"Yes."

"Why did you wait all these months to follow up?"

"I told you. My father's note was delivered to me only a week or so ago. Maybe it was something my father wished, to give me time to adjust to his loss. I really don't know."

"Would it surprise you that earlier this evening, the man in this picture was identified as Daniel Towson?"

"What? That's ridiculous. I told you, it is my father and me having dinner at Scoma's. Who said it was Towson?"

"First, let me ask you a question."

"All right"

"You told me that you had to leave the museum for an appointment, but actually were met there by two people and drove off in a car that belongs to Towson."

"No, that's not what happened at all. Yes I had an appointment and yes, I was met by two men at the museum, but that wasn't planned. Just as I was leaving, these two men came up to me and warned me about digging into my father's death. Simon, I am really scared."

"Lauren, you are making it very difficult for me. I can't help you if you are not prepared to tell me the truth." I waited for a long moment, and then turned to walk away.

"Simon, please wait." I turned back and she looked so forlorn that I realize she is having a hard time coming to grips with whatever is behind this.

"Why don't you start by telling me about the two men who forced you into the car this afternoon?"

"Simon, that's ridiculous. I just told you. I was leaving the museum for my appointment at the bank, when these two men came up to me and told

28

me that I had been seen with you, and that my father's work was none of my business, and I should leave well enough alone."

"Was there a specific threat made?"

"No, just a strong suggestion that I go home and drop it."

"You said that you thought this Dr. Froehlich stole your father's invention and then maybe had him killed. Tell me about that."

The evening was getting colder and a salty breeze started to grow from across the plaza. Lauren shivered. "I think that maybe it's Froehlich."

"Give me one reason that I should believe you."

"Simon, I really am scared. Please help me."

I took her arm. Obviously, she wasn't going to answer my questions right away, so I guided her back to Scoma's where we had left our cars. She asked me to follow her to her hotel, where she parked in the garage and then came back out to where I was sitting in the car, waiting. Just as she got in, a large black sedan ripping down Bay St swerved towards us. There was brief crump as the sedan turned into us, straightened and then took off towards the Embarcadero. It was over in an instant and the street went quiet again. Lauren turned her white face towards me. I made up my mind and drove, making several random turns while I watch keenly through the mirror for any tail. There was no one following.

The light in my garage comes on as the door opens. The damage from the collision is relatively minor, fortunately.

"You are staying here tonight. Would you like a drink or bed? The guest room is up two flights in the front of the house. You will find a robe, some pajamas in the dresser and a hot bath if that is your preference."

"Thank you, Would you mind? I really am worn out. I promise that I will answer your questions in the morning."

In the front room, I can hear her footsteps on the floor above, moving between the bedroom and the bath. I pick up the mail that had been pushed through the door slot and dump it in a basket on the reception desk, for tomorrow.

My bed calls to me, so I take a small glass of brandy and head upstairs. Before I sleep, my thoughts whirl between truths and lies, bad guys and good guys, and those that could be both. I think that of all the people I met today, Edith Towson strikes me as the only true innocent. I hope that this bears out in the days to come. But what should I do? You never know when a client first tells you a story, how much is put out there to gain your sympathy, and how much really happened. But first I have to figure out if Lauren is going to be a client, or an adventure. The best that I can come up with is that I will work on this tomorrow

.

# 2 FRIDAY - SAN FRANCISCO

The brandy in the glass from the night before glows in the morning sunlight. I barely tasted it when I fell deeply asleep.

Although the house was quiet, I suddenly remembered that Lauren was in residence so I put on a robe to cover my nakedness. Stopping for a quick hair and tooth brush, I stepped into my old sandals and padded down the stairs to the kitchen.

"I found the coffee" says Lauren from the pantry doorway as she walks into the kitchen in a matching robe and bare feet. She seemed much smaller in the robe; it almost made a double circle around her slim waist. With it so tight, there was little showing above except for her chin. But her hair had been brushed, and it shone in the sun. "I can't find anything but Special K. Do you have any muffins or toast?"

"In the freezer," I reply, shifting gears from staring at her hair.

She crosses in front of me in a bee line for the refrigerator. A healthy clean scent follows her. I moved into the pantry and dug out marmalade, a wedge of cheddar, and a grapefruit, which I halve at the counter. She returns with a couple of English muffins which she put in the microwave to defrost and then retrieved butter and milk from the fridge.

"Thank you, Simon. I really was a wreck last night and really appreciate your hospitality."

"Just pour me some coffee and leave it black if you please." I felt the need to keep her at arm's length. "The cups are..."

"Yes, I found them. Go to the table. I set it out in the bay window."

After a minute, the muffins defrost and she pops them efficiently into the pre-warmed oven, slices the cheddar thinly, and finds a saucer for the marmalade pot. We move to the table. I take a swallow of my coffee and slather butter on the muffin. Tomorrow I will cut back on the butter, but not today.

"Lauren, you talked a lot about your father's problems last night. Not to be crass, but your father is beyond help. Tell me more about yourself. How

31

about your starting somewhere at the beginning. I really would like to understand more about Lauren Sylfern. Last night, that car was not just passing by, it was intentional. Before I get any deeper, I really need some background."

Settling herself into the chair and pushing the muffin plate away, she absently picks up a few crumbs from the table, pushes them into a tiny pile and then spreads them out again. "About two weeks after my father died, I was visited by two men who identified themselves as Government Agents. They said my father had worked on a number of sensitive projects during his tenure at Los Alamos National Laboratories, and they needed to be sure that nothing of a classified nature was in the house. I didn't have much choice in letting them into the house, but as they searched I stopped one of them and asked to see his I.D. again. He brushed me off and continued with their search. I thought that their credentials came from the National Security Agency (NSA), so I called my office in Washington and asked a colleague to see if he could check with the NSA and verify that they had sent agents to my home."

"I was told that any information about the NSA was above my pay grade, so I should just cooperate. The agents left after about 20 minutes, taking a small package which appeared to be my father's computer hard drive. They offered me a receipt for it and I took it. A couple of minutes after they left, one came back and said he had left his notebook on my father's desk. I didn't think much of it, but after he left for the second time, I went into the office and found that the receipt was also taken. I'll tell you, Simon, it was really strange. They were polite and efficient, yet I felt intimidated, though it was nothing I can specifically put my finger on."

"Lauren, that is tactic that all agents are all taught early. Never give a suspect a chance to think up an excuse or a defense. But for you, maybe it was just the idea of strangers invading your home and disturbing your father's office,"

"I guess that is it, but I definitely got the feeling that they were after something beyond classified files."

"Did you ever verify their identities?"

"No, but I think that in the flurry and distractions that followed my father's death, I had more important things to occupy my mind."

"Did they ever come back?"

"No. It was only that one time."

"Anything else?" I asked as she got up and poured us some more coffee.

"Yes, one more thing," she related. "The same afternoon after the two agents took my father's computer drive, I received a call. It was a voice that seemed familiar to me, but identified itself as being an Agent Frederickson of the FBI. He told me that my father's work was very important to the security of the country, and that anything that I knew about it I should never discuss with anyone. He told me that I would be under surveillance for a very long time and that I would suffer the same fate as anyone else that threatened the US under the Patriot's Act."

"Did you check on Frederickson?"

"No but what he said certainly scared me."

"OK, so let me understand. Your father was a scientist and he worked on secrets at Los Alamos. He died and you were warned to keep a wrap on anything you might know. Is that it?"

"Well, if you put it that way, I guess it sounds reasonable. But I don't understand how Towson fits into this? And why did you meet him at the Cliff House?"

"Before we get into that, I need to know the rest of your story. What exactly is your job at State?"

"I work as a liaison between the State Department and the Commerce Department. It is an innocent enough group that is involved with the movement of technology between public and private entities. In short, we research buyers of government technology and also do the same for sellers to the government of new technology that can be modified for government operations. We also verify and grant export licenses for private technology. In my job, I work with a group of both researchers and military specialists that protect both ends of the information exchange."

"And what exactly do you do for this group?"

"It really isn't important. I am just another grunt in the office."

She still had not answered my fundamental question. "So once again, what do you want from me?"

Lauren stopped playing with her muffin crumbs on the counter and looked up to me. "I need some help with finding out what happened to my father. I also need some protection. If I am right about being watched, I am worried about what 'they' might do to me."

"Well, the second issue is simple. Go back home and then to work. The chances are that if you act as if nothing is wrong, nothing will go wrong. And for the first, forget about your father's business. Whatever happened is done. If the police are finished with the case, you might stir up a hornet's nest with an inquiry. Also, it may be expensive. You said your father died in an accident?"

"Yes. My father was driving and we skidded on the road, I fell out of the car and the car went down into a gully. I must have been out for a while. By the time I came to, my father was dead. I left the car and tried to find some help, and eventually made it back to my hotel. He had been talking about Froehlich when he lost control of the car, so after it happened, and I was trying to cope with the accident and his death, I lied to the police and said nothing about being in the car. I believe they thought I had been there, but I suppose that they took pity on me and stopped asking me questions.

"Do you think that the accident was set up?"

"I don't know for sure, but it could have."

"Let's assume, for a minute, that it wasn't an accident. Do you think that someone wanted him dead?"

"Well, there is Froehlich…"

"What about his work. Was he working on something that presented a danger to someone, or that someone could gain from by his death?"

"No, or at least I don't think so. But if they are watching me even now, after all this time, there's got to be some reason. I never thought it had anything to do with me, but maybe it is something that I don't know is important, or maybe someone thinks I might know something."

She is probably being paranoid, and I'd best stay out of it. "Lauren, I am a P.I. and I find missing people, help gather evidence on others, and try to stay out of anything more important than injured egos. I don't think I can help you. Even the incident with the car last night, in the cold light of day, I would say it was a coincidence. Let me ask you something. How much digging have you done on this Froehlich?"

"Well, I did some research at the office and later at home."

"Did you search public sources, or use your government channels?"

"Both."

"That's probably it. If Froehlich is that important to U.S. Security, you probably triggered an alarm at one of the agencies, which led to your encounter at the museum. I would take the warning seriously and drop it."

She seemed to deflate for a minute, then disappears into the guest room, reappearing carrying her cream suit. "Do you have an iron?" she asks.

34

"Yes, it's in the little closet behind the guest bath door."

While she busies herself, I thought about her story. For me, the problem is whether there is any connection between Lauren, Towson and the key. Since Towson and Lauren appeared almost simultaneously, there might be one. Besides, she really gets under my skin. So maybe I'll do a little checking before totally breaking it off.

My old office shared facilities at Ft. Myer in Washington with a variety of information-based agencies and a few consulting firms. I decide to call in a favor, and dial the number which I'd hardly forget, namely my former partner's office.

"Commander Carson," the familiar voice answers.

"Hello Jim"

"Simon; where the hell did you spring from?"

"I'm still in San Francisco. Jim, I wonder if you've got a minute to give me a hand."

"I'm really surprised that you, of all people, are asking me, particularly after you left me flat and then no word for three years. You know, not all of us spend our time lolling on the beach,"

"Jim, you know that I wouldn't ask unless it was important."

"Important to whom?"

"Jim, I am not going to snow you. I don't have access to the kind of personnel files that you do, and I need some background to help me decide to take a case or not."

"Who's the client?"

"Jim, I can't tell you that. But I can say that she  ..."

"Of course, it had to be a broad."

"Jim. She says that she's in trouble, but I don't know how serious. There are four people who come up in her story, and I need to find out about them. Two of them work for the government, one used to. Can you help?"

"Four, no less; Ok let me have them, this squares us for Tokyo."

Immediately, I flashed back to a back alley next to Shinjuku Station, where we had crossed a cell of the Yakuza syndicate who were trading Afghanistan opium for U.S. Naval secrets. We had been following a gang member from our embassy onto the Manunouchi Line to Shinjuku Station, where he jumped off at the last minute and tried to lose us inside this huge node on the Japan National Railways system. He ducked out a service exit and was about to meet his contact in the alley when three yakuza spotted Jim where we were hiding and opened fire with automatic weapons. Jim was pinned in a doorway while rounds chipped away at his hidey-hole. I climbed an outside stair to a second floor perch, where I was able to spot and then pick off two of the gang before the third fled. As the last guy took off, however, he put a round through the right eye of our pigeon, breaking the one thread we might have kept to the gang. Jim came through with just a few cuts from flying brick shards. So yes, he owed me.

In five seconds, the competition was back. I am so glad that I am out of that crap. But I do need Jim's help so I play along. "Thanks. But I may need more in the future, so I'll introduce you to a UC Berkeley girl the next time you come to town. I assume that's still your taste."

"Only if she's a Phys. Ed. major. All right, who's on the list?"

"First is Lauren Sylfern, next is Daniel Towson, then Ernst Zilbern and last Johann Froehlich."

"Froehlich? Are you in fast company! Is this the same Froehlich that works at the White House and is worth a gazillion dollars?"

"You tell me, Jim. On Froehlich, I don't really need to know a lot, just a brief summary of recent activities."

"You know that he's tied to a number of National Security programs, so the minute I tap his file, bells will start ringing over at NSA."

"OK, I don't want you to get into any trouble. If you would just help me out with the other three, it would be terrific."

"When do you need this?"

"I really need Sylfern and Towson soon. Could you call me with the two and then hold on Zilbern and Froehlich until we can get together?"

"Are you planning to come here any particular day next week?"

"Sure, let's plan on Tuesday. I will give you a firm time when you call back. Thanks, Jim."

"Simon, a word in your shell like ear. The Admiral wasn't very happy when you dropped out. He doesn't ever say anything, but the word is that your name is not to be mentioned in the office."

"Yeah, well I didn't have much choice. How is our favorite sea dog?"

"Ornery as hell, as usual. I hope you don't expect me to give him your regards?"

"No, I agree that wouldn't be a good idea. Jim, please call me as soon as you can."

Jim and I came into the office at almost the same time. Both of us came from the Navy Fleet. When I finished my SEAL BUD/S and SQT training, was awarded my Trident and assigned to the Teams, as much as I enjoyed the physical challenge, I wasn't sure that this form of Special Operations was something that would keep me going long-term. Initially, I had been slated to Team 4 in Little Creek, but I expressed interest in, and was eventually offered a place with Naval Intelligence. After a training tour, I met Admiral Lewis, who was putting together a special group which I joined. Jim, from his first day, looked to command. He had some good support at the NSA and was looking to rotate back there when he ascended at least one more notch in his drive to flag. He wasn't a bad partner, just ambitious. But maybe I too could be considered to have a similar M.O. during those days. It wasn't until my wife died and I had to get out. Well, I'll just wait for his call. Jim worked fast, so I guess it wouldn't be more than a half-hour or so.

It was still early, but I thought that I would like to verify one other bit of information. I called Directory Assistance and asked for the telephone number of Daniel Towson. There was no listing, but there was one for an Edith Towson on Vallejo. Taking the number and writing it on a pad next to the kitchen telephone, I dialed it.

"Hello" answered the voice I remembered from the house last night.

"Good morning. I am sorry if it's early, it's Simon Chess. I dropped by your home last evening."

"Oh yes, Mr. Chess." The woman recognized, but did not seem overjoyed to get my call.

"I wonder if it would too great an imposition for me to ask you one additional question concerning your husband."

"Very well, but please understand that this is quite disturbing to me, so please limit it to one question."

"Did you have to identify your husband's body after the accident?"

"What an impertinent question," she charged. "I told you last night that the car went into the bay and was badly crushed. I was shown his wallet, watch, and wedding ring. And yes, they offered to show me his remains, but I had no desire to see him like that. So the answer is no, not exactly."

"Thank you. You have put up with me enough and have only one more small question."

"Very well, but this will have to be the last."

"Do you know if your husband had any dealings with either Ernst Zilbern or Johann Froehlich?"

"Why ever would you want to know that? My husband dealt with many people in his business. I know who Johann Froehlich is, and it is very possible that my husband did know him, but whether or not they worked together, I can't say. My husband was an Industrialist; he had many associates in various ventures. As far as Zilbern, I don't think so. Who is he?"

"He is, or rather was a scientist at Los Alamos, in New Mexico."

"No I don't think that he ever worked with people over there. Mr. Chess, My husband was primarily in the import-export business. Some of the products that he dealt with involved governmental licensing and military support. Anyone in that field probably knew Daniel. But I can't ever remember him mentioning either gentleman. I'm sorry, but I can't help you. Does this have anything to do with his death?"

"Thank you. I don't think so, but there are a few coincidences about when and how he died that I need to clear up before I can answer that question. You have been very patient with me. I won't bother you again."

"Do you think that my original suspicions were correct concerning my husband's accident?"

"Right now, I don't know what to think. But I can say that I will certainly let you know if I find out something."

"I take it you are going to keep looking."

"Yes, I am." I suppose that in spite of Lauren's inconsistencies with her story and a few fibs thrown in for good measure, I will help her. Why the hell does she have to be so damn attractive?

"Mr. Chess, I am sorry for being so abrupt with you. Your appearance with the picture took me by surprise. I was not convinced of the facts as told to me after the accident. I may be old, but I am certainly not feeble, and I am extremely well connected as well. If you can find out the truth about Daniel's death, I would be most appreciative."

"Thank you. I will keep that in mind." She is one tough bird, I will say that.

"Simon," Lauren called from kitchen. "Where are you?"

"In the office."

She comes into my office and glances around. "What a dismal little room. Simon, you really need to get a decorator up here."

I grunted. She was right, but I like it this way.

"So what are you going to do now?" I asked.

"I was hoping that you had an idea. Could we do whatever we do together?"

"Well, I need to take care of a few things, so why don't you wait here while I do some errands. There are a bunch of books downstairs, and my assistant, Stephanie should be arriving soon."

There was a noise from downstairs. "There she is now. Come down and meet her."

As I come down the stairs with Lauren behind me, Stephanie passes into the Reception room.

"Hi Stephanie" I call out.

"H; Oh you have company."

"Yes. Please meet Lauren Sylfern, a new possible client. Lauren, this is Stephanie Zalinski, my office manager.

"Well it's always good to meet a new client, especially early in the morning." Stephanie said coyly as she glanced at her watch. "Did you make coffee?"

"Yes, I enlisted Lauren's help as it was early when she arrived."

"So what's the problem?" asked Stephanie.

""I'll fill you in later," I interjected. "Steph, would you see what you can find about a Daniel Towson of San Francisco? Lauren and I will be up in the office."

We return upstairs again and just settled in my office when the doorbell rings and I can hear Stephanie walk over to answer it.

A man's voice asked for me.

"Do you have an appointment?" she asked.

"He'll see us." I could hear the door being pushed open and footsteps clomped about on the floor below.

"You'll have to wait down here," Steph said, raising her voice in some alarm. "Please wait here, NO, don't go upstairs."

There was a muffled sound, and a thud, and the footsteps sound on the stair.

The door to my office was open and its frame fills with two men dressed in dark suits. They look a lot like the same two thugs that I met at the Cliff House yesterday, but I couldn't be sure.

"What do you want?"

"Don't be stupid" the larger of the men exclaims." Just hand it over."

I try to keep my face as bland as possible. "I told your boss before; I really don't know what you are talking about."

Lauren suddenly jumped up. "I know you. You came to my house."

One grabs her by her arms. I started to reach for my side desk drawer where I kept the Glock. "Hold it right there" the other says, as he produces a large black pistol, which he points in my general direction.

"Lauren, please stay still."

Lauren stops struggling and said, "Simon, these are the two men who took my father's things."

"Who are you?" I ask. "Let me see some ID."

"We're government agents. Just move down the stairs. Do it now."

I drop my hand and start to push my chair back. "Slowly," the man says to me. I turn my back and walk towards the stair. I can feel the breath of the guy behind me, as he follows closely. This is not good cop-craft. When I reach midway down the stair, I stop abruptly so he falls into me. I reach between my legs, grab his crotch and squeeze hard. He yells instinctively and tries to grab my hand. I shift to his ankle, levering it up through my legs. Down he goes on his back, his arms flying up toward the ceiling. His hand with the gun points up at the ceiling. I spin slightly to one side, step over his arms and chop at his wrist, striking the radial nerve to briefly paralyze his hand. Grabbing the hand, I twist it backwards and free the pistol, while stepping sideways to shift my weight, letting him slide down the stair on his back. The treads catch him and spin him around on his slide until he hits the newel post with his head. The one behind Lauren was trying to free his gun from inside his jacket when Lauren suddenly stomps down on his instep, crunching the metatarsal and causing immediate excruciating pain to radiate up his leg. His gun catches inside his pocket as I take two steps up the stairs and shove Lauren to the side, ramming the heel of my hand into the bottom of his nose, breaking it. The blood spurts from his broken nose as he finally clears the gun from his pocket. As it starts to swing up at me, I remember the lesson 'foot trumps fist.' Grabbing the railing I launch my feet into his face, right to his smashed nose. He falls back onto the stair and the gun drops from his hand to clatter down the steps.

I run down the remaining steps and pick up the gun which had lodged against his partner's body. With the safety released. I point it up the stairs. Lauren recovers her footing and looks back to check on the one she hurt. The man is moaning and holding his face, all the fight having left him. She turns back to me and exclaims breathlessly "You sure treat your guests roughly."

I ignore her for a moment. From downstairs, Stephanie calls out "Simon, are you OK?"

I am still breathing hard when I answer "So far."

The gunman at the bottom of the stair isn't moving. The one above me continues to moan. I pull him upright by his lapels.

"Now, let's see some ID." I dig out his thin credentials case, and flip it open.

'National Security Agency' with an eagle in a blue field stares prominently from the middle of the plastic card, together with a photo and the name 'Walter Morris.' Below the name is printed 'Central Security Service.'

"It looks like genuine NSA," I said to Lauren.

'But why the gun?' I think to myself. From my experience, the NSA guys are not usually cowboys.

"What are we going to do?" said Lauren.

I slip the two credentials into my pocket and check on the other one. Reaching out, I feel his pulse; strong and regular." Just out for a bit," I say to no one in particular.

"Lauren, until we can clear this up, I think we need to get scarce."

Stephanie is standing by the stair. "Steph, give us a few minutes. Then call the police and report a break-in." I reached into the downed agent's pocket and slipped out his ID which I pocket. "I will take both of these. If the police ask where I've gone, say that I went to make a report at the local station." Then I replace the man's gun in his coat pocket and lead Lauren out the back door.

Once outside, I scan for backup, and not seeing anyone, I flash out to the rear street barely slowing at the corner for oncoming traffic. We can't go to the police. It would very difficult to explain what I was doing attacking two armed government agents.

We rocket up to the top of the hill and turn towards the center of the city. "Best to be in a crowded place" I explain to Lauren. At Mt Marcy Park, old people are practicing Tai Chi in the plaza. Taking a table behind one of the potted trees, I pull out the IDs.

"I still don't understand the guns."

Nothing appears to be unusual. Along the side of the plastic card, hidden by the holder, is a bar code, with a magnetic strip just below it. The magnetic strip is less than 1/16" wide, and would be all but invisible, had it not been for the bright sunlight. I assume that the card doubles as a door entry. The bar code probably wouldn't yield more than a name and ID number. But you never can tell. These days, an awful lot of information can be coded into such a strip.

"What key were they asking about?" asked Lauren.

"I don't know. I suppose it has to do with that Towson fellow who brought me to the Cliff House. He asked me to return a key which I don't have." I looked blandly at her.

"A key?" She asked. "What kind of key?"

"I have no idea. I think that they got me mixed up with someone else."

"What has the NSA to do with Towson or this key?"

"Who knows? But we have to find out. I don't want any more NSA folks coming around. Lauren, do you have a cell phone?"

"What kind of question is that? Everyone has a cell."

"Not me," I retort. "There are times I really like my privacy."

She opens her purse and takes out the phone. Flipping it open, I punch in the number for my office. Stephanie picks it up after two rings.

"Oh Simon, the police came and took both men away. One of the cops is upstairs, taking photos. A second car arrived and they're all upstairs. They said that they hoped to meet you at the local station. What should I do?"

"Stay cool. Did you get a call from Jim Carson?"

"Yes, he left a number for you to call back."

"Thanks, Steph. I'll call you later" She started to say "Wait" as I closed the telephone.

I re-open the phone, and dial the number Steph had given me. Carson answered immediately. "Simon, what have you gotten yourself into?"

"Why do you ask?" I replied

"The NSA has been here like flies on a carcass. They wanted to know if I knew where you were and why you called me. Hey, I really don't want to be dragged into anything. What's going on?"

"Jim, I really don't know myself. Do you have any of the information that I asked about"

"Yes and no. I have some material but I can't send it to you. Can you come get it?"

"Yes, I will. Let's meet tomorrow morning. Can you get out to our favorite hidey hole?" I was referring to a grungy coffee bar in Arlington.

"I have more control here at the office. Why don't you come here, say about 9 or so?"

The thought of going back to the "Office" stirs too many unpleasant thoughts. But Jim is helping me so I'll deal with it. We agree on the time.

"Simon," he says, "Keep me out of this. NSA isn't like the Fibbies; they just love invading privacy."

"Thanks, Jim. This is important, or I wouldn't ask."

I close up the phone and hand it back to Lauren. "Now how about some straight answers?"

"Simon, what do you mean?"

"Are you sure they are the same ones that took your father's things?"

"Well, they looked like the same men. At least, I think so."

"And what do you know about your father's death that you aren't telling me?"

"I never accepted it as accidental. I know that Froehlich stole inventions from my father and my father knew about Froehlich's betrayal to the Germans. With the kind of position that Froehlich has, the information my father had could undermine his credibility and bring him down. Also, I

43

suspect that Froehlich knew about some new work that my father was working on and probably decided to take him out and steal his secrets again."

"But what's the connection to Towson?"

"I'm sorry I didn't tell you about him when you first asked. He scares me. Towson is an arms dealer and a thug. I wouldn't put it past Froehlich to use Towson to get at dad, or me either."

"Lauren, are you sure that it was Towson that you saw at the Cliff House?"

"Oh yes. I remember him from my last encounter. But at that time, he was acting very kind. I just didn't recognize it as an act."

"Would it interest you to know that Edith Towson, who I met yesterday evening before coming to the restaurant, told me that Towson died at about the same time as your father? She also identified him in the photo from Scoma's."

"Are you sure?"

"Yes, absolutely; it upset her very much, and I believe her."

"Simon, I wouldn't lie to you about that. I don't remember him at the dinner."

"Do you know Edith Towson?"

"I've never met her."

"Why do you think that she would tell me almost the identical story about her husband that you told me about your father?"

"I don't know. Maybe she is confused."

"I think we should go together to her house and see who is confused. But meantime, tell me again exactly what happened last year."

"I told you. My father came out here for a meeting, and I came with him. I traveled with him a lot to meetings like that. When I was a child, my mother would go with him, but then she got sick and died. My father seemed so lonely that he would take me for company. Most of the time, I was not invited into the actual meetings, but I always went so my father and I could spend time together. Our visit here was no different, except that my father was upset about something. I know that he had tried to get a passport and couldn't because his work involved National Security. But I think there was more to it than that. I remember that after the meeting, we all went to Scoma's. There was my father, Alattin and a few of other men;

44

I think they ran software companies. Anyway, we went to the restaurant together, but then we had to leave because my father was due back at the lab the following morning. Alattin and the others stayed at the restaurant. My father decided to take a detour to Twin Peaks, like I told you. I argued with him, but he was determined. Then there was a fence and I was out of the car on the ground, with the car down in the trees. I went back to the car, but it was burning, and my father was still inside. There was nothing I could do. I ran away. Oh, Simon, maybe I could have done something but I was so scared." I could see tears starting up again, but this was no time for sympathy.

"Who is Aladdin?"

"No, it is Alattin, with two 'T's. Alattin Akan is a friend of my father's from the lab. Actually, he is a friend of mine as well. He is not much older than I am and a very brilliant mathematician that worked with my father on some of his cryptology developments. He comes from Turkey."

"Lauren, I need to make reservations to get to Washington."

"I'm going too," Lauren said. I search her face for a motive, but then nod and call U.S Airways to book two seats on the evening flight.

"You know; you really should get yourself one of these," commented Lauren as she returns the phone to her purse.

I grunt and then say, "Ok, we're on for tonight. Meantime, let's go back to the museum see if we can find out more about who might have taken the horse."

We drive to the museum across town. It had just opened. Inside at the desk, I ask for the manager. In a couple of minutes, we are ushered into his office.

"Good morning" I say. "Yesterday afternoon, we were here looking at your collection. I checked a package in your checkroom, and when we retrieved it, something was missing from it."

"Did you report it?" he asks.

"Only to the guard."

"Just a minute, let's get the attendant in. He picks up the telephone and dials, asks for the check room attendant. "I'm very sorry sir; we have had no problems with our checkroom before. Can you tell me what was taken?"

"Yes, it was a large wooden horse sculpture, not terribly expensive, but a personal memento. I had just purchased it in Gump's, and checked the bag."

"Of course, sir, please just wait a moment." In another minute, there is a knock on the door and in comes the Cloakroom attendant that I had seen the previous day. She was small and obviously Hispanic, but very young. "Rita," the manager says, "This gentleman claims he left something with you that seems to have gone missing. Do you know anything about it?"

"Yes sir. I mean, no sir. Just as I told you yesterday" she turns to me, "the shopping bag was still here and I don't think anyone touched it. Oh wait," pointing at Lauren. "You were there too. You gave me a paper to put in the bag. Remember sir, you took the bag later."

The manager turns to me "We can call the police if you like. What was the value of the missing item?"

"But sir" adds the now frightened attendant, "Oh sir, I am so sorry. I was told to say that nobody touched it if you came back. Please, sir, I thought it was a joke. I really didn't think I was doing anything wrong." Tears start forming at the corners of her dark eyes.

"Rita, please tell me exactly what happened," the manager asked gently. "If it is as you say, there won't be any trouble."

"Oh I don't know what I am going to do. There was a man; a young man, very good looking, who came into the museum right after you. He said that it was your birthday, and that he was a friend of yours. Mr. Chess, right?" I nodded. "Well sir, he gave me a picture in a silver frame and asked me to put it in your shopping bag and give him the horse. He told me that you were a good friend of his, and he was playing a practical joke on you."

"What did this man look like?" I ask.

"He was young, and tall, but not so old. Oh, sir. I didn't mean that you look old. But he was much younger than you and he laughed when he talked to me. He is a very nice looking man, and I thought that he couldn't be telling me a lie."

"But what about the horse?" I ask.

"Oh sir, he gave me $20 said he would borrow the horse and give it back to you at dinner. Oh, and he told me that you might be a little upset, but that it would be all right. He said it was only a little prank. He wrote a note to you on the back of the picture."

"Rita, you have to understand that the museum trusts you to care for people's possessions, and you did wrong. Please go back to your job and we will speak about this later." The manager opens the door and the tearful girl runs out of the room, sobbing. He looks back at me "I'm so sorry sir. If you will fill out a form, we will take full responsibility for your loss and refund the value of your horse. And please accept my apology for the inconvenience."

"No need. I will get my horse back. Thank you for clearing up the mystery."

As we left the museum, I used Lauren's phone once more to call Stephanie.

"Oh boss, the police just left, and I looked through your office. Nothing seems to be missing or disturbed. Also, I researched Daniel Towson, and found that both the Chronicle and the Examiner reported him killed in an auto accident last year. His survivor is his wife, Edith. Would you like the address?"

"No, I've met the lady. Did the paper tell you anything about what he did?"

"Yes, he owned Turkish-American Import-Export, Ltd. a holding company that is based in Greece."

"Stephanie, would you see what you can find out about Towson's wife? Also, there's a fellow by the name of Wayne Hudson, who works at the Cliff House Restaurant? I have Lauren's telephone with us. I need to get to Washington to meet with folks at my old office who have some new information for me. Please call me when you learn anything."

"What about the police?"

"If they call or come by again, tell them that you haven't heard from me and don't know where I might be."

By Towson's house, I stop Lauren from getting out. "Lauren, would you mind waiting while I speak to Edith Towson privately before we have a confrontation. It won't take long."

In the daylight, the house looks quietly elegant. The bell double clang is almost mournful. No one comes to the door. I walk around toward the back. A gardener is pruning some bushes by a gazebo. He looks up as I approach. "Buenos Dias, Señor. Lo siento; La Señora no está aquí."

I switch to my halting Spanish and inquire if the Mrs. Towson is expected back, to which the gardener shrugs and says that he comes each day and

47

gets instructions on what to do, but no one was there when he arrived this morning.

I thank him and return to the front. I try the door and am surprised that it is unlocked. I carefully step inside and close the door behind me. There is no sound but the clock ticking slowly in the front hall. The place appears to be empty. Walking softly back into the kitchen area I see that it is spotless, no pots, no dirty dishes, and no evidence of any food preparation. Finally I return to the front of the main stair and call upstairs. But there is no answer. I start up the stair just as the telephone begins to ring. It rings 8 times and then stops. I guess there is no answering machine, or it is turned off.

At the top of the stairs is a cross hall which has several doors leading to bedrooms, I suppose. Near one end, an open door looks into a central bathroom. Across from the bathroom is a double door. I am fairly certain that this must be the Master Bedroom. I turn the knob and push against the door. The room is shaped like an "L" with a sitting area at one end, and the sleeping area along the long side. A door from the sitting area leads to a large walk-in closet, which appears to have been divided into a men's area and a women's area with drawers and cupboards between. Even though she had told me that her husband was dead for more than a year, his side of the closet still was full of clothes, as if she was waiting for his imminent return. Out of the closet, the facing door apparently leads to the Master Bath as well as back to the hall. I open the bathroom door.

Edith Towson was indeed home, but not taking callers. She was draped across the lip of the large stall shower, her hands stretched out on the floor. Her head was thrown back and dark blood had run out of a neat hole in her skull to pool on the marble floor. She was nude, and there was a bar of beauty soap next to her inside the stall.

I looked around. The room is spotless. Whoever did it had carefully closed the shower faucets, wiped them clean, mopped up any water, removed any towels except for some clean ones stacked across the room on a heater-rack, and departed as he entered, closing the door and removing any traces of his presence. Poor Edith, she seemed an innocent. I wonder why she was killed.

I leave everything as it is and return to the bedroom to search for any helpful information. There is nothing in the end table drawers or the small desk in the sitting area. The closet is also totally devoid of material: No passport, no letters, no files, and no personal trivia of any sort.

48

Returning downstairs I look in the library and through it into a small office. This must have been Mr. Towson's home office. But it too is empty. It was like a stage set, ready for the curtain to go up.

I opened the front door carefully and peek out. There seemed to be no one in sight. As I walk down the portico stairs, the gardener calls out "Wait, Señor." He must have left his chores and come around the corner of the house as I came out. I ignore his call and keep going back to the car, where Lauren is waiting patiently. The gardener peers at the back of the car as we exit the driveway. I cannot remember if I had closed the front door of the house or not. But I thought that we had better make tracks if he goes in and finds Edith.

Lauren turned to me "What did you find out from Edith Towson?"

"Nothing; Let me ask you something. Are you sure that you never met her?"

"No, what makes you ask that?"

I pull the car over to the side of the road and stop. Looking at her square in the face I tell her "She was dead, shot in the head."

There are very few cars on the street. The seconds moved by very slowly. But Lauren seems to be in another place. I do not want to prompt her so I just wait to break through into today's moment. Lauren stares at me but no tears, no outward emotion of any kind. "Did you see who did it?"

"No." I start the car again and we drive down the hill towards the Convention Center, and then City Hall. Lauren's telephone rings. But she doesn't answer, instead she flips the face open and says "It's your office" and hands me the telephone.

"Steph?"

"Simon. Please, you need to contact the police. They called here twice looking for you – a Lt. Jurgens from Central." She reads me a telephone number and I take a pen from the console and note it on a scrap of paper. "They told me that there was no trouble, but it was very important for you to show up, since they needed you to clear up the office incident."

I hang up the telephone. There was something gnawing at me. If it was Lauren's father in the car that went off the hill last year, why did Edith Towson claim it was her husband? Could it be that she didn't know that her husband was still alive and he wanted to conceal his existence by killing her? But why, and what has this to do with Lauren, or with me?

49

I think that I had better call Jurgens and see about the NSA incident. I borrow Lauren's phone again.

"Central, Sergeant Sweeney" the voice answered.

"Lieutenant Jurgens, please."

"Jurgens - Homicide" an aggressive voice answered.

"Lieutenant, this is Simon Chess."

"Chess - Yes, you need to come to my office right away."

"I'm sorry Lieutenant, but it really is not possible. Can you tell me what you need to know over the telephone?"

"Look Chess, this isn't a question of choice. I think you would want to come in rather than we come get you. Understand?"

"Lieutenant, I am certain that you are interested in my welfare, but..."

"Chess, I don't care what you think; if you want to avoid a charge, you'll come to my office, and do it now. Where are you?"

"As I said, I am unable to come right now, but if you will just tell me what the charge might be, I will contact my attorney and we will both come to your office together."

"Listen to me. You are a licensed PI which means that if you don't cooperate with me right now, I'll pull your ticket and your days as a PI will be over. Get your butt over here."

"Lieutenant, I do want to cooperate with you, but I have left the city and won't be back for a couple of days."

"All right, so you want to play games. First there's an assault charge on two Federal Agents, which is a felony both here and in DC. Want more?"

"Lieutenant, two goons attacked me in my office. I had no way of knowing that they were agents."

"Chess, I'm sure you can clear this up, but you need to come in. I will expect your face here in 30 minutes or a BOLO (Be On the LookOut) will go out and you will be arrested on sight. Do yourself a favor and work with me, and I'm sure we can figure out a way to make this go away. Otherwise, it gets bumped up to the D.A. and then it's out of my control."

"Lieutenant, I really wish I could come in. By the way, if you're homicide, how come you got tapped for a simple assault case?"

"Chess, I want to make it easy for you. You've helped the police before and most reports I've got say you're a good stick. I'll give you 2 hours. After that, your ass is grass."

I re-call Stephanie. "I need to stall Jurgens when he calls again. I can't deal with him until I get back from Washington. Please tell him you don't know where I am and can't reach me because I don't have a cell phone. Both of us are now going directly to the airport. I should be back tomorrow or the next day. Did you find out anything about Wayne Hudson?"

"Other than his address, and the fact that he works part time for the Cliff House Restaurant, nothing, although before he worked there, he had a Charter Business. He ran tours and day fishing out of the marina. No record except when he was a juvenile."

I thought we might take a swing past his house again. When I ring the doorbell, a dog next door barks, but there is no one home. As it is approaching lunchtime, I thought we would swing by the Cliff House again, to see if he was at work. We needed some lunch anyway and if there was a connection to Towson, or whoever the Grey Man was, we might pick up something there.

Out to the coast, the weather was much clearer than the previous day, and all the street spaces are full, so we parked down the hill and walk up to the restaurant. Inside, all was normal – but no Hudson. At the reception desk I am told that he had not shown up that morning, and they had to call a substitute.

We ask for a table against the wall near the kitchen, and are rewarded by a strange look from the hostess, but she takes us to an empty area near the kitchen door and drops menus on our place-settings. After ordering, we sit back with glasses of Riesling and some sourdough bread and wait for lunch. Lauren had said nothing about the death of Edith Towson. Nor had she mentioned Wayne Hudson.

"Lauren, there are some issues that we need to get straight between us, if you want my help. First, if you lie to me, I won't take on your problem."

"Simon, I haven't lied to you. But you have to understand that this is very hard for me. My father was more than just a father, he was my best friend. I miss him terribly."

"Sure, I understand that. But you haven't been straight with me about Edith Towson."

"It's true that I don't know her, but I do know about her. Edith Towson knew my father and I think that they were in love many years ago. In those

51

days, her last name was Andros, and her father was in the Greek Resistance during the war. When my father was rescued by the Americans, they went to Cyprus before coming to the U.S. since there were some papers that had been smuggled out of the Soviet Union that he was asked to decode. My father told me a few years ago, when he got a call from her."

"So what happened?"

Well, my father, who was still quite young at the time, went to Cyprus with the Americans and met a group of the fighters. Remember, that the war was still going on, and the Greek Resistance was still waging a guerrilla war on the Germans. Dad was taken to Andros' house, where he stayed for a few days while he worked on the papers. It was at that time that he met and fell in love with Edith. When he finished his work – he never really told me much about it – he was evacuated to the U.S. and the Andros family stayed in Greece. The very first time that I ever heard her name was when she called our home in Albuquerque."

"So how did you meet Daniel Towson?"

"I told you the truth about Daniel Towson. I did meet him when he called on me after dad died. He asked me if my father ever solved the transcription that he was working on in Cyprus, but nothing more that I remember.

"Did he say anything about his wife and her old relationship with your father?"

"No."

"Yesterday, when I mentioned his name, you recoiled as if you were frightened of him. What was that about?"

"My father mentioned something about him being in league with Froehlich. I thought that you might be with them as well."

"Tell me more about the dinner on the night your father died. Do you remember anything that was odd or that bothered you?"

"No, there was some talk about my father's new work, but nothing unusual. You said that Edith Towson recognized her husband there, but not my father?"

"Yes. She was very shocked, because she also saw you in the picture, and had been told that a young woman had been in the car with her husband. Maybe she didn't recognize your father after all these years."

Lauren thought a moment. "I guess that is what happened, but it still is strange about the identity of the dead man. I wonder if she was covering for her husband and knew he was alive."

"I don't think so. It seems to me that she was still distraught over his death, and I don't think she was faking the tears."

"Simon, I'm sorry if I didn't tell you everything in the beginning. I still wasn't too sure of you. Why did you meet Towson here yesterday?"

I think that she's still holding back. "It was a case of mistaken assumptions. But it isn't important. The real question is what I asked you a few times already. What do you want from me?"

"I need to know the truth about my father's death. Also, I need to know why I am being watched and followed. If I am going to get on with my life, I need answers to these two questions first."

"Lauren, can you afford to hire a Private Investigator like me?"

"Yes, at least for a while. My father left me my house free and clear, and I have some savings from translation work that I do in addition to my work at State. My father did some computer security work consulting after my mother died and made good investments, so I have a nice nest egg. I could spend up to $50,000 on this investigation. Do you think that it will cost that much?"

"Nowhere near that, but no more lies, or I will drop the case."

"Agreed; so why Washington?"

"I have asked for some background research from my old Navy office. Listen, we can accomplish more if we work separately for now. If you are being watched, I would like you to keep as low a profile as possible. Go back to Albuquerque and dig through all your father's remaining files and papers. See if you can come up with anything that would have stimulated someone to take lethal action against him. I will join you there when I am finished in D.C."

Lauren agrees to my approach, although reluctantly. After lunch, we again drive past Hudson's house again, but there still was no answer to my ring.

"Stephanie," I said as I call, "Will you dig a bit deeper into Wayne Hudson? I learned at the restaurant that he only had a part-time job there. His house is far too costly for him to afford it. Can you find out if he works anyplace else as well?"

Before getting to the airport, we swung by the garage where Lauren had parked her car the night before. Just before getting out of the car, I voiced one additional nagging question. "You said last night that you had flown here to San Francisco to catch Froehlich. How is it that your car is not in New Mexico?"

"Oh Simon, this isn't my car, it's a rental. Don't you know you can rent almost anything these days? Really!" She took off. As I drive, I again I feel that peculiar sensation of being watched. I check the mirrors, but no car stood out. I thought I would drive an erratic pattern to draw out any tail. After several turns, I found myself nearer the Presidio and on a dead-end street. I stop next to a house in mid-block and look in my mirror. In about 10 seconds, only one car, a dark chocolate sedan passed on the street, but with the dark side windows, I couldn't tell who it was driving.

I back up and started down the short street. When I get to the "T" I picked up my original route. The feeling seemed to be going away. Lauren is waiting for me at the terminal.

"I thought you agreed to go straight to Albuquerque."

"Simon, I am still worried. What if they are waiting for me at home?"

"You shouldn't be in any danger. The important thing is for you to act natural, do your normal routine, and don't put out any disturbing waves. If anyone should ask, you consulted me on the issue of your father's death, and then returned home. You know nothing about any incident at my office. OK?"

"Will you call me when you are coming? I'll pick you up."

"See you then." As she goes to find United for an afternoon flight, I move up in line to pick up a boarding pass. It's too late for a direct flight, so I had to fly through L.A.

I know that at the Security point, sometimes there are alerts placed but usually the TSA agents are either too busy or untrained to follow through with any type of effective watch. I guess that Lieutenant Jurgens didn't follow through with a BOLO yet. Once through Security without a hitch, I settle down to wait for the flight.

# 3 *SATURDAY - WASHINGTON*

Night on an eastbound plane passes faster than day travel, but with no relief to the cramped seats, stuffy air, the bangs and bumps of passengers moving up and down the aisle, and stale coffee. Occasionally, a light would be turned on by a nearby passenger who decides to read or work on a laptop – its staccato clicking offsetting the periodic cries of a hungry or wet infant.

I keep going over Towson's face as he casually made his threat. I saw expressions like those at my old Navy office. The ones that lived on the brink of disaster so many times that it no longer mattered. "Take him out with extreme sanction" was like ordering lunch. There comes a point when the value of life has been compromised so many times that it is only expedience that prevails. It's why I finally had to leave, and do not relish going back into it, even for a visit.

In the beginning, the Teams were exciting. Growing up around the sea like I did in Cape Cod, I gravitated to underwater adventure. When I got out of college, I owed the Navy four years, and Coronado, California seemed like a great place to escape to and the idea of becoming an elite SEAL excited me. I survived the initial three-week Indoctrination Course (INDOC) and qualified to endure the extraordinary physical and psychological challenges of the 25 week Basic Underwater Demolition/SEAL (BUD/S) sequence. I think that I didn't Drop on Request (DOR) out of sheer determination never to quit. Then it was on to 26 weeks of SEAL Qualification Training (SQT) before finally earning my Trident (NEC 5926), After spending a couple of years as a SEAL in NSW Special Operations (Navy Special Warfare), I lost my zeal and was very lucky to catch the attention of Admiral Lewis, who offered me a billet in his new ESCORT (Embassy SpeCial Operations & Reconnaissance Team) team. I might still be there if it wasn't for my wife's death, and she might not have died but for my ignoring the impending danger to her.

The plane touches down at Reagan just as the sun is starting to come up. I eat a soggy breakfast croissant and have some watery coffee at the airport, while I wait for a time when I know that Jim will be in his office. Shunning a rental, I wait outside for a Virginia Taxi to take me near the

Pentagon to Ft. Myer. There was the usual crunch of traffic heading for the bridges on the GW Parkway even on a Saturday, but it is a short drive, As we pass the Pentagon, I wonder how my old Navy buddies are surviving, if at all. In a tiny organization like ESCORT, almost nobody cared about rank, except for a few like Jim, The Admiral is one of the few rare stars that are less concerned about their own futures than the success of our mission and the protection of his staff. Even though I was out, and even though I still harbored ill feelings towards the government bureaucracy, my attitude did not extend to Admiral Lewis, who I always respected and admired.

The office is concealed inside a nondescript building on Navy property. In front of the office door, there is no sign, just a black podium with a speaker button and magnetic card reader. I swipe my old ID, and then push the button. The door clicks open and I go into a short hall. Bright fluorescent lights shine down the blank walls. After two minutes during which my body is scanned and my identity verified, the inner door clicks open. I walk into what looks like a typical corporate reception room, but for a lack of identification logo and any visible office equipment on the desk. The receptionist is a pretty brunette; a little thin for my taste, but with an eager look that some would find disarming. She is about 25 and has a wide smile and dark blue eyes. She asks us for my identification. Her demeanor is infectious as I smile back and hand over my Driver's License and Navy ID. She glances at them and puts them into her desk drawer. "These will be returned to you when you leave. Please take a seat. Would you like some coffee or tea?"

The suggestion 'or me' doesn't escape my notice, but I decline which brings a tiny pout from glossy lips. She returns to whatever she is doing behind the counter-desk, and occasionally glances at me and smiles some more. The chairs in the Reception area are firmly attached to the floor, should anyone decide to use one as a weapon. None of the cushions are detachable, and there are no crevices in the upholstery. It's business as usual. After ten minutes of waiting, a door opens and Jim comes out: tall, fit, and tanned, with a slightly superior air and a forceful grip. I'll bet he still plays rugby on weekends and smashes racquetballs in the evenings. He is carrying nothing and has no jacket on.

After greeting me coolly, he ushers me through a third door into a small conference room. The receptionist gives me a little wave as I go in. The room has no other door but the one we came through and is intended to prevent uncontrolled access to the main office. The walls hide steel plates over lead sheeting and have an electric radiating grid to inhibit eavesdropping. In the corner of the ceiling behind a pinhole, there is a camera which is both live monitored as well as recorded to disk. Before closing the door, Jim asks the receptionist if she will come in and give him a hand. She jumps up and comes around the desk, all legs and wiggle. Once inside, Jim ignores me and says "Gina, I was playing racquetball this morning and strained my wrist. Could you give me a hand with this ointment? I can't manage the cover with one hand." He looks over to me as he says it, with a slight emphasis on the word "cover."

"Sure, Jim" the girl says as Jim holds out a tube of aloe gel to her. Off comes the cap and Jim winces with pain convincingly so she drops the cap on the table and takes his wrist in one hand, while squeezing some gel into her other. An odor of eucalyptus permeates the air. Then she drops the tube onto the table as well. She pulls up his shirt sleeve and while she is rubbing the stuff on his arm, he leans to the side so she has to stretch across the table to keep rubbing. Up comes her short skirt and her blouse pulls across her chest, giving a nice view of thighs and nipples pressed into her blouse fabric. I reach out as if to steady her and palm the tube and cover. Jim keeps leaning over the table as she finishes. He makes a motion as if to scoop up the tube, and slides his hand into his pants pocket.

Gina tugs her skirt down, straightens her blouse, and prances out of the room. Jim and I both watch her wistfully for a moment, then turn to the business at hand. I start to say "Jim did you?" But he interrupts me abruptly with "Thank you for coming so we could update your annual security clearance."

I thought that I had better follow his lead. Clearly something was amiss and he did not want to open the door wider. "Thank you, Jim," I replied.

"Colin telephoned me and gave a good report on your background update," Jim continued.

My antennae rose very quickly at using my office "Legend" name. There were listeners with a particular set of interests, but not from our agency, or he would not have used that name.

Jim takes a small recorder out of his pocket and turns it on. Placing it on the table, he asked me the routine clearance questions, which I answer concisely. After about 10 minutes, Jim picked up the recorder, thanks me again and releases the door behind us. After seeing me into the Reception room again, Jim retreated into his office and I picked up my IDs.

Gina looks up at me before I go. "Are you coming back?"

"I don't think so."

"Do you need directions or a suggestion for dinner?"

I looked at her almost violet eyes and thought that it might be a very nice interlude if I were to take up the implied invitation. But I have some fish to fry that can't wait so I give an internal sigh and say goodbye. "No Thanks. I used to live here."

"That's too bad," she replied, "Well, if you need anything, please call."

I smile at her and leave. Returning to the street level, I direct a taxi to the Library of Congress. Once there, I inquire at the main desk for the Digital Collections. I know that since 1954, the Library has been amassing a huge collection of rare documents, maps, music, sound recordings and many other categories, stored either on disk or microfilm. As I reach the Collections Desk, I ask for newspaper files for the previous year in both San Francisco and Washington, since I knew these were stored on film. The librarian directs me to a small private Reader Room, and shortly, delivers a stack of microfilm cassettes.

Libraries are great places when you have to examine documents, primarily because everyone is looking at something. Microfilm rooms tend to be well lit and have a great deal of privacy. Also a public microfilm or microfiche reader has all you need to read a microdot or tiny bit of film. These days, many libraries are digitizing their files rather than filming them, so before long, the library may no longer have private spaces like this.

I ignore the cassettes for the moment, take off the tube cap and use a corner of my nail to pry off the plastic center. Under it is a bit of film, which I put under the glass of the reader. Jim's words leaped out to me.

"You have stirred up a hornet's nest at NSA. We had 2 agents here last night that were out for your blood. The Admiral was cool, but after the NSA left, he asked Tom and me to look into both you and Lauren Sylfern. There is a police report that you beat up a couple of their agents and stole some documents. If you're into something like this, please stay away from me. I can't afford the contact. Now you owe me. Under the tube's main label are the files for the three people you asked me about."

I went back to the tube and saw that the label had a detachable corner which, when pulled open, revealed several micro-sheets wrapped tightly around the aluminum tube of ointment. Taking the first sheet, I placed it on the reader glass.

"Daniel Towson was born Stendhal Xyso, in Istanbul, on July 6th, 1922. He was educated at the Istanbul Bilgi University, receiving an early Law Degree at age 19. He graduated near the top of his class, with a minor in International Politics. It is not known precisely what he did in the war, except that he fought against the Germans on Cyprus. After the war, he discovered that his entire family was dead, killed by the Greeks during an abortive raid. He returned to Istanbul and started a small import-export company [see Turkish-American Export-Import, Ltd.] shipping arms to the Arab nations from caches stored by both the Germans and Allies during the war throughout Northern Africa, Greece, Italy, and Southern France. After Israel was granted partition in May, 1948, he sold the new Israeli state weapons to fight the Arabs. With the earnings from these ventures, he shifted his business to more legitimate cargos: Oil, Grain, Rice, Cotton and other Middle East products, constructing a small fleet of ships to carry them, and building markets in Western Europe and the U.S. He seems to have skirted the periphery of the drug trade because there are no links to major drug shipments either to the U.S. or to Europe. He emigrated to the U.S. in 1956, and continued running his ventures from both Washington and San Francisco. By now he has acquired a wife, Edith (Efterpi Andros) who was born in Cyprus from Turkish parents. There is one daughter, who seems to have left home at age 16 and is now living in New York. Towson was reported killed last May in an auto accident. In the police report, it seems that he was accompanied in the car by an unknown young woman. His ashes were dispersed by his widow. There's more on his business if you need it. In terms of friends and associates, he had some dealings with Ernst Zilbern, and also he acted as an agent for Froehlich, but we have little data on exactly what he did, since those records are over at NSC and have not been shared with the rest of the community.

Ernst Zilbern was born in Germany where he trained as a mathematician at Heidelberg, obtaining his PhD in 1935. He worked at various German laboratories on cryptology. He was captured by the Polish Resistance but returned to Germany to work at Peenemunde. He served for a time with the Allies in Cyprus. At the conclusion of hostilities, he was brought to the U.S. under Operation Paperclip, and immediately engaged in code work at Los Alamos National Laboratories in Taos and at Sandia National Laboratories in Albuquerque. In New Mexico, he married and had one daughter, Lauren. Three years before his death, his wife contracted cancer and eventually died of it after a two-year battle. Zilbern's work remains highly classified. He died in May, of last year, coincidentally the same day that Towson died. There is additional coincidence, both died in San Francisco of auto accidents.

Laura Sylfern was born in New Mexico in 1977. Her father, Ernst Zilbern, changed her name to Sylfern. After completing school at Albuquerque Academy in 1995, Lauren went to Stanford University, and received a B.A. in European Languages and Political Science. After graduation, she took a job with the U.S. State Department and got an M.A. in Ancient Mid-Eastern languages from Georgetown. She is currently on leave from her assignment with the classified LIAS-X program. She continues to live in Albuquerque in her father's house and also maintains an apartment in Georgetown. She has top secret clearance and is a linguist. Her file lists 11 languages with fluency and a dozen more with varying levels of expertise. She has no flags on her file, but several NSC and NSA inquiries. No details are available. There is no direct connection to Towson or Froehlich. On the personal side, Lauren Sylfern has no known relationships. Until he died, she was devoted to her father and traveled with him frequently.

Johann Froehlich is German and worked with Zilbern during the war at Peenemünde, escaped and came to the US also under the Paperclip program. There is a gap between 1944 and 1945 which is classified with eyes-only so I couldn't get a peek at it. The CIA believes that he was recruited for some negotiations with the Greeks. Once in the US, he worked at Oak Ridge, Army Ordnance, and eventually left to form a company, ZeroLoss that created both industrial and military codes, as well as code generating and decoding machines. He did some of the fundamental research associated with modern long-primes as factors for NSA and industrial codes. He holds patents on several processes for constructing long primes. In the process of becoming wealthy, he also became friends with many members of Congress, including the current President. Upon the President's election, Froehlich was appointed to the National Security Council and currently serves as an ex-officio ombudsman and advisor to the NSC and the National Security Advisor to the President. He lives in Bethesda, Maryland. His wife of 38 years died 6 months ago, and he has no children. There is a very tenuous advisory that he utilized Towson's company to disperse ZeroLoss's patented code generation devices, but there is no second source verification.

Simon: I can't do anything further. I do not have a lot of freedom of action. Watch out for Froehlich. He has a reputation of being vindictive at best and murderously aggressive at worst. Try to get some resolution with your problem with the NSA, otherwise, you may find yourself in real hot water.

The rest of the film had addresses, telephone numbers, bank account numbers, passport numbers, and a few passwords. I decide not to destroy the film to preserve these, even though tradecraft dictated that I do so. But there just wasn't a safer way for me to store the information. I slide the film under the tube label, reseal it, and replace the cap cover. It was not yet lunchtime, but I felt like I had lived another whole day and a night.

I mount a film of the SF newspapers and found the story about Towson's death. But there was no mention of Zilbern's. There is no explanation for the double history, except that Towson had to have been involved in Lauren's father's death and used the accident to cover up his own disappearance. Not that there seemed any reason for it on the surface, unless somehow there was a connection back to Froehlich. If Froehlich was as lethal as Jim thought, maybe somehow Towson had to hide from him.

My next step has to be to dig more into Froehlich, without arousing his suspicions. The only lead has to be through the NSA. I still know a few people there who might be persuaded to help me unofficially. Somehow, if NSA is after something Zilbern had, it follows that Froehlich may very well be running that operation. And if he is, and they could reach out to San Francisco to Lauren in my office, we were both vulnerable. I wonder if Froehlich was connected somehow to the key that Towson was after. Once I get the NSA backtrack started, I really need to get on to Albuquerque and check on Zilbern's associates there. But first, it is to NSA Headquarters. Jean had a good friend who still works there, who might be able to help me. Several taxis are waiting at the curb.

"Interested in a long ride?" I asked the driver.

"Where to?"

Fort Meade, Maryland."

"That'll be twice the rate for me to get back." He replied.

"OK, then take me to BWI Airport at the fixed price."

"OK Joe, you can't blame a guy for trying."

"I want you to take me to NSA Headquarters. Once we get there, I will need you to wait for me and then take me on to BWI."

It will be a long ride through DC northeast into Maryland. Up 295, we exit at Pawtuxet Freeway and then into the NSA Security Zone. At the gate, I take out my ESCORT ID, The taxi driver's license and insurance card are scanned as well and we are cleared into the holding area for visitors. As I walk to the main entrance, I can't think how many times I have walked this path when Jean worked here.

I again show my ID and ask for Marcia Flynn, who works in the NIARL, the National Information Assurance Research Laboratory. Marcia used to be a close friend of my wife's and was mostly responsible for keeping me whole during that crisis in my life. The guard checks the Intranet directory and makes a call. It a moment, he looks up and asks me to wait.

It takes about 10 minutes while I look at the displays of NSA's dual pride: Electronic Intelligence and Crypto-Analysis. Pictures dominate the multicolored images: giant antennas and computers sifting through reams of data to find pearls of wisdom for America's decision-makers. I remember Jean's descriptions of the conflicting agendas and personalities which dominate this place. She used to wonder how such bright people made such bad managers. But here comes one of the really good people. "Hi Marcia, it's been a while."

"Simon. My God, I've missed you." She says as she runs into my arms and wraps me up with hers. Kissing me roundly on the mouth and holding me for a long moment, she pushes back and then whacks me a good one, right to the chest. "What do you mean, strolling in here like you had a meeting – it's been three years and not a word. Tell me."

Before I can say anything, the memories come back – Marcia, Jean and I. Oh poor Jean.

"Marcia, I missed you too, but I didn't miss the office, or the work."

"Yes, I know. You look tired. What's going on?"

I almost can't bear to see her, so vital, so alive. Why the hell did I ever think that this was such a good idea? But I need her help, so I forge ahead. "Marcia, can you come out of here for a little while and talk with me?"

"Yes. It is Saturday, after all. What's the matter?"

I drew her over to one of the displays. But with cameras in the ceilings and bugs everywhere, it made no sense to say anything that would put her on the spot.

"Can you have lunch with me someplace away from here? It's nothing important, but the building brings back bad memories."

"Sure, why not meet me at the Bangkok Kitchen –it draws a lot of other office and military folk. But it's not in the building."

"Well, I was thinking about someplace farther away, where we are not likely to meet anyone you know here."

"Sure. I can drive us. Do you have a car?"

"No, I came in a taxi. If I send him off, would you take me to the airport after lunch?"

"OK – I'll pick you up at the gate on the way out." She turns and heads back towards the security doors. I go out to Visitor's and pay off the taxi.

It's been three years since Marcia Flynn was part of my life. She was more Jean's friend than mine, anyway. Sure, I knew she was drop-dead gorgeous, but as vibrant and outgoing as she was, Jean was quietly and peacefully beautiful. Where Marcia was tall, had flaming red hair and deep green eyes with a slight mist of freckles, Jean was dark and petite, almost like a fragile Dresden doll, but one made of spring steel and fired porcelain with luminous pure white skin and a melting smile ; black hair like mine but long and lustrous. She hardly ever raised her voice, but made her points with quiet, efficient logic. Yet in the middle, she could be ribald as well, and it never failed to throw me for a loop. Maybe she wasn't the first girl I loved, but she certainly was the last. Jean Marisa Villeila: born in Cuba to a family that emigrated to the US when she was 5, her father always believed that he would return to his great mansion on the Isle of Pines, so he never became a citizen. But mama knew otherwise and made sure both she and Jean were naturalized as early as possible. With a scholarship to Harvard and a major in Mid-East Studies, she graduated 6th in her class went on to her Masters, after which she was recruited by the NSA. I was assigned to her soon after joining the Teams, and she taught me how to blend into the Islamic culture when I needed to. What a God-damned shame that she got caught in the meat grinder in this very building, and was taken away from me. Now seeing Marcia, it is very hard to cram my anger and grief back into the box.

Marcia waves at me and honks the horn from a white Mercedes convertible. "Nice ride," I comment.

She smiles a thank you and then zips out of the compound.

Marcia is one of the real people that somehow actually manage to work for the government; so bright that NSA overlooks her fundamental irreverence. I first met her when I started dating Jean. One day, while I was waiting for Jean to show up, this tall, stunning redhead walks up to me and announces that if I didn't treat Jean right, I would have her to deal with, and that I certainly would not enjoy the experience. She then strode off, leaving me standing there with my mouth open. Born right near here in Maryland of a privileged family, her dad was a chemist with DuPont Chemicals. As she was finishing a Ph.D. at MIT in mathematics, she was recruited by the NSA and became one of their lead analysts and creative thinkers in a very short 5 years. She was a good friend to Jean. After the 9/11 march to Iraq and then after Jean was killed, she became a compassionate and genuine supporter to me. None of my SEAL training prepared me for the torment and guilt that I felt, and Marcia waited it out with me until I had to leave here and go west to hopefully, find some peace. I should have known that you carry your burdens with you, no matter where you are.

Today, she takes us to the Elkridge Furnace Inn Restaurant, a beautiful pre-Revolutionary compound on 16 acres along the Patapsco River: Elegant and quiet, it serves well to ease tensions and to be a perfect backdrop to our conversation.

I order a Caprese Salad with Grape Tomatoes followed with Cabernet Gnocchi, while Marcia has Crab and Artichoke Dip served with Purple Potato Chips followed by Calves Liver Persillade. Accompanying our lunch, we order a bottle of Verget 2005 Pouilly Fuisse.

"After you left ESCORT, you seemed to drop off the planet. How about filling me in on the in-betweens?" Marcia asks, between bites of the chips.

"I settled in San Francisco, and took on some private investigations."

"Do you mean you traded your talent for peeping through keyholes?" she said, with a slightly aghast expression on her face."

"Well, not so much; more like helping attorneys make their cases, and digging into histories for disenfranchised widows and orphans."

"What about your love life?"

"Pretty empty. I really haven't wanted to put myself out in the field since Jean."

"Ok, I'll dig more into that later. Truthfully, you look like hell."

"Being back here is not something that I wanted or was prepared for."

"OK, I do understand. It takes a lot of time, and some of the issues probably will never disappear. So tell me what you didn't want to say at the office."

Before I answer, I look closely at her. There are some people who never seem to age. No matter what it throws at them, life metes out only light jabs. Three years had passed and she still looks feisty. If she weren't so incredibly valuable, she might have been fired for her support of Jean's objection to the made-up Iraq intelligence, but she is also a survivor. So here she is, three years later and still the same. But behind the clean and wholesome look is a grandmaster strategist. It is this quality that I need right now. "Without really understanding why, I seem to have drawn the ire of a couple of powerful Washington types. So before I ask for your help, I wanted to give you a chance to walk away."

"Don't worry about me. Tell me what's going on, and if I can help, I will, but first, does it involve the NSA?"

"I think that it might. Yesterday, two agents from your Central Security Service visited me at my office, with decidedly unfriendly intents."

"Did they accuse you of anything?"

"No, but my client and I were fairly straightforwardly attacked."

"That's not their usual M.O. Do you know who sent them?"

"It might have been Johann Froehlich."

"You don't start at the bottom and work up do you? Froehlich has a lot of influence. But he has no operational role at the NSA so it would have to be someone else. I can look into that back at the office. Is Froehlich one of the two that is pissed at you?"

"Yes, I think so. That is actually part of my problem. I am not sure of his involvement at all. It's one of the things I need help from you with."

"Who's the other one?"

"Daniel Towson."

"I know about him, arms merchant and part-time dealer for the CIA. I wouldn't exactly call him a friend to the agency. OK, so what can I do to help?" She said, as she crunches down on the last chip and pushes her plate aside, taking another small swallow of the wine and then waits while the waiter pours another glass for each of us and clears our places. "Simon, you know that you can count on my help. I was really heartbroken when you picked up and moved to San Francisco, although I do understand why. Let's put that behind us and go forward from here. Tell me the story, and then I'll pick at it. "

I relate the events about the key and the threat by Towson. I also tell her about Ernst Zilbern, as well as the conflicting stories of the auto accidents. Finally, I tell her about Edith Towson's death, and the apparently missing Wayne Hudson.

"The link to Froehlich is tenuous at best. What aren't you telling me?"

I wish sometimes she wasn't so quick. To keep Lauren's importance in perspective, I decided to tell a partial truth. "I got a call from Ernst Zilbern's daughter. She thinks that Froehlich had something to do with

Zilbern's death the previous year. She was in my office when the two NSA agents attacked us."

"Are you working for her, or do you have some other interest?"

"I took her on as a client, and only a client. But I haven't decided if she's telling me the truth, which is one of the reasons I am here."

"Do you think that Froehlich had Zilbern killed?"

"I don't know. I only know that I was threatened twice – once by the NSA and by Towson directly. Who killed who is not important, it's more a question of why."

Marcia considered while she scooped up her Calves Liver and I focused on the Gnocchi. "First of all, as I said, you should know that I will help you. I understand why you haven't called over the past three years – it must have been awful for you."

"I just wanted out of everything that reminded me of Washington. It had nothing to do with you personally."

"What about now? Have you been able to come to terms with her death?"

"Marcia, there are times when I think that I have, but then something triggers a memory, and all the pain and anger comes back in full force."

"Simon, like you, I always questioned who was behind her assassination. But the files are sealed, even from me, so I never found much to go on."

"I wish sometimes, that I had insisted she leave the agency and never accepted the exile that they sent her to. I think she would still be alive if I had been more insistent."

"Simon, you have nothing to be guilty about. I should have been a better friend to her."

"Marcia, let's make a pact."

"What do you have in mind?"

"As soon as I get this job done for Zilbern's daughter, let's see if we can work together and dig into who might have had Jean killed. This may help us both towards closure."

"Simon, my experience is that it really doesn't help with closure, but if nothing else, we can get the bastards. So now tell me about Froehlich and Zilbern."

"Their relationship goes back to World War II, and maybe even farther. I don't know. It started in Germany and continued in Cyprus and later here in the U.S. They seemed to have been friends as well as scientific collaborators. But then there was a falling out. Zilbern's daughter is convinced that her father was killed by Froehlich. Can you do some quiet digging?"

"Of course; I have access to several types of data – files on individuals that for one reason or another are important to all intelligence organizations, raw data collected from Electronic Intelligence (ELINT) and Human Intelligence (HUMINT) sources that gets filtered, sorted, and analyzed before it is coded for storage and access. We normally deal with thousands of requests for information on domestic and foreign individuals, organizations and institutions, so one more inquiry wouldn't be a problem. But with someone so highly placed in our government, our inquiry has to appear legitimate and appropriate. So we have to have a plan."

"The NSA has a method for dealing with any request. First, we need to establish a valid inquiry. I think that we can use the President's National Security Advisor for that purpose. Normally, an inquiry from him constitutes an authority to establish a working group and initiate action without any further validation. I can generate this myself and issue it to our HQ via his hacked communications. Once it arrives, I will then receipt it and log it. It would have to be something that would include Froehlich, without specifically identifying him. In fact, the inquiry should be something that would allow us to include Towson, Zilbern and any other person that surfaces relating to our special interest."

"What a minute. You are suggesting subverting NSA security protocols for a personal investigation. This could get you into major hot water."

"Simon, let me worry about that. There are so many convoluted agendas around our office, that one more wouldn't raise an eyebrow. There are far more sinister politically generated investigations in the works every day. To cover myself, I will leave a note in the file covering the hack as a breach test, and who knows; something might come out of this that would be useful to the agency in the long run. So let's get back to the inquiry."

"What about Cryptographic Security?"

"That's too general. It has to be really narrow to pull this off. Since I know something about Froehlich's work, what about 'Advanced Code Key Migration to the Private Sector'."

"Actually, that sounds really good."

"Sure; the President's Advisor would certainly be interested in anything that strengthened private sector security codes, and he would want the NSA to keep watch on migrations and developments in that direction. It is a perfect net for both legitimate and personal inquiries."

"So once you have created the inquiry and surfaced it through a legitimate channel, what comes next?"

"I will need to create a Task Group and charge them with the responsibility of research. I will select someone for the Chair who is particularly strong at empire building, but has no interest in challenging the source of the request– a typical bureaucrat. From there, it will be a simple task of letting the Chair assemble the research group, put a budget together and get it approved. At that point, computing resources will be released to that charge number for the work. Actually, this type of inquiry could occupy the group for a very long time without raising any antennae. If the Chair selects the group members, those chosen will be weaker than he is. From there, it will be a simple matter of filtering – separation of the real issues that we are interested in from the phony issues under the Mission Order. I will set up a filter to separate our high value research from the cover work, As such, the bureaucracy will be satisfied that we are meeting the needs of a powerful interest, while the group itself will divert all their unrelated research results through my prism to us. This will be a classic case of managing the available resources to multiple goals. With the infusion of high security around here, no one talks to anyone else anyway, particularly about anything important, so even Internal Security will not have any special interest."

"This seems to be overly complicated," I remark.

"Oh yes, but you see this is the way NSA justifies its work. Within our bureaucracy, larger is better; yet an organization whose goal is protection against subversion can't recognize it internally. By giving our operation a phony goal we can justify its existence with busywork, while underneath, we use the same tools to follow the real investigation in total secrecy. If you like, I can even assign you as a temporary contractor to this new office. We can re-vet you and put you in the information loop. In this way, you can do your own research if you like, and do it right under the nose of the people who are after you, and they will never suspect."

"The problem is that I can't stay here. I have to leave for New Mexico to see about the connections from that end."

"Oh, that's not a problem either. I can give you a secure laptop and an encrypted satellite phone so we can communicate. This way, you can get access to the research as it surfaces." Marcia stopped and looked very self-satisfied. "But do you really have to go to New Mexico right away, tonight?"

"Yes, I have to search from that end as well."

"Look Simon, it has been three years. What about it if you waited until tomorrow morning to go west, and spent this evening with me. It's 2:00 right now. If you stayed, you could catch the first flight in the morning, and still get there by mid-morning. So we could still enjoy the evening, and you could get there in time for a full business day's work tomorrow."

"Your offer is very tempting."

"Ok, it's settled. Let's hit the road." With that, she gets up and walks to the car. I pay the check and follow her.

The drive to her home is quick, if not actually death defying. She handles the car like everything, with confidence. She had lowered the rag top, and the wind pulls at her hair, throwing it into a raging flame streaming behind her head. She would look exactly right standing on the bowsprit of a Celtic ship about to ravish the English coast.

Her home is a rough stone French Country house overlooking the Rocky Gorge Reservoir. There is a conservatory in the back and tall planters with cypresses flanking the front door. Near the conservatory is a swimming pool that was also edged with stone, with a rock outcropping at one end, out of which dropped a falls. The door leading into the house has leaded glass panels whose crystals sparkled in the sunlight. She made one small detour to turn off the alarm system, before disappearing down a circular stone stairway to get us some wine from her cellar.

Once the wine is opened and poured, she points me to the conservatory and then disappears upstairs to change out of her business clothes.

The glassed-in space is warm, and sunlight filters through translucent screens. Many of Marcia's orchids are still blooming, and through there is no noticeable scent, the colors are riotous and alluring. A couple of white metal chaises and loveseats are arranged in a conversational grouping. I sink into the deep cushions of one of the chaises and kick off my shoes. I can hear squabbling finches outside. With my feet up and a half-glass of fragrant red Beaujolais warming my belly, I lie back and in no time at all, fall deeply asleep.

# 4 *SATURDAY NIGHT, WASHINGTON*

Rustling branches just outside the conservatory wake me; the birds had apparently quieted for the evening, I feel a clean, cool duvet on me and a breeze coming in from an open window. Marcia must have thrown the cover on me as I slept. A pair of slippers is waiting for me by the side of my chaise. I can't remember how long it had been since I felt so luxurious.

I start for the house, when I hear voices coming from inside. One was a woman, surely Marcia and the other a man. Not wanting to disturb her, I retreated into the conservatory to wait. After a little while the front door opened and closed, and then Marcia appears.

"You should have come in," she says. "I would have liked to introduce you to a friend of mine who lives next door, a curator from the Smithsonian; John Crawford. He works at their Museum Conservation Institute lab in Suitland and likes the peace and quiet living up here."

"Maybe another time." I surprise myself with my retort. I somehow am angry. "Marcia, I think that maybe I should try for that evening plane. Would you take me, or I can get a taxi." Immediately I felt like an idiot. But idiot or not, I have to get out of here.

"Well, you'll just have to wait. I've invited John to dinner, and he really is a nice fellow. He's been through a rough patch recently and it wouldn't hurt you to get out of yourself for an evening." With that, Marcia stalks out of the room and in a moment, I hear the sounds of pots banging in the kitchen. Now I feel really stupid. I follow the sounds into the kitchen, where she is stomping in from the pantry with a large pan, drops it onto the stove, and then starts chopping garlic vigorously with a large cleaver.

"Marcia, I'm sorry. I really didn't mean to..."

"Of course you did. You are angry and I happened to be present. That comes from living alone. Now you've gone and let me into your private space, and you'd like to push me back out. But being mad at me won't bring you peace of mind. Simon, we both loved her."

"If only I had been a good husband, it's my fault."

"It's not your fault. Really, it's not your fault. You didn't kill her. I think we both know that she had made too many enemies. We tried to protect her. But we couldn't and she died. You have to find a way to let your anger go. It eats at you and tears at your good nature. In time, it can make you a bitter old man focused only on the past. Does it make you feel better thinking that you were helpless? I sure as hell wish that things had been different, but they aren't and there is a hell of a lot of life left. So let it go."

"Marcia, I think what really gets to me is that when I do have a good time; I feel guilty. I mean that you just came to me with a tiny little domestic announcement like inviting a friend in for dinner. To me it seemed like an invasion of my privacy. I am truly sorry that I sniped at you. Please forgive me."

Marcia put down the cleaver and comes over to me, puts her arms around me, holding me while she said "There is nothing to forgive. It's not your fault." We stand there for a few more moments while I begin to feel tears start behind my eyes. After a time I let go of her and go around to the other side of the central counter.

"So, you've invited your friend John for dinner. Do you think that maybe it isn't so wise for us to be seen together, particularly after putting together this subversion plan?"

"Simon, the best possible thing that we can do is to act absolutely normally, and give no one any other idea."

"Of course, I understand that. Remember where I worked."

"John knows that I work for the NSA, but nothing more. He is a dear man and a specialist in ancient art and sculpture. He has no connection to you or to me, other than our being neighbors and friends."

"OK. So what's for dinner? I am actually hungry."

"I am throwing together a Caesar Salad, some veal piccata and a little pasta with oil. I have some nice fruit and cookies for dessert, and we'll have espresso to finish, perhaps with a little Sambuca. Will you go to the cellar and select a dinner wine?"

"If that is what you call 'throwing together', what would you do for a real dinner?"

She points me in the direction of stone steps leading down. I find myself in a small wine cellar with racks on the sides, a floor-to-ceiling refrigerator in the back, and a rustic table in the center. A wrought iron candelabrum illuminates the cool space. The cellar is extremely well organized. There are labels on the shelves covering both regional and varietals, and the refrigerator is divided into Whites, Sparkling Wines and a few Rosés. I close the refrigerator and search through the racks for a Tuscan red, finally settling on a Ducale Resservo Chianti Classico that is about 12 years old. Using the opener attached to the edge of the table, one push and the foil is cut, cork is drawn and dropped in a hopper below the machine. As I come up the steps, Marcia is back to banging pots.

With a mouthful of something, she points me up the stairs; I get the hint about cleaning up. So up I go. My shirt is a mess. I've been in it for a day and a half already. Back in Marcia's closet, I see one of her outside work shirts that looks like it will fit me, and it does. My feet go back into my socks and shoes, and then to the bath to comb and wash. As I head down the stairs, the door chime sounds, and Marcia points to the door as she plunges the salad spinner in her hands, drying the Romaine. On my way she passes me with a "Nice shirt" jibe, but there's a smile in it.

I open the door to a thin lively man in his 60s, nearly my height, sporting a wild mane of white hair, ferocious white eyebrows, kind blue eyes and an ascot. His shirt is buttoned right up to the top covered by a light blue blazer, which hangs loosely on his frame over dark blue slacks. His feet are pushed into leather sandals with no socks.

"Good evening," I offer, "You must be John."

"Yes, of course I am," he says sprightly, "And you are Simon. It is a pleasure. I hope that you will not mind the intrusion of a third wheel to your tandem."

"It's good to meet you. Marcia tells me you are a friend, as well as a neighbor. I'm the stray that she took in tonight."

"Yes, she does do that, doesn't she?" Then with a chuckle, he darts directly towards the kitchen calling loudly "Marcia, I have arrived bearing gifts."

"Come on in and have some wine," Marcia calls from the kitchen. He gives her a hug and hands her a few flowers. I could swear that they came from her planter, but she seemed pleased to receive them.

She finishes pounding the veal paper-thin and puts out flat bowls for dipping in flour and egg. Lemon is sliced, and the capers are ready for the pan. Pasta is in the pot, veal dipped and sautéed, and thin lemon slices are placed between layers on a platter. I carry the veal, John the salad and Marcia brings up the rear with the pasta and a foil bag with garlic bread. I pour the Chianti from the sideboard.

As we sit, John asks me what I did. I replied with my standard PI history. "It's not too different from what we do," he says. "We try to see behind the obvious, to discover the how and the why, and the place that it might fit into an overall puzzle of intersecting agendas." I glance at him when he uses the word 'Puzzle,' but see that it is not a metaphor but just a description of his work.

"How many times do you find pieces that don't fit?" I ask.

"Oh, it happens all the time. In fact, it is rare that everything fits in an organized way. It's like looking through a prism. From different viewpoints you can only see single colors, and almost never see the whole white light source. The trick is to look from as many different viewpoints as possible, to assemble the most logical and the simplest answer."

"You mean like Occam's Razor" I comment.

"Exactly; the simplest answer is usually the closest to the truth."

He then launches into tales of archeological puzzles that have been solved or which are yet to be solved. I am fascinated by his stories. My investigations seem so mundane, compared with this kind of detective work. While he speaks, I find myself daydreaming about what it might be like, unearthing history. Marcia was also enthralled. She sits at the table, leaning forward on both elbows as John related the construction of whole cloth from tiny clues.

Finally, John stops with a little embarrassed laugh and makes a self-deprecating comment about monopolizing the evening, but Marcia puts her hand on his arm and thanks him. He smiles back and jumps up to bring plates and utensils into the kitchen. I follow him and ask him how he got to be buried in the Smithsonian. John laughs at the 'buried' remark. "When I was at school, I wanted to play football. Oh, yes. I know I don't look the type. Well anyway, I had every hope of becoming a true Tiger – you know, Princeton Tigers? Well, when I wasn't on the bench, I was usually down at the bottom of a pile with my face in the dirt, or mud, depending on the weather. My coach got so tired of calling for the stretcher, that one day he said to me 'Crawford; you spend so much time buried in the ground, why don't you just go be an archeologist and get paid for it?' I think that was my last day on the team. Actually, the idea kind of appealed to me. So I went around to the A&A department and took an introductory course. That summer, I went on a dig to Polis in Cyprus. It was hot and dirty, and the living conditions were abysmal, but I couldn't get enough. Just the thought of assembling a culture from a few tiny pieces of evidence was thrilling. I was hooked. It seemed only like a moment until I woke up one morning with a brand new PhD. in my hand. I worked at the Cairo Museum for a while, and then the Vatican, but really wanted to come home. The Smithsonian offered me a research job and I grabbed it."

"Do you ever miss football?"

"Hell no. Well, maybe a little. I was sort of hoping for a boy when I got married – someone I could play ball with, but it turned out to be a girl, and she is wonderful. She is 13 now and at the stage where she is trying to decide to be either a giggly girl or a stay a tomboy. I think that she switches every other day." John didn't mention his wife, but with Marcia's comment before, I decided not to ask.

We busy ourselves with kitchen chores until Marcia makes coffee and we retire to the living room. The meal had been absolutely perfect – taste, presentation, and company. Living alone as I had been for quite some time, I really had lost the art that Marcia wields so effortlessly, to bring us to a state of relaxed comfort, yet with minds still alert. I had not let anyone get close for so very long.

"John, thank you for coming tonight," I said out of the blue.

"Oh my dear fellow," he replied. "This woman means a great deal to me and I haven't seen her so radiant for a long time. It is really quite a treat. Thank you."

"John, tell Simon about some of your new acquisitions," said Marcia as she called from the kitchen.

"Oh yes. My goodness there are two pieces sent to us about a year ago from an anonymous donor. One is a golden helmet with an unusual script around the base. It looks a little like ancient Greek, but more probably an isolated example of one of the Hittite languages: perhaps Etruscan or even Luwian. We have made no success at all with the translation so we have been searching for other examples without success. The helmet design is finer than Anachean. I'm not sure if you know that in 1995, a Hittite seal was discovered in the excavation at Troy, and there is a great similarity between that seal and this helmet. So there may be some justification for identifying the helmet as Trojan. But without its provenance and not being able to translate it, we are still somewhat at a loss. A mystery, you might say."

"The material itself is a further puzzlement. It has the luster of gold but not the softness. To date, it has defied assay. Gold was always in use back at the time this apparently comes from, but a helmet of gold would have been ceremonial, not a war helm. Bronze would have been the material for war, although Hittite alchemy had created varieties of wrought iron as well. You know that they had created a rudimentary blast furnace, so much higher temperatures could be reached. But getting back to the helmet, if we only knew where it came from, we could have more clues as to its identity and significance. For some strange reason, however, the donors simply sent it to us in a box, with no return address or contact name."

"The second piece is a breastplate of apparently the same metal as the helmet. The symbols and text on it are very similar to that on the helmet, So far, all we can tell is that it is very old. It certainly is worth a great deal. Most artifacts that we receive from donors are accompanied by various tax forms so that the value can be included in annual deductions. I have never received anything like this before."

"When did they arrive at your doorstep?" I asked

"Last March, just over a year ago," John's obvious enthusiasm for the piece was dampened by the missing provenance.

"John, it sounds like you could use a detective, not for the archeology, but for the owner's identity." I laughed as I said it, but realized that I might be not too far from the truth.

Marcia comes into the room and looks towards me "Did John tell you about the armor? Why don't you give him a hand with it?"

"Sure," I reply, "But first I have a few queries of my own that need to get resolved."

"Marcia, I have to be going. Thank you so much, and Simon, it was a pleasure meeting you." John rises to leave. Then he turned back "Simon, if you do have some time, come over to the lab and I'll show you the artifacts. Maybe you can help if it interests you." Then he gives Marcia a kiss and a hug and bounces out the door.

As the door closed, I asked "Have you known John long?"

"Oh yes. When I first came down here and bought this place, I was very lucky to find John here. He helped me when Phillip walked out on me – Oh you didn't know Phillip. I was involved with a man who I worked with, but it didn't survive office politics. He and I broke up and I was depressed for a quite a while. John looked after me and encouraged me to get out again. He is quite a man. No, I am not in love with him, but he dispenses strength with his integrity. I value his friendship a great deal."

"What happened to his wife and their marriage?"

"John doesn't talk about it; I just hope that somehow, they will work it out. I know that he is miserable without her, and their daughter, Emily as well."

"Marcia, I am sorry that you too had a rough time. But you seem to be stronger for it. I know I haven't fully acclimated to Jean's death. It really is good to feel alive, and I do feel alive tonight; mostly thanks to you."

In response to my comment, she reaches out to me and wraps her arms around me with a big hug. I reciprocate and she pulls back for a moment to look at me directly, then leans forward and kisses me softly on the lips. I feel myself respond to the kiss, but then pull away and she backs off with a little embarrassed laugh. Then she walks back into the living room and picks up the last of the coffee service for washing. From the kitchen she gives me directions upstairs to the guestroom. I stop in the kitchen doorway and thank her again for a genuinely delightful evening, then turn and head upstairs.

In the guestroom, the bed covers have been pulled back, and a pair of pajamas has been laid on the footboard. After a long shower, I turn out the light and just before falling asleep; think how nice it would be to have an unexpected visitor.

# 5 *1154 BC THE CITY OF TROY*

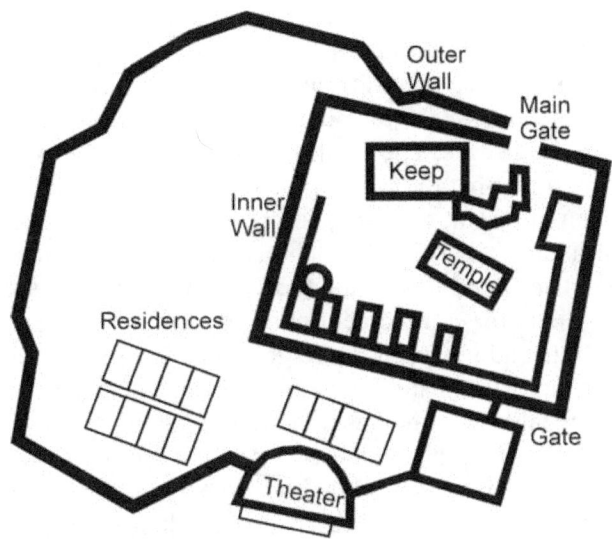

It was the ninth year of the siege. The well no longer flowed clear and cold as it had for generations. The encroaching sea had left it brackish and hardly quenching. Only fighters and children were allowed a small bowl three times a day. The rest had to suffice with sponges that were kept in sluices to hold the rain when it came. The smell of corpses was everywhere, but particularly when the breeze turned from the South, for that is where the dead were stacked against the outer wall. In the night, children with swollen bellies cried in their sleep, as their mothers died next to them.

Yet the gates stayed closed and the people's spirit remained optimistic. Where once 10,000 cheered the games, now barely 2,000 manned the battlements. Strategically placed armor stuffed with straw, which were periodically relocated, gave the illusion of more warriors. On the south wall, the remains of the old theater pushed into the market square. It reminded Anastheus of his days down in the pit, backed by the Chorus, bringing joy and pain to the people of the city, as he related the tales of pride, conquest, might and tragedy that he had been taught as a boy. He had a gift of memory, so could recite long passages even today. Not a tall man, Anastheus made up with intelligence his lack of physical heft. At 23, he was still full of hope for his future and when the younger boys cast stones against the wall in contests, he would yearn to join them. His parents had not the time before their deaths from starvation to arrange a marriage for him, so he remained without attachments. His older brother was lost to the war, and his sister, given to an armorer, now had but one living child.

Anastheus was in a hurry. He was called to Council. The armies outside had kept their fateful promise: to stay and see the entire city dead and the buildings torn down in payment for our daring to challenge their king. They would give no quarter to the populace, even though we are cousins and nephews to the Greeks. The armies of Sparta and Athens had joined together in a great lie: that the wife of the king of Sparta had been stolen by our Paris, son of Priam, our king, and brought here as chattel. Their king Menelaus claimed Paris had stolen his gold and other treasures as well. No one outside our gates understood the real truth: our ships contested with theirs for commerce; our allies in the Cyclades and Dodecanese, Crete and in Cyprus were growing stronger and challenged the Greek merchant traders and the Spartan King, Menelaus had squandered his wealth so there was none left to pay his army. For the lie of honor betrayed, their king had gathered his wife's former suitors and told them the lie, prevailing on them to defend Helen's honor. So they came to restore Helen back to her husband, defeat us and loot in the process. Even though the great Odysseus and the Cypriots did not believe the story and would not participate in the trumped-up war, it made no difference. A carefully crafted propaganda campaign had convinced the Greeks of our kidnap and theft, and so they came. At first they could not defeat us, because we had too many allies that continued to supply us, so the Greeks took them on one at a time, and overwhelmed them, cutting our resources to the bone. Now it was almost over.

He passed the old theater and turned into the temple grounds, where the altar of Zeus stood, a testament to the loyalty of the people. Waiting inside the temple were three men. One was our priest, who proselytized our glorious destiny. The second was the keeper of the histories, a seer of great learning who had studied in Alexandria and Babylon. The third was unknown to me. He was not a large man and frail with a furtive look like a rat that gets caught out in the torchlight. He stood behind the other two.

"We're glad you came so promptly" said the old priest. "Are you feeling well?"

"Yes. I am hungry most of the time, but no less or more than others. I wish it wasn't so difficult on the young ones. They don't have much resilience. This morning, as I was coming up the steps to the temple, I saw another child dead with a swollen belly, held by a wailing mother. I wish there was something I could do."

"There is something." The old priest looked at the other two, who both nodded. "We have a mission for you."

"What kind of mission?" Anastheus asked.

The seer turned towards him and added, "You must know that we cannot last more than a few more days. With no food and little water; we cannot hold out."

"How can this be true? You both have told the people to stand fast, and that we will be delivered. How could you yesterday tell everyone to be courageous, yet now you say the opposite? Which is the lie? Forgive me, but I will not do anything for the likes of you." He turned to leave, but the priest put a hand on his arm and gently, but firmly, pulled him back.

"Leave me alone" Anastheus said.

"Please wait, and hear me through."

Anastheus stopped, but folded his arms and waited for the priest to finish.

"You need to understand that we have a deeper responsibility than to the lives of the people. If and when Troy falls, you know that the Greeks have vowed to destroy everything here and to enslave any survivors. We have a responsibility to the future, to save as much as possible when we are overrun. We need your help in preserving our heritage."

"You speak to me of heritage. How can one person, no matter who they are, keep a heritage alive?"

The learned seer spoke again." We have created tablets that are made of a new metal, created by our smiths. This metal is as immortal as the very gods themselves. On these tablets, we have engraved our alchemy, our medicine and our mathematics, partly derived from Alexandria, but made new by our own discoveries and the teachings of our elders. We charge you to take these tablets, take responsibility for their contents, and hide them where only one true to our gods and our people will ever find them." As he spoke, he reached under his robe and pulled out a sheaf of thin metal leaves, which had been bound together along one edge. He handed them to Anastheus.

Anastheus took the package, leafed through some of the pages, and then put them down on the altar plinth. Then he spoke to the priest "You speak of being true to our gods, yet you show your cowardice by your words. I may be only a youth, but I have learned through your preaching, that our gods demand better from us. Why should I believe anything that you say now?"

"Because in your heart, you know that we have no reason to hope. Our allies have been defeated and no longer can supply us with food and arms. We have no friends who are able or willing to fight on our behalf. All we can do is to protect the seed of our culture for the future. That is something one person can do, if you will do it for us."

"But why me? I am not strong like a warrior. Certainly, I am not powerful enough to protect these treasures from being stolen."

"Anastheus; don't be modest. Military prowess would be useless in this type of mission. You are an actor; no one would ever think that you had anything valuable. You can pass among any class without drawing attention, like a chameleon that changes color with his background. You are intelligent with a good memory and a strong will. This is what we need now, someone that can pass unnoticed through our enemies."

"But I can't escape the city."

The third man finally spoke. His eyes darted to all corners of the temple, and he took tiny steps forward and backwards, like he was guarding his food bowl. "We have secured a way for you to leave the city without being seen, even if it means sacrificing all of us." Through this, the third man made his identity known as our medical arts leader, a Shaman of the spirits, who toiled in the dark grotto beneath the keep. "The Greeks are not happy with their war, and their alliances are breaking for lack of financial support from the people. But they fight on so long as Menelaus is their king. We have crafted a way for them to win, but all they will succeed in gaining are these piles of rocks and our dead children. Our treasures are those of the mind, and you can preserve these."

"So it is not only your words that are traitorous, but your deeds as well."

"Don't be stupid, Anastheus. Give up the idea that somehow Zeus will come to help us at this late hour. You need to face reality. All we have done is to make sure that when the city is taken, you and the tablets will escape. Don't you realize that by setting this in motion, we have sealed our own fate as well? We shall die so that you can live and keep our heritage alive. Does that make us traitors?"

"No. But everything I have known will be destroyed without my lifting one finger to stop it."

"For you no less than for us; Anastheus, accept this mission. You will be fighting a different battle with your wits than staying and losing by the sword."

The Priest Keeper spoke again, "One thing you must promise us. It is something that will be harder than anything you might do in your life to come. You must see that the tablets are kept hidden for as long a time as possible, until they can be used to rebuild our culture."

The Shaman added "Someday, you will marry and have children. You may be a merchant or a poet, but whatever you do, and wherever you go, you must protect these documents. At the right time, whether it is you, or someone else that you choose, an opportunity will come up to allow them to be revealed. It may take many more years than your lifetime, but you choose. Remember us and remember the sacrifice of all here for our future. We are sorry to have to burden you with these tasks, but you are the best available candidate. You must do it."

As he spoke, suddenly a great shout arose on the walls. "We have won the day, the invaders are gone." The shout was picked up again and again by many in the city, passed from one to another in gleeful abandon.

"Quick, the play has begun. You must get your possessions together and prepare to leave. You will know when." The priest and seer looked at one another with resignation.

The four of us came out of the temple and into the square. Up on the battlement, the guards shouted down to us "It's true, they have gone. They have left their war machines and disappeared. Praise great Zeus the deliverer." Anastheus ran back to his hovel, where he wrapped a few pitiful clothes, his spare sandals, goblet, bowl and knife into a small bundle. The council of three returned to the temple to prepare for their fate.

"Open the gate and send out a scouting party," called the General of the Army to his men. So, for the first time in nine years, the bronze bars were lifted from the gate and it was pushed open. Out went seven soldiers led by a captain. The giant doors were reclosed and again barred.

Anastheus mixed with the crowd as they surged against the gate and in the square; some rushed to the temple to thank Zeus for their deliverance. Water bowls, their most precious possessions these days, were used to wash the feel of Zeus' statue, and the last of the scented candles were set out on the altar.

After almost one full hour, the soldiers pounded on the gates, seeking re-admittance. As gates were again opened, the captain entered, announcing that the invaders had gone.

The great gates were then opened wide. People flooded out of houses and shops, each seeking to be the first to breathe the free air outside the wall. Anastheus forgot his charge in the excitement, and was swept out with the crowd. The departing army had left on the field all their machines of war: siege towers, catapults, and great rams. Several horse idols, clearly honoring Poseidon, the Greek God of the Sea, remained in the camp as well: a little larger than a normal horse, they stood with small altars before them, still wreathed in incense. These horse idols were mounted on skids, so that they could be dragged into battle, giving spiritual support to the troops. The Greeks had taken all their small weapons with them, but they had abandoned many jars of wine and baskets of food in their encampment.

As evening fell, the gates remained open and musical instruments appeared, leading circles of dances and revelry. The Greek jars of sweet wine were rolled into the city and cracked open; people filling themselves with these gifts. The fresh vegetables, dates, figs, salted lamb and olives, which the city dwellers had been denied for so long, was taken up and consumed in a feast of thanksgiving. Young girls braided their hair with flowers, and were chased by young men, who had put away their swords in their joyousness. Old men smoked their pipes and shared with one another stories of their bravery and encounters with death all these many years. Old women in circles talked again of their hopes for grandchildren. Girls shared secrets and boys who would be men strutted and wrestled to impress the girls. The three leaders stood on the temple steps and watched their flock with heavy hearts for they knew what they had devised for tomorrow.

As the night wore on, the excitement and filled bellies overcame many people and they lay down in open doorways and slept. Anastheus, thinking that the threat was gone, forgot for a time the charge that he had been given and joined in the contests. He was still young, and almost for his whole adult life he had known only the life of a captive in a besieged city. So he put his bundle back in his room to sing, dance, spill wine and hail the unwon freedom.

Very early in the morning, when the peace of sleep took even the city's dogs and birds, there was a stirring in the Greek encampment. At each of

84

the invaders' horse altars, the tails slowly raised and trapdoors dropped down from the horses' bellies, followed by solitary figures. These dozen wraiths crept into the city and went about their assigned missions. Two ascended to the gate towers to disable the bronze chains that held the great bars, so it would not be possible to drop them ever again. Two stole into the main tower, where they started piling tables and benches for a fire. Four went into armories to seal the doorways with wood and piles of debris, which would also be set afire. The last two mounted the steps to the temple, and from there descended into the grotto.

Anastheus slept lightly, since he had an aversion to strong wine. The young maiden who lay with him on his narrow pallet shifted in her sleep and untwined her legs from his as she rolled over on to her stomach. Anastheus looked at her soft, smooth back and buttocks, and began to stroke her. She moaned in her sleep and spread her limbs. As he ran his hand over her downy skin, he warmed to his youthful passion. She turned on her back, and her white skin glowed pink in the early dawn. Though she was still asleep, her mouth opened slightly in expectant desire. He looked at her face with its unusually white skin and the black mane of her hair and realized that he did not know her name; but it did not matter. She had chosen him in the maiden's dance last night as she whirled around the fire and thrust her body out in an appeal for fertility. She was beautiful then as she stopped in front of him, opening her arms as her chest heaved and sweat ran down her belly and ripe thighs. Even with the rite passed and the seed planted for a new life, she was still beautiful. He was about to move between her open arms and legs again and crush her soft breasts with his chest, when he heard the clink of the gate chains just outside and remembered his conversation with the three leaders. He stopped moving and listened, but could hear nothing more. The girl made a small mewing sound and then drifted back to sleep, snoring softly while remaining open in welcome for him. But the moment passed as he recalled his charge and mission.

His clothing had been thrown aside last night in their mutual eagerness to join together. He felt around the pallet and located his tunic and sandals. Then he stood up and pulled the cloth over his head, tying it around his waist with a bit of rope. He stepped into his sandals and moved out of his room into the open market plaza. Although there was nothing moving nearby or in front of the inner garrison walls; some small unfamiliar noises must have triggered his sense of order. "The tablets must be where they were left, on the altar to Zeus. I had better get them." He said to himself.

As he broached the temple, the sounds of men reached him. The door down to the grotto was ajar and he could see candlelight bouncing off the walls. At first he thought it must be the Shaman, but then the voices coming out of the grotto startled him. They were not familiar voices and they spoke harshly and with accusation in a language that was not of the city. He hid himself behind the door.

Soon the doorway filled with the shadows of two men. One turned to the other and said in Greek, "Did you find the tablets?"

"No, they must be with the other old one. I killed the one below but could not find it. You best go look in the priest's quarters behind the statue and I will search here."

Anastheus, who had studied Greek and Egyptian in his childhood years learning the plays that were popular with the people, knew by these words that the Shaman was dead. One of the intruders went to the side of the temple and disappeared out a door. Anastheus felt around for some kind of weapon, but there was nothing handy. He crept up the steps to the statue of Zeus and watched from behind the statue's legs. The remaining man was searching in alcoves between the columns. Then he climbed to the altar and gave a cry of triumph as he saw the tablets on a high plinth above the altar. He ran to the top step around the base of the Zeus statue, and slid them off the table. Then he started back down the steps. When he passed, suddenly Anastheus struck out with his foot and caught the thief between his legs. The man tumbled forward and clattered down the full stairway to land on his face. Jumping up, Anastheus ran down the steps and picked up the bundle. Then he looked down at the Greek. His head was tilted over on one side at an angle that could not be assumed if he were alive. His neck was broken. "I killed him." Anastheus stood on the steps as he looked down at the intruder, rooted to the spot by what he had done.

Then he heard footsteps coming from the priest's apartment and he thought again of his mission. Clasping the bundle to his chest, Anastheus retreated out of the temple and made his way across the plaza. The sky was still dark, but there was a hint of light in the predawn. Beyond the plain, through the open gates he could see that the horizon was no longer a clean straight line. A saw-tooth foretold the coming of a fleet. He thought; "I'll have to hide these, or they'll be found. But I have to find a place outside the wall." To one side of the main gate, there was a small alcove where a soldier could sit, keeping watch through a small slot between the main gate and the man-sized door within the great gate. Within the alcove there was a high window where the soldier could reach out and cover the hinge of the smaller door with a spear. The slot was too small to squeeze through, but just large enough to put a blade in to cut someone attempting to dislodge the hinges. In the slot, there was a recess within the outside wall that a stone could be pulled in to close it from arrows. It was into this niche that Anastheus placed the tablets, and then securely replaced the stone cover. "When the Greeks exhaust themselves with destruction, they will leave and I shall return for them," he thought to himself.

He then crept out through the gate. As he slid from one war machine to another he concealed himself, flitting through the shadows. A crackling sound behind him drew his attention. From the tower there rose a pyre with black smoke and from within the walls came shouts and cries as the innocents woke to the new threat. As Anastheus neared the water, he could see the visage of many ships draw closer, attracted by their cohorts' sign. Their hulls were black in the sunrise, and the sails too, were black. From each ship many oars struck out and propelled them, with the force of thousands. The Greeks had returned in force.

Anastheus found a small boat with a triangular sail. He pushed it out until it floated gamely, and then climbed aboard, using the single oar at the stern to propel the boat in the windless morning along the shore towards the South, away from the Greek Armada coming in from the northwest. "I must find an ally somewhere. I will remember my vow." He said to himself as he sculled the boat toward the headland.

As the ships neared the city's shoreline, Anastheus was already around the headland and heading south across the warm sea, unseen.

# 6 *1873 THE ARCHEOLOGICAL DIG AT TROY*

The great man sat under the canvas canopy. Around him were all the signs of a discovery in the making. A ramp with cobbled paving stones had been unearthed right where he had calculated, but the rings of steep furrows which arced away to the east and north still held their secrets. He knew because he trusted the Poet.

This was the third time that Heinrich Schliemann had come down from Germany, never a doubt in his mind that Troy would be found here in Hissarlik, on this spit of land, further back from the sea than anyone ever imagined, and he was going to prove he was right. But it wasn't only the poetry of Homer, the lure of the city, or its treasure that drove him. It was the jeers of his contemporaries. In his life, first as a grocer's apprentice, then as a commercial agent, he never fit the traditional academic model for an archeologist. But he knew that right here in this place, was the source for Homer's Iliad, the greatest drama ever written. The old city of Troy lay here, covered by newer cities and then by a thousand years of nature.

"What matters," he thought, "is to find my vindication."

For months, his partner railed against him for ignoring the upper levels of the dig where all the signs pointed to the Homeric City. To the east, wire stretched across the site where the government owned its part of the site. But that side mattered not at all. It was here that he knew he would find the proof. "Dig deeper." He drove his local crew to cut down and down, into the Turkish, through Roman and into the Greek, the Hittite/Trojan and past it through the late Bronze Age and the five successive Western Anatolian cities, all built upon each other. But he found nothing that supported his faith in Homer. So he started again at the bottom and dug out each layer through the five and the one, and then it was time.

Schliemann was an imperious sort, with a stern, thin face and a drooping mustache, which did little to offset his hollowed cheeks or prominent cheekbones. In recent years, his hard belly had softened, but not his expression, worn by decades of battle with his contemporaries. His straight hair was combed severely, hiding the beginning of baldness which showed only with receding temples. His hands remained strong and calloused from years scrabbling in the harsh climate of his digs. His eyes remained sharp and accusatory, challenging anyone who doubted his right to be called a professional.

The night grew quiet as the workers left for their tents, supper and straw beds. The wind from the west slowed and died as the land cooled. Just as it started again to waft back towards the sea, he dropped down into the pit with his torch. The smoke stung his eyes as he held it against the side of the pit just above the last tier to be excavated. Something in the dirt wall caught his attention: a glint of yellow in the dark brown clay.

Climbing up the ladder to the surface, he grabbed a pick from the workers' pile. Back down into the hole, he struck at the side of the yellow reflection. The corner of a stone emerged which pressed on a yellow box that was canted on one corner. Pulling at the stone proved fruitless, so he again struck with the pick into the side of the hole. Clay showered down on his feet and on the box from above, concealing it for a moment. Then as he worked with the pick, another stone came out of the wall, and another. As the debris was cleared with his boot and his shovel, he could see the beginnings of a wall, with large cut stones disappearing down towards the pit's floor. Again and again he struck with the pick, each time, revealing a bit more of the wall. The box suddenly came free and the large stone which held it dislodged, landing on his ankle and driving it sideways against the floor. In some pain, he levered the pick's point under the stone and pulled on the handle. The boulder gave way and turned over. His foot came free and he spun around to grab at the box.

Holding it up to the torch, he saw that it was a flattish metal box with a cover, about 3 centimeters long and 2 wide. Intricately carved and engraved, it seemed to be made of gold. His knife came out in a flash. Working at the corners of the cover, he freed the last vestiges of clay from the gold and then digging with the knife point along the lid, he forced it open, ignoring the dents his knife made in the carvings.

The cover sprang open. Inside, lying on a bed of crushed pearls was a necklace of precious stones, strung on gold wire, worked into a clasp in the middle. There were clear aquamarines, blood sapphires, God's tears of amber, emeralds of deep green and black onyx. Between these larger stones, there were small topazes and amethysts of different hues. At the clasp, blue round sapphires shone, and in the center was a large diamond. The close-fitting box kept the stones as they must have been more than 2,000 years earlier when a royal hand closed the box for the last time.

Finally, he thought, this is my proof. The necklace and box were not Greek, but a cross between Greek and Persian, or maybe Egyptian. The animalistic figures on the box reminded him of an Abyssinian temple wall he had seen in Babylon. He concealed the necklace and box in his robe and stood up.

"There's more" he thought.

He returned to his tent, where his new young wife lay asleep. Placing the necklace on the bed next to her face, he lay beside her too excited to sleep and remembered how they scorned and mocked him. How they called him a charlatan and a thief for presuming education. Though he spoke 13 languages fluently and was rich from his merchant trader's life, he had no place in their field of work. Better to leave it to those who paid their dues to the universities. But he ignored them and financed his own digs in Mycenae and the Peloponnese. His obsession cost him his first wife, who finally got fed up with their nomadic life and returned to Russia. But here was his chance. His partner, Lord Calvert, owned the rights to half of this site, so he became Calvert's collaborator and partner, eventually supplanting the more schooled archeologist in this demanding quest for Troy.

Finally, he thought of his pregnant new wife lying here, of how he found Sophie through an advertisement in a Greek newspaper and how he brought her here to his tent near the sea. It gave him some peace, and he finally slept.

In the morning, he concentrated the work on revealing more of the wall. As the day grew warm, it gradually emerged from the marl, revealing its design with a straight corner end on the right and a niche on the left. The end of the wall had large vertical holes bored into the stones, apparently to hold a long rod. Every third stone was notched back past the holes, so that it resembled a joint, where something fit into the notches, like a door or gate.

Schliemann tried to imagine what the doorway opened into. Digging deeper into the hard earth became backbreaking for the workers, but they knew also that something was different. Opening before their eyes in this deep pit, was a part of history unknown before. As they cut down along the wall surface, the stones appeared to grow in size. Finally, the picks struck stone at the bottom of the hole – apparently the floor of the wall. When the clay was hauled out of the pit, the cobbles of the floor were revealed. They sloped down away from the wall towards the plain.

Sunset found the exhausted workers grateful for their dinner and their beds.

But the man couldn't stop. He started higher up in the niche and cut channels through the covering clay back to the wall, stopping only to dig out the spaces between the channels. Finally a niche was revealed.

Later that night, he stole back to the tent, where he unfolded his robe from his newest discovery and placed the object next to his bed. Fantastic thoughts tore through his consciousness. A new challenge assailed him. He could not rest. He placed a small torch into the ground next to the bed and carefully opened the bundle. The fire glinted off the golden metal before him. It made shadows on the letters engraved there and shone brightly along the edges. What appeared to be a single tablet was actually a large number of very thin metal foil leaves, inscribed with text and diagrams. "Tomorrow, I shall start to make a copy of these leaves, so that I can hide the original as I study and decipher the contents. Taking a flagon of wine, he poured himself a libation of sweet nectar and sat to wonder at the images before him. But the shapes started to swim and float in his view and his eyes grew heavy. "Tomorrow" he repeated, as he closed his eyes for a moment, then a moment more.

Deep into sleep, he did not notice a shadow that crossed the tent, and two hands that carefully lifted the metal, enfolding it in the rough wool. The torch burned on, but reflected off nothing but the skin of the sleeping master.

# 7  *SUNDAY, NEW MEXICO*

The early morning was overcast as Marcia drove me to BWI. I thought that I would feel awkward after the kiss last night, but it really was strange, I feel like it was the most ordinary morning in the world, being taken to the airport by her. The airport, as usual, is a confused agglomeration of passengers, employees and security, the latter trying to do a good job under impossible circumstances. But eventually, I get on the plane and we take off. I felt a little unsettled after yesterday. I am sure now that it has to do with loyalty coupled with lingering guilt.

Before leaving the house, Marcia had handed me a slightly large cell telephone. "This combines the technology of satellite communications with some sophisticated encryption, so it should be safe to use. I have a matching one. To reach me, touch my name on the menu and it will automatically reach me. I am not going to give you the actual number because it will be different every time you call – much like a multi-code garage door opener. But when I answer, if you need help, say your name is 'Chess'. No matter where you are, your telephone will transmit a GPS location and do so even when the phone is turned off. Even if the internal SIM card is removed, it will still transmit. I will figure out a way of reaching you."

The approach to Albuquerque usually takes you either down a nice easy ramp from the west mesa to the irrigated valley, over the Rio Grande onto the airport. The approach from the east drops like a stone from the 10,000 ft Sandia Mountain down to the runway. Today, we take the elevator route. The runways are exceedingly long, as they share both passenger aircraft and some of the giant cargo transports serving Kirtland Air Force Base. Kirtland is also home to Sandia National Labs; one of the places where Lauren's father worked.

The terminal looks a lot like a pueblo village, in pink adobe with turquoise windows. The blue contrasts with the orange tile floors and the whitewashed ceiling beams, to let you know that you have indeed arrived in the southwest. As I walk through the building, I use my new telephone to call Lauren, then go to wait outside Baggage Claim.

When Lauren shows up she jumps out of the car to give me a hug. There is a childlike vitality about her that is infectious. She takes me to her home, which turns out to be a sprawling adobe in the valley near the river, turned inward upon itself like an old Spanish Casa, surrounded by a high wall. Inside, the thick adobe walls keep the interior cool and quiet from outside noise. The house is entered by a double gate in the wall, which leads through a high Portal into the courtyard. A pool sparkles in the sunny interior courtyard, totally concealed from the street. Around the pool, the roof extended over an open Lattia corridor which has French doors into each room. The walls are stained a soft orange-red, which reflects warmly the sun. Lauren leads me around to one of the guest suites with its own closet kitchen and large bath. The bed is constructed from bark-stripped cottonwood trunks, and a heavily patterned Navajo rug dominates the brick floor. In the corner of the room is a tiny Kiva fireplace, also adobe, whose rounded sides and chimney project into the room. Light filters through plantation blinds and heavy cottonwood Vegas split the bundled twig ceiling into several sections. A deep cottonwood chair stands in the corner, with another smaller rug on it, and the comforter on the bed is soft beige. It is a room where one could sink into.

Lauren suggested that I take a short nap while she prepared lunch, but after a wash-up, I join her in the kitchen which, in spite of the rustic surrounds, is replete with modern equipment. It is a bit too early for wine, so I settle for iced tea while she prepares a lunch of stir-fried chicken fajitas in flour tortillas, accompanied by guacamole, salsa and sour cream.

"So what did you find out in Washington?" she asks.

"I discovered that our problem goes deeper than simple murder, and that there is a connection between Froehlich and Towson. Also, the tenuous link with Cyprus and the War is a little stronger. But I don't know exactly where that goes yet."

Lauren considers what I said for a moment then reacts "So you agree that Froehlich really was behind my father's death."

"The fact of murder is less important than its motive. What you need to do is tell me everything your father said about his relationship to Froehlich, and particularly before they came to the U.S. Let's start backwards. Just before coming to the U.S. they were both stationed in Cyprus, right?"

"Yes, but I know the motive: it was ego. Froehlich stole from my father, got rich, and wanted to conceal both the theft as well as the original act that would undermine his prestige if it came out. So long as my father kept quiet, Froehlich was willing to let it alone – but then something must have

94

happened to threaten Froehlich, so he had my father killed. It's as simple as that. Don't you believe me?"

"Lauren, I know what you believe, but if we are to get to the bottom of your father's death and the current attacks, we have to take a methodical approach."

"Sure; meantime, who knows what Froehlich plans against us."

"OK. Let's follow your train of reasoning. He kills your father; it is declared an accident. There are no clues which lead to him, except for the wild accusations of the murdered man's daughter who probably is driven by grief. If this were all true, why would he still have anything to gain by going after us, or conversely, what would he lose by leaving us alone?"

"But maybe he thinks that I know things about his past that can come back to roost."

"Exactly; that is why I have to know everything that you know." Lauren stops talking and thinks about what I have said and then she nods. "All right, now let's go back to Cyprus. Tell me what happened there."

"He told me that something needed to be decrypted, and that he had to go to Cyprus to take care of it. He also said that he never was able to complete his work."

"Did he say anything about working with Dr. Froehlich while he was there?"

"Yes, but he never wanted to talk about it. He made some comment once about Froehlich betraying him, but I always thought it had to do with the killing of the Polish Resistance patrol."

"What about Towson; one of the things I found out was that Towson is Turkish, and could have been there at the same time. Did you ever hear you father talk about Standahl Xyso?"

"Who is he?"

"That is Towson's birth name."

"Well yes, I heard the name, but not in any particular reference. Let me ask you something, Simon. You said that Towson was after something that you had – a key?"

"Yes, that's right."

"Do you have the key?"

"No, I told you before. I am not at all sure what he was talking about. Why do you ask?"

"Well, if Towson is after a mysterious key, maybe it has nothing to do with my father's death."

"That might be true, but I have a hard time believing in coincidences, particularly if they are so close in time. In my experience, when two events occur almost simultaneously, I have found that they tend to be related in some way."

"Maybe you have the key and don't know it."

"Why, Lauren, are you focusing on this key?"

"If you think it is connected to my father, maybe you should search for it. Then, if you get it to Towson, he'll leave you alone, and we can go after Froehlich, or whoever killed my father."

"I'll keep that thought in mind."

"Simon, you know, thinking about things my father said to me that seemed unconnected or odd at the time, I remember one time when I was about 13, we were playing a word game, you know, 'Hangman', where you keep guessing letters and every time you miss, another part of the hanging body is added until either you guess the word or the body is finished and you lose. Well, my father had decided the word and I was doing the guessing. There were many spaces left, and the figure was almost complete when my father suddenly looked up at me and said in an astonished voice "Allegory" but I knew that wasn't the word and asked him what he was talking about. He said that when he was in Cyprus, he had a word puzzle that he had to figure out, but the letters didn't mean anything. But he never considered allegories. He said if only he had, maybe he could have solved the translation."

"Are you sure he used the word 'translation' and not the word 'decode' or 'decrypt'?

"Oh yes, he said it was a translation."

"So what do we do now?"

"Lauren, we need to approach it from your father's professional associates. What I need you to do is to make a short list of people that your father worked with and trusted. Maybe he trusted someone with more than just National Secrets. Then I think we should go see them and try to discover anything that might lead to motive or opportunity. What bothers me is the attraction our inquiries will create. I am less concerned for myself.

Ultimately I know nothing. But I think that you know more than either you have told me, or even more than you think you know yourself."

"I can take care of myself" she retorted.

"Not against a personal vendetta, particularly if the resources of our secret agencies are involved. I would feel a lot more comfortable if you recognize that the deeper we go, the more we will be perceived as a threat to whoever we are after."

"Ok. I know you are probably right, but I'll be damned if I will let him get away with it and if I have to take some risks, then I'll deal with it."

"I know that you are focused on Froehlich, but he may be only part of your problem, or he may not even be involved at all." Lauren shook her head. "Yes, I know what you believe. Just try to keep your mind open to whatever facts that we uncover – and above all don't ignore the risk."

Lauren goes off to find some paper. When she returns, she starts to make a list. After looking at it for a time, she crosses out some names, leaving only three. She shows me the remaining short list of names. The first is Tom Yancey. Tom, as Lauren explained, is a biochemist who has been looking to build a code model based on genetic manipulation. According to Lauren, he believed that the genetic sequence could be utilized in developing new cryptographic formulas which were both unique, yet able to be replicated. He worked closely with Zilbern on code key development from a unique, if radical perspective. He works at Sandia Laboratories.

The second was Alattin Akan, a relatively recently arrived mathematician from Turkey, who worked on computer models to simulate randomness using far more advanced processes than current methods of random number generation. Alattin was one of the men at the fateful last supper that Lauren attended with her father, and had been a good friend to both Lauren and his father since he arrived here in the U.S.

The third was Eleanor Frankel, a psychologist who works on memory retention and neural networks. Frankel was a resident of Santa Fe and works at Los Alamos as well. Of the three, Lauren knows Frankel the best – she was a kind of stand-in aunt and one who Lauren took typical growing-up women's problems to. Although the three of them were confidents of Zilbern, Lauren is not overly fond of Yancy; she found him cold and unfeeling. From her description of Yancy as an 'Adonis' in appearance, I think that she probably had a crush on him and was rebuffed at some point in the past.

"With Frankel as your favorite, let's try her first. Call her and see if she is available for dinner – we can pop up there and meet at a nice restaurant."

Lauren disappeared and I withdrew my new cell phone to call Marcia.

"Miss me already?" she exclaims.

"Sure" I reply. "I got a few names from Lauren Sylfern for your search. They were all co-workers of Ernst Zilbern, and might have learned something that could have contributed to his death. Also, all three have connections to cryptology, which would make it possible that they had connections to Froehlich or the NSA. Lauren doesn't know of any relationship with Towson. Also interesting is that one of the three -Akan, was at the dinner where Edith Towson identified her husband." I pass along the three names. In addition, I added Jim Carson at ESCORT, the late Edith Towson, and also asked her to see if an agent at the FBI was named Frederickson.

"I started the paperwork on the Task Group, and got a preliminary budget approved. This afternoon, I will select a Chair and be assigned a Security Liaison. Should I start the process of getting you aboard in your role as a consultant?"

"OK, but please be careful. I don't want your identity to be linked with mine. Why not try use work name – Colin Lessant. No one knows that name outside of my old ESCORT group. It shouldn't raise any suspicions, at least not unless the Navy gets into the loop."

"Colin. That's almost as nice a name as Simon. But I like Chess better than Lessant."

"Marcia, will you let me know when I get access to the group database?"

"Yes, but you should be aware that access is a two-way street. If you access our site from a public computer without encryption, your network header will point the NSA right back at you. In a few seconds, software may be downloaded to your machine that will transmit everything, including keystrokes back to the NSA and possibly to whoever might be tracking you through their portal. It would be much better if you used one of our secure laptops, which contains very strong encryption. When do you think that you will be back in San Francisco? I can get you a secure laptop delivered there,"

"I don't know; probably the day after tomorrow."

"OK. Today is Saturday. I will have a machine delivered to you on Monday morning. What I will do is encrypt the password and get it placed on your computer before it leaves here tomorrow. Then the next time you call, I will give you the key for access."

"Marcia, one more thing: This whole business started with some sort of old key. It was lifted before I could take a good look at it. Is there any way that you could see if an old key comes up in your researches? It looked like gold, yet it seemed old. Anyway, if it comes up, could you include that in the data search?"

"Sure, a mysterious key; maybe it goes to a treasure box somewhere. Sure, I'll add it to our keyword matrix. Now, tell me more about Lauren Sylfern."

"Retract your claws, my dear. It is not seemly."

"You just watch yourself out there in the wild west. I would hate to have to do surgery to remove a Cupid's arrow!"

"This is business, as I have already told you."

"I think that is a direct quote from *The Godfather*, but don't mind me."

"I'll talk to you tomorrow. Goodnight." Marcia makes some kind of gargled sound and hangs up the telephone.

"Lauren," I called out, but there is no answer. I repeat it louder, but still no answer. The house was all on one floor, so I figured that she was back somewhere and the adobe walls are very thick. I walk to the rear of the house where the master bedroom, the doors to the courtyard standing open. Starting there, I walk around the yard, looking into each room and calling her name. No answer. By the time I get back to the kitchen, I was starting to get concerned. I find the door to the garage and look inside. Her car and a couple of bicycles were inside and the outer door is closed. Back in the foyer, I go out the front door and through the outside gate; but no Lauren.

Inside the house, the land line telephone starts ringing. I run inside and locate the phone. The voice at the other end says "No more games. Now we make a trade. Bring the key to the Plaza by the Cathedral in one hour and you may have her back." It was Towson.

Before I can say anything, the connection was broken. How did he know where we are and was able to kidnap Lauren so quickly? I know if Towson grabbed Lauren, I have to deal with him, but without the key, it's a no-win. He would have both of us. The key was important to him, so maybe I should tell him the truth. But that probably wouldn't work because then Lauren would be a goner, and probably me too. Just then there was a knock on the door. I went to the door and opened it. Two men stood there,

holding there flat little wallets open, so I could see their identifications.
"Federal Agents," they said. "May we come in?"

I opened the door and both walk in. They were wearing dark suits and ties,
unusual for the more relaxed New Mexico culture.

"We need to speak with Miss Sylfern," the nearer one said. "And who are
you?"

"My name is George, and I live down the street. Lauren asked me to come
and take care of her plants while she was away. She said she was going to
San Francisco and didn't know exactly when she might be back. I'm sorry,
but I don't exactly know where she is now."

The leader said "Do you mind if we look around?" and before I could say
anything, the other one disappeared out to the courtyard. In another
minute, he returned and shook his head. "George, is that a first or last
name?"

"It's Frank George. I can't give you any ID since I left my wallet back at
home, but you are welcome to come back to my house and I will get it."

"That won't be necessary. Fred will just take your picture." After calling
Fred back, he comes around with his cell phone and snaps a photo. I guess
the image got transmitted somewhere to be checked against their database.
I knew that in a minute or two, an alert would be transmitted from the
office if the NSA had shared their search with Homeland Security or
Justice. I thought that I might have to get out of a jam if that happened.
While I was waiting, I get another cup of coffee from the kitchen. The
leader came into the doorway, and I tensed.

"Ok Mr. George. Thank you for your help. Here's my card. If you see Ms.
Sylfern, please give us a call. We need to speak with her in connection
with an ongoing investigation, so it is important that she contact us as soon
as possible. Let's go, Fred."

I release a held breath. I guess NSA didn't raise a flag. I walk back out
through the entry and see both of them disappear through the gate. As soon
as it closed, I start searching for Lauren's car keys. Finally I find them on a
hook inside the Garage. I need to find wherever the Plaza is. Just outside, I
search in the tiny glove compartment for a local map, but there is none.
Then I noticed the flat panel in the center of the dash – a GPS Navigation
System. It boots up and asks me for a destination. I struggled through the
supposedly intuitive menus until I found a directory for Albuquerque. I
tried "Plaza" but got a question mark. I tried "City Center" and a map
displayed of the downtown area. Off to one side, there was a small square

that was labeled "Old Town Plaza." I scroll the screen to that area and click on the map. The image expands and shows a cathedral right next to the green square, so I guess it is what I am looking for. Back to the 'Destination' screen, I type in 'Old Town Plaza'.

The GPS thinks a minute and gave me a view of the street that I was on now with a blue line leading to the left. As I moved in the car, the map flowed with me and the blue line showed me turns and distances. The "Distance to Destination" started rolling backward, from 11.3 miles. On both sides of the street, which the GPS said was Rio Grande Boulevard, there is a mixture of large estates and congested developments, all strung together in no apparent order. Everything had walls, and some had impressive gates at the curb. One that I passed has a race car in sheet metal imbedded in the driveway gate with fancy hubcaps in the wall pilasters. Another had horseshoes. The road twisted and then it opened to four lanes, with some businesses added into the residential landscape. I passed under a highway, which the GPS identified as Interstate 40, and continued south.

Soon I came to a fork in the road. The GPS pointed me to the left into a very narrow street with shops on both sides. It looks very old. The destination indicator had scrolled down to under a mile, more slowly now as I drove cautiously between parked vehicles and pedestrians loaded with large bags and cameras. Suddenly the road opened on the left to a large plaza, faced by an Adobe church on my side. In the center of the Plaza was a white bandstand, elevated a few steps from the street level.

Four people are standing on the platform. One is Lauren, and one is Towson. I hadn't realized how tall he was. The other two I didn't recognize. I decided to see if I could talk my way out with Lauren. Finding a space to park on the street, I climbed the few steps, Towson said "I'm glad that you took me seriously. Now, let us conclude our business and you can be on your way."

Lauren's skin is a little pasty but she looks to be unhurt. Towson is ignoring her as he waits for my answer. "I'm sorry, as I told you; I do not have this key that you asked me about."

"Mr. Chess, I have not been completely honest with you, for which I apologize. The key is quite important to me, as I mentioned previously. It was stolen from me quite some time ago, and I had thought it was gone for good. Then I learned who had it, and arranged for its return. But unfortunately, you wound up with it, probably without even knowing it. All I want is for it to be returned. I would most appreciate your helping me."

"Mr. Towson, why is it so important to you?"

"Oh, so you have discovered who I am. Well so much for the better. The key is an antiquity that rightfully belongs to the people of Turkey, where it was found. It belongs in a museum. I want to return it."

"You can certainly prove your good intentions by letting the girl go."

"Of course; she is free to go at any time."

"Does the key match a lock somewhere?"

"Actually no. We in Turkey have lost so much of our archeological history through looting and corruption, that it is just one more artifact that I would like to see back where it belongs. I meant you no harm, but was justifiably upset since I thought that you had been responsible for the key's theft. Now I see that I was wrong. So I beg your assistance in reclaiming this lost piece of our history."

"I really am sorry; I do not have your key."

"Let's stop this foolishness. I know you had it. So where did you put it? It was not in your office or car."

"Yes, I did have it, but I hid it. It's in my safety deposit box at my bank."

Towson looked at me hard, and then spoke to his goon "Let them both go for now, we can always find them again." He then said to me "You understand how it is. I will give you one more day. You have my telephone number and I will expect a call by tomorrow night that you have retrieved it and have it available for me."

With that pronouncement, he takes the two men and leaves the bandstand. Lauren is shaking a little, but holds herself together and returns with me to the car. "I wonder how he knew we were back here in New Mexico" I say more to myself than to Lauren. "Lauren, did you tell anyone that you were coming back here?"

"No, I didn't even check out of my hotel in San Francisco. Do you think that they were following me to the airport?

"It's possible. How did you pay for your ticket here?"

"My credit card; when I left here for San Francisco, I bought a round-trip ticket. I just charged it. But that was before I met you. When you left me at the airport, I showed the United Airlines people my return coupon and they booked me on my flight – oh wait, there was an additional charge for the new flight, so they did run my card at the airport a second time"

"That must be it. But if he got the information that way, he must have some agency help somewhere along the line. Well, we will find that out tomorrow. Meantime, let's take care of the interviews here and then go back to San Francisco tomorrow."

Eleanor Frankel had been unable to meet us for dinner, so Lauren had arranged a late lunch with her up in Santa Fe. Although it was still early for our lunch, we decided to drive up anyway.

Santa Fe is the state capitol. It sits at 7,000 feet, about a thousand feet higher than Albuquerque. In the main Plaza, the buildings are decidedly western, but exclusively surfaced in stucco with rounded corners; either adobe or made to look that way. The center of the plaza is planted in ancient cottonwoods. Everywhere we turn, there are art galleries and shops.

We walk around the plaza and stop into some of the shops as we have some time before our reservation. Tourists are everywhere. Finally, we head down a side street to Casa Sena, set in a courtyard within an old adobe building. The restaurant has a series of small dining rooms. We have a glass of wine while we wait for Eleanor Frankel. It is still warm, so the heaters are not turned on in the courtyard yet, and diners flow in and out. Soon a slightly dumpy, 70ish woman in a print dress strides in, whereupon Lauren jumps out of her seat to embrace her: Eleanor, I would presume. She bulldozes her way into the room, trailed by Lauren and plops into a waiting chair, sticking her Earth Shoes under the table and smoothing her dress over plump legs. Lauren introduces me and Eleanor pulls out a pair of glasses on a black ribbon. She tilts her head back and examines me through the lower part of the bifocals.

"Well, you don't look like a thug." She exclaims as she peers at me like a pinned butterfly under a glass. I think I like her. "So what are your interests in my Lauren?" she begins as an interrogator would challenge a suspect.

"Good afternoon, Ms. Frankel. I am very glad to meet you. Lauren has..."

"Oh sure, give me the line. Did you learn that in dancing school, or at some afternoon tea?"

"If you would let me get a word in, I was going to say that Lauren tells me you are like her mom, and she really needs a mom right now."

Frankel starts and then turns to Lauren "What's wrong, honey?"

"Oh Aunt Em, we've been looking into dad's death. It seems that we have stirred up people who were connected with dad. I have been threatened and even kidnapped this morning, but Simon rescued me. But now, we're being watched. What scares me is that it is possible that these people killed dad last year."

I picked up on her pet name "Aunt Em?"

"Oh yes," said Lauren. "When I was younger, my father took me to see the Wizard of Oz so many times; I decided that Eleanor was my 'Aunt Em'. I always call her that."

"Lauren, first of all are you all right?"

"Yes, no one hurt me; they just scared me."

"Did you contact the police?" Eleanor asks.

"I don't think they will help, you see, it is the NSA and Towson."

"Towson!" comes out in a gasp from Frankel. "What's his involvement?"

I interject "It was Towson that took Lauren this morning. He promised to let her go if I traded him for something that was left to me which got lost."

Eleanor looked at both of us. "What is it that Towson wants?"

"A key," Lauren and I said almost together.

"Oh my God, Ernst told me, but I thought that he was just exercising his imagination; oh dear me."

"Em, what are you talking about?"

"All right, I promised him that I wouldn't say anything, but I guess I have to now. Ernst told me that when he was in Cyprus many years ago, during the war, he was given a task of decoding an inscription that appeared on two ancient artifacts: a golden key and a suit of armor. The artifacts were unusual in that they were Greek in style, but were made of an unfamiliar metal, much harder than steel and golden in color. Your father thought that they dated back to at least 1000 BC, and came from the eastern Mediterranean. He wrestled with the inscription for weeks, but made no progress. Somehow the armor got stolen from your father, but he still had the key with him when he was moved to the U.S. He continued to ponder it for years. He came to believe that the key did not open anything, but was a metaphor for a cryptogram key. It occurred to him that perhaps it could be used somehow to translate the inscription on the armor. But he no longer had the armor to test it against, and therefore could not decode it or translate the material. He never learned what happened to the armor and assumed that whoever took it would need all the pieces to solve it. He took the key home with him to New Mexico, and put it in a safety deposit box. I wonder how Towson learned about it."

"Did you ever see the key?" I asked.

"No. As far as I know, Ernst kept the key hidden because he knew that the artifact would be valuable to someone. Even the code itself was unique and he thought that if he solved it, the information might be valuable. According to him, the code was not only foreign in terms of language; it seemed to be undecipherable. This was quite a statement, coming from him."

She then turned to Lauren "Didn't you help him with his key research?"

"No, I'm sorry. I wish that I had, but he never told me about it and I never heard about any armor either."

Eleanor looked at Lauren with a puzzled expression. "That's funny; I could have sworn that he said you were as stumped as he was, but that you might have some thoughts about the writing style."

"No, it wasn't me. Dad hardly ever talked about his work, except in generalities, and nothing at all about his time in Cyprus. Only that he was there and also had been reunited with Johann Froehlich again after leaving him in Germany."

"Froehlich! Was he in Cyprus too? You know that it was he that betrayed the Polish rescuers to the Germans back before Peenemünde. Ernst also believed that he stole your father's long-prime invention. I wouldn't be surprised if he wasn't behind the theft of the armor, and now the key. It would certainly fit Ernst's suspicions."

"I know about the betrayal, and dad told me about Froehlich's theft of his prime generator."

"Eleanor, I take it you don't think too much of Dr. Froehlich," I commented to Eleanor.

"I should say not; especially after he got Towson involved with his various schemes. I tell the two of you, neither Froehlich nor Towson should ever be believed or trusted at any time. They have only one thing in common: self interest."

"Eleanor, can you please tell us more about Towson?" I added.

"Daniel Towson was a snake. Are you saying that he is still alive?"

"Yes, Aunt Em. He is very much alive."

105

"But his body was found last April."

"Em, the person who died wasn't Towson, it was dad. I think that Towson and Froehlich together faked Towson's death." Lauren said quietly.

"Lauren, you father died, but he was lost off a boat that was on its way out of the Golden Gate Bridge. As I understand it, he fell overboard into the current and his body was never recovered. I spoke to the boat captain. He was interrogated by the police, but released when no one found any evidence of foul play. I tried to reach him later, because I wanted to visit the spot where he fell over. But no matter how I searched, the captain no longer had a boat, and seems to have also disappeared."

"Em, you're wrong. Dad died in the car. I was with him. He lost control of the car and we went off the Twin Peaks road. I got thrown out of the car, and knocked out. When I came to, the car was on fire with dad inside. There was nothing I could do." Tears started to form in the corners of Lauren's eyes and Eleanor came around the table to hold her.

"I'm sorry, Lauren, that is not what I learned from your father. He called me that night and told me that he had been in an accident, but was able to escape the car. He said that he wandered up to the road, and was picked up by some passersby. When he spoke to me, he was calling from someone's house. He said that he was waiting while the two men went back and tried to find you. He was very worried that you had been thrown from the car and he couldn't find you. He wanted me to know that he was all right. That was the last I heard from him."

"Em, why didn't you tell me about this before? I've had nightmares about that night for a whole year. In my dream, I can see him calling out to me, but I can't get to him. Em, it's been horrible."

"I'm so sorry, but your father was worried about your safety, and begged me not to say anything, especially to you. He thought the car was tampered with and if you knew, you would start digging, and they would come after you as well. I promised him, no matter what happened. That seemed to give him some peace. When reports of his death came out, I assumed that whoever arranged the accident tried for him again, this time succeeding. I kept mute to protect you."

"Eleanor, how do you know about the drowning?"

"Some weeks afterwards, I received a call from the Police, who told me that they got a tip about that night. When they investigated, they found that Ernst was on a boat where there was some kind of meeting. The boat captain claimed that a rogue wave knocked him overboard. The Police could find no evidence to the contrary, so they had to drop it. The Lieutenant told me to leave it alone. When I questioned him, I was told that the file was closed and sealed, and that some pressure from Washington was exerted to keep it that way. I was also told not to repeat my conversation with anyone."

"Do you know who else was at this meeting?"

"No, I got the distinct impression that this was not a subject for discussion."

"What is the boat captain's name? Maybe I can do some digging and locate him."

"Wait a second, I will think of it -Wayne something; Wayne Harter, or Holder; something like that." Eleanor seemed lost in thought.

"Could it be Wayne Hudson?" I asked.

"Yes, that's it, Hudson."

"When did you talk to him?"

"It was about two weeks later after Ernst disappeared. Hudson was still being interviewed by the police, so I found out where he kept his boat and went down to the marina to speak with him."

"Was he a skinny older guy that looked more like a bookkeeper than a salt-water sailor?"

"Exactly; do you know him?"

"I had the opportunity to meet Mr. Hudson briefly, a couple of days ago. He is a manager at the Cliff House Restaurant, where, coincidentally, I also met with Daniel Towson, though not exactly on friendly terms."

"Well, he's the fellow I'm talking about. Interesting that he was no longer in the charter boat business. And you say he knew Towson?" Eleanor shuddered.

"The last time I saw Hudson, he was getting into Towson's car. He hasn't been home again since then."

"Knowing Towson, I wouldn't be a bit surprised if Hudson is feeding fishes as well. Well I think that clears up the question of who engineered your father's death. So Towson is still alive. That is one nasty character." Eleanor turned back to her meal, did not speak about it again until after dessert was served.

The meal is remarkable. La Casa Sena bills itself rightly as the finest restaurant in New Mexico. For appetizers, Lauren has local goat cheese, crusted with piñon, Eleanor orders a lump crab cake, and I enjoy mussels with garlic in a green sauce. Before the main course was served, we had an Intermezzo of granitas: Pomegranate, Chile, Mango, and Jalapeño. As for main dishes, I pick grilled venison, while Lauren eats sea bass and Eleanor trout, baked in adobe.

During the meal and dessert, we stay away from the topic. Lauren and Eleanor catch up. I watch the warm interaction between the two of them and wonder why Lauren stayed out of touch with Eleanor for so long.

Both ladies order dessert, sharing a Lavender Crème Brulee with a bowl of fresh raspberries on the side. I resist for a bit, but then break down and try a piece of their Buttermilk Almond Cake. With coffee, I decided it is time to explore Eleanor's obvious hatred of Towson.

"Eleanor, I know that it worries you, but whoever killed Ernst is no doubt behind the threats to Lauren. I need your help to keep her safe and solve the problem. So can you help us with anything more about both Towson and Froehlich?"

Eleanor looked at Lauren fondly and then nodded.

"I first met Daniel Towson in 1965 or 66. He had been here for about 10 years by then. I was introduced to him by a small group of people that were taking the Turkish side in the conflict over Cyprus. Towson, but I think he had a Turkish name before that, was strongly pro Turkish, and was looking to put together funding to support the overthrow of archbishop Makarios, the Greek leader of the Orthodox Church in Cyprus. Towson believed that Cyprus was ethnically Turkish, and should be politically part of Turkey, while Makarios demanded self-government. Makarios had been exiled by the British, but continued to fight for self-rule. By 1959 he was able to come back to Cyprus and was elected President. Towson wanted to put a plan together to eliminate Makarios, blame it on the colonial Greeks, and reintroduce Turkish rule on the grounds of restoring stability."

"You have to understand that Towson believed fervently in the Turkish cause. Cyprus was very important to both Greece and Turkey because of its physical location, as a way-station to the eastern Mediterranean and Suez. The UN had a peacekeeping force in Cyprus at that time. With occasional flare-ups, status quo was generally maintained. But by '71, tensions had built up to a point that a Greek based military Junta seized power and started a strong anti-Turk campaign of ethnic isolation, supported by 98% of the Greek Cypriots. Makarios himself continued to lobby against British colonial rule. In July, 1974, Turkey retaliated by invading Cyprus and attempted to set up its own rule. Towson's weapons and funding aided in this invasion. I believe that he saw this work as a patriotic act, and not merely to increase his wealth."

"In spite of the UN's chastisement, Turkey continued to rule Cyprus. Even when Makarios returned to Cyprus with the support of both the UN and England, he was unable to restore independent government. Three years later, Makarios was dead. It was reported that he had a heart attack, but evidentially, his heart was removed and his remains were buried without the heart and without any autopsy. I thought that Towson might have had a hand in this, because the sequence of events were almost exactly what Towson had been planning almost 10 years earlier. It's difficult to be sure, since Makarios was an enemy for not only the Turks, but anti-independence Greeks as well."

"Once Makarios was dead, the partition between Greeks and Turks settled again into an uneasy peace, with the Greeks still occupying the south and the Turks the north. The south has prospered, while the north is still under embargos by the UN as a continuation of the illegal Turkish partition of the Island. I would believe that if Towson is still alive, he would be continuing in his fight for unification, but under Turkish rule.

"Towson, aside from these 'terrorist' leanings, developed many alliances in the US for his Turkish causes, as well as for the causes of a variety of warring factions around the world. You will remember that the U.S. considered Turkey an important part of our cold war against the USSR. Turkey had been persuaded to host military bases there, far closer to the underbelly of the Ukraine and to Moscow. But Towson's help in Turkey weren't the only activities that earned him U.S. friendships; he also sold lots of arms to Israel while the U.S. looked the other way. He was brought into the political insider track for his "aid" to Israel and was given a unique position as advisor and agent for insurgencies in a variety of locations. In real terms, this meant that he fronted for the CIA by diverting arms to insurgencies in Afghanistan, Nicaragua, Iran, and Iraq."

"Do you think that he had the support of the Turkish government?" I queried.

"Who knows? Turkey has been a friend to the US for many years. As I mentioned, we have vital military bases there, created in the early '60s and remaining to support our pro-Israel and anti-Russia policies. I doubt whether Turkey would overtly support or protect Towson. Their country made a big mistake in invading Cyprus, but world markets and the politics of the Middle East have eliminated the possibility of sanctions."

"So you think that Towson would do anything to re-strengthen Turkey's role in the world?"

"No question about it. I think that he would use all his political contacts and businesses to reawaken a new Ottoman Empire."

"Do you know anything about his personal life?"

"Not much; I know that he brought a wife to the U.S. and maintained a home in San Francisco, but not much more."

"Ok. That gives me a good picture of Towson; what about Froehlich, and his relationship with Towson?"

"Froehlich is another story completely. Ernst worked with him during the war in Germany, but after the war they really didn't work together, even though they were in very closely related fields. The best way to characterize Froehlich is that he is an opportunist, with a capital 'O'. When Towson was spouting his wrath against the Greeks, Froehlich listened and supported the ideas of conflict, but never overtly. He worked to develop strategies which would ensure conflicts escalated, because the more conflicts there were, the more nations and industries would want to keep confidences and secrets from one another, which was his business. In a way, he is worse than Towson because he always hides behind others who do his bidding."

"Near the end of the War, the US put 'Operation Paperclip' into action. This was a plan to capture or 'liberate' as many German and Axis scientists as possible, getting them to move to the US instead of to Russia – who incidentally had a very similar plan. At the top of Paperclip's list was Werner von Braun, for his work in developing the V-2 rocket and rocket fuels during the last 3 years of the war. Von Braun also had a hand in their nuclear program and most of the advanced engineering done by the Germans, including the jet plane and related metallurgy. The Paperclip list was an updated German list, Osenberg, which was put together in 1943 to identify German engineers and scientists then in the military or in concentration camps, who could be put to work in Research & Development for Germany. This list was discovered by the US Intelligence corps who renamed it the Black List. In May, 1945, Operation Overcast was implemented to evacuate as many German scientists as possible before the Soviet Union could get them. In July, 'Overcast' resettlement camp in Bavaria was renamed 'Paperclip' and the scientists were offered one-year contracts in the U.S. Froehlich was given the job of verifying the identities of these scientists and worked with Colonel Tofloy of the US Army Ordnance Branch to transport those scientists who accepted these contracts. Among them was your father, Lauren. Actually, a total of 127 of them did accept and were moved to the US, settled in several different Army installations around the country. These 'Paperclip Scientists' were eventually offered visas and were given permanent status here, integrated into the US culture and most became citizens. Froehlich maintained contacts with many of them and as their work grew in value, both in rocket designs and nuclear engineering, his reputation rose with them.

"Are you saying that Froehlich, by himself, invented or created nothing?"

"To be honest, I don't know for sure. You have to understand that much of this information came from Ernst. He was embittered by the treatment that he received from Froehlich and from the U.S. government when your mother became ill. I don't know Froehlich myself, but I trusted you father."

"I do know that Froehlich's work on long prime code key developments was created primarily by Ernst, for which Froehlich got the credit along with the cash. Although they had broken with one another just at the end of the war, I think when Froehlich received patents for code key developments that Ernst had designed, it was the final straw. I was actually surprised that your father didn't act on his grudge, and expose Froehlich for the charlatan and thief that he was. But I think that you father had other things on his mind. He continued his work at Sandia and Los Alamos through your mother's illness and death. From that time until he died, he never mentioned Froehlich's name again and I seriously doubt if they ever spoke again."

"Aunt Em. If Froehlich is behind this interest in my father's most recent work, why would he be a threat to me? With his connections, he could gain access to almost anything that was done at Los Alamos."

"Don't be naïve, my dear. Froehlich would borrow, steal, connive and subvert anything and anyone to get what he wanted. Your father had a lead on some new technologies that had just been discovered. He was following the trail back to Europe where it had been developed. I believe that if Froehlich had a clue as to what your father was after, he would be on it in a flash. But, as I said before, Froehlich's Modus Operandi is string-pulling. If Towson could be manipulated, I would bet that it was Froehlich behind the curtain."

"Do you know any of the details of this new research that Ernst was interested in?" I ask.

"No, only that he said something odd once. He said that it was 'discovered' not 'invented'. Your father, Lauren, was quite precise in his language. If he said 'discovered', he meant just that. It meant that something was already there which was found, not something new that was created. That's all I can tell you because it is all I know. Lauren, you must know that your father loved you more dearly than life. If there was anything he found that was important, he would have found a way to see that you got it, even if he were to die suddenly like he did."

"But I have found nothing." Lauren thought for a minute, but stayed silent.

"Maybe you haven't looked in the right place."

"Lauren, I have a question for you." A suppressed idea that had been bothering me for a few days surfaced again. "Why did you come looking for me last week? I mean it's not like I was a unique PI or anything."

"I told you, Simon. I was looking for Froehlich. . I recognized you from the file that I obtained at State. I thought that I would ally myself with you. Your background in Special Operations would be helpful to me. When I saw you with Towson at the Cliff house, I thought that I better find out more about you if I was going to trust you."

It didn't ring quite true, but then her agenda was somewhat singular, so I was just a means to that end.

After thanking Eleanor and making small talk about future get-togethers, we leave the restaurant and Eleanor left to find her car. It was evening by the time we drive back toward Albuquerque. Lauren put the top down on her Porsche, and we flew through the desert.

When we reach the house, Lauren puts the car in the garage and closes up for the night. I plead exhaustion and excuse myself to the guest room, although I think that Lauren wanted to stay together a little longer. I lie down and set a mental alarm for about 2 hours.

The house is quiet when I wake. I pulled my green and brown nylon camouflage jumpsuit out of my briefcase and slip into it. My sneakers are black. From two small cans, I dig out my cam paint and apply it to my face, neck and ankles. First I put on a coat of dark and medium brown, and then cover it with blotches of green, to help break up the recognizable shape of my body. Then I creep quietly out of my room into the courtyard. I thought that I should check around for any watchers, to validate Lauren's story.

At one end of the courtyard, there is a small concrete planter set against the outer wall. Next to it is a large cypress, so the wall is in deep shadow. I wish I had packed my Night Vision glasses, but will just have to settle for awareness. There is almost no breeze so I wait until I hear a car coming down the street and then as it passes, I slide over the wall on my stomach, dropping quietly onto the mulch bed outside the wall. I lay there for about 15 minutes, to see if there is any movement nearby, but there is nothing that I can see or hear. Then I rise and walk slowly around the property, stopping every 10 feet or so to listen and merge with the night sounds. I sense no one. If anyone was there, I do not encounter them.

After about an hour of reconnaissance, I slip over the wall into the courtyard again and back in the guest room. My camo suit is rolled into a tight tube and cam paint is scrubbed off. My last act is to lock the door and dig out my sat phone

.

# 8 *SUNDAY NIGHT, ALBUQUERQUE*

"This better be good."

"Marcia, I'm sorry to wake you, but I wanted to wait until there was little chance in being overheard."

"What time is it anyway? Oh, it's 2:30. Simon, is this normal for you to wake sleeping ladies for something as trivial as a case? Have you put Ms. Client to bed?"

"Yes, but not in the context you're hinting at; she went to bed alone some time ago. I've been out an about to check on any watchers."

"So what is it that couldn't wait until a respectable hour?"

"There are no full time watchers, so either Lauren is lying, or the interest in her is sporadic."

"Simon, I would vote for the former option. From what little I have dug up on her, the story that she told you doesn't seem to be either complete, or entirely true. But when you get the laptop tomorrow, you will see the file I put together. OK, so that's her. What was the other news?"

"I discovered that there may be two new motivations – one is Turkey and Turkish interests and the second are new code systems that could have been 'discovered' as opposed to being 'invented'. The code business may be the key to connect the NSA's interest. But the Turkish connection may be behind Towson's involvement. It seems that Mr. Towson is particularly interested in protecting Turkish history. At least, as he told me, he wants the key to return it to the Turkish people as an archeological artifact which rightfully belongs to them."

"Do you believe him?"

"There is certainly a strong element of truth, validated by Eleanor Frankel, who we met today. Apparently she has some history with Towson and his avid pro-Turkish activities over the years."

"Do you think that there is a chance she is working with him?"

"If she is, she certainly covers it with apparently genuine animosity for the man."

"You know, anger is a perfect cover for a lie."

"I think that in this case, her obvious love for Lauren is driving her attitude. But there are a couple of contradictions that Eleanor brought out during our conversation that add to the question of Lauren's veracity. She was particularly interested in Lauren's denial of any knowledge of the key, yet Ernst told Eleanor that Lauren, as a specialist in Middle Eastern languages, was consulted on the possible translation.

"As I said, Simon, I would seriously question anything that she said, and also think that we need to investigate her motives."

"Well those are my contributions and questions. How are things going at your end?"

"I would rather talk about something else, like the fact that I really miss you. I was really surprised to feel that today, but I do."

"Marcia, I don't know what to say."

"Well, you could say it was nice, or dumb, or even interesting."

"Well it is nice. Thank you."

"There are times when you are quite thick. All right; today, as I told you, even though it was a Sunday, I set up the group. By the end of the day, the chair was fully aboard. I picked a fellow called Smithson, a good Yale Eli: ambitious and vacuous. Smithson is in the process of picking his group of analysts who owe allegiance to him for one reason or another, and is putting together the mission profile. My original query which I sourced to the President's National Security Advisor, asked us to report to him on any efforts to subvert our code security and migrate our technology to the private sector. We formalized the study group mission; however; we limited it new crypto-systems, as opposed to Government systems commonly in use. When Smithson queried me about his group mission as a possible conflict with NSA Security, I realized that he really is as stupid as I thought. I explained to him patiently, that Central Security is concerned with security within the organization, not from outside, except for facility issues. God, what a dummy; I guess that is why he succeeded so far on the Peter Principle."

"Anyway, he went happily about assembling his new empire, which, by the way, now numbers about 65 analysts of various types. We have all the hardware, Cray time, and budget we need to move ahead. The Queen Ant is certain that he is fielding a great responsibility dispensed by the Kingmaker NS Advisor. But he also understands that his program is totally under the radar, so he can't even hint of his importance to all those that he would like to impress. While this is disappointing to him, he'll get over it."

"Initially, we set up taps on everything that went to and from the list of scientists and their friends that Smithson put together, supplemented by our short list. To keep it honest, we included Froehlich to the list, as well as his friend Towson. I think that Smithson didn't care what we did or who we investigated, so long as he was the head of it and could be seen as a valuable leader in the organization."

I took the opportunity to break in when she took a breath." But have you uncovered anything yet?"

"Well, no. We just got everything in place, and the ELINT data is starting to come in. We started with the usual keywords to signal diversion to our databases, but today I added a number of the special words that we decided on. I'll add Sylfern, Frankel, Akan and Yancy in tomorrow – no today. It's already tomorrow today."

"I have to get back to San Francisco tomorrow. Towson is certain that I lied to him about the key, so he will be watching me."

"Where are you staying tonight?"

"At Lauren's house, why?"

"Do you usually stay at client's houses when you are on a case?"

"No, but she is a special case."

"Well, good for you."

"She is a client. Marcia, you have to understand, I have clients, and they sometimes are women. I don't sleep with clients, and particularly young women who are depending on me to protect them."

"Simon, I know how it is. Besides, while you are there, I am here, and there's always the professor."

"Stop, won't you? He's too nice. Not like me."

Marcia laughed out loud. "Ok, you win."

She was still laughing when she broke the connection.

# 9 *1945, PEENEMUNDE*

There were no explosives left. There was little fuel. Alcohol required thirty tons of potatoes for each flight. When explosives ran short, concrete blocks were substituted. When fuel became scarce, the storage chambers were left empty, so the lighter V2 projectile would still fly, but only damage the will of the people, not their structures. Yet production didn't stop.

The head of research still pushed development of the next two generations. First would the long cannon, which would deliver tiny self-propelled projectiles to their targets with the added impetus of the main cannon. These guns would exceed 120 meters in length. But before these were put into production, another generation was started. This version of the V2 would attack from space. But to do that, a metal was needed that would resist hotter temperatures. Experiments were made with graphite and tungsten but they were difficult to procure. New engine nozzle designs were experimented with that circulated the liquid fuel itself to cool the combustion compartment. But so far, none of these experiments were successful. Even the Fuhrer was kept in the dark of this research, so the R&D team might survive his mania if the project didn't succeed. But the word went out.

"Find the most exotic materials or science possible to meet this high temperature challenge."

From Scandinavia to the Middle East the orders were given – look, listen, get the information. Bring it back to the Fatherland and contribute to finishing this war. America, with its great resources and industrialization could not be beaten without it. The new German rockets had to withstand the higher heat to generate more thrust. Current models could reach up to almost 70 miles into the atmosphere. But the trajectories were not high enough and enough fuel could not be stored to deliver a large explosive payload 3,500 miles. New metal was needed for the combustion chambers and the nozzles. Without it, Germany would lose.

Into the camps in Italy, Poland, and throughout Germany the search was started. It was thought that the Jews might know. Their merchant networks can help. Those at the top were willing to do almost anything to achieve this goal. Even if it meant giving amnesty to get the information, it was considered a smaller price.

So from Greece, Spain, South America, Africa, Japan and even agents in China, Portugal and America itself, the search went on. Back in Peenemünde, the launch vehicle was designed, engines engineered and machined and test beds created. All awaited the final metal. But none came.

Then a hint came from Cyprus, from the hated Turks. There may be a metal there that could serve the Fatherland. There may be a technology that is very old. But so far, it could not be found and the science which spawned it cannot be located.

A key scientific agent was dispatched to Cyprus to discover the source and secure it. Local Greeks exposed him and he was shot. In retaliation, anyone who might have any information about the agent's capture or information he may have uncovered was seized, tortured and finally killed before revealing anything. Even among the Turks themselves, there were a few that owed alliances to Germany or had relatives that could be threatened. But none of these avenues yielded fruit.

So the search went on. Meanwhile, Peenemünde had to be dismantled and moved. The previous August, a massive air raid by the Americans and English, called Operation Crossbow, killed hundreds of foreign prisoners working in the development and production facilities, as it was targeted at the sleeping quarters. The head of engine development was also killed in the raid.

A new laboratory was being built in Austria, in underground bunkers inside the Alps. Gradually these facilities took shape in spite of the bombing raids on transportation centers and on convoys carrying people and materiel to the new location. All had to be done in secret, for fear of more directed raids on Ortler Mountain, the new site. So construction and equipping proceeded very slowly, but it did move forward. Until the new labs and production lines were completed, the work continued here.

Just this week, word came that the test stands in the Alps were completed, and a new, higher velocity wind tunnel had been finished there, so plans were implemented to relocate the Lab to the Ortler Mountain site.

Frederick Almsteder was in the lab when the evacuation order was received. It was still winter: February, and the snow was deep around the main tunnel entrance. Almsteder was not one of the main scientists in the lab, but was responsible for testing new materials for the nozzles of what would eventually be called the V-4. A young man when the war started, he aged rapidly in this stressful environment where there was no day or night and no relief for the massive pressure to succeed where there were no antecedents to rely upon. Privately, he abhorred the treatment of all the Jews and political prisoners brought here from those horrendous camps and bullied into assembling the rockets. Even the scientists among them, men who he once admired while at school, were beaten and badgered to cooperate in the laboratories, and when some refused they were put into the most dangerous of jobs like mixing explosives, or taken outside and shot in front of the others as examples. But publicly, he had little choice. The SS that ran security for the lab were always present. Frederick hoped that their development work would make a quick end to the war, as had been promised by Von Braun and others. Yet year after year the war raged and neither the English nor the Americans showed signs of yielding. Attacks all over Germany had increased so that each day, somewhere could expect bombs. With dwindling resources for pilots, planes and fuel, now when bombers flew over, there were almost no fighters defending even this important location.

Today was his turn to evacuate. He went to his quarters and selected some warm clothes for his journey. Others were collecting their few remaining notebooks and models. All of the large hardware had already been dismantled and moved. The lead scientists were already gone as well. This would be the final train, and it was scheduled to leave soon.

Frederick was leaving the lab when the teletype started chattering, and a thin strip of paper started to emerge from the side of the machine. It was all in 5 letter groups, a code that needed a translator with a book, or the code decrypter machine into which the message would be typed and out of which would come the plaintext. But there was no cryptanalysts left at the lab. They had all gone east.

"Frederick, get out. The train is going to leave any minute." His friend Konrad shouted.

"But there is a message coming through. I can see that it has a high priority prefix and is coded Utmost Secret."

"Frederick, I believe there is a duplicate receiver at Ortler. Perhaps they will get the message there. Leave it and come now, or you will be left behind, and the demolition charges will kill you."

"It is only another minute or so more. There are at least 500 groups already, so it can't be much longer." Frederick gathered his bundle and stood anxiously by the receiver."

"All right, but if the train departs, and you are left behind, don't blame me." The voice receded as Konrad carried his travel parcel down the tunnel towards the entrance.

But still the machine chattered. Then there was a sharp toot as the locomotive signaled its intent to leave. Frederick tore off the message, taking as much as had already come out of the teletype, and grabbed his bundle. As he ran towards the entrance, he could still hear the teletype clattering behind him.

He emerged from the tunnel to see that the engine was already half way out of the station. Behind it, the cars were accelerating as they retreated along the empty platform. Frederick started running. His clothing parcel slipped out from under his arm and fell to the concrete. But he didn't stop. He had to catch this last train. A few soldiers stood by the end of the platform and stared at him. They stood next to a truck piled with rolls of detonation cord. He kept running. After all those months in the lab, he was seriously out of shape and pain started in his chest as he ran. The closer he got to the train, the faster it went.

He reached the end of the platform and leaped down to the tracks, hopping over snow piles, switches and debris scattered in the rail yard. Potholes and bomb craters littered the landscape, yet he still ran. In his hand, he clutched the last message, one that he was determined to bring with him.

A burst of wind pushed him along as he ran. Then the train slowed over a trestle and he sprinted closer. There was only 50 feet separating him from the last car and the train seemed to be slowing. 'I'm going to make it' Frederick said to himself between gasps for breath in his all-out run. At the back of the last car, the center door opened and an officer came out onto the rear platform.

"Get away. This is a restricted train," shouted the officer, as he started to reach under his holster flap covering his pistol.

"But I work in the laboratory," Frederick tried to shout, but the wind blew his words away and all the officer saw was a hatless man, running towards the train, clutching something that blew in the breeze.

"It looks like a bomb fuse," the officer thought. So he drew his pistol and pointed it at Frederick as he gained on the train – only 20 feet to go.

"Wait" Frederick shouted as he tried with all his breath to make the words heard. But only a gurgle came out of his ragged throat. One shot is all it took. Frederick fell between the rails; all his breath whooshed out of him and he lay facing the gravel between the ties. His last thought was that if only he had waited for the whole message. Then he died.

The message tape fluttered in his hand and then wafted out across the yard, to vanish for all time. Back at the lab, the chattering teletype machine finally spit out the last groups and went silent.

As the afternoon wore on, dust motes hung above the empty desks. The great assembly halls, metal stamps, cutters and benders which shook the very walls, were quiet. In the tunnels where prisoners labored in agony, nothing remained but empty beds, drying from sweat-soaked bodies.

Footsteps came in from the laboratory to the dormitory. "Are they gone?" a man asked.

"Yes, all but we two." The other turned the corner and came into sight; a small man with jet black hair and a kindly face.

The first man, taller and more Aryan, with blonde hair and an imperious nose, reached his bed and fussed under it, digging out a small parcel of clothes he had sequestered. "Let's get out of here. We need to start heading east. The Russians are only a day away and there are German patrols in between. We must cross the river to them."

The second man also took a small bundle of clothes from his footlocker. "But don't you think it would be better to head west? There we will be sure to be given the opportunities that we are looking for."

The first man turned. "But we agreed. The Russians have already promised me a laboratory and all the assistance I would need to continue our research. They also promised that we could use their far-flung network of agents to continue the search for metals and guidance technologies. The Americans have no interest in this work. They only want a bomb. I want to reach out to the stars. You too have the same dream. Let us do it together, in the east."

"Very well; I shall go with you, but I still believe that the Russian mind will surely turn to the bomb, and I don't trust that they will fulfill their promise to you. We should give the Americans a chance."

"I will never rest until I reach my goal," the first man said with utmost resolve.

The two of them picked up their bundles and walked out of the Dormitory into the common hall, then passed the communication shack. The first man turned into the door.

"Where are you going?"

"I want to see if any new messages came in about our worldwide hunt."

He looked on the desk at the log, but nothing was there from today. Then he glanced at the Teletype machine. A small coil of tape with the end torn off, was sticking out of the slot, He cut the tape off at the end of the message and stuffed it into his pocket. Then turning back to the door, he took a small codebook from the open safe, and put it in his other pocket. "Come, let's be on our way."

They walked out of the main entrance, and were immediately accosted by a small patrol that was guarding the demolition men, who went about setting charges to bring down the mountain and seal the entrance.

"Who are you?" the patrol leader asked.

"We missed the train. My friend here couldn't keep up. Perhaps you can show us the way to the main station so that we may catch another," the first man said. He pulled out his identifications with the bright red ''Wissenschaftler' [scientist] stripe diagonally across his photo.

"There are no more trains. We are protecting the site until it is sealed. Once it is secured, we have been ordered south." The patrol stood by while the demolitions men completed their tasks, and then they pulled out in their truck stringing cord behind them. While they waited with the patrol, there was a brief 'crump', and part of the mountain came down on the railroad tracks, sealing the main entrance tunnel. The patrol got into their truck and escorted the two scientists into the back.

The smoke was clearing from the explosion, as the truck bearing the two scientists drove east, intersecting the Oder River between Poland and Germany, and began moving south towards Berlin, to join the retreating army.

For two days, they traveled, stopping frequently as the Allied bombing raids continued along the Polish border. After traveling about 130 miles, they turned west and took the road through Angermünde on a line toward Berlin. The town was deserted, and they searched through the village for any food which might have been left behind. With only 43 miles to go, the patrol leader decided to not chance coming upon an Allied or worse, a Russian patrol this close to Berlin. They chose the local church as a place to sleep. The following morning, they would make a break for Berlin itself.

The soldiers, weary from the many months in battle and without full rations, lay down on the hard stone floor of the church or on the few wooden pews that were still intact. At the east end of the church, the altar

124

windows were gone, and the cold wind permeated their sodden clothes, making sleep a fitful choice. The two scientists had fared better in their months at Peenemunde so a brief period without food was only a small hardship. After the guards were overcome by exhaustion, the taller scientist shook the shorter. "Come, we are east of Berlin. If we leave now and continue further east, we should meet a Russian military patrol very soon."

"No, I told you, we would be far better to go west. I do not trust the Russians."

"Well, you stay here, then. I will go on my own."

"Go then. I will take my chances in Berlin."

"You are foolish and idealistic. Very well; but do not say anything to the soldiers. In the morning, you can say that you slept and know nothing of my whereabouts."

"Go. I will say nothing. I wish you God speed."

The tall scientist crept out of the church set off on his own.

In the morning, when the patrol awoke, the leader questioned the remaining scientist, but true to his word, he revealed nothing. The patrol reorganized and moved out of the church. Their truck was still standing in the square in front of the church, but they had very little diesel fuel and were unsure if there was enough to make the remaining distance. They started out anyway. About two miles out of the town, the truck finally coughed a few times and died. So they started walking through the snow along the road, hoping to meet some other soldiers with a truck, or some spare fuel. For three miles they slogged through the deep drifts on the road, until they came upon the railroad tracks leading towards Berlin. While they waited, sitting on the tracks, a truck appeared from the southwest, driving slowly as the driver searched for the pavement under the snow. The men stood up as the truck drew near. It had started to snow again and was difficult to see anything in the flat morning light. The truck stopped nearby and from out of the rear came khaki colored uniforms, not grey. It was the enemy. But the Germans were too tired to fight, had almost no ammunition, and were ready to go home, so they put up their hands, even though no weapons were leveled on them.

From the front cab of the truck, an American officer stepped down and signaled to his men to take the German's few guns. Then the officer announced in German "We are an advanced patrol, on our way to Peenemünde to rescue the scientists and prisoners held there."

125

The leader of the patrol came up to the officer and said "They have all gone. The facility is destroyed. You will find no one."

The American came up very close to the Patrol Leader and said "Are you telling me the truth? We have been told that several scientists have still remained in the area."

The scientist then spoke up "I am sorry, Captain, the Sergeant is telling you almost the truth. I am one of the scientists from there, and seek asylum in the United States. We were taken by this patrol as we were leaving and forced to go with them. My associate escaped last night but I do not know where he is."

From inside the truck, a familiar voice spoke out "I am here, my brother. Last night I lost my way in a snowstorm, and met this truck on the road." He said nothing about his trying to go east, so nothing more was added.

"Very well," said the American Captain. "Let us return to our unit. Our truck should not be recognized in the snow. It is a two day drive."

The Americans rather kindly helped the rescued patrol into the back of their truck. When it was his turn, the scientist climbed in the back with his countrymen, personally grateful that it was the Americans that found him and happy that he was reunited with his friend.

Inside the truck it wasn't much warmer than out on the road, but at least the wind was cut off and some heat radiated from their bodies huddled together. The Americans got back into the truck and it turned southwest towards Berlin.

# 10  *1889, TURKEY*

It was the last time that the Schliemann would visit the site before his death that year. His health had deteriorated, and he left most of the work to his most recent partner. His mausoleum was already built and waiting for him in Athens. It was his ears that bothered him the most. An operation for a serious inflammation of the inner ear was unsuccessful, and he lived constantly in pain. The site at Troy was savaged over the intervening years since his first excavation. There was always the lure of gold, gems, and artifacts that could bring high prices among the black market collectors throughout the world.

Hundreds of holes pockmarked the site, and evidence of wholesale theft of reliefs, sculptures and even stones from the walls. All that could be identified with an origin here at Troy were taken and sold to the highest bidder. Such a tragedy, he thought. The nobility of Homer's great story, the beautiful poetry of the clashes between tribes and the intervention of Gods on all sides, were trampled into dust and sold for hard currency. The Turkish government did very little, particularly as this site was so far away from any major city. So it was left to the robbers and desecrators to make the most of the opportunities.

Yet he still believed in the legend. He toiled with the goal of unearthing marvels which would firmly place him in the annals of great archeology. The grotto lay somewhere at their feet. The altars which gave homage to the protecting patrons: Zeus and Athena were also not yet fully revealed. But a stair leading to what appeared to be a main altar still supported his footsteps as he climbed to the top.

At one time, a great statue of Zeus stood here, protector of the city and ruler of the skies overhead. Where the statue stood, only a large, flat, smooth stone remained as testament to its history and the support of so great a weight.

He no longer had money to hire many workers, so he toiled alone in the night, scraping with his digging stick, around and around the platform stone, looking to bring it fully into the torchlight. After only a few tries of ramming the point of his iron bar down into the resisting marl, he would have to stop, the dizziness in his head making it difficult to continue.

He was hoping to make one last discovery before his health failed completely. But it eluded him. As he worked, he thought of Sophie, his wife, who had toiled beside him for many years. She also helped him smuggle treasures from several locations here and in Mycenae. 'But not for me alone' he said to himself 'It is for the great Berlin Museum where my story shall be told with my finds.'

A new torch announced that he had company. "Heinrich, are you coming to bed. It is late." She called up to him.

"Yes, Sophie, I'll be along soon. Here, can you help me with this stone?"

"Of course," she replied, picking up another digging iron and joining him.

They both worked together, digging deeper along the edge of the stone, until the bottom corner was revealed. "Let's try to lift it" He said, as he put his bar under the edge of the stone.

"Heinrich, it is much too heavy. Your heart will give out. Let's wait until the morning when we will have help."

"Sophie, my dear, I am going to go anyway one of these days. But I just need to see what is here. You know, when they erected a statue on an altar, frequently they would bury some treasure that the God would particularly admire, as homage. The God would protect the treasure and in doing so, protect the temple around it and usually the city as well. So this is an important place for us to look."

At the word 'treasure' Sophie perked up. While she loved her husband, she also loved beautiful things, and periodically resented so much of their fortune being used to finance these digs, year after year. While they did find some special carvings, masks and jewelry here and in other places, even after these were sold, there was little left. If Heinrich died, Sophie, so much younger, would still have to live for many years and it was no joy to do so without money. So she toiled onward.

Little by little, the altar stone was revealed. It was thinner than Heinrich thought that it would be, due to the size of the statue that originally must have been on top. But then again, the size was only an estimate, based on other cities. They shifted their efforts to clearing the stair side of the stone. If they could lever the stone up, or even slide it out in that direction, it would be free to move on to the broad top step, and perhaps even slide down the stairway. So they worked for two more hours, until that side was clear.

Back to the rear, they worked with the blade of their digging sticks to cut a slit between the stone and the clutching marl. It was hard, like raw concrete, and with the tread of so many feet upon it, had compacted into something that almost was as hard as the stone itself, so the work was backbreaking. The dark was waning, and the first hint of approaching dawn crossed the sky, shading the stars from their bed of darkness.

"Come here and help me try to push the stone out," he said to her.

They both pushed their iron blades deep into the slit between the stone and the marl and levered back together. At first there was no movement and the sweat burst on his forehead, causing him to stumble and wait until the nausea passed. Then he started again, and she added her weight to the iron. Together they pushed, then pulled, then pushed again. There was a crack,

The stone split into two pieces where they had placed their points. They shifted over towards one side of the split and pushed again. The hairline spread across the stone. One further push and it rotated out over the stair enough to look beneath. There seemed to be a hollow under that half of the stone. By alternating at the rotated stone, they worked it until it hung over the top stair. She then reached under with her bar and overcame the fulcrum.

The stone crashed down the stair, taking the edges off the marble treads as it continued towards the bottom. On hitting the last step, the stone split into three pieces that tumbled upon one another. Both waited at the top for the noise to summon someone. But all was still quiet back at the camp.

Now the hollow under the altar was fully revealed. It was too shallow to stick a torch into it to see, but not so shallow as to prevent him from lying on the floor and reaching under with his arm. He grasped something rounded. Pulling with all his might, he worked the item out from under the stone. Then it lay at his feet.

A golden helmet, worked with precious stones that glinted in the torchlight. It had a raised crest and a nosepiece made of two slanting projections falling from the brow. It was engraved with tiny script, intertwining leaves and grasses that looked like the braided manes of horses. Inside the helmet, the remains of what at one time was a leather head cover had completely rotted away, leaving only the metal loops where it had been threaded to the helmet. At the crest, at one time there must have been plumes or feathers fitted into a receptacle along the top.

It looked more like a ceremonial helmet that a war helm. What neither could understand was that the metal was still bright, the works clear and precise, and the loops and holes unaffected by all these thousands of years.

"This wasn't a dry tomb, like one found in Egypt that kept metals from turning black. It looked almost exactly as if it had just been placed there that morning. Sophie took the helmet and wrapped it inside her robe. He lay down alongside the altar stone and again searched with his outstretched arm. There was something else there – larger though flatter than the helmet. Again he pulled and twisted and swore, and soon it was out.

A breastplate of the same design and material as the helmet lay on the stone. He lifted it up and put it on his chest. The metal seemed to mold itself to him so it fit perfectly. Again, the inner portions which once were of leather had long since crumbled to dust, but the metal was perfect.

Pulling it off himself, he held it up to the growing light. From a recess in the front of the breastplate, something fell to the ground and clinked on the stone. A golden key, one unlike any he had ever seen before. It looked to be of the same metal. The workmanship was, if anything, even finer than that of the armor.

They both looked at the hole in the ground and the broken altar stone.

"There is no way that we can hide what we have done." he said.

"I will find a way," said she. "This morning, when the workers arise, I will give them some coins and have them fill the hole, returning the stone pieces to some semblance of its original look, and then spread sand on top to cover the cracks. Meantime, you take these things back to our hotel, and we shall find a way of getting them out of the country."

The day dawned. In their hotel room, they started to pack. Knowing that the government would search their luggage for artifacts, they secreted some bracelets and a few coins in a large toolbox that they carried with them, never knowing exactly what they might need at a site. In the main section of the box, there was a recess for trowels and smaller tools, as well as an inner compartment for shards, which were unearthed by the thousands in their digs. Most of these had been shipped back to Germany. The breastplate and helmet he covered over with a thin layer of clay, so they appeared to be very crudely made, and then brushed with silver paint. As they lay drying on the balcony, he carefully packed the bait in the tool cabinet, and covered it with dried palm fronds which had been shredded. Sophie threaded packing twine through the loops on the breastplate and stuffed a scarf up inside the helmet, securing it with woven twine.

The August morning was hot, and there was no breeze to abate the heat. The boxes and trunks were packed, and passage had been booked to Athens. The steamer was waiting at the ferry dock in Canakkale, about 20 miles away, so it would take about 2 hours to get there, carrying all their belongings. He thought to himself that he would just have to endure. "Are you ready, my dear?" he asked his wife.

"Yes, let me help you." Together, they strapped on the breastplate and put the helmet on his head. He had fashioned a broom handle into a spear, with a knife tied to one end. All decked out, he looked just like he hoped, a caricature of a Greek warrior from Agamemnon's army. They strutted out of the hotel and into the waiting carriage. He mounted the driver's seat and with an imperious gesture, pointed the spear forward. All the workmen standing around to watch their departure broke out into applause. Down the hill to the coast road they went, with him sitting erect on the top.

When they reached the dock, the authorities were waiting. A Turkish Army Captain instructed his crew to open all the boxes, trunks, packages and cases. In the toolbox, a soldier found the cache of small treasures. He hurried to the Captain, who took out the bracelet, coins and some other small jewelry. He put everything but the coin in his pocket, wagged his finger at the master and shook his head in disbelief at the master's appearance. "It looks to be meager pickings this time," the Captain said, as he laughed at the old man in his made-up warrior's appearance. The old man ignored the barb and waited, maintaining his proud posture, saying nothing. Calling together his men, the Captain instructed the patrol to close all the parcels and cases, and load them onto the steamer. As a final gesture, he tossed the coin to Schliemann saying "At least you won't leave totally empty handed" and laughed. Then with a final wave, he turned and marched his troop back to the Customs Shed.

The traveling party ascended the gangway and was escorted to their cabins. Once inside their cabin, the Schliemann collapsed on the bed, while his wife removed the armor and helmet. His entire body was sheathed in sweat and he could not stand for his exhaustion, so he lay, while his wife called for tea.

Soon, a double blast on the steamer's whistle signaled their imminent departure. As they moved into the channel and headed west down the Sea of Mamara, he turned to his wife. "It is done; we have succeeded beyond our dreams. Sophie, will you promise me one thing?"

"Yes, of course."

"I will not be on this Earth very long, so when I finally depart, will you take these things and bring them to the Museum in Berlin? I should like a plaque to read "Donated in the memory of a great archeologist. Will you do that?"

"I should love to, but what if I am unable to live without selling these few things that we have left?"

"Sophie, you have been with me for many years. During that time you have grown to love archeology almost as much as I have, and you have built up a reputation too, for being extremely reliable in your excavations. You will have a future on your own, and you need never apologize to anyone for your husband. Yes, if you need to sell them, then do so. You should know that each year, I deposited sums from the sale of the artifacts that we found with the Jewish merchant moneylenders in Athens and Alexandria. By now the profits that were made on these deposits have amounted to a tidy fortune, which should keep you well for the rest of your life. So you should be able to keep the armor."

"Thank you, my dear husband."

Now the steamer was in the channel, and the boilers were all making as much steam as possible, as they headed towards the last stage of his life.

# 11 MONDAY, NEW MEXICO

A ray of sunlight pries open my eyelids. The morning dawned cool and clear, here at 5,000 ft. The sun crept over the rim of Sandia Mountain and lit the mesa to the west, gradually flowing down into the valley and then over the river which placidly flowed south towards the Gulf. In the yard outside my window, skinks and geckos run riot up the walls and over boulders. A tiny vole sticks his nose out from under a Pampas Grass plant and sniffs the air, twinkles his nose and shoots across to where an agave had pooled water on its lower leaves. A road runner appears on top of the wall, cocks his head, then jumps down into the yard and struts across with a unique mechanical gait as she listens to the scurrying of her lizard breakfast. In the house, it was quiet. As the sun warms the roof, there was no change inside under the cool adobe and thick wooden ceiling. Light sneaks through spaces in the twig shutters.

There are just too many lies. While I wash, I remember my very first lesson in the Teams: There is no visible enemy. Enemies are friends, look like friends, and act like friends. Friends are enemies, look like enemies and act like enemies. Vietnam taught us that anyone could be anything one moment and the opposite the next. No one wore uniforms. If I don't remember this lesson, I was told, I would be dead inside 6 months. All I could do was to pay attention.

Marcia is my first call today. She answers and then practically shouts at me, "What's going on. Your name is on a 'Seize and Hold' list as a potential threat to National Security. The order came from the NSC office. What happened? You must have pissed off someone higher up. The only positive note is that this is strictly NSA, so it is definitely a move to keep it in-house.

"If you can keep an eye on this order without exposing yourself, please feed me any reports. I expect to have to deal with them directly, particularly if I return home."

"You could always come back here, and use my house." Marcia offered.

"No, I really want to keep you at a distance, particularly in NSA's mind and anyone behind them. Besides, I still have a couple of Zilbern's associates at Los Alamos to track down."

"Be careful. I don't want to lose you."

"Don't worry. But you might want to think again about letting me access your data, they're sure to trace the authorization back to you."

"I've got that covered. But after the incident in your office with the CSS agents, you might want to get some official status to protect you. Have you thought about getting sanctioned by your old office?"

"To tell you the truth, I would rather avoid that. It would straitjacket my inquiries, besides forcing a confrontation with some very unpleasant history."

"I understand. But you should think about it. If you are tagged, you may need a friend in court."

When I hang up, I have more questions than answers. I dress and join Lauren at breakfast, for which she has already made us a couple of burritos and some strong coffee. During breakfast, I ask her about the other two associates of her father – Akan and Yancy. She says that as far as she knows, both still work for the Department of Energy in Sandia and Los Alamos respectively. I think that I might get better answers if I do it alone.

"Lauren, I need to talk to both of them, but the highest priority is for me to get the NSA off our tails, particularly after what happened in my office. I think that the best way to deal with the NSA is to go to Washington and confront them at Headquarters before returning here to interview Akan and Yancy. Will you give me a lift to the airport?"

"Yes I'll do that, but who at the NSA will you confront?  And even if you do, aren't you opening yourself to arrest? Maybe if I came with you, they would more likely to believe that this has to do with my father, and not you."

"No for three reasons. I still have some people at NSA who might be able to intervene on my behalf, and if it is a rogue operation there, I don't want to expose the real substance of our inquiry. Thirdly, it is more important for you to search through your father's papers again and see if there is any clue to the key or to your father's work."

"But I've been through all his papers."

"You need to do it again. This time, you have an objective. For example, scientists are notorious documenters. Did your father keep a diary of work and ideas?"

"I don't know. He was always scribbling something."

"Look around for it or maybe for a notebook. If we could find more hard information from your father, it would really help fill in the blanks."

When she leaves me at Departures, I go in and arrange to take a rental car for the day. After picking up a map, I head first to Sandia National Laboratories. It is just east of the airport, secured by Kirtland Air Force Base perimeter fences, gates and Air Police. On the way out there I stop in the Lovelace Hospital parking lot and use my satellite phone to see if I can reach Yancy. Fortunately, I catch him in. When I explain that I was looking into Ernst's work, I identify myself as an investigator from the Navy so he agrees to see me. I stop at the Kirtland Gate and find he left word of my arrival. Showing my Lessant Navy ID, I am admitted.

Sandia's laboratory buildings are all of one model, 4 stories with a central corridor spine and labs opening on either side. Security inside the lab buildings is good, but not ultra-restrictive. That is kept for the high energy and test site facilities, scattered behind the lab buildings and over the several thousand acres of open desert. Although it is operated by the Department of Energy, the original concept of communication among researchers grew out of the AT&T Bell Laboratories Basic Research Model, is still carried on here. Many of the intellectual pursuits evolved into product research which drifted into the private sector out from under DOE. These necessitated special facilities for prototype design, pilot plants, and small scale production facilities. Scientists are still encouraged to collaborate, so perhaps I could get some information from Yancy.

Tom Yancy was a contradiction: An Adonis nerd; complete with a pocket protector in his white shirt, bow tie, and a dozen pencils and markers. His grip is distracted, but his voice was anything but nerdy: strong and deep. He is about 6'-2, sandy haired and broad shouldered, with a wide flat face and a straight nose. He could probably have posed for one of those Greek statues I have seen in the museum. It didn't mesh with the pocket protector, but it proves that looks aren't everything. I look almost directly level into his version of blue eyes. I do notice that the back of his head was beginning to go bald, and his grey hairs are a bit more profuse than mine.

"So what can I do for the Navy?" he asks.

"It's really not for the Navy, more for Lauren Sylfern." I watch his expression change from full attention to marginal interest.

"I am afraid that I don't know Lauren too well, I met her some time ago but then she was merely a precocious child. She hung around the lab when she was a teenager, but since Ernst moved up to Los Alamos, I didn't encounter her at all. Ernst was devoted to her, and to his wife. It was so terrible for them when her mother died, and I know that Ernst tried his best. But what do you want from me?"

"Perhaps if we could sit somewhere and maybe have a cup of coffee, I can explain."

"I really am quite busy. Why don't you try me again in a couple of weeks?"

"I promise I won't take very much of your time, and it is important."

He did not invite me into the secure area, but we moved into a small coffee lounge off Reception. There were vending machines and little knots of people with their heads together at a few tables in the room. On the wall of the lounge, there was a large blackboard which was covered with equations and graphs. A cloth cover was rolled up and pinned to the top of the blackboard. He pointed to a small table near the kitchenette and getting a granola bar from a vending machine, sits down. I got a cup of vile looking coffee from an urn on a side table and join him at a scarred plastic table.

"Can you tell me anything about Ernst's work here?" I ask.

"May I see your ID again?" I pull it out. He holds up the ID photo up to my face to match, and then he produces a tiny card reader out from his pants pocket which he runs along the long side of my card. On the face of his reader is a small screen, which displays my name, security clearance level, and agency affiliation, as well as a small duplicate picture of my face. It does not say that I was retired, just that I have Q clearance and work for the Navy.

"Mr. Lessant. I am glad to meet you. Please forgive my suspicion, but we always need to be sure who we are talking to."

"Don't give it another thought," I reply. "I am pleased you are so careful."

"Ernst and I were like two people gnawing the same ear of corn from opposite ends. He worked on mathematical systems to create unique code keys and code systems, from which both institutional and military encryption and decryption can be created. I work on biological equivalents. I utilized his math models to analyze the probabilities of mutational control and replication. He used my biology to define chaos and randomness in his prime structures. I believe that most of our goals were very similar. Where they differed, however, was in terms of application. He looked to develop new systems, where I looked to a new understanding of differentiation models, and methods for both controlling and identifying controls over mutation."

"I understand the mathematical foundation for cryptosystems, but how can biological organisms relate to the subject?"

"Genetics is very similar to cryptology. A stem cell starts off identical to all the other stem cells in an embryo, but then changes to a specific functional cell which is differentiated from other cells which starts off identical in every respect. How does this occur and what are the mechanisms for storing the 'keys' to specific differentiations? If we could control the level of differentiation, monitor and potentially hold fixed positions as the structures change, and then replicate it, we have the fundamental for storing unique information in a way that cell biology will keep secure until it is needed. If you think about this not as biological development, but as information storage and retrieval, how different is this from encrypting information with a code key, and using either the same or different key to decrypt the information. With our understanding of the biological code, we would have in place a new approach for transmitting information that would be totally immune to computer attack. This type of system should be far more reliable than any type of artificial coded media storage, no matter how abstruse. If we extend this basic concept into mutation management, particularly if we can develop the ability to control the gene activation, we might even have the fundamentals of a biological computer that we could use for computational implementation. Of course, this would not have the time-dependent flexibility that numbers systems have, but being immune to unauthorized decryption somewhat makes up for that."

"Ernst believed that the impetus to change, in a deterministic sense, creates the opportunity for the analysis of life itself. Our challenge is to make these systems viable and to ultimately pay the bills. For both of us, the entire concept was very interesting. It is equivalent to a one-way code that could never be lost, yet also never be broken, without the determinant key. It is sort of a method whereby you can conceal information, but cannot get it by any other means other than with a unique key. For example, if institutional intelligence is stored using this type of model, even if the host organism ceases to be viable, the information remains intact, similar to other permanent storage media. But it also would be incredibly easy to replicate, and therefore easy to "transmit."

He stopped for a moment. It seemed like his exposition was part of a speech he had given many times. "This was the substance of Ernst's latest work, particularly the work that we collaborated on. Does this help you?"

"Yes and no. I begin to see the importance of the work, but not anything that would cause his death, unless you are so far along in the research that it became important, either competitively or economically to others?"

"You think that his death was not an accident?"

"That's one of the reasons I am helping Lauren."

"On this biological side, we did not have competition on that kind of level. The computer model, however; was getting close to a prototype which could be evaluated by others. But for Ernst's work on the evolution of more sophisticated keys for current crypto-systems, I believe that he was on the verge of a breakthrough. Most of the codes in use today are based upon extremely large prime numbers as factors in inducing the code. In order to generate these huge but precise numbers, it takes a Cray supercomputer and once the factors are combined into the codes, it is virtually undecipherable. Industrial codes are limited in the length of the key, so have a lower level or overall security, while governmental codes have a longer basis. This has been done intentionally, to make it possible for institutions like the NSA to access industrial codes and decrypt them if necessary for national security reasons, but not the other way around."

"I believe that Ernst had come upon a new cryptology system that was a whole order of magnitude more complex than current systems. The problem, I believe, was that the sources for this approach were outside the U.S. So the problem for him was gaining access and control over the source for the new technology."

I pondered this for a moment. "What source?"

"He never shared that with me. He only said that it came from outside the U.S. and he had to find a way to access it. I know that he tried to obtain permission to leave the country, and was very angry when it was denied. I tried to get him to share the information, particularly as we had worked so closely for such a long time. But he was very reticent on telling me anything more. I think that his attitude resulted from an earlier incident when he shared information and got burned by the person he shared it with. It was unfortunate that due to the work he did, he was not allowed to travel outside the U.S. I don't think that he thought that he was in any particular danger, but I do remember him saying that he had a friend in Washington that he was going to talk to, and he was going to get his take on the problem."

"Did he say who his contact or friend was?"

"No, I never knew. But when he left for San Francisco last year, his plan was to go from there directly to Washington. I recall that he took his notebooks with him to San Francisco. Oh, yes; he took Lauren also. He told me that if he brought Lauren, that there would be less suspicion than if he traveled alone. I know that frequently, he was assigned minders by the NSA since his work was so important. When he didn't come back from San Francisco, I got worried, and then I heard that he had died, I always wondered if there was something behind the 'accident'. But then there was no inquiry or follow-up so I let the issue drop. Tell me, why are you asking these questions? Is Lauren in some kind of danger? Although I don't know Lauren now, as I told you, Ernst was my friend, so if there is anything that I can do."

"Thank you. You have helped a lot. I will trace the Washington contact and see if there is any connection. As to Lauren, I don't think that she is any particular danger, but there are still some open issues with respect to the NSA." I thank him for his help, and leave after assuring him that if I discovered anything, I would let him know. I wonder if the contact that Yancy spoke of was Froehlich. Yet Ernst was furious at Froehlich for stealing his invention. But who knows how desperate Ernst Zilbern was to go after this new system. Another fact I verified is that Ernst kept notebooks.

Next it's off to Los Alamos. In order to get there, I drive up to Santa Fe, through the western portion of the city, and northwest towards Española. At the fork in the road in Pojoaque where Camel Rock Casino sits, I hang a left and head towards the mountains where Los Alamos overlooks the Rio Grande Valley.

The altitude at Los Alamos is close to 9,000 feet. I start to feel that I am getting closer when I see great communications dishes line the road and blockhouse buildings sprouting antennas, littering the verges. I had called ahead and reached Akan, who readily agreed to meet me, but outside the research lab. At the Coffee Booth in tiny downtown Los Alamos, the air is very quite cool under the trees and there are still patches of snow on the ground.

Alattin Akan is tall for a Turk. He has the light coffee skin of a Persian, and the requisite mustache along with prominent eyebrows and a thin face. But he is almost as tall as I am, so at home, he would stand out in any local crowd. His eyes and hair were black, with not a single white hair marring the sleekness. He is dressed in a soft green pullover with short sleeves, and khakis.

"Call me Alattin," he remarks to me by way of introduction. There is only a slight hint of an accent which is reminiscent of Slavic, but with softer gutturals. "How can I help?"

I explain to him that I am trying to resolve some of the last days of Ernst Zilbern's life, particularly his last work. Alattin volunteers nothing. "I am following up a possible threat that was made on his life. I understand that it may be related to a new discovery that he was seeking."

"How much do you know about it?"

"Not very much at all, but I would like to know more."

"I was wondering how long his discovery would remain un-noticed," he mused. "Last May, he came upon some clues to a new code system, which gave great promise. It was based upon some writing that was on a very old key. Have you found the key? I understand that it was lost just before he died."

"It is possible that the key was found, but now it seems to have vanished again. Can you tell me more about the key?"

"Have you ever seen it?"

"Only once, but very briefly."

"I thought that you might be attempting to decode the inscription."

"Then you have seen it also."

"Of course I did. Ernst asked me to see if I could help him translate the inscription, which appeared to be a combination of formulas and instructions. Even with my knowledge of Turkish and Greek as well as a couple of the Persian dialects, I could only make out a couple of the words. Lauren, his daughter, helped us with her knowledge of ancient Middle Eastern languages, but parts of it were just gibberish to us. I suspected that the inscription was only part of a puzzle."

"Where did Dr. Zilbern find it?"

"Find it! No, it was given to him during the war. At least that is what he told me."

"Do you know where?"

"I believe it was in Cyprus. He stopped there to do some decryption work involving the key just before he relocated here."

"You said that Lauren helped you and Dr. Zilbern?"

"Oh yes. But she didn't get any further along than we did on our own."

"Do you also believe that the key was old?"

"Oh it is old, all right. I told Ernst that it probably was at least 1000 BC, and came from somewhere in Turkey or Greece, or maybe one of the Aegean islands. I suggested that he show it to a language expert at one of the museums, and get scholars involved in the research. That's when he brought Lauren in. Ernst was concerned that the translation might reveal something important, so he wanted to keep as few people involved as possible. He consulted with no one on the outside that I know of."

"Do you know if he photographed it, copied the inscription, or somehow left a record of it?" I was grasping at straws.

"Oh yes, he had an extensive diary, where he tried to copy as best he could the markings on the artifact. I saw it several times. It had a lot more in it than the drawings of the key. He was always fascinated by anything that was used in history to encrypt information. He had pictures of charts and engravings as well as maps, because he was also interested in how codes and passwords migrate around the world. He called the key a 'shibboleth'."

"I have heard the term before, but am not sure what it means."

"It is one of Ernst's favorite stories, because it illustrates how tiny differences in interpretation can have a huge impact on results."

"Back in biblical times, the Gileads had secured the river Jordan and wanted to limit access by their conquered rivals, the Ephraimites. As each refugee passed through the Gilead guards, they would be asked to pronounce the word 'shibboleth'. If they pronounced it without the 'h' as 'sibboleth', they would be seized and killed because only their rivals would pronounce it that way. Over 42,000 Ephraimites were caught by this method. The concept of language migration and its use in creating simple, but effective codes was something that intrigued Ernst all the time that I knew him.  As to the key itself, I have not seen it for over a year."

"Thank you. Can you tell me about San Francisco on the last day of Ernst's life?"

"Oh, so you know that I was there. Well, it is true, although no one has ever asked me about it before. As you probably also know, I am a mathematician and worked with Ernst for several years. When the system of long primes was developed for codes, Ernst had gone further than anyone in designing a method for generating these numbers quite easily on small computers. The government was very concerned that it would no

141

longer be able to decrypt industrial versions of these codes, because new code keys based on Ernst's approach could be change far faster than any decryption attack by NSA computers. A great deal of pressure was placed on both of us to bury this research.

When Ernst started work on the key, he believed that he was on the track of an ever more important discovery: a code key system that could not be broken through brute computer force. Using the key as a reference, even though he did not understand it fully, he worked on the supposition of this type of system. The deeper that Ernst went, the more possibilities he felt that it had for commercial exploitation. In his first major invention – the long-prime development, he made the mistake of seeking advice from an old friend, who stole the idea under the guise of investigating it. Ernst's friend became very wealthy as a result of this theft. So this time, he decided to present his concept to a group of software companies with the idea of setting up a bidding war among them. In addition, he thought that he could raise some venture capital to move his idea out from under the Los Alamos umbrella. So long as he stayed here, he was subject to rigorous security limitations on travel and communications."

"Ernst and I had dinner with a small group of these people. Oh yes, Lauren came too. Ernst talked about his approach, and shared some expectations. Those that were working on similar research were quite annoyed at losing advantage that they might have had and jealous of the Ernst's progress towards a commercial goal. Ernst, who was never much of a businessman, was interested in the financial side of it, but as a scientist, his main focus was on solving a very thorny problem."

"We broke up after dinner; Ernst was planning to go to Washington to consult with someone because he had to leave the country to complete his research and was being prevented from doing so by the government. We left the restaurant together, but separated immediately afterwards. Lauren was going back to New Mexico. I was staying in San Francisco for a few days. Another person at the table was also going to Washington, and offered Ernst a lift. But he only had a two-seater, so Lauren couldn't go with them, as I remember. I offered to take Lauren myself, since I wanted an opportunity to talk to her privately, but she wanted to go with her father. So in the end, Lauren and Ernst drove away together in their rental. That's the last time I saw him.

"Alattin, has anyone come around asking questions along these lines?"

"Right after his death, there were some men here from the National Security Agency, looking through Ernst's papers. They took his hard disks as well as papers. But they asked me nothing about San Francisco."

142

"What about his diary? Did that ever turn up?"

"No. I believe that Ernst left it at home in Albuquerque."

"Can you tell me who the other people at the dinner were?"

"I can get you a list. I had one in my calendar, and it should still be there?"

"I really would appreciate it. But tell me, do you remember if Daniel Towson was one of the people at the dinner?"

"Why yes. How did you know?"

"Could you tell me what you know about Towson?"

"He came to the dinner actually without an invitation. I am not sure how he knew. I had not met him before. But he and Ernst knew one another – I think from the War. Towson, I believe, runs an Import-Export business. If I remember correctly, he was at the dinner representing some overseas interests in Ernst's work, He said very little during dinner. Why do you ask about Towson? Do you think that he had something to do with Ernst's death?"

"I don't know, but what I have uncovered so far points me in that direction. Frankly, it is too early to tell if anyone participated in or arranged his death. What about a Wayne Hudson – was he at the dinner?"

"No. I have never heard of him."

"Are you familiar with Johann Froehlich?"

"Certainly; he was responsible for exploiting Ernst's creation of long primes. I didn't mention him to you because Ernst's problems with Froehlich are old business as far as I know. Tell me: do you believe that Ernst was murdered?"

"I don't know, but the more I look into this, the more questions I have. Before I leave the subject of the dinner, do you remember who it was that offered Ernst a lift to the airport?"

"Why yes, it was Daniel Towson. I thought it odd, since he and Ernst did not seem to either have much in common, or any affection for one another."

"Thank you. That helps me a lot. I wonder if you might tell me more about yourself."

"Me? Oh I am a nerd who is absorbed in abstruse mathematical concepts. I came here from Turkey many years ago; in fact it was Froehlich that put a good word in for me at Los Alamos. So I have him to thank for being here.

I am not married, and am now a citizen. Los Alamos works closely with the Berkeley Livermore Laboratories in California, where I did my post-doctoral research. Here I do a bunch of odd things, some on my own and some to provide theoretical and computational support to other scientists. Ernst was a typical client of mine. He needed a sounding board for his theories. He also needed someone to help him with mathematical implementation when he had some of his insights. He was roughly my father's age, so I sort of adopted him as a pseudo father; my own having died in the Cyprus conflict. I really miss him."

I start to ask another question when he interrupts me.

"Oh I remember one thing that Ernst said when we parted that night. He said that he was afraid that when he asked his 'friend' for help, that it might be the last person that he would ever ask anything for again. It didn't mean much to me then, because it was such an offhand comment, but now that you have brought up the specter of possible murder, maybe he was being prophetic. To your anticipated question, I guess this would mean that yes; he was concerned for his welfare that night. Also, he was always very precise with his language. When he used the term 'friend' I am certain that he was being sarcastic. I think that he had reached a kind of last resort. But then again, sometimes idiomatic English leaves me bewildered"

"One last question, Alattin; did he have any income other than his salary at Los Alamos or Sandia?"

"No. I remember that he was particularly broke after his wife's long illness. But I believe that as a result of the meeting with the software crowd, that he would have received some venture capital, had he lived. Why do you ask?"

"I wondered about Lauren's resources, particularly going forward with this investigation."

"I don't think you need to worry about being paid, Mr. Lessant."

"No, it isn't that. I was just looking at various motives for getting rid of Ernst, that's all."

"I would say that money wasn't a genuine motive unless you consider future potential."

I thank Alattin for his help and again promise to keep him informed. As I was leaving, he asked me a last question. "Do you know Simon Chess?" I ask him to repeat it and he says the name again.

144

"Why do you ask?"

"Well, Ernst told me that Chess was one other person that he might go to for help if he needed it. He said that Chess had done some special investigations and rescued some friends of his. Anyway, if I was you, I might search out this Chess fellow and see if he was contacted by Ernst."

"Thanks. I will do just that."

I head back down the mountain aerie towards Santa Fe. On the way, I call Marcia, but she was not answering, so I left a callback message. As I pass the Pojoaque Pueblo, a lone car joins me on the road. I casually notice it as I pass, since, unlike others, it doesn't seem to be waiting for pueblo gas. I don't think much about it, until a couple of miles down the road; suddenly the car is alongside edging me towards the shoulder. As I glance over, a man is holding a badge emblazoned with 'FBI' out the window. I slow and stop at the next turnoff—the Nambe store parking lot. The other car parks just behind and off to the left, and two men get out. One takes a position off the right rear side of my car, and the other one comes up, stopping just behind the driver's door.

"FBI; put both hands out through the window," he instructs, sliding his badge and ID to where I can see it. I do so, and he snaps plastic flex cuffs on my wrists. Then he says "Get out slowly and stand facing the car. You know the drill." I obey, and he uses a foot to pull mine away so I am leaning against the car. The other man opens the passenger side, searching the front seat. Then, finding only my map, he closes the door and comes around to a spot behind me where he waits just out of reach. The first man digs into my pockets and comes out with my wallet, rental keys and my house keys, along with a small amount of cash. He tosses the wallet to his partner.

"Which is it, Lessant or Chess?"

"Both" I say, but nothing more. The man with my wallet pulls out a cell telephone and makes a call. He says "We've got Chess," listens for a minute, then holds the telephone towards me and takes my picture. After listening for another minute, he closes the phone and motions me to their car. "Come with us," he says.

I don't seem to have any choice. He takes a second set of flex cuffs and threads it through the ones on my wrists and through a handle on the inside of the door. They don't bother with my feet. The man with my car keys goes back to the rental and opens the trunk. Finding my small bag inside, he opens it, rifles through my clothes, and tosses it into the trunk of this car. He then gets into the rental. The other agent starts the FBI car and we travel in tandem South again through the outskirts of Santa Fe, and then on I-25 to Albuquerque. I try to open some conversation or make innocuous comments about the weather or baseball, but all my efforts are ignored.

As we pass through Albuquerque, we turn east on Central Avenue. I wonder if we are heading back to Sandia Labs, but instead, we turn into Kirtland Air Force Base. Then it's around the administration building to one of the large hangars. The agent in my rental peels off in the parking lot as I am driven through an inner gate onto the apron, to a Gulfstream V jet. As soon as we stop, the driver comes back, cuts the flex to the door handle, and motions me into the plane. As I go up the access stair, the plane's engines go into pre-start and the turbines begin to spool up. Once inside, I am met by a male cabin attendant who motions me to one of the overstuffed lounge chairs and belts me in. The engines light off and the plane turns left and head for the end of the 11,000 ft. east-west runway. Stopping momentarily at a hold point just off the east end, we wait for a Southwest plane to land. Within 30 seconds, we are racing down the broad expanse and lift sharply off. Almost immediately, we turn left in a half circle and point east as we climb out. In no time at all, we are higher than most passenger aircraft, into military airspace as we pour on the fuel and race away from the Sun.

# 12 *1890 NAPOLI*

It was Christmas Day. The bells throughout the city peal out their welcome.

As he lay in his hotel, Heinrich Schliemann contemplated his fate. His original plan was to return to Athens after coming out to Halle for a last attempt at surgery to relieve his ear inflammation. Although the surgery was partially a success, it left him exhausted and weak, unable to travel much further. Still, he pushed himself to brief visits to Paris, Berlin and Leipzig, before returning to Naples to see Pompeii for a last time. He tried to get home to Athens for Christmas, however; the trip proved far too strenuous for his condition. At Sophie's urging, and finally her demand, they would stay here in Napoli over Christmas, and then, when he recovered, go on to Athens. He hoped that he would be able to see his mausoleum once more before it claimed him for eternity.

Sophie came in to his bedroom as he listened to the bells. She brought some new flowers. "Wherever did you find these on Christmas morning?" He asked.

"It was a miracle," she replied. "I stopped to get some bread for our breakfast, and a flower seller was hawking just outside. But these are a poor substitute to those we have growing at home. I know that I put my foot down about finishing the trip there, but perhaps I shouldn't have?"

"No, you were right to insist that we stay here. I believe that my time has come, and actually I look forward to it. Will you sit with me for a while?"

"Yes, indeed I shall, for as long as you like. If you think you are strong enough to listen, I have to tell you a story. Something strange has happened, and I want to share it with you."

"What happened, my dear?"

"While I was walking back from church this morning, I was approached by a man who no sooner had greeted me when he demanded that we return the last treasures we found. When I feigned ignorance, he told me that he was representing the rightful owner, and that we had no right to keep them. I believe that he was speaking of the armor and the key. He was so

147

confrontational, that I almost ran to find the Caribinieri. But then he calmed down and said that he would explain so that I would understand how important a discovery these artifacts were, and why we had to return them. Honestly, I don't know if I should believe what he said. Would you like to hear what he told me?"

"Yes, but speak softly, lest prying ears overhear of our treasure. Are they still in Athens?"

"No, I didn't trust our agents there; particularly because of the jewels on the armor. While you went on your last trip, I arranged that they be shipped here. Right now, they are in our closet in the next room. Would you like me to show you?

"No, no; I will get to wear them again soon enough. So tell me what this man said to you."

"First, he asked me to go into the church again, so that he could tell me the story in the sight of God, so that I would know that he was telling the truth. I agreed, and we turned around and re-entered the nave. We sat on a pew in one of the side chapels. Then he started talking, like he was reciting a poem that he had memorized. I kept very quiet while he spoke, and listened very closely so that I could remember it and repeat it to you.

"When he finished, I was so astounded by the story that I decided it would be better if you heard it directly from him, so I brought him here. Right now, he is waiting just outside the room. Do you think you are strong enough to listen to him?"

"Yes, particularly if you believe his story."

"I won't say until after you have heard it as well." Sophie went to the door and brought in the visitor. He was not a large man, but appeared to be very intense. He wore a red fez on his head, and was dressed in a white cotton tunic and slacks, which ballooned slightly at the waist and ankles. His eyes were black and they burned like onyxes as he looked down at Schliemann.

"Who are you?"

"Who I am is of no consequence; it vitally important that you and your wife return the armor which you stole from Troy."

"I am afraid that I know nothing about any armor."

"You wore it the morning you left for Greece. You tried to disguise it but we were watching, and we know the truth."

"I am not going to admit anything."

"Please tell Dr. Schliemann the story like you told me," Sophie asked.

"Very well; perhaps after you hear my story, you will understand why it needs to be returned to our safe keeping."The man looked out to the window, and then began to speak in a slightly sing-song manner:

*Before the time of the Trojan War, we were already far older and lived in the predecessor city to Troy. We are called the AFAR People. We established our capitol in 4200 BC, at which time we were known as Hurrians. In Ukesh we lived in peace through the coming and going of nomadic peoples. In the third Millennium BC, we were besieged by the great Akkadian tribes, but won them to an alliance and so continued to live in security while they built their empire throughout Mesopotamia. During this time, we created writing on clay which is called Cuneiform. We developed music and glass as well as great new philosophies on the origin of peoples. We survived by trading our inventions for protection. When the Egyptians arose as a civilization, we sent ambassadors to teach them mathematics and science. We infiltrated ourselves into the Egyptian culture, and blended with them, becoming priests and healers. Our scholars gave them medicine, surgery, metallurgy, and in particular the refining of Bronze and Gold. We were the priests who brought the ideas of the Single God, Amun, and the solar year calendar. During the great Exodus of the Semites from Egypt, many of us went with them and helped to keep them alive in the desert by divining for water and cultivating of fruits and vegetables in portable wagons, so that they could still move yet feed their multitudes. As they moved to their future homeland, we continued moving north, and settled in the place that was known as Ilios which became Troy.*

*There, we flourished for a time, but an invasion from the Hittites decimated our numbers, and we were again forced to align ourselves with the Greeks; assimilating ourselves into the Greek city-state that Troy had become. Within the walls, we gradually assumed positions of responsibility for metal working, religious leadership and medicine practices. Our old sun worship and that of the underworld fueled the newer creations of Zeus, Poseidon and Hades, which became inculcated in the Greek culture. These Greek-Trojans grew strong and vied with the trading cultures for dominance of the seas. Those in the Greek states who found themselves losing their hold on the trade routes became angry and jealous of the Trojans, so became their enemies. Athens, Mycenae,*

*Minoan and Egyptians lost great fortunes to the Trojans, who became rich and powerful.*

*Eventually, the Spartans could not tolerate losing commerce to this small city-state, so they took the lead to destroy our city and capture its treasures, including our sciences. The Greeks made up a story that the Trojans had kidnapped the wife of the Spartan king, along with looting his treasury. Their goal was to weld both the Spartans and the Athenians in an alliance to fight a war. For 6 years, they laid siege on our Trojan city, but could not make the city yield. They had not realized how many allies continued to supply food and arms to our besieged people. So they attacked and subdued the allies of Troy, until there were none left. For three additional years the Trojans held out and the Greek people started to rally against the war. They had sacrificed enough for their merchants. The king was pressured to recall the army and leave Troy, but the Spartan king was embarrassed at having to admit failure, and the merchants were in favor of continuing, as they has unlimited access to trading so long as the Trojans were occupied with the war. So Menelaus got his generals together and they devised a plan to defeat the city in a single massive stroke. The plan was to convince the Trojans that they had given up and had departed, and so induce the city to open the gates whereupon the army would return and complete the conquest.*

*Our people actually created this plan. We had infiltrated the Greek encampments and understood that Troy could hold out no longer. Had we known of the Greek people's growing resolve to end this war, we would have waited, and rebuilt the city after the army was recalled. But knowing only that our city would be totally destroyed, we assigned one of our own to take responsibility for our future. Our leaders reduced our most important discoveries in mathematics, metallurgy, astronomy, geology and medicine to a Book of metallic tablets, and created three pieces of Trojan armor as the keys to deciphering our ancient language and to this Book. This armor is what you both found under the altar stone at Troy. Our descendants have always kept watch over these items, including the Book which you discovered some years ago. I was the one that recovered the tablets from you, but not the armor– the breastplate, the helmet and the key."*

Schliemann interrupted the story, exclaiming "I found the Book. It was in the wall niche at Troy. I brought it into my tent, but fell asleep and when I awoke, it was gone. From that time until now, I thought that maybe I had dreamed the whole incident. It was your people that took back the Book."

"Yes, I retrieved it while you slept. But let me continue."

Schliemann waved his hand to indicate that he was to go on.

*According to the instructions that my predecessor gave me, our items were to be kept hidden until someone revealed himself as the "Rightful Seeker." This person would then be given the task of revealing the secrets to the world. At the time of the Book's exposure, people would come to understand why knowledge is more precious than treasure. Neither Greece nor Rome, nor any present country in Europe has earned the right to these discoveries, since many of them will again violate civilized behavior. We believe that the culture at Troy, for all its faults, was a far more honorable culture than any today. Perhaps if the Trojans could live again, it would be a sign that other cultures could return to their basic beliefs, and rise out of greed, treachery, acquisitiveness and vindictiveness to express in concrete deeds, the essential goodness of mankind."*

The man stopped. "Now you understand why it is so important to return the armor and the key."

Schliemann sighed "I believe you, but I am so sorry that we no longer have these items. We had shipped them to Athens, but it seems that they never got there. Neither of us knows where they might be."

The Turk then looked between Sophie and Heinrich and said "Very well. If you no longer have them, I will take my leave and continue my search." Then he thanked them for their time and left.

After he had gone, Sophie asked her husband "Well, what do you think? Do you believe his story?"

"I really don't know if he is telling the truth, or merely fabricating it to get a line on the armor – it is quite valuable. Yet if it were true, it would speak volumes to those of us that have sought to reveal greatness through learning. It is much like the story of my own life. By revealing my true nature, my colleagues should finally understand the truth of my greatness."

"I am glad that you didn't reveal their location. Remember, after you are gone, these will be the means for me to secure my future. Do you think that he believed you?"

"I do not think so. For this reason, you will need to guard our possessions very carefully for the short period of time I have left, and then afterwards, until they can go to the Berlin Museum."

That evening, in the hotel room, the man sat in his chair, his wife next to him. As crowds of people surged through the town reveling in the Christmas Story, he rose to look out the window. Suddenly, he was overcome by a faint and collapsed to the floor. His wife screamed, and there were running feet outside the room, followed by a banging on their door.

"Please get a doctor," she cried. Several ran off to do her bidding, while three stayed to carry him to the bed. He lay there, breathing with difficulty, his heart beats counting down. Then he roused himself and reached out to his wife. She ran to his side and grasped his hand in both of hers.

"I'm finished," he exclaimed between breaths.

"Yes, my husband, I believe you." She replied.

"Will you care for our discoveries and see to my honor?"

"Yes, my love. That is exactly what I shall do."

He fell back again. The doctor soon arrived but with a few perfunctory gestures, echoed what she already knew; that he was dying.

The day waned. The new day came and there was no change. The heartbeats came slower, and the man frequently groaned in his coma. Then, as the clocks struck one, his breathing finally stopped, the heart counted down slowly to zero, and the man who had wanted his whole life to be recognized as a great discoverer, a great scientist, a valuator of the greatest of Greek Poets, died with his wife and her memories enfolding them.

# 13 *MONDAY WASHINGTON*

As soon as we are off the ground, the attendant cut off my cuffs. I try to draw him into conversation, but he merely prates inanely about the latest contest on Reality TV. Although there are some magazines and a small library aboard, I don't feel like reading but instead just close my eyes. I suppose that I am being taken to a more senior agent or Assistant Director for questioning.

I have learned over the years, to not anticipate, but to simply be careful and wait for an opportunity to regain control. Back in the Survival Evasion Resistance and Escape (SERE) course, I had been trained to deal with a probable capture. Beatings, water boarding, sleep and food deprivation were the expected norm. Hopefully, I will never have to experience it for real.

I recognize Andrews Air Force Base in Temple Hills, Maryland, just southeast of Washington, as we land. We turn onto the apron and follow a jeep to a hanger, where we stop just short of the overhead door. When the aircraft door opens, the attendant ushers me out. As I reach the stairs, he hands me my bag, and a bulky envelope. A sleek limousine pulls up and the driver opens the rear door. My bag is taken and deposited in the trunk. As we drive through a security gate, I open the envelope and find all my pocket possessions, including my NSA satellite telephone. I turned it on, but there is no signal. I can only assume that the car body contains some jamming system to prevent external electronic eavesdropping.

We drive over the bridge to Alexandria, past National Airport, but keep on until we near the Pentagon, where we pass Ft. Myer and my old office. At the Pentagon City complex of office buildings, we park in a Restricted Zone beneath one of the buildings. The driver leads me through a rabbit warren of tunnels. Around a corner from a row of shops, there is a small elevator, which the driver activates with a card key. He hands me my bag just as the door closes on me.

The elevator ascends to the top floor, where the door opens directly into a small reception room. The receptionist, a tall man in a business suit, comes around the desk, welcomes me by name, and escorts me inside through a pair of large double doors. Large windows overlook the complex. In the center of the room there is a circular conference table with deep armchairs. Seated in one of the chairs was a smallish man in a very well-cut pinstripe suit with a small American flag lapel pin. He stands and holds out his hand to me.

"Colin Lessant, I am so glad to meet you after all this time." He says in a voice with a trace of European accent. "My name is Johann Froehlich."

I look closely at him as I return the greeting. Except for the cut of his clothes, I would never pick him out of a crowd. He seems supremely ordinary. I imagine that he lulls people with this impression, which fronts an enormous intellect. Even his eyes aren't particularly sharp, in fact they are watery yellow-brown, and look weak and unassuming. From what I have learned about this man, he is anything but.

"Colin, if I may call you that, I should like to tell you that I have always admired your work for Navy ESCORT. I was very sorry to hear about your wife and I know that it prompted your resignation from the service. But I would be remiss, if I didn't tell you that your efforts and dedication to the cause of freedom and democracy are appreciated among the very highest levels of our government."

I identified his accent. It came from the slight mispronunciation of the words "have" and "of," which came out like "haff" and 'uff'. German or Austrian, I thought. If I hadn't been told his history, I would have surmised Austrian, since the words were pronounced very softly, rather than gutturally. But so what; I took in what he said as an attempt to flatter me before he drops the other shoe.

"That was a past life," I remarked in an offhand manner. "Now I am more 'Private' than 'Public' and I use my real name: Simon Chess. May I ask you why you had the FBI bring me here?"

Froehlich sighed. I guess he would have preferred more lulling and less confrontation. "Please sit down. I should like to consult you on a couple of problems. These are less the nation's problems, and more my own. Will you help me?"

Well that's a new twist. Ask for help before shooting the helper. "Tell me what you want, and then I will tell you if I will help you, but don't count on it." I offer.

"Yes. Well, my problem involves someone that you already know, Lauren Sylfern." Before I could say anything, he holds up his hand and then continues "Don't be alarmed. I know that Ms. Sylfern retained you to

154

assist her, and this will not compromise your commitment at all. In fact, I may assist you with your investigations on her behalf."

I decided to shut up and let him do the talking.

"I would imagine that you have learned some facts from Lauren about my relationship with her father, Ernst Zilbern. Yes? Well I'll tell you the story from my perspective, and you can decide if I am worthy of your assistance."

"As you know, I am German by birth, but American by citizenship. I grew up in Germany after the First World War, during a time of great economic hardship, mostly blamed on England and the U.S. In school, Aryan heritage was glorified, as was the notion that Germany would again grow strong. When Hitler came to power, I hailed him as a new hero like so many of my fellow young men. He ended the depression and gave us new hope. As a young man at the University, I confess I wore my *Deutsche Jugendbewegung* (German Youth) uniform with pride. I earned my doctorate in physics and mathematics, and looked forward to helping to build the technological revolution I could see in our nation's future. But when Poland and Czechoslovakia were invaded, I began to have doubts about the Nazi goals. By then, the Gestapo, with the assistance of the Reichstag, had suppressed our personal liberties. Government control was cloaked in the fervor of National Security. Anyone who spoke out for freedom was branded as unpatriotic. With the increasing centralization of authority, reprisals against dissents were swift and final. This is the environment and culture in which both Ernst and I grew up."

"I was assigned to a team headed by Von Braun, to work on the development of the first rocket designs. These became the V1s that rained on England. Once the VI program went operational, our team began developing the V2, with the V3 and V4 on the horizon. I worked in several laboratories, and became acquainted with Ernst as we both were assigned to work together under von Braun. Eventually, we were both relocated to the lab and factory complex at Peenemunde. There, we worked on many of the propulsion and guidance designs. Peenemunde, in the extreme northeast corner of Germany close to the Polish border, was as far away from any potential escape opportunity as one could get in Germany. Everything at the lab was done under the close scrutiny of the Gestapo and the Schutzstaffel (SS)."

"As the war continued, I became increasingly convinced that Germany would ultimately lose. I convinced Ernst that we should take whatever chance that might be presented to escape together before we died in the more frequent bombings. He finally agreed, but we could not decide whether we should go east or west. Finally, an opportunity presented itself.

After the raids on Peenemunde killed many of our personnel, the government decided to move the lab to Austria. On the day of our departure, we hid until after the last train left, and then tried to make our way east. As luck would have it; we were captured by an American patrol and were brought to a camp where we were eventually offered contracts to come to America. Both Ernst and I had vowed to remain together, so we accepted the agreements. But before our final journey to the U.S., we were both sent to Cyprus, where Ernst was given a task of deciphering some information on ancient artifacts that had surfaced there. These were delivered to the Americans by Standahl Xyso, who we know as Daniel Towson. I was sent along because we had worked closely together and had an established pattern of mutual support, although it was Ernst who was the expert cryptographer leading the translations. Unfortunately, someone stole the artifacts from our camp.

Since the artifacts were gone, there was no need for us to remain in Cyprus, so we were shipped here. Both of us were resettled in Tennessee, but our work diverged and we separated: Ernst to New Mexico and I to Oak Ridge. In Los Alamos, Ernst worked on the next phase after nuclear fission – the Hydrogen fusion bomb. He met and married a local woman, and they had one daughter: Lauren. I stayed in Oak Ridge for a time, and then moved to Redstone and Huntsville in Alabama to work on guidance systems for missiles and orbital vehicles. I married a woman that I met in Tennessee, but we were never fortunate enough to have children. When Lauren was born, I thought that finally Ernst finally accepted his new country and gave up blaming the west for the German depression and for splintering Germany into two separate countries. I was very happy for Ernst. Although we were far apart, I thought of Lauren as a surrogate daughter and tried to keep in touch. I did not have much opportunity to work with him again, but we did have some brief business dealings. Some years later, his wife became ill and eventually died. By then, the gulf between us had grown so wide that I never saw him again, until we lost him last year."

"Thank you for the history lesson, but what does it have to do with me?

"First, I want you to know that I care a great deal about Lauren. Second, Ernst and I had a falling out over his invention and my business. I need some help from you to intercede with Lauren on my behalf."

"Why is it so important to you right now?"

"I am only alive for another year. I have been diagnosed, and it is fatal. It would be far better for both Lauren and I if we were to talk while there still is still time."

"Why haven't you simply gone to see her, or called her?" I asked.

"I have tried without success. She won't see me or speak with me. I believe that her father poisoned her with the idea that I had stolen Ernst's inventions. That isn't true. I bought them from Ernst. At the time, neither of us believed that crypto-systems would grow to the huge business that exists today, so my company succeeded beyond my expectations. The greater my success, the angrier Ernst became. I offered him a share in it but he refused and would no longer speak with me. I need to clear this lie with Lauren before I die."

"I must tell you that Lauren believes a totally different version of your story."

"That makes me very sad. Ernst was a genius in his field. While the NSA was building more powerful computers to use in creating new long-prime code keys, Ernst took a radically different approach and was able to greatly enlarge the then-known primes. Further, he was able to generate them extraordinarily fast and with small computers. Do you understand how important long numbers and particularly primes are, in terms of codes and data encryption?"

"Yes I do, at least generally. I know that primes are unique in that they are numbers which are only divisible by themselves and the numeral 1. Primes are multiplied together generate the keys for codes. The longer the number, the more difficult it is to resolve the right set of prime factors."

"You are correct. Essentially, the issues of code creation and analysis are based upon very long numbers in that manner. But finding primes takes enormous computing power. Many codes in use today are viable for only a few minutes, so it is impractical to have systems where it takes weeks to generate a new set. Further, in order to satisfy the needs of government, a whole order of magnitude is required over industrial and commercial keys to further reduce vulnerability to brute force computer attacks."

"Huge numbers are needed to create immense keys. They are good as they go, but not totally invulnerable. What Ernst developed and what I built upon is an inexpensive and non-reversible method of developing very long keys, which could be used for digital communications. The foundation for his approach is partially the development of a true random number generator, and partly from the development of small, extremely fast computers with lots of desktop power. Patenting these processes made me wealthy, although not terribly popular among the NSA contingent, since the key systems I developed made it far more difficult to break the messages which resulted. If you consider the analogy of a lock, my keys were not totally pick-proof, but impractical to attack since they could be changed almost instantaneously and very easily. By the time a code was broken, it would be out of date and not used again. Initially, great attempts were made to deny me the right to publish and to capitalize on my approach. You may recall that when public-key systems were authorized by the government, a lower security level was assigned to non-governmental entities, which made them easier for the government to attack. Well, my system removed that limitation on private industry, so there was a huge lobbying effort by businesses that wanted these systems, to get them and to allow my approach to be marketed. Pressure was applied to Congress, and the security bans were released. The President, operating under the same pressure, signed it. But the NSA retained one important restriction: No newspaper, TV or Cable entity was allowed to publicize it. So my systems went into common use, but were kept relatively quiet. Congress also prohibited me from marketing outside the U.S., but information leaked anyway. As a result, the NSA has a much harder time of decrypting electronic surveillance."

He continued; "Their difficulties prompted the NSA to lobby for far greater latitude in monitoring plaintext like email, internet communications and voice communications as well as encrypted text and voice. Congress and the Administration gave them what they asked for. It was pitched to the public as part of the "War on Terror," but in reality, it was partly NSA's method for dealing with their own inability to break a lot of the messages encrypted with these new keys. I don't think that the people over in Ft. Meade like me very much. Fortunately, I have a lot of personal support from the current administration, the companies that I have helped, and a large number of people in Congress who are beholden to those companies."

"Dr. Froehlich, forgive me but I have a hard time believing you to be some sort of innocent; either with regard to Ernst Zilbern or the NSA. For example, it was very easy for you to reach out to the FBI and drag me here, when a telephone call might have accomplished the same goal."

"I am sorry. I have been in Washington perhaps too long. Here the demonstration of power is usually the only way to get someone to listen."

"I also believe that you could have gone to see Lauren at any time during the past year. Why didn't you? By not doing that, you allowed time to harden her resolve to bring you to heel for the death of her father."

"Simon, I had nothing to do with her father's death."

"I'm sorry, but look at this from my perspective. You drag me here and spin me a story about how important Ernst Zilbern's research is, which tells me that you are very interested in it. Second, you tell me that you have no friends at the NSA, but you impress me with your insider power by calling the FBI to dance to your tune. The plea about your concern for Lauren insults my intelligence. Lastly, you obviously have researched me, based upon your commentary about my 'good' work at ESCORT. This would have led you to my real name and my recent history as well, so your initial comments to make me feel appreciated were equally phony. Yet in spite of all these things, you plead innocence and ignorance. It doesn't wash."

"Simon; I am no innocent. Nor would I want you to feel that I am not respectful of your intellect or ability. I appreciate your directness in confronting these apparent inconsistencies. I have no wish to plead the cause of a dying man either. But I will tell you that I have tried on numerous times to re-establish communications with Lauren. I went to her house, I sent emails, I telephoned and I sent emissaries. She was totally unreceptive to any of these entreaties. Ernst hated me. Somehow, he saw me as representative of all of our government's callousness at the time of his greatest need: when his wife was dying, and later when he wanted to follow the trail of his newest discovery. I also think that he was carrying anger from our days in Europe many years ago. I can't be responsible for his attitude or influence over Lauren. I can, however; do my best to rectify half truths."

"What is so important about Zilbern's discovery?"

"If Ernst had discovered a radically new approach toward code design, particularly if it was a concept that could not be broken by any brute force method, there would be many public and private entities that would pay dearly for such a level of security. I would say that extraordinary efforts on behalf of acquiring and controlling this knowledge would be expected. Cyber warfare is not a new idea, but has been growing in huge steps since the proliferation of small personal computers. Such a new code system could potentially render a computer safe from hacking, as well as provide transactional security at a level previously unimaginable. The Internet highway, which is vulnerable at so many levels to data and identity theft, could actually be made secure as well, so the possibilities are endless. Although few practical codes have ever been invented that could not be broken, this would be a revolutionary step in progress. As such, it would be very, very valuable."

159

"So Ernst's actions then would be of great interest to the government, and particularly the NSA, as well as to corporations and particularly financial institutions, plus foreign governments and private interests?"

"No question of the interest. But the circle of people who knew what Ernst was tracking down was quite small."

"Would you say that Daniel Towson was in that circle?"

"Towson is a bastard, and I am sorry that I ever met him." Froehlich got up from the table and started pacing "As I mentioned, I met him in Cyprus during the war. Afterwards, he extorted my help with his search for weapons that he could sell to the warring Middle East, and to others, particularly in Latin America and Asia. With the need to supply weapons to Israel without raising the ire of our oil producing sources, pressure was put on me by the CIA and the White House. I reluctantly helped him for several years, but was finally able to get him off my back. I was very glad that he died last year. But in answer to your question, Towson knew about the source for the new code system, but I do not believe he recognized it for the potential that it has. So I would put him outside the circle primarily out of ignorance. But that point is moot since he is dead."

"But you know that he is not dead."

He stopped in his tracks. "Of course he is. The FBI reported him dead last May. I saw the police reports. Believe me, if he was still alive, I would still find him slithering around here, looking for more favors."

"I met him just yesterday, and he made a threat on Lauren's life, as well as mine. Also, his wife was killed a couple of days ago. I am sure Towson did it to conceal the fact that he was still kicking. Lauren believes that if you didn't have her father killed, it was Towson."

"Simon, you must believe me when I tell you that I know nothing of this. I'll admit that at the time Ernst's death, coming at the almost the same time as Towson's death, seemed suspicious – the auto accident and all, but then when he never showed up again, and I was just so grateful to whatever provenance looked over me and removed him. Your information is new. Tell me, you spoke to him?"

"Yes, several times. The first time I was threatened since he thought that I had something he wanted, and when he didn't get it, he threatened Lauren."

"What was the item?" Froehlich asked, expectantly.

"I would rather not say right now, except to tell you that Towson's interests seem to be tied with his loyalty to Turkey."

"Yes, that sounds just like him. When I first met him, he was trying to get back to Turkey."

"Can you tell me more about Towson from your time in Cyprus?"

"Let me think. When I got to Cyprus, things were still in an uproar. The Germans were no longer in total control of the island, but the fighting between the Germans and Cypriots had mutated into a fight between Greek and Turkish factions over control of the island and the establishment of either colonial or independent rule on the island. I was sent there to help Ernst. Evidentially, the Turks claimed the artifacts we were working on originated in Turkey, stolen by the Greeks. The Greeks believed that the Turks had taken these treasures from Athens. Ernst was convinced that these artifacts were from a much older civilization in the Middle East. As it turned out, when the armor was stolen from Ernst, the thieves missed one small item: a key. We had studied some tiny writings on it, but came to the conclusion that it was meaningless text, set out to confuse anyone. Obviously, it was a key to something. But what, we never knew."

"What happened to the key?"

"Ernst took it and kept it with him when we continued on to the U.S."

"This must be the same key that Towson is after. I briefly had it myself, but then it was stolen from me. Towson thinks that I still have it."

"How does the NSA figure in on this?"

"Two NSA agents tried to seize both Lauren and me on Friday. They came to my office, but we were able to escape from them. I have no idea who sent them, or even why. I will tell you that Lauren believes you set them on us."

"Although I don't have many friends over there, let me make a couple of calls and see if we can get to the bottom of that question. If you will just wait here, I will be right back." He got up and left to another room. I still don't trust him, but he makes a good case. While I waited, I walked around the room. There is nothing personal in the room. Even the bookcase held only leather-bound classics. No novels or journals. Finally, after about 5 minutes, he returns.

"Simon, I made a call to my friend, the Security Advisor to the President. I asked him to put the question to the NSA Director. We will have to wait for the answer. I have a meeting to go to. Can you fend for yourself here in DC for a couple of hours? I would like to meet you for dinner. Would you do that?"

"I really can't since I need to get back to San Francisco. You don't have any problem with my leaving, do you?" Froehlich shakes his head. "Can you give me something to prove that you are telling me the truth? This key business seems to be too trivial to be the cause of these threats. After all, it is only an old key. Even if it was somehow connected with riches, everyone involved except for us is already immensely wealthy, so I cannot imagine this being the sole cause for kidnapping, killings, and extortion."

"Why don't you draw Towson out? I will try to get you some help. Have you any idea where the key might be?"

"Well, since Towson doesn't have it, and I don't have it, there has to be a third element in this somewhere."

Froehlich terminates our meeting by rising and escorts me to the door. He sounded reasonable, but that's something true of all great manipulators: they always sound like they are telling the truth, even if they contradict themselves in the same sentence. Well, now, at least, if he is in with Towson, my message is clear about not having the key. I wonder who does have it. Or if they have it, do they know what it means? I wish that I had looked at it longer. I still said nothing about Marcia's study group. Speaking of which…

"Where are you?" Marcia asked.

"Actually, I am just outside Dr. Froehlich's office in Pentagon City."

"Can you come out?"

"I wish I could, but I was on my way back to San Francisco when Froehlich had me picked up and flown here."

"Are you all right?"

"Yes, no problem. Marcia, any update on Towson?"

"Towson made a lot of calls to someone in Turkey over the past two days. But it's really strange, as his voiceprint doesn't match that we have on file. Maybe he had someone else make the calls. We don't have an ID the recipient. But one of the U.S. calls was to Albuquerque, to Lauren Sylfern's home number. It was very short, and we missed the conversation."

"I wonder if he made another threat, or was looking for me."

"How did you get to Washington?"

"Froehlich had the FBI give me a ride. I didn't have any trouble except for a wayward rental car now at Kirtland."

"What did Froehlich have to say?"

"I think that we could be wrong about him. He spun me a pretty convincing story about his relationships with Zilbern and Towson. If we are to believe him, Towson extorted his assistance somehow and he was very unhappy to hear that Towson was still alive. He also claims innocence with regard to stealing Zilbern's discoveries. I don't see much of a motive for going out of his way to lie to me, so he could be telling the truth. Do you have any new information?"

"No; Froehlich interceded with a CIA probe into Towson's arms dealings. Following that, however; the CIA had a lot of business with Towson's company. In fact, his organization was part of a plan to get arms into a number of locations in Africa and the Middle East. The CIA also used him as a contractor for some nuclear fuel shipments to Israel, along with parts and pieces to help them build their reactor. The only connection we can find between Zilbern and Towson was in Cyprus at the end of the war. If you're finished there, can you come to see me?"

"No, I need to get back to San Francisco to pick up the trail on the missing key and to protect Lauren. I believe the key is an integral part of this puzzle."

"I sent the computer to your home, so it should be there when you arrive. When do you think that you will be back east again?"

"This should be over in a couple of days at the most. Either I will get myself out of the soup, or be the soup. Whichever, I should wrap this up by Friday, and will call you. How is your group getting on?"

"Oh they are happily searching for security leaks. But one thing did come up, just a few minutes ago. Our group administrator got a new assignment to add to our tasks. Talk about an odd quirk of fate, he was instructed to include 'Chess' in the list of potential threats, and to locate you. The interesting thing is that the directive came from the NSC. We immediately put you under surveillance, including your telephone, email, fax, and IP. The only open line you have is this one. What happened?"

"Maybe I was too quick to give Froehlich a pass. He called the Security Advisor while I was there and told me that he was trying to clear any action against me. So much for Washington doublespeak. Listen, I have a couple of errands to run here, and then I will figure a way to get home.

Also, you can forget about my access to your group's database. They will now be watching for any access by either Simon or Colin. So just keep some distance from me/. I'll call you later."

When I am outside the building, I know that I have to make a detour. I need an operational umbrella. Governmental agencies are extremely daunting. Even though Marcia had offered her not inconsiderable help, I still need to get some support from my former Director. So it was back to ESCORT.

This time, when I am admitted to the Reception Room, I ask for the Admiral. The receptionist replies that I am expected. I should have known. I am escorted into the inner sanctum and to the corner office, where Vice Admiral Robert Lewis is at the helm, directing the world-wide efforts of this relatively secretive group of analysts, agents, and staff. Even dressed in mufti, old habits are very hard to break, so I march into his office and come to attention directly centered in front of his desk.

He commanded instant obedience and respect simply by his bearing with or without a uniform. He sat so erect and so solidly, a typhoon could not have budged him.

Born just after the end of the Second World War, Robert Lewis came from an all-Navy family. His father was a Chief Petty Officer on the Iowa, a battleship-hard gunner's mate, who retired with a severe loss of hearing from the 18 inch guns. It made him bark loudly at everyone. Robert was a good student at school, with a penchant for history, and a body for middleweight wrestling, that earned him a high school letter, even though his stature was a relatively short 5'-8." With his father's insistence, he entered the Naval Academy in 1966 during the middle of the Vietnam War. At Annapolis, he was shielded somewhat from the growing anti-war sentiment. But during his first summer cruise as part of his study program, he was thrown into it when he was in a group showing the flag in France, and saw many public displays of anger and anti-American demonstrations. It cut through his idealism about America, and changed it to a commitment to strengthen America's role and image in the world. While many of his classmates sought the heroic romance of flight or sub-school, he opted for Intelligence. Fortunately, a strong sea-daddy friend of his father's recognized that young Lewis had the capacity for deep selection, and steered him into more politically attractive jobs, starting with Navy Air. He went along and threw himself into aeronautical engineering and flight training with the same enthusiasm and commitment he made to his classes at the Academy and on the mat. When he got his wings, he already had garnered a Masters in Aeronautical Engineering, and was put on track for the Astronaut program. By 1975, he was set for a Skylab tour, but a cutback in funding reduced the crews and aborted longer term involvement. He was left on the beach along with most of the rest of the prospective Astronauts. Meantime, he had married a Navy brat and they had started a family. Two more girls were added to his shipboard complement by the time he was in his 30s, and he was being wooed by several large Aeronautical Contractors to leave the Navy for stratospheric income and power. Then came the Islamist Revolution in Iran and the siege at the U.S. Embassy. The CIA screwed up, and the NSA had no clue. On top of the lack of proper intelligence, when the rescue mission flopped, Lewis believed that something additional needed to be done. Military Intelligence had become an oxymoron. Organizations responsible for vital intelligence assessment and support had become bloated with funds and staff, yet couldn't find their way to the head. He lobbied with many of his friends and supporters to start a new, tough, small intelligence organization within the Navy that would support operations rather than spend most of their time cozying up to Congress for funding increases. He got his wish. Deep Selected for Captain at 36, he was given the authority to start ESCORT. Within five years, it was so successful that his billet was made 2-star, and he attacked the job with a ferocity that he took to everything else in his life. At home, things were not so smooth. One of his daughters contracted meningitis and died, and his wife lost a major battle with Leukemia. His remaining daughter was like her father, and is bringing up three children and keeping a Navy Pilot husband in line at the same time. With another star on his shoulders, Admiral Lewis takes each day as if it is a personal challenge.

"Mr. Chess. Twice in one week after three years is a record, even for you. I didn't think that you would ever choose to tread these decks again."

"Thank you, Admiral, for seeing me. I know you have little time, so I will get right to the point. I am at odds with some powerful forces within the government. Somehow, I have drawn the ire of the NSA, FBI, the National Security Office, and even the San Francisco Police. I need some cover."

"Yes, I understand that you are a 'person of interest' at the present time. I would guess that your next words will be something like 'I am innocent' or some other drivel."

"No Sir," I say loudly. "I know how to take my lumps when I have done something that I shouldn't have. I offer no apology. But I do want to understand better what has stirred the nest, and I believe that whatever is behind it has something to do with National Security. Can you give me some cover?"

"Before I answer that, I will tell you that you had no business asking one of our staff to be your bloodhound. Yes, you should know that I was informed the minute you showed up here and went through that ridiculous pantomime with Jim Carson. Our security boys enjoyed the leg show, but I am very glad that Carson chose to give you information that had nothing to do with this office, or he would now be in Greenland escorting icebergs. You should have come straight to me in the first place. I don't hold it against Carson, he acted out of friendship. But you do remember that in our business, there are no friends."

"Yes Sir." I replied. After that, what else could I say? "Sir, the reason I resigned have not changed."

"Yes, well, we all give up our personal agendas here. I did not take your resignation lightly. You were a valuable member of my team. But that is in the past. I will offer you help, but it is on my terms, which you may accept or not, but I will not negotiate. Is that understood?"

"Yes, sir, I do."

"As of right now, you are back on the payroll, TAD as my assistant to liaison with the NSA. Your task is to identify an operative within the NSA who is subverting the office for a personal agenda of stealing their new code research. As this position will necessitate your acting independently, this order should absolve you temporarily of any charge that the San Francisco Police Department should be compelled to levy on you. Also, this will satisfy any FBI inquiry. It might also help you with the NSA, but we'll have to take that one step-by-step. You will have access to our research and analysis. However; this is not to be considered a license to act irresponsibly or independent of my authority. I will expect accountability and regular reports. Got it?"

"Yes, sir, I got it. But have any idea about what's got the NSA stirred up?"

"There is a very strong movement to strengthen the privacy by major corporations that believe they are vulnerable to governmental intrusions through weaknesses in their communications integrity. Further, there are hints that there are some new technological advances that the military-industrial complex believes are being denied to them by the government. They have put a lot of pressure on agencies within the government to seek out these new technologies, and to unveil the researches. Several prominent Congressmen have been lobbied or even hired to administer this pressure, with expected results. Fortunately, this office is somewhat buried and therefore immune to most political pressure. But ultimately, we report to the CNO (Chief of Naval Operations) and the Joint Chiefs, so we need to be circumspect. Somehow, you were identified as an intermediary with access to those who are thought to be denying what these companies seek."

"Thank you for your confide4nce, sir."

"Don't screw up and get yourself killed. I would then have to assign somebody else."

"Aye, aye sir."

"Go home and try to pick up the link there. I will give you access. Do you have a secure telephone and computer?"

"Yes to the telephone, but not yet to the computer."

"We'll get one to you. Now get to work." He opened a drawer in his desk and took out a folder with a broad red stripe diagonally across it, but didn't open it yet, waiting for me to go.

"Sir, did you set me up?"

He looked at me very severely and then his eyes crinkled and he said, almost kindly, "Well, my boy, you are finally thinking clearly. That is a very dumb question but a good deduction. If I wanted you back here, I would have just pulled you in directly. There are times that one should be underhanded, but you don't gain the loyalty of your men by acting that way with them. You are dismissed."

"Aye, Aye sir, and thank you." I don't know why, but it always feels like I am being dismissed by my father. On the way out, I stick my head in Jim's office, but he is not there.. My new ID is waiting at Reception along with an envelope containing a credit card and an airline ticket for an evening flight to San Francisco. I wonder how it was arranged so quickly – but that's my old office for you.

# 14 *MONDAY NIGHT - SAN FRANCISCO*

The evening fog has persisted as we descend over the lower bay to San Francisco Airport. The whine of flaps and clunk of wheels-down tell me we are close, but there is no sight of the ground until a brief glimpse of waves a moment before touching down. By the time we taxi to the terminal, most of the passengers are anxious and they jump into the aisles as the seat belt sign goes off. I am in no hurry, so I wait. I hope that my rental in Albuquerque will be eventually returned by the FBI – or I would have one hell of a bill next month.

When the taxi reaches my house, I don't see anyone lurking, but with satellite imagery, it really isn't necessary. I will just have to take a couple of chances. I go up to my armory on the third floor. The pistol that I keep in my office desk drawer is good for general work, but I really need to be better armed if I have to deal with more from Towson. Behind a large piece of electronic equipment in my lab, a hidden door reveals my emergency stores and armory. I select two weapons: a K-Bar knife and a Glock 19 Auto made of polymer, with 9x19 clips. It has big stopping power, very compact for concealed carry, and is highly accurate. The minor annoyances of brass ejection straight up and back and a single safety system which cannot be activated with a round in the chamber are tiny drawbacks that don't outweigh its small size and simple operation. I pick an ankle holster – it is not as easy reach, but since I don't usually wear a jacket, it works better for me in the long run. I take two extra clips of 9mm ammunition and a sheath for my knife, one that fits down under my belt in the small of my back. I know that K-Bars are a little out of date, but it has always been a good friend so I stick with it.

Now, at least, I will be more prepared the next time someone comes at me. I have a Gemtech silencer for my pistol, but I decide it I won't need it. This isn't a case of stealth. I pocket a couple of other small items, including a lock-pick set, and some flex cuffs. One special item rests in a plastic box. It is a special credit card that I had made several years ago, but haven't used for some time. Imbedded in the card is a microchip that contains a small computer and a wireless communications set. When the card is swiped, the computer spits out a different name to the card reader, and the communicator activates, reading the data transmitted by the reader to the host, canceling the transaction and sending back an approval to the reader-receiver. It isn't strictly illegal, but an internal record is made in the card of each transaction, so later, I can dump the card memory and issue checks to the vendors. The benefits of avoiding NSA probes outweigh the drawbacks, and I slip it into my wallet.

Back down to my bedroom, I take a shower and dress in a long shirt and chinos, with an extra pocket sewn inside for my spare clips. First, I need to figure out what is causing the attention from NSA. Surely, by now Towson knows that I don't have the key.

I think one place to start is at Towson's house. My earlier search had been too cursory. If Edith Towson had been murdered to conceal Daniel's faked death, that was one thing, but if not, then maybe there was something in the house that could connect the dots.

I park a couple of doors down, and come back through the back yards. The door to the conservatory is unlocked, so I carefully check around the edges for any wires, particularly at the hinges. I cut the glass, just to be sure and feel around for an alarm circuit. Finding none, I open the door. Inside I find another door to the back hall. This one is locked and alarmed but I do not want to risk a window, so I use my tension wrench and turning tool and have it open in about a minute. With Edith dead, I reason that the alarm system is probably off. Alongside the door, there is keypad, but all the LEDs are dark. I open the alarm keypad and bring out a multimeter from my small bag of tricks, touching the voltage sensor to the exposed contacts but the circuits are dead. Motion, pressure or acoustic sensors are probably equally inactive,

On the first office off the library the desk yielded nothing but some ledgers which appear to be for household accounts, a checkbook with no accompanying register, and a few unpaid bills, neatly sorted by pay-date. In the bottom drawer, there are a few photographs, but no one that I recognize, except for Edith Towson herself in small groups of people and one with a young girl; I suppose her daughter. The telephone is still connected, but there is no answering machine. I check each book on the shelves. Most of them are classics, but at one end, there is a well-thumbed set of Robert Ludlum's thrillers with the paper jackets removed. I see no apparent false book-boxes. The office yields nothing.

I climb the stairs and start searching in the master bedroom. In the master closet, I discovered a safe in the floor that takes a key. After inserting my tension device, I discover that the design uses a safety deposit box lock, which made it inviolate to my equipment. I search in likely places for the key, but no success. Finally, I spot Edith's jewelry box on a shelf. It too requires a key, but has very flimsy lock. Inside, there are some very attractive and quite expensive trinkets but no key. I tap the walls in the closet looking for hidden compartments, but all the walls seem to be solid. The bathroom is my last venture in this suite. Here, one of the drawers in the vanity reveals a safe deposit key.

Back in the closet, I try the key and the door springs open. The compartment is almost empty, except for a single folder, and a passport case. The case holds passports for Edith and Daniel Towson, as well as a packet of traveler's checks for each – amounting to $10,000 each, and a few miscellaneous plastic cards. One is for a club of some kind, but I couldn't read it since it is printed in Arabic. I continue to dig through the folder when I hear a sound downstairs. I quickly close the safe, keeping the contents in my hand, and shut the light off in the closet.

I creep out of the closet and through the master bedroom to the hall. Sequestering myself behind the door, I listen. Downstairs, I can hear footsteps and some whispered words, but nothing I can make out. Then one set of footsteps moves to the stair and I can hear the slight squeaking of rubber soles on the wooden treads. They reach the upstairs corridor and then go quiet. I wait, but just to be safe, reach down and pull the Glock. There is a slight creak from the other end of the hall. Behind me, the windows appear to be both closed and locked. The steps come toward the master suite. I flatten myself behind the door and put my shoe out as a wedge so it would stop the door. I must make some sound that I am not aware of, because the footsteps stop just outside and a soft "Phut" sounds as a bullet crashes through the door showering me with splinters. Immediately following, a voice calls out "Frank, up here" and a foot collides with the door. It flies open and bangs against my shoe. A hand reaches around to pull at the door. I smash at the hand with my pistol, eliciting a yell and a second shot. But this shot goes wild as he recoils. I slide sideways and another shot punctures the door, lodging in the wall at chest height. I fall to the floor and spin, firing upwards. My shot misses, and the intruder drops back into the hall. "Frank, get up her now" the gunman yells. I throw myself across the room and land on the far side of the bed. Rising to the top of the mattress, I train my Glock on the doorway. Three more bullets buzz into the room and then a man dives in, ending up on the floor on the other side of the bed. I reach under the box spring and let off a couple of rounds. The first bullet crashes into the wall base, but with the second shot, there is a flat thud of a bullet hitting solid flesh, followed by a yell and a groan. I shift my aim back to the doorway, through which I can hear someone else running out in the hall. The noise from my pistol is still echoing in the quiet room when the footsteps in the hall stop just to the left of the door jamb.

The standoff continued for a full two minutes, before a voice calls out "This is the police. Come out. Backup is on the way; your best hope of getting out is now, before you wind up a stain on the carpet. Just stand up and throw out your gun, and you won't be hurt."

Local cops don't usually shoot first, so I assume that the police announcement is a false flag. Perhaps I can give him a turn. "Just a second; don't shoot; I am coming out," I call out. I raise myself off the floor just enough to reach the top of the bed, and inch by inch, I slide along the mattress, keeping a weather eye on the doorframe for any movement. I keep the Glock pointed towards the door just in case. When I reach the other side of the bed, I risk a glance down at the other fellow. He is lying in an expanding pool of blood, but the wound is in his thigh, so I thought that unless I nicked the femoral, he should be OK. He is conscious, but obviously in a lot of pain. His gun is not visible; probably under the bed, because I see both hands. Pointing the gun at his head, I drop down on top of him, and roll off onto the floor, eliciting another loud groan. "I am not going to wait much longer. I will give you 10 seconds, and then I am coming in" the voice outside calls. I grab the wounded man around the shoulders and roll him on top of me, just in case I need a shield. He screams, but at least he is now partially covering me. He reaches for his leg as I dig into his jacket pockets looking for an ID. But no wallet, no badge, no police. I call out to the fellow in the hall "Your partner is dying in here from an arterial shot. If you want him alive, you'll back off. I'll come out"

"Look, I don't want to kill you, but don't force it. Throw out your gun."

I scrabble around under the bed and locate the other gun, popping the clip out. "OK, here it comes" and I throw it out into the hall. As soon as the gun hits the carpet, I get up and run to the dressing table. Taking the chair from inside the knee space, I throw it through the bedroom window. Then I slide sideways behind the window drape next to the smashed window.

The sound of the breaking glass brings the partner into the room in a rush, waving his gun around as he runs. As he reaches the window, he leans out to look down and I shove my gun into his armpit. The pain hits him like an electric spark, and he drops his weapon onto the floor. He tries to come back at me with the other hand, but he gets tangled up in the drapes. I take a step back into the room and wait while he untangles himself.

"Take care of your friend," I say. "Get a pillowcase and make a tourniquet for his leg or he will be dead by the time you tell me your name." He follows my directions and grabs a pillow, dumps it and ties his buddy's leg. Then he rips the small lamp off the end table and sticks it through a loop and twists. His friend groans, but the blood flow starts to drop off.

"Now who are you both, and don't tell me the cops, 'cause you blew that one when your buddy shot at me through the door without a warning."

"You're Simon Chess; right? We were sent to bring you to our boss."

"So why the gunfire?"

"Jerry is stupid sometimes."

"Who's your boss?"

"Mr. Towson."

"And where were you going to bring me?"

"Hey Chess; we're strictly hired help. He took us on to bring you in because you owe him big money. He said…" a startled expression comes over him and he pitches forward, smoke coming from a neat hole in the back of his head. I drop to the floor as another round buries itself in the ceiling above me. I crawl to the door and into the hall. There were lights on all over the house, so I keep close to the floor as I crawl down the stairs and back through to the conservatory. I realize that I left the folder and passports upstairs, but had put a couple of the cards in my pocket. I am not going back up there. It is time to leave. When I move through the conservatory, I keep a low profile. At least there are no lights on out here. I manage to get out into the yard without drawing any more gunfire. Behind the house, there was a hedge and a wall. I gradually make my way out to the hedge and then crouch below the top of the wall, as I work my way back to a spot under the broken bedroom window. From a point next to the wall, I can see clearly through the upstairs window. I can imagine that if someone stands on the wall, it would an easy shot into the room with a rifle; particularly after there was no glass, and the room lights were on. I search around on the ground but don't see any brass. 'Professional hit' I think to myself.

Not wanting to leave nice footprints, I move to the hardscape and then around to a neighbor's yard. Over one more house, I find my car still parked in the back driveway. I checked the doors but everything seemed as I left it. Before getting in, I check underneath for any stray packages. I don't believe that Towson wanted me dead yet, but it is never a bad idea to be cautious.

I need to find Towson's base, now that I am sure of my adversary. I have to carry this to him rather than always being on the defensive. Moreover, I have to find out more about that damned key.

Marcia answered the call on the second ring. I recognized that it forwarded to another line, so I was doubly careful to wait until I heard her voice before volunteering to talk, but her voice comes through just fine.

"Hi. I want you to know that Towson sent a couple of his boys to bring me in tonight, but I got away from them. Can you find out if Towson has any offices or other places in San Francisco? I would like to make a house call."

"Yes, I have a list. None of them are in San Francisco proper, but across the bay in Oakland, there is a warehouse near Jack London Square which is owned by his company, and there is another warehouse, probably a bonded facility near the Naval Supply Depot down by the docks. He also has a house up in Berkeley near the Fairmont."

Marcia gives me the addresses and telephone numbers of the three locations. "Are you OK? Did you have much trouble with Towson's men?"

"Only a little, but I am starting to get pissed."

"Simon, try to stay cool. Whatever you do, don't take on the role of white-hat cowboy. I'd like you in one piece, please. By the way, did you get the computer yet?"

"Yes don't worry and no on the computer. I am away from the house, but I will be going back there soon. There is a slight chance that I may miss it, depending on how the rest of the evening goes. I will call you tomorrow morning"

I wonder how they knew to find me at Towson's house. They probably tried me at home first, and then had a list of places that I had visited. On the way home, I try Lauren again, but still no answer. I decide not to leave a message. I hope that she is OK. When I arrive home, there is a car parked in front of my house, Even though there's no bubble light, it has a spotlight turned inward at the driver's door, and a City Government license plate. There are times I wonder about out illustrious finest as they try to conceal their presence. But now I am ready for them. Better them than more of Towson's hoods.

I go around to the alley and park in the garage. Back inside the house, I put my Glock in a drawer along with the K-Bar and go to the front door, turning on the outside light. When I open the door, the two guys are walking up to the door. "Chess ?" one asks.

"Yes, and you are…"

"Jurgens, Lieutenant, San Francisco Police, Homicide." He holds out his wallet card and badge.

"Come in, Lieutenant, I am glad that you are here, it saves me some gas."

He leans toward me. "Don't be a smart ass. I should arrest you right now and then we can pick this up at the station."

"Sorry, Lieutenant, but I have a 'Get out of Jail Free card'."

"Show me." As I reach to my back, the second officer steps sharply away to the side, expecting a weapon. I pull out my recently renewed Navy ID. "I am on official Navy business on a matter of National Security. I am really sorry that I couldn't tell you before, but the investigation is ongoing." Jurgens takes the wallet and looks carefully at the picture, agency and ID number.

"Well it's your picture, but who is Colin Lessant?"

"It's my office name. In my business, we run the risk of vendettas, so all field agents use office names to protect their personal lives."

"So which is it, Lessant or Chess?"

"Lieutenant, do yourself a favor. You never heard of Colin Lessant. If anyone ever asks about me, it's Chess. Got it?"

"Sure, sure"; he responds sourly.

 He pulls the card out of my wallet and turns it over to see my fingerprint and a miniature DNA scan, as well as an original signed request for cooperation from the Secretary of Defense. He tosses it to his partner. "Check both of him out. Did you beat up on the two NSA people or not?"

"Lieutenant, it was a misunderstanding. They made the first move and never showed IDs."

"What about Edith Towson and Wayne Hudson?"

"I found Edith Towson dead by execution with a gunshot wound to her head. She was in her shower at home – and the front door was open when I got there. Hudson, I know nothing about, except that I contacted him about a lost item of mine. The last time I saw him, he was getting onto a car in front of his house. I can give you the plate number. Has something happened to him?

"Chess, it seems that anyone who you meet, somehow winds up dead. Hudson was found yesterday morning, floating in the bay. He had also been shot. Do you own a gun?"

"Yes, a 9mm Glock."

"Get it for me."

"It's upstairs. I'll be right back."

"No more disappearing tricks, OK?"

"Absolutely, Lieutenant; I am happy to cooperate."

"Stop shoveling and get me the gun." Before I can start up the stairs, his partner returns from the car and nods his head. Jurgens tosses back my credentials.

His partner starts up after me. "I'm sorry, Lieutenant, but I have some items that are classified, and would prefer if your man stays here. I'll only be a moment." I continue alone and go to the attic, where I procure a second Glock from my armory. It's clean. I take a fresh clip and slide it into the grip, and return downstairs. Jurgens takes it, ejects the clip, smells the barrel and produces a handkerchief which he pushed down into the firing chamber and then examines it. There is nothing but a light coating of oil on the cloth.

"I'll take this for our lab. Now tell me why you are investigating Towson and Hudson. The body count sucks. It makes our citizens uncomfortable, and my bosses pissed off."

"Lieutenant, all I can tell you is that I believe Edith Towson and Wayne Hudson were killed to conceal the fact that someone who is supposed to be dead, isn't."

"Are you talking about Daniel Towson?"

He was smarter that I gave him credit for. "Yes, he is certainly one that I would question for the murders, but there is more to it,"

Jurgens appears to want to ask more questions but I wave him off. "Lieutenant, I just returned from Washington. I am exhausted. It was a very long flight and I have been going since very early this morning. Would you mind?"

Jurgens got the hint. He moved to the door. "You need to come down to my office and make an official statement. I don't want any more work for the Coroner from you. You work with me, right? You find something out about these murders, you tell me, right?"

"Lieutenant, I couldn't care less about the murder angle. It's all yours."

"When can I expect you at the station?"

"I will call you tomorrow morning."

"Chess, I want to make something really clear. This is my town, and I don't want Feds leaving bodies around with no explanation. Anything else that smells bad, your ass is mine. I'll pull your P.I. license and lock you up until your buddies in Washington can spring you. Got it?"

"Right, Lieutenant; but if you grab Towson, you'll let me know also, OK?"

"Sure – you'll be the first one I'll call."

The door closed on both of them.

I pour myself a single-malt and was just starting to relax when the doorbell rings again. This time I look through the side glazed panel first, before opening the door. On the step is a young man with a computer case under his arm. He shows me an NSA ID and asks for mine. After signing some papers, I take ownership of a new laptop. When I turn it on, the login appears with a request for my Navy ID number, assigned to Colin Lessant and then a request for a new password. An email icon leads me through the Internet to a secure site at the NSA, containing a dozen files waiting for me, as well as a message from Marcia. The message gives me my clearance password to access the files, together with a contract and new National Security form which I had to sign digitally and return. With bookkeeping taken care of, I send a personal note to Marcia. It takes a couple of minutes for my clearance to be validated, but then a 'cleared for access' flag shows up next to each file and message. The top message includes a GPS log of hits for each of the people on the inquiry list. I try the one for Froehlich, and it brings up a map in real time, showing him at home in Bethesda. I check Towson, and get a map which places him in Albuquerque, but his icon is dated with the previous day's date. Lauren also had a locator, and shows her at the present time on a flight to San Francisco, scheduled to arrive later this evening. It also shows her with a reservation at The Palace Hotel for tonight.

There is an option to integrate all the subjects on one map, as well as pointers for each subject to a list of communications and audio files. I could also call for an alert to be transmitted to me based upon on proximity among subjects, as well as if the subjects contact one another. One interesting icon was a track on me, as well as on several people whose names I do not recognize. I guess these were network contacts for each subject, as the computer back at NSA constructs a social network for the contact group. For each contact, there is also a list of data taken from a variety of files including state DMV, DOD, FBI, Police, Bank and Credit Card files. I could also initiate satellite or special surveillances, including Humint, through this channel, although before approval, I would undoubtedly have to secure authorization for the use of National Reconnaissance Office Keyhole Satellite assets, however; there is a link to state and city traffic cameras well. This is a very powerful tool for the work I have to do, and a bit frightening in its intrusion potential.

But it's time to call the day. Before bed I go up to the attic and carefully clean and oil my Glock, refill the clip, and place it on my night table. No more surprises.

# 15 *1932 PHALERON*

For the past 5 years, Sophie Schliemann lived in a small house that she built here in Phaleron. It stood by the sea, southwest of Athens. White stucco with a blue tile roof made it indistinguishable from others in the neighborhood, but for a large stone patio flanked by old olive trees. Before coming here, she had arranged that all the artifacts, treasures, gold coins and pottery be transferred from various places in Europe, to the Staatliche Museum in Berlin, where her husband had given most of the artifacts in 1881; adding to them periodically over the remaining 9 years of his life. The collection at the museum, which bore their family name, Schliemann, was pledged by the museum to remain permanently on view.

Up through this day, in her 80th year, she recalled with love, the many years that she and her husband spent toiling together, scheming together, and protecting each other, for the sake of his good name. For the last 40 years since he died, she had administered digs in Greece and the Peloponnese and used the wealth from some of the finds as well as part of her remaining fortune left to her by her husband, to finance orphanages and sanatoria. Many of her donations went to build extensive research facilities for tuberculosis.

Today, she sat alone on her porch, wondering if it were to be her last day. Her heart had been acting up lately, and almost two weeks ago she finally was unable to do more than sit on her porch and wait. It was a typical winter day, perhaps even colder than most, but she loved sitting out in the bright sun with a light wrap spread over her. Her doctor had told her that she would never leave this place again.

In her musings, she failed to hear someone come into the house and stride out to the porch. When she finally roused sufficiently to see who was standing beside her chair, she did not place the man, but somehow he looked familiar. He was nearly as old as she, very thin, but fit, though his hair and pencil mustache were steely grey. He wore a conservative blue suit and a Fez. Thinking that perhaps it was another of the recipients of her largesse, she held out her hand in welcome, but the man did not take it.

"Do you remember me?" the man asked quietly, speaking in Greek.

"No, I do not believe I do."

"Do you recall on the day that your husband took ill, I came to speak with you?"

"Oh my God, it is you, of course." She started to get up, but fell back into the lounge chair. "What do you want?"

"Many years ago, I told you a story. It was about the origin of some relics that you found and hid. Do you remember?"

"Yes, but the story was nonsense. I only know that you wanted to steal what we had found, so you spun me a tale of old civilizations and old science. Are you here now to finally apologize to me for those lies?"

"Not at all; I am here because you will die soon and I need to know where you hid the three items that I asked you about on my last visit 40 years ago. I was unable to trace them after you left Naples for Athens. I had assumed that you sent them along with the rest of the stolen items to Berlin, but they were not in the shipments. Most recently, when you again scheduled new shipments to the Berlin Museum, I followed them and our agents at the Museum searched, but to no avail. Where are they?"

"They went along with the rest. I do not know anything else."

He looked sharply at her "You are lying. I know that you have kept them with you for these 42 years. Mrs. Schliemann, you have no longer any need for them, and they will do far greater good if returned before the next war breaks out. Germany will not be a safe place for them with the oncoming Nazis. If they don't destroy them out of ignorance, it will be a real surprise. The Russians may want them as well. The only place where we think that they will be safe may be in the west."

"They are not yours." Sophia's eyes blazed as they used to when she was angry at those who attacked her husband.

"Madam, they are indeed ours, and have been so for a far longer time than your few years. I am the 110th Keeper since the fall of Troy. And before then, there were 76 more stretching back to before 4000 BC. So don't think that 42 years means anything to me. But I am the only one that lost direct control of them and now that you are dying, I would like you to please return them to me."

"Tell me again, what exactly these items are."

"You know as well as I do. They are a helmet, a breastplate, and a key. Fortunately, since we recovered the Book from your husband, it is still within our control."

"Book? I know nothing about any books. Tell me about it. I won't tell anyone, but I wish to know. I am dying, after all."

Don't you recall my telling you that when your husband dug the Book out of the niche in the Troy battlement; that he had fallen asleep and we took it back?"

"No, I do not remember the details you told me about." Sophia held up her hands as if in supplication. "I will make you a bargain. You tell me about the book, and I shall tell you where the other three artifacts are hidden."

"That is a fair bargain, but you must tell me first. If you do, I shall take your trust as a sign of good intention, and will fulfill my part of the bargain."

"Very well, but you must give me assurances that they will be placed in the Berlin museum along with the rest of my husband's legacy."

"That, I am sorry to say, is something that I cannot do. As I told you, the information contained is too important to be used by the growing National Socialist Party."

"You must acknowledge that these items are my husband's property, discovered at the cost of his life. I have sworn to extol his name through the artifacts that he discovered; when no one would give him the respect he was due."

"I can only assure you that once their purpose has been attained, we will see that they are placed in the museum as you request."

"When my husband smuggled them out of Turkey, as you know, he made rough clay covering to hide their true identity. After we reached Athens, they were placed in the tomb that we had built, which now holds his body. They are still there. I had the clay coverings removed when my husband was buried. The key is back in its pocket within the breastplate, just as we found it."

"Thank you. We will not disturb his tomb. As long as I know where they are, it will be enough for us. Now for my part of the bargain: Do you remember anything of what I told you last time?"

"I do remember that you claimed to be descended from an old Mesopotamian civilization which has long disappeared. Your people went to Egypt and to other places collecting and dispensing scientific information and new discoveries. You told me that the Book your people created was done to protect your culture from destruction in the siege of Troy. Yes, I remember that it really is such a nice story; something to pass

181

to your children as a kind of fable to teach them to take the right paths in life. It isn't real, is it?"

"Oh yes. It is real, and it does exist. I can tell you that it rests where it will be the easiest to find, but also the where it will be the most difficult. If you solve this riddle, you will find our great Book. That is all I can tell you but for one error that you made in remembering our story. Yes, we wrote in it what we had learned during our sojourn in Troy, but remember that our culture goes back thousands of years before that time. In earlier times, our diaries were on papyrus, stored in clay tubes. Originally, these were deposited in the Library at Alexandria, so that while we were in Egypt, the great scholars' works would be available for research. Even then, the Book contained far more than only science. It also contained literature, medicine, agriculture, music and many other creative pursuits; all carefully recorded and  stored in the library to be made accessible to anyone who need but ask."

"Then the library was burned; not once, but at least four separate times. Many of the scrolls were lost. It was then that our ancestors decided to copy the remaining scrolls onto metal. Bronze was too heavy since it would take many strong men to carry such a book. Other metals were also either too soft or would not survive the temperature of future fires, as would undoubtedly occur over the coming years. Our metallurgists devised a new metal that was extremely light, flexible and could not be melted by any known burning. The armor that you have in your crypt is also of this metal, since it gives clues to the Book's existence."

For many years this book was kept at the site of the rebuilt library, but then it was moved to Troy, as the AFAR relocated there to construct our own city. During a more peaceful time in Egypt under Ptolemy, a new Great Library was constructed in Alexandria. Some keepers in those days believed that this library would be a good place for the Book, but it was left in Troy, as the Temple of Zeus constructed there was not to be disturbed. As it turned out, the new library in Alexandria was burned several more times. It is thought by many historians that the last burning was done by the Roman Emperor, Julius Caesar as an expression of his power over the Egyptians, but we know that it was burned by the Egyptians themselves, in a ploy to raise public anger against Rome."

"So the book exists. On its sheets are inscribed the best of the ancient world's heritage of learning, including those of our own scientists, who labored alongside many recognized scholars. Since your husband unearthed our Book, we have taken the opportunity to add to it. In order to protect the data, all of the information is put into an unbreakable code. The key to unlocking the code is on the breastplate, the helmet and the key. No single one of them contains the whole key, but it is only when all three joined that the key can be used to decipher the Book. "

"I want you to understand," she said "my husband and I always believed in the burden that is borne by historians and archeologists. It is we that gather and preserve the past for the future. I see that you are of the same character."

"In the time that you have left, please do not repeat anything of what I have told you. We do not know how many enemies of truth may continue to plague mankind in the following generations, only those that we know about today. This must not even accidentally get into the hands of new Caesars, regardless of what culture they spring from. You must promise me this."

"I do, on my word as a scientist. May I know your name?"

"I'm sorry, but I have no name to give you. I am just the 'Keeper'."

"But where are you from?"

"For now, I live in Cyprus, but I shall probably move soon. I have lived in many places."

"Thank you. I must rest now. These exertions have made be very tired."

"Of course. Goodbye."

The man left the way he came. When he was gone, Sophie struggled to stand, and she walked very slowly into a room that she used as an office when she was not so ill. As she sat at her desk, she took some notepaper and wrote a long letter to her daughter Andromache, living in Paris. Then she took another envelope and wrote a note to one of her grandsons, Alex, who was serving in the French Army. Enclosing the note in one of the envelopes, she wrote her grandson's name on it, sealed it, and put it in the other envelope to Andromache. This she left on the table by the entry for the mail.

Her tasks completed, she returned to the porch. Next to her chair was a new book that she had been reading earlier that morning. Picking it up, she found her place and continued reading about the most recent adventures of Hercule Poirot.

# 16  *1945 CYPRUS*

In the cave, the scientist bent over his task. There was no electricity. In the dark, a couple of candles burned at the corners of his table, but when these were gone, he would have to confine his working hours to daylight, unless they could get more wax. As it was, they were starting to burn olive oil lamps. But the lamps tended to smoke so it was difficult to work for long periods.

Before him on the table had been laid three items: A breast plate, a helmet, and a key. All three had come from Athens, but they were not Greek.

"Have you gotten anywhere with the translation?"

"Yes, but I have only small clues as to its meaning."

"What have you made out so far?"

"There is a book that contains secrets of the AFAR, but I am not sure what AFAR means. But my translations say that the book can be opened with a key. It also says that the key is to 'pull out the truth.' It doesn't say how this 'truth' is to be pulled out. I have looked all over the breastplate and the helmet, but there is no place that would take the key.

"Let's get the Greek back in here and see if he can tell us anything." The shorter man said.

"We have tried before. He just doesn't know anything except that these were to be delivered to the Americans. He knows that we are both German, so he totally refuses to talk to us. I guess he thinks that we are working for the Nazis."

"Did you try analyzing the metal itself?"

"I don't have the tools. But I agree with you, we should try to get more from the Greek."

The shorter man went out and returned with a man that looked unlike a typical Turk – very tall, but thin, with a wiry build but no mustache, and his skin was quite light in tone and his hair was very fine. If you saw him on a street in northern Europe, you would think him to be Scandinavian.

Also, when he spoke, it was evident that he was well educated. The two American soldiers that brought him in were also dressed in civilian clothes, though both also looked Greek or Cypriot. One of the soldiers said "We'll leave him with you, and wait outside."

"What do you want of me?" said the Greek.

"Where did these artifacts come from?"

"You are Germans. I will tell you nothing."

"Yes, we are Germans," said the taller man as he sat at the worktable. "But we have left Germany for America. The Americans sent us here because they believe that we could decipher the symbols written here on this armor, and help them find the book."

"I don't believe you. You are dressed like Americans, but underneath, you are still filthy Nazis."

"No, that isn't true. How can I prove it to you?"

"You can let me go."

"No one is keeping you here against your will."

"The guards out there told me that if I tried to leave, I would be shot."

"I will tell them you can go. But if we do let you go, where shall you go?"

"I will return to Istanbul, which is where I am from."

"You are Turkish, not Greek?"

"Filthy Greeks? No, I am not of them."

"Will you tell us your name?"

"I will tell you nothing" Under his breath he muttered "sons of swine."

"I can understand how you feel" the shorter scientist said.

"You understand nothing! How can you understand what it means to have no family, and no home? You, with your swagger and superiority; you think that only true Aryans are worthy of respect. I will see you in hell."

"You know only your own tiny existence. You are like a worm that only knows how to eat and doesn't have any idea that you could be a beautiful butterfly, if you gave it a chance." While the scientist spoke, the one at the table snorted "Let him go. You can't trust these people anyway. We need help but we can get it in America. We don't need this one."

"You are going to America?" the Turk looked at both of them wide-eyed. "If I help you, what will you do for me?"

"What do you want?"

"I wish to go to America, too. I think that in America, I could start a business and be rich."

"You help us and we shall speak to the American soldiers on your behalf, and ask that you be allowed to come with us. Will you help?"

"Yes I will, but do not think me a fool. I will want assurances. You will not get the opportunity to double cross me twice."

The shorter scientist called to the guard. When he came in holding his weapon at the ready, the scientist asked him to go get the Major. In about 5 minutes, the Major walked into the tent."

"Major, this Turk has asked us for a bargain. He will trade the detailed knowledge of these artifacts for an opportunity to go to America. I must tell you that in order for us to do our job, we have to learn as much as possible about these pieces, and we do not have much time."

"Very well," the Major replied. "We will have to conduct a security assessment. If there is no problem, I will arrange a place for him onboard our aircraft, and secure permission for his entry into the U.S."

"Thank you sir," the scientist said, as the Major left their workspace. Then the scientist turned back to the Turk. "Will that be acceptable to you?"

"Yes, so what do you want?"

"First, please tell us your name."

"Standahl Xyso."

"How did you come by these artifacts?"

"I was paid to go to Athens and bring these things back to Turkey. They came from a tomb there which I broke into and found these in a casket. But when I reached Cyprus, I learned that my contacts had been killed by the Germans, and so I have been stranded here. I thought that I would help the Americans and maybe earn their gratitude, to be paid with a Visa and transportation to the United States. I know that is the place I want to be. Europe is finished. America is the power for the next generation, and I want to be part of that. I don't know much about these pieces, but I was told that they are important to our future."

"How did you learn about them?"

"When I was at University in Istanbul, I made friends with a small group of fellow Turks that believed, like me, we have to work for peace. I broke with them only because I believe that so long as this war is with us, the least we can do is to profit from it."

"So you are a pragmatist."

"I suppose you could call me that. When the war broke out, and it looked like the Germans were going to take over Europe, my friends and I wondered if America would come into the war and with their resources, take the offensive. But it didn't happen, and things got worse. Then America came into the war and we hoped it would be over soon, but it still drags on."

"My friends and I formed a Resistance cell and were planning some attacks on German supply shipments, but we were and held captive. While in the garrison waiting for interrogation, we heard that the Germans were searching for some metal that they could use in a new type of rocket that they were building. In Turkey, there were rumors that some ancient artifacts made of a unique metal had been stolen by a German archeologist and smuggled into Greece."

"My friends and I were tortured and put in cells down where the water seeped in all the time. It was very cold. Every day we were taken out and beaten. Sometimes, they would come in the night and drag us out into the yard where the wall was full of bullet holes from executions. We would be lined up against the wall and the soldiers would aim their machine guns at us. Then they would give us one last chance to give them information."

"When the Germans started pulling out, word was passed down through the prison that everyone was to be killed. I managed to escape with two others before the executions started. We decided to locate these artifacts and see if the Americans wanted to buy them. According to the rumor, they could be found in a mausoleum with the name "Schliemann" on it. So while my friends were trying to contact the Americans, I located the crypt and broke into it, finding two caskets inside. In one of them, I found the armor on the corpse. I took them and started back towards Istanbul. If the Americans weren't interested, I planned to return them to Turkey, but when I got here, the Americans told me that they would study the artifacts and then make me an offer. I brought them here at great risk."

"These were very old relics. Inscriptions at the tomb said that Schliemann was an Archeologist. That's all I know. We heard that these originally came from Turkey. Once they have been studied, they should be brought back there."

"But you brought them to the Americans to sell. What changed your mind?"

"At first I only wanted the money, but now, after the killing of my friends, I think that they should have died for something besides cash. Will you help me get these items back to where they belong?"

"I am only the translator. I have no control over what the Americans do. I cannot make that promise to you. I will promise that I will speak to the Americans on your behalf."

"Thank you."

"Do you need any money? I may be able to get some funds from the Americans for your contributions here."

Xyso replied "Oh, I don't need any money. Along with these artifacts, I found a cache of gold coins, some of which I sold to get me this far, and some of which I will use to start a new business."

"Can you show me one of these coins? Maybe if I saw it, I could identify the source for these other pieces. That would speed up my investigation."

Xyso went out and returned carrying a small box. He put the box on the worktable and then opened it. Inside the box was a very old coin. On one side was a profile of a soldier wearing a helmet similar to the armor. On the other side of the coin was a bird of prey, flying over a landscape. He looked at the coin under a magnifying glass. There was no writing on it at all, on either side.

"May I keep this? I will pay you for it." The scientist said.

"If you get me to America, it would be my payment." Xyso thanked the scientist for his help, and departed for the village, saying "I shall return before you leave. Then I shall come with you."

Just then, the Major returned to ask if the Turk had helped. The scientists told him that he had, but it still was impossible to go further in the project without a more comprehensive laboratory and metallurgical assay equipment. The Major replied by telling him that those resources were not available here, so they would close up the shop and call transport for their onward trip to the U.S.

The taller scientist announced "I had better go into the village as well, if we are going to leave. I need to get a few things for the trip."

"Be careful. I will send an escort with you" said the Major.

"No need, I speak both Greek and Turkish, so I will blend in." With those words, he crept down the hillside, carefully sliding from one boulder to another, until he reached the main road. The lane was not much more than a double track through the hillside, and empty but for an occasional farmer with a donkey cart laden with vegetables for the market. When he reached the village itself, he stopped at a tavern to have a drink, where he saw Xyso in a corner with a glass of wine. The scientist quickly left the tavern and walked toward the center of the village, where he searched for and then entered a small shop up a dark, narrow alley. There was a boot which swung on chains in the evening breeze over the main entry. As he entered the cobbler's shop, a bell mounted at the top of the door struck against a metal clapper announcing his presence. A young woman of indeterminate ancestry came out of the back room and announced that the shop was closed. The German ignored her and requested to see Wilhelm. He spoke in Greek to her. The girl first said that there was no Wilhelm in the store, but after the scientist insisted, she looked him over and then apparently made up her mind, retreating into the back of the store.

"Yes, who is it that comes to see an old man in the night?"

"I came from the cave in the mountain" the scientist replied in German. "I need to get a message back to the bunker. Will you let them know that we do not have the information, but I will arrange for a shipment this week."

"Yes, I can send the message, but you must leave immediately. I cannot afford to be seen with a visitor after the shop is closed, particular a German."

"I also need you to arrange for the shipment."

"How big is the package?"

"It is small enough to fit in a box just under one meter long, a half meter high and a bit wider."

"I will get a crate, but it must be disguised, and I need to have an address."

"Just mark it 'Hazardous Biological Samples, Keep Cool'. It is to be addressed in care of Herr Franz Hauptman at Zoo Berlin. Put a Red Cross on the crate so it will pass through the lines without inspection."

"You must have this shipment to me by tomorrow evening, or there will be little chance of it's getting through. The Partisans are very active now. I can't be sure if any trains or truck convoys are still running."

"I will bring you the package tomorrow." Before leaving the shop, he purchased a pair of boots, to explain his visit. Then he returned up the hill

190

to the camp. It was dark when he reached the cave. His fellow scientist had fallen asleep with his head on the workbench. He roused his friend and escorted him to bed.

Once his friend started to snore, the scientist took a very small Leica matchbox camera and carefully photographed the helmet and breastplate from all sides, including the backs and inside. He searched for the key but couldn't find it, concluding that his partner must have secreted it somewhere. He put the camera into his travel bag, hidden in the toe of a sock. Then he took the helmet and breastplate and stuffed them into a basket, which he slung on his back. He moved quietly back through the encampment and down the hill once again.

Just as he turned into the alley, someone leaped out of a doorway opposite and grabbed him around the neck. With the basket on his back, he couldn't get his arms up to defend himself. An arm was around his neck and his face pushed into the wall of the building. A smell of sour wine assailed him as a voice sounded with lips pressed to his free ear "Traitor! Now you shall pay." The arm pressed harder into his neck under his chin. He struggled, but the man was very powerful. The assailant pulled the scientist's head further and further back, until the scientist started seeing black blotches and flashes of light. He tried kicking out at the wall of the alley but he was weakened by the lack of air. Again the man grunted as he forced his knee up against the lower back of the German and pulled on the neck putting a huge strain on his spine. "I'm going to die" he thought and in a supreme effort he raised his leg and kicked out against the wall. His captor fell back to the ground but still clung on his throat. The scientist tried to roll backwards to break the grip, and in doing so, cracked the head of the man beneath, on the cobbles. The grip loosened and the scientist grabbed a ragged breath before rising up again and throwing his head back into the man's face – driving his head back to the stones, while breaking the man's nose in the process. The grip on his neck released and the scientist rolled off.

There was almost no light in the alley as the scientist stood up. He peered down at the fallen man. Suddenly a knife glinted in the man's hand and it surged up towards the scientist's chest. He fell back and the knife just grazed across his chest instead of through his neck. Then the man stood and advanced, holding the knife in front of him tossing it from hand to hand as he approached. The scientist backed up until he came into contact with the wall and realized that he could not escape. He tried to kick upwards, but the man sidestepped and gained another step. Although his face was in shadow, his teeth gleamed as he smiled in the looming darkness. Just as the knife hand cocked for a final strike, there was a sharp crack of a piece of wood hitting bone and the man collapsed to the street, the knife clattering on the cobblestones. The scientist slipped down the wall in a feint. Then the sharp pain of a slap in the face woke him.

"What….Who…?"

"Shut up, you fool. It is me, Wilhelm. Who do you think?"

"Wilhelm. I brought you…"

"Yes, yes. But you said you would do it tomorrow. Why did you come back tonight?"

"When I got back, it looked like we were packed and ready to leave in the morning. I had no more time."

They rolled the unconscious assailant face up."Xyso!"

"He must have been waiting for you. Here, give me the basket and go back to your camp. I will take care of him and get this off to Germany."

"But he is supposed to be going with us tomorrow."

"So he will be missing. Do you think that anyone will care? One more missing Greek" Just go before you are missed."

The German walked slowly back, rubbing his sore neck. When he finally arrived back to the camp, it was past 2 in the morning, so he crept into his tent and peered into the steel mirror he kept with his shaving accessories. There was a red mark extending all across the front of his throat. He wrapped a scarf around his throat, and with his clothes on, fell into bed.

Between the stones under the worktable in the cave, in a small crevice, lay the third artifact: a golden key.

# 17 *1945 BERLIN*

The walls along the north side of the Zoo kept the river from filling the basement, but the dampness still came through and made moldy slime along the stone floor. The Reichmarshal had commanded that his personal treasures be moved from the museum to this place, where they could be hidden for as long as he wished, no matter how the final days of the war played out.

On the west side of the garden, the tram no longer ran. It had been bombed by the Allies. Almost anything that moved these days was bombed. But overhead, the animals in the zoo seemed to be spared. That is why this location was chosen. Already, the cache at Schloss Neuschwanstein had been discovered, as well as other caches in Linz and in Austrian mineshafts. The Russians were assembling 'Trophy Teams' at the same time as the West had put together 'Monument Men' to liberate these treasures. As Franz strode through the main hall, he thought to himself "We stole from them, now they are going to steal from us. You can call it anything for the masses, but we who are the guardians of our Aryan heritage know the truth. It is stealing."

*Obersturmbannführer* (Senior Stormtrooper Leader) Franz Hauptman was responsible for this cache. He had been personally assigned by Hermann Göring to protect the Reichmarshal's interests. That which the Fuhrer had not specifically chosen for himself was shipped to various locations around the country and to Austria. But first, Goring made his personal selections. The most precious of those were moved here. Hauptman knew that if it took his whole life, he would guard these rooms and protect the contents until Göring came to claim them. Even though Goring was not in his SS chain of command, the Reichmarshal was responsible for the Luftwaffe and very close to the Fuehrer, so no one questioned his orders.

Franz wore civilian clothing, and had taken on the title of Assistant Habitat Master for the Zoo. He took his job very seriously; toiling every day to see that the creatures in his charge were fed as well as he could, despite the shortages of the war. The longer he managed their care, the more sympathy he felt for the innocent beasts. He wheedled straw and silage from farms around the city, even calling on troops to displace the remaining farmers in order to get foods for his animals, birds and aquarium stocks. Most of the farmers were dead or gone to military assignments, and usually the remaining family members were too young or afraid to argue. But it still was most difficult.

Today, he was sorting the last delivery, when suddenly the drumming of footsteps sounded on the access stairs, and there were shouts from the guards. Franz thought that perhaps the city was already being invaded. Quickly, he closed up the box he had opened and ran to the door. As he started to pull it open, a great push from the other side sent him sprawling. He started to curse and grabbed for his glasses, when he suddenly recognized the intruder. It was Hermann Goring himself, followed by several high ranking Luftwaffe officers.

"Hauptman, stand in front of me," Goring shouted imperiously. "What do you mean by leaving my treasures strewn about?"

"I'm sorry sir," Franz trembled in answering. One word and he was history. "Sir, what would you like me to do?"

"Do? Do? What do you mean Do? I told you to put these things in a bunker. Do you have potatoes in your ears?"

"Yes, sir. A Bunker. But sir, there is no bunker, here; only these storage rooms."

"Don't make excuses. I said a Bunker and I mean a Bunker. In two weeks I expect a bunker to be built here under this storage room: built so that no one can ever find it. If it is not build properly and by next week, your bones will be the first artifact stored in it. Do you understand?"

"Yes, my General. I shall do it now. But I have no people to help. They have all either been killed or disserted."

"Don't bother me with details. I want it built, do you hear?"

"Yes sir, right away sir. May I beg of you a paper that I can use to requisition supplies and workers?"

"Sergeant, get me some paper and a pen."

A younger man ran out and returned in a minute with paper. He also produced a pen, with which Goring wrote a few lines and then signed it. One of the other escorts produced a large ornate stamp, which he used to stamp on top of the General's signature. The general turned and strode out, calling over his shoulder as he left "Two Weeks." Franz picked up the paper from the floor. It said that he was authorized to act in the name of General Hermann Goring to procure people and materiel for construction.

Over the next week, a small army descended into the basement of the Zoo building. By hand they excavated a pit, lined it with paving stones from the street outside, and caulked it with cement which had been procured from an army unit building city defenses. The entrance to the bunker was in the floor through a trapdoor. To the wooden trap more stones were mortared. The whole assembly was raised and lowered by means of a pulley and a ring mounted in an overhead beam. Once the space was completed, a single electric line was run through the floor to a pair of ceiling lights in the new bunker. Crate by crate, the treasures were carried down through the trapdoor and deposited. When all was moved, the trapdoor was sealed. Franz placed the original catalogue of artifacts in the bunker with the goods and closed the trap himself. He had made a copy of this list, which he hid in his rooms. Dirt was scuffed on top of the stones that hid the door, and the lights turned off. The men who had labored with such difficulty to dig and construct the bunker were brought out to a requisitioned truck to be paid off.

Hauptman took care of this himself. Reaching into the truck body, he withdrew a machine pistol and opened it on the workers. The noise of the gun was loud, but not so loud as to mask the screams of the victims. One by one, they all fell to the earth, blood streaming from their twisted bodies. Two men had started to run, but their legs were cut down. When the rest were dead, Hauptman strolled over to the two still crawling across the plaza where the tram once ran. Two bullets in each head finished the job.

He walked the machine pistol over to the riverside and leaned over the guard-wall, dropping it into the river. He ordered the few remaining soldiers to gather the dead and dispose of them in an abandoned building nearby. Then he strolled home, a Habitat Manager again, where he took a bath in cold water and buried his uniform in the back yard, but not before he took the note that Goring had written and secreted it with the catalogue copy.

He dressed in overalls and a work shirt that had a patched sleeve. He had a small meal of cold tinned imitation ham and a boiled potato, washing it down with water. There was no coffee. He then went back out to the zoo building, into the administration block, and began his vigil, waiting for either the Allies or the Russians, whoever came first.

## EASTERN BERLIN – SAME TIMEFRAME

Colonel Sergei Gorchakov entered the city just behind the advancing paramilitary corps. He was a large man, wide across the shoulders and

195

chest with coarse features on his square Slavic face, and a residual harelip which was partially concealed by a brush mustache. His army officer's shoulder boards had blue flashes, which identified him as belonging to the intelligence services. He wore straight black boots with rounded toes and heels, which he unconsciously clacked together when he was impatient; which was most of the time. He sat in the right front seat of a 2-1/2 ton American truck provided to the Russians during the latter part of the war. Occasionally, he would reach inside his coat and adjust his crotch, which was squashed by his expanding belly. On the seat next to him was a worn black leather satchel with two straps buckled at the top that carried his documents and orders. Inside the satchel also was a narrow flask of vodka, which was now empty, eliciting more impatience than usual from its owner.

His unit drove their tanks down the main streets from the east, paralleled by single engine light aircraft that spotted residual German fighters still clinging to tiny footholds in churches, markets and office blocks. Occasionally the Russian pilots would see some gun barrels sticking out of windows and call to the tanks that would fire on the buildings, flushing out the few kids remaining from the once glorious polished troops of 6 years earlier. Most of those teenagers had no uniforms, few bullets, and no helmets to protect them, so they were methodically shot, torched with flamethrowers, or blown up by artillery. Street by street, the Russian army advanced neither giving quarter nor recognizing white flags. The remembrance of German cruelty in their motherland was too near for anything but wholesale retribution. Unless the citizens immediately showed obedience to the advancing troops, they were gunned down and ground into the dirt.

When Gorchakov and his special team got to the museum in Western Berlin, the balance of the company continued deeper into the city while he detailed one platoon to ascend the main stair. Waiting for them was a group of soldiers from the Allied Army. Gorchakov accosted the group and demanded to see their leader. An American Lieutenant Colonel introduced himself. Gorchakov then gave the American a folder of orders, announcing "I have come to take back that which was stolen from The Soviet Socialist Republics. You will immediately turn over to me all the artworks, so that I may compare the catalogue with those from our museums."

The weary American soldier calmly responded. "I am sorry Colonel, but all the items here have already been consigned to the Allied Art Treasure Commission, and your nation, as a member of this commission, may apply for the return of these treasures, but only after they have been verified that your country is the rightful owner."

"Do not interfere with my orders," Gorchakov retorted heatedly. "I am here with my men to insure that nothing further is stolen from our motherland. Stand aside."

"Colonel Gorchakov," the American said with great patience and politeness "As I said, you may apply to the Commission, and also, you may detail a representative to stay here with us and witness these last articles loaded for shipment."

"Get out of our way now, or you and your men will suffer the consequences." Gorchakov signaled to his men. The men slipped their machine guns off their shoulders and held them loosely in the general direction of the smaller Allied group.

"Now sir; this is not the time or place to be squabbling over trinkets. We have both fought a war as allies. Do you really want to challenge that alliance and risk your government's exclusion from sharing in these spoils?" The American strode out to the entrance and waved a small convoy over to the museum. Six trucks and two jeeps turned into the courtyard and took positions encircling the Russian trucks.

Gorchakov followed the American outside to the steps, but seeing the now larger American force, retracted his demand. "We are always ready to work together for mutual peace and understanding. He smiled, showing the steel fillings in his teeth that had turned brown. It gave him the look of an old hyena. "Give me a copy of the catalogue covering the items that you have packed."

"Of course; Sergeant, give a copy of our Bills of Lading to the Colonel."

Gorchakov gave the signal to his men to stand down. The American colonel waved the support convoy on. His men then returned to loading their own trucks. As boxes started coming out of the building, Gorchakov took out the new list that the Americans had given him and laid it side-by-side with one he had brought from home. He checked off each of the items with a fat pen that looked lost in his hand, as he found them on the American's list. When that list was exhausted, he looked at his original catalogue. There were many missing entries. Surely, the Americans could not have overlooked items that were supposed to be here.

As the loading continued, Gorchakov moved his men quietly to the side of the museum, by the employees' entrance. As each museum worker came out the door, he or she was met by one of Gorchakov's men who escorted the worker to a space between two trucks where soon, a small group of trembling men and women had been herded. Gorchakov took out his pistol and summarily shot one in the head. The smell of burned hair mingled with the sticky sweet smell of blood as the man slid to the ground.

"Tell me where the hidden art is located. I wish to know right now, or one by one, the rest of you will join your nameless colleague."

"He is not nameless. That is Herr Steiner, the curator of paleontology," a youngish woman said, staring defiantly at Gorchakov.

"And you are?" drawled Gorchakov in very guttural German.

"I am Madeline Kirsch. I look after European Paintings."

"You have no more paintings," said Gorchakov as he raised his pistol again.

"Wait, I will tell you. You need to go to the Zoo."

"The Zoo? Is that some kind of insult?" Gorchakov asked as he cocked his Tokarev pistol, pulling the tiny hammer back until there was an audible click.

"No, Sir. Please. About 6 months ago, a detail from the Luftwaffe came here and took away a lot of the art. When they invaded my collection, I heard two of them say that they were to be taken to a new storage place inside the Zoo."

Gorchakov turned them loose with a warning about talking. He detailed two of his men to load the corpse into one of the trucks for later disposal. "We cannot get to the Zoo right now, as there are too many watching the western part of the city. But we will be back." The trucks moved off to the East Zone, leaving behind only another large bloody stain on the cobblestones.

# 18 *TUESDAY SAN FRANCISCO*

The shrill telephone rouses me from a dreamless sleep. The clock said 6:45 and I was still not ready to get up for the day. But the Caller ID said the Palace Hotel, so I assume it was Lauren.

"Where have you been?" She asks accusingly. "I worried about you all day yesterday."

"Lauren. Good morning. I had to go back to Washington and take care of some things. Where are you?"

"I'm here, at the Palace. Can you come over and meet me for breakfast? I have some good news about the missing item."

"OK. I will be there in an hour. Get us a table in the Garden Court?"

I showered and dressed, taking my Glock from the Kitchen drawer and strapping it to my ankle, as well as slipping my K-Bar into my waistband. Before I leave, I stop up in the attic and get some cash from my safe, and then write a note for Stephanie.

I head into town, which is going about its normal Tuesday morning rush. Even at 7:15 when I leave the house, Montgomery and Market Streets are crowded. I leave the car with the Valet, and stroll through the registration area to the Garden Court. Lauren waves to me from a table set under a Palm tree, next to one of the huge columns. There already is coffee on the table. Was it only 6 days ago that all this started, right here?

"I was worried when I couldn't reach you and thought that I had better see for myself that you were all right," She says.

"Why would you be concerned? I told you that I was going to Washington."

"Yes, but I got a call from Alattin, who said you stopped to see him, so I realized that you didn't go directly to Washington like you said. Then, when you didn't call or come back, I wondered if something happened to you."

"Lauren, I wasn't lying to you. While I was waiting for the flight, I suddenly got the idea to follow up with Drs Akan and Yancy while I was still here. After those meetings, I carried on with D.C. What did Akan tell you?"

"Not much, but he offered to be a backstop for me if I needed one. Did you accomplish anything in Washington?"

I think it would be better if I kept the meeting with Froehlich to myself; at least while Lauren was so sure he and Towson her primary threats. "I tried to clear up the NSA angle. One less agency after our hides will give us some room to maneuver."

"I am really worried about what Towson might do. Simon, will you promise to stay close to me until your investigation is finished? I can't imagine what I would do without you." Lauren looked like she was going to cry. A single tear leaked out of the corner of her eye as she looked up at me like a wronged puppy.

"Lauren, don't you think it's about time that you were straight with me?"

"Simon, what do you mean?"

"First, there is the key. You gave me a great story about not knowing anything about it, yet both Eleanor Frankel and Dr. Akan were certain that you helped your father with the translation, being an expert in ancient Middle Eastern languages like you are. Then there is the whole business of your father's double death."

"I told you. I was knocked out of the car and when I woke up, it was on fire. I thought that my father was inside. I never heard about the drowning episode until Aunt Em told us about him.

"I've got some news for you. Police Lieutenant Jurgens was waiting for me when I came home from Washington. He's with Homicide and was working on the death of Edith Towson. He told me that Hudson is also dead."

"Simon, I swear to you I don't know anything. I am getting really scared. With everyone connected to my father's death being killed off, I wonder when it will be my turn."

"Lauren, I do want to help you, but if I can't trust you, then we might as well call it quits right now. Now tell me what you know about the key."

Lauren kept quiet for a couple of beats, and then continued softly "I did help my father, or at least I tried to, but got nowhere. The key had a jumble of words that made no sense. I'm sorry I didn't tell you, but it really meant nothing to me at the time – just another puzzle that my father was interested in, but that we couldn't find the solution. I can't believe that anything like this key would be the cause of all this killing."

"Lauren, both Hudson and Edith Towson had to have been dangers to someone, probably Towson: Edith because she knew that her husband was still alive and Hudson because he was connected with your father's death. If what Eleanor said was true, I would imagine that last year, Hudson took your father on a midnight cruise; probably unwillingly, and he wound up in the drink. It doesn't explain what you told me about the auto accident, but does explain Eleanor's version of the story."

"Simon, I told you the truth about the accident."

"Maybe what really happened goes something like this: Towson or someone working for him fixed something in your car that made your father lose control. When it went off the road as planned, you were thrown out of the car unconscious. Towson must have been following and arrived right after, found your father maybe alive, and then dragged him out. Maybe he put someone else in the car. He probably needed your father to help him get the key, or his diary, or whatever. So he took your father somewhere, got or didn't get what he needed and deep-sixed him with the help of Hudson. Meantime, the car needed a body that could be identified, so he could go undercover, for some reason. By the time you woke up, Towson was gone with your father, and somebody was dead in the car. How he arranged to have himself identified in a second accident, I don't know. I would guess that now he's after you because you, like Edith, knows that his death was faked. But what connection would you have with my missing horse puzzle unless you are still lying to me about being in the car? If you lied, you would still need me if you thought I had the key. But I really don't have it, Lauren. There is no simple explanation, particularly about you and your father."

"Simon, I swear to you, that night was as I told you and I am certain that Towson is still alive."

"So tell me again why my puzzle horse is in the middle of this?"

"Let me ask *you* a question. You say you bought the horse in Gump's, so unless there was some kind of conspiracy, you must have been the victim of a mistaken identity – the person at Gump's was supposed to give the horse to someone else – maybe an agent of Towson's, but you wound up with it. Maybe it's just a big mistake."

"That could be true, but since the horse was stolen, and Towson is looking to me to give him the key, there has to be a third party. Otherwise, the horse would not have been stolen in the first place."

"So the horse had my father's key in it, and it was stolen at the museum?"

"Yes, it has to be the same key."

"You know, Simon, when I was small, I found it in a box on his desk. I used to play with it, trying it in the doors in the house, until one day, my father found me with it and scolded me for taking it. He told me that it was a very old key, and was in his care for safekeeping. Except for the time that he asked me to help him with the translation, I didn't see it again. But how did you wind up with it?"

"When I was here at the Garden Court last week having breakfast, it was slipped into my pocket. I found it when I went to pay for the horse, and decided to put it inside. I wonder why Towson wants this key so badly."

"Well, let's find the horse, give it to him, and be done with this. Lauren looks around the restaurant with a fearful expression.

"All right, but now you have to describe it in as much detail as possible for me. Remember, I saw it for maybe ten seconds before stuffing it in the horse."

I call the waiter over and ask him if he could get me paper and a pen. When he returns, Lauren takes them and starts to sketch. In about 10 minutes, she turns it around to me. It looks something like what I remembered. A key, about 5 inches long, with a paddle handle on which was a cloud and a lightning bolt on one side and a horse on the other. The shaft was straight, but with holes bored along the barrel, each of a different size and each in a different position. The shaft was not round, but octagonal in cross section. Around the cloud were a scrawl of text and some diagrams, very tiny ones. Lauren couldn't reproduce the text or diagrams.

I stare at it for a while, and then have an idea. I excuse myself while Lauren goes back to the dessert table for a sweet to finish off breakfast. I go back up the few steps to the waiting area outside the restaurant, pull out my telephone and call Marcia. I ask her to research the key, giving her its description. She asked me to email the sketch after scanning it with my new computer.

"John Crawford" the kindly voice answers when I call.

"John, this is Simon Chess. We met at Marcia's house the other evening."

"Of course; how are you Simon?"

"I'm still pursuing faint trails, probably like you."

"I'll bet mine are older than yours."

"I think you might reconsider the bet. I ran across a very old key which is part of my puzzle. Maybe, if you have a few minutes, you could look at it and give me an opinion."

"Dear fellow, I would be glad to do so. It would give me a break and maybe help me see my own problem in a new light. Can you send it, or if not, a photo might work?"

"No, but I have a sketch."

"A sketch would be better than nothing. Just send me a scan. By the way, are you planning to be here in Washington soon? I called you a couple of days ago about my armor; you remember the artifacts I told you about. Well, I've made a little progress with the analysis and thought that you could help me find my source."

"I have a feeling I'll be in town soon, so I'll be glad to help you. Meantime, I'll send you the sketch."

John gives me his email address and promises to reconnect later that day. He says it will take him a few hours for his research. I go back into the Garden Court, collect Lauren and we head back to my house. On the way, I tell Lauren about sending the sketch to a friend at the Smithsonian. When we are back at the house, I take the sketch to my new laptop. On the side there is a narrow slot, just wider than a sheet of paper. I insert the sketch into the slot. It is taken in and then returned from the same slot. On the screen is an image of the sketch with a menu. I add a brief note to John and Marcia and type their email addresses. In a moment, an acknowledgement is received.

Back in the kitchen, Lauren has another cup of coffee and then settles in the bay window. "You know, Simon, this is really a lovely place you have. It really makes me feel at home."

I don't pick up on the invitation, but ask her if she can think about why Towson that would need to kill her father. I then leave her in the kitchen and go to my office. I open my laptop again and log onto the NSA portal. Lauren's issues have to take a back seat to the key recovery, to get Towson off our backs. If Lauren had it, I could think of no reason why she would keep it from me. If Froehlich had it, then he would have reacted differently to my questions. So who was left?

Maybe the best thing that I can do was to try to cast some bait. I take out the note that I had left myself with Towson's number on it. Then I log onto the GPS locater map. Towson's telephone rang a long time before it was picked up.

"Yes, Chess, do you have my key?"

"Mr. Towson, I am really tired of this game." I said. "Can we meet somewhere and I will give you what I have?"

"Well, you have finally come to your senses. Give me you cell number."

"I'm sorry, I do not carry one. Just call me here at home when you are ready to meet." While I speak with him, I looked on the map. The symbol marked "Towson" had started blinking, but the location is in Albuquerque. I guess it would be a while.

"I will have a telephone dropped off at your home in an hour. As soon as you get it, call this number and I will set up the meeting." The telephone clicks off.

I call to Lauren and say that I had an errand to run. On the way out, I tell Stephanie to expect a package, but to just leave it unopened for me. Then I drive back to Gump's. The counter with the puzzle boxes still has one like my horse. As the salesman is wrapping the replacement I purchased he comments, "Didn't you buy one of these last week?"

I tell him that I had given it to someone, but wanted one for myself. He then said "You know what is strange? Just after you left, another man came in and asked me if your name was Simon Chess? I told him that it was the name printed on the credit card receipt. I guess someone recognized you and wanted to be sure."

"Did he give you his name?"

"No, and he didn't buy anything either."

"Can you tell me what he looked like?"

"A thin gentlemen, very well dressed. I would say that he looked Middle Eastern, perhaps Lebanese or Greek. But he spoke English with hardly a trace of accent."

"Can you tell me anything else about him?"

"Well, he was in the next room when you bought the puzzle, and as soon as you left the counter, he came over. I think he was watching you."

"Thank you very much. Here, let me give you my card. If he comes in again, or anyone else comes into the store and asks for me, would you be so kind as to give me a call? You see, I am a Private Investigator, and sometimes a client brings out the worst in the people we look into."

"Of course; I will be happy to do that. After all, I made two sales to you already. Shall I hold one of these horses in the back, just in case you want another one?"

I shook my head and thanked him again. Whoever followed me, if I never saw him the first time, he had to be a professional. On the way back to the office, I stop at an old hardware store on Mission Street, and make a small purchase. Then I return home. Inside, Stephanie has a package for me. She told me that it had been left on the doorstep after someone rang the bell. I take it upstairs, greeting Lauren on the way, and then open it in my office. There is a new cell phone inside.

Towson's number is preprogrammed into the phone. He answers on the first ring. "Meet me at the place where you and Lauren had dinner. Make it 4:00 this afternoon, and bring it with you."

It was not quite lunchtime. I call the Admiral's office in Washington and report in, telling the aide that I am still on the track of the code key, but had not made any progress yet. Then I call Marcia.

"Simon! I just had a call from John. He found something interesting about the scan that you sent him. He asked me to have you call him. This key is attracting quite a crowd."

"One more thing; do you remember when we were sitting at dinner? Well, John mentioned something about the artifacts that had surfaced at his office for analysis. I had an idea that the key might be related."

"Well, he is quite excited about it. Give him a call."

"I will. Now, please tell me anything new."

"Well, we've verified the link between Towson, Zilbern and Froehlich. They were all in Cyprus together, but Towson was still using his birth name, Xyso. I understand that when Froehlich and Zilbern returned to America, Xyso was denied passage and entry, so he made his way back to Istanbul and started his import-export cover business dealing in arms. We don't know where he got the money, but it was enough for him to buy an old tramp steamer. Our first records of Xyso coming to this country are in 1956, after his business was running well. He seems to have had Froehlich's help getting a green card. Froehlich signed a sponsor agreement attesting to Xyso's (now Towson) character. Since then, there have been periodic contacts between the two of them. But a year and a half ago, all contact ceased.

"What about the other three scientists whose names I gave you?"

"All checked out, although the Turk, Akan who is the only other foreigner. But he came over as a young man, and took his degrees at U.C. Berkeley. There have been no alerts, other than annual security screening for his work at Los Alamos. He seems to be clean as well."

"Tell me about you." I said. "Is everything OK with you at the office?"

"Not really. I am very sorely missing you and wish that this were over so you and I could pick up our suspended relationship."

"What I mean is are you under any suspicion at work, or have there been any strange folks hanging around?"

"If you mean have there been any strange men in my bed, the answer is no. Not even under it. But there is a Personal Trainer that I keep in the hall closet with my tennis racquets."

"Marcia, I really don't know what I am going to do with you."

"Oh, I'll give you a big hint!"

"Not now, please. Look, I am on the trail of the resurrected Mr. Towson again. In fact, I will be meeting with him later this afternoon."

"Be careful. Towson is an arms dealer, after all. He is used to violence."

"OK. I'll be careful. Thanks, love."

"What a nice name; Goodbye, dear."

I hung up with an involuntary smile on my face. Lauren shows up and tells me that I look goofy. Then she leaves me a mug of coffee. I do some paperwork for a while. After all, I have some real paying clients to attend to. I make a few phone calls, and answer emails that had been piling up. Lauren comes in again, this time with a corned beef sandwich and a cold beer. I hadn't realized that I was hungry. I do not tell her about the plan to meet Towson later

Before she goes downstairs with the dishes, she asks me "Have you heard more from Towson?" she asked.

"Yes, he is still demanding his key."

"Simon, it's not worth your life or mine to really know what happened to my father. I would rather drop the whole thing. I am really worried about you. I can't see how keeping this key will get us anything at all."

"But I told you, I don't have it any more."

"Yes, well. I'll tell you one thing. If I had it, I would give it back and be done with it. It's brought nothing but grief."

I chalk up Lauren's comment to frustration. "There is one thing, however; I think that we will be done with him today."

"Why? What have you done?"

"I did speak to him earlier today and agreed to meet him later, so I will just do that, and try to convince him that I no longer have the key, nor know where it is."

"I doubt whether he will believe you."

Later that afternoon, I drove down to the wharf, but this time, I had a package with me. I find a parking spot on the street and walk down the alley to Scoma's. It is already 4:15. Towson is waiting for me about halfway down the alley. "Let me have it." I hand the bag to Towson. He pulls out the horse and then looks back to me. This was the first time that I had seen him standing next to me, and he was about my height. "What kind of game are you playing?"

"Just look inside. It's a Trojan Horse."

He tosses it back to me and commands "Open it." So I fiddle with the various parts and soon the saddle flips up. He takes the horse and pulls a key out of its compartment. It was the one I purchased at the old hardware store. He stuffs it into his pocket without much of a glance, as I try to keep the relief from showing on my face. "Will you now keep your side of our bargain? I ask.

He turns from me and nods to his two men standing next to the opposite wall. They both start across the street when a taxi zooms down the alley forcing them to jump back. I take off up the alley and then west towards Ghirardelli Square. As soon as the taxi passes them, both men start running after me. I sprint, jinking between shoppers and sightseers. The two men are about 50 feet behind me, coming fast. I duck into the wine shop at the northeast corner of the Ghirardelli and head up the interior stairs, emerging at the plaza level. Without looking back, I sprint diagonally across to the office block on the southwest corner. Both of the men emerge from the wine shop and spot me before I can reach the building. Into the office block, I run up the stairs two at a time and then past art galleries and offices. Up another flight brings me to the exit on Powell, where I turned back east and run to the corner of Larkin. I can't see either of them as I crouch down behind a stone planter in front of the office windows.

In another few seconds, one of the men appears at the door where I came out and searches the street. Before the second man shows, the first one ducks back into the building and I could hear him climbing the outside stair and running along the balcony just above me. I push back against the cold brick façade of the offices. Above, the footsteps continue past me. Then there was a shout from inside the building and the man above stops and returns to a point directly above my hiding place, but where I am hidden by the concrete balcony. When he retreats west towards the stair, I start running again the opposite direction, turning the corner and tearing downhill towards the water. I get to the garage entrance about half way down the block and turn into it, careening down the driveway ramp. The garage is packed with parked cars. I find a big SUV parked in a stall next to the wall and duck down between the front wheel and the concrete block wall. My breathing is ragged from the exertion, but I wait and soon it slows when one of the men appears at the garage entrance. "I'll look in here. You go around to the entrance on the west side."

The man walks slowly down the ramp towards me. I can see he is holding a gun. When he gets to the end of the car row where I am, he kneels down to look under the cars. But next to the big tire, I doubt if he can pick me out. He moves to the next row. Each time a car zooms up the ramp, he conceals the gun by his side, but as soon as it passes, it comes up again.

When he reaches the last car in the next row, he turns around and starts my way. The first I see is the profile of his gun as he passed in front of the SUV. I launch myself at the gun and chop at his radial nerve. He gives a brief shout and the gun falls to the pavement. I reach out to grab his arm, but he recovers and takes a step backwards. I fall forward across him and he brings an elbow hard down on the middle of my back. I tuck and roll, winding up facing away from him on my feet. Before I can spin, he is on me. He tries a grab for my head, but misses when I drop my chin as I fall forward onto my hands, kicking backwards. It catches him in the diaphragm and he involuntarily folds forward. I scissor both legs up to his neck and then roll, dragging him down as his head connects with the concrete. It is all over.

At the garage entrance, I look out up and down the street, but his partner had moved to the opposite door. So I cross the street walking slowly down the hill back towards the water, I put my hands in my pockets, and try to blend in with the other afternoon tourists.

My car is still sitting outside the alley where I left it. I take a chance by opening the door and jumping in. As I clear the area, no one apparently follows. I get back to the office in a somewhat foul mood. 'That's two puzzle boxes I am out already.'

As I open the door, Stephanie stops me and tells me that Lauren had decided to go out, saying she had some errands to take care of and would be back by 7. Steph puts on her jacket, bids me goodnight, and leaves.

I think it is too late to call John, so I decide to do a little more research on Towson-Xyso's company. Marcia had told me that there was a facility in Oakland near Jack London Square, so I thought I would start there. I drive over the Oakland Bay Bridge, drop off the freeway near the railroad yards and drive along the Embarcadero towards the Jack London Square. I do not have a clear idea of what I am going to do if I find him.

Jack London Square is a misnomer – more like an outdoor mall. This afternoon, it is alive with tourists. Reminiscent of Fisherman's Wharf, it's not quite as Honky-Tonk. Next to the mall is the Oakland Amtrak Station. West of the Square stands the Naval Supply Depot. The gate to the depot ends my search in that direction. But I stop at the guard shack and show my I.D. and I ask if he might know where Turkish Imports has their warehouse. But the Shore Patrol guard doesn't, nor his Chief. I turn back east and cross over the arching bridge to Alameda. The residential developments have pushed out the warehouses that once served the Navy and Army bases nearby. So back across the short bridge, I start to search north. There, street after street of warehouses line the Nimitz Freeway. I drive a spiral pattern, looking for anything out of the ordinary. Then I see my quarry: "Turkish American Imports" it said, in bright white letters on a red background. Next to the text are a white crescent moon and a star, like the Turkish Flag. The sky is growing dark and the chain link fence has razor ribbon coiled on top.

I drive along the fence, and see that it ends at the high wall of a windowless building fronting on the street. The building has a large double-truck overhead door into which is set a small man-door with a window. On the other side of the building, the fence continues. I follow the fence to the corner, around the corner and down a side street. At about 100' spacing, tall floodlights are mounted inside the fence, casting bright mercury vapor illumination on the fence and street. Through the fence, there are railroad sidings and several warehouse buildings with dock doors. The roofs have large industrial skylights. There are no other doors or windows that I can see or material piled in the yards. It is very neat and orderly.

In one corner of a nearby warehouse, a tall silo extends up about 75 feet, with a ladder on the side. But it is too far from the fence to get to it. So I would have to go through the main door or the fence. I cannot see any indication that the fence is electrified, but there are warning signs that the grounds are guarded by dogs.

I decide to wait and see if anything moves in or out. After an hour or so, the constant lack of stimulation lulls me into a kind of semi-stupor, which makes it difficult to pick up small changes in the scene. So I do not see the difference in the skylights as the lights go out in one of the warehouse buildings. I was staring at the fence, rather than through it so I almost totally miss an overhead door opening in the warehouse, and a large black sedan comes out. As soon as it clears the door, the door starts back down. The car meanwhile, crosses the yard and enters the back of the gatehouse. I had turned my car around and backed it up against a garbage dumpster on the street, but if the limo drives towards me, I would be discovered. In a moment more, the overhead door starts upward and the car noses out into the apron. As it passes the door, a light within the gatehouse illuminates a driver, a front seat passenger, and a figure in the rear seat. I cannot tell who it is, but the car could not be mistaken for anything else – it is a Mercedes 600. At $145,000, it represents the high end of their sedan line. Not your average soccer-mom's transportation.

The car reaches the street and luckily for me, turns away from me. As it gets to the next corner and turns toward the freeway, I follow. Fortunately my SAAB doesn't stand out at night, particularly with my headlights off. I had disconnected the 'always on' feature shortly after I got the car. The sedan crosses under the elevated freeway and turns left, to the on-ramp with me not far behind. It heads north. There is a reasonable amount of traffic on the Nimitz, and also when we get to I-80, so I am not too concerned with being spotted. But to be sure I occasionally turn off the lights and switch lanes before turning them on again. We cross over the Vallejo Bridge continuing north. Then I almost lose them when they take an abrupt turn at the exit towards the Vallejo business district. Now on Rte. 29, we descend and work our way towards the water again, ending on Harbor Way. Here I have to keep the lights off because there is no other traffic. Across the water from the marinas, Mare Island is brightly illuminated as ship repairs go on into the night. The limo turns into a covered dock. It has the same Turkish-American company sign on the top of the building.

Where the covered dock meets the land, there is a gate and fence. But the fence does not reach the dock building itself. Instead, it ended at riding poles, which allows the dock to rise and fall with the tide. Attached to the dock is a narrow catwalk used for maintenance. The catwalk wraps all the way around the water side. Along the top edge of the building, floodlights hang out over the catwalk, but tonight they are off. At the shore end, the catwalk ends just inside the fence line. The gangplank that spans from the dock to the shore is wide enough for a truck, and looks quite sturdy.

The doors on the dock are closed tight. I stroll over and discover that the gate to the gangplank is not locked, but a hinged 'U' on the pipe had been slipped over the pipe to hold it in place. I folded the hinge back and pull on the gate. The gate hinges do not make a sound. Once inside the fence, I re-latch the gate and cross the gangplank. Reaching the entrance to the dock building, I step over onto the catwalk. There are wood handholds above the catwalk, so that a person could move crab-wise along the face of the dock – which is exactly what I do. At the corner I work my way along the length of the dock until I reached the seaward side. There are two large doors for boat entry, but they also appear to be locked. At the seaward corner there is a ships ladder leading to the roof which I climb and lay flat on the slightly sloping roof. Casting about, I see several hatches between the skylights, which probably allow for ventilation of the dock area. Crawling to the nearest one I try lifting it. It was locked down. I move to the next one in line. This one appears to be unlocked. I lift it just slightly and peer inside. The interior is dark, so I open the hatch fully and slide through, catching a short ladder which is pegged to the interior ceiling. I swing my feet up and grab the ladder, using one free hand to pull the hatch closed again. Then I walk upside-down along the ladder like under my old school monkey bars, until I reached the side wall. Near the shore end of the roofed dock rests a large cabin cruiser. It must be almost 120 feet long, with several decks and a flying bridge. Near the stern, which faces the shore, a pad holds a tiny helicopter cabled to the deck. The rotors are folded over and also lashed. The interior lights of the cruiser are on, and occasionally a small pump would cycle, sending a wash of fluid out a side scupper. With a high freeboard, it looks like it could handle most of the oceans, even in the worst of weather. A boat like this probably needed at least 5 or 6 crew, and would easily hold a dozen passengers in comfort for a long cruise. The decks are of wood, probably teak, and the rest of the ship is painted white, except for a bright red plimsoll line. On the small stack which rose just aft of the wheelhouse is the same logo that is on the building.

I drop to the floor as quietly as I can, and start making my way around towards the stern. Large round portholes are spaced regularly along this side. The one closest to me has been swung up and out on its top hinges. Through the porthole, I hear soft music playing, and voices. I crawl along the dock to the porthole, which was across about 2 feet of open water. Crouching on the deck, I listen.

"No, I was going to go back to Washington, but without the key to unlock the information on the armor, the full decrypt would not be possible."

I did not recognize the voice. The responder, however; had a voice that I could not forget. "I got the key, so we can start the final phase."

"Let me see it," said the first voice.

"We need to settle accounts." It is undoubtedly Towson and seems insistent. "You promised me an equal share in the development. I want our contract finalized."

"Don't talk to me about contracts. If it weren't for me, you would still be crying in your beer about being wronged. I told you then and I'll tell you again. There's a huge fortune to be made once we find it. I know that all you care about is your legacy, but the Book's contents are priceless. We'll both be rich beyond our dreams. I've got everything set for turning the Book's formulas into money. You'll be able to make any kind of legacy you want to. But I expect your complete loyalty."

"But you agreed on a contract."

"You can't be worried about money."

"I want my name back."

" Are you an idiot? Remember, this is something you came to me with and I agreed to help you. If there are a few casualties along the way, so what!"

"I took care of getting the key from Chess."

"You know that the key has to go with to the armor."

"Yes, I know. But I have expenses."

"You need to stop whining and handle your end. There will be more than enough for both of us."

The unknown voice grew muffled, I suppose he had turned and walked farther away from the porthole. Then Towson said "Very well, I will show it to you. " There was a sound of shuffling paper and then the other voice said sharply "You stupid fool. What do you take me for? This is not the key."

"Of course it is. I got it from Chess."

"Did you actually look at it?"

"Well, no. Let me have it back for a minute." There was a break in the conversation for a few seconds, and then Towson continued "Damn him! Chess must have switched it."

"Where is he now? I hope you didn't do something stupid again like kill him."

"No, he evaded my men."

"That's one bit of decent news in the middle of your foul up. Take him and make sure you get the real key this time. Or do I have to take over again like I did with his wife the last time we tried for the Book?"

"I'll get it this time."

"Just get the key – then I don't care what you do to him. Maybe I should get someone else to do your job."

"But you still need me."

"What use is a partner that won't deliver?"

"Don't threaten me. I still have information that will be vital down the road."

"Just don't think you can run this on your own, either. If you cross me, I'll squash you."

Towson moves off as does the other man. I wait for a few minutes, but they do not return to the room. I look through the porthole. The cabin is empty, but there are two wineglasses on the table, and some papers. I thought that if maybe I could get to the papers, I might be able to identify their owner. I raise myself; step carefully across to the boat, grab the porthole cover then I swing my legs into the room.

"What the hell was that?" comes from the next room as I hit the carpet a little harder than I had hoped. I quickly rise and search around for a hide. There is a large armchair behind a desk, so I cross the room and crouch behind the chair, hidden by the desk. Footsteps came into the cabin and stop in the doorway. Then Towson's voice exclaims "I thought I heard something fall in here, but I don't see anything."

I wait until the footsteps retreat out the door and then reach over the desk to look at the papers. The top paper has the US Presidential Seal on them and the contents consist of an order directing the National Security Advisor to recover of a list of documents. Before I could turn the page, however; the voices get louder again. I thought my luck might have run out, so I ran to the porthole and dove out, clearing the narrow fissure of water and landing in a forward roll on the dock. Then I slide back to the water edge. Someone blocks the light from the porthole, as I lie flat. If they look straight down, I could be seen. Instead, the light shines again as whoever walks away from the porthole. Then I hear the sounds of a telephone call being made and an order given to search the dock. I crawl to the seaward doors, but they are secured on the inside with a padlock. I could not go back the way I came in, since the bottom rung of the ladder is too high for me to reach. So it is into the drink. I roll into the water. From my position, I can see the gangway doors open up and several people run into the dock. I submerge just as the interior lights go on. From underwater, I could see that the exterior floodlights have been turned on as well, as they shimmer at the surface beyond the doors. I swim under the boat doors and out into the bay. As I surface just outside the doors, and can hear people running around inside the dock.

Water has always been a friend to me. From the time growing up in Woods Hole on Cape Cod when I explored every inch of Eel Pond and Great Harbor, up through my SEAL days. Keeping a very low profile in the water, just my eyes above the surface, I swim close to the marina boardwalk. I thought that I would wait to climb out until the furor died down back in the dock.

It is cold in the water, but not much different from my numerous long swims in Coronado. My clothes actually act a little like a wet suit, as they are clinging to my body and make a tiny barrier of warmer water next to my skin. About 100 yards from Towson's dock, I cling to the bottom rung of a ladder and watch. With the relatively thin skin of the dock walls, I can see the lights moving around the sides. Just as I am about to pull myself out of the water, I feel something brush my leg and then my hold on the ladder is broken by something seizing my lower body and dragging me down.

As I am pulled deeper; my feet have swept upwards away from my assailant. I butt my head backwards, and crack it sharply against the glass of a swim mask. My assailant releases me briefly, but before I can react, he locks a grip around my chest, pinning my arms. We sink deeper until I can feel my feet sink into the muck at the bottom of the estuary. I don't have much more time as his grip tightens and I am being forced to expel the residual air in my lungs. Tucking my stomach I bring my knees up and over my attacker's head, locking my ankles behind his neck. Then I straighten my torso and legs, forcing him to somersault forward towards the bottom with me now above him. My calves have dragged the mask off his face, along with its attached air hose. The silt stirred up by our gyrations has made it very difficult to see, but I can see the mask floating up from his face. The intensity of my squeezing drives more air from me, as I grapple for the mask. I know he must be going for his knife, because that is what I would do. I don't have any options, so I go for the mask anyway, and catch it, jamming it to my face and forcing water out with a last expulsive clamping of my diaphragm. I raggedly inhale the dry, cold air from the attached tank. Some residual water inside the mask comes in with this first life-saving breath, but I suppress the urge to cough and take a second breath. The straps have torn off the back of the mask, so I take one more buddy breath and then let go to reach for my K-Bar. As it comes out of the sheath, his hands, which had been pulling on my knees, slide off to dangle in the water and he floats limply. I relax my knees and pull myself down to his body by grabbing his hair. Reaching his chest, I spring the harness release and pull his tank set off his back, along with the regulator, buoyancy compensator vest and mask. Air bubbles still flow from the mask as I jam it against my face again and clear the water from it once again. Then, holding the mask by one hand, I slip the tank over my head and re-snap the harness around my own body. It is very tight as I am slightly larger than him, but it won't be needed for very long. Then I check the mask straps. They aren't broken, just slipped through the buckle. I re-thread the ends and seat the mask properly on my head. Turning in a slow circle, I cast about to see if I have any more visitors, but except for the now sunk body below me, I am alone.

I swim another 100 yards hoist myself from the water and scramble up a ladder to the quay, leaving the SCUBA gear in the water. Then I made my way back to where my car is parked. By that time, I am thoroughly cold. Once I reach the car, I turn on the heater and then drive to the marina's entrance. I wait there in the darkened car, away from any streetlight, until the two men appear, coming from the dock. They are too far away for me to get a good look at Towson's partner. I follow the limo up to the freeway and then to the Oakland Airport, where someone jumps out and disappears into the terminal. With my clothes in such a sodden condition I can't follow him. So instead, I call Marcia, even though it is very late in Washington. "Marcia, can you do something for me?"

She answered sleepily, but comes wide awake when she hears my voice, "Of course. What's wrong?"

215

"Well, I went for a swim that I didn't plan, so I am wet and cold. But right now, I am at the Oakland Airport. A man who sounds like Towson's boss just went in for a flight. I believe that he is going to Washington. Could you check the passenger manifests for all flights over the next couple of hours, and send them to me?"

"Certainly; you get home and get to bed. I will take care of it right now. Should I be looking for anyone in particular?"

"I don't know who it is, but whoever, he is in up to his eyeballs. I am going home now. I should be there in under an hour. I will take a hot shower and go to bed, but call me if you find out anything. I want to also tell you that I finally found the reason the key is important. But I'll tell you about that tomorrow."

"Shall I come and scrub your back?"

"Thanks, but maybe not tonight."

When I get home, all was quiet, so I lock the garage and shed my wet clothes onto the kitchen floor. While the shower is heating up, I put a glass and a bottle of scotch beside my bed and pour myself a large draught. Then I am in to soak the heat into my body, and fall into bed.

As I sleep, my dreams kept moving over the landscape of joy and fear, pleasure and pain. I was drifting on the sea in a raft, searching for survivors and trying to pull them aboard, when the waves come up and covered my mouth and nose. I couldn't breathe. The sound of the waves pulling at me mixed with my calls for help. I thrashed to surface out of the deep, but I could not break free of its hold. I can no longer tell if I am dreaming or awake, as I am pushed deeper into a dark pool. The sounds around me grew muffled and my heart pounds in my chest as I struggle. Then I felt myself drift down. There is a siren pull of the dark, and then quiet.

# 19 *1949 EAST BERLIN*

It was four years that Colonel Gorchakov waited. Finally the Eastern Zone of Berlin was created by a treaty with all the allies and the Russians had their own zone. Now he could finish his assignment.

The four years had been hard on him. There was little food on the Western Front where he had been assigned, and with the German cleaning out every farmhouse and village in their desperate retreat, there was nothing left to forage. Even his rank afforded him very little in the way of luxuries. His family back in Moscow fared not much better, and when letters arrived, they were full of pleas for help, which he had none to give. But with the war finally finished he wanted to go home with something more than hunger pangs.

It was a bitter October day. The morning had been rainy with a bit of sleet mixed in, and the sky was gray. The wind still blew from the North, bringing with it a harbinger of winter. Unfortunately, the Zoo was in West Berlin, and he had to bring transport to the western zone to reach the art treasures secreted 4-1/2 years before. He assembled a special crew of GRU (Glavnoye Razvedyvatel'noye Upravleniye – Army Intelligence) that all spoke English, and assigned a Major to take responsibility for the mission, although he would join in the recovery.

As the afternoon wore on, it became colder and darker. "Perfect" thought Gorchakov as they mounted three trucks, which had been thoughtfully provided by the allies several years ago. The trucks had been repainted with American insignia and equipped with U.S. military number plates. They drove through the Brandenburg Gate like tourists returning from a visit to the east. When they were stopped, their forged papers passed inspection with no trouble. From there, they turned southwest and headed in the general direction of Zoo Berlin.

Across from the ornate main entrance to the Zoo, tram tracks were still being cleared of war debris. They crossed and drove up to the gate. Gorchakov came out of the truck, along with the Major and a guard. The balance of their team waited.

217

As it was late, the gate had been closed for the night, so Gorchakov pulled the bell cord. He rang it again and again until a light went on in the building and when a man came out to ask what they were doing there. Gorchakov said "We're here to bring a consignment of food and supplies from the commissary."

"But it is very late," the man exclaimed. "Can you return tomorrow?"

"If you don't want it, I will take it back," replied Gorchakov.

"OK, OK I will get the gate." The man unlocked the gate and swung both leaves back. Gorchakov signaled the trucks to drive in. Once inside, they closed the gate and his troops dismounted and entered the main building. The zoo attendant went in with them, led them to his office and then asked for the manifest.

"What is your name?" Gorchakov asked.

"I am Franz Hauptman. I am the Assistant Habitat Manager here at the zoo."

"Show me where the art is stored, Hauptman." ordered Gorchakov.

"I do not know what you are talking about, sir. I am only an animal keeper and grounds manager here. This is a zoo. There is no art here."

Gorchakov withdrew his pistol from his holster and pushed the barrel against Hauptmann's forehead. "You will tell me right now or I shall kill you and tear apart your zoo until I find it myself."

"Sir, I beg of you. I know nothing about art. I would give you anything if only I knew what you are talking about." At this, tears started rolling down the cheeks of Hauptmann's face.

Gorchakov turned to his men "Such is the great Aryan heritage – a weakling who only knows how to shovel shit for other animals. He's not worth killing. Search this building from attic to basement. Anything that looks like art crates must be reported to me at once. Be aware that the storage rooms may be concealed."

The men spread out through the building. When they came to a room with a closed door, they smashed it open. Windowed cabinets were splintered with the butts of rifles, and cases holding reference books were systematically ripped apart. In the veterinary laboratory, all the equipment was upended or smashed. True to their orders, every room was opened, razed and then left empty or wrecked.

In the basement, the storage rooms were opened, but were found empty. Everything had been removed.

As the soldiers were waiting in one of the storage rooms for the others to finish searching, Hauptman held onto a large iron ring anchored into the ceiling. The ring was of black iron and looked out of place in the middle of the ceiling. The soldier finally noticed what he was using for support and sent for Gorchakov.

"And what is this for?" he demanded, pointing with his chin at the rusty ring.

""It is used to swing crates that are too heavy to lift when we need to load these storerooms."

"Why is there only one? If crates needed swinging, there would be a whole line of these rings along the corridor as well. But there's just one. Why?"

"Sir, they pull the crates down the hall on a cart, but to get them into this room, they have to swing them, because the cart is too wide for the door."

Gorchakov examined the ring. It looked like it had not been used for a long time. But still he was puzzled. He looked over at Hauptman who was leaning against the wall, apparently indifferent to Gorchakov's curiosity.

He then studied the floor stones and noticed that some of them were sharp edged and dark, while others were lighter with worn edges. Following the edges of the worn stones, he discovered that it defined a rectangular shape. Kneeling down, he called one of his men to bring a knife. He started to probe until he found a loose stone. Then he dug along the edge of the loose stone and pried it up. Under the stone was a smaller iron ring matching location to the one above. Immediately he understood and called for a rope. He tied the rope to the ring in the floor, threaded it through the overhead ring and then had his troops pull on the end. There was a loud creak, and a trapdoor opened an inch, then two. But it would not rise further. He had the men drop the door back in place and probed further. A second loose stone revealed itself, under which was another iron ring. This was near the front edge of the trapdoor. He threaded the rope through the second ring and back through the overhead ring and down again through the first ring, making a crude pulley. Then when his men pulled the rope, the door opened fully, revealing a flight of steps leading down. He took a flashlight from one of his men and switched it on, descending into the pit. As he reached the base of the stair, he cast around to discover more than a hundred packing cases, art boxes and smaller packages, one of which he kicked open with his boot. Out spilled a number of gold coins. On the top of the crates lay a dusty clipboard, with a list. He scanned

219

through the list. While it was written in German, he recognized items that were on his old list. At the bottom, he read the descriptions of two final items, evidentially added later than the rest. He tore the paper off the clipboard and stuffed it into the breast pocket of his uniform.

Gorchakov re-climbed the stair. Hauptman glanced at him and then bowed his head. "I have failed you, my General." Gorchakov pulled out his Tokarev and shot him twice, once in the top of his head and the second into small bit of the white skin of the nape of his neck that showed above his shirt.

The body was dragged down to the bunker, blood smearing the stairs and floor. Then the soldiers proceeded to systematically strip the room of everything. With Gorchakov watching, they worked silently, carrying boxes and cases up the stairs and out to the trucks. When everything was loaded, the men released the rope, dropping the trapdoor back into place, removed the rope and replaced the loose stones. Gorchakov scuffed dirt into the joints to conceal the door again and left the shell that was once Hauptman down in the dark.

They drove slowly through the streets of West Berlin and finally stopped near the Brandenburg Gate which would lead them back to the Russian Zone. "We must wait until morning, and join an American convoy heading east."

So for the rest of the night, the men waited. Some slept, and some smoked. But the hours went very slowly, and the night was very cold. As the sun came up, Gorchakov turned to his Major and said "I will go and watch for a convoy by the gate where you can see me. If I see one, I will take a cigarette out and light it. This will be your signal to bring the trucks. Fall into line behind the convoy, and when you pass me, I will jump in."

Gorchakov got out of the truck and walked to the gate. As he stood there, he saw several people standing around, looking for a lift to the east. Traffic was growing and a variety of vehicles, all heading to the gate. Finally, he saw a group of three military trucks. Two of them had red crosses painted on the sides. "They must be bringing hospital supplies," he thought to himself. Standing in full view, he pulled out a cigarette and lit it.

After a minute or two, none of his trucks came around the corner, so he put the cigarette out and lit another one, this time flourishing the match. The hospital convoy grew closer. Up ahead, there seemed to be some holdup at the gate. He quickly ground the cigarette under his boot and ran to the corner behind which his own trucks were waiting. The trucks were gone.

The street was empty. On the ground, there were small piles of cigarette butts and a couple of oil spots, but no trucks.

Behind him, the slowdown at the gate cleared, and traffic started moving again. Gorchakov started to panic. He turned back toward the gate and ran up to the lead hospital truck. It was driven by an American soldier, but next to him was a nurse also in army uniform. "Please," said Gorchakov, "can you give me a lift? I have an assignment in the Russian Zone this morning, and my jeep broke down."

"I'm sorry," said the nurse. "We do not have any room. These supplies are very important to the Russian hospital so we need to go there immediately, no detours. Sorry."

"Please. If I don't get to my appointment, I will be in real big trouble." The truck drove on a few more feet. Then it stopped and the passenger door opened.

"Get in." the nurse called.

"Thank you so much. You have saved a life today" said Gorchakov. He continued to himself "But for how long, I couldn't say."

# 20 *SATURDAY - SAN FRANCISCO*

The smell of rust was first. The sweet acrid odor stings my nostrils and brings me to waking. I think I opened my eyes, but there is nothing but blackness, with dampness just behind the rusty stench. Next I feel the ear pressure, not like being underwater, but the blood in my head tells me that I am upside down, or nearly so. I can't seem to move and feel hardness pressing in on my arms and legs. Where the hell am I?

I can move my feet a little, so I feel around. My toes slide along the wet surface – I am barefoot. But I couldn't tell what it is. Maybe if I bent my knee. Ok but it doesn't get me anywhere. How about my hands? One seems pinned under my chest, and the other one is above my head. No, nothing.

OK, I am breathing, and it is dark, and I am wedged, but I not in any particular pain. What the hell is it? I feel around with my free foot and could sense nothing. Likewise with my free arm I reach downwards, but for a few rough spots, there's nothing to push or pull against.

How did I get here? I can't seem to remember but waking just a moment ago. Do I know who I am? Along with the name, pain came rushing in. It grabbed me starting at my head and radiating to my chest, throbbing at first but then squeezing my temples inward like I had a steel band that someone was tightening around my skull. Along with the pain came a rush of claustrophobic fear.

"Quiet", I shouted in my head. "You've been in tight spots before. Use your brain. Think it through and solve the problem", Quill used to rail at me. "What is the point of the exercise?" He would add as he punctuated each word with a rap of his wood Boku rod on the dojo mat. "Let go of what is not in your control. Breathe evenly, use your senses."

I took a breath, held it for a few seconds and then in a controlled exhalation, release it slowly. Air stirred against my toes, while the smooth cold dampness confined my shoulders and arm as they pressed against my body. My breath railed against the quiet and the blood coursing through my ears made a flat dead leaf rustle.

I arched my left foot and probed the wall of my confinement. There was nothing. As I pulled my right foot upwards, the grip on my shoulders seemed to ease and suddenly gave way and I surged downward for perhaps a couple of inches before the friction again grabbed me.

This time, when I felt again with my outstretched arm, I could feel a joint. It must be some kind of pipe – like a storm drain. I realize that I have a reference point in my space. My touchstone to figuring where I was, how I got here, and how I might escape, was a small joint in an otherwise smooth-walled cell. I reached out again and reassured myself that it was still there.

The air grew colder. The damp moisture had leeched the heat from my skin and I am seized with fits of shivering. There seems to be less pressure on my arms – or maybe it's just that I can't feel them so much. The dark is almost worse than the confinement.

I remember the drown-proofing that I went through at BUD/S. They tied my hands and feet and then dumped me in the pool. The first time I hit the bottom I flexed and pushed off, slowed by the water, but my face came up enough to take a breath before starting to sink back. The second time I sank slower, but I became disoriented as to which way was up. Since the lights were off in the room. I started to get furious about not being able to see. The more I struggled, the more it seemed hopeless. Then I realized that if I relaxed and did things slowly, I might have enough air left to float. So I shoved down the anger and let go the fear. Slowly, slowly, I came back up, but not so I could breathe – my face was in the water. I twisted back and forth until gravity turned me over, but the water was still over my face. Quickly, I bent, lifted my face and breathed out, which sank me faster before I could breathe in.

Nothing worked. I was drowning. I porpoised again and again, finally breaking the surface and taking one breath before I tilted and sank back. I couldn't last much longer. Spots were growing with bright outlines in my vision – ragged and scary. But fear was the killer, so it had to go. I will beat this.

The pipe has to be a drain pipe which probably gets larger as it descends. That's an idea. If I could get somehow past the joint, maybe the next section will be wider. But how? If only the inside was wet, I could slide.

I try twisting my body, using the joint to push against, but I can't seem to get enough leverage on something so shallow. If I could get my second arm free and stretch it out. I take a deep breath and force as deep an exhale that I can. I pull my arm up from my belly, where it had been caught under

224

my rib cage and slide it up to my chin. But that compressed my chest further and I couldn't inhale. I had to get my arm up over my head, no matter what got broken in the process. When I pulled my arm up, my body moved with it so I held fast onto a lump in the pipe and pushed against it while I pulled my arm up over my face and freed my elbow from under my chin.

Then, as my arms came up and over my head, I could breathe again. I took a deep breath. This time, when I exhaled, my weight overcomes the friction of the pipe and I start to slide. Past the joint, my arms over my head and my toes pointed. The roughness of the joint tears at my skin and I leave a few patches as I slide downward. But this actually helps, since now blood is flowing from cuts on my chest and arms, which lubricates the pipe wall. I slide down past another joint and all of a sudden the pipe is larger and I am sliding less and falling more. Now I have to slow down or I will surely land too hard on my head and break my neck in the process. Another joint moves by and I try to grab at the lip on the joint with my fingers, but it is no go and my speed increases. I let my arms come back to my chest and then join my hands, pushing my elbows out to the sides of the pipe. At another joint, the flanges catch my elbows and slow me a little, but at the expense of a major skin tear along my arms. I strike bottom with my head, barely feeling anything as my senses leave me.

Consciousness returns to find me still in the dark hole, but no longer confined, and no longer inverted. There is a throbbing in my head which I find comes from a large egg on my skull. If there was some light, I might be able to determine if I could see or not. But there is none. From my fetal position, I start to uncoil and begin to feel around. Every muscle and joint screams with pain and stiffness. Because of the terrible throbbing pain I feel in my head, the raw tears on my skin hardly bother me at all,

From what I can feel, the pipe is much larger, so I must have fallen into a horizontal part of the drain system. The diameter is not quite wide enough for me to stand up. But at least I can sit or lie down and try to stretch out my muscles. I do not feel any air moving and the pipe seems relatively dry. I do some experimental twisting and flexing, and have no particularly sharp pains adding to the ones in my head and neck. My fingers all work, and when I stretch my back to reach out to my toes, those parts of me are also unbroken. A stray thought appeals to my sense of the ridiculous. Here I am, doing PT inside an underground pipe. "Hooyah, I cry," but there are only echoes in response.

I apparently still have trousers and a shirt on, although both are in rags. I am starting to feel very thirsty but no hunger yet. I wonder how long I have been in here. It must be less than half a day. Even though I cannot stand fully erect, it seems that the pipe slopes downwards. Should I go up or down? If this is some kind of storm drain, it may continue to get larger as it descends, but either way, I should be able to find an access manhole.

I decide on downhill. If the pipe gets larger, I will be able to stand up and not be forced to crawl. I take a couple of steps, but dizziness knocks me over and I realize that I must have some kind of concussion. There seems to be enough air, so it's got to be coming from some place.

I crouch even though all my back and chest muscles scream, and start duck-walking along the pipe. About every 30 steps I come to a joint; with a raised flange on each side. I start counting the joints as I go along. I keep at least one hand in front of me as I go along. I really don't want to run into anything, particularly with my face. After 30 joints, there is a sudden change in the sound of my steps, like a hollow echo. I reach out to the sides of the pipe. On my left, is the pipe wall, but on my right there seems to be just space. I move towards the space and reach a wall corner; it is a branch in the pipe. Since the pipe I have been following continues past the branch, I can only think that the branch is incoming, and if I take the stem leg of this 'T", I will be going back uphill. I take a few steps up the branch and confirm that it ascends. So I turn back. There is a difference now in the pipe. The floor is wet, and becoming somewhat slippery. I have to go slower as I crouch along.


Then it comes to me. Usually, they put manholes at places where debris can get stuck, like at a branch connection. I turn and work my way back up, slipping along as I try to keep my footing. Back at the Tee, I feel up along the top of the pipe. Sure enough, there is a space where I can stand up fully. Standing, I again stretch my aching muscles, before searching upwards. The opening seems to be about 4 feet wide and is circular in shape, but smooth on the sides. There is no ladder or any projections that I can grab onto to hoist myself up. I squat and then jump as high as I can. My hand touches something sticking out from the wall. When I land, a sudden shooting pain in my neck and a flash of light tells me that this may not be a good idea. I lean against the side of the pipe for a moment or two until the dizziness passes. Then I try again, gathering myself and leaping as high as I can. This time, I smack my hand against an iron bar and grab it. Swinging under the bar, I pull up and take hold with my other hand. Then I do a pull-up and my forehead touches a second one, higher up. Alternatively pulling up and grabbing, I work myself up the iron ladder until my feet are on the bottom rung. After resting a minute or so, I start to climb.

After ten rungs further, I reach a circular cover. I tried pushing up, but nothing moves. I search around the edge for a latch, but there wasn't one. Most of these are held by their own weight, to make removal easier, I suppose. I felt the other side of the shaft with my toes. There seemed to be a small recess on the other side, opposite the ladder. I pushed a foot into the recess and reached around with my hand. I inverted my body and pushed against the recess with my feet, while doing the same with my hands on the top rung. Using my back, I pushed upward against the cover. I pushed as hard as I could and then there was a slight metal rubbing sound, and I could feel the cover move a little. But when I pushed, the pain in my head jumped tenfold and I cried out as it tore through me. But this was the way and the only way, so I couldn't give up.

I rested for a moment, and then shoved with my back against the cover. It rose about two inches and shifted to one side. I almost fell back down the shaft with the muscle release, but was able to catch myself on the ladder. This time when I reached up, I could feel an opening along one edge. But no light came through. Air did. I could feel it wash against my nose as I stuck my face up against the small slit.

Back to spanning across the shaft, I pushed again with every bit of strength I had, and this time the cover slid sideways, tilting up from my back and tearing my shirt and more skin in the process. But I didn't care.

Pushing up, I emerged from the hole and then, grasping the sides of the opening, I rolled out onto the ground. As I lay on my back, breathing hard, I looked up. Of course there was no light. It was nighttime and had rained. It was also much colder. The air chilled me through. But I was out. No matter the cold. I had to lay back and close my eyes.

I must have slept for some time, because when I woke, the sky was lightening. I was a mess. My clothes were in rags. I raised my head and looked around. I was on an embankment adjacent to a road, but there was nothing to give me a sense of where. I sat up and again had to fight down nausea and dizziness. Across the street is a tall fence with razor ribbon on top. On my side, there is an open plot of land with a lot of debris and garbage in piles, scattered around. Beyond that, there are a couple of warehouses. With the daylight, the air was getting warmer. I still I had no clue.

I tried to stand up but wobbled badly on cramped and sore legs, back and arms. Finally I was able to stand relatively straight. I pick a random direction and start to walk along the road. When I come to a corner and look up, there are no street signs. Then dizziness hit me and I have to sit down again. I think that if I only could close my eyes for a little while, this would pass.

I must have slept again, for the next thing I was aware of is being shaken. I opened my eyes and tried to focus on the large figure in front of me. I recognized the cop's uniform. But before I could say anything, I was jerked upright, dragged to the side of a car and unceremoniously dumped in the back.

"Call in another wino for the tank" a voice said. I couldn't see because I was on my stomach with my head down on the floor and my legs up against the inside rear window. "This one's pretty far gone. Maybe we should take him to the hospital, came from a different voice.

"Hell no; let's just get him to the station, and let them worry about him." The car started. I must have fallen asleep again, because the next I knew, the car was stopped while the second voice picked up the earlier theme "Look Al, he really is in a bad way. If you won't take him, go have some coffee and I'll bring him to the hospital."

"All right, you're too soft. Next time, one of these bastards'll shiv you from DTs."

"Al, lighten up. This sucks."

We move out again. I rouse myself to ask a question, but it comes out a croak, and not much more. The voice that was Al's called out to me "Shut up, asshole. You're lucky my partner has a broad's heart."

After a while we stop and the door opens. This time, some other hands reach in from both sides and pull me out onto a cot. Then I am strapped down and the cot is raised with a jerk. Again I seem to lose it; this time for only a moment as I watch the sky disappear and be replaced by regular ceiling tiles and lights. Two people slide me off the cot onto a hard table and I am covered with a cloth. It smells of disinfectant and burned cotton. I am strapped down and a bunch of voices are around me. One sticks a needle in my arm and another starts attaching wires to my chest and legs.

I doze again, to be woken by someone staring down and asking for my name. I reply "Water" and I am given a straw in a flask to drink. Then I am asked again for my name. Finally, I am able to say it out loud: "Simon Chess."

"Mr. Chess, you are in the Highland General Hospital. Do you have a home address?"

"Yes, in San Francisco, on Vallejo."

"Do you have insurance?"

"Lady, I…oh never mind. Yes, I have insurance, but my wallet is gone."

"Is there somebody we can call? I need your insurance card."

"Would you call Stephanie? I'll give you the number."

"Is that your wife?"

"No, but a close friend. I am not married anymore."

"Mr. Chess, are you taking any drugs or medications?"

After the usual medical history questions, two orderlies wheel me down to a brightly lit room. Something they gave me started to work and I drift off again.

"Simon!" Then I felt a warm embrace and kisses.

"Stephanie. How did you get here?"

"The hospital called. What happened? You look like you were run over. They said you have a concussion. Where have you been for two days?"

"Steph. I don't remember exactly. I woke up in a storm drain. Can you please tell me what day this is?"

"Saturday. A storm drain? How..?"

"The last thing that I remember is going to bed. I think I forgot to set the alarm, I was so tired."

Stephanie pulls a chair over to the bed. "On Friday morning I came to work as usual. When you weren't there, I looked upstairs, but everything was neat and clean. I thought that perhaps you had taken another trip. But when you didn't call, I started to worry. There was a call from somebody called Marcia, but she didn't leave a number. Also, Dr. John Crawford called from the Smithsonian in Washington. He was surprised that you had not called him and asked that you please reach him soon. By Friday evening, I was a little frantic. I called that Lieutenant Jurgens and asked him if he knew where you might have gone, but he said that he was no longer interested in what you did, so long as you stayed out of his hair. I even tried Lauren Sylfern in Albuquerque. What happened?"

"Can you just get me a robe or something and a wheelchair? Find something that makes you look like a nurse. Wheel me out to your car and let's get out of here."

"But they told me you have a concussion and are seriously dehydrated. You should not get up."

"Please, just get me home."

Stephanie leaves and I turn off the monitor machines. I decide to leave the IV set in my arm for now. In a minute, Stephanie comes back with a short coat around her shoulders, wheeling a chair. The coat has an ID tag hanging from the pocket. She is also carrying a white robe, and dragging an IV trolley. With her help, we move the drip to the trolley and I wrap the robe around me. She takes my chart from the foot of my bed and places it in my lap, then wheels me out into the corridor and past the nurses' station to the elevator. No one pays any attention.

When we reach the garage, Steph helps me into her car, and I pull out the IV from the heparin block in my wrist. She has a light blanket which she pulls around my shoulders to hide the robe, and then drives us out through the security station. Fortunately, nobody stops us.

We drive over the Bay Bridge into San Francisco. As we pass the front of my house, we both look for any sign of a watcher, but there seems to be no one. We turn the corner and into the alley. There is a car pulled in front of the garage. The engine is on but there's no one inside. I tell Steph to back out and pull into the driveway next door. We sit for a minute. I can't imagine who might be still around. Towson probably had me dumped after he interrogated me. He undoubtedly used Rophenol since I remember nothing.

Someone comes from across the alley stands by the car, looking at my house. Before I can form a plan to deal with him, he gets into the car and drives off. I guess it was just a coincidence. Stephanie enters the code in the security pad. It opens and I get out, go through the garage and into the house. Steph parks in her usual spot and comes in after me.

"Steph, I almost lost a lot more than a couple of days, mostly due to my own carelessness. I must have been drugged and shoved into a storm drain to die, and it doesn't make any sense, unless it was Towson looking for his damn key again and finally realizing that I don't know where it is, decided to terminate me. I know I should probably go straight to bed, but I don't want to give up more time. By now he thinks I'm dead, we have a tiny advantage. So go make some coffee. I will go up and shower, get warmer, and then sit with me so I can talk through everything I know, and you can help me look at it with an independent eye. It is about time I plan an offensive."

# 21 *JULY 4, 1962 - MOSCOW*

In the United States., Independence Day was in full swing. Parades and picnics mark the celebration of the signing of the Declaration of Independence 186 years earlier. In Washington, the young president had just returned to the White House from laying a wreath at the tomb of the Unknown Soldier and honoring fallen comrades at Arlington Cemetery. In New York, and Boston, barges towed out and anchored in the Hudson and Charles Rivers respectively, were being readied for massive fireworks set for tonight.

Here in Moscow, there was no celebration. General Gorchakov was in a hurry. He had just left the Kremlin with a mission. It was called Operation Anadyr. Everything about the mission, including its name, was a deception. To all accounts, the 60,000 troops engaged in the operation were scheduled to leave for the northeast corner of the USSR in a couple of days, to engage in a training exercise in the Arctic. Protective clothing had been issued as well as insulated covers for their small arms and warm felt boots for their feet. Even though it was summer, thousands of hearts were not looking forward to a cold and wet summer in the arctic.

But Gorchakov knew. As soon as the troops were loaded, they would be diverted first northwest to the Baltic; there to rendezvous with and board merchant ships bringing Intermediate Range Ballistic Missiles, launchers, and support equipment to the Soviet allies in Cuba. The missiles themselves had started their journeys in a series of shipments beginning last month. Overall, the plan was to bring five full missile regiments to the island to bolster Castro's defense systems against a threat of invasion from the United States, and to point a ballistic finger at the Americans in response to the US's similar installations in Turkey. The story, however; given Cubans was all about Cuba. Chairman Khrushchev had told Castro back in April that they would give him assistance to protect his dominion from U.S. aggression. At this moment, a small armada of 86 ships was being put together for the trans-shipment of personnel and equipment, which was to continue through the early fall months.

Gorchakov had lived under a cloud since the end of World War II and was sidelined from any involvement in Korea or any other international military campaign. If it wasn't for his father-in-law, Sertin Kolyevitch Starkov, who was in the Politburo, Gorchakov would have been sidelined even more distantly, probably to one of the Siberian Gulags. He had failed in his mission to Germany in 1949, although somehow the art shipment eventually did turn up. Currently, it was sequestered in a secret storage room within the Lublyanka Prison complex under KGB (Komitet Gosudarstvennoy Bezopasnosti or Committee for State Security) headquarters, inside the Kremlin.

This was Lieutenant General Gorchakov's last chance to regain his former star-status, and to be placed on the promotion path again. This new job of his needed someone of his current rank, so his father-in-law had lobbied for him to be promoted secretly. But he knew that it was only provisional, and that he had been jumped at least one rank from his former Colonel level. As a man of 50, it was still possible for him to reach high status again, but only if he succeeded.

June in Moscow can be cool, but today, it was a balmy 72 degrees and the smells from the Moskva River were almost tolerable. He decided to walk over to Army Headquarters, only 8 blocks away. As he walked along the Teatral'nyy Proyezd, he thought about the intervening years, and what the loss of face in the military meant to his ambitions. He never did figure out who was behind the diversion of the art which he took from the zoo in Berlin, but bluffed his way to survival when the crates showed up again on their way to Moscow. No one in the crew ever divulged more information as to where the trucks had gone, or how they got back on track. They told any who asked, that Gorchakov had been detained at the border, and held while the rest of the team was allowed to go through. They added that a couple of the trucks had broken down and needed repairs before they could reach Moscow. The delay cost them a week in transit. Gorchakov chose not to look too closely at the gift horse, and went along with the story. But he was never allowed to see the boxes nor their contents again.

He would never forget the trip from Berlin to Moscow. When he got through the Brandenburg Gate, he left the hospital convoy and begged a jeep to take him to his old unit. But the unit was already on its way elsewhere, so he got assigned to a different army unit being rotated back to the motherland for re-education. They had been too long outside the boundaries of their country so could no longer be trusted to maintain loyalty to the party and to Stalin. They had been scheduled for weeks of lectures and rallies. The government had to continually reinforce the mission of those who risked their lives for meager rations and lack of support. Stalin had been brutal in his demands of sacrifice from all military units, and he demanded total loyalty at the point of his gun. Gorchakov was anticipating a very difficult time of it when he reported his failure. After his two weeks of re-indoctrination, he was allowed to transit on to his headquarters. As he strode into the building to meet with his boss for the first time in a month, he was envisioning the future; years of penal servitude (if he were lucky). But when he finally was seen by his General, the man slapped him on the back and welcomed him home, although he was also chastised for not accompanying the shipment as he had been ordered. Gorchakov said nothing, but secretly reveled in the fortunate turn of fate. Even though the result of his mission was good, his personal future was in doubt. Until this new assignment surfaced, his rank remained the same and his assignments were menial.

Now, his new responsibilities occupied all of his time and energies. With the complex bureaucracy, even though his orders came as a directive from the Secretary of the Communist Party and the Premier of the Nation, minor functionaries still impeded progress and demanded their due in terms of red tape, delays and bribes. But everyone knew these processes within the government, and no one was willing to take on reforms. So Gorchakov had been supplied with a large sum of ready cash to grease the functionaries to execute their orders.

Once inside the rabbit warren of Army Headquarters, he hurried to his office. Inside, waiting for him, was his aide. Like most generals, he did comparatively little work himself, but trusted the details to his aide. Major Sertin was extremely hard-working, but would never rise above his current station, as he had few political or family connections. The good Major had a huge sheaf of papers to be signed, covering training plans, requisitions, travel orders, logistical arrangements and embarkation schedules. Since the majority of the actual trans-ocean travel would be via non-military ships, Gorchakov also had to sign commission papers for many of the ships' masters so that they could be paid on top of their regular stipends. He knew there was a second reason that he was chosen for this assignment, beyond the prodding of his father-in-law. With his slightly tarnished record, it could be anticipated that he might fail. If he did, then he would be branded as a rogue, take the brunt of heat from any foreign reactions to this black operation, be cast out and executed. This way, if he succeeded, the political leaders would take full credit for the victory, but they would use him as their scapegoat if it failed. Gorchakov knew this was the way of governments.

In spite of all the secrecy and advanced planning, it was inevitable that word would get out. With more than 80,000 people involved in such a massive undertaking it was extremely likely that the American CIA would find out about the mission. So Gorchakov had also set up a parallel disinformation plan. Unfortunately, this plan detailing the arctic maneuvers was very short lived, and his only other alternative was to document all the shipments as farm machinery, going to their Cuban ally. He couldn't hide the troops, however; or the Castro's voice once he had received the missiles, even though they weren't totally under his control. One component which was missing completely from his plan was a setup that would blame someone. So he worried.

Gorchakov would accompany the missile shipments in October, to see them set up in their launchers, so that full credit for this accomplishment would be his. To his mind, this mission was the right thing to do. Long-range Mutual Assured Destruction philosophies were self defeating, in that no one with half a brain would ever use ICBMs. But Short range was something else. With only 90 miles to cross, it would be very difficult for the Americans to react quickly enough to forestall the attack. Even if Russia pushed the Cuban button, the U.S. would be forced to retaliate on Cuba, rather than on his Motherland. This venture had to come off without a hitch, or, as Gorchakov thought using a western colloquialism "I will be toast."

As Gorchakov worked diligently on his assignment, his dutiful major had different agenda. So when Gorchakov closeted himself in the inner office, the Major picked up the telephone.

"I need to meet you tonight."

"Your favorite café, say about 10 O'clock?"

Major Sertin hung up the telephone. By 8:30, Gorchakov finally came out of his office. "Yevgeney, I am going home. Tomorrow we must put the papers together for the next shipment. Have you contacted the GRU to get the false documents if the ships are stopped?"

"Yes General. They should be here in the morning. I have taken care of it."

"Goodnight then, Yevgeney Stoyisnachky."

"Goodnight, General."

By 9:15, the office was quiet. Here and there a light burned, but between vodka and bureaucracy, occupants would probably be asleep. Office cleaners did not come every night, so tonight there would be no further visitors. The major closed the front door to his office and locked it. He turned out the main light and took a small flashlight from his bottom drawer. Inside Gorchakov's office, there was a safe bolted to the floor. The

234

general thought that he had the only combination, but Yevgeney was very enterprising over the years in getting combinations to all the safes that he had contact with. In a moment, the safe was open. Inside, there were the true manifests of the shipments that were going on the merchant ships, as well as some of Gorchakov's personal papers. He took the most recent documents out of the safe and covered the one window to the street with a blackout drape. It was a simple matter to spread the manifests on the conference table and photograph them using the illumination of the desk lamp. Once these pictures were taken, he turned to the personal papers. Among them was an old, beat-up folder. He opened it and a few papers slipped out onto the table. They looked like a catalogue of some kind. He found a magnifying glass in the desk and looked at them under the glass. The list seemed to be of art and artifacts with origins in Greece, Turkey and France. At the top of the list was a German Military seal that looked like the Luftwaffe. It had an Oval wreath surmounted with a flying eagle with a swastika in its claws. He remembered that Gorchakov said that many years ago, he had slipped some valuable artifacts out from under the noses of the Allies in Berlin, when he discovered a secret cache assembled by Hermann Göring. The major did not believe him at the time, but looking at this list, decided that it must be true.

He spread the list on the table and photographed it as well. Then he carefully put everything back into the safe exactly as he had found it, and closed the door. Secreting his tiny camera in a small pocket sewn under his belt, he picked up his jacket and draped it across his shoulders, unlocked the front door and went out.

When he got to the checkpoint at the main building entrance, his briefcase was searched, and he was patted down, but the film canister was under his belt, so could not be felt. He drove his car to a residential block in the eastern portion of the city, where he parked next to a small neighborhood café. On the way, he checked for tails, making random turns along his route. He was quite sure that by the time he reached his destination that he was clean.

Inside, the air was heavy with acrid tobacco smoke. It hung like a blue pall over the 20 or so patrons at small scarred tables or perched at the bar. Arguments were in progress over football games. A TV suspended over the bar displayed a political speech, barely visible through the grime on the glass. No one looked up as he strolled in and sat at a vacant table, ordered tea and spread a newspaper from his pocket on the table. The waiter returned with a tall glass filled with black liquid which steamed on the tray. He half-heartedly swiped a corner of the table with a dirty bar towel and deposited the tea, dropped a small bowl with loose brown sugar, and collected a few rubles from Sertin, who sat alternating between sipping his tea and scanning the newspaper. Soon another man, taller and dressed like a street-cleaner came in and took an adjacent table. Sertin let his sleeve brush over the top of his tea glass and upset it. The dark liquid splashed on the table and dripped to the floor. Sertin took his napkin and mopped at the tea, while the waiter ran over with his bar cloth and Sertin pushed his chair back to avoid the spreading pool of sweet tea on the table, bumping his neighbor. Excusing himself, Sertin picked up the dry parts of his newspaper and disgustedly strode out of the café. When he got back to his car, he checked his jacket and found that the drop had been accomplished: the camera cassette having been lifted by the street-cleaner.

About 10 minutes after the drop, the worker stood, drained the last of his vodka, and wobbled out of the café on unsteady legs. He walked slowly away, periodically stopping to lean against a building wall for support, while he searched for a tag. Eventually, he reached his beat-up grey-blue Lada. He drove around randomly for a half-hour and finally ended up around the corner from the American Consulate. In the confines of the front seat, he pulled off his work jacket, combed his hair, put on a tie, and squirmed into a sport coat that had been lying on the back seat. Then he cleaned his face with a small moistened towel from the glove box, and got out, striding purposefully the rest of the way to the government sanctuary. As was usual, he was photographed by the KGB team stationed across the street from the main gate.

Inside the consulate, he mounted the steps to the third floor, and walked down a hallway, which got narrower as he proceeded. Finally, he came to a door at the end of the hall where a sign announced "Electrical Switchgear, Danger: Authorized Entry Only." After knocking, he was admitted to a room filled with communications equipment.

"I picked up this camera from my contact at Army Headquarters. It must be important, since he called me out of our normal schedule. Will you process the film?"

The sailor to whom he was speaking took the camera and disappeared into an adjacent darkroom. When he returned, a tiny 16mm film strip was mounted in a holder and brought into the meeting room. The projector was turned. Although there was no caption, the forms on the screen appeared to be cargo manifests of weapons that were being consigned to several merchant ships of Russian and other registries. The lists included IRBM missiles and support equipment but the destination missing.

"We had better get these to Langley," said the agent who retrieved the drop.

"Scan the images and send it. Let's use the highest priority code. Obviously we need to find out where these missiles are going, and track the ships. Once it is sent, put the film in the next diplomatic bag."

They continued looking at the film until they came to the last three sheets which were different. They saw the German Luftwaffe crest on the documents and recognized that these were a list of art and archeological treasures. "Let's send these as well in the diplomatic bag, but separate them from the manifests. These last appear to be old, so must have been included for historical purposes."

Everyone went about their work, and in due course, the material joined a large flow of incoming high-priority information reaching the Central Intelligence Agency headquarters in Langley, Virginia. Because of the high priority code, a copy also found its way into NSA files. There, it was catalogued and stored, but no action was taken.

In Langley, the shipping manifests reached the desk of a median level analyst, who reviewed them and decided that without a destination on the manifests, these were just one more shipment of weapons that the Russian military moved around regularly, so took no special notice and made no particular mention of it in his daily report. When the diplomatic bag arrived from State, the film was logged and stored for future analysis. No one would take notice of these items until October, when everyone would scramble to cover this gross error in judgment.

# 22 *SATURDAY NIGHT– SAN FRANCISCO*

When I come downstairs, I am feeling a little better; at least I am clean and warm. I don't seem to be able to remember much about the time period when I fell into bed on Thursday until I awoke in the storm drain sometime Saturday morning. If I had to guess, it was probably some drug like rohypnol or some other depressant administered to keep me quiet before interrogation, which would account for the memory blank. Towson probably got what needed and decided he had no further use for me.

Stephanie had made me a small dinner. While I eat and work to fill in the blanks, she sits quietly with me. After some time, she put her hand on mine. "Don't worry. It will come back. Just work on what we are going to do now."

"As far as I can see, I have two priorities, first to find the key, and second to find the man behind Towson. I wonder if he works for the government. Whoever he is, he had an educated voice and an aggressive authoritarian manner that Towson defers to. I also need to find about this 'Book' that Towson and the other man mentioned on the boat. They seem to believe it is their overall objective. But what has this to do with Zilbern's death? Marcia is digging out lots of information, but how much has relevance?"

While she marshals a response, Stephanie goes back into the kitchen and heats up some coffee cake for the both of us. I really don't understand why she didn't remarry after her divorce four years ago. I know that she is popular and spirited. I suppose that she is not coquettish enough for jocks and not aggressive enough for the young business set. With brown hair, hazel eyes and a somewhat diminutive 5'-2" frame, her lack of glasses belies her intelligence, but she also conceals it behind an open smile. Zalinski was her maiden name, which she took back on her divorce from a 30s something attorney, who dumped her for his boss' daughter. Stephanie came from a Wisconsin farming family and was taught as a child the values of loyalty, clean living and a healthy diet. She really loves San Francisco and spends a lot of spare time working in animal rescue and a local food pantry, when she wasn't looking after me.

"Stephanie," I call out to the kitchen, "I have kept you out of this mess because it was getting dangerous. But I can't go it alone, and I don't trust Lauren. Maybe you can bring a fresh perspective to this puzzle."

"Sure, boss. I'd be glad to help, if you think I can."

I go through it all again. I skip over some of the stuff with Marcia, but other than that, I give it to her as coherently as I could. It takes a long time and several cups of tea to get it all out. But I will say one thing for her; she listens patiently. At the end, she asks me one question. "Could the key not really unlock anything, but instead be a metaphor for a code key?"

"Why didn't I think of something that simple? Of course; the key is undoubtedly part of a code system. Towson's boss indicated as much."

"Simon, another point you should think about. It seems to me that if this is something that is very old, and it turned up in your pocket, it would seem that whoever put it in your pocket had a specific reason to do so. It wasn't a mistake. There is some reason that you were intentionally meant to have it. If you can figure that out, maybe you will be halfway to the solution. How many times have you told me about Trojan Horses? Maybe your being given the key was a way to get you to look into its source, and find the connections, which would then solve a larger puzzle."

"Sure, I've been looking at it from the viewpoint of who stole it from me, not who gave it to me in the first place. Lauren and Towson are only one side of the question. But if it weren't for her, I wouldn't know it was Towson who was after the key. He would have been just a 'nameless grey man'. And one more thing, Lauren had nothing to do with the NSA agents who arrived at our office. If Froehlich is an enemy, then I have to put aside most of what he told me. He could have had me eliminated almost any time, particularly if he has the NSA's help. So we have several different forces at work: The key owner, Towson, Lauren, Froehlich, Towson's boss and whoever was behind the NSA attack."

"So that brings me back to the NSA. If this were their operation, Marcia would know about it. So it has to be a rogue NSA op. or another setup like Marcia's, where someone is after something and set up a blind to cover it. That means somebody who has insider leverage over the NSA is involved. Froehlich said he had too many enemies there and made a good case. What about Marcia? No, she has been a really good friend. So I think we can put Marcia on the 'friend' side of the list. I need find out the identity of this new Mr. 'X'. What about the people that worked with Zilbern? Maybe they found or were part of whatever Zilbern was working on and wanted it for themselves? I would say that Eleanor can be eliminated. She seemed to

240

be a genuine article 'aunt' to Lauren, however; she did know about Towson and the key. But Alattin Akan knew about the key as well. He seems to be genuinely interested in Lauren's welfare, so I question whether he would be a threat to her. None of the others know anything about the key."

"Steph, we have to start ruling out people. I will see what I can find on Eleanor Frankel and you dig at the other two of Zilbern's co-workers. If we can put them outside, I can start on the key giver. While I'm at it, I wonder if Marcia got anything from FAA records on X's Oakland departure Thursday evening."

"Simon, you should leave this for tonight, and try to get some sleep. Concussions just don't go away in a few hours by themselves. How about you go to bed and I will work on the research."

"Sure. Truthfully, I do feel groggy. Wait a minute. There's something else I just remembered. At the boat, when the Towson and X were talking, they said two other things that caught my attention. Mr. X said something about having taken care of Jean, you know, my wife. Also, Towson said he was tired of the deception and wanted his name back."

"How did your wife die? Simon, you never said much about it. Maybe it is important to share that with me." Stephanie looked at me with some concern.

"You are right, Stephanie. Maybe beyond our immediate problem, you can help me understand why I feel so damn guilty. You know that Jean worked for the NSA. Well, in 2001, right after 9/11, the NSA was given a job of creating intelligence that would stand up to UN and press scrutiny, showing that Saddam Hussein was behind the 9/11 attack and had Weapons of Mass Destruction that he 'pointed' at Israel, his Arab neighbors, and at the U.S. This scenario was supposed to prove to the world that if Iraq was left on their own, the U.S. and its allies would soon find themselves besieged with satchel nuclear bombs, biological pathogens in our water supply, and a military attack on Israel. The CIA was also asked to find some people who could be put out as verifiable 'intelligence assets' so that the administration could initiate a war on the grounds of eliminating a terrorist regime. One faction in the Saudi government was approached to contact their fellow countryman Bin Laden, to generate intelligence that he had an Al-Qaeda stronghold inside Iraq. This part of the propaganda was extremely difficult to prove, since it was widely known that Saddam had ruthlessly rooted out Al Qaeda from Iraq, since Al-Qaeda was primarily anarchistic so would threaten any government's stability, Muslim or not. Although oil access was partly the goal of this

241

new U.S. effort, a second major goal was to drive a wedge into the faith-based regimes in the Middle East, by establishing a model democracy in their midst."

"The NSA and the CIA put together a series of intelligence briefings and based them on a single unsubstantiated interview with a Middle East 'expert'. The Secretary of State was unconvinced, and neither were a number of people within NSA and the CIA, particularly those who were non-political. Jean was one of these. She tried to expose the false leads and manufactured intelligence prepared by her colleagues. The Administration first tried tarring her with an anti-patriot label, but it refused to stick. They also tried to shut her up by sidelining her from access to the intelligence stream. But that just made her more determined. At the direction of the Administration, she was finally ousted from her job and sent to Israel on a mission to supposedly set up closer coordination between the Mossad and the NSA. In reality, she was taken out of the game."

"When the ultimatums were issued to the Iraq government, she again tried to get the truth out by contacting local media. But then, while she was in her hotel in Jerusalem, a bomb was placed under her room and she was killed. Her body was never recovered because the bomb destroyed everything. I got a phone call late one night, telling me what happened. I still get nightmares about it. I had just spoken to Jean. She had been telling me that she was going to resign because she was sick of the whole sorry business so she wanted to come home. She was telling me of her decision when the telephone went dead, and I knew something had happened, but it wasn't until the next evening that I was told. I think it was the worst time of my life."

"Oh Simon, I am so sorry. Is that why you left the Navy?"

"Yes, well not right away. First, I tried to find out details about what happened. It seemed just too convenient for it to be a non-specific terrorist bombing, which is what the Navy told me. When I tried to visit Israel for myself, they wouldn't release me. I did not hear a whisper, so after a couple of weeks, I got angry and confronted my boss, who told me to fall into line or ship out, so I did the latter. I never regretted leaving, but now I am a little sorry that I went back. Hopefully, when this is over, I can leave for good. The problem is; it's never for good."

"After you left, did you try to do any digging on your own?"

"Initially, I had some help from others that knew us in Israel and Washington, but all leads petered out and the official version stuck."

"Did you ever consider that whoever was behind the action against Jean and then helped to push you out of the loop may be connected to our current problem?"

"You know, I really never connected those dots until now. I always thought that if I only had kept Jean with me and not let her go to Israel, she wouldn't have been killed. That made me responsible and guilty."

"Simon, consider this. The termination order was issued here in the U.S. Somebody whose interests were tied up with the war, the oil, and the money like your Mr. 'X'. Now here you are, stirring the pot again, and who shows up at your door? The NSA; with orders to detain you. Perhaps the source is the same. I think common sense says that they are related."

"So what you are proposing is that the central theme is politics, money and power."

"Doesn't that make more sense?"

"Stephanie, you certainly can get through to the heart of issues. I think that you are on the right track. I have been looking at this from the very narrow scope of a bad guy and his personal agenda. But this could be much larger."

"One more thing Simon. You said that Towson was tired of the deception and wanted his own name back. How did he sound when he made that statement?"

"He sounded frustrated."

"I wonder what he meant."

"Well, Towson was an assumed name. His given name was Xyso. Maybe he wishes he could go back to his Turkish roots."

"Well, I can understand wanting to take back a real name. I sure didn't want to keep my husband's name after the divorce. As soon as I could, I dropped it."

"Steph, I don't think it was that kind of frustration. This seemed really important to him."

" If it is more complex than you originally thought, we really need to be armed with as much information as possible. I'll go and do a little research. You get some rest."

"Thanks, Stephanie. I have a feeling that you have helped uncover some of my fears, and illuminated some hidden agendas. But you are right about another thing. I have to sleep."

The telling of Jean's story made me exhausted on top of the aftereffects of the last couple of days. Stephanie said that she would take care of the dishes and probably stay in the guestroom since it was so late. I thank her and just collapse on my bed.

During the night sometime, I think Stephanie came in and got me out of my clothes and into the bed properly. I wasn't sure, but was just so tired that I didn't resist one bit.

# 23 *SUNDAY SAN FRANCISCO & WASHINGTON*

From my bed, the doorbell rouses me. I hurt everywhere; even my teeth. The bandages on my arms and legs give me some protection from blankets and sheets, but the deep pains in my leg muscles and back push through my unconsciousness. I hear voices from a distance and then a staccato tapping like someone is running. Then I am engulfed by fragrant hair and arms and kisses, while my face is wet by tears.

"Simon; Shit! What did they do to you? I'll kill them. Oh Simon. I am so glad you are OK. Stephanie told me. Crap!"

"Marcia?" I croak. My throat was still very dry.

"Stephanie called me and she was so worried. I do not want to lose you. I had to come. Oh Simon" she hugs me again. It hurts, but it feels so good, too.

"Marcia, can I have some water?" I manage to get out.

Marcia goes into the bathroom and returns with a glass, which she holds for me while I drink it all. "Thank you. I was so dry"

"Are you sure that you are all right?"

"It looks worse than it is. I'm OK now. You know, you really didn't have to come." Marcia's face closes up and I could see that she was hurt by what I said, so I added "but I am really glad you did. I cheated the reaper again."

"I called her back late last night, after she heard from the hospital and decided to come see for myself. Simon, maybe it's not too late to stop your digging. I don't think that Stephanie would ever tell you to quit, but after the incident here last week with the NSA agents, and then the murders of Edith Towson and Hudson, it is getting very close to home."

"On Tuesday, I thought there was only Towson but remember on Thursday night I asked you about the flights from Oakland?"

"Yes. I didn't get the chance to tell you that I searched passenger lists, but there was no one that I recognized. Why are you so interested?"

245

"That's what we need to talk about. Last night, I laid out the whole package to Stephanie. Well anyway, after going over it again from the beginning with her, we both believe that we are involved in something a lot bigger than a couple of killings. It even relates to Jean."

"Before you tell me, I wanted to tell you something as well. On Friday I saw a new order from the Director to leave you alone."

"Oh, I wonder if Froehlich spoke to him, or if this is another red herring. On Thursday night, I followed Towson to his boat. He met with someone who seemed to be the senior partner in this key business. He also made a reference to Jean's killing. If the man, who I am now calling Mr. X, was told that I was dead, it could prompt such an order, provided he was in a position to influence or give it himself. Marcia, let me ask you something. Do you think that the Director of NSA could be in league with Towson?"

Marcia stops talking and goes over to the window to stare out while she thinks. Meantime, Stephanie called from downstairs that breakfast was ready and for us to come down. Marcia goes into my closet and returns with a bathrobe and my slippers. With Marcia walking close to me, I work my way down the stairs to the kitchen, but not without a few moans and groans.

I don't know where she found them, but the counter in the bay window is set with a bowl of fresh flowers, and three placemats, so we can all look out into the garden. I sit on the stool, which fortunately has a soft cushion. Steph has brought in a pillow from the couch to use on the stool's wood back, for which I am very appreciative. Marcia sits across from me and takes my feet into her lap.

Stephanie puts down plates of scrambled eggs and sausage with buttered toast. Coffee and OJ are poured already. I dare not tell her that food doesn't particularly interest me this morning; I think that it makes her feel good to do something nice for me. So I paste a smile on my face, thank her for the breakfast, and dig into the eggs – but with small bites.

"Steph, I just told Marcia about our conversation of last night. She said that the NSA order against me was lifted on Friday. Marcia is still thinking about my question about Towson's connection to the NSA."

"I don't think it reaches to Director. General Sheppard doesn't seem the type. He's an Army 3 star, with a huge technology background, and did a lot of good, reforming NSA's technological competence. He's a political appointee, and he owes his job to the current administration, but I doubt whether he would be in favor of personal vendetta, but even if he did, I think he might use technology first. You know; drain your bank account, cancel your credit, phony your record, pull your clearance, isolate your access – those kinds of things. Frankly, I think that he's far too intelligent a man to get into bed with the likes of Towson. I wouldn't say that of the former Director, who was a real nasty bit of work. But he's gone for a couple of years now, so I think that the new Director is not a good suspect."

I ask her "What about the connection between our investigation and Jean's death?"

"I don't see any, other than sending her to a place where she might be exposed to something like what happened."

"So what about your former Director?"

"Well, Jean was a thorn in his side, so getting her out of town where she could no longer stir up trouble was probably his decision. He was smart enough to do that on his own, without outside help."

Stephanie then spoke up. "Well whoever X is, from what you said, Simon, he is apparently in charge. If he took some responsibility for Jean's death, then he had to be part of both administrations, and is still in a powerful position. He also sees you, Simon as a threat."

Marcia looks hard at Stephanie and realizes, like I did, that there was more to Stephanie than just another farmer's daughter. "Stephanie, would you like to come to work with me at NSA? I think we could use another bright person out there."

"Not a chance; but thanks for the offer. Simon, do you think that John Crawford has something which can bring some additional light into this?"

Marcia added "Yes. He was convinced that you found a link that could 'unlock', as he put it, the armor artifacts that he was working on. You should call him."

"Why don't we both call him right now? The telephone in the office has a speaker on it, and we can all conference together."

"You guys go make your call. I will clean up breakfast. Marcia, if you are going to stay to help out with Simon, then I will go home and change my clothes. Simon, please call me if you need me to come back today. If not, I will see you tomorrow."

"Steph," I go over and give her a hug "I can't tell you.."

"Just go make your call. You're a good guy, Simon, and I'll do whatever I can to help – Go now, Shoo!" she scoots us out of the kitchen and we go back to my 'public' office downstairs.

"Good morning John, this is Simon and Marcia."

"Oh my - Marcia, are you out in California? I am so glad you called. I have to tell you. Oh dear, I left my notes at the lab. I hoped you would call during the week. That sketch you sent Simon fits right into what I was telling you about the two artifacts that I have at my lab. Did you find the original?"

"No, not yet; but what do you mean it fits?"

"Where should I start? Remember when I mentioned to you last week at your house? No? Well; these two artifacts donated to the museum are both in such excellent shape and so old that they are simply remarkable."

"Were you able to date them and figure out where they came from?"

"That is part of the mystery. Normally, when we get something like this, we take a tiny scraping from the inside someplace where it will never show, and do an assay, but in this case, so far it has been impossible. You see, the material is so tough that we can't get any scrapings, even with a diamond drill. I have never seen anything blunt a diamond drill before. We are positively baffled by the material. It looks like gold and acts a little like it, in that it is flexible and electro-conductive with virtually no resistance, as a matter of fact. The script and etchings on it are as sharp as if they had been cut today. I can't imagine how they were cut, there's no tool marks at all – it is almost like they were struck by machine. Well, anyway, we have been trying to decipher the script with no success. It seems as though there had to be three sections of the script. There is a reference in Greek and Aramaic on the Breastplate about the three factors and about a book. There is no question that the text on the armor is in a code. Our people have postulated that it is a three-factor code which is exceedingly complex. There is no way that we can even begin without the actual key, although a photo or really detailed drawing might also suffice."

"John, let me ask you something. Do you have the two pieces securely locked up when you are not working on them?"

"Well, yes, we have a good security system. It is, after all, the Smithsonian, and we are keeper of many very valuable archival sources. Why do you ask?"

"The key has caused at least two, possibly three or more deaths. Someone is out to acquire it along with your armor."

"Oh that is a problem. Well, we do have a special clean-room lab inside MCI where secure studies can be conducted. It is a vault completely fitted out with a laboratory. I will just have to transfer the armor there. It really is an inconvenience, Simon, but if you think it is necessary..."

"John, it is of utmost importance that you take extraordinary measures to protect these items. Let me ask you another question. What is this reference to a book?"

"Well, there is a reference it. But it is not clear whether the word is 'book' or 'tablets'. It seems that either would work in translation. Oh I wish I had my notes. Let me try to remember exactly. The inscription in Greek and Aramaic both say '*The key draws out truth. The book is the graven Tell beneath which the ages lie for rebirth in prosperity. Discover the book where it has always been.*' That is as much as I was able to get from the helmet, but the translation is not very precise. There are some questions whether the word 'draw' means to draw like with a stylus or if it means to 'draw' something, like pull it out. But whichever it is, or even if there is a third meaning, the key inscription is absolutely essential. But let me ask you both, how are you involved in these artifacts?"

"John, it is too long and complicated to explain now, but somehow, I got pulled into this, and it involves both our government as well as private interests. This is far more than a scholarly endeavor. John, whatever you do, please keep these items secure. I believe that they are very important. Also, if you find out any more, and especially if you find out more about the book, please let me know right away. Thank you, John. Oh, and one more thing. Do you have any idea who might have donated them to the museum?"

"Well actually no. They arrived via FedEx, but we tossed the box."

"Can you tell me when you got them?"

"Well, yes. They were delivered just over a month ago. Just a second, let me think. Yes. They arrived sometime on March 15th. I remember their arriving as I was contemplating the onset of the 'Ides of March'. You know that I have always believed that Caesar was a victim of his own thirst for power, and Shakespeare just added drama with the 'Ides' warning. But if he was really killed on..."

"John, please let's get back to the package?" Marcia interrupted gently.

"Oh yes; March 15th; well that is when we have them logged into our system. Usually, it only takes a couple of hours for anything that arrives to be recorded, so I would assume they came that that morning, sometime. Will that help you?"

"Well, it will tell us when they were sent, but without the tracking data, we don't know much more. Tell me, once they got into the museum, how did you personally get them?"

"They were sent directly to me. It is strange. I am not that well known, since I spend most of my time down in the basement, but these were addressed to my attention, so actually, I unpacked the box myself. I must say, they really were a surprise. There wasn't a note or anything, nor was there any information about where they had been found or by whom. That type of provenance is always helpful in my research."

"Has anyone followed up with you, asking about your progress?"

"No, at least not directly, but I did get a memo asking me to let the Director know if there were any new discoveries. It had something to do with upcoming budgeting. He was looking for some good PR to help sway more potential donors; nothing specific. I get a memo like this a couple of times every year, so it's not unusual."

"Thank you very much, John."

"Let me know if you learn anything more about the key. Also, Marcia; are you planning to be away for long? I am only asking if you need me to water your plants and check on the house."

"I'll probably be out here for at least a couple of days. Thank you for offering."

"Are you working together on this investigation?"

"Yes, particularly on trying to find out about our adversaries. You might want to keep pretty mum about our call. Simon got attacked a couple of days ago and just got away from them yesterday, so he's a little banged up but OK"

"Oh my goodness. I will certainly keep quiet. Simon. Was it bad?"

"It could have been a lot worse, but fortunately whoever did the attacking didn't use all their marbles or I wouldn't be here now."

"I am certainly glad to hear that. I also suspect that Marcia is even more pleased. Is there anything else that I can do?"

"No thinks, at least for now. But like Marcia said, not a word to anyone, at least not yet."

"I'll be as quiet as a museum mouse, and they are far more discrete than the churchgoing type."

"Thanks, John. I'll call you in a day or so."

I go up to dress, while Marcia comes up and disappears into my little office.

When I am dressed, I join Marcia. Actually, I am really pleased to see her. I felt a little embarrassed at my abrupt departure from her during my last visit, but I will get over it. Right now, it's nice to see her – hunched over the laptop with her red hair flying about wildly.

On a spur-of-the-moment urge, I reach around her shoulders and hug her, while I plant a kiss on the top of her head. She leans back and upside down, returns the kiss on my mouth. In spite of the various aches and pains, I feel instantly excited by her lips and darting tongue exploring and sending chills down my back. Before I even realize it, I slide my hands down from her shoulders to her breasts and begin kneading them, feeling the nipples grow hard under her tee shirt. Her hands grab the back of my head, pulling me down to her mouth harder. I reach through the open neck of her shirt and capture one breast fully in my hand, as she moans against my open mouth and pushes back in her chair so that I can reach down with the other hand and begin stroking her between her thighs. She moans against my neck and then seizes my hand and pushes up out of the chair. Leading me to the bed, she pulls me down to her. For the next half hour, we are totally absorbed in one another's bodies. Finally, with an explosive release, we lie quietly together.

"Simon?"

"Huh?"

"Breakfast was good, but this is so much better."

"It certainly is great therapy for aches and pains."

"I'll give you a new pain if you don't shut up. Come on, let's get back to work."

Both of us pull on our clothes and go back into the office. This time, before Marcia sits down at the desk, she takes hold of my head and gives me a little kiss, then drops back into the chair. "Would you get us a couple of cups of coffee while I continue here?"

I go back to the kitchen and brew a fresh pot. I think we will both need it to keep our hands busy. We'll never know when another attack of randiness may arise. While I am in the kitchen, I find a note that Stephanie

251

left for me, saying that she found while doing some research on Towson's company, tax filings by a "Mortimer Stark Larson, L.L.P" with a K Street address in Washington, D.C. The note contained their contact information.

I suppose it was the joy of not being dead that drove me to seize the moment with Marcia. But now I feel just a little bit embarrassed. It's not like I haven't had any one night stands in the past three years, but not with anyone that I really cared about. The amazing thing is that I don't feel guilty about it. With other women, I always felt like I was betraying Jean. Today, it was different.

I take the note along with a carafe of new coffee, some milk and sweetener for Marcia and a small plate of biscotti, into the office.

"Frankel can be ruled out," she says. "I was curious what a psychologist would be doing working at Los Alamos, but she is cross-trained in neural networks, so I will bet she has a role with the integrated science approach used at the labs these days. Also, she is far too close to Lauren and was to Ernst, so I don't think she has anything to do with this."

While Marcia is working on her NSA laptop, I have been checking out Yancy. "I think Yancy is also out. He is strictly a scientist with perhaps only delusions of grandeur pertaining to his DNA models. While I look at Akan, you concentrate on the NSA order."

I found that he had arrived from Turkey as part of a scientist exchange between universities. He was both a cryptologist as well as a computer systems analyst. So he would certainly have an interest in following up any references to a new code, or to new sciences. I wonder if he knew about the 'Book'.

She tells me that there were hundreds of telephone intercepts back to telephone numbers in Turkey. All of these included the original audio track, as well as a written text and translation. She scans a few, but the ones she looked at were conversations with friends and family in Ankara and several other towns, as well as some with colleagues at Universities in Istanbul. But nothing that seemed to have anything to do with the artifacts or Zilbern. By narrowing the list with keywords "KEY," Marcia retrieves 5 calls, all related to his work in advancing the NSA prime key systems. She switches to "treasure" and gets one hit. It was a short conversation with someone in Istanbul, remarking on the treasures of the Hagia Sophia that were going to be exhibited in the U.S: nothing suspicious surfaces. She then looks at another list – this one of emails between Akan and family as well as other scientists around the world, regarding his work. Here the list was quite diverse, but again nothing that particularly stands out. We crosscheck emails between him and Towson but none fit. But there were a few between him and Froehlich. The contents were technical, however, relating to Akan's research. Just on a chance, I ask Marcia to look for any activities between Wednesday and Saturday, but again, nothing out of the ordinary, and nothing suspicions. "Well, I think we can eliminate him as well" Marcia says. That's 3 down and two to go.

Based upon the conversation that I heard on Towson's boat, I thought that we should use Jean and other analogies for her as keywords in our first search. A few hits come up both audio and email. One of the audio intercepts was between Towson and an unknown. Towson asked the unknown if the "trail was finally cold on his wife." The response from the unknown was "there was nothing to open that issue again." Could that reinforce the fact that either or both of them had something to do with Jean's death? I can understand that Jean might have something to do with the unknown, especially if he was involved as our Mr. X in the NSA, but with Towson? Why would Towson ask about her unless somehow she was involved with him as well? Was I somehow in this long before I knew that I was involved? Was Jean somehow involved without my knowing? What if she had to die because she knew something or acted on something that was a threat to them?

Maybe this is something we don't have to undertake solely on our own. I could ask the Admiral to reopen the investigation into Jean's death, and if he does, then maybe it will help draw X out into the open. Marcia thinks that so long as Mr. X thinks that I am dead, I would be relatively free from immediate danger. But if I open this door, who knows what may come in.

This seems reasonable, but we have to draw out the adversary, to get any further. So I compose an email to the Admiral, outlining what I had discovered, and asked him for help in possibly re-opening Jean's assassination investigation. I suggest that perhaps our counterparts in the Mossad can help with the inquiry.

Marcia has been looking into the Oakland Airport logs, to see if any private aircraft left on Tuesday night. Oakland logged 4 corporate flights out that evening and one charter. Two were owned by Silicon Valley software companies, one owned by the Bank of America, and one by a local Oakland real estate developer. The charter was a G4 bound for Alaska carrying four fishermen on a week's salmon expedition. Just on the chance, I ask Marcia to crosscheck military records and the tower log. She told me that the military records would take some time, but the tower logs she could get at right away, through the FAA.

While she works on those links, I get at another gnawing question. Why wasn't I killed outright? A bullet would have been certain. But it could be the difference between doing something yourself and having others do it for you. They would not necessarily have the same motivation. In the storm drain, my body would eventually be found, because it would clog the pipe. But what if the goal was to put me somewhere where I would not be found for a few days? This speculation isn't going to get me anywhere.

Marcia was still tapping away, concentrating on the screen, so I get up and go out to the Reception room, where I ring up Lauren. "Simon, I thought you had dropped into a hole in the earth."

"That's quite a metaphor." I decide to share with her the events over the past couple of days.

"Oh Simon, I am so sorry. Are you really OK?"

"Yes, except for a few bumps and bruises."

"Who did it?"

"I am pretty sure it was Towson."

"Towson!! But he didn't want you dead. Well, I mean he would not have wanted you dead."

"That's a strange statement coming from you." What do you mean, he didn't want me dead?"

"Well, all along, he had made lots of threats, but never really carried any of them to finality. Doesn't he need you alive to deliver the key to him? What good is killing you? He would lose the only person who could possibly lead him to the key."

"Lauren, how much more do you know about Towson?"

"Simon, really! I only know from what I can infer from his actions. I don't know any more; really I don't. Have you any idea of his motive?"

"Lauren, if I could get inside of his head, I might have a clear picture of what's going on. But let's leave that for a moment. I need to pick your brain again about your father's connection to the key. I suspect he was studying the other two artifacts in Cyprus, but couldn't resolve the puzzle. How much more do you know about that?"

"As I said, he kept his own counsel most of the time about what went on in Cyprus. But afterwards, he didn't ever see the armor again. All he had was the key." He told me that it was stolen from him the night before they departed for the U.S."

254

"You told me that it was in his safety deposit box. In order for me to have been given it, He must have taken it out at some point near his death. Did he give it to you?"

"No, I told you. The last I saw is when he decided to put it away. Did you check with the bank – maybe they have a record of the last access to his box. Father did have several friends in archeology. Maybe he showed it or gave it to one of them to study. I think that he was closest to Eleanor, but he didn't give it to her either."

"What about Alattin?"

"I doubt it. But he did know some people at the Smithsonian, He also knew people at several schools like Yale and Stanford that have archeology programs with field research teams in the Middle East."

"Did you ever hear the name John Crawford?"

"No, I'm sure. Did you say Crawford? Where does he work?"

"He is a researcher at the Smithsonian."

"No, I'm sorry. Simon, I have to go. Would you like me to come to you and we can work on this together. I'm sure that I can help find out."

"No, after this last attempt on my life, we should keep a little distance between us. I don't want to have to worry about you as well. Let me call you. And if you find out anything more, or you have another Towson contact, please call me."

I was not surprised to hear Lauren's reaction somehow. I never really believed that she was an innocent bystander. But if she is part of Towson's plan, then I had just made John into bait. This gives me a few twinges, but it certainly would be the test of Lauren. If John is left alone, then Lauren is probably OK. But if he is approached by Towson or any of his men, then Lauren is guilty, without a doubt.

I decide that the next episodes would most likely take place in Washington, so Marcia and I should return. I am sure now that Towson would want to bring the three artifacts together. This means a visit to the museum laboratory. Besides, if the investigation reopens Jean's death, I want to participate as well. Lastly, X is no doubt a Washingtonian, so that means we go.

I call Stephanie at home and tell her that we will be going to Washington today. She says that she will be over within the hour, as soon as she finishes watering her plants. Before we hang up, I suggest that she should probably plan to bring a bag and stay here for a few days. With me gone, she will have more security here than in her own apartment.

When I get upstairs, Marcia is sitting at her laptop, staring off into space. Then she spots me and says "I matched all the logs and records with a very interesting result. There was a single military aircraft that left Oakland for Andrews on Thursday night. There is no record of the passenger, and the authorization was the Department of Defense, so it could have been anyone in the Military or possibly evens a contractor. The aircraft landed at Andrews, and there is no matching motor pool request for a car, nor a gate log for a departure. I would guess that whoever flew had their car waiting at Andrews and drove it out without needing a special pass. That would only mean someone with a lot of seniority."

I shared my thoughts on returning to Washington. She agreed and got us tickets on the next direct flight this afternoon. By the time I got a bag packed and got myself back downstairs, Stephanie showed up.

I went back up to the attic came down with a pump shotgun and a box of shells, which I hand to her. She looks a bit aghast when I brought them down, but I explain that this type of weapon is the best defense for a novice. Someone who has no experience with pistols is just as liable to shoot themselves as they are to do damage to the surrounding landscape and would be very unlikely to hit an intruder. But a shotgun is different. The act of cocking it is usually enough to scare anyone off. And if she did have to use it, a general shot in someone's direction would do enough damage to stop an attack. She took and expertly opened the breech, checked the alignment and cleanliness of the barrel and loaded it with five cartridges, explaining that as a girl in Wisconsin, she was quite familiar with using a shotgun on the farm and for pest control. After setting the safety she found a spot near her desk where it was out of sight, yet very handy.

Upstairs, I pick up my case and a few bits and pieces from my safe... I thought that I might stay at Marcia's and use that as a home base while I stake out John's office.

Stephanie offers to drive us to the airport, so we don't have to leave my car there. Marcia calls John to invite him over to her house for a late glass of wine tonight. She expressed concern about my flying with the concussion but I set her somewhat at ease since our nonstop flights would give me a chance that to sleep– although it was tougher on my dwindling bank account. I guess that's why credit cards were invented.

On Sundays, SFO airport is flooded with tourists, laden with paintings of cable cars, Coit Tower and the Golden Gate Bridge in the fog, as well as sourdough bread by the carload. While Marcia gets us boarding passes at an automated kiosk, I stop at the Boudin Bakery in the airport and wait in line. Enticed by the fresh bread smells, I pick up two loaves for us. I pass up Ghirardelli Chocolates and order two decaf lattes at Starbucks, accompanied by one somewhat irresistible blueberry coffeecake. Then it was into the crush of people, vying for early spots in the line. I can never understand why people were so competitively eager to get into that toothpaste tube called a luxury passenger aircraft, enduring the stink and noise, but then shoving and pushing to get off when they arrived. It makes no sense.

Fortunately, we are traveling first-class, so we enjoy the gracious hospitality of plastic imitation food with box wine to lull our sensibilities with the notion that we are 'first class' people.

It was evening when the plane touched down. It also was more like a controlled crash, slamming down on the hard concrete and elevating my headache. Outside, Marcia and I look for a taxi, but we had hardly started walking to the stand, when a horn toots and there's John waving at us. Like the good friend he is becoming; he wasn't going to let ceremony stand in the way of his picking us up. As we put our small bags into his trunk, he looks at me and notices the bandages and bruises "Simon, how terrible it must have been. Let's get out of here."

"Thank you, John. As I learned in the Teams, the 'only bad day was yesterday'."

When we reached home, she helps me into the house and points me upstairs to the bedroom, where I clean up from the trip and find a spot in one of the guestrooms for my clothes. With my face washed and hair combed, I feel a little better, but my ears still ring.

Marcia and John are in the kitchen when I come back downstairs. I am a little embarrassed by how I feel, and make a small joke of it by announcing "Hi Honey, I'm home. What's for dinner?" as I walk into the kitchen. Marcia was sitting at the kitchen counter with a glass of wine. John was standing looking out into the night. Then Marcia turns to look at me and I could see that she had been crying. "Simon, I lost you once, and I almost lost you a second time. I don't want to lose you ever again. Do you understand?"

"Yes I do understand, really. But I am not going anywhere."

John looked a little embarrassed, but he came over and shook my hand, holding it a little longer. "Yes, I agree. Let's not lose you over this business."

Marcia gets up from the counter, walks over to me and gives me another warm kiss – not passionate, but very tender. This gentle compassion is another new side to her that I had not seen before. She breaks her comforting hug to give me a glass of wine. I probably shouldn't take it with my head and all, but I said to myself 'Hell, I am not going to be a victim' and smile as I took it. The smell was of cherries and oak, with a little plum thrown in. "What is this?" I asked Marcia.

"It is a pinot from Fallon vineyards in the Central Coast region of California. Actually, it is quite inexpensive for a Pinot Noir."

"It's wonderful. Guys, please sit down, both of you. I have been thinking along the lines of setting a trap for our criminal friends, and need John's help. John, I also want you to hear more about the story that is beginning to come out, which may explain your artifacts."

Even though it was late, Marcia announced that we needed to have a proper supper, so she disappears in the general direction of the pantry. John had, as usual, brought some flowers for Marcia before he came out to BWI. She brings out some brie, crackers, and pâté from the refrigerator, with a few cornichons which she slices thinly to balance the pâté. As we sip and crunch, I tell John in some detail of what happened over the past four days. I talk freely about the snooping I did on Towson's boat and the storm drain experience, which I truncate for both out benefit. I also share my suspicions of Lauren. In addition, I talk about the story of the key with all three of the major players in Cyprus, and the circumstances of Jean's death. This third telling is a lot easier for me. I also relate the connection of the artifacts to the deaths of Hudson, Edith Towson, and Zilbern.

John listens intently with no questions, although I am sure that many cross his mind while I was talking. At the conclusion of my story, John says, "I understand your motive in sharing my identity with Sylfern. You have dangled me as bait. I just want you to know that even though you didn't ask first, I agree with it and will work with you to bring this into the open. I also better understand your concern with security."

I ask John to tell us as much as he knows about the armor so far. His eyes light up as he talks, both for their historical value as well as from the clues towards the 'Book' and advanced crypto-analysis. He also highlights the possible relationship of the key as the third factor in the code, and the book's potential value to society. "It's not only from the viewpoint of a historical treasure, but also in terms of hints to gaps which might be filled in science and mathematics. I would hate to speculate, but it seemed that these issues are more important than the historical documentation of a lost or ancient civilization."

"The breastplate is particularly fascinating. Although its size is smaller than one that would be created for today's human frame, it has a unique property of apparently fitting almost anyone who wears it. If I were a mystic, I would say that it senses the size of the wearer and molds itself to their proportions. We tried several different people in the lab, and all claimed that it fit perfectly, although when we made measurements, there seemed to be no differences that we could tell. Initially, I thought that it was made for ceremonial usage; however, after our failed efforts to assay the metal, I have come to believe that it is a functional war device. It is extremely lightweight, but there are no attachment loops for equipment such as blades or arrows. On the interior, there must have been a leather jerkin which was strapped to the body, since the small loops for ties are in place, but the leather itself rotted long ago. There is a front pocket which was probably used for coins or small personal items."

"The helmet is just as unique. Although the design is apparently Hittite, the metalwork is exceedingly fine and ornate. Bird plumes undoubtedly adorned the top, and the cheek pieces have deflector panels for swords or arrows, but the face otherwise, is open. So either there is a piece missing, or the helmet too, is ceremonial."

"The inscriptions are the most puzzling of all. The breastplate gives some clues by a kind of Rosetta-Stone inscriptions in Aramaic, Greek and an ancient language which has only recently has been identified as ethnically Hurrian. The Hurrians were pre-Babylonian cultures living in the Tigris-Euphrates regions. Unfortunately, we know comparatively little about them. While these give rise to the notion of a 'book', the details are sketchy at best and undoubtedly are in a code of some sort. Perhaps if we had the key, or really good drawings of it, we could continue to decipher these inscriptions."

We sit with our own thoughts while Marcia brings dinner to the table. She has whipped up a Boeuf Bourguignon over egg noodles with roasted vegetables and a small salad of mixed greens. The bread that I had bought has the crust just brushed with olive oil. She had switched our pinot out for a young Côte du Rhone burgundy, to compliment the same wine in the beef. After appropriate compliments to the chef, we fall to it.

As we eat, I outline my plan. "John, tomorrow morning, when you go to the museum, I would like to go with you. Marcia, can you get John a GPS locator so that you can track him?" She nods and said that before we left in the morning, she would stop by her office and pick one up for us. "When you go to the museum, I would like to come too, so I can see this armor as well. Would you mind?"

"Marcia, the one thing I do not want to do is to identify you to any third party. So long as your involvement is unknown, there is a good chance that you will stay safe."

"Simon, I have been thinking about that. I think it is too late. If X has the kind of access to the NSA as proven by the past attack, the moment that I put you in to my group as an agent with access, the link to me was exposed. No one at the NSA in our little blind group has contact with you; only me. X would have learned that if he was watching you. So long as I don't overtly look for him, I doubt whether he will take any direct action against me. But let's put that aside and talk about this Lauren baiting."

"Ok. I gave Lauren with John's identity and his connection to the armor. Considering how fast their reactions are, if nothing happens tomorrow, then we need to find another way. I would offer Froehlich as a backup. He has a lot of old irons in the fire – code keys, animosities with the NSA, ties to Zilbern and Xyso-Towson, Cyprus, and Germany. But let's give it one more day. Meantime, tomorrow I will get to a place where I can see who comes around, while still remaining out of visible range. While this is going on, I will bait another hook for Akan as well. I believe that he has a greater interest than he has indicated. Let's just see who comes out. If we do get a bite, I will take the job of reeling in the line back to its source. Marcia, tomorrow morning, you check on new intercepts."

"Sure, but let me do that tonight. We need every advantage that time will give us." We both go into Marcia's study and she logs on to the NSA site. There are intercepts on three telephone calls from Lauren and one received by her. Both of the first two are scrambled, so we got no clear voice. The third was a call to reserve a flight to Washington for tomorrow morning from Albuquerque.

"Well, that certainly confirms that Lauren Sylfern is deeply in it. I did not see a scrambler set on the telephone in her house, but she could have used another line. "I should have trusted my instincts earlier."

"Don't blame yourself," John said. "The damsel in distress is always a worthwhile ploy. It gets us almost every time."

Marcia chimed in, "Simon, I think you should wait on Akan until we see what transpires with Lauren. She is coming to Washington tomorrow, so let's see what happens with her first."

I agreed. If she shows up at John's door by herself, then there are a number of plausible explanations, but if she shows up with reinforcements, we have to be prepared for enemy action.

On that note, we quit for the evening. John would drive along with us the following morning while Marcia picked up the Locator, and then John would take it with him to work. I would follow behind John, and Marcia would monitor events from her office. John wished us a good night and went home. I stayed with Marcia and helped her with the cleaning up, and then we both retired to bed. She suggests that we sleep in her room together, but I put her off for tonight. I still feel a bit squirrelly this development in our relationship, and don't want to push it.

# 24 _MONDAY- WASHINGTON_

At 6, the alarm wakes us and we hurriedly dress. By 6:30 we are having coffee with John, and then drive to Marcia's office, waiting while she goes into the building and returns with a GPS Locator which had a distress button should we need immediate aid. She also gave me a compact digital camera with a transmitter, whose photos would show up instantly on Marcia's computer. Then John heads to the office, while I follow behind.

Morning traffic was already heavy, and I ended up losing John as I drive toward Suitland, Md., where the Museum Conservation Institute is located. John had directed me to the spiral shaped building on Silver Hill Road, just off Suitland Parkway. As I turn off the road into the driveway, the guard takes my Drivers License and verifies my visitor status with the information he had received from John a few minutes earlier. I was directed to the correct building and parked. From the parking lot, I have a direct view of the front entrance, without being in view of other visitors. From an initial survey, there are three entrances to the property, including a rear service entrance, so all I could properly cover was the front. After I get settled, I call John. We had agreed on some emergency words to call me into the building or to indicate that he was leaving. I could see his car near me in the employee lot.

As time went on, more employees arrive and I get a couple of dirty looks at being parked without a valid sticker. But after a couple of head wags and a pointed thumb, I am ignored. A few visitors show up and I take their photos. Around 11, a large SUV pulls up to the entrance, and someone got out of the back concealed from my view. I snap some candids. Marcia had agreed to run each through photo recognition software against her database, DOD and NCIC. At 11:45, the man comes out carrying a briefcase, and jumps into the SUV, which immediately drives around the entrance circle and out through the guard's gate. As it turns, I get a photo of the front plate. At 12:30, John comes out a side door and walks over to his car carrying a bag. He leaves it on top of the car and returns to the building. After he disappears, I casually stroll over to the aisle where his car was parked and sweep up the bag as I pass. When I return to my car, I find that the bag contains a ham sandwich, some chips, and a soda – Lunch for the help. In a little while, the effects of morning coffee and lunchtime soda takes its toll on my bladder, so I walk up to the main entrance and ask the Receptionist for the bathroom. She gives me a funny look, but then I guess she assumes I am a waiting driver. She just points to the Men's Room. Then it was back to my stakeout.

At about 4, a car drives up to the visitor's area and parks. Out comes Lauren. She locks the car and walks purposefully into the main entrance. John calls me. "Lauren Sylfern is here and is asking me for a meeting. She said that she has some information about the armor that I was researching. I will meet with her. Do you want to listen in?"

"Yes, please. Just put your cell on speaker."

All I hear for the next few minutes is a hiss and some background music, which I assumed to be John's computer. Then I hear their voices coming into the office. "I don't really know what I can do for you, but come in." says John.

"Dr. Crawford, I think that I can help you instead." says Lauren very confidently.

"Really, how could you do that?"

"It was my father that had first tried to decipher the armor that you have. I still have his notes on the information that he got from the two pieces, as well as information about the key, and detailed drawings of it."

"So what do you propose?"

"I will give you my father's Diary in exchange for your sharing with me the final meaning of the inscriptions on the helmet and breastplate."

"What about the Key itself?"

"Oh, I don't have it, but I do have a good idea of who might. We don't need it anyway. My father drew a detailed diagram of the key."

"Will you bring me the diary?"

"Yes, but first, I would like to see the two artifacts. I want to verify for myself that they are exactly as my father described in his diary. Then, I will give you the diary itself."

"I am sorry, but I can't allow you access to our secure laboratory, and I won't bring up the artifacts up to this office." John sounded adamant.

"Then I cannot help you. I will not compromise my father's work and have spent considerable effort in protecting his diary."

"Can you return tomorrow morning and I will think about your terms tonight?"

"I'll tell you what I will do. I will be back here at 10:00 tonight. If you let me in, I will give you access to the Diary. If not, then I shall return home. But I will leave you with one more word. Several people have been killed for this information. Without my drawing, you will never be able to finish your translation. I am not asking for much, and it is within your power to grant this without anyone ever knowing. So the decision is yours. I will return at 10. I hope by then you will have decided to be reasonable."

With that, I heard footsteps moving away and a door closed. John picked up the telephone. "Did you hear?"

"Yes. We need to talk about this. Why don't you meet me at Marcia's this evening at 7:30, and we will council."

I then hang up and call Marcia. She already knew about Lauren's visit from the photo I transmitted, but not the substance of the conversation. I offered to clue her in when I saw her and asked her to bring another GPS locator or two, and a couple of pinhead bugs.

As it was still an hour before John would leave for the evening, I settled back again to wait and watch. I couple of additional visitors show up just before 5, and I duly record their images. Then John comes out and walks toward his car. As he opens the car door, a man comes out of an adjacent car and accosts him. The man speaks in a low voice and then returns to his car and drives off. I tried to get a couple of photos, but wasn't sure how much I captured. Meanwhile, John stands at his car door for a few seconds, apparently upset, and then enters his car. The engine starts immediately, and he goes towards the guardhouse. I follow, but decide not to telephone him, as we were going to meet soon anyway.

He drives directly home with me close behind. He stops at his own house, and closes the garage door behind him. I waited for a minute or two but when he doesn't come out, I go back to Marcia's and wait for her. She arrives in about 20 minutes.

As I come inside, Marcia is waiting in the hall. After being kissed and mussed, she breaks away and goes in search of wine. I join her in the kitchen again. I tell her of the conversation between Lauren and John, as well as the incident in the parking lot. We both wait to speculate on our next step until John joins us, which he does at the appointed hour.

As I open the door, I am shocked at John's pale appearance. He just stands at the door for a few moments, appearing not noticing that I had opened it,

265

and then walks in without a word. I follow him into the kitchen where he embraces Marcia and holds onto her for the longest while. Then he stands back and says in a wooden tone "They've taken her," whereupon he sits at the counter and shakes his head a couple of times. Marcia takes him gently by the chin. "Who?'

"Emily, my daughter; the fellow in my parking lot told me, so I called Karen and it's true. I have no idea what I am going to do."

"John," I said, "Tell us the whole story, please."

"When I was leaving the office, a man came up to me in the parking lot and said that I had better cooperate, or my daughter would disappear. I didn't believe it, but he had said it like it was nothing to him. What am I going to do?"

"What do they want?" I asked.

"I don't really know. I guess it has something to do with the armor. Lauren Sylfern asked me. Well you were listening, Simon, you know what they asked. It wasn't such a big thing – just show her the armor, give her access to the translation and she would give me the diary. But what is so important that they would take Emily?"

"Marcia, I sent you a couple of photos of the man who talked to John in the parking lot. Did anything come out?"

"Yes, nothing clear on the man, but we got a plate number. It is a Government Plate, issues to the Executive Branch. I don't know who, but if it were a motor pool car then we would have a record of who signed it out. This is a personal car. It will take a little longer, but we will find out who it belongs to."

"I don't care who it belongs to. I only care about getting my Emily back. I have to do something, but what?" John was stressing at a higher pitch. "I don't give a crap about this armor. They can even have it if it means so much to them. Nothing is worth her life; Nothing!"

"John, let us see if we can find out more. How about the guard's log? John, is it electronic or a journal?"

"It's put into a database. We always keep records of visitors, especially to the Institute. There is a lot going on in there in terms of sensitive artifacts and items from foreign governments."

"OK, John, don't worry, we'll get her back. Marcia, can you log into the guards database, and also, we've got to find out who is assigned to that car/"

"We also have to come up with a plan to deal with Lauren. She will be coming by John's office in a little over two hours, and we have to be ready for whatever she asks – particularly if she is connected to Emily's disappearance."

Marcia disappeared out the door to the study. All thoughts of dinner flew out the window. "John, can you find out the exact circumstances of Emily's abduction? I mean do you know somebody at the school who might have some information?"

"Let me call Karen."

"Is that your wife?"

"Ex. She and I were divorced a year ago. Emily was in private school and even with joint custody; we both thought that it would be better if she didn't have to shuttle. I go see her when I can, and she comes here whenever there is a break from school. I just hope that she doesn't blame me for this."

"Go call her and see if she knows someone who might know. Have the police or FBI been called?"

"No. I don't want to bring them in until I know what's going on."

"Give me the address where your ex-wife lives and I will see if I can get some quiet protection and a tap on her line. Meantime, just call her."

"OK." John gives me the information and goes to call. I pull out my cell and dial my Navy Office. When the duty officer answers, I tell him that I must speak with the Admiral right away. He puts me on hold and within 20 seconds the Admiral is on the line.

"Admiral, Simon Chess. I need your help. I am working on the assignment, but someone who is helping me with the code key problem has just had his daughter kidnapped. I need some agents up to his wife's house and a tap put on her line."

True to his instantaneous focus on the important stuff, he immediately asks for details. He tells me to expect a call back. No questions about the investigation, the people, nothing – just action. I really appreciate that from someone who is stretched in so many different directions as he. Before I knew it, he was gone.

By then, John is back. Karen had given him the name and telephone number of the school monitor who was on duty at the end of the day. We call her together. She said that a man in a dark suit came up to her and flashed some credentials in her face saying "Federal Agent" and requested that she point out Emily to him as the kids came out of the building. When Emily appeared, the man spoke to her briefly and they both left in his car. The Monitor didn't catch a license plate or name, just that it was a dark sedan with tinted windows. A few minutes later, when Karen Crawford came up in her car, the monitor had to tell her what happened. She went in to speak to the headmaster, and then left.

We thank the monitor and then go in search of Marcia. She is sitting at her desk. On a pad next to her, she had written "NSA" with a big question mark. She was still focused on her screen, so we don't want to bother her. Finally, she looks up and said "I don't believe it."

"What? Marcia, what? The NSA took Emily?"

"No, not the NSA. The car is assigned to the President's Security Advisor, or rather, to his office."

"Froehlich?" I asked.

"No, he doesn't drive an official car any more. No, it's somebody from the NSC staff. I doubt whether it is the boss, but somebody there is very interested in the armor."

"Or the Book" I added.

"Yes; or the Book. Well this brings a new wrinkle. I hope that this is a private action and not something cooked up by the White House."

"You know, if the White House wanted the armor, all they had to do is to call the Smithsonian and they would have ordered me to give it up to them." John added.

"Well, no. If they had ordered it directly, then there would be records, and if someone later used the information, it could be traced back to the President's office."

"Marcia, let me ask you something that has been bothering me. Do the agents who work for the NSC staff carry credentials?"

"No; most of them are staffers and have no powers aside from influence. Even the Advisor himself has no operational powers; but he does use NSA or FBI agents on occasion, as well as CIA, DIA, ONI, and other staffs through their courtesy. Why do you ask?"

"Well, I have been wondering about the two 'agents' that tried to grab Lauren and me in my office several days ago. They carried NSA credentials, and I haven't seen anyone follow up the beating I gave them."

Marcia quickly replied "Let's deal right now with the two items on our Most-Immediate Agenda – Emily's release and Lauren's demands. One thing seems to be certain. They are connected. Simon, your bait worked in spades. The problem now is to figure that with that tiger loose, which end to we grab for?"

"John, you have to go meet with Lauren. Agree to anything except giving her the artifacts, just in case she asks. I will go with you for security. Let's get you wired, so we can listen. Next, you have to tag Lauren with a bug. If she is connected with the lifting of Emily, there will undoubtedly be a follow-up meeting and we have to know where and with whom. Marcia, let's split the tasks; I will take the field with John, and you manage the Op. Center. While we are getting back to John's lab, can you see if you can get any further hits on the visitor? How about surveillance cameras at John's office in the parking lot? Or maybe traffic cameras on nearby streets? Marcia, are there any National Reconnaissance Office Keyhole assets in the area? What do you think?" "

Marcia goes back to her screen, while I go in search of something quick for us to eat before we had to go out again. I find some roast beef in the fridge, and slice off a few slabs of the remaining sourdough bread and add a slice of tomato to mine, but I think not for Marcia. I dig out some bottled ice tea and I bring a plate in to her. She makes a face, but bites into hers anyway. John was about half done with his when I come back into the kitchen. He is chewing mechanically as he stares at the window. I take a few bites and then my phone rings. It was the Admiral.

"Our team will be at Karen Crawford's house in 15 minutes. There is a technical crew right behind and a Hostage Negotiator is available. If the talk gets to money, you're covered. Another team is headed to you to support interrogation and custody, should there be a target. They will be just behind you at the MCI office, but for backup only. Arrival is pegged at 21:45. Local cameras have been appropriated. The MCI had been alerted that a test intrusion is to be implemented, and they will instruct guards to not interfere. You are tasked as Op Lead. Don't screw up. Call me later." And he was gone again.

At 9 we take his car and I lay hidden in the back. I had taken one pinhead bug and dipped it in Vaseline, should we get a chance to get Lauren to drink it. I had a second one on a little metal burr that would attach to any clothing if brushed against. This one was also magnetized, so maybe we could get it on her purse or belt.

By 9:30 we are in the parking lot. The guard barely looks at John as he flashes his I.D., and never looks in the back of the car. We park close to the entrance, and I wait with John for our quarry's appearance.

At 10 promptly, a dark blue sedan drives through the gate, barely stopping. Although there are just a few cars in the lot, the car stops near to us. Lauren gets out and walks toward our car. I urge John to get out so that she will not see me. He stands next to our car, blocking her view inside.

"I see you have decided to be cooperative. It certainly is the right choice," said Lauren by way of greeting.

"You will get nothing and see nothing unless Emily is brought to me safe" replied John.

"What are you talking about? Who is Emily?" asked Lauren, as she stands there with her mouth slightly open.

"Don't give me that crap." said John angrily. "You took my daughter, and you can go to the devil if you'll get any cooperation whatsoever from me without bringing her back. And do it right now." John was pretty mad. I did not expect this level of bravado from him.

""Dr. Crawford, I really don't know what you are talking about. I came here to make a simple exchange. I need to see these pieces that you have, and I am willing to give you the diary for them. Please, this is very important to me. I really don't know what.you mean your daughter was kidnapped? Oh my God, I really didn't know. And you thought that I was responsible? Oh no. I am really sorry. Did you call the police?" the tremor in her voice was very real – either she was truthful or was a better actress than even I thought.

Crawford wasn't buying. "Ms. Sylfern, the coincidence is just too pat. You come here this afternoon with no warning, make a veiled threat, and then the next thing my daughter is taken from school and I am warned to cooperate. So tell me, how stupid do you think I am?"

"No, no. I'm so sorry. I have no idea about your daughter. Please, you have to believe me. Oh God, it must be Froehlich. He must have had me followed and connected me with you. He must know that you have the armor. Oh, but you don't know about him. Look, here's the diary." She digs into her bag and pulls out a notebook with a speckled black cover, the kind that school kids kept many years ago. It was dog-eared, had a lot of papers stuffed into it, kept together with a heavy red rubber band. "If it would make you believe me, you can have this – no strings. I would just like to see the two pieces, that's all."

270

I decided to join the conversation, so I opened the back door of the car and stood up.

"Simon! What are you - oh; you thought I was behind this – is that why you didn't call me? Oh Simon, truly I want to see an end to this and find out who killed my father. I also want to make sure that if Froehlich is behind this, that he pays. He stole from my father when my father needed mostly was a friend. Now he is after something bigger – something that you, Dr. Crawford have. Please believe me." She again pleaded.

Just then two other cars came through the gate. They circled around on either side of us and stopped about a yard away on each side. The rear door of one opens and a dark suited man got out. He walked over to us and stopped, taking in the three of us very slowly. I do not recognize him.

"Chess - You don't get the message very well, do you? And Lauren Sylfern; well, that's expected. Crawford, we have a package for you, and we want a simple trade: The armor for the package. We obtained this package at school this afternoon. Are you ready to make the exchange?"

"As I told your friend here," John said, pointing to Lauren, "First I see my daughter safe and in my hands, and then you can have whatever you want."

"It doesn't work that way. You go in now and get the armor. Bring it out and give it to me. Then you will get your daughter back. We don't negotiate; just do it. And I will take the book you have, Ms. Sylfern." He held out his hand. I took a step toward Lauren and pulled the book from her hand. "This is not part of the deal. As Dr. Crawford said, show us Emily."

The man stared at me and then pointed to the other car. There was a scuffling sound from inside and then a girl's voice cried out. John jumped and took a couple of steps toward the man, bringing his hands up as if to grab him. "Don't be a fool. Mess with me and she's dead. Just be a good boy and get what I want from your lab."

John kept walking towards the man. "She might be dead already, but you aren't. I'll take care of that right now."

The man reached into his jacket pocket and pulled out a gun. He pointed it at John, but included all of us in his look. "Don't be a dead hero." He warned.

Then he turned to me and demanded the diary again.

I opened the door to our car and tossed the book in the back. The gun fired and the bullet whammed off the door I had just opened, ricocheting off into the night, leaving a deep dent in the door. I said quickly, "John, go in and get the armor. It will be all right. Don't worry."

John nods and turns toward the building. As he walks to the entrance, the gunman's attention moves to John, but with the other car in full view, there is nothing I can do. He disappears into the building. The three of us stand there, waiting for John to get back. So long as they had Emily, I couldn't make a move. Finally, John appears at the door, carrying a large package. As he gets closer, I could see that the armor was covered in bubble-wrap and taped. John holds it up to his chest and walks towards the gunman. When he gets closer, the gunman points to his car and John starts in that direction, but as he passes me he whispers one word "Watch" and I tense while he carries on towards the car. Just as he passes the gunman, he turns abruptly and pushes the package into the gun. It fires, and the gunman gave a shout as he starts to crumple to the ground. I run towards the second car, crouching to pull my gun from my ankle holster. With the gun in my hand, I continued running towards the other car. The engine turns over and one of the side windows starts to open. I fire two rounds into the hood, hoping for the radiator. Then I run to the far side. John meantime, uses the package as a battering ram and smashes it into the face of the downed gunman. He then holds it in front as he races to the other car. Through the open window, several shots ring out, clanging off the package. John's shield works, however; and he keeps coming until he reaches the car. The engine starts and the car began to move - with John running alongside holding the package over the side window.

The car accelerates leaving John behind. Meantime, I take aim at the driver through the windshield and let fly another two rounds. The first ricocheted off but the second penetrates and must hit someone because there is a cry from inside. I pull the door open and throw myself across the seat. From the back, a gun appears over the seat-back and I make a grab for it. We wrestle for it and the hand pulls back. A shot goes off and a bullet tears through the seatback but just ticks at my clothes. I couldn't fire back because of the girl; then a voice in the back said "The next one goes into her head. Throw your gun over the seat."

I eject the clip and do it, keeping the clip in front. But at the same time, I dig into my waist and pulled out my K-Bar. "Now, get out of the car and walk away. I slide to the ground and then stand up. As I back off, the rear door opens and a man comes out, pulling a girl of about 13 through the doorway onto the ground. Then he grabs her by the hair and drags her upright. John is about 100 feet away on the other side of the car. He started walking toward this car, still holding the package in front of him.

"Give me your keys" said the man with Emily. He starts to move toward John's car. "I said, give me the keys." He is dragging her along as she tried to keep her feet.

"I don't have them," I say as I watch the kidnapper for an opening. My knife is still at my side, but I shift to a throwing grip as I keep that side of my body away from the pair.

The man turns and called across the roof of the car to John, who is closing. "You; stop there and toss me the keys" John wasn't hearing a thing. He just keeps walking.

"John, do it" I said loudly. He stops and looks at me, I repeat it more quietly "John, just do as he says, toss him the keys." I nod to John and he finally understands. He stops, put the package down on the concrete and then reaches into his pocket. Emily stops struggling and turns towards me. I look at Emily and mouth "Stand Still" and she nods, quite possessed. John pulls his hand out of his pocket and holds up the keys.

"Just toss them to me easy. And no funny stuff."

John tosses the keys high and to his left. The gunman has to reach up to catch them. As he stands up, I throw the knife. If flashes and catches him in the throat. Dropping the gun, he grabs at his neck, but the knife had done its trick. A great gout of blood spurts from a torn carotid and the man starts to collapse. Emily tears herself loose and runs to me, as blood sprays her hair and back. The man hits the pavement and gurgles as he tries to breathe. But it is over for him. John runs around the car and as Emily reaches me, she is swept into his embrace. "Daddy" was all she could say as he holds her tightly.

Lauren stood rooted in the same spot. She hadn't move a muscle from the time John batted the first gunman until this moment. I could see tears streaming down her cheeks. "Oh I am so sorry. Please forgive me. I never wanted this to happen. Please, I'm sorry."

"It's OK Lauren, it's over for now." I said.

John releases Emily and looks up at me.

"John, you did great. But what was in the package?"

"Oh, it's the armor. I forgot to mention it but we tested it in our archeometallurgy lab and found that it was an extraordinarily tough. This armor would stop a bullet even better than Kevlar. I doubt whether there is even a scratch inside."

"John, you're a pip: Mild mannered scientist and all."

"Simon, I only know that they weren't going to get away with this. Not my Emily, Not ever. Listen, I have to call Karen. Emily, I need to call Mommy and tell her you are OK. You are OK aren't you?"

"Yes, Daddy, my hair hurts, but nothing else. And they did give me some ice cream after picking me up from school. But that man is dead. And so is the other one in the car. Don't tell Mommy about the dead people, she will be very upset."

"OK dear. But let me call her right now." He turned away and took out his cell phone.

Lauren, who had been standing by crying, came over and takes Emily by the hand. "Hi, I'm Lauren. You must be Emily. Can we be friends?"

"Sure Miss Lauren. But why are you crying. Did the bad people have you also?"

"Yes, in a way they had me too. But they don't any more, that's all that matters. Your daddy and Simon saved us."

"Thank you, Mr. Simon."

While we are standing there waiting for John to finish his call, another car turns into the lot. A large Mercedes limo drives over to near where we are and stops. The rear door opened and out pops Dr. Froehlich.

"I was wondering when you would show up." I said to him as he walked over to us. I assume you know each other?"

Lauren stared at Froehlich as he greeted her. "Lauren, I haven't seen you in many years, not since you were a girl. I am sorry to meet you again this way, but it's nice to see you, no matter what prompted it."

"Dr. Froehlich."

"Yes, indeed," I interrupt her, "What are you doing here?"

"Yes. Well Simon, I received a call this evening from an old friend of mine, your boss, who asked me to come and make sure you all were OK. The admiral and I go back a long ways. Simon, I see you've had a bit of trouble."

"Just a minute while I check in;" I walked over to the car that had held Emily and looked in the front seat. The driver was still alive, but bleeding from my bullet, which had gone into his shoulder. I thought he would keep. I walked over to the first gunman, but he was dead. The car that he had been in was gone. I pick up my phone and call the Admiral. "Good evening sir, I am reporting in that the girl is safe, one of the opposition is dead, one got away, and the last is still alive and disabled. The armor is safe, and our side is unharmed."

"Well Done. Our team will be there in a few minutes to sanitize the area. I want a full written report on my desk tomorrow, but for now, go home. I will send protection details for you all. Have the artifacts returned to the MCI, and call me in the morning."

"Aye, aye sir, but don't hang up sir. Did you ask Dr. Froehlich to some here?"

"Oh, he showed up already? Yes, I did. You can trust him. He and I have worked together in the past and I trust him implicitly."

"Thank you, sir. I will do just that."

"Dr. Froehlich, I have regards to you from the Admiral. John, this is Dr. Johann Froehlich, formerly of the National Security Office. Lauren, I think that you need to settle your issues with him."

"Simon, it will be a long cold day in hell before I ever forgive him for what he did to my father. So just count me out." Lauren had gone rigidly erect.

"Lauren," said Froehlich "I am sure that I can help you understand what truly happened in the past, and maybe you will forgive me." Lauren stood still, with her lips compressed, saying nothing more.

A van turns into the lot followed by a flatbed tow truck and several men pile out wearing what looked like ABC protection suits and gloves. They pick up the body, put it into the van, and then come over to the other assailant's car. They take the wounded driver out of the front seat and put him on a gurney, wheeling him over to the van as well. But before they close the doors, I walk over. "Who are you working for?" I ask. His eyes looked at me with both anger and defiance. "None of your business," he said.

I look down at him and said "Look, you will either tell me now, or the boys here will take you somewhere and you'll have to tell them then. At least now, you won't suffer any more."

"Go to hell." The fellow turns his head away and grimaces.

The cleanup crew closes the van doors and then they search the ground, picking up all the brass, and then hose it down with detergent spray. The car is loaded on the flatbed and that area is also policed and sprayed. John starts walking back to the lab with the package when Froehlich stopped him. "Will you let me see these once more?" he asked.

In the light which streamed out of the Reception Room onto the apron, John tears off the tape and unrolls the bubble wrap. "Lauren," Froehlich called "Come and see. It is what your father searched for since 1945 when last we saw them."

In spite of Lauren's truculence at Froehlich's presence, she was drawn to the package. John takes the last wrappings off the armor and we all look at it, glistening in the light. It looks as it must have just the moment it was completed by the armorer so many years ago. The helmet's raised crest missing only the plumes which once grew from it. The breastplate was more like a tunic, with a fitted-in waist. Tiny inscriptions worked into twisted braids fill the plate and around the face opening in the helmet. The figures also ran down the helmet's nosepiece. At the sides of the helmet, the wearer's ears would be protected by flaring of the cheek-plates so that a spear or sword blade would be deflected away from the ears. There were no scratches on it anywhere. John turned it over and the inside had nothing either except for a couple of silvery smears where the bullets had left a little of themselves where they caromed off.

"So this is it" I said. "I'll admit that it is beautiful, but to have so many deaths associated with it…"

"Yes" confirmed Froehlich. "I remember when they were stolen from our cave in Cyprus. We woke in the morning, your father and I, to find nothing on the worktable and no sign of their ever being there. The only record we had was the diary that your father kept, where he tried to copy down all the inscriptions. But without a starting or end point, there was no order to the writings. So we never got even a good beginning. But your father did have the key. I didn't know it then, but I learned from him later that it had been dropped by whoever took the armor. He found it in a crevice in the floor. If it hadn't been so bright and shiny, it might be there still. But he did find it, kept it. I never saw it again, although years later I asked him about it. But by then, he was no longer speaking to me."

"You really expected an answer, after what you did?" Lauren's voice was cold and low.

"And exactly what did you father say that I did to him?" Froehlich asked.

"You stole the equations that created the large primes that founded your big company, got rich, and got yourself an important position in the government."

"No, my dear; I never stole them."

"Don't give me that. My father would not have lied to me."

"Lauren, things were very tough for you both at that time. He was having a very difficult time when your mother took sick. Her medical bills were piling up, and you were off at school, the Albuquerque Academy, as I recall. It was so expensive, and you were doing so well. I was not a wealthy man, but my wife and I had no children so I offered him what money I had for you, and to help your mother, but he wouldn't take charity; he was very proud. He thought that his work was good, but never realized how valuable it really was. I made a deal with him. He got the cash to help pay for your mother's illness and your education, and I got the equations. I know that it wasn't enough, particularly when the government refused him the insurance that he was entitled to. But by then, your mother had died. When my business started to take off, I tried to convince him to join me, but he refused to speak with me. I suppose that in the stress of having to deal with your mother, he forgot my original offer. The single time I did reach him, he accused me of stealing from him and making millions, while he still struggled. I tried to talk to him but he wouldn't listen. Maybe you will listen."

"Lauren, I put 10% of the stock of my company in your name when it went public. I had wanted to give it to your father, but I knew that he was too proud to take it directly. So it went to you, even though he tried to make me out a thief. Lauren, that stock now is worth almost $100 million, and is still growing. I tried to tell him, I really did. Lauren, I am so sorry that he was so angry at me. If only he had listened, we would have been able to work together, and he would have been free to pursue anything that he wanted to do for the rest of his life. But he was so angry over my decision to betray Germany at a very bad time in Germany's history. This was not a good discovery that he made, it was a great discovery. But Lauren, your father had his own mind. When he decided to do something, he just went and did it, no matter what the consequences or barriers. It made him great, but it also made him bullheaded. I am really sorry that you never got the benefit of his work, but you have it now, if you want it. If not, then do with it what you like. It's your decision."

Lauren started to cry again. "If only I knew. Oh my God, if only I knew. Now what am I going to do?" she said the last more to herself than to anyone else. She reached out and touched the armor. Then she looked up at John. "Put these away again, and keep them safe. We will find the key and you will be able to solve the puzzle. I am so sorry." Then she walked away towards her car.

"Lauren" I called, "Wait; we need to be together in this."

"Later," she mumbled. "There is something that I have to do first." She got into her car and drives off. The van and tow truck had left by then, leaving everything almost as it was when we arrived. Froehlich repeated Lauren's cautionary note and John nodded, going back in the building with Emily in tow.

Froehlich and I remain in the parking area, both with our own thoughts."Have you made any more progress towards finding the key?"

"No. We thought we had, but Lauren was our best lead. Now that she's a dead end, we are back to identifying who gave it to me. We do have the diary though, so perhaps it may help John. I assume the Admiral brought you up to date?" He nodded. "I think that whoever dropped it on me wanted to expose the characters in this plot, but for whatever reason, could not do it on their own. That would be the only reason that I was brought in. I would be the bait and I could take care of myself, so I was an ideal candidate. If they had gone to the authorities, they would have been laughed at. With Lauren after it as well for her own reasons, the key would have done exactly what it did do, brought the two of us together with just enough information to follow the trail, but not enough to stimulate an official investigation. I still do not have much of a clue who started this. For a while I thought it was Lauren, but she would be very unlikely to choose me to help her, geographically speaking, that is. So it had to be someone that knew of me, and also knew of the three artifacts. Any ideas?"

Froehlich said "Actually I do, but I am not ready to share yet. You might find it too farfetched. So let's keep with the realistic probabilities. Back in '45, the people in the OSS knew about the discoveries, because Ernst and I were sent there before we were transported to the US. There are still quite a few of them around, but it would be virtually impossible to find out who knew then and is still active. I would have assumed that anyone who was in the OSS and later in the CIA or a sister organization might have come across your name and work. It could be any of the alphabet soup that has an operational black ops unit. Too many potentials to find a solid lead there. What about starting where you were given the key? "

"The first time it was in the Palace Hotel. But it was at the Asian Museum that it was lifted again. Do you think it was the same person?"

"If it has not turned up so far, I would say yes. Suppose it was given to you to draw out Towson, Sylfern and anyone else connected, but then taken away to protect it from falling into their hands?"

"That would fit. But that would mean I have or had some kind of guardian angel that I never saw or recognized. Someone would have to be awfully good to follow me around without my getting even a hint?"

"Obviously, the reason for starting was just that – starting. Suppose you totally dropped it now. If you are still being monitored somehow, they would expect you to continue pushing until it was solved. But if you do nothing, or go off on a tangent somewhere and leave this behind, I'll bet that they will give you another nudge back. Maybe you'll get the key again, or something else. After all, right now things are somewhat at a standstill. The armor is locked up, Lauren is off soul searching, Towson is casting around with no leads, and your job with the Navy can't get going without another lead. All the other players are dead, and the key is untraceable. Whoever X may be, if they are anxious now, backing off will give anxiety a chance to fester, leading to a possible mistake or exposure. Why don't you just leave this for a while, and let's see what develops."

"Dr. Froehlich thanks for your advice. Maybe I will do just that. I only have one bit of unfinished business – a tiny lead here in Washington. I will take care of that today. Do you need anything from me?"

"No, no my boy. You have already helped me by bringing Lauren and me together again. I think that when she has had the opportunity to get over her shock, I will be hearing from her."

I have been thinking about another related subject all the time we have been talking, and decide that maybe now is the time to bring it up. With what the Admiral has told me about his trust of Froehlich, and when I saw myself with Lauren, maybe Froehlich is an answer to the bigger question. So I decide to go for it. "Dr. Froehlich, before you go, there is one thing more that maybe you can help us with."

"Yes, of course. What is it?"

"I believe that this armor and key business is related to the death of my former wife Jean. Let me try to explain the logic, and please help me see it with independent eyes. We have been laboring under the assumption that Daniel Towson is our bad guy, behind all of our troubles, and that it is his passion for the book, maybe because of his loyalty to Turkey, or maybe his greed, I don't know. But Towson as our antagonist does not answer a couple of fundamental questions."

279

"First, I want to tell you about my wife's death. You may know that my wife was killed in a Jerusalem bombing of her hotel. Initially, I thought that it was done by our government to shut her up from speaking out knowledgably against the drive for war with Iraq. After all, she was systematically stripped of her good name and job by someone in the administration, and then conveniently died. The Palestinians terrorists were blamed. If they did it, OK. But if they didn't, then there had to be an NSA connection, first because they sent her to that hotel, and had a need for her silence. If it had been a terrorist act, then why stop me from participating in the investigation?"

"Within a day after starting this case, who shows up at my door? The NSA, with a very aggressive attitude. What possible interest would they have in this investigation, other than some casual mention of a sophisticated new code? So the common denominator is the same, although the connection is pretty weak. Towson would not have the clout to call upon the NSA for personal purposes. "

"Originally, Dr. Froehlich, I thought that maybe you were behind Towson, but now I see that I was wrong. The real fallacy in my logic is that if Jean was killed for some deeper purpose, I just don't understand it. A dominant player in the administration would have had nothing to fear from her."

"Last week, I followed Towson to his boat in Oakland, and found out that he really reports to X. The question is: is the armor, key and book the real goal or is it another blind? I would guess that it is valuable and perhaps even useful, but for whom? And why am I involved at all. John said tonight that if someone powerful wanted these artifacts, they could just have taken them with no fuss at all. So why all these sidetracks? I am convinced that we do not see the true enemy yet, and we need your help to find it."

"My boy, since you and I spoke last, I have been attempting to find out who set the NSA agents on your heels, with no success. I also have been concerned about a growing consolidation within our administration. I did know about your wife's killing. A few years ago, Admiral Lewis failed in his own investigation of who was behind it. He also was convinced that she was destroyed by our own government, or at least by some highly placed persons in it. I know he mentioned nothing of this to you then, but I believe that he knew you had to leave the agency to mend on your own. His inquiry was very quiet, so virtually no one knew. I agree that we have to identify both the real motives and persons behind all this. However; I do not believe that direct investigation will yield anything further at this time. I think that we have to create an atmosphere of comfort for whoever is at

280

the head of the table, and watch for inconsistencies. So long as you do nothing to alarm him, you should have no concerns for your safety."

"Dr. Froehlich, I am far less concerned for myself than I am for John and Marcia. Oh, you don't know about Marcia."

"Yes, my boy, I know of your relationship, and I know her work."

"She has become very important to me personally, as well as professionally. I believe that both my friends are potentially at risk, and would not want to expose them further, regardless of the cost."

"Until the key surfaces again, or Dr, Crawford somehow completes the translation, you need to take a break. Why don't you take your lady on a trip?"

"I think that you have the makings of a great idea. But before I take your suggestion, I do have one tiny lead left to follow up on. At his boat, Towson made an offhand remark about his identity. I think that I should check that out, which I will do tomorrow."

John had come back out of the building again, and walked to the car. "Let's head back to Marcia's," I said.

He nods and looks into the back of the car. Emily is sound asleep. As we drive out and headed home, I make a couple of calls. The first to the Admiral "Sir, we are heading home now. I need to take some time off after my bout with the storm drain and a concussion. I will pick up again in a few weeks." He said that it was fine, so long as he got his report in the morning as promised. Then I call Marcia, stopping her questions by saying that we were on our way back with Emily, and I would fill her in when we reached home. I also said, for the benefit of anyone that might be listening, that I was really sick of the whole business, and wanted to end it, but that I would talk about it when I got home.

Later that evening, after John begged off and disappeared home, Marcia is anxious to know that everyone is OK, particularly when I describe the gun battle.

"So what is our next step?" she asks.

"I think that we need a break."

"Simon, don't you think we have a little advantage? I think that we should press on the offensive."

"Actually, this isn't my own idea. Dr. Froehlich suggested that since we really don't know the motive of the attack, other than obtaining the armor,

281

that we should give them a chance to make some mistakes. Also, so long as John has the artifacts locked up in his lab, they are quite safe unless they openly reveal themselves by officially taking custody of them."

"Well, that makes sense, unless it is Froehlich himself who is behind this."

"I would say it was very unlikely. I trust Admiral Lewis, and he vouches for Froehlich."

"Well, I trust you, Simon, so that is good enough for me." She gives me a hug and looks straight into my eyes. "So what does Herr Froehlich suggest?"

"He thought that it might be a nice idea if you and I spent a little time together, like maybe on a vacation."

"Oh *he* thought! It's good that you fell on your head or I would give you a shot."

"Actually, I think so too. How about it?"

"Are you suggesting a weekend at No-tell Motel?"

"No, how about a month in Europe?"

"Not too bad – tell me again how it was your idea."

"Marcia, I don't know exactly where we might be heading, but the only way we are going to find out is if we spend time together, outside of our work life. Does it really matter who suggested it?"

"Of course not, just so long as we act on it. I will put in papers for a leave of absence tomorrow morning."

That night, I slept fitfully, unsure about the decision that would immerse me in a new life. I frankly don't know if I am ready for it. I wonder if I am being fair to Marcia, but I believe that she understands. I know that I need to move on.

# 25 *TUESDAY - WASHINGTON*

Mortimer Stark Larson, L.L.P is located on K Street, Northwest, in an 11 story modern office building with an imposing lobby; a testament to the wealth generated by Beltway Bandits. The main reception room is on the top floor, with a marble foyer and heavy glass doors, which are so perfectly balanced as to move with the slightest touch. A reserved, severely coiffed receptionist offers me coffee from a silver carafe poured into a Limoges China cup with accompanying tiny sweet rolls, while I wait.

Earlier in the morning, I had telephoned, and was surprised how easily I was able to get an appointment with Nathaniel Larson, the Managing Partner. The use of Towson's name worked its charm, however; so here I sit.

After a very short wait, I am gathered by a well-tailored woman in her 50s, who leads me past a glass fronted conference room lined with hundreds of books labeled "U.S. Tax Code" to the end of a carpeted hall and through a walnut door with bronze handles. It all was clearly designed to impress a visitor of the firm's solid foundations.

Larson is a small man in his 60s, with a fringe of white hair framing sharp hazel eyes and half-spectacles. He smiled as he comes around his desk and his clasp was dry and firm. Leading me to a small sofa, he perched on an adjacent straight-backed chair.

"Do you know Mr. Towson well?" he inquired, in a Boston Brahmin accent.

"I am afraid that I don't, however; we have had business dealings."

"Would you be so kind as to tell me when the last time was you saw him?"

"What a strange question, Mr. Larson; why do you ask?"

"Mr. Towson is a man who enjoys his privacy. I should think that someone might use his name in vain, and without his personal permission."

"If you are asking me how I know him, then please ask me the direct question."

"Perhaps I might have another reason for inquiring. You know that reports were circulated that he died last year."

"Yes, I had heard that, however; they are not true."

"So you have seen him recently?"

"Well, he certainly looked fit this past week in San Francisco."

"That actually, is a relief for me to hear it. His company has been a long-standing client of ours, and this year, he has been even more private than usual. To tell you the truth, I was worried that the reports of his death might be true. Well, thank you, Mr. Chess. You have made a positive contribution to my day today. Now, how can I help you?"

"I am a Private Detective who has been retained by a client who is contemplating a joint business venture with Turkish Export-Import. I was asked to inquire as to the health of the company, and the likelihood of their following through on any venture my client might enter into."

"Well, Mr. Chess, I cannot reveal to you any details of the company's financial health other than our required SEC filings, but I would say that with Mr. Towson at the helm, it a singularly strong organization. If you have researched the firm, you must certainly know that there are no pending lawsuits or breach-of-contract actions against the firm, and their history over the past 30 years has been one of consistent growth."

"Yes, well thank you for sharing that with me. But I am concerned about one thing that you said at the beginning of our conversation. It is important to my client that Mr. Towson personally involves himself in this venture. If you have not seen him for quite some time, would you say that he has become reclusive or aberrant in behavior?"

"I would not want you to get any negative impression from my remarks. Mr. Towson must be concentrating on something quite important these days. Perhaps it is the venture that your client is developing."

"No, it must be something else. But let me ask you one further question. I understand that Mr. Towson is very emphatic in his regard for the Turkish culture, and for the rights of Turkey to have any historical treasures returned that are now in others' hands. Would you agree?"

"Oh most certainly. Although Mr. Towson is a U.S. Citizen, he is very passionate about the thievery which decimated the Ottoman heritage, and he has always worked valiantly for their restoration to his birth land."

"Would you say he was fanatical about this passion?"

"I think that it depends on your perspective. For a displaced Turk whose family was destroyed by foreigners, it might not be called fanaticism; but instead perhaps strong concern for right. But in terms of action, I would say that he has been generous to a fault with funding and repatriating stolen art, artifacts, historical documents and other symbols of Turkey. But please excuse me. I have spoken out of turn. Mr. Towson is not a fanatic. He is a loyal American, but most decidedly a Turkish American. I would leave it at that."

"Thank you, Mr. Larson. You have been very candid and extremely helpful. My client too, is a patriot, so he will certainly understand Mr. Towson's position. Mr. Larson, please forgive me for one small additional question. Do you know Edith Towson?"

"Why no, I can't say that I have ever met her, and Mr. Towson is very spare with personal commentary."

"As a last question, is your firm or you yourself of Turkish heritage?"

"No, however my wife came from Istanbul. Unfortunately, I lost her to cancer about 10 years ago."

"I am very sorry. I was asking, since it occurred to me that perhaps Mr. Towson preferred to associate himself and his company with other people of similar heritage."

"No, I don't even think that he knows about my wife's birthplace until after she died. No, he has associates from all over the world, but a large fraction of his business is associated with Turkey and Turkish products."

"Thank you, sir, for the generous time you have given me. I want to reassure you that the Daniel Towson that I know is certainly alive and active in business."

"Good day, Mr. Chess. Please let me know if your client needs any consultative assistance. We would be very pleased to build a supportive relationship with your venture. Can you share your client's identity with me?"

"I am sorry, but I am not able to do so at this time. But thank you and good day."

I am mystified why Towson has isolated himself from his CPA for a year. Obviously, the firm continues to retain Larson: very strange behavior for a successful businessman.

# PART TWO – THE BOOK

# 26 *FIVE WEEKS LATER*

The group was somber. They sat around the granite table in a wood paneled room and stared at one another. Although there was no head to the table and all the chairs were alike, one of the men led the group by their deference only. When he spoke, the others kept silent, yet when any other spoke, they might interrupt or argue.

The leader finally spoke. "We may have failed." The others looked at him and at each other while nodding. "The best candidate for 'Seeker' seems to have lost interest in his quest. I am afraid that if he doesn't pick up the query again, we may have to take back the armor, and save them for the next generation."

One of the younger keepers interjected "Would you again discuss his selection?"

"Surely; you weren't here when we picked him. Originally, we gave the task of Seeker evaluation to a woman who was one of us. But in her investigation, she fell in love and then married her prospect. Unfortunately, she was murdered by those who sought most for their own power though the Book. Before she died, she sent us a report telling us that he had passed all of her initial tests. At the moment when she would have led him to the key as the first step in the last test series, she was kidnapped, tortured and killed."

"How did the archeologist wind up with the armor?"

If you will remember from your studies, Keepers always search to find the proper Seeker. One who will take our knowledge and share it for the benefit of everyone, not use it to gain power or wealth. The artifacts were originally discovered by Schliemann who came to Troy to reveal its greatness. He was the best candidate at the time – strong, independent, already wealthy, and searching to give back to the world whatever he could find. But in the end, he was just as selfish as so many others in the past. As you remember from your studies, we guided his hand to our city in Turkey, and gave him reign to find our Book directly. But when we tested him with treasure, he forsook the book for his own riches and for personal glory. Remember that in the previous generation, we had tried with the general in France, who sought to overthrow royalty and give freedom, learning and self determination to Europe. But he fell to personal power and crowned himself emperor. The next tests were of the revolutionary in Austria, who sought to rebuild the failed German state and provide a strong educational foundation for the people. They located our three pointers. But his candidacy ended with the reign of terror to exterminate anyone who threatened his power base. Then we looked to the ideals in the Soviet Union: those of communal state and shared wealth drew us to engineer the pointers to them, rather than to the West. The West seemed to have some good ideals, but they were so wedded to the goals of individual wealth, we decided they were not ready; nor suitable. So we again had to retrieve our artifacts."

"Gradually, over the generations, we learned that many brilliant, far-seeing individuals of great talent and promise also joined their dreams to conquest or power. So we always keep an eye on humanitarians and less worldly truth-seekers who demonstrate ideals when surrounded by expediency."

"The archeologist came to our attention from his passionate defense of those who support the restoration of artifacts to their homelands, and the aggressive pursuit of thieves who deal in black market art. When one of our investigators inside the Smithsonian proposed him as a possible candidate, we arranged separately that he be given the armor as the second piece of our puzzle. What is particularly interesting is that both candidates are getting to know one another. If we had not retrieved the key, the confluence might have led prematurely to the discovery of the book and its location. So while we consider re-energizing our primary candidate, we should also carefully watch the secondary, particularly in the event that the primary is also killed."

Another at the table spoke for the first time." Why have you hesitated from pushing forward?"

"My primary reticence is based upon the dangerous ground that we would again place our candidate. In fact, both of them would face similar peril. He has endured great pain and only now is getting a brief measure of happiness. I am reluctant to put him in jeopardy again."

"But Keeper, you must. We are bound to our tasks, whether they are pleasant or difficult. That is what I have been taught and that is what you have demanded of us during my time here. Is it not?"

"Yes. You are, of course, right. In addition, their work together is accomplishing a secondary task, the illumination of a sub-rosa structure within the U.S. Government which subverts information for personal profit. So we must, despite our misgivings, continue on this path. Take the key and find a way to have him discover it again."

"I will do as you ask."

# 27 *THREE WEEKS LATER– LONDON*

It was one of those sparkling days that lie on the fulcrum between the foggy cold of spring and the humid swelter of summer. In the park, the nannies wheeled their prams and prated to one another while their charges balled, snoozed or wetted as their case might be. Older children not quite of school age played or chased ducks around the pond, and old men sat on benches and dreamed of imagined exploits as they waited to die. Gardeners scurried about: digging, replanting, pruning and fertilizing. In their wake the colors danced in the morning breeze and reflected sparkles of sun into my eyes.

I sat serenely on the ancient wooden bench and contemplated my full belly and my full heart. I had not felt this way for years. In fact, I never thought that I would ever feel this way again. Each day astonished me with new joys. The glint off the silver at the breakfast table no longer just reflected the light, but was a prism to memories and pleasures. I heard sounds in the trees that were not there a moment before. We were weaving an intricate web of new insights into each day's occurrences with each other.

"A Shilling for your thoughts" she says as I missed her approach.

"What happened to the penny?"

"Inflation.  Good morning, darling" Marcia sits beside me and throws her arm around my neck for a squeeze and a kiss.

"Did I ever tell you that I love you?" I responded.

"Oh that. Yes, but I thought it was all 'pillow talk' You mean that even after last night, you still love me?"

"Well…" I get a cuff on the ear.

"What shall we do today?" I ask. 'Shall we scare up a car and go off with a picnic?"

"Yes, that sounds like fun. But talk about scaring. The last time you drove here, it wasn't only me being scared, but I think everyone else that we encountered on the road thought that we might do a crasher at every turn."

"Hey, it wasn't so bad. That tram, for example, only had to turn aside a little bit!"

"Yea, I think that whoever was standing on that bus wound up in somebody's lap. But what the hell, maybe they made newfound friends. How many hubcaps do we have left on the car after your encounters with the curbs?"

"Well, there was the one in the Cotswold's, and that particularly nasty one on the Single Track up in near Lake Windermere – I would guess we have two left. Doesn't Hertz require evidence of where we took their vehicle?"

"That's what Odometers are for, my dear. Yes, let's go up to Oxford and do a punting picnic."

We get up from the bench and took hands as we cross the green toward Hyde Park Corner. There are the usual soapboxes of all sizes, surmounted by speakers of every persuasion; each passionately exhorting. We stroll along, taking notice of everything and nothing at the same time. Then something from one of the speakers pierces my subconscious.

"I say to you, the spirit of man is buried in the soul of the horse. Its truth is the key to the future. To unlock the spirit of mankind, seek the key and it shall be revealed to you. Do not look to your church, or your government. But look within the horse's hidden soul."

"Marcia, do you hear what I hear?"

"What's that, dearest?"

"He is talking about the key." I take hold of her hand more firmly and pull her towards the speaker, who had taken a swig of bottled water and was beginning again, holding something aloft.

"We were put on this Earth to be keepers of the book, to be guardians of the flame and protectors of the future. Look to the good that is within you. Come and take this treasure of the mind and make it your own." The man voice was at fever pitch, but no one was apparently paying him the slightest attention. On the adjacent podium, another is warning about the devil hidden in each television, a third about the evils of secondary education, and a fourth something about bodily fluids. Strollers pass by ignoring the irrelevant noise.

In his hand, he holds a wooden horse. It looks just like the one which had been stolen from me so long ago. Stunned, I ask him if I could look at his horse.

"Oh this old thing. I got it in a pawn shop. It's nothing. But I like exercising my lungs every morning, and am always interested in who might stop by to hear me rant." the voice was quite educated, and the attitude somewhat ironic.

"May I see it?" I asked, holding out my hand.

"See it? You can have it for two Pounds. I paid a little less, but deserve to make a profit, right?" I fish into my pocket and drop two Pound coins into his hand. He gives me the horse and then disappears into the morning crowd.

"Have you been taken in again?" Marcia asked.

"Actually, this is going to sound weird, but I don't think so at all. If I am not mistaken, it looks just like the horse that I told you about: you know the one that I put the key into back in San Francisco." I looked around, but the speaker had disappeared. In his place, another had mounted the soapbox and was starting his oration.

"What a nice prize, Simon. We didn't even have to go to a carnival. Oh well, bring it along."

"Marcia, I'm serious. Let's stop someplace and let me open it up. Who knows, maybe the key is inside?"

"Simon. Wait. Let me have it. We should get rid of it. I don't think we should open it up. Simon, look at you. You're happy and relaxed. We both are. This trip has been wonderful for us, and to tell you the truth, I have found something that I never want to lose again. This could be Pandora's Box for us. Do you really want to start up again?"

"Sweetheart, I have no choice." The horse, and all it brought back, broke my day into pieces. I feel that I have to open it. It doesn't matter what is inside, or even if there's nothing. But the horse is now inside my defenses, and the enemy that is inside is not going to stop until we deal with it.

We pass a tea shop and go in to find a small table in a corner. Sunlight plays through the blue and white curtains onto the horse's flanks and on the starched table linens. The hostess brings tea in a Royal Doulton pot, a smaller pot with milk, a plate of scones, Devonshire cream and strawberry preserves, as well as a large pot of hot water, strainers and two Doulton cups.

As Marcia pours the tea, our conversation keeps breaking down into silences, as the thoughts of what the horse implied takes more and more of our attention. "You know, it doesn't really matter if it's empty, but I think that we both know that is not going to be true."

I reach for it, and methodically manipulate the pieces. When I take hold of the ring to give it a pull, I said a silent prayer that it would be empty, and that we could fill it with new memories. Marcia, seeing my hesitation, puts her hand on mine in support and smiles with those lustrous green eyes. I pull the ring. The saddle pops up, and the velvet bag is revealed, just like it was when I had placed it there all those weeks ago Of course, inside is the old key..

Marcia looked down into the compartment and then reaches out and picks it up. From what I can see, it is very finely crafted and golden in color. On the paddle-shaped handle, there are fine etchings of symbols and letters. Rows and rows of symbols are braided together around the rim. The barrel of the key is not round, but octagonal, and on each face there are holes bored into it, varied in spacing and size. The handle bears a raised crest of a horse on one side, and a lightning bolt on the other. Marcia dips into her purse and comes up with a steel nail file, which she lays against the edge of the key. Filing with as much force as she can muster does nothing to the key, but the ridges on the file are flattened. Finally she lays it on the starched tablecloth and we look at one another.

"Simon, I think we need to get back to our hotel. The picnic can wait."

"No! We're going on the picnic, and I will not think about this key today." I pick it up and put it into my pocket. But it was an empty promise.

The joy seemed to go out of the morning as we walk back to our hotel. When we are in the lobby, I stopped at the concierge and asked for a magnifying glass. Inside our room I go to the desk and look at the key under the glass. Yes, the engravings are very sharp and precise. I can't understand them, but knew instinctively that this was the same key. We have to go home and finish what we started. "OK, let's do our picnic," I say gamely.

Marcia looks at me with love and understanding as she replies "No, I think not. I had better make reservations for home, and we'll deal with this."

"I'll at least put off calling John until we are home. But you're right, I'll help pack. Try to get us a ride today, but if not, then we'll have a nice day, dinner, do a show, and then head home tomorrow."

Marcia smiles at me and dials British Airways. While she is on the telephone, I put the key into a watch pocket sewn into my pants at the belt line. She ends her call and tells me there is nothing available until the morning, so we make early dinner reservations at Simpson's on The Strand, and then I call downstairs to have theater tickets booked. There is a new Webber musical that recently opened in the West End, and tickets, though few and expensive, are available. I book two stalls and Marcia starts packing. For the balance of the day, we actually did a picnic and laughed, but in the backs of our minds, the questions loom before us.

Dinner proves to be its usual treat at Simpson's, which is why it's a favorite of mine. Large round-belly carvers wheel around large round-belly salvers filled with roast beef, lamb, pork and fowl, offering slices as they pass. Savory gravies accompany each slice, along with generous puffs of popovers, and mounds of mash, cabbage, and other hearty vegetables. We skip dessert and head to the theater, arriving just as the Overture starts. In spite of our stall seats, we have to wait until the applause before being allowed in, and then settle to a musical fantasy for a couple of hours.

It was quite late when we walk back to our hotel, forsaking the cabs that jingle by. When we get to our room and readied for bed, we are both quiet. As we slip under the duvet, Marcia slides over and hangs on to me, as I do with her, hoping that we never would be apart, and whatever we face, it would be together. We fall asleep that way, holding one another.

# 28 *TUESDAY - WASHINGTON*

We are assaulted by the sweltering heat at BWI as we come out the Arrivals doors. Marcia had telephoned John Crawford when we got off the plane, who agreed to pick us up outside Customs. After warm greetings, we put the bags in the Boot [forgive me: Trunk] and John chauffeurs. It is around noontime so there was not a lot of traffic on the way home. I have no one to call. Stephanie was on extended leave and as I had shut down my office before we left, there was no one else who needed to let know that we were back. Stephanie had found another job but had promised to return if and when I needed her. I assumed that eventually I would call the Admiral, but not just yet. When we reach Marcia's house, I carry the bags upstairs, and then we sat down to our first glass of wine.

"You both look radiant" said John, as he toasts us. "Simon, this past month has actually erased some hardness from your face. Frankly, I expected you both to stay longer, at least until fall. Something must have happened to change your plans. Can you share it with me?

In answer, I reach into my watch pocket and produce the key. I hold it up and then toss it over to John. He looked at it with open-mouthed wonder. "Where on earth..?"

"John, you wouldn't believe it if I gave you the details. Let us say that it was given to me, for what purpose I can't say. But now I am turning it over to you to rejoin the other two parts of this puzzle."

"Simon, it is wonderful" he said as he turns it over and holds it in the sunlight streaming through the window. "It looks very much like the sketch that you sent me, but...there is no question. This key is from the same source as the helmet and the breastplate. The script on it is so tiny, I will need a microscope to read it, but read it I will. You know, I have the diary that Lauren gave me that fateful night when you rescued Emily. But even the diary only hinted at the three-factor code that had been created, but from what I was able to decipher, that the key itself was needed to finally solve the hidden message."

John continued to peer at it through the reading glasses that he had carried in his pocket. "I wonder what the holes are for. I'll bet that the inscription, once we've decoded it, will tell us. Simon, I would really like to work on this right away. I still have half a day. Would you mind if I took it down to the shop right now?"

"Let's do one thing before you take it. Marcia, do you have a digital camera here in the house?"

"Yes, dear; the resolution is really high and we can take a variety of images, rotating the key as we do. Once it is photographed, I can take the image files to the office and we can create a full 3D image as well as a model in pretty much any size, just in case the key is lost or stolen again."

She goes into her study and returns with a Nikon D-80, with a macro lens. Laying the key on her desk, she puts a scale next to it and then takes about 50 pictures, as she slowly rotates the key. Then she takes a few shots of each end, and returns it to John. He pockets it. I offer to drive along with him to the MCI office, but he waves me off. "I can't believe anyone knows that you have the key again, so I should be safe for the few miles until I get it down to the lab."

I accept his explanation a little reluctantly, but walk him to the door. Marcia runs out to give him a kiss, and the door closes behind him.

Once he is gone, I decide that it is time to call the Admiral.

"You're back among us. Where does the search stand?"

He never takes the time for pleasantries. In some ways, it is refreshing.

"Sir, I would rather not describe it on the telephone. May I see you this afternoon?"

"Yes that will be fine. I'll see you in my office at 3."

Before I could say another word, the connection is broken. I come back into the study, where Marcia is uploading the images to her office site, and putting them on a smart-drive as a backup.

During our time in Europe, I had told Marcia everything about my days on active duty with UDT and then ESCORT. Marcia accepted all with no objections or comment, even though she knew that it might give us some problems later. We had talked about our future, and both came to the conclusion that once this book business was completed, Marcia would extricate herself from the NSA, as would I from the Navy, and we would look to a life together that did not involve the government. Fortunately, neither of us had to find employment for some years to come. Financially, we were in very good shape. Marcia's parents had seen to her welfare through a lifetime of judicious investments, and the bonuses that I had received from my successes in ESCORT, though no match for Marcia's, were safely squirreled away, so they could carry us through a bad patch or two. Although we had not seriously talked about it, I have grown to trust her implicitly, although I knew that she did not like some of the violent episodes in my professional past. But what she missed in a violent undercurrent, she more than made up in insatiable curiosity and determination.

She also shared with me more about her work at the NSA, even though their company motto was "NSA-Never Say Anything." Many programs that they had undertaken bothered her regard for personal liberties, and I saw that she continued to struggle with the directives to indiscriminately monitor Americans' communications. I assume that eventually, she would either come to terms with it or resign. But our future together, whatever it might be, will have to wait until this business was completed. Then we will see.

Marcia had decided that if I was going to town to meet with the Admiral, that she would stop by her office as well, and see where the land lay. So it wasn't entirely with light hearts that we parted in the driveway,

The drive to DC was without incident, and I arrive at the office about 2:45. Gina was in Reception, and made a few oblique references to getting together, but I was immune. She must have sensed it, because when she told me that the Admiral was ready to see me, she was all business.

He was in his usual chair, with a few files on his desk. He absolutely floored me when he rose behind the desk and offered me his hand. "I am very glad to see you looking so well. She is a lovely and fine woman, and I wish you both well."

"Thank you, sir" I stammered, more out of astonishment than anything else.

""Now sit and give me a report."

"Yes, Sir." I told him of the encounter at Hyde Park Corner, and the curious man who handed me the key. The Admiral blinked a couple of times, again something that I had never seen him do. Then he asked me if he could see it. I told him that I had given it to John Crawford. He immediately put his hand up and stopped me from saying anything else. He picked up the telephone and barked into it. "Get Recovery and Protection teams out to Smithsonian MCI to keep an eye on Dr. John Crawford and get a team out to his family to protect his daughter Emily, and his ex-wife, Karen Crawford. Do it now." Then he hangs up and turned back to me. "You should have gone with him. So long as these

301

artifacts are not under proper guard, no one connected to them is safe. Now, have you documented the key, in the event it is lost again?"

"Yes, sir. We did a multi-image scan and will..."

"Where are the files?"

"Marcia has them. She's taken them to the NSA to build a 3D-Model."

The Admiral made another call, giving orders to protect Marcia as well, and to get copies of the files from the NSA.

"But Admiral, do you really consider this necessary?"

"Mr. Lessant, [he always calls me that when he is annoyed at me] these artifacts are vital to National Security. It has come to my attention that the artifacts themselves are not so important, except perhaps in an archeological sense. But they lead to a find that can very well determine this nation's future in years to come. I have been assured by several very important members of our government, that this document must be found and secured. This is not simply an interesting puzzle, it is vital to our national interests, and you had better consider this in your future work to find it."

"Aye, aye, sir, but we don't even know what is on the document. How can you say, sir that it is a vital national priority if no one knows exactly what it is?

"Young man, a month ago, there were several interested parties in this hunt, all of which were ruthless in their pursuits. Since that time, the continuing work on the transcription of the armor by John Crawford and his team at MCI, have led us to believe that this book contains solutions to many of science's great puzzles and new technologies as yet undeveloped. Our metallurgists still cannot render an accurate assay of the metal used in the armor. Imagine what is hidden away in the book of these same people? What incredible benefit it would bring to our nation and to our people if we were to find it and re-discover its secrets."

"Mr. Lessant, you must take responsibility for this mission. For whatever reason, you have been given a great opportunity. Someone wants you to have this knowledge, and your government agrees. You are to work on this and this alone, until it is found and delivered. Do you understand?"

"Yes, sir, I do understand."

"We will give you support and your team will get the best technical assistance that is available. You will find this book. Now, get up to the MCI lab and make sure that it is secure. Frankly, I would rather that they were brought to a lab that is in our direct control, and not have a turf war start with the rest of the military and civilian agencies. So for now, they will stay within the Smithsonian's umbrella, but with our protection."

"Aye, aye, sir. I will do my best. But Admiral, I have a question on a related but different subject that I wonder if you would not mind my broaching.

"What is that?"

"Just before we left for our vacation, I asked Dr. Froehlich to look into the possibility of a force within the government that had personal agendas relating to the book and its information. I also gave him a potential connection between the death of my former wife and the attacks on me by the NSA. He told me that he would speak to you about this, with the idea of reopening the investigation into Jean's death, and who might be Daniel Towson's senior partner."

"Yes, he spoke to me about it and we have again looked into the incident in Jerusalem. We are now convinced that a contract party was involved. The Mossad discovered that the explosive used was C-4. The tag chemicals in the explosive identify it as U.S. and from military stocks. It was placed on the ceiling of the floor below her room and shaped to explode upwards. There is no question that she was the intended victim. It was also timed for early morning, when she would be certain to be in her bed. I am sorry to say that we have been unable to identify the contractor or financial source. The anti-American character bias was given to the Israeli media immediately after the incident, and was traced back to this country, but the trail went cold. Considering the fear that was being publicized about Muslim Jihadists, it would be surprising if some enterprising political opportunist did not seize on the incident and turn it to an advantage. The motive for the killing has not been made clear yet. I believe that we will need to wait until a new leak surfaces. Until then, all roads are currently dead ends. Based upon analysis of her remains, she was full of drugs, which indicates that she was probably questioned under chemical inducement. I am sorry that there is no further evidence, although your report on Towson's conversation at his boat does lead me to believe that your Mr. X has a history which includes action against your family."

"The identity of X is certainly someone in our current administration, with ties to the military. The logs which would have shown his arrival at Andrews were erased, as well as all FAA en-route controller tapes. There is no record of the flight, except for the initial fix by Ms. Flynn on a military flight plan filed for Andrews. The NSA connection was traced to the NSC (National Security Council) office at the White House. But the requesting officer there, a Colonel, by the way, has been reassigned and is not available for interrogation. There is a memo that was unearthed by the JCS (Joint Chiefs of Staff) which assigned that officer to his NSC post, but it was a normal in-chain of command appointment, proposed by the Secretary of the Army and approved by the National Security Advisor. His vetting was carried out by the FBI. Formerly, the officer served in the Defense Intelligence Agency as an analyst."

"I believe that you are correct in your assumption that a Mr. X exists, but possibly as a euphemism for a small group of powerful individuals, acting in concert, but for what underlying purpose, I do not know. I am not a conspiracist and am persuaded only by facts. But the facts are clear that there are some parallel activities, not in our overall nation's interests,"

"If this type of group exists and they are after the Book as we are, I think that I should incorporate them into our search criteria."

"What you need to do is keep your eye on the ball. Multiple agendas will only serve to diffuse your work. I will take care of collateral objectives for now."

"Aye aye, sir. Thank you for your confidence in me."

"Nonsense, you've earned it. Now get out of here, I have real work to do."

I leave the office, after picking up a few replacement articles for the ones lost the previous month, including a new satellite phone. On the drive back from the office I call Marcia.

"Simon, I am so glad you called right now. The office is in an uproar. I need to see you. Can you get away?"

"I'm out of the office now, but I have orders to John's Lab. What's going on?"

"Just a minute; I need to go somewhere where I can talk without being overheard. I'll call you back. Give me your new number."

As I left the parking garage, a dark sedan fell in behind me. After a few blocks, I realized that it was probably my protection detail. I was on the freeway by the time Marcia called back.

"Simon. It's a hornet's nest out here. We've been found out. The Security Service has been loosed on groups mandated by any non-NSA initiator, and our investigative group was identified. The Group leader is running for cover, and I'm not sure if our covert purpose will be discovered or not. In the short run, it means that the group is being disbanded."

304

"Mr. X again?"

"I don't know. I only know that it's not just my group, but a large number of special-interest groups. Evidently, a variety of blind groups have been created like I did mine. This looks to me like a general sweep of operations to clean house of superfluous bureaucratic empires."

"How will this affect you?" I queried.

"Well, so far, just the group leadership is slated for interrogation. Since I am outside their regular channels – relegated there, by the way by my Group Task Force Chair in order to consolidate his position – I might get a breather, but eventually, the finger will point to me."

"What are you going to do?"

"If I resigned right now, it would be like drawing a bright spotlight. The real problem is that your access to this channel for information will be cut, if it isn't already. Fortunately, I think that since you haven't used it except briefly, quite a while ago, Security will probably pass it for the meatier dish of insiders who were merrily investigating everyone else. If it goes according to normal, with a little help from me, it will resolve itself into a turf battle between Security and Mission. Security will win, the group will lose, a few heads will roll, and it will go back to business as usual."

"Will the investigation of your group get as high as the National Security Advisor? After all, it was he that you set up as the initiator for the group."

"No, I don't think that anyone wants to take him on. I think that the link between him and the group will remain unchallenged. About the worst that will happen is that the Director will send a note up to the White House, saying that Internal Security will continue to serve as the official investigators for any concerns of the Advisor or the NSC. The Advisor will think, as he undoubtedly does anyway, that the NSA has a screw loose somewhere, and deep six the memo. At least this is how similar communications have been dealt with in the past."

"Marcia, I'll get along without the link, but thanks for worrying. The Admiral has given me pretty much a Carte Blanche as to the book search, so I can shift the access point to his office. But I am really concerned about you. With all this peeking through keyholes going on, please don't do anything that could pick up a tail."

"Too late. I've already downloaded some very interesting audio files from your old friend Towson. Not that it should come as a surprise to you; the conversations involved our Mr. X and mentioned Jean again. According to the file, Towson was told that Jean was an agent of some kind. But I will tell you more about that tonight."

"Was there anything on the tape that could give you a clue to X's identity?"

"No, except that it came from Washington. Simon, please be careful."

"OK, darling, I will just do that. I will see you tonight. But first, I have to get up to Suitland to see John." Interesting, I thought. Towson was still on the trail. But at least he doesn't appear to be farther along that anyone else.

I turned into the MCI lot with my escort still behind. Like me, they were held only briefly at the gate while credentials were checked. The main difference for me was the badge that I am been given. The previous time, it was a red Day-Only Visitor's badge that erased itself in 24 hours. This time, the badge was a green Contractor Badge, with an embedded code to allow me access into the lab itself without an escort. I ask the Receptionist for directions and am shown to the elevator. There are no floor buttons, only a card-key slot. I insert my key; the doors close and the elevator descends. I can't tell how many floors we pass since there are no illuminated numbers, but eventually, the car reaches a stopping point and the doors open. Since this is part of the Smithsonian Institution, I expect to see a somewhat dingy corridor with dusty naked light bulbs in the ceiling and bookcases filled with forgotten artifacts. It is anything but.

The door opens on what looks like a hospital corridor. The floor is terrazzo in a muted brown shade. The walls are plasticized and completely clear of any signs. Across from the elevator there is another card slot directly in front of me. On either side of the foyer, there are locked entrance doors. The ceiling lights are diffuse and bright. When I insert my card into the slot, the doors on my right open and a series of green lights embedded in the floor illuminate a path leading off down the corridor. I follow the lights and as I pass each one, it goes out. The lights lead me through several intersections to a steel door sent in an end wall. I card this entry and it opens to the secure lab.

Inside the door, there is an anteroom with several coated paper clean-room suits on a shelf in sealed packages. A sign informs me to don a suit, boots and gloves before entering. I find one suit that seemed to be large enough for me and put it on over my street clothes. The suit has Velcro tapes to seal it, and integral booties. Once I am suited up, I move through the air lock to a small chamber whose floor is some kind of open mesh. When I step on it, it begins to vibrate and hidden UV lights turned on in the walls and ceiling. When the vibration stops, the door opens to an inner anteroom where I have to step on a sponge mat impregnated with a fluid of some kind. Then the final doors open the lab that looks like a cross between an operating room and a kid's electronic-toy dream. Large pieces of equipment line the walls, and the operating room clusters brightly illuminates the three artifacts on the table. A large suspended binocular microscope is focused by John on the key. The image is shown on a large plasma screen mounted above the table.

"Hi Simon; this key is absolutely fantastic. Can you believe that it is more than 4,000 years old?"

"Hi John" I replied. "How far along are you?"

"The key gives directions in code, for the combining of the texts from the three components, to make a plaintext translation. The main part of the problem was that the text symbols on the key had to be subtracted from those on the armor, not added to them. This is the meaning of the directions to 'draw out the truth.' Each of the component elements of the key became resolved into a discrete logarithm. So our first discovery is that this culture of 4,000 years ago knew higher mathematical concepts. The factor which was included in the key symbols required that it be used to reduce the product of the other two factors, thus making a third factor to open the code. In addition, the key had regular physical place locations on the armor, where special characters would be visible through the key's holes. So the code was a combination of three independent factors, coupled with a positional reference which would require all three artifacts to be present at the time of decoding. No two artifacts alone would be sufficient. Also, it meant that a drawing or photograph alone of any of the artifacts could not be substituted for the real metal item. When I figured this out, it was possible to apply the numeric factors and produce a plaintext transcription. It's like your puzzle box. Looking at any part of it gives you no clue as to where to start, but once you have a starting point, the rest falls in line quite readily."

"So what does the translation say?"

"I have no idea of the complete translation yet. But I can say for sure that I am very close to completing the process in generating the text itself. I tried taking the first part of it and submitting it to one of our most sophisticated computer translators, but with the exception of an isolated word or two, not much progress has been made. There is an inference component that I added to the translator, which looks for common word associations with the translated words, but so far, nothing coherent. At least I know that I am on the right track."

"Are you about done for the day?"

"Well, I could stop. It is monumentally exciting, but very tiring. Imagine a message so clear, with so much promise, from so long ago. It boggles the mind."

"Do you have any clues about the book?"

"Well, the word 'Troy' and 'Trojan' comes up a few times. I can only assume it refers to the ancient city of Troy that Schliemann found in Turkey. But there is another reference, to 'Keepers' or 'Protectors'. I think that it means the book is kept in trust by a succession of Keepers, who were responsible for its safety and secrecy. But where the book could be, I don't know. Originally, I suppose it was in Turkey. If the 'Troy' reference is right, it was kept at that location, or maybe it was created there. I don't know yet. But you know, at least if you believe in Homer's Iliad story, the city was destroyed by the Greeks. So if the book was there, it could be anywhere. But I guess we'll find out more lately. The problem is I don't think this armor will tell us anything more about where the book might have gone. If the armor came from around the same time as the book, it can only tell us as much as was known 3,100 years ago. Probably the best we can hope for is that it will tell us something more about what the book looks like, and the people who took responsibility for it. We'll then have to use that point in time to project the ensuing history, but it will be, at best, only an estimate. One thing is clear, however; that you should strongly consider. You are the one who was chosen, by someone or some group, to seek out this book. I got the armor, but you got the key. Neither of which could be translated without the other. So perhaps it was meant that we both work together. After you lost the key, it was given to you a second time. So somebody is determined that we should have a shot at finding this book. What I don't understand is why they didn't just give you the book itself? Maybe it's some kind of rite of passage. That may get clearer as we go along. Now, you said something about getting out of here?"

"Yes, I certainly did, Ollie. Lead me home!"

John laughed as we exit the lab, slog through the sponge, discard the suits in a flash box, and retrace the corridors to the elevator.

"John, I would be very, very careful about saying anything about what you had found so far. I have a bad feeling that any word about being closer to the book may lose it for us."

"Of course, but this is a scientific discovery of epic proportions. I hope that we have the opportunity to disseminate the details soon. But I trust your instincts, Simon. Now, do you need transportation?"

"Hang on a minute and I will tell you." As we leave the building, my ESCORT car was parked in the nearest Handicapped Parking spot. I walk over and speak to the driver. "I was wondering if you could help me out and drive my car home. I would like to ride with Dr. Crawford."

"Sure, Captain. The Admiral gave us orders to keep you safe, so we will follow you." I toss him the keys and head over to John's car. John is a very careful driver, and makes no unexpected turns or stops along the way. I ask him how Emily is doing, and he replies with a great smile, that she is terrific. In fact, since that night in the parking lot, he and Karen are talking again, taking their cues from Marcia and me, and both seem to have put aside whatever the series of events that led to their breakup. Emily was tickled with the rebuilding relationship, and John was looking forward to wherever it went.

I had noticed the reference to my Navy rank. I was a Lt. Commander when I resigned and would have to talk to the Admiral about how I got bumped up. Not that it really mattered to me. This navy business was strictly short-term although the extra $2,000 per month can't hurt.


On the way home, John continues speculating what might be contained in the book. While I keep an attentive expression on my face, I am thinking of where it could be and who might have it. John's question about why not give me the book directly rambles around in my head. The only answer that I can come up with is that he must be right about its being some kind of test for me. But why me; after all, who am I? I am not a scientist or diplomat, or philanthropist. John keeps talking about medical advances and quantum physics, while I ruminate about that last question. Well, suppose it wasn't 'me'. Suppose there have been many who were given hints or oblique directions as tests, and they all failed. Maybe it wasn't the person, but circumstance.

There is no question that John is right about one fact. Someone wanted me to try for it. But to what end? When we get home, John drops me off. Marcia has not come in yet, so I use my own key to get in, and disarm the alarm system. As I walk though the house, I am constantly touched by her presence. The furniture, art, colors and style are eclectic and feel so integrated that the overall gives a sense of peace. Nothing is jarring, and there is humor in it as well. A painting of a court jester is set adjacent to that of a dour matron. A bold abstract is across from a Southwestern Indian adobe pot. But somehow, it all fits together.

It is amazing to me sometimes how little things like art tell so much about someone. Almost without thinking about it, a comparison of Marcia and Lauren pops into my mind. Marcia has chosen a job that is intensely secretive, yet she is extraordinarily open in her demeanor. Lauren give the impression of innocence, yet is immersed in fabrication and secrecy. Both are physically beautiful, but Marcia's genuineness shines out of her eyes, while Lauren is like a plaster model in a store window. Now that Marcia has come into my life, I can't imagine how barren it would be without her.

I go down to the wine cellar to select a bottle for dinner. While I am considering the options, I hear the front door open and footsteps moving across the front hall. I am just about to shout to her, when a man's voice calls out "The alarm is off. Someone must be in the house. Find them," followed by more steps running toward the back of the house and up the main stairs. I stand very still and wait, holding onto the wine bottle that I had picked. I can hear doors being closed and two voices calling back and forth to one another. "Keep looking," the commanding voice repeats. Then another: "Nobody here, Jack. Maybe they went next door to Crawford's." The voice from the front door says "find Chess' laptop and the other responds "I've got it. It was in the bedroom closet." The first voice then announces "We've got what we came for, let's go." The footsteps recede, a door closes and the house goes quiet again.

I wait another minute or so and then climb the steps back to the main floor. There is no sign of anyone here, nor any sign that anything was amiss. When I cross to the main door, I open it and see an empty driveway - no ESCORT minders. I am halfway down the driveway, when I realize that I still am holding the wine. As I am about to turn back to the house, Marcia's car appears. "Coming to meet me? Where are the glasses?" I lean down and give her a kiss, glad to see she is safe at home. But I guess my expression is not what it seems because she asks "What's wrong?" so I tell her of the invasion and theft of my laptop. She drives the car to the house, gets out and comes back to me with a hug. "I'm so glad that you didn't have a confrontation."

"Did you see the security car out in the road?"

"No, there was no one near the house. Let me call John and ask him as well."

He reports that they are still sitting out in the driveway. Marcia goes into the study. Pulling out her laptop, she logs in.

"This will give them a surprise" she says as she keys in a code.

"What did you do?"

"I initiated a self destruct sequence on your laptop. In about 30 seconds, the computer will fry itself. No point in giving them a chance to access the drive."

"What happens if someone is using it?"

"They will get a hell of a surprise, but it shouldn't hurt anyone."

"Too bad."

I return to the kitchen, open the wine and am glad to be drinking it instead of having to use it as a weapon. After joining me in a glass, Marcia starts dinner while I go watch some news on TV. After dinner, we move to the conservatory.

"If the material in the book is as important as John suggests, How many will want to use it for profit?"

"Right now, I am more concerned about our vulnerability. Even if I hadn't triggered the self-destruct mechanism, the laptop has a lot of self-protection built into it. Any attempt at removing the hard disk, or bypassing the password would have resulted in instant erasure of all data and programs as well as the triggering of the acid capsule that would turn the motherboard to mush."

"Whoever 'they' are, they know about us both, and are willing to move against us, even here. You know, if they get desperate, kidnapping and torture isn't unheard of."

We decide to start a habit of setting the alarm. Even if we can't completely stop someone from invasion, the alarm cameras and audio monitoring will at least give us some clues as to who invaded our home.

I go out and talk to the agents who seem to have returned to the house. I don't recognize either of them, so I ask for IDs. They tell me that they received a call about a possible intrusion next door, and they had gone to backup Crawford's detail, but it turned out to be a false alarm. So after being reassured that everything was normal, they returned here. I told both of them that when they take a protection assignment, their first responsibility it to their protectee, not to any other collateral problem which might crop up. Both appeared to be chagrinned and apologetic, so I let it go. They screwed up and now they know it.

With no reports to the contrary, I decide not to call the office and report the invasion and laptop theft. Instead, I set the alarm and go upstairs. Just before going to bed, Marcia gets a telephone call, and tells me that she has an early meeting with the Security people in the morning

# 29 *1999 MOSCOW*

February 11 was an especially bitter day, with the temperature hovering at about 15F. below zero (-25C.). The sky was the same color as the piles of dirty snow, scraped from the sidewalks. Across from the yellow headquarters building, even the statue of Dzerzhinsky appeared to be shivering. In Red Square, there were no visual differences between men and women, as all were swathed in heavy coats, scarves and fur hats. No concessions to fashion could be seen at this time of the year. Even the teenagers flexing their hormones hid inside their coats and boots.

It was nearly dark, when three men strolled across the square towards the building. "Is all ready?" one asked.

"Yes, our brother has prepared the electrical closet. At his signal, the circuit will be closed, and the short should ignite the insulation. It will quickly spread to the main distribution panel and should put the building out of commission for quite a while."

"Did you get the key to the vault?"

"During my last shift, when the guard was getting coffee, I picked a lock on one of the Security Safe drawers. I also have the key to the vault room in my maintenance set. It is up to us to get through the prison section to the storage room. Do you have the gas?"

"Yes, the carbon monoxide will act extremely rapidly and cause unconsciousness, but will oxidize and should not leave any lasting traces. Hopefully, any casualties will be attributed to PVC gas."

The three men waited by the entrance, making it appear that they were seeking shelter for a few minutes in their trek across the open square. As they waited, alarms suddenly started sounding inside the building, and these were echoed with sirens mounted on the corners of the old Baroque building. They could hear shouting inside and people yelling "огонь [fire]." In a moment, the front doors were thrown open by a crush of people, stumbling over each other to escape. The three men waited for the crowd to pass them, then kept close to the wall as they slid in through the main doors. The guards who normally protect access had joined in the rush to escape the wood paneled corridors which was originally installed when the building was built in 1898 for the All Russia Insurance Company. After all these years and a lack of maintenance, the wood was so dry it would ignite at the slightest instigation. The men passed through the inspection point and into the heart of the building.

The upper floors of the building had, for many years, been the headquarters of the feared KGB. Since Gorbachov and then Yeltsin came to power, the KGB was officially abolished, but the new FSB (Federal'naya Sluzhba Bezopasnosti) performed the same domestic functions under its new name, administered by many of the same men in their old offices. They avoided these upper floors, where the administration managed both internal and external State Security and instead took the stair which led down to the basement levels. In these depths, the tombs and cells of the Lublyanka Prison remained as they had been for 80 years, creating nightmares for people throughout the country. Down through the medium security sections where interrogations were held; they passed through the political prisoner levels to the lowest level. It was said that this was the tallest building in the country, because from this basement, you could see all the way to Siberia.

On their way, they had donned gas masks to disguise their appearance. Guards who passed and challenged them were told that they were searching for the fire source. Smoke was emanating from somewhere at this level, and they occasionally found people who weren't so quick to leave, unconscious on the floors. The walls here were of rough stone: the same material as the floor. It was as if they had descended to a Victorian pit. Rooms with heavy oak doors opened off the main corridor. Most of the cell doors had no windows. At one such door, indistinguishable from others, the men stopped. A key was produced which opened the cell. They left it open as then entered a tomb-like room with a large iron vault on the back wall. A key was inserted into the vault door and turned to a sharp 'click'. The three of them then pulled on the door, but it was stuck shut. At least 50 years had elapsed since this door had been shut for the last time. They pulled hard, first one, then all three, but the handle stayed in place and the vault remained sealed.

"Hold there! What are you doing here?" shouted a question from the corridor doorway. They turned to see two army uniforms, with blue FSB flashes on their shoulders, both men carrying AK-47 Kalashnikovs pointed in their direction.

"We're ordered by the Minister of Security, General Barannikov, to retrieve some important documents that must be protected from the fire," the leader replied. "Come give us a hand."

"Let me see your orders" shouted the army captain.

"There was no time to write the orders. The General directed us to come here at once, right after the alarms sounded. "If we stand around arguing, we will all die and the documents will be lost. I am Major Starkh. Help us right now, Captain – get your ass over here!"

The captain inclined his head to his sergeant saying "go help, I will stay here." The sergeant put his weapon next to the door and grabbed the vault handle. The four of them strained at the door. There was a slight rusty creak, and the door opened a fraction. "Captain, it will take all of us. Be quick." He considered, then put down his Kalashnikov as well and joined in the struggle. Gradually the force of 5 overcame the years of rust and disuse, and the door was dragged open. The leader ran into the vault and began to search among the boxes. Meantime the captain went back to the cell door and reclaimed his weapon. As he pointed it at the group again, he was abruptly hit from behind, groaned and fell to the ground. Two others grabbed the sergeant and one jammed a portable mask on his face, releasing gas from a canister.

From behind the captain, their compatriot who had started the fire appeared. "Quickly, we must leave. The electrical room has been discovered and the fire brigade has arrived. It will be put out in a couple of minutes so we have to be away."

From inside the vault, the leader reappeared with two parcels in his hands. One was round, about double the width of a football. The other was flattish, about 1 meter by 1 meter by 50 centimeters deep. As soon as he carried them out, he joined his brothers in getting the door closed again. Then he locked it. Outside the room, the alarms ceased.

"It's time to change," he said.

The three pulled off their work overalls, which hid army uniforms with the same blue KGB/FBS flashes on their shoulder-boards. Two took the parcels and walked together, escorted by the third, with the captain's weapon. The arsonist joined returning employees and went back to his job in maintenance.

When the three reached the uppermost level of the prison, they were again stopped by guards.

"Where are you going with the packages?"

"We are going back upstairs. We brought them down where they would be safe, and now we are taking back to the third floor, where they came from. Stand aside.

The guards looked from one to the other. They knew that on the third floor was the office of the FIS Directorate, and it would not be good for their futures to stop these officers. So they both fell back and allowed the small party to pass. When they reached the front door security station, the leader produced a forged paper bearing the crest and signature of the Director, giving permission for the three to take out two parcels, with express orders not to inspect the parcels. The Chief security guard, however; ignored the orders and went to his workstation, returning with a large knife. Despite the verbal and written warnings, the guard cut the twine on the large round parcel and pulled aside the paper covering to reveal a bit of gold metal inside. 'Ah, he thought to himself, a personal treasure that the Director is taking out in case of more fires: Very smart.' He then saluted the three officers with their parcels. They walked out of the building and down the stairs to the square.

"Take these home," the leader said. As the two men crossed the Square with the packages containing their old treasure, the Keeper stood for a moment on the steps, ignoring the cold, and remarked to himself that the Soviets could never be regarded as possible Seekers. They are passionate and have the potential, but not under this regime."

# 30 *WEDNESDAY – WASHINGTON*

When the telephone buzzed, I looked over at the clock. It was just past 6."Simon," said John Crawford. "You have to get over to my office right away. It's very important."

"John, what's wrong?"

"No, no. Nothing is wrong. But it is really very important; I can't talk about it on the telephone. "

"Simon? Is everything OK"

"Yes. It's John. He has something important and wants me to come right away."

"He's at home?"

"No, at work. You stay; I will go and call you from there."

"Remember, I have an early meeting with Security. I guess they finally got around to me after all. I have to go, although I would rather come with you."

"Not to worry. I'll be fine." I give her a quick kiss then strip on my way to the shower. Dressing in casual clothes, I wave to the minders at the door and drive to Suitland. When I get to the front door of the lab, John is waiting for me and jumps in the car.

"Let's get away from the cameras and microphones here and go have breakfast someplace. I am famished. Last night, I couldn't sleep, so I came back to the office. I got an idea – but I'll tell you more when we are somewhere else."

John is agitated, but apparently from excitement rather than worry, so I ask nothing. We drove into the Suitland town center and find an IHop. Inside, we order breakfast. When the waitress leaves, John looks furtively around and then hoarsely whispers to me "I solved the riddle of the message" and then sat back with a self-satisfied smile on his face.

"Wow," I comment. "OK professor, give."

"The book contains all that we expected and more. It appears to be a compendium of discoveries which go back to well before Egypt was a civilization, backed with explorations throughout ancient times, to Europe, the Americas, and Asia. Every aspect of discovery and creativity was catalogued and stored in the book. The code which was so impossible to decipher before all three artifacts were put together, as advanced as it is, serves only to conceal the nature of the book, not its location. It speaks of a people called the Hurrians, who seemed to start their civilization in the Mesopotamian valley. For some reason they changed their name to the Afar People, and took on a role as some kind of super-librarians dedicated to preserving discoveries for future humanity. There is a modern AFAR nomadic people living in eastern Africa, however; these do not have any apparent connection to the historic Afar."

The waitress waddled out from the kitchen with a large plate of pancakes and sausages for John, and a smaller dish of scrambled eggs for me. John poured a half-cup of syrup on his, slathered butter over it all, and started in from one corner of the plate. I wonder how he manages to stay thin. In between bites, he continued with his story.

"The code was designed as a test of ability to understand the incredible array of the world's talent recorded in a collection of topical papers – which, by the way are on paper-thin metal plates. According to the text, these plates are virtually indestructible. Each decade, a panel called Keepers assigns individuals to write new pages in the book, so that the contents not only cover ancient science, but also new science as it is created and verified. Simon, the treasure is so stupendous as to exceed the wildest of imaginations. Its value certainly can be counted in monetary terms, but its true value is in solutions to so many problems that have plagued humans since rocks were thrown at animals for food and clothing."

"John. This is wonderful. But is there any hint as to where the book is located?"

He looked quizzical as I guess he was deciding which was more important: the information or breakfast. "Yes, but only cryptically. Simon, you have to remember that the armor is itself several thousand years old. All that it could tell me was a description of the required qualifications for those that were chosen to keep the book. You will have to do the job of seeking. By the way, there is a reference in the text for a "Chosen Seeker" who the Keepers are supposed to wait for and bequeath the book to."

"The Keepers came to the City of Troy in the 13th Century BC and lived among the Trojans for about 200 years, until the fall of Troy in 1154 BC.

Those that escaped joined the returning Greek army. Their plan at the time was to set up a base in Athens. They actually engineered the defeat of the Trojans. Without their intervention, the Athenians and Spartans would eventually have destroyed everything and everyone there. As it was, the army took many prisoners when the city fell, and among the prisoners were the AFAR. But the First Keeper escaped with the book before the city fell, so their long-term plan was pinned to the Keeper's survival. The armor was buried in the City, under the main altar of the Temple to Zeus. It must have been found during one of the digs, perhaps even by Schliemann himself. But if he did discover the armor, then there is no record where it might have been stored in the intervening years."

"When I did some separate research, I found a CIA reference to a cache of art including Priam's Gold and other Schliemann's finds discovered in the Soviet Union after World War II. In 1962 this information reached the CIA, however; no one acted on it. These pieces were put on display after the fall of the USSR, but Boris Yeltsin declared that they are considered the property of Russia, so there is no plan to return them to Turkey. The armor could have been part of that store, but how they got out of Russia, and then came to my doorstep is still a mystery. Simon, this is all I have at this time. What shall I do with the information?"

"Don't say a word. Continue your studies. You must have other things that you're working on. It is particularly important that no one in our intelligence agencies learn of your success yet. It will come out eventually, but I am certain that we need to bypass normal channels for now. Is that OK with you?"

"I don't understand."

"John, there is someone high up in the government who has a personal interest in your work. So long as you still have challenges, you will be left alone."

"Do you know who?"

"Not yet."

"Simon, I trust your instinct in this; but what about Marcia?"

"I think that it is time for Marcia to leave the NSA and for us to go back to Europe. My guess would be that this morning, when she was sent for by her Security folks, she would be put through the wringer about breaches. Depending on the outcome, it will give her an excuse to quit. I have to follow this back to Greece. I don't want to leave Marcia here, so our romance, while true, gives us perfect cover."

"Simon, I trust your judgment. I will tell you, however; that family is very important to me. I won't risk Emily's life for some artifacts."

"I wouldn't have it any other way. But I think that chapter is closed. It didn't work the first time, so there is less likelihood that it would be repeated."

John sponges up the last of the syrup with a bit of pancake. The pervasive odor from the griddle and the ammonia smell from the waitress' table rag next to us are making it hard to keep down my breakfast, so I am really glad to get out of there. I drop John back at the lab. Then I call Marcia, but her telephone is unanswered. It was 8 by then, so I assume she is in her meeting. I thought that I would go directly home. In the rear view mirror, I see my minders behind.

I will have to find a way of breaking with the Admiral. I certainly can't drag them along and still act independently. I am certain that if I go to Europe with the Admiral's blessing on the Book assignment, it will get back to X. I hate to lie to him, but we have to keep our information close.

When I return home, I assess our situation. I still had a lot of little toys back at my office in San Francisco, but will have to do without them. I can't bring a gun to Europe, so I would have to get another after I get there. I use my satellite phone and call a local travel agent. I ask her to book a tour for both Marcia and I anywhere, so long as it starts in Athens. I used our real names, and pay for it with my regular Amex card. While I was waiting for the agent to call back, I try Marcia again, but there is still no answer.

The travel agent calls, telling me that if we could leave that night, she was able to get us on a cruise with air connections to Athens and transfers to the port of Piraeus the following morning. The cruise began in Barcelona, but has stopped in Athens for two nights as part of its schedule. From Athens, it would continue cruising around the Mediterranean and eventually wind up in Istanbul, three weeks later. She asked me if I wanted an extended tour beyond Istanbul, because there was a connection to a slow trip on the Orient Express, lasting an additional 2 weeks, ending in Venice. I tell her to go ahead and add that as well, and the very happy agent hung up, counting her big commission.

I then try Marcia a third time, but this time, the telephone forwards to a recording which says that the number is no longer in service. I begin to get worried and am thinking about driving down to her office, when I hear a crunching in the driveway. I open the door to see Marcia stop in front, jump out and run toward me with a bright red face. "They fired me" she shouts into my chest.

"Oh, dear, I am so sorry." I said into her hair.

"Sorry. Shit. I am pissed," she leans back. "They had the unmitigated gall to march me out of the building, confiscate my ID and then close the door in my face. I can't believe it. I will get them. You can be sure of that."

"Don't worry about it. The timing couldn't be more perfect."

"What do you mean, Perfect! Perfect for whom?"

"Why for us, my dear. Come inside and I will tell you all about it. Oh, and by the way. I am so glad to see you. Thank God you are OK."

"OK? You're damned right I am OK. Those sons of ..."

"Marcia," I interrupted. "John solved the riddle and we are off to Greece together – tonight."

"What? John solved it? Do you know where the..." she looked back at her minders, who had joined with mine at the foot of the driveway "OK, inside it is. Greece?"

"Athens; John said that the Book trail needs to be picked up there."

"Athens sounds great. But what about the NSA? You don't think I am going to let them get away with this kind of crap, do you?"

"Sweetheart; if we suddenly disappear in the general direction of Europe without a good reason, we would be tailed, harassed, and beset along the way, courtesy of 'X' or Towson. This way, our trip can be pitched as an escape after your prejudicial termination from work. It couldn't be a more perfect cover. Besides, I have another idea, but I am not quite ready to talk about that."

"OK, I understand." Her chest gradually stopped heaving as she took it in. We walk together into the house and shut the front door. "So when do we leave?"

"We are booked tonight on a flight which connects with a cruise ship out of Piraeus, but we will skip off the ship and stay in Athens."

"Do you think that we can pick up our interrupted vacation along the way?"

"That's part of my other idea. But I am going to wait until we see what we can find in Athens before I say more." As I spoke, I pointed at the walls and ceiling, and then holding my hands out with palms up, I shrugged my shoulders. Marcia is certainly a quick study. She nods and points to her ear. There is a very real possibility that her house has been wired for sound.

We walk through the foyer when another call from the travel agent comes in, confirming our second two week add-on. She tells me that she'll courier documents over to us this afternoon. Then we start packing. From inside the closet, she says "Simon, I can believe it. The NSA has been a part of me for so long, that I can't believe it is over. Thank you, Simon."

I keep packing. Her words have touched me and there is nothing more that needs to be said.

When we finish packing, the doorbell brings in the courier, who has arrived by motorcycle. I sign for the documents, and then close the door. My satellite phone rings. It is the Admiral.

"I am sorry to hear that your girlfriend was fired. She was a good worker over there. Maybe we can use her here."

"Admiral, she is really distressed over this and wants to get away. I am going with her. I know that you have me following this book, but Crawford hasn't made any significant progress yet, so until that happens, I am like a fifth wheel. I need to go with Marcia, but I will change plans the moment John makes progress."

"You're going on a cruise?" he asks.

"Yes sir." Of course he knew already. I wonder what else he knew. "We leave for Athens tonight, then tomorrow to Piraeus and the boat. I was just going to call you."

"Well I am glad you didn't ask me. I would have said no, and you would have told me to go to hell, which would leave us in another stand-off. This way, I can be magnanimous and wish you well. Are you going to make an honest woman of her?"

"Sir, she is a very honest woman. But it is certainly on my mind. I know that you have some concerns about an agent's value after marriage, but I hope that if I decide to go through with it, I hope you will give me your blessing."

"Of course, my boy. I was so sorry when your wife was killed, and am very happy for you. Full Speed Ahead."

"Aye, aye sir, and thank you, sir." I hung up, not without some misgivings for lying to him. But I am sure he already knows the exact truth. It is uncanny how nothing escapes him.

# 31 *THURSDAY - GREECE*

Fortunately the First Class seats that the agent booked for us allowed us to lay full length on the plane, so it was a relatively comfortable, though a short night. The flight attendants on the Air France aircraft seems unusually friendly and courteous to the likes of us Americans, and breakfast is actually edible. Even the croissants are flaky. Coffee, though, is the usual airline fare. I am not sure exactly what is wrong. The look says coffee, but the smell and taste leaves a lot to be desired. It must be the water.

When we land in Ben Epps Airport, it is just another sunny Athenian day. We suffer the access bus, with its cadre of armed guards escorting us to the terminal. Inside, Customs is a breeze, and while we wait for our bags, I share a plan that I developed. "What we need to do is to find a couple that can take our place on the cruise, so no one will be the wiser when we stay in Athens."

"That makes sense. But how do we go about dealing with passports and check-in at the ship?"

"It really should be quite easy. When people get to the dock to board a ship for the first time, they show passports and travel documents to board. Once on board, their passports are traded for credit cards to use as shipboard IDs. So long as they are with the cruise, the cards are good for everything, including inter-country passport control, local IDs and shipboard re-entries. At each port of call, the Customs and Immigration people only check the passports in the ship's safe, and do not compare them with the actual passengers. Usually this is a formality, since cruise ships bring a lot of buyers to the various ports. All we have to do is to use our documents to get the cards, and then switch passports before exiting the boat. We can then turn over the cards to our pigeons, and they're good for the trip. They will never be found out, so long as they don't draw special attention anywhere. If their own passports are actually the ones in the vault, when they get to the final debarkation point, they will be returned and the credit cards shredded, so no one will be the wiser."

323

"You've thought this out pretty thoroughly. But what will happen when they turn in IDs that don't match their passports?"

"By then, the cruise is over, and we can give them a cover story. Also, the passports will have their actual pictures, so the cruise line won't hold them back."

"OK. So we are looking for a young couple, close to our ages and looks, that wouldn't mind a vacation and playing a part in this scam. Not so easy, McGee."

We both start searching around the airport. Marcia selects Baggage Claim, while I take the Check-in counters. There are a lot of couples about, but none are even close to our appearances, particularly with Marcia's red hair. After an hour, I am getting quite frustrated. Then I see Marcia coming towards me with a young couple in tow. "Simon," she calls to me. "Come and meet Tom and Rita Coleman from Cincinnati. They are on their honeymoon and were just bumped from a flight to Paris."

"Hi Tom, Rita. Did Marcia tell you what's going on?"

"Oh, yes," breathes Rita "and I am so sorry that you have to hide from Marcia's father. He must be an awful control freak."

Marcia picks up the story. "I was telling them how father is very dependent on me and constantly demands my attention and presence. If he finds us on the cruise, he will have his people take me back and we need to get away. If you take our trip and give us a break. It will give us time to get married. After we are married and return to the U.S., he will have to let me go."

"You really will give away your cruise?" asks Tom. "This is no scam?"

"No, Tom, we don't want a thing from you. We'll go with you to Piraeus where the ship is waiting, check you in, and then you're off while we stay. Please help us."

The two of them take a couple of steps back and talk quietly, then come back with smiles on their faces. "We'll do it, we don't believe it, but we'll take a chance. It's a lot better than fighting for days over our missed flights and a broken reservation in Paris."

"Great. Let's go."

We get our bags and then the four of us take a shuttle to Piraeus, which takes about an hour in the heavy Athens traffic. When we get there, we find the ship and follow the plan exactly. At the check-in desk on board, there is a crowd of both new arrivals joining the cruise like us and those leaving for a day in Athens. It is a fairly easy trick to show them our passports, palm them and hand them the Colemans'. We also hand the Colemans' bags to the ship's Porter. They don't check the tickets against the passports before issuing the on-board cards in our names, only checking the reservations. We use the cards to get off the ship and hand them to Tom and Rita. Then use their new cards to get through gangway security. At the end of the cruise, when Tom and Rita exit the boat, I told them all they have to do is drop the cards in the waste basket, and innocently ask for their passports with their proper names. With 'Simon and Marcia' safely on the ship, we take the shuttle back to Athens and find a hotel. There are stiff penalties for registering under phony names, so we use our real names and trust that the trail to the ship is followed and whoever comes looking, doesn't pick up on the switch.

On a chance, since it is summer and many have left Athens for cooler climates, we tried the Royal Olympic, a 5 star – 5 story glass box at the foot of the Acropolis, in front of the Temple of Zeus and near the Plaka Market quarter. The hotel is clean, cool and comfortable. Both of us decide to take showers. We order a small light lunch while we luxuriate in the big garden tub, and then after eating, stretch out on the oversized king bed and take a nap.

At about 5, we wake almost together, and find that in our living room, a bottle of local wine has been left by the management. Since no one in Athens eats before 10, we share a glass of wine and map out a strategy.

"If they found me in London, they can certainly find me on their home turf. Perhaps we should just be conspicuous for a couple of days, and see if anyone contacts us."

"Don't you think it is a bit risky to be publicly in view? It might bring the dogs back on our scent.

"I wouldn't want to make the newspapers. But let's try some sightseeing in places where these 'Keepers' might be lurking."

"I'll make a list." Marcia gets out the guidebook starts making notes. After a few minutes, she copies her short list onto a fresh piece of hotel stationery. "We have a lot of time until the city wakes up for dinner at about 9:30 or so, so why don't we start at the Zeus Temple across the street?"

"That works for me" I reply. The temperature is close to 90 with some humidity, so we dress as lightly as we can, barring impropriety. Out the front door, we cross the Odos Athanasiou Diakou, a divided roadway which separates the hotel from the temple grounds, and walk towards the block where the temple once stood. All that remains is the foundation outlines, and a couple of clusters of isolated columns. One corner of the building is a testament to the Hadrian reconstruction, but the rest is gone. At this hour, with the heat of the day still upon the city, most but the short-term tourists are still napping. We walk slowly around the building site, and then out to the triumphal arch, through with we see the outer edge of the Plaka District. Above the Plaka, looming over the district is the Acropolis with the Parthenon pointing east towards us.

As we approach the arch, a lone man who has been leaning against it pushes off from the column and approaches us. "English?" he asks.

"American," I reply.

"I take you to special discount shops in the Plaka."

"No thanks." We start for the crosswalk to negotiate the 8 lanes of traffic on the separating street.

"No charge" he adds as he catches up to us. "My name is Stefano. I help you find anything that you look for."

Marcia responds to his offer "How about an old book?"

"There is one very special bookshop that my cousin has. Come, I show you. If I am with you, he give you a special price."

Marcia looked at me with arched eyebrows. I nodded and gestured to our new host to lead the way. I wish I could have brought a weapon, but we'll just have to be watchful. Traffic lights seemed to be more a request than a demand. We waited for an opportune moment and then dash across the wide boulevard. Upon safely reaching the other side, Stefano leads us into the rabbit warren of narrow twisting streets in this 1,000 year old market. I decide that if we turn into a particularly lonely alley, I will cut this adventure short. Around the corner from a well-populated café, a bookshop is marked by bins filled with old books, maps and drawings, flowing out on the street. Stefano leads us inside, and disappears into the back of the store, presumably in search of his cousin. After a few moments, he reappears, leading an elderly short and very fat man with a dark olive complexion protruding out of a rumpled shirt and black pants with a torn pocket flapping as he approached. His only bright spot was a carefully trimmed white moustache which was waxed to points

His voice was surprisingly deep and he spoke English with a decidedly British accent. "Good evening. How can I help you?" He inquired.

Marcia answered his question. "We were searching for a rare book that was written in Troy many centuries ago."

"I have some old books, but I am afraid that none of them are that old. Books of that age would have been written on papyrus or acanthus leaves. Our oldest books here date from the 18th century, but I would be very pleased to show them to you."

"No, this book was inscribed on metal leaves."

"I am sorry but I never heard of a book with those characteristics. Where did you learn about this book?"

"An archeologist friend of ours told me about it."

"Then you must go to the National Archeological Museum here in Athens. Perhaps someone there will be able to help you. Would you like some coffee?"

"No thank you. But we appreciate the suggestion about the museum." Stefano, who had been listening to their conversation, pushed off the overflowing rack he had been leaning against, and piped in "I would be pleasured to show you the museum."

Marcia flashed a brilliant smile at him, which immediately caused him to flush in adoring lust. "No thank you, Stefano. We have many sites to visit first and have an introduction from our archeologist friend in Washington." Stefano was crestfallen. To have such a beautiful woman turn him down flat was clearly not something he was used to.

I looked around the store and decided if I saw something that Marcia might like; I would buy it as a thank you to the old man, and to recapture Stefano's faith in us. As I scanned the titles, I saw that books were not arranged by language, but by general subject. I didn't see anything that particularly interested me, so I started looking through the folios and prints. One particularly intrigued me – a set of 'Spy' prints from Vanity Fair Magazine showing caricatures of British political leaders in the first half of the 20th Century. Picking it out, I waited until Marcia was absorbed in another part of the store and purchased it. Stefano offered to have it delivered to our hotel, so Marcia wouldn't know. I offered him some money for the service, but he refused it, saying that he was entranced by her and would be honored to offer this small service.

With our business concluded, I waited until Marcia was done, and we left the shop. It was still too early for dinner, so we continued our wandering. Deeper into the quarter, we pass another café, where bouzouki music wafted out the front door. I suggested a coffee, and Marcia readily accepted. As we settled into the somewhat smoky atmosphere and ordered sweet coffee, I excused myself. I had a mission. Telling Marcia that I would be back in 5 or so minutes, I left by the front door, retreating from a raised eyebrow.

About a half block from the café, I had spotted a jewelry store called Byzantino, which seemed to specialize in old Byzantium pieces. One necklace caught my attention, but I had given Marcia no sign of my interest when we first passed. I ring the bell and am admitted by a young, well tailored clean shaven man, who was casually, yet elegantly dressed. Pointing to the necklace in the window, I ask him if I can see it more closely. He unlocks the window showcase and brings the piece in, placing it on a black velvet cloth which had been placed on the counter.

It was one of the most beautiful and carefully crafted gold necklaces I had ever seen – a ¾ circular shield of yellow gold surmounted with twisted braids of yellow and white gold, fashioned into flowers. At the ends of the shield, rectangular gold blocks surmounted with beads, connected it to a necklace of fine gold strands, perhaps 30 or more, woven into a flat braid. The craftsmanship is so fine that I expected it to be way beyond my budget, but I am surprised when a reasonable price is quotes. I make my mind up immediately, and ask the shopkeeper to wrap it for me. As he is wrapping my treasure, the young man explains that unlike many of the jewelry stores in Athens, all their pieces were made in the store, and were one of a kind. I thank him and walk back to the café, the necklace burning a hole in my pocket – but that is for later.

When I re-enter the café, Marcia is no longer alone. Two men were vying for her attention. Both are extremely disappointed when I show up to reclaim both the girl and my coffee. But they put on brave faces and back off without even a whimper, although one of them claps me on the back and sighs.

As we sit there, I thought about a decision that I have come to, as of yet unvoiced. But sitting there with the soft melody emanating from the Bouzouki and the warm coffee puts me in a frame of mind that I always want to keep with me.

"Marcia," I said, although it came out like a bit of a croak "I realize that we came here to Greece on a particular quest. But I have found something far more important to me."

"What's that?" I could tell that she sensed something was coming, and realizes that I am a little nervous.

"What do you think of the idea that since we are here in Greece, that this would be a really great place to have a honeymoon?" As I ask my question, I reach into my pocket, produce the tissue wrapped package, and place it on the table in front of her.

"Honeymoon? Oh Simon, Oh yes, yes." Big tears started to roll down her cheeks as she opens the wrappings and takes out the necklace. "Is this what you really want? Are you ready for this? Do you really want to marry me?"

"Yes, yes and yes again. Marcia, I love you. I am so glad that we are together, and want to stay together."

"Do you think that we can be married here in Greece?"

"When we get back to the hotel, I will talk to the Concierge. I really would like to find a little town somewhere outside Athens. Do you much care if it is Eastern Orthodox or would you prefer somewhere else?"

"It doesn't matter to me. I would be happy even with a Buddhist ceremony, so long as it is legal. A small town church sounds perfect to me."

I put the necklace on Marcia's neck which she insists, in spite of her casual attire. I stay in a euphoric fog all the way back to the hotel. Depositing Marcia in our room, I call down and ask the Concierge for a few minutes of his time. He invites me down to his office. After telling him of our marriage plan, he gets very excited about helping us. He tells me that they have had many weddings in the hotel, and a few up at the Acropolis and at the Temples, but he never met a couple that wanted to do it in a small town, surrounded by local villagers. He tells me that he will look into nearby towns that we could go to.

About a half hour later, the telephone rings. It is the Concierge. He tells me that there is a small town south of Athens on Cape Sounion. The town is called Legrena, and it has a lovely Greek Orthodox Church. He also says that the town has a very old temple to Poseidon, in case we decide to have the wedding there. But I reinforce our earlier decision. He then tells me that he has telephoned the church, and the priest would be willing to have us come and speak with him, and follow with a small wedding on Sunday after Mass. There are several weddings scheduled for that day, but as it is normal for weddings to be sandwiched back-to-back during the summer months, they will make space for us. The town will be turning out for weddings that bracket ours, so we will have our town-witnessed ceremony. The only problem that the priest sees is that there is no sponsor and we will need a license. If we go tomorrow, the priest has offered to help to find a sponsor for us. I quickly share the information with Marcia, who nods with shining eyes. So I ask the Concierge to arrange it. To pave the way, the concierge calls and asks the priest to post a notice of the impending marriage on the church door. The only holdup might be the obtaining of the license, but the Concierge assures me that he has a cousin at the Ministry of Foreign Affairs, and will go with us first thing in the morning to walk the papers through. He asks me if I can get a letter from the American Consulate saying that they have no objection to the marriage, but when I say that I can't in time, he brightens up again by suggesting that a few more Euros should overcome that problem as well.

So with that in the works, we decide to find a place for dinner. On the way out, we stop at the Concierge's office and I generously cover him with banknotes for his help. He waves us away, saying over and over that it is not necessary, because it will give him so much pleasure, but on the other hand takes the notes and slides them into his desk.

Above us, as we cross the main street again, the sky is turning dark and bright lights illuminate the ancient Parthenon, Propylea and Erecthium surmounting the Acropolis. Visitors sometimes walk up the inclined ramp at night to see them up close, but the hill is home to thousands of hungry cats and itinerant thieves, so daytime is a better choice.

As we stroll along, my antennae are still tuned to the people around me. I don't know if we are being followed, but my senses go on heightened alert. Marcia senses the change in my hand pressure, and looks over to me in question. I say quietly to her that it is possible that we are being followed, but that this is a characteristic of any tourist area. Vendors, thieves and beggars are known to follow a tourist for long distances, looking for just the right opportunity to snatch and grab, or just to turn on the charm for a valueless product sale or handout. So even though I am alert, we continue our stroll. But I keep us to the more populated streets to reduce our risk as much as possible.

Before leaving the hotel, the Concierge had recommended a place for dinner, and also said that we had an appointment to see his cousin at 10 in the morning and the priest at 2. He arranged a car to drive us. I stop a passing taxi, and give him a piece of paper on which the Concierge had written down the restaurant address. We are whisked away, hopefully to a good restaurant and not to necessarily another cousin's den.

The restaurant is just opening at 9:30 when we pull up. The taxi driver tells us that he will return at midnight, since we are expected to take at least that long to have a decent meal. The restaurant is expecting us and as we are shown past a table full of delectable desserts, we find ourselves in a

330

miniature garden. The restaurant backs up to the north side of the Acropolis, and is set high into the hillside. At the back of the restaurant, catacombs make up the setting for the kitchen and service areas. Where we are, Athens spreads out in front of us, and hot pita bread with just-made Hummus and Tzadziki made with local yoghurt and chopped cucumbers are served to whet our appetites.

Our dinner is simple, but extremely well prepared. I particularly love Moussaka, the national dish of ground lamb, potatoes, eggplant and tomatoes, covered with Béchamel Sauce and baked. Marcia opts for baked lamb with tomatoes, made with baby lamb chops and very ripe local tomatoes. We share a salad with feta, lettuce, kalmata olives and tomatoes, sprinkled with lemon juice and very light oil. For dessert, we have Ghalaktoboureko, which is cream of wheat custard in philo, served with honey, and sweet Greek coffee. By the time coffee comes, it is close to 12, and we are ready for bed, although full to the brim. The taxi arrives on time and returns us to the hotel.

Back in our room, it is so refreshing to have no messages, no emergencies, and no surprises, but that of each other's company, which continues to surprise and delight us.

# 32 *FRIDAY – GREECE*

After breakfast, we are picked up by the car that the Concierge had arranged for us. When we get to the Ministry, he is waiting for us. We follow him in and he speaks to the Guard. In a few minutes, a man comes down the main central stairway and welcomes us in English. He is of small stature, but struts like a pouter pigeon, making sharp jabs with his chin as he walks along the corridor. This functionary ushers us to his office, where we are crowded into three small chairs in a tiny room with a huge desk. From behind the desk the Concierge's cousin tells us that normally the process of obtaining a Marriage License for a foreigner is handled before the foreigner leaves their country, since it takes many weeks to get the paperwork completed. He starts enumerating the various documents that we will need: Birth Certificates with an official translation (that alone takes two weeks), Letters from the U.S. Government stating that there are no official impediments to the marriage, translated with a Diocese Seal, and a current passport. Further, he explains, not all applications are approved. Although Marcia begins to get agitated, I sit and listen, recognizing that these are tactics to raise the ante. When he completes his litany, I thank him for all his help, and tell him how we realize that he has gone out of his way even to see us on such short notice. I tell him that in America, both Marcia and I are very busy with our volunteer work for local charities and have been so deeply committed to our work that we simply forgot to take care of all this paperwork in advance. Marcia looks at me out of the corner of her eye as if to ask if I had taken leave of my senses, but plays along.

I believe that he understands my references when he says that he too has a number of local charities that he works for, but has so little time because of his important job, that he is forced to substitute money for the time that he is unable to give. I tell him that I am so grateful for taking this extra time of his, that I would be glad to help him contribute to these charities in his name. We settle on an appropriate amount, and he takes a Marriage License form out of his desk drawer. With our passports in front of him, he fills out the form and then has us sign them. Opening another desk drawer, he withdraws three large stamp pads – green, blue and red - and half a dozen rubber stamps. Carefully examining each one, he inks them and stamps in various locations on the form. From another drawer, he takes out a metal seal, which he uses to emboss on top of his own signature, after which the concierge adds his signature as Witness. Two more stampings; this time with the blue Greece national seal, completes the process. Then he folds up the form and hands it to us in exchange for a rather thick wad of Euros. We thank him for his assistance and depart.

The concierge leaves us at the car and returns to the hotel with another libation of notes filling his pants pocket. Marcia shakes her head and we get into the car. "Business as usual?" she asks me.

"Field work always needs some help" I answer. Then we are off to the Sounion peninsula.

We drive out of the city south until reaching Piraeus, then turn southeast along the coast road for about 40 miles. With a population of three million people, Athens itself sprawls, but the further we travel, the more rural it gets. Vineyards line the left side of the two-lane road and stony beaches on the right. Although the road dips and turns, the trip is smooth and comfortable.

The town of Legrena is spread out with perhaps 150 houses. It has two main attractions: a beautiful crescent beach right at the tip of Cape Sounion on the Aegean, and the ruins of a Temple to Poseidon, which brings many tourists each year. Off the main road, in the center of the town is a brick and stone Eastern Orthodox Church When we arrive, the church is empty, but the bell by the main church door brings the priest out from a small house set on the north side of the main church building. He is wearing his black cassock, but has a large white napkin tucked into his collar which flows down, under his black, scraggly beard and almost covers his large cross on its chain. He is thin and has smiling almost black eyes, which peer up at us. He points to the door of the church, where there is a document pinned to it, I can read both our names on the document, so I assume it is the notice of our impending wedding. The Concierge had told us that in the city, we would be required to take out an advertisement announcing our wedding, but in a small town, it could be posted on the church by either the Mayor of the town or the Priest.

He welcomes us into the church and invites us to sit at a pew, while he stands in front. With very little Greek but for tourist questions, I am loath to ask anything. But he laughs and tells us that with all the tourists in Greece, it is necessary for everyone to speak at least 5 languages. We assure him of our intent and thank him for officiating. He tells us that he has found a couple in the town who will act as our sponsors on Sunday, and just wanted to meet us ahead of time, since Sunday will be a madhouse. He invites us to come back with him for coffee, but takes our decline gracefully and sets the time for us on Sunday next. As we are leaving, he looks down and sees his luncheon napkin still tucked into his collar. With a little embarrassed laugh, he pulls it out and holds it behind his back with one hand, while offering the other. We smile along with him as he suggests that we visit the Temple, particularly if we are looking for a 'gift of the gods' for our wedding; because we will undoubtedly find it there. When I give him a puzzled look, he replies that Poseidon has been around for far longer than the Christ, so he would be foolish not to respect the contributions that came from the antecedents of modern Greece. I assure him that we will go to the temple and thank him for his courtesy.

The driver, who has been patiently waiting in the parking lot, nods and sighs when I give him our new destination and pulls out of the driveway, while the priest waves goodbye with his napkin. We turn left on the main road and continue towards the southern tip of Cape Sounion, where the old temple has stood since 440 BC. From the main road, a small loop leads to the temple itself. It stands high on a cliff overlooking the sea, with a new concrete bunker-like Administration and Concession Building close to the road.

Most of the Doric columns that made up the outside row of the temple are still standing, although some may have been re-erected. The platform is wide open, and there are fallen sections of columns and friezes littering the site. Behind the main columns, the cliff face thrusts out into the Aegean, We pick up a snack at the concession counter and walk out to the temple, carrying our coffee and pastries. When we get to the site, there are several guides who approach with bundles of postcards and offers to explain the temple in a half dozen languages including Chinese, Japanese and Korean. I wave away the guides but one is quite persistent, following as we walk around the ruins, explaining Poseidon's role in Greek mythology, history and culture. When we get to the altar area, the guide grabs my hand and pulls at me, pointing to the stone floor. He tells me that right here in this spot is where the great statue stood, that faced its twin across the sea in the City of Troy. I tell him that I understood that Zeus was the patron of Troy, not Poseidon – I remembered that from John's discourse on the armor.

The guide looks at me strangely. I guess he was not used to tourists contradicting his explanations. He tells me that if I knew that, I should also know that Poseidon was the twin brother of Zeus, and that that they had a third brother, Hades. After they arranged their father Cronos' death, the three drew lots to divide up the kingdoms of the earth. Zeus won the leadership of all the gods and took the sky and sun for his realm, Poseidon the sea, and the worst lot, which was the underworld, became the domain of Hades. So by twin, the guide had meant his twin brother, Zeus. The guide continues on to tell me that the treasures of Zeus have been never distributed to the world, but Poseidon's had been already given. He then let go of my hand and walked away.

I returned to where Marcia was examining a relief carved on one of the fallen friezes, and we make our way back to the car. With the hour approaching 4, we start back for Athens, taking a northern route this time. The driver explains that by the time we get back to the city, the traffic will be particularly bad, especially as this afternoon begins the weekend.

The drive back is quite a lot longer, and we do not arrive back our hotel until after 6:30. This time, when we enter our room, there is a blinking message light. With great trepidation, I pick up the receiver and hear that there is a message from John. I ask Marcia if she told John where we are, and she tells me that she had, but gave him express directions to not contact us unless it was extremely important. The message is innocuous, just that he called and would appreciate a call back. As it is lunch time in Washington, I return the call, but to his cell telephone.

He interrupts my questions. "Simon, thank you for calling I hope you are enjoying your cruise and want you to know that everything is all right, but that I will have to relocate to a new lab, so that we would not be able to reach one another for some time to come."

"Do you know where you will be?"

"I am afraid that I cannot say, but your friend Robert may know." I presume he is referring to the Admiral. He then continued "He has offered to keep an eye on Emily and Karen since I won't be able to leave my location once I am installed."

"John, thanks for telling me. I'll leave you a message when we know we are coming home."

"That would be perfect. I am sorry, but I have to go."

"Wait, John. I wanted to give you some news. Marcia and I have decided to get married."

"Simon, that is wonderful news. You couldn't have made me happier. When?"

"The day after tomorrow."

"Oh I wish I could be there for both of you. Please take some pictures, if you can." With that, he hangs up.

Marcia puts in a satellite call to Karen, to make sure that she is all right. Once she is assured, she lets her know that we are enjoying the start of our cruise, and will be getting to Crete tomorrow for our first major stop.

After we go to bed, and later, when the lights are off and Marcia is softly snoring next to me, I think about our day, Sounion, our omnipresent guide, and the peculiar message from John. It rattles around in my head as I try to interpret his cryptic comments. I guess that John was forced to move with the armor to a safe house somewhere, and is being guarded continuously. Also, that our plan for him to delay revealing the decryption was necessary, and he is worried about the safety of Karen and Emily. That part is clear, but I don't understand why he would have to relocate. It seems that the subterranean lab at MCI was quite secure. Maybe it has something to do with the inevitable turf war that had to surface between the Navy and the other intelligence services over who gets to claim the armor's secret and the lead on the book. But of course, there is Towson and the unknown factor.

Then my thoughts turn to the strange conversation with the guide. The only element that would make sense is if, somehow, the hotel's Concierge was persuaded to direct us to that town and temple, and then it would follow that our 'guide' was making allusions to our search. But that would be far too much fantasy for my imagination. We'll just have to take it on face value, and realize that anything which even remotely smacks of our search, or a book, or Trojan history sticks to my heightened awareness. With that, I decide that it would be far better to get some sleep.

# 33 *SATURDAY - ATHENS*

Marcia wakes this morning with an idea. Nudging me, she starts talking before her eyes are open. "Simon, Let's see if we can pick up anything at the National Archeology Museum. If there are any people who have a long-term interest in historical artifacts, we will find them there.

"Good idea. Get me coffee."

"But darling, if we get an early start, we can drop hints about recently discovered armor and see if anyone picks them up."

"Good idea. Get me coffee."

"Come on, today is Saturday. Remember that tomorrow, we won't have any time to do anything else but get married, so by Monday, three days of the cruise are gone already with nothing to show for it. Let's go, Move it."

"Great idea. Please get me coffee."

"What a grouch. Is this our future? You demanding coffee before wishing your almost new wife a good morning with a big kiss?"

"Yes dear." With that, I get whacked soundly with a pillow. "I don't have to take that" and come back with a similar weapon. We bat each other a few times and then dissolve into laughter.

"Actually, you are right. That is a good idea, and one that I will be very happy to go along on, but first..."

"Yes I know, get me coffee."

She leans over me and grabs for the telephone, but not before it rings. Instantly, the mood evaporates. But it is only the concierge, wishing us a good morning and asking if we would like to order coffee.

In about 15 minutes, the waiter arrives with coffee, rolls, cheeses and sweet butter. There are also two fresh oranges and a grapefruit. With breakfast laid on, we plan our morning: First to the Museum to drop some hints, and then some touring. Marcia has never been up to the Acropolis, and would like to walk though the Parthenon. So with our morning planned, we dress and take a taxi to the museum.

After two hours there, looking at artifacts, and asking questions of museum workers, we inquire if there are any curators of Trojan history in the museum. A surprisingly young man meets us in the exhibit and talks to us for more than an hour about various finds at the Trojan site, and leads us around to show some of these artifacts in the museum. He makes special note to us about some of the recovered Trojan loot; I guess because we are Americans "Unfortunately," he says, "there is still a battle going on between Greece and Turkey over the ownership of many of these items. It's like the Trojan War is still going on, but this time, it is the Turks that are laying siege to the Greek's store of treasure. This has been ongoing for 50 years, non-stop – much longer than the original Trojan War, if one were to believe Homer."

"Have you heard of any other finds in Troy that can be traced to older civilizations before the first city was built?" I ask.

"Periodically, these rumors crop up, but so far, they have all been dispelled. About 50 years ago, there was a story going around that a great Hittite set of armor had been found at Troy, and that it was of a very unusual metal, even harder than the iron and the early steel that the Hittites smelted. But they never turned up. These stories continue to surface from time to time. If only some of them turned out to be true. Imagine what we could learn from artifacts like these. Oh well, dreaming is not productive in my line of work. What else can I do for you?"

"You have been very kind." I give the curator a hotel card with my name on it. "If you hear of anything, we are going to be here for a few more days, and would love to help in a search."

The curator disappeared into his offices, and we leave the building. "I would have sworn that there was a spark of interest when you talked about a search, but I guess no takers." Marcia pulled me along, "OK, enough work, let's go to the Acropolis,"

We choose a taxi from the line waiting at the entrance to the museum grounds, and ask to be taken to the foot of the Acropolis ramp. It's only a 5 minute taxi ride, and by then we want something for lunch. So rather than beginning our climb immediately, we go into the Plaka and pick a Souvlaki shop, where a huge cylinder of shredded pressed lamb and pork is turning slowly on a spit. The cook slices down the edge and the meat falls into a pre-warmed pita, to which is added some sauce and a few onions and peppers. The whole mess is wrapped in wax paper and handed to Marcia. A second is prepared and handed to me, and two cold beers are taken out of ice, uncapped and shoved into our other hands. We turn back to the ramp, munching our sandwiches while vainly trying to let the juices fall on the pavement.

It is a long climb, but the view as we ascend is fabulous. The Plaka is spread below, a twisted warren of tiny streets and alleys. Beyond it, there is a large open space with the Temple of Zeus and gardens behind. Beyond that we can see our hotel. The buildings on top of this Limestone monolith don't start to make their appearance until we are nearly at the top. One can imagine the Panathenian parade, starting miles away at the city gates in the walls, stately walking along that path, bearing the new clothes for Athena, circling the Zeus temple and then climbing the stairs to the Propylea, where the final steps lead through its portal to the mesa of the Acropolis. From there, the Parthenon, painted in all its red, blue, gold and green glory, would shine in the sun and deep within it, the Protector of Athens would reflect the gold of the sunrise down the long axis of the temple. Three times they would parade around the building and then go inside to pay homage to Athena Parthenos, while others would dress its larger Athena Pallas in the center of the main Acropolis square. Then for days, there would be athletic contests and other games to honor their patron.

This afternoon, it is a hot and dusty climb, but even with the colors gone, the Parthenon was starkly impressive. Standing on an enlarged plinth, the stately Doric columns rise to the roof, where once the frieze ran around the building depicting the annual procession. At the ends of the building the pediments showed the birth of Athena at dawn on the east side and the contest between Athena and Poseidon on the west side for who would be the patron of Athens. But to see these epic dramas and the frieze, one has to go to the British Museum in London, to view the prize of Lord Elgin. Many agree with the notion that he preserved them, while easily as many claimed he stole them. But whichever, they are certainly not here today.

Since I had visited here previously, I see that the rest of the south columns had been re-erected, and the building looked to be almost whole; however, there is still no roof. While I waited for Marcia to sate herself on the majesty of the architecture and history, I took a seat on one of the stylobate steps that lead up to the temple. I become aware of the many tourists and locals who regularly visit the site, bring picnics, and enjoy the views. Tour groups abound in every hue and language. I become aware also, of someone standing behind me, on the topmost step. He seemed to be looking at me but when I looked at him, he turned away. Finally, the man stepped down towards me. "Are you a tourist?" he asked.

"No, not exactly, why do you ask?"

"It is only that you look familiar. Is your name Chess?"

"It might be. Who are you?"

"Who I am is not important. But what I have to say to you may be important to you. Is that your lady? Pointing with his chin over to where Marcia was peering at one of the remaining sculptures high on the wall.

"Yes it is. Why do you ask?"

"She is very beautiful and tomorrow, you are getting married?"

"Why yes. How did you know?"

"Tomorrow, after your wedding, be sure to visit the Temple of Poseidon again. And this time, hire a guide. He will show you things that you could not see in the museum." With that, he steps down from his perch and strides quickly down the hill path.

I realize that it is the contact that I had been hoping for. But if he found me, who else might find me? I decide to say nothing to Marcia until we are back at our hotel.

After getting her fill, Marcia pulls me over to the Erecthium, where the Maiden caryatids hold up the roof, and then to the Propylea and the site for the Athena Pallas statue. By then, the sun is starting to set and we tiredly walk down the hill, this time directly to our hotel. When we get into our room, Marcia is still bubbling about the buildings. She doesn't seem to be tired at all, yet I am pooped. But I put on a game face and suggest we go downstairs for a drink before resting up for dinner.

"I have to find a dress for tomorrow. What time do the shops close?"

"At three on Saturday, but there are some that are open later right here in the hotel."

"I have to go find something. And don't give me that 'I need a nap' routine. You go as well and get something a little more appropriate."

"Do you want me to come with you?"

"Not a chance. Now go."

So up I get and down to the mall level. In a men's store, I ask the clerk what would be appropriate to wear at a wedding. He asked if I was a guest or in the wedding party, and I said that I was the groom. It didn't faze him one bit. He then asked where and when the wedding was planned for. I told him tomorrow in a small town outside Athens. That got to him. He suggested that with the hot weather, a white open collar dress shirt and white pants or black pants would be just fine, as well as appropriate shoes. I looked down at my feet, which were stuck in sandals. He shook his head and asked if I knew my bride well. He told me that there were many arranged marriages still throughout Greece, so I shouldn't be surprised at the question. But then he said as long as I did know her, it would be OK to wear what I had on, but to get new socks. After twenty minutes, I was fully armed with wedding clothes, and went back up to our room. There was a small parcel on the table, with a return address in the US. A courier delivered it while we were shopping.

When I opened it, out fell a small box and a note, which turned out to be from John. It said "You will need these. I had them made by cutting an old relic with a specialized torch developed at NASA. Love to you both, John" I opened the box to find two golden rings, one slightly wider than the other. From his note, I gathered that these came from the inside of the breastplate, and were two of the rings that held laces to tie on the armor. I tried the thinner one. It fit almost perfectly, while the other I would bet would fit Marcia. How absolutely incredible of him!

I put the rings in a drawer and lay down on the bed. I thought about staying awake long enough to see Marcia safely back in the room, but just fell asleep with my old clothes on, and my new clothes spread out on the bed beside me.


## SATURDAY EVENING

I awake to find that the clothes I had left on the bed were gone and the room is too quiet. I call out, and am very relieved to hear her answer me from the bathroom, telling me not to come in. As my heartbeats gradually returned to normal, I lay on the bed and then remembered the rings. "Marcia, you have to come out. I have something to show you."

"That's nothing like what I have to show you" she said. I waited, and then she came in from the bathroom. The dress is white, and reached her knees, but on top it's strapless; a sheath of white silk, with a thin diamond necklace choker, and her hair swept up and piled high on her head. She wears no makeup, nor did she need any. It is the most beautiful vision I had ever seen. Her 5'-10" height is accentuated by tall white heels, with slim pointed toes.

"You are so beautiful," which made her lovely green eyes tear. She is Aphrodite, the bride of Poseidon, with the flaming hair and regal bearing. But she isn't Poseidon's bride, she/s mine; or at least she would be tomorrow.

343

"Come, let me show you." I opened the night-table drawer and took out the rings. Handing her one, she tried on the wider version, which was only a tiny bit large for her finger, but would work quite well.

"Wherever did you get these?" she asked.

"They came from John. He cut them from the breastplate. They are at least 3000 years old."

"Oh, my God. They are beautiful. Let me see yours" and I hold it out to her. "Perhaps we will be able to etch something inside." I said.

"Oh no. These are ours, but not permanently. When we are old and die, they shall go back to the armor."

"Yes, of course."

She returns the rings to the drawer and goes back into the bathroom, re-emerging in a robe. "May we eat in our room tonight? I don't feel much like going out."

I agree with her, and we order up a light supper. Even though it is well before the dinner hour, the kitchen accommodates us and sends up an assortment of small specialty plates with a bottle of Rosé. After dinner, we put the table outside our door and turn on the TV. The BBC has no news of interest, so after a while, we both start to doze and turn out the light. I realize that I had forgotten to tell Marcia about the contact up at the Parthenon, but it will wait. Tomorrow is our wedding day and perhaps a new day of discovery.

# 34 *SUNDAY - GREECE*

At breakfast, I shared with Marcia the contact that I had received at the Acropolis and added my concerns. I lost one wife and I want to be sure that I would not lose another. The thought crossed my mind that perhaps we should take care of the book business first, and see that it was safely home, before starting a new life. But the radiance that I saw in her face last night dispelled any further thoughts in that direction.

The morning passed quietly, as we took our breakfast. Marcia made a passing reference to the bad luck created by a groom seeing his bride the morning of the wedding, but then she said that that this tradition went back to times when arranged marriages were the norm, and children were not encouraged to see their prospective spouses until the family contracts were fulfilled. Today, I had hired a rental car so that we could manage our own fate. As the morning wore on, we pack up our clothes and documents, and took to the road south. As we moved out into the country from the enclosing city, I saw no tail. The car that I had rented was a convertible, unusual as a choice for many Greeks, due partly to high pollution levels in the cities. So we attracted stares along the roadway.

When we arrived at Legrena about noon, the full day of weddings is already underway. The priest had offered us his house to change, so Marcia disappeared into the bedroom with her clothing bag, and I changed shirts out in the living space. The room was tiny; whitewashed plaster both outside and in, with a few simple pieces of furniture: a reading chair, a small couch and table, and a bookcase. In the corner was a card table that would barely seat two, a couple of folding metal chairs and a coffee pot. The stove was a two-burner camp stove, and the refrigerator was barely waist height. There was a small black-and-white TV set on a folding table, and a small portable radio stood on the kitchen table. I assumed that the bedroom was equally sparsely furnished, mostly from castaways and donations. I am surprised at the menial level of existence, since the area's homes are quite large and well landscaped. But when a person chooses to live on faith and the kindness of others, it portends a difficult existence.

There was a bride and groom just coming out of the church when I walk across the yard. By custom and after guidance, I go around to the front and wait patiently for my bride to arrive. One of the previous guests had retrieved a bouquet from one of the morning weddings, which she hands me to hold, with a little bow and a smile. The guests are all chattering and exchanging digital images with one another as I wait. Then Marcia comes around the corner of the building, radiant in her white strapless sheath, with her flaming hair wrapped with a bit of lace on top of her head. Several of the guests 'ooh' at the Vogue Bride suddenly transported to their tiny village. They part and make an aisle to me, except for raised cell phones for pictures. I hand her the flowers, and we walk together into the building. When we reach the altar, the priest is waiting for us, along with another older couple: our sponsors. The priest asks us for our rings and license, which I retrieve from my trousers pocket. He looks at the license briefly, signs it, seals it with an Archdiocese embosser and hands it back to me. He holds the rings over our heads and blesses them. Then he puts them on the third finger of our right hands. The sponsor then takes the rings off our fingers and swaps them between us, as the priest chants. Three times, the rings are swapped while the chanting goes on. Finally, on the third swap, we have our own rings back. The priest then joins our right hands and holds them together, telling us to remain while he prays. Then he turns back to the altar and takes two thin crowns linked by a white ribbon and places them on our heads. The sponsor swaps them three times like he did with the rings. Then comes the blessing of the wine, and we are told to drink from our common cup, three sips. He then removes the cup, removes the crowns which are put on the altar for the next couple, and separates our hands. When the chanting stops, he whispers to us that we are married, and can leave.

There were no vows, and no kissing, but we did anyway. With the kiss, the guests break out in applause. Taking her hand, we leave the church by the front door. As we walk back to the priest's house, we can see the next bride making her way up to the church door where her nervous groom waits.

Back in the house, we both change into casual clothes, and Marcia carefully wraps her dress in tissue before putting it into her bag. I take out a small bundle of Euros and leave it on the kitchen table with a Thank-You note to the priest. We are then into the car and drive down to Poseidon's Temple. I don't feel much different: it was so quick and I didn't understand a word of it.

When we get to the temple, the lot is full of Sunday tourist cars and busses. I find a narrow spot against a boulder, and we climb out. The concession stand is surrounded by young families with children, clamoring for sweets, mixed in with some old folks with bright yellow nametags, who look lost without their groups. Past the bunker, the walk is lined with hawkers of cards, photos, maps, and mementos of ancient Greece. There are also many guides with license badges on their caps and pamphlets under their arms, lying in wait for anyone traveling by themselves. I did not see the guide that accosted me a couple of days ago, so we pressed on.

When we reached the Temple itself, the colonnade stands out against the sky. Marcia and I sit on the stylobate and wait, holding hands. Both of our thoughts were somewhat remote from the book and our tasks ahead, as we look out over the water, and feel the sun and its brightness reflecting off the white marble. Then a shadow passes, and I look up at our guide from the other day.

"So you have returned. What is it that you are seeking?"

"We had hoped to find a book here."

"This is no place for a book" he said as he laughed out loud. "This is a place to enjoy the rapture of old Greece."

"I'm sorry, but we were told to come here today to satisfy our quest."

"And what will you do if you find this 'book'?"

"We will take it back to our own country, and see that it teaches our children," Marcia adds. "We have just been married, and plan to have many."

"Well, congratulations to you, then. Very well, come with me and we will see what we can find together, Mr. and Mrs. Chess."

"Simon, 'Mrs. Chess indeed!'"

The guide has already moved off so we follow after him. On the seaward side of the Temple, the guide leads us on a narrow path between the boulders, and down the cliff. I am glad that we had switched to our sneakers, or we surely would have ended the marriage too soon with a fall into the Aegean. We help each other down until we reach an apparent dead end. There is a narrow gap between a projecting rock and the cliff wall, into which the guide slips. It would be impossible to see from the water and a casual tourist or even devout explorer attempting the path would be deterred by the path's apparent end. We both sidle around the rock and find a tiny slot canyon which goes back into the cliff for about 20 feet. Then the canyon also disappears; ending in a flat rock face. The guide leaves us there and returns back to the entrance of the slot, disappearing around the rock. When there is no movement for a moment or two, I think that maybe this was a dead end in another sense, as well. Then a door

347

slides open in the rock face, which is filled by another man. Although there was nothing familiar about him, the HK4 pistol with a long black silencer pointing at us is all too familiar to me.

"Good afternoon, Mr. and Mrs. Chess. My name is Daniel Towson. Please come in."

"Do we have a choice?"

"Yes, of course. But it might be unhealthy for you both."

He looked well versed in close work, as he stood in the doorway just outside hand or foot range. While the pistol was pointed at Marcia's torso, his gaze flicked back and forth between the two of our faces, looking for the slightest hint of pre-movement. It wasn't worth it. I began a step towards the door, and he immediately backed up and re-sighted on Marcia's face.

"I will explain everything to you. Please come in. It doesn't look like much on the outside. Please go to the end of the corridor, through the double doors." He follows us in. Once we pass through the outer doorway, it slides shut. From the outside, it must again resemble a rock wall.

The corridor is hewn from the native rock. On the stone floor are oriental carpet runners which muffle our footsteps. Along the walls at regular intervals, wrought iron sconces illuminate the rough ceiling and walls. As we walk, we pass several inset doors. All are closed. At the end of the corridor, double doors stand open, leading into a large circular room with no windows, but illuminated by rows of electric sconces, like torches, along the wall. In the center is a large circular marble disk, which serves as a table. Around this table are 12 chairs of some dark wood, yet covered in bright cushions. On the floor are scattered more oriental carpets, mostly red and black Turkish Bokhara designs with their large elephants' foot motifs. Against one wall is a shelf, on which stand several bottles of wine, glasses and a somewhat out-of-place white refrigerator. Towson opens the refrigerator and brings out plates of stuffed grape leaves, bowls of pistachios, olives and a plate of soft cheeses, which he places on the table, along with a basket of the omnipresent pitas. Three glasses of light red wine are poured and he indicates chairs for us.

"Before we get started, I want you to tell me what exactly you are looking for."

I look closely at his face, but get no indication of receptiveness or aggression either. "Why would I say anything to you? First of all, I don't know who you are, but you aren't Towson."

"I am Daniel Towson." Doubt can be read on my face like a flashing sign. "I know you are surprised and curious, and I am being rude. This will take some time, so please, eat and drink."

"You greet me with a pistol and then suggest refreshments?"

"Forgive me. We have to be very careful. Would you please show me your passports or other identifications?"

"Very well, but I would like to know exactly what you want of us?"

"That's quite simple. I want to be assured you are who you say you are, and why you have come to Greece. Obviously, you didn't come here just to be married. I also want to know who you are working for."

I looked at his face and saw no resemblance to the Daniel Towson that I met in the U.S. But we have come here on a quest, so I believe that we'll need help to get to the next step. I had retrieved our passports from the hotel in preparation for our wedding, so I handed them to Towson and he looks at both carefully. Then he hands them back to me, and puts the pistol he had been carrying into a drawer in the serving counter. Then he looks at me expectantly.

"We came here seeking answers to a puzzle."

"That's quite generalized. I'll ask again, but only for one last time. Why did you come here?"

"Look; I came here with good intentions. You made the approach to us, not the other way around. Obviously, you want something. So just tell us and stop fencing with me." I smacked the table and pushed myself up. "Marcia, let's go."

"Sit down, Mr. Chess."

"My friends and I were given a key, and a couple of old archeological pieces. Although we do not have them any longer, they have opened the door to our search for another part of a puzzle. We thought that we could find it here in Greece."

"Do you make your search for someone else, or for yourselves?"

I thought for a moment. John had talked about the search for someone to use the book for the good of the world, so I could have parroted it back to this Towson. But somehow, I guessed that he would sense the exaggeration and throw us out. I decided to tell him the truth, and see where it led us. "Initially, my search was to help someone find if her father's killer. Then it became a search to thwart someone who was

349

threatening me. Now, I really can't say. The whole idea of our search is mostly because I am curious as to where it will lead. Without the search, I would never have found Marcia and with it, maybe I can find something useful, as well as putting some old fears to rest."

Towson turned to Marcia. "Why are you involved in this?"

"I believe that there is an undercurrent in our country that is exceedingly corrupt. Perhaps any discoveries we make will not change this, but we are going to try. Maybe this sounds righteous, but it is not meant to be so. I despise those forces and have an idea that our search will bring out the very worst. Our exposure may be just the ticket to pull their fangs. Besides, look at what it has brought me personally. That is something I wouldn't trade for anything."

Towson shifted his gaze to encompass both of us. "Unfortunately, noble causes will not get you closer to your goals."

"You mean to say that the Book is not here?" I interjected.

""No, this is merely a meeting place for us who watch over our old secrets."

"Can you tell us more about it?"

"I will tell you that we do manage and protect the Book. As you know from your work with John Crawford, the book comes from an ancient group of people who called themselves the AFAR. Exactly where they came from and how they came to be associated with a venture such as the Book is not terribly important. But it was started as a way of recording all the greatness that humanity developed; either on its own or with divine inspiration, it matters not. What is important is that at one point in history, we believed that a record needed to be created, because societies in which great discoveries were made inevitably destroyed themselves. The first permanent book was begun approximately 2,000 years ago and has been added to quite regularly.

"For 112 generations since Troy, we have had two charges: protect the Book, adding to it as new discoveries are created, and replicating ourselves with the next generation of Keepers. Our ultimate ancient charge is to find a "Seeker," who is prepared to use it for the benefit of mankind. Our search is not limited to any single country or culture. As the world becomes more populated and cultures proliferate, we need to constantly expand our search, and this means we need a younger group of Keepers. I have been instructed by our group to offer you an opportunity to join our work. We had two initiates, but both are now gone. One of them, Simon, was your former wife, Jean."

"She was one of you?"

"Yes. In fact, it was part of her job to evaluate you as another candidate. But then she was killed."

"What happened to her? The official story is that Palestinian Terrorists set off a bomb in her hotel, but recent events are pointing to a more personal agenda."

"She was sent there, as you both know, to get her out of Washington. We do not know exactly who identified her as one of us, but she was discovered captured and tortured in an attempt to get her to reveal the location of the Book and the rest of our clan. When she resisted, she was killed. I am so sorry, Simon. I am responsible, since I brought her into our enclave, and gave her the assignment which ultimately led to her death."

"Do you know who gave the termination order?"

"No, we do not. But we do know that it came from America, although the contractor was from Lebanon."

"You do know that whoever had her killed is still out there, and we will find him."

"I am certain that you will. But let me continue. Simon. We gave you the key as a test. One of us placed the key in your pocket in San Francisco, to see how you would react."

"Mr. Towson, is Lauren Sylfern part of your group?"

"No, we know of her through her father's interest in our documents. Although he was German, and actively working on weapons projects for the Nazis, we believed that he hated the war, and was interested in putting science to more constructive uses. Thus he became a candidate. We gave him the opportunity to study the armor and key just after the war, when he was directed to Cyprus by your government. Unfortunately, before he was able to effect a translation and decoding, the armor was stolen. We are not certain who was responsible for the theft, but the final result was that it was sent to Germany, where it was hidden for a time, before being taken again by the Soviets and sequestered for another 40 years. We never really understood why Stalin did not put a team on the armor. Eventually, we learned of its location, and were able to re-acquire it."

"I assume you sent the armor to Dr. Crawford."

"Yes, we did. Dr. Crawford was another one that we have been watching for some time. When he resisted the urge for personal glory which would have followed his revealing of the inscription translations, he continued to rise in our estimation. But he and the armor seem to have disappeared."

"They have been sent to a secure site, administered by the intelligence agencies."

"We hope that he is safe. If and when he surfaces again, we have already decided to offer him a role in our group. I see that you both are wearing rings from the armor."

"Yes. John Crawford was able to remove them from the inside of the breastplate and sent them to us." said Marcia as she rubbed the ring with her other hand and turned it on her finger.

"It seems to be slightly large for you. Before you leave here today, we have special tools here that can shrink it to fit better."

"Just don't mess with it too much. After all, it means a great deal to me."

"Don't worry," said Towson, as he pushed a button which brought a man to take our rings away. She looked sharply at the new man, but he held up his hand as if to tell her not to worry.

"Mr. Towson, thank you for your story and invitation. I think that Marcia and I share your concern for your Book, but I am not sure if we want to take on any responsibilities associated with it without making a joint decision. Tell me, if we were to accept, what specifically would you want us to do?"

"We Keepers are spread out around the world. Six times a year, all of us travel to one of our secure sites to coordinate our work. But aside from the meetings and our continuing search for a Seeker, we have no specific duties. Occasionally, as we did with you, we have to actively participate in someone's life for a brief period, but for the most part, we maintain a watch over any efforts to learn about or seek out the Book."

"I have a question for you" said Marcia. "You talk about this work as if your goal was peaceful, yet you personally have been an arms dealer and death trader for many years. How can you resolve this contradiction?"

"Yes, I have sold arms, and did so without remorse. I have no apologies, however; I will say that I ceased this business about 20 years ago, and have kept my Import and Export business strictly in the venue of non-lethal products. My arms dealings preceded my role in this group. Back at the end of World War II, I discovered that of the two scientists that came to Cyprus to study the armor, one of them attempted to return it to the Third Reich. I tried to stop it, but was foiled in my attempt. My actions came to the attention of the Keepers, and they started keeping tabs on me, until they eventually offered me a position."

"But what about the people on your boat in Vallejo? They were not benign."

"My boat was sold a few years ago, when I moved most of my holdings back to Cyprus. I still kept a warehouse there, and my company uses it, but not the boat. The boat was sold along with the dock. You mean that someone has been using it in my name?"

"Yes. Both the boat and dock bear your company name and logo. Just before coming out here, men there tried to kill me."

"I will look into that. I have a Manager in Oakland that I will have to ask."

"I followed someone who has been claiming to be you. He went to the boat and met someone else, who he seems to be reporting to. Have you some idea who either of these two people might be?"

"No I don't."

"Doesn't it bother you?"

"I said that I would look into it."

"I have another question or two for you." I continue "Why isn't Edith here with you? I should think that when you relocated to Cyprus, you would have brought her with you."

"Yes. Unfortunately, Edith and I separated some time ago. I understand that she was murdered, which makes me sad. I also understand that the police had you as a suspect but then dropped you. Can you tell me how that happened?"

"I suppose it was that my gun didn't match the bullets taken from her body, I arrived at her house after the killing, and had no motive. Do you have any idea of why she might have been killed?"

"Perhaps someone thought that they could get information about the Book or its location from her."

"Yes," I said. "I suppose that is the case. One more question, please. Where is the Book?"

"Of course I knew that you would ask. It is in a safe place. In our group, only the most senior Keepers know the location of it, just to be secure. But if you accept this responsibility, after initiation, your trust will be tested for five years. Then, if you are elected to the brotherhood, it may be shared with you."

"Mr. Towson," asked Marcia, "Why, I wonder, is there a subterfuge connected with your identity? I mean, of all the people that someone could have impersonated, why you?"

"Good question if you are telling me the truth about an impersonator," answered Towson. "Since the Book could be traced back to Turkey, and most everyone knows my history and sympathies, wouldn't it be likely for me to get potential cooperation from others that have a similar desire to return to Turkey what is rightfully ours?"

"Yes, that could be it. But the other man who took your name has been identified as the real Daniel Towson by people that know him. Can you prove that you are Towson and not the imposter?" Marcia realized, as I did; that something didn't ring true and challenged him.

"I can't prove it, except that those of us here are the brotherhood of Keepers, that have a special purpose, and I am one of those. I do not much care if you believe what my name is, but just that you understand our responsibilities, and that we are offering to share this with you."

"Do you mind if we went back now? Oh, by the way, why are you located here, in this cave?" I questioned.

"Above us is the stone base of the great Temple of Poseidon, god of the Sea and brother to Zeus. The twins have guided us for thousands of years. It is only fitting that we are sustained by the power of the Temple above us. Though the Greeks identified with these two gods, these brothers are Turkish in origin. The worship of Zeus and Poseidon dates back to even earlier than ancient Troy. The Greeks, with their entire military, could not defeat the noble Trojans in honorable warfare, so they resorted to using our Gods against us in treachery. But enough of these Greeks; you must decide whether to join us or not. Your future depends on your choice."

"Is that some kind of threat?"

Towson dropped his easy countenance and his face became suffused red again. "I am only relaying what I have been instructed to tell you." He pressed the same button and again the minion appeared in the doorway. But this time, he was holding a pistol, which he pointed towards us. "Now I am going to speak for myself," said Towson. "I know that you are here under false pretenses, no matter what the others say. You are right. I am not Daniel Towson. I am his brother, Rashid Xyso. You made a big mistake when you killed my brother and his wife in your greed to obtain the Book. Our family will be avenged when you have a little accident on your wedding day. Now get up and go out into the hall." He reached into the drawer behind him and pulled out his gun as well. Then he nodded towards the doorway as his man backed up to remain out of arm's reach.

"I did not kill your brother or his wife. If you are indeed Rashid then the man in America who tried to kill me, and who killed Edith must really be your brother Daniel."

"No, Daniel is dead. Edith is dead, and you must now pay. Now move out towards the entrance."

"But you know the truth. If he were dead, you never would have told us that you are him. Your motive for killing us must be something else. What are you hiding?"

"Just move out into the hall and stop trying to confuse the issue."

"I am curious. You spoke of the Greek treachery in defeating Troy. Was it not the plan of the AFAR people that ultimately lost the day for the Trojans?"

"That is a lie! It was the Greeks who betrayed us. They did it then, and have been doing it ever since."

Marcia faced Rashid and spoke in a reasonable voice. "But the translation of the armor tells a different story. If you are true to your oath, you must know that the Greek king was treacherous and the people were duped into believing a lie. You have a right to be angry at the leadership, but not all the people. Rashid, we are not your enemy any more than the ancient Greek people. The AFAR were protecting their history, as you are still doing today. Simon and I are with you in this. Please believe me."

"After what you have caused today, how could I not avenge my brothers?"

"What are you talking about?"

"I will show you and maybe you will feel some remorse before you die." With that he waved his gun for us to move down the rock corridor and then stopped at the second door on the right. Shoving it open, he pointed inside. As the door opened on oiled hinges, we could see a half-dozen bodies, sprawled on the floor, with puddles of blood everywhere and spatters on the walls up to the ceiling. They had been surprised, because several looked like they had been sitting at reading desks or in lounge chairs. No one was alive. Marcia gave a little cry when she saw the mayhem in that room. Towson pointed to the bodies. "If you hadn't come

355

here and drawn attention to us, this never would have happened. Look at them. They didn't have a chance."

Marcia, spoke, her voice shaking with sorrow. "But we had nothing to do with this. Yes we came here again, but we were directed here by one of your own. Mr. Xyso," added Marcia. "I work for the U.S. Government and have been investigating the death of your brother. I am convinced also that it was faked. We had nothing to do with either your brother's death, or his faked death, whichever it is. Why did you set up this elaborate game with the cave and the book? It would have been far simpler to ambush us somewhere."

Towson's gun wavered a little. Before he could firm up his resolve, I added "Rashid, we never told anyone of our visit here. The only ones that knew are the concierge at our hotel and the driver that brought us here on Friday. Perhaps someone learned of our visit from them. But we never knew about this hiding place until the moment that your guide brought us. Please understand that your friends are victims of someone else's dirty work. Did your brother know of this place?"

"No, he never knew."

"Did Jean know?"

"Yes, but I can't believe that she told anyone. Besides, if she did, why wait until now to attack us. No, it had to be you."

"If it will make you feel that you are avenging these terrible deaths, then go ahead and kill us too. But you will never be sure. The one that really did it will be free to do it again, perhaps even worse next time."

Towson pressed a stud on the wall, and the door slid smoothly into a recess. He indicated that we should go through first. With his associate as a backup, there wasn't much I could do. I gesture to Marcia to go in front and I follow behind, more slowly to give her an advantage of a little more distance. Towson stayed back behind and the other man remained inside the door.

When the passage became narrow, I stopped and turned back to Towson. "What exactly were your instructions regarding us? I think that I should know."

Towson raised the pistol to my head and replied "I was told to give you our invitation and then to send you off with a small additional clue."

"Do you think that this invitation would have been offered if there was any doubt of our trustworthiness?"

"No, but I cannot leave my family unavenged, so you have to die. It is our way."

"I am really very sorry for the loss of your sister-in-law. I too am very angry at her wanton murder and will do my best to track down the killer. Rashid, I have killed in my work, and I have killed on the battlefield, but I have never killed an innocent old lady in her shower for no reason at all. I do not know for a fact that your brother murdered his wife, but I do know that he threatened Laura Sylfern and tried on two occasions, to have me killed. So I would put him at the top of my list for Edith's death. I am afraid that is all I know now. I do understand your pain and I do understand honor. Your revenge is misplaced. Look into the eyes of my wife of only a few hours, if you don't believe me."

Towson gestured with the gun to continue my last steps. I turned and walked on until we reach the large boulder, where I sidle around it. Although now I am out of his sight, I take a few steps and then turn and wait for him. When he reappeared around the rock, he looked oddly at me for a moment, and then lowered the pistol. "Why didn't you run?"

"I told you. I did not kill either of them. You must trust what I say."

"You could have run. I would have if you were pointing a gun at me and threatened me the way I did. But you waited. I don't understand. But I do believe you. All right; let's leave it at that. I will do what my brothers asked, and then we are finished. But if I find out that you have been lying to me, nothing will stop me from finding you and carrying out my promise."

Marcia, who had walked on was waiting near the head of the path. She came back down when she saw Rashid drop his aim I held out my arms to her and she walked fully into them, giving me a hug. Then we both turned to Rashid. He said "What you seek is where it has always been," and then he started back towards the cave.

Marcia called out to him "Rashid, you have forgotten our rings."

He nodded and motioned to the other man to come. Then he took the rings and returned them to Marcia. She put hers back on her hand and gave me mine. Then we walked up the path along the cliff edge, towards our future.

357

# 35 *MONDAY – TURKEY*

On Sunday evening, we took dinner back at the hotel. Neither of us wanted to go out again. The drive back from Sounion was uneventful. As we left the Temple grounds and drove past the edge of the town, several people who must have been guests at the church waved to us.

"Where do you think the book is, Simon?"

"If it is where it always was, my guess would be that it is back in Troy, where everything started."

"I can't imagine that it would be still there among the ruins of the city. How could they have continued to add to it if was not accessible?" asked Marcia.

"Perhaps Troy is not the final location, but it is the only place that I can think of to pick up the trail, based on what Rashid told us. I think that we have to go there to find out if we are right or not. But we have to decide what to do about our friend, the Admiral as well. We can't keep ignoring the fact that he expects to hear from us. I can't imagine that John has been able to stall for very long, and certainly our cruise switch will be found out. So we need to have a plan to help get John out of his hole, while still being left relatively free to go about our own search without interference. We have to assume that Daniel Towson's associate, Mr. X has an ear to the ground in Washington in one of the agencies– yours, mine or the Company. So whatever we do, if we alert the Admiral, it may bring on the dogs. Do you have any ideas?"

"If I was back at the agency, I would set up a smokescreen of some kind as a diversion. What about if you played it straight to the Admiral – tell him that your wedding went well, and that you are ready to get back in the saddle, as it were. Say that you need to find out from John if there has been any progress, so you can pick up the trail. Hopefully, you can convince him that John will trust you, so he will put you back in touch with him directly. Then talk to John and have him tell you about the Greece connection, like it was the first time. You can then tell him that you will start here. That should get him off the hook with the Feds, so while they let him get back to the Smithsonian, you and I can fly off to Istanbul and hike

359

to Troy. If they come looking for us here, we will have just gone off for a couple of days into the hinterlands, and they will watch our hotel while we fly away."

"That sounds like a good plan. Let me find a cell phone and I will start it going."

With Marcia listening, I find my Navy Sat. Phone. When the Admiral answers, I give him the story and ask for the contact. He growls congratulations to us on the wedding, makes a nasty comment about jumping ship but then calms down after hearing my offer to follow through for him. He tells me to wait one, and then John is on the line. "Hello, John, it's Simon, do you have anything new to tell me?"

"Simon! Oh my. Did you both do it? Are you married?"

"Yes, and it was wonderful. Marcia sends her love" she nods vigorously "and your present arrived just in time. They are wonderful."

"Well, don't tell anyone. The guys here would be furious to learn that I sent you the rings. But tell me, are you well?"

"John, we are terrific. Now listen. If you have made progress, that would be great. Please tell me what you found and we'll be off on the trail again, while you should be free to return to the MCI."

"Yes, yes. That would be different. I have been locked up here and ..."

"John, please. Just tell me what you found."

"Simon, this is an open phone."

"No, it's encrypted."

"OK then. Let me tell you. I just finished the decoding. The book is everything that we thought." He then goes on to repeat the translations that he told me about a week ago. I didn't stop him as he told me (and everyone that was listening) about the probability that Greece was the key to finding the book. When he finally wound down, I broke in. "John that is great. Since we are here already, we will pick it up. Are you now finished with the armor?"

John says that the code will keep the NSA working to figure out a way to incorporate this new approach into a cryptology system, particularly by adding the quirks of a lost language and a key into the equation. John also says that the armor will keep the analysts at CIA and the metallurgy labs busy, so he can't imagine anything else that he could contribute. I tell him that I will put in a good word for him with the Admiral about letting him get back to work.

Later, I use my special chip credit card to book flights to Istanbul, and reservations at the Bosphorus Istanbul right on the Golden Horn. The flights are for the following morning, so we finish our dinner, and with linked arms, follow crumbs back to our room for the night.


## MONDAY

It was still dark when the alarm wakes us, and we groggily search for our bags and begin to pack. As per the plan, we decide not to check out of the hotel this morning, so that whoever tracks us here, will probably stay here, at least for a couple of days, unless they have access to our travel records. Last night, before coming upstairs, we stop at the Concierge's office and tell him that we are taking a couple of private honeymoon days, and if anyone asks, we are just out of our rooms. Another application of Euros seals the bargain.

Before we leave the hotel, I get another idea. For the benefit of further disinformation, we write some notes about meeting a contact at the Archeology Museum. We add a brief postscript about the "Macedonian Connection to the book" which, we say in the notes, that Philip of Macedonia's threats to attack Athens in 352 BC split a faction of the Book Keepers, who voted to move the book into Macedonia. We were going to see if we could pick up the traces in the north. We took a little map of Greece and circled Macedonia very heavily, and put an explanation point next to it. Marcia also got a list of a couple of local travel agents and wrote their names on a hotel pad. We then crumpled the map and let it slide behind the desk in our room; then ripped the top page off the pad with the agents' names. Our hope would be that if anyone came looking with an eye to following us, there would some oblique clues to follow.

We take our small overnight bags with us, leaving our larger bags in the room and our clothes in the dresser. A taxi outside the hotel takes us to a car rental office. Driving our new rental, we go directly to the Airport and leave it in long-term parking. It won't be discovered for several days. Inside, we suffer ramped-up security, which includes body and bag searches. Our army convoy escorts the bus out to our Turkish Airlines flight, which takes just under 2 hours to fly the 350 miles, so it is still early when we land at Atatürk Airport. The approach carries us over the center of the city, with the Golden Horn just on the left.

Customs clearance takes almost no time at all, and we come through the security gates into a yelling, pushing crowd of drivers, people searching for loved ones, and a liberal assortment of pickpockets. Since we have no checked baggage, we quickly find a taxi outside and roll up the windows against the humidity and heat. The hotel is a high-rise pair of white towers overlooking the Golden Horn and across to Old Constantinople/Istanbul. This side of the strait is Europe, while the older city is in Asia. Inside the main hotel entrance, the street noise disappears. It is too early in the day for our room to be available, so we leave our bags at the bell desk and stop in the Breakfast Room for coffee. Both of us order American Coffee and some pastries, which at today's exchange rate, costs almost $100. While we nibble at the rate of ten dollars a bite, we decide to postpone Troy until we can get a car and driver, and concentrate the balance of today on exploring. Marcia has never been here.

Our first destination is the great red church: Hagia Sophia. The monument, which is no longer a church but a museum, is set towards one end of a long park, with the Blue Mosque with its 5 great minarets at the other end. Hagia Sophia is enormous; with the dome so high that it feels like it could rain inside. The colors are incredibly bright, and the Quran verses tiled on the walls, dome and pendentives mix with Byzantine images of Christ, Saint Sophia and the Virgin. As usual, parts of the interior are being repaired: an enormous scaffold stretches along one side of the dome up to its peak. The dome is so big that even hard-soled shoes on the marble floors do not echo. As expected, there are several tour groups huddled together around their guides, and many different languages can be heard. It is almost impossible to walk through this structure without looking upward, as it was intended. As we stroll around the building, that crawly feeling started gnawing at my senses. I have learned to trust it, so while Marcia wandered, I took every opportunity to check for a tail. But with all the people in the vast building, it was impossible to tell if anyone was specifically watching us. I try all the tradecraft tricks, but never see anyone.

After the great Hagia Sophia, Marcia demands that we go to the Grand Bazaar, which is nearby. I was glad to find an opportunity to see if the feeling stayed with me when we changed venues. With taxis plentiful, we find one quickly. The driver's only question is where do we want to start? He points out that the Covered Market has nearly 4,000 shops, and that they are arranged by streets – all covered. So it is like a small city indoors. In 5 minutes we are standing in front of a pointed arch over the high doorway. Inside, we get some sense of what the driver meant. Street after street are covered by continuous barrel vaulting, while shops with glass fronts line cobbled walks.

Just inside the door, I delay us for a few minutes while I see if anyone comes to the same entrance looking for us. Marcia doesn't mind, as the section that we entered was devoted to dishes and pottery. Store after store show brightly colored pottery, bowls, platters, dinner sets and every conceivable serving piece by the thousand. Marcia picks a likely store and waves to me as she gleefully accepts the invitation of a 'puller' stationed just outside the door. While she drinks coffee and views a succession of dishes that were brought out, I waited outside, partially concealed in an adjacent doorway of a store that was not yet open. Although several cars drop off shoppers, no one caught my attention or stood out. If they were there, they were very, very good.

Marcia comes out and asked me if there was something bothering me, but I shook it off and follow her like a wayward puppy, through one shop after another. By the time she was done, I was loaded with an armload of odds and ends, which then were crammed into a brand new Kilim Wool Bag. The wheels on the bag made it a lot easier to roll, but not very well over the cobbles. Finally, I called a halt and balked at Marcia's next purchase possibility – a huge lamp. "That's it," I said. "I quit."

"Spoiled sport!" she called out, bargaining with me to hit only one more street. "Love, we can't possibly carry another thing."

"They ship." She replied, smugly.

OK, one more, but it had better be the last. So up one more street, our bag bouncing and rocking, probably was breaking every dish inside the bag. This was a street of booksellers and art dealers. One shop advertised ancient art. "Marcia, if it is truly ancient art, we will be stopped at the border, so anything we buy here, will most likely be phony."

"Fake or real, look at these things!" she said, walking through the displays of Greek and Turkish tiles, pots, coins and brassware. "You know, Mr. Chess, I have not bought you a wedding gift, so I am determined that you shall have my choice. Will you wait outside, please?"

I turned around and dragged my bouncing bag out through the door. Soon, Marcia came out of the shop with her prize, wrapped in paper. It was long, flat and heavy, but I couldn't see what it was. "OK, let's go" she said, so we started walking towards the entrance when we had come in. As we turned a corner and spotted the exit down at the end of our street, I saw two men standing near the door; one on either side. They appeared to be waiting. Although I had never seen them before, I took the safer of choices and grabbed Marcia's hand to turn back the way we had come. She pulled away and pointed towards the exit, but then sensed something was wrong. I spoke to her in low tones, as the vaulting carried echoes "I think we are being followed. Come with me."

She immediately dropped her objection and comes along. Fortunately, with a lot of people in the market, it appears that we had not been spotted yet. We walk until we found a broad avenue with lots of people. Then search for an exit. After two more streets, I motioned Marcia to continue and muttered "One more block" while I ducked into a doorway and waited. Across the street was a clothing store. After carefully looking back down the street, I cross, entering the store and make a couple of small purchases. Then I return to the street and join Marcia. Handing her a black chador, I put on a pair of sunglasses and a beaded skullcap. There was nothing I could do about the bag or the long package, but it would have to be enough. My shirt was white with an open collar, like hundreds of others here. Marcia covered her head with the chador, which fell to her ankles and completely concealed her western clothing. She held it closed with one hand in the Muslim style, while she dragged the bag with the other. Now attired more like locals, we started looking for a way out. I asked Marcia to walk behind me, drag the bag, and to keep her gaze lowered. I, however; stood upright and military straight with my long parcel on my shoulder like a rifle as I strode confidently along the avenue. In tandem, we came in sight of an exit on the north side of the market. At the door, standing on either side, are two more men. Both look like security as they carefully scan all the pedestrians walking towards them. I decide to take a chance. As we approached the doors, I take a firmer grip on my package, and Marcia subserviently follows behind. As we draw close, the men look hard at both of us, but then their gazes pass over to others. I pushed through the door, letting it close on Marcia as she struggled with the bag and the door in true Mideast fashion. No one pays the slightest attention. Outside, the entrance opens to a cul-de-sac where taxis wait. As the taxi pulls out, I do not see anyone come out after us.

"Simon, were the two men looking for us?"

"I don't know, but if so, we evaded them. I can't be certain, but I thought that we should not take any unnecessary chances. I am sorry about the rudeness at the door."

"Don't be ridiculous. But I would hate to have to wear this thing all the time. Who do you think they were?"

"I have no idea. I thought initially that they might be security, but who knows? We have to stay alert."

Back at the Bosphorus, I turn on the TV to a local station, as we open our bags, and Marcia gave me her prize: a long rod with a point at one end, and a flat blade at the other. It seemed to be made of iron, and was quite heavy. "Thank, you, dear. But what is it?"

"A digging stick; for a Private Investigator, you certainly have much to learn. You know, this could actually be the stick that Schliemann used at Troy. At least that is what the fellow in the shop told me in an aside. Who knows, it might even be true."

"Well it certainly looks old. I will cherish it and we can use it in our back yard to root out roots. Thank you."

"Shall we try to get to Troy tomorrow?"

"Yes. Maybe if we show ourselves, someone will find us like they did at the Temple."

"OK. You make arrangements, while I take a shower and get prettied up before dinner." Marcia started to walk to the bathroom, when something catches her eye on TV – a picture of two people. "Simon, come look. Isn't that the couple that we switched places with at the boat?"

"Yes, I think so. Wait a minute" I switched channels until I found BBC broadcasting in English. The news is still on."

> Delphi Cruise Lines reports that the young couple has been missing since their ship, the Mycenae, departed the island of Santorini yesterday. Authorities on the island have found no trace of the two Americans, who joined the cruise in Athens. Simon Chess and Marcia Flynn are U.S. Government employees on vacation. Ms. Flynn resides in Laurel, Maryland; Mr. Chess in San Francisco, California. Shipboard security found their stateroom torn apart, so it is assumed that the two were abducted. A spokesman from the cruise line provided a statement that a full investigation is underway, and that they are taking every precaution to protect their guests while on cruises. Your reporters will be following this story and attempt to interview other passengers at their next port of call, Kusadasi in Turkey.

"Oh Simon. I have a terrible feeling about this. Do you think..?"

"Let's not speculate. I hope that their true identities are discovered and that they are then released."

"Maybe we should tell the cruise line about their real names, so it will be reported correctly and the abductors will realize their mistake."

"Marcia, it can work two ways. If they find out, they might just kill them right away, but if they are unsure, they might give them a little rope to see where it leads, but you could be right as well."

"Oh Simon, what a mess this is. I never thought.."

"Our best bet is to keep going. Once we find the Book, this will be resolved as well. Let's not let our imagination run riot. I know it sounds callous, but we have to keep going."

"Yes, I know you are right." She continued her walk to the shower, but her mood was no longer bright.

The hotel recommended Changa, a restaurant located across the Bosphorus in the Taksim quarter. The concierge reserved a table for us, which was waiting as we arrive in our taxi. The restaurant is located in a wonderful turn-of-the-century townhouse with hand painted walls and original Eames tables and chairs. In the middle of the dining room is a large copper artichoke chandelier, and the walls are filled with art from local Turkish artists. Upon entering the restaurant, we walk across a glass floor, beneath which we can see down into the cellar kitchen where the chefs ply their arts as we look over their shoulders.

The menu is an exotic fusion of old Turkey and modern Europe. Marcia starts with fried zucchini flowers stuffed with Lor cheese, basil and pine kernels while I have smoked mullet and pomegranate in a turnip soup. For main dishes, I have Roasted Loin of Lamb in Quince Sauce with a red cabbage salad while Marcia has Grilled Grouper. To accompany our meal, the waiter chooses a delightful light red Turkish varietal wine from a nearby vineyard. Because Turkey has been a Muslim country for so long, the variety and availability of local wines is limited and the cost is exceedingly high, but for this dinner we splurged. We share some home-made assorted truffles for dessert, to accompany with our sweet coffee.

After dinner, we take a short walk to the center of Taksim, and stroll through the eclectic neighborhood of old Istanbul, mixed with new shops and galleries. Then we decide, since it appears to be nearby, to walk across the bridge to our hotel. But as soon as we leave the quarter, we are besieged by beggars and children, so we snag a passing taxi and travel back to the hotel, unmolested.

# 36 *TUESDAY - TROY*

This morning, the telephone announces that our car and driver have arrived and will be waiting for us downstairs. As a thoughtful addition, the concierge has also arranged a guide to accompany us to the dig at Troy. We hurry to meet in the lobby and invite him to join us while we have a light breakfast. The guide turns out be an archeology student named Nasîr Topal who is studying at a local university, earning some additional money by providing guide services to interesting sites in the area. He takes out a detailed map of Western Turkey and shows us our route today. It takes us out of Istanbul to the west, along the northern coast of the Sea of Mamara, to the town of Kilitbahir, where a short car-ferry ride will take us across the narrow strait to Canakkale. From there, we will drive south and west about 18 miles to Hissarlik, where Schliemann found Troy.

As we finish our coffee and begin the trip, Nasîr tells us something about Troy. "Many Christians believe that Troy was visited by St. Paul, where he had a vision of the coming Gospel, but that it probably isn't true. At that time Troy, or 'Troas' as it was called, referred to the general region in addition to the city itself. It was in this region that Alexander of Macedonia first defeated the Persians, at the Battle of Granicus. The first city of Troy was established by Ilus, son of Tros, around 3,000 BC. Although the city was named for the father, it was also called Ilios or Ilion, which was morphed by Homer in titling his classic, the Illiad: the story of the great battle between Troy and Greece. Heinrich Schliemann, back in the mid 19th Century, always believed that Homer had described a real city, and that Troy was not a myth, unlike most of the other archeologists at that time. He also believed, based on his studies of Homer, that it should be found near the town of Hissarlik, in modern Turkey. In spite of a great deal of opposition, Schliemann followed his hero Homer and found the city."

"Unfortunately for the Turks, Schliemann, while a great student of Homer, was a terrible archeologist, and looted much that he found at the site. He and his wife, Sophie conducted digs throughout Mycenae and the Cyclades, and amassed a great fortune in artifacts, many of which were smuggled out of Turkey and now reside in Berlin. In his dig at Troy, he was so obsessed that he completely bypassed the Homeric Troy and trashed many artifacts as he pursued his agenda. Eventually he had to abandon Troy due to ill health, leaving it to the professional scientists who manage the site today under the auspices of the government. In addition to the treasures sent to Berlin, many of the artifacts taken from the site are still hidden in private collections or in museums outside Turkey."

The overall drive to the ferry is nearly 150 miles. Once we reach the car ferry, it is a short 15 minute ride across the narrow strait, and then along the south road to the ruins.

From the plain, the city sits on a slightly elevated hilltop, where remains of the walls shadow the hillside. On the southwest side, a cobblestone ramp leads up to the main gate. From there we can see the first trenches where Schliemann dug deep into the wall to uncover earlier Troys. Nasîr tells us that there were a total of 9 cities, built one on top of another. Near the gate is an inventive reproduction of the enormous 'Trojan Horse' of myth. Nasîr tells us that no one is sure how much is real and how much is myth, but that researchers keep finding support to Homer's story of the Greek subterfuge.

Marcia and I notice that, like other historic locations, there are many groups wandering around the site. No one takes any notice of us as we explore the ruins. Of all the gates, the Eastern Gate is in the best condition.

Since the lair in Cape Sounion was situated under the Temple of Poseidon, I ask Nasîr if he can show us where the temple of Zeus was located. He tells us that he doesn't know exactly if there was a Temple to Zeus, but there was an Athena temple. Unfortunately, he says, all that is left is a single decorative metope from that structure: the temple itself was completely destroyed over the centuries. He leads us to the seaward side of the city, where Troy 7 foundations can be seen. A marble metope – a marble slab over 6' wide and nearly 3' high from a column entablature is mortared into the wall. It shows Helios, the sun-god, driving a chariot with four horses across the sky. Sunbeams radiate from his head as he illuminates the world. The structural wall itself is made of stone blocks, closely fitted together and assembled with no mortar. Marcia asks if we can sit and rest for a while. Nasîr leaves us and goes in search of a toilet. He tells us that he will return in a half-hour, when we should start back to Istanbul.

We look closely at the stone carving, made probably around 400 BC by the Greeks. "I wonder if this temple re-used the older Zeus temple erected by the Trojans."

"What I wonder is how we are supposed to be contacted, and by whom. Or maybe this is another misdirection."

A small group of five men approach. They are wearing jackets, but the weather is certainly too warm for this type of clothing. As they come closer to us, two separate from the others and walk up to where we are sitting by the metope. The first one looks at it for a short while and speaks to me "You must come with us. We have been sent to escort you further." He indicates the path and waits while we stand up.

"Who sent you?" I ask.

"Those who you have been searching for sent us. We are your escort." He leans forward slightly to help Marcia to her feet, and his jacket swings open slightly, revealing a large pistol in a shoulder holster.

"What about our guide? He will be back for us soon." I reply.

"Don't worry about him, our associate here will wait for him and tell him that you have found some friends and will be continuing with them."

"But we still owe him part of his fee."

"We will take care of him, just come with us, please."

"Where are we going?"

"To a secure location."

"Why are there five of you?"

"You are very important to us, and we are simply insuring your safety. Now please; let's be on our way."

As we start together, two of the men form up on me and two on Marcia. Although none have overtly threatened us, I am fairly sure that their term 'escort' is probably not the right word. I reach under my shirt around the back and both of my escorts go on high alert, reaching into their jackets to hold their gun butts, though none are brought out. I finish scratching at my back for a moment, and then drop my hand to my side.

We come to a narrow opening in the wall, where one of the men steps in front of me and the other falls back. I grab the forward man and pull him towards me, stepping sideways so that I can help swing him into his partner behind me. As he falls, I reach into his coat and grab his gun. Before he can react, he crashes into his partner's chest and the two of them struggle for balance. I take a step through the opening as one of Marcia's escorts sidesteps my guards and launches a kick to my crotch, but only succeeds in connecting with the doorway. As his leg ricochets back, he lands lightly on it and sends a kick at me with the other leg. This foot connects with my backside. Marcia meanwhile turns and kicks upwards at the man on her left, but he grabs her leg and pulls her off her feet. I am off balance when my second guard shoves his partner out of the way and comes up with his gun, firing a round in my direction. The bullet smashes into the transom above the door as I thumb the safety off the first guard's weapon and fire the gunman. I nail him squarely in the right shoulder but before I can move my aim, my guard backhands a punch to my diaphragm. It connects, but is too weak to cause any damage. I start to spin with a flat leg toward Marcia's last guard, but he takes a step back and pulls out his own gun, pointing it directly at Marcia's head shouting "Enough."

I immediately let my gun drop, raising my hands as the two men on the ground push themselves up and regain their composure. The one holding the gun turns to me and we are marched toward the parking lot. "Mrs. Chess will travel in the first car, while you, Mr. Chess in the rear car, please."

"We would rather be together," I say.

"Just get in and no trouble." The man replies as he pushes Marcia toward the lead car. The guard that was shot is helped into the front of the first car by the driver, who then starts shoving Marcia into the back seat.

"Get your hands off me" she says, but he ignores her and shifts a grip to her arm, pushes her into the car, and gets in the front. Three of us get in the second car and we set out in convoy, leading out of the site and back toward Canakkale.

Just outside the town, the lead car turns off the main road into a smaller side alley, while my car continues straight. "Where are they going?" I ask in some alarm.

"Just keep quiet." The leader turns his head and speaks to me. "You will cooperate if you wish to see your wife again. Do you understand?"

The car stops at a garage door of an unidentified building. The building appears to be some sort of warehouse, with covered pallets arranged in rows. As the car stops, the rear door is pulled open. Above us on a balcony, is an office area, with an open metal stairway leading up to it. My escort points up the stair and remains below. At the top of the stair, a man comes out of the office block and waits for me. The lights which hang above us cast shadows on the man's face, so I don't recognize him until I am almost at the top. It's Towson. He has finally caught up with me.

"Come up, Mr. Chess. We will talk, and then you will tell me what I want to know and then perhaps you will get to live another few hours." The slight Eastern European accent is more pronounced that it was when I spoke to him last, back in Albuquerque.

"Mr. Towson." I reply to him. "You don't look much at all like your brother."

"Just come with me." He walks along the catwalk and through a door. Inside, there is a desk and two chairs. He sits behind the desk and indicates the other seat for me."

"Where is my wife?"

"Ah, the delightful Marcia. Be prepared to never see her again. But that will be up to you. It will depend on how you answer my questions."

"Mr. Towson, my wife is important to me. You know that so I won't lie. I will tell you what I know, but what I do not know, I cannot tell you."

"We shall see. First of all, you need to understand that I am unwavering in my determination to acquire this Book that you have been searching for. I believe that you have information that can help me achieve this goal."

"All I know is what your brother told me, and I quote: 'The book is where it always was'. We came out to Troy, since that was the origin of the book, but have not found it. Your guess is as good as mine."

"Your friend, John Crawford, told me that it was in Greece, yet we followed you to Troy, a far less likely location."

"Is John all right?"

"I am afraid that he has had a slight accident. It is of no consequence. Now I want all the information that you have."

I think that if I had something to hit him with at that very moment, he would be dead, but for Marcia. "I am telling you the entire truth, as best I know it. As you know, I met a man at the Temple of Poseidon on Cape Sounion who claimed that he was the Keeper of the Book. I suppose that it was you that destroyed the other Keepers?"

"Go On," he waves his hand, urging me to continue.

"After you killed everyone there, you didn't stay around long enough to check if there were any more of them about. You missed a couple. One of whom calls himself Rashid Xyso. He says that he is your lost brother, and wanted to talk with you about your family, some of which are still alive and living in Turkey."

"I don't care about what anyone told you, except for the Book. I am determined to have it, at whatever cost. At this point, you are my best option, so you remain alive. Your wife, on the other hand, is meaningless to me, so I advise you to stick to my questions and cooperate fully."

"Mr. Towson, or Xyso, or whatever you call yourself. I am your best option. If anything happens to me, the book will be gone for another generation at minimum. Likewise, if anything happens to Marcia, I will be of no help to you, since my life would be ended with the same result, as far as you are concerned. Your only chance at the book is to help me find it. I have been promised to be brought inside the circle of those who know where it is, who are known as Keepers. I will help you, but only if you release Marcia right now, and let me continue my search - Your choice."

"Mr. Chess, do not underestimate me. I will kill your bride."

"Don't underestimate me, Mr. Towson. I will survive, and you will die. I probably will kill you anyway. I understand that you tortured and killed my Jean some time ago. Once I learned this, I vowed to make sure her killers did not live out another year. I do not much care about this Book that you are obsessed with. So again, you choose."

"I don't know anything about your Jean. But that is beside the point. You will tell me what I want to know, and you will do it now."

"I will make you just one bargain. Marcia is set free and I will help you find the Book, and make you a promise not to kill you until after the Book is secured."

"You in no position to bargain."

"Actually, I am. You have reached a dead end. Without help, you will never get any closer. You should have learned that after you killed all those people at Poseidon's Temple."

Towson sat for a few minutes while he considered my offer. "Shall we bring out your wife and see if losing an eye or hand changes your attitude?"

"Towson, do your worst. If your interest is the Book and nothing else, then take my offer."

Towson gets up and paces around the room. Finally, he stops and looks down at me. "Very well; I shall accept this bargain of yours. The moment, however; that I believe you to be working against me, Marcia will be summarily terminated. Do you understand me?"

"Yes. But do not ask me to shake hands with you."

"I care not. But you certainly have balls, my friend." He gets up and goes to the door, opens it and calls out to his men to bring the girl here. Almost before he finishes, I can hear the sound of running footsteps, and Marcia appears in the doorway.

"Simon, oh I was worried." Then she turned to Towson "And you, you bastard, you can go to hell, and I will see to it."

Towson laughs out loud. "Great spirit, no matter how short lived," he comments to no one in particular.

I tell Marcia that I have agreed to work with Towson until the Book is found. Marcia looks angrily at me and then back to Towson. Finally, she understands. Cooperation only means "the better part of valor," so she sits back until we have an opportunity to act otherwise.

"I think that our next step is to get back to Troy. That was the direction that your brother..."

"Don't call him that. I have no brother."

"Well, whoever he is, he told me, and I quote: 'the Book is where it always has been.' Since it was kept in Troy before the Greeks destroyed the city, I can only assume it is still somewhere there."

Towson snorted. "I have maintained an agent there for the past year, since I learned of the Book's source. You know, of course, that the armor code was deciphered more than a year ago by Ernst Zilbern. He had copied the inscriptions on both the armor and the key during his time in Cyprus, and used it to finally crack the three-factor code. His daughter helped with the translations, and together they resolved some of the ancient history of the Book."

"Just as a matter of interest, not that it is important, but did you have anything to do with his death?"

"Actually, I did not. I believe that he accidentally was swept off the boat and landed in San Francisco Bay. The boat captain told me, and it made me angry since I thought that his death would interfere with my search for the book. But it worked to my advantage. It meant one less person competing with my interests."

"So you have an agent in Troy. Are you sure you can trust this agent?"

"I ...I assumed that...he is paid a great deal...Frederick!" he calls out. One of our escorts comes in. "get Klaus up here by this afternoon." Frederick nods and disappears. "I shall interview him and re-assure myself that he is doing his job."

"What else have you done at Troy?" I ask.

"I had sensors placed there. If there were any meeting or activities at night after the site closed, I would know."

"How did you learn of the Poseidon connection?"

"That's not important. I know that Schliemann found the Book in his dig, but his wife claimed that it was stolen by the Keepers. That information was put in a letter to her son just before she died, along with a brief history of the AFAR. She told her son in the same letter that the book was returned by the Keepers to Troy, but I think that she was only speculating. Although I do not know where it went, after it was recovered from Schliemann, it is unlikely that it was re-hidden at Troy, since the site was then, and continues to be an active archeological excavation. Perhaps it was brought somewhere that had special significance for the Keeper clan. After all, they had a charge to both keep the Book safe, as well as add to it as new science evolved over the years. This had to be done where they had access to a workplace and laboratory for making new pages, as well as a place to assemble the data."

"Chess, you were chosen by the Keepers for some special purpose. The logical location for you to pick up this thread would be back in Troy. Go there see what you attract. Marcia shall remain with me for insurance."

"Don't bet on it," Marcia interrupted. "Where he goes, I go, or there is no deal."

"Do not think me stupid. You will not survive the day, should you decide to play me."

"Mr. Towson; we can accomplish both our goals far better without threats. Right now, you need us, and we are willing under the present circumstances, to work with you. So leave it at that. Just get us back to Troy, and follow as you will. We will eventually reach a day of reckoning between us, but not today."

"Towson nods and then recalls his men. "Before you go, let me repeat something I said. I have spent the better part of my life in this search. If I get one small hint that you are not cooperating, you and whatever families you have will be killed in a particularly painful and protracted manner. Do not take this threat lightly."

They lead us to the rear of the office block, where sleeping rooms have been set up. Besides the small bed, there is a TV, a hot plate, a small refrigerator as well as a bathroom, but no telephone or window. We are locked in.

"Simon, what are we going to do?"

"The first thing is to not panic. We are alive, no broken bones, and no drugs yet. Let us not try to plan anything but instead go along with our bargain for now." I point to the ceiling and walls and to my ears, to indicate listening devices.

I find some packaged meat and cheese in the refrigerator, some bread in a cabinet, and water to drink. "Not like last night's dinner" commented Marcia as she chewed the slightly stale bread and mystery meat. We turned on the TV and tuned it to the BBC station we had listened to yesterday. During the news, we saw a brief story on the abduction of Tom and Rita Coleman as our namesakes. I thought to myself, Towson mentioned nothing about this.'

# 37 *WEDNESDAY – TURKEY*

The door is slammed open and two men come in to drag us out. A third man covers us with a gun.

"Put the gun away Edward. There is no need for violence." says Towson from the doorway. We are taken to a car in the alley behind the warehouse. When one of the men open's the driver's door, I tell Towson "It would be better if we arrived alone." He looked at me sharply, and then waved the driver away.

Towson hands an envelope through the driver's window, containing our Passports, wallets and money, but not our cell phones. We drive past him out the alley. Marcia immediately starts looking in the glove compartment and the door pockets for a map. "How are we going to get backup?" she asks.

"We'll have to find a telephone somewhere. As we drive through Canakkale, I see a sign with a boat silhouette. "Maybe we can find one at the ferry." I turn towards the water and follow more signs until the ferry terminal appears. Marcia stays while I run inside. The cacophony in the high-ceilinged room is outrageous. It seems that everyone is shouting at once for tickets, coffee, family members and business associates. I find an information desk and ask for a telephone, but the attendant doesn't understand me, so I make a phone sign with my hand and she points me towards the toilets. I find a row of pay boxes, but have no local coins, so I go over to a news seller and pick up a newspaper. Putting a 5 Euro note into the seller's hand, I am rewarded with a dirty look as he makes change. With my coins, I go back to the pay boxes and pick an open one. The door to the booth is broken, and the phone is torn off its wire. I look for another open box, but all are taken. I walk back and forth, hoping for someone to end their conversation. Finally, a very stout woman throws her receiver down and grabs at a half-dozen packages that she has crammed in with her. I offer to help her but she will have none of it. She pushes her fat through the door and then turns around, grunting as she clutches at thin air while trying to reach for her parcels. Finally, with a supreme effort, she succeeds and drags them to her bosom, where it flows over the parcels and conceals her hands in its folds. Her black dress stretches to the breaking point as she waddles out of the area, muttering to herself, her rolled black stockings knotted below the hemline rubbing at each other while her brogans smack on the floor.

Into the booth I am assailed by a combination of sweat and urine, overpowered by the imitation floral scent of dollar toilet water. Ignoring the glaze on the receiver, I insert a couple of coins into the slot and dial the Operator, to ask for an English speaker. I ask to be connected collect to the Admiral's home number, as it is still night in Washington. When he picks up the phone and the operator asks permission to connect the call, he grunts. "Where the hell are you?" he asks. "The news reports..."

"Admiral. I will explain later. This is important. I am in Turkey, on the trail. I am on my way with Marcia to the digs at Troy. Towson caught us and is forcing us to cooperate with him. We need backup. I am afraid that if I don't come up with the Book, Marcia will be killed, as well as yours truly."

I will always have to hand it to him for bypassing appetizers when there is meat at the table. "Tell me what you need."

"I think that the Book may be in Troy. We will be there in an hour. If you could send an extraction team for us, it would be great."

"I will get someone there, but it will take a couple of hours. Where is the site?"

"It is near the town of Hissarlik in Western Turkey, right near the sea. I am now in Canakkale, about 20 miles away and will be driving there."

"Very well; how can I contact you?"

"You can't. Towson took our telephones and we have no access."

"Stall them as long as you can. I will send the troops."

"Thank you, sir." The connection broke before I could say anything further. With some hope, I return to the car and see Marcia driving around the square in front of the terminal. She stops as she reaches me "The police made me move" and I jump in.

"The cavalry is on its way." I say as she picks up the pace towards the west.

"How are you going to attract the Keepers' attention?" she asks me as she drives, rapidly overtaking and passing donkey carts, overloaded mini-trucks and bicycles on the road.

"Slow down. We need about 2 hours for help to arrive. Until then, we are on our own. I think that our best hope is to start where we left off, at the Temple of Athena, which previously was Zeus's altar. If there is no clue there, then we will make up something until we are rescued."

So back to Troy we go, where we park and walk through the site again. As we reach the Metope from the Temple, we take a seat on a couple of broken column pieces. Several groups come by with their guides: First one with a German speaker, then French, and then English. I half listen to the guide as he explains the artifact.

"The symbol of Helios is the most common and most important god for the people of the time. The Sun brought light that grew the crops, and gave warmth to the peoples of the Earth. Each culture had a representation of the Sun-God, and many were very similar. In Rhodes, the Great Colossus was built to Helios, and the Greek Apollo was based upon him. Even the earliest depictions of Christ were as Helios, with the Sun's rays streaming from his head, as you see here. Later, the halo replaced the rays in Christian images. Your own Statue of Liberty is a modern Helios, based on the Rhodes Colossus, with the same rays in her crown. Bartholdi wanted to make a connection between ancients and moderns with his representation of liberty. The source for all these ideas came from Egypt. The Sun God Ra with the Sun itself sitting as a crown on his head represented the source for their civilization. Everything sprang from it: The Nile with its annual floods, the Pharaoh's divine power, and the growth of their culture. They worshiped the Sun, just as we did in his name Apollo."

"Athena, in her role as protector, was born from the forehead of Zeus, her father. The place where all knowledge springs is the head of the people too, so her birth though unconventional, could be considered prophetic. Now, let us go to where the altar probably was placed, and see if you can feel the energy rising from the earth and descending from the Sun."

As the group moved off I signaled to Marcia to join them. We attach ourselves to the tail of the guide's charges as he walks up through the gate towards the west side of the City. "Here is where the altar stood, with its great statue of Zeus facing southwest towards his twin brother Poseidon on Cape Sounion in Greece. If you stand and face that way, you can imagine the energy flow between the two brothers: rivals yet sharers of the Earth's realm. Their third brother is down deep in the Earth, Hades: the master of the Underworld. There are no statues to him here, but it was thought that he was to be located at the point of an arrow, where the feathers were these two, and the point was in Egypt. The message is clear. Egypt is the land of

379

evil, while Greece and Turkey are the opposite poles. If you follow that arrow, you shall surely die, so remain here with the living."

As the group attentively followed their guide, I hold Marcia back and we stand on the broken stone at our feet. I walk around the altar several times while I think. There has to be a clue here. This is ridiculous. I don't understand that no one has come to contact us, and there is nothing here. I feel very frustrated, like we made a totally wasted trip. But Towson came here also, and even if he followed us, he would not have come unless he had a reason. From where I stand, I look out over the ruins of the city walls and the ridiculous wooden horse which I can see back at the gate. From here, it seems to be laughing at me.

Marcia is looking around also, but it appears we have come to a dead end. If it hadn't been for the fellow we met in Sounion, would we have come here? We might have anyway, because the armor came from here. Well, if the armor came from here and was a coded message, would it make any sense not to have some sort of clue here also to the location of the Book? But it would have to be a clue that was placed here after Schliemann's time, since before then, the book was here.

I look down at the stone. It is cracked in several places. In spite of the guards, people had scrawled graffiti on it. But I could see that attempts had been made to erase it by the government by scrubbing the stone with detergent. One part of the graffiti, however; had been scribed in place with a sharp tool. It was an arrow. I guess the guide's story about the arrow inspired someone to draw it. I looked where it was pointing, but it wasn't anyplace to speak of, kind of vaguely south southwest. I don't think too much of it and call Marcia over.

"We could go back to Greece again. Maybe we can get more help from Towson's brother," Marcia offers.

"Whatever we do, we have to do it soon, because Towson is not going to leave us alone if we don't come up with something."

While we are talking, Marcia is tracing the graffiti patterns with her toe. The arrow particularly attracts her and she runs her toe along the shaft, and then bends down to dig out the dirt that has filled in the deep groove. "Hold up there, what do you think you are doing? You can't dig here. It is forbidden," comes from a roaming site guard.

"Oh, I'm sorry sir, Marcia exclaims. "We were just resting for a few moments after our long walk around the site." She looks up at the guard with her deep green eyes and wild mane of red hair, like Athena reborn. "It is really unfortunate that people disrespect your history by putting their own personal marks on a place as sacred as this." She points down at the altar stone and the incised arrow as she shakes her head in disbelief.

"Yes, it is." The guard replies "That particular mark has been there for as many years as I have worked here, and I came here as a young man."

"Why do you think anyone cut an arrow into the stone?"

"I wonder too. I think that maybe it pointed to where someone was going, or where they came from. We have tried to erase it, but it's too deeply cut into the stone. Someone must have put it here to stay." The guard touched his cap and gave a tiny little bow to Marcia. Then he walked away, muttering to himself.

Marcia had knelt on the stone, so I help her up, and we start toward the car. Both of us are so focused on the implications of our failure, that we don't immediately hear a pounding noise coming from the sea.

As the noise grows loud, it finally attracts our full attention. It is a helicopter. It starts to descend onto the site, but as it approaches, guards appear and try to wave it away; but it continues to descend. On the side "NAVY" is printed in bright white letters near the tail rotor. It is an SH-60 Seahawk attack, search and rescue bird, complete with bristling rockets and gun barrels. The helicopter lands and a squad of Marines in full gear jumps out. Our backup has arrived. The guards crowd around the new arrivals, but they push through and start walking to the site. "Lieutenant," I call. "I believe you are here for us."

The officer moves toward me, followed by his squad. They all look like they just came off the high school football field, but there was no game in their eyes and in the IARs (Infantry Automatic Rifles) that they hold at the ready, barrels down but fingers in the trigger guards. As the lieutenant reaches me, he salutes and says "Captain Chess?"

"Yes, Lieutenant, have you come for us?"

"Yes, sir. The Admiral's compliments; please get aboard. Men: Defensive perimeter!" The group encircles us with weapons pointing out. Marcia and I walk into the protected center of the group to the helicopter, and climb aboard. As soon as the last man is aboard, we take off, heading back out to the Aegean. We sit in webbed seats and are strapped in as the machine tilts over sharply and points southwest. It is far too noisy to speak, but the Lieutenant shouts "30 minutes." I nod vigorously, whereupon he returns to his seat. The marines safe their weapons and snap them into a rack in the center of the ship.

For a half hour, we clatter across the ocean. We had been passed helmets, but the noise is even louder inside. Through the open door, we can see some ships, and then a carrier appears under us like a huge flat Greek island, with a sailor flagging us down to a circular spot painted on the flight deck. As soon as we touch down, Airedales jump out of recesses along the deck and tie us down, the engine is cut and we freewheel while the marines debark. A navy officer is waiting near the island as we approach. He salutes and says to me "Welcome aboard, Captain Chess, Mrs. Chess. Please follow me, and mind the knee-knockers." He leads the way through the hatch which stops about at knee height and into a passageway, up three sets of ladders (stairs) to the 'O-5' deck, where he leads us towards the forward side of the island and knocks twice on a doorjamb. "Enter" comes from within. The officer pushes the door open and holds it for us until we go through, then pulls it closed.

"Come in, Captain Chess, and Mrs. Chess. The Admiral sends his compliments. Welcome aboard the Harry Truman, I am Captain Starr, the commanding officer." I feel the urge to salute, but quell it as he sticks out his hand in welcome.

"That certainly was a welcome rescue, Sir" I say as I take his hand. Marcia's turn is next, and she flusters the captain with a kiss instead of a handshake. "What's the flap about? I got a call to pull out the stops and get you out of there."

"Do you know anything about our mission?"

"No, and truthfully, I don't think I want to know. I've got my hands full with this interdiction role that we are playing here in the Eastern Med. We are trying to cut the drug traffic out of Afghanistan for Europe, and it is a gigantic headache. Our task force is designed for attack and defense, showing the flag, and as a platform for protection against threats to our NATO allies. We are not structured for this assignment, but we're doing our best. But enough about my woes; tell me how I can help you."

"Captain, you got us out of a jam. We both really appreciate it. If you don't mind, we didn't eat anything this morning, nor much last night. Would someone show us to the mess?"

"I'll do you one better. I'll have my aide show you both to the Wardroom, and we'll put it on the ship's tab."

Before Marcia can add a word, there is a knock on the door. "Enter" says the Captain, and in walks a civilian dressed in casual attire. "I understand that this is Mr. and Mrs. Chess," he says as he holds out his hand.

I take it while the captain adds "This is John Edwards, of the CIA. He is assigned to us as part of our interdiction force, if we capture drug runners that need interrogation." I can see that Edwards does not meet with Starr's approval, but in today's Navy, there are all sorts that one has to do business with to survive.

"Good day, Mr. Edwards. Yes, you have us."

"I wonder if you might tell me what the hell you were doing in Turkey. You don't belong to The Company."

"Mr. Edwards, I am afraid this is a 'need to know' issue, so you will have to forgive me, but I would rather not say."

"Chess, let's get one thing clear. You are operating in my patch, and I will not tolerate any poachers. So answer my question,"

"Get off my case Edwards. I am not in your chain of command in either direction, so butt out."

"Chess, I will remember your name. Whoever you work for will hear from the DCI (Director, Central Intelligence). I will just wait here with you until you leave." Edwards stands against the wall until the captain waves him out.

"Well, that was interesting," says the captain with a twinkle in his eye after Edwards leaves. "Oh well, let me get you some lunch." He picks up the telephone, and a moment later his aide opens the door. I thank the captain. Our trek takes us through the enormous Hangar Deck and around a maze of passageways until we reach Officer's Country. Then a side door leads us into a large conference/dining room with an adjoining kitchen and lounge. A white-jacketed steward takes our order.

Soon, we are delivered coffee, some fresh-baked rolls with side dishes of cheese and some chicken salad. We attack our lunch, and then push the plates aside, declining the proffered ice cream and cookies.

"I have an idea," Marcia started, "You know I have always been good with cryptograms and puzzles. I see this as just that, a series of events and clues which are designed to give us dual messages, only one of which is the correct plain text. Consider the Poseidon site as a piece to the puzzle. In going there, we were pointed at Troy, It is always important in any cryptogram to consider that the instructions themselves are a clue along with where the instructions lead you. So the instructions that 'pointed' to Troy were as important as the fact of Troy itself. We looked at Troy and found two clues. The first, oddly as it seems is validation that our competition was not ahead of us, but the second clue is how to use the

Troy reference as a 'pointer'. The guide told us when he was explaining the significance of the twin brothers: Poseidon and Zeus. Both pointed to each other, but both pointed another way as well: and that way was...?"

"Of course; it means something. Let's get a map." In the corner of the wardroom there is a large bulletin board with an operating area chart on it. We both go over and look. By drawing a line between Troy and Sounion we establish a base. Taking a line perpendicular to that base from its midpoint, points directly at Egypt. "Egypt was the tip of the arrow, the third brother to Poseidon and Zeus. I find it interesting that our Poseidon contact was also a 'brother' to the Troy contact. So the notion of brothers is also a clue. Marcia continues with her thought. "While you are thinking Egypt, consider this: It came to me while we were flying from Troy – that graffiti on the altar stone. The arrow which has been there for so many years; it pointed in the same direction as we flew "

"Egypt!"

"Exactly. Simon, you have been looking at this from a detective's viewpoint. Think of it as a cryptographer. As detective, you sift through evidence and arrive at a logical deduction. As a cryptographer, you search for patterns: behavior, interrelationships, substitutions and keys. In this case, the evidence points to Towson being an evildoer, hell bent on destroying everything in his path to search for the Book. But his actions, if perceived merely as keys to the cryptogram, can characterize him as a pointer that has value in achieving *our* goal, not his.

"So you are saying is that if we discard the ins and outs of the story and look at the pattern it creates, we will have a better chance at succeeding."

"Yes, that is just what I am saying." Marcia sits back and looks at me with a self-satisfied smile on her face.

"So that means we have to go to Egypt."

"Yes. But where in Egypt would the Book had been hidden and remains until today?"

"Oh my God. You mean...," and we say it together "The Library at Alexandria."

Marcia continues, "After all, like Edgar Allen Poe stated in his story 'The Purloined Letter', the letter was hidden not is some secret hiding place in the floor or behind a picture, but in a pile of other letters. Our Book is undoubtedly hidden in plain sight with many other books, in the place where it continue to evolve: the Library."

"But the Library was destroyed by Julius Caesar." I commented.

"Well maybe not Julius, but certainly it was destroyed; not once, but several times. Yes, but each time it rose from the ashes. Remember that the book was supposed to be written on thin metal plates that were indestructible. So if it was in the Library, wouldn't it have been rescued and brought somewhere like Troy until a new Library was built? And remember also the offhand comment made by Towson that the Keeper left Troy and made his way south? I read about a new library that was recently built in Alexandria to resurrect the original Great Library. There was a worldwide architectural competition for its design, and the goal was to make it the greatest library in the world. Would it not be the perfect place to place the book now?"

"Yes, of course it would. I wonder if we can get the captain to ferry us there."

"Well, he was given special accommodation orders by your Admiral. Let's ask him."

I picked up the telephone in the Wardroom and asked to be connected to the Captain. In a moment, he was on the line. "Captain, would you be able to arrange a transfer for us to Egypt, preferably Alexandria?"

"Just a moment. We have a flight group that is going to Egypt to deliver some new aircraft. I am sure we can divert a couple of them to Alexandria before going on to the Egyptian base. Let me check....Yes. The day after tomorrow the mission is scheduled. Can you wait that long?"

"Is there a possibility that we can do it sooner?"

"Let me get authorization from your Admiral. I will get back to you in a couple of minutes." I replied that we would wait here for his call. The call came in less than 5 minutes. "I'm sorry, Chess, I can't do get you on the delivery mission, but if you can be ready in an hour, I am placing two F-18 Hornets at your disposal. We will get you there this afternoon. The Admiral was insistent."

"Thank you sir, he does get that way sometimes. We are ready. Shall we wait here?"

"No. Let's get you to the Ready Room to meet with the pilots. They will brief you there on procedures."

"Thank you again, sir."

"The Truman is always ready to support our Navy team. Goodbye and Safe Voyage." I passed the information to Marcia, who remarked to me that she always wanted to see what it was like in a fighter, but hoped that she didn't ruin her image by throwing up on the pilot.

In about 10 minutes, a crewman from Flight Operations comes in and escorts us up under the flight deck. He pointed out that the catapult cylinders above our heads carried live steam, pressurized to nearly 1000 psi. A pinhole would decapitate us instantly. We look at the overhead suspiciously, as the crewman laughs at our discomfiture. "Don't worry, we've never lost a guest, only a couple of Green Berets, but those crooked legs can't stand up to our SEALS anyway."

Up in the Ready Room, large armchairs arranged in stadium seating face a lectern with several large plasma screens on which were depicted satellite imagery of the Eastern Mediterranean and Northern Africa. Symbols represent our task group, other NATO and allied warships, and merchant shipping, as well as designated foreign naval vessels and a few unknowns. Another screen projects weather information, sea-state data, wind and visibility up to 70,000 ft. Other smaller screens listed tactical operations information: loading data for each aircraft, and a list of operational missions and flight personnel. I noticed that our names were listed beside the pilots of two F-18 dual-seat aircraft. In a few minutes, pilots stroll in. How young they look. Two come over and introduced themselves with supreme assurance. We are briefed on intra-aircraft radio procedures, warned not to touch anything, and are fitted Nomex flight suits which are extremely tight, as well as with parachutes. "You probably won't need the suits, but it is better to be prepared, in the unlikely event that we need to make any sudden moves or have a fire. They asked us if we had ever gotten airsick, and Marcia said yes, but not lately. They gave us bags just in case, but said that if it happens, it would be during high-G maneuvers, far too fast for us to react, so we would most likely be pinned in our seats by our suits and straps. They told us to try to throw up in our own laps, because it obscures their vision through the canopy. They also walk us through emergency evacuation and ejection, but warn us not to stick out anything if we booted, because it would be torn off. I am quite familiar with the drill, but for Marcia, this is all new and she looks a bit queasy.

So armed, we walk behind them up to the flight deck to the holding area where two beasts lay in wait for us. Ladders hang over the side from the cockpits. Marcia mounts one and the crew chief at the top helps to get her and her gear settled and strapped in. I move to the other aircraft and did likewise. Fighters are not designed for 6'+ bodies, so for me, the fit was quite cramped. The pilots come aboard and went through pre-start. Helmets on our heads, put there by the Crew Chiefs, have built-in microphones and speakers, which monitor the operations and launch circuits for the pilots, catapult operators; as well as broadcast communications on speakers mounted in the island, so that all would know what is going on at every moment. With a word to me about holding my tongue on the circuit, the carrier turns into the wind and sped up to about 30 knots. The ship's speed made the wind roar down the deck in a 65 knot gale, shaking the aircraft and us like a blender. Since there were no other flight operations, we were directed to the forward catapults, where we stopped while being hooked up, and then, as the engines spool up to full power, the canopies come down and the launch officer touches the deck. I am slammed into the seat back by an unseen force so hard, I can't breathe. The deck disappears and the plane dips slightly towards the water before pointing upwards at a 45 degree angle and transforming itself into a rocket. In moments, we are up in the clouds. Suddenly the world turns upside down as the pilot makes a 180, by then already a couple of miles from the ship. As we level off, I look to my right and Marcia's aircraft was less than a wing length away and only a few feet behind. We straighten out, heading towards the sun. The pilot reduces thrust as we reach altitude and it seems like we are going to drop from the sky, but Mach meter next to the Airspeed indicator read 0.8, which translates to about 620 mph. The pilot's voice comes on the intercom and asks me how I am doing. When I reply OK, he says that we are going to put the pedal to the metal, and again I am slammed into the seat as the afterburner kicks in and the mach-meter spools up to 1.5, or almost 1,200 mph, the transonic insertion happening without my notice whatsoever At this speed, the aircraft is quieter and smoother. The pilot tells me our total flight time would be well under an hour.

It seems like only a few minutes passed until we slow and join the approach pattern for the El Nozha International Airport at Alexandria. Our pilots receive permission to land and come in over a large man-made lake, reclaimed from the Nile Delta Marshes. We land with less than a 2,000 ft. roll-out. We taxi to a private terminal and the pilot pops the canopy. I found that I am stuck in the seat by my suit, parachute, and stiff muscles. Marcia already has stripped out of her suit and is waiting for me. "Sissy," she called out to me. "We better get you to the gym before you will be of no use to me at all."

We thank the two navy pilots, and give them our gear. I think Marcia's pilot is in love. When she stripped out of her helmet and suit, he stood open-mouthed, like a panting puppy and stared at her, unable to say anything. Then, when she gave him a hug and a kiss on the cheek, he fumble-footed around and dropped his helmet.

As we walk to the small terminal servicing private aircraft where a Customs officer is waiting, Marcia and I both turn back for a moment and wave to the two fighter jocks, only one of which had re-entered his plane while the other still stands on the tarmac, rooted where Marcia had kissed him.

# 38 *WEDNESDAY EVENING – ALEXANDRIA*

The city bakes in the summer sun. It is the time of Ramadan, and the populace works and fasts through each day, as they look to the fourth prayer with the setting sun and celebrations. Ramadan derives from the beginning of the revelations of the Quran. It is a time of scorched earth and paucity of food supplies. The fourth month of the Islamic Calendar, marking Ramadan, would be celebrated for another week. Since the Islamic Calendar did not mesh with the Gregorian calendar adopted by British Parliament in 1751, Ramadan occurs at a different time each year. This year, it coincided with the coming of summer, so it was closer to its tradition.

We came into the city from the south. The great harbor of Alexandria stretches two arms east and west to encircle both navigable waters and shallow sandbars. It is on this eastern arm that the new Bibliotheca Alexandrina has been constructed: a joint project of the Egyptian Government and UNESCO. We decide to search for a hotel near the library, but with almost 800,000 visitors a year making pilgrimages to see this new wonder, we are not sure we would be able to find one close by. Once we are through Customs, an easy venture with our brand new Truman supplied Passports, already stamped with Egyptian visas (courtesy of our reluctant CIA colleague), we instruct our taxi driver to take us to the Library, from which we will cast about for a hotel.

The library building is almost circular in shape, with a steeply slanting roof which slopes back from the street down towards the water, like a huge canted telescope mirror. At the airport, we had picked up a small brochure on the library, showing a plan of the various components: museums, stacks, planetarium, manuscript library, art galleries, conference center, restoration laboratory, and a children's discovery center. Twelve levels hold millions of volumes with a total capacity of 8 million; and with the ability to expand as needed. But with advancing digital media, it is expected that with the digitizing of newer volumes that are accumulated each year, paper will gradually be superseded, except for volumes and records that should remain in their original form for research and posterity.

The exterior looms above us as we leave our taxi. The outside walls are made of grey granite, with inscriptions in 120 languages around its surface. We start searching for a hotel. Nearby, on El Gueish Avenue, we see the Renaissance Alexandria Egypt. With 10 floors, it is fairly new and close enough to easily walk.

Since it is after 4:30, we have a reasonable chance at a room, particularly as the kind Captain Starr loaded us with Euros. The desk clerk looks sourly at my request without a reservation, but when we slide over our passports, his mood changes as the inserts drift to the floor behind the counter. Remarkably, a room is made available, but not with a view of the sea, unless we are willing to wait [translation: more Euros] but he is disappointed again when we accept his first choice, and like most Americans, don't ask to see the room before booking it.

Upstairs, the room overlooks the top of the kitchen. We don't expect to be here for very long, so we drop our small bag and go out in search of some clothing for both of us; the previous set still either at our hotel in Athens or in Towson's Warehouse in Canakkale. At this rate, I say to myself, we will have papered all of Europe with our clothing before we are done. The taxi driver had recommended that we go to the central Souk, Alexandria's Market in the geographic center of the city.

The Souk is a warren, similar to Istanbul, but surrounded by many streets of outdoor vendors: carts and stalls with cheap goods. We had been directed to bypass these and focus on the better stores closer to the center. I wait for Marcia while she picks out some casual clothes, and a *djellaba* cloak with a headscarf. I pick one out also; in dark green, while hers is white. Her biggest problem is finding something that will fit her tall frame, but eventually, we are both outfitted again, and put our stuff into another new rolling bag. The sun is starting to set and throughout the city and we hear the calls of the mullahs to fourth prayer. This evening, as the celebrations and feasting grows louder, we take the quieter choice of a small dinner served in our room and then bed.


## THURSDAY MORNING

This morning, we rise early and walk out to the harbor. To the west, we can see a fort, built from the stones of the Great Lighthouse of antiquity. To the east, at the base of the enclosing land arm, is the library, dominant in its circular shape. As we walk there, we stop at a café and have coffee, *fuul* and *t'aamiyya* which are fried concoctions of vegetables and sesame paste stuffed in a pita. The vendor has a huge vat of cooking oil in which they are fried, so the food arrives hot and flavorful, though not my normal breakfast choice. This morning, we wear our djellabas and sandals, so we blend in with the Egyptians, except for our height and Marcia's crimson hair which is only partially concealed by her headscarf.

Inside the library, we orient ourselves to the ultra-modern building, and bypass the main reading rooms for the antiquities center. There, the arrangement is very similar to that of the Library of Congress. Nothing is allowed out onto the public floor, but research can be done in a series of tiny rooms with glass walls, so very little can be hidden. We decide that the security of the reading rooms and research facilities precludes our being able to begin a realistic search. So we opt for the Antiquities Museum; a portion of the library devoted to artifacts and old manuscripts. After walking around the showcases, we search for a curator's office. One of the guards follows us with a very suspicious look on his face, perhaps stimulated by our dress more than our manner. Finally, as we look through manuscript displays in one of the specially humidified rooms, he comes over to confront us. English is his first choice.

"Are you looking for something in particular?" he asks us.

"A very old book," Marcia tells him.

"This section of the library is for antiquities, but not books. You will have to go to the manuscript section in the main library."

"This is a book that may have survived the ancient Library, and then was brought here from Troy. We are searching for the book, but we are also searching for the Keepers of the Book." I add to Marcia's statement.

"I said we have no books here in the museum, but you may speak with a curator. If you wait, I shall see if one of them is available. Please wait here."

The guard comes back in a couple of minutes and calls for us to follow him. We go behind a display of mummies in their wooden boxes, and through a door which the guard opens with his key card. In a corridor, we are taken to an office, and left inside. As the guard closes the office door, I can hear the lock click

Inside the office, there is a computer terminal, a small research desk with a couple of uncomfortable chairs, and a reading lamp. There are no windows. There are also no apparent visible air ducts opening into this room, but it is not uncomfortable. After a moment or two, the outer door opens and an older man, probably mid 70s enters, studies both of us with only a nod as a greeting, and then without speaking, goes over to the computer terminal and begins to type. With the first keystroke, a picture of the library appears, together with a login script. Then a second and yet a third protected page appears. Finally, he keys in a statement or question, and the screen blanks a moment. Both our photographs appear on the screen. He looks carefully at each photo and back to us, pointing to our djellaba hoods and waving for us to remove them. Then he looks again. The background of the photos appears to be the Poseidon Temple Keeper facility. He turns to us with an expression devoid of emotion.

"Tell me exactly what you are looking for."

I immediately answer "We are seekers of the Book, and search for the Keeper."

"And where did you learn of this Book?"

"We learned it first from the key, then from the armor, then from a Keeper, and then followed the ancient arrow to this place, at the tip of the arrow." The man looks at her for a very long time, and then at me.

"And what shall you do with this Book, should you locate it?"

This time, I answer. "It is deemed that a Seeker shall come and the Keeper shall bequeath to the Seeker the knowledge and wisdom of the Book, for the benefit of mankind."

"Noble words, but just words; I believe that you want to find this mythical book for yourself, so your quest is ended. Please leave now." He gets up and turns off the computer terminal. Then he opens the door to escort us out.

I stay rooted in my spot in the little room and continue: "So many have died to protect the Book and its secrets. These are not for one man alone, because they represent a time capsule of great discoveries. Our country is not perfect by any means, and our leaders are equally imperfect. But we have men and women who also aspire to doing good works. This may be the right time for the works to be discovered. If your enclave will trust us, then we shall make whatever effort to honor that trust."

"But can you speak for others?"

"Frankly, no, I cannot. All I can promise is that we shall try."

"I shall consider what you have said, and speak to others. You understand that I already am at risk by revealing myself to you. If your words are deemed to be true, you shall hear from me tomorrow. Now please go. You probably have been spotted here, so you are not safe. But if you survive the night, perhaps tomorrow."

With that final word, he departs, leaving the door open for us. Having come so close, I am reluctant to go, but Marcia persuades me that there is nothing here for us tonight, and we were better off doing as the curator told us and let the next move be theirs. So we go back the way we came, and arrive at the main reading room, then out to the central reception. When we get outside, it is still late morning, so we decide to go back to the hotel and shed our djellabas for more comfortable clothing. I guess I am not used to the lack of air movement from neck to ankles.

Inside the hotel lobby, we are about to enter the elevator when a voice calls to us. Johann Froehlich is standing by a lounge chair, waiting for us.

"Dr. Froehlich, what are you doing here?"

"Good afternoon Simon; Marcia, we have never met. I am Johann Froehlich. It is a distinct pleasure to meet you at last. Yes I was waiting for you, for you both, as a matter of fact. Marcia, I know of you from your very fine work at the NSA – stupid people for letting petty squabbles get you ousted. Do you mind if I call you Marcia? Simon, I congratulate you on your investigation. You have sacrificed a lot to undertake this, but I see from the two of you here together, that you both have gained a lot as well."

"Thanks. But why are you here?"

"Actually, your Admiral asked me to help you. He was ready to send troops in, or a team as a backup, but this is a sensitive matter and needs acknowledgement by these Keepers, that they will do the best thing by making the Book available to you. Force and arms will not do it; only diplomacy. The Admiral believes that my track record in power diplomacy is good, and if you needed some assistance in convincing these people of your sincerity, I could help. Besides, we have an additional problem that I need to share with you both. Can we sit somewhere, perhaps in the bar?"

The bar is empty, due to the time of day and Ramadan, although there is a barman arranging glasses and bottles. He ignores us as we take a small corner table for the three of us. "Our Mr. X has surfaced again. I believe that he is not a single person, but a small group of people that are attempting to subvert normal channels in the executive branch of our government, and turn huge profits from a number of expedient ventures."

"Do you think that these are government people or corporate?"

"I believe the primary thrust is private, although there are a couple of important government people paving the way."

"Where did you learn this information?"

393

"To answer your question, I have to give you some history. About 10 years ago, I was invited to a meeting set up by the State Department, with several CEOs who were discussing the rise of China and India as competitors to American Industry. During our meetings, we listened to a number of experts who predicted that our future markets, particularly international markets, would be served in the future by primarily non-American manufacturers due to a weakening dollar and the availability of cheap labor outside the U.S. I found it very informative and accurate, as the future unfolded. Most of the representatives at those meetings responded by investing heavily in overseas production and partnerships with foreign companies who needed investment capital.

There was a general perception that concentration of political power within the corporate sector would be healthy for the country. These organizations wanted a stronger voice in the government, and sought out many different approaches to achieve this. In order to achieve this kind of control, there needed to be a compliant Administration and Congress, and a less restrictive Court. There also needed to be national diversion through fear. I am afraid that I saw too much similarity between what was proposed at these meetings and what I experienced in Germany during the late 20s and 30s. I was not in favor of a corporate run government, where profit substituted for a republic. I dropped out of these discussions, but they have continued, and possibly have engendered a new under-government that is extremely well heeled and growing in power. If these forces are supported by senior government bureaucrats, then they would present a formidable foe. I am not certain if this exists, but little events that have occurred have led me to believe that there may be some that have picked up these ideas and are running with them."

"Do you have any specific evidence or anyone in particular that might be behind such a movement?" I queried.

"No, but I will say that if we are successful in recovering this Book, and if it is as valuable to future research as I think I could be, then it will certainly draw out these parties. All I want to do is to let you know so that you will be watchful and prepared."

"Dr. Froehlich," said Marcia "I will be very frank with you. You have a reputation of getting what you want, and doing it by whatever means available. I don't trust that you are telling us the complete truth. What are you concealing from us?"

"My dear, you are extraordinarily perceptive and I commend you for that. Yes, I confess I do have an ulterior motive. After hearing of this great tome and its contents, I should like to see it myself, and help secure it for our society. You must know that as a scientist, I have always cherished new ideas. Among other things, they have given me a lifestyle that I could have never hoped to achieve without invention and innovation. But to see it, to touch it, even for a short moment, would give me great pleasure. Marcia, you are wrong about one thing. I feel a responsibility to the country that took me in, and I feel a responsibility to my deceased former partner who spent so many years searching for it – however misguided he may have been. My one error with Ernst was to betray us to the Germans and get those Polish Resistance people killed. I regret this and have so for 60 years. But it happened out of the ignorance of youth; if there can be a defense. Now, may I invite you to dine with me? It would give me great pleasure to have the company of two beautiful people like you both."

Marcia and I look to one another for objections, but finding none, she speaks first. "We accept your invitation. What time would you like us to meet you?"

"Let us say 8:30. That will give me a chance to lie down for a little while. At my age, it is one of life's pleasures that I both appreciate as well as employ."

We continue our walk to the elevator. It was open and empty. When we got up to our room, however; it was also open, but not empty. In the room, waiting for us, was the curator from the library museum. As we walk in and I see him standing by the window, I say by way of greeting "You turn up in the oddest locations."

"You both must be very careful. There are people around the hotel and in the library that have been asking about you. Have you checked your clothing for a listening device or GPS transmitter?"

"No, all of our clothes are newly purchased, except, that is, for our shoes. I take off my sandals and look carefully at the stitching and straps, then turn them over and examine the soles. Nothing looked out of the ordinary. Marcia did the same with her sneakers, with a similar result.

"Did you bring anything with you from Turkey?"

"No, nothing" I said, at which point Marcia jumps in "Simon, our documents!" We empty our wallets on the bed. Nothing seemed amiss. Passports, ID cards, everything are examined in excruciating detail, but nothing. I am feeling much more relieved as I start to put my wallet back together. Then I notice something odd. My American Express card has been used quite a few times, with the result that the magnetic strip on the back has gotten worn. This card's strip is almost unmarked. I look at the card, and see that it is my card, and it is my signature on the back. The front of the card is scratched where it has been swiped by readers, particularly the older ones. But the magnetic strip is virtually new. I look at the edge and see something unusual; the stripe is slightly separating from the card. I use my fingernail and pick at it and then the whole edge lifts from the plastic. I realize that it not bonded into the card. I pull it off and hold it up to the light. The strip is slightly translucent and I can see a couple of small squares, infinitesimally thicker than the rest. Back to the card, I can see that under it the original magnetic strip is still embedded in the card. I take the strip and hold it out to our guest.

"It's a GPS transmitter" our guest said. "You have been followed since you left Turkey."

"It must be Towson." As I explain to the curator, I take Marcia's card and look at its strip as well. Sure enough, her magnetic strip is a phony as well. "Daniel Towson is a Turk with designs on the Book. He captured us in Troy and forced us to spend the night as his guest. I suppose he put these little gems in our wallets while we were asleep. Yes, if he is on the trail, we are certainly in for a rough time." I turned to the curator "You had better get out of here so you won't be caught."

"Don't worry about me. Here, let me take those strips. I will keep them with me for a while when I leave you, and confuse them. But for now, I have something for you." He reached down alongside the table and picked up a briefcase that I had not noticed before. I opened the case to find, inset within sponge rubber, a golden metal book. It was quite thick. I held up the case to the curator "This is the Book?"

"Yes. This is a product of history. Guard it well."

With that, he goes to the window, opens it, and steps out onto the ledge. Then he takes hold of a thick wire which was hanging down outside which has a hook attached to it at waist height. He clipped a carabineer on his belt to this hook and gives the wire a jerk. The wire goes taut and he is pulled out of our window, up to the roof.

Marcia and I take the book out of the briefcase and open the pages. It was fantastic. The tiniest writing, formulas and diagrams had been painstakingly created. I put it back and close the case.

"I guess we need to be on our way" I said.

"What about dinner with Dr. Froehlich? Do you want to call the Admiral?"

"Yes, let's have dinner with him. I think that so long as the curator, or should I say the 'Keeper' has the GPS strips and stays away from us; we should have a temporary break. But I will call the Admiral as well."

"Simon, do you think that Froehlich can help us?"

"I think we can use all the help we can get. Do you believe him?"

"Let me say that I am impressed by his sincerity. I am particularly interested in his views on Mr. X and his friends. If Towson is only one of our threats, then I don't know what we are going to do. Froehlich has a lot of powerful associates who might help us as well. Do you think that Froehlich could be Mr. X?"

"Sweetheart, I really don't know. There are so many possibilities, that regardless of the risk, we have to trust someone." I had purchased a burn phone at the souk, which I now use to call the Admiral at the office. "We have succeeded," I said. "Get us out of here."

"Can you get to the airport?"

"Yes, but we will not be alone. Your emissary contacted us."

"He is a real friend. Trust him."

"Thank you, sir. We should be ready at about 9. But there is a small problem. We were tagged with a GPS Locator in Troy by Towson and I would expect some company here very soon."

"Very well; we have a team on the way, but it will take four hours. Can you get to our CIA office in Alexandria?"

"Sir, I think that they would be less than helpful. One of them gave us a veiled threat on the ship and accused us of poaching. I would feel more comfortable if we waited for your team."

"Yes, I got the word from the DCI – you are probably right. LZ in six hours at the Airport: we'll be there." I hang up.

"Simon, do we wait here until dinner?"

"Yes. I just wish that I had a weapon. Let me go downstairs to the Gift Shop and see if I can find anything that may be of some use."

"All right, but don't be long. I will worry." I look out into the corridor, but, except for a housekeeper pushing a cart, it is empty. Down in the lobby, the desk clerks are servicing a couple of check-ins. In the Gift Shop, I search through a lot of decorative junk, but there is nothing. Even a ball of string could be useful, but none to be had. On the wall, next to some Arabian knickknacks, there are a couple of phony daggers. I asked to see them. The rhinestone studded sheaths conceal a cheap metal blade about 8 inches long and curved, but there is no edge on it at all. Well, for the price, it is something. I bought two. Also, I see a couple of weighted Lucite

397

paperweights, with pictures of the old Alexandria Lighthouse imbedded. I pick up a couple of these as well. There is also a jewelry-making kit. I didn't care too much about the plastic jewels, but there is a nice spool of tough bead wire in each kit. I also asked for a small sewing kit to repair buttons. It comes with a pair of threaded needles. I paid for the purchases, put one of the paperweights in a pocket, and tuck the fancy knife into my pants, then back to the room. I use my card key to go in. Marcia comes out of the bathroom and asked "Did you find anything?"

I dumped my bag on the bed. Marcia fingered the items and laughed. "Great, you bring a knife to a gun fight. That's really evening the odds." Holding up the sewing and jewelry kits she added "Not that I meant to needle you, but what're these for?"

"I owe you a bridal gift. I thought I could make you a necklace."

She looked at me and screws up her face for a retort but stopped when I added "no, the wire is useful in close-up work. The plastic jewels will also be good if we have to bribe our way out."

"Oh yes. By the way, what is the state of our cash?"

"We've got nearly a thousand Euros. Let's split them between us." I gave the dagger to Marcia and instruct her on how to hold it underhanded and stab upwards. Even with no edge, the point should have good effect. I also show her where to aim for. She understands immediately how to punch holding the paperweight to save her hand. I unthread the needles from the kit and stick them into the inside of my belt, to use as crude lock-picks if necessary.

"Well, my dear," I said "we are as ready as we can be."

"What about our Souk clothes?"

"Let's leave them here along with the bag."

"Simon, I never thought I would say that I was tired of buying clothes. Between clothes and rental cars, this is going to cost us a small fortune. How about I make some calls and start getting things sent home?"

"Good idea. Also while you are at it, I don't think there is any point in keeping our hotel in Istanbul as well."

"But your digging stick! All right, I will call there also."

While Marcia uses the cell, I telephone downstairs and tell them that we will be checking out in the morning. I also order a wake-up call and a car for the airport for a 7 AM pickup tomorrow. Maybe if someone asks, they will be encouraged to wait until then. Not that I really believe it.

As the calls are completed, there is a knock on the door. I look though the security pinhole and see a waiter carrying a tray. "Marcia, did you order anything?" I ask.

She answers from the bathroom "Yes, a bottle of wine and some appetizers."

I look back out of the peephole but can't get a good look at the tray, so I open the door. The waiter, a thin short man with his omnipresent mustache and black hair bows slightly and then, carrying his covered tray, walks softly into our room and looks around for a place to put it down. His jacket is white and is far too large for his small frame, which I think is a little odd, but not enough to stimulate suspicion. I point to the desk, where the briefcase is lying. The waiter picks it up and moves it to the floor, balancing the tray in his other hand. Then he turns his back to me as he places the tray on the desk. I go over to the bed where the end table holds my wallet and money. When I turn back, the waiter is holding a pistol in his hand and the briefcase in the other. He waves me down to sit on the bed, while he watches until I am seated. Then he backs up towards the door. I can hear Marcia moving around in the bathroom, unaware of what is going on. I dare not call out, since she would come into the line of fire with me.

As the waiter reaches the door, he realizes that he can't open it against its spring, without putting something down. So the briefcase goes on the floor again and he reaches behind him to open the door. I realize that it's now or lose the book, so I start to rise, but the waiter anticipates my move and insistently motions me to sit again. Then he opens the door and holding it open with his foot, reaches down for the briefcase. At that moment, Marcia comes in from the bathroom. The gunman spots her and twists to cover her. I launch myself across the room and get about half way when there is a shot and a bullet whizzes just past my back to lodge in the carpet. Marcia jumps back into the bathroom as the man scoops up the case and backs out the door, then turns to run down the corridor. I follow, while I hear Marcia trotting behind me.

The stairwell door is close by, and is just starting to close as I ram my shoulder through it. Above, on the next flight of stairs, the man is climbing. I head up the stairs as fast as I can go, taking two risers at a time. On the next floor, the stairway door is closing, but I can hear footfalls up another flight, so I ignore it and keep climbing. Five more flights we ascend and then I hear the door opening and the sound of something heavy hitting the floor. As I come around the landing, I can see the man lying on the top steps while standing above him is Marcia, holding the briefcase.

"I was wondering when you would get here," she says.

My breath is ragged as I step over the body. "How?..."

"The elevator, my darling. It was opening just as I came out of the room, so I took it to the top floor and waited in the stair doorway. When I saw him round the landing, I leaped into the stairway and crowned him. The lighthouse did the trick." She held out the heavy glass globe that I had purchased in the gift shop. It had a big bloody splotch on one side, with a hairs stuck in the middle. The gun was under the body, so I rolled him over and picked it up, pocketing it for a future need. He was still breathing, but out for a while. Under his waiter's jacket were a dark suit coat, and a thin I.D. wallet inside the breast pocket. Opening it, I see a photo of the same man, over which was an embossed shield: a blue circle with a small globe in the center with two red satellite orbits crisscrossing the globe, which partially covered a yellow torch. Around the rim of the shield were written the words "Defense Intelligence Agency, United States of America."

"He is apparently one of ours, but why the gun?" I looked at the other panel of the I.D. It identified the holder as Angelo Ramirez and had another color shield; this one of the Department of Defense. "I wonder how Mr. Ramirez got the word on us, and the order to seize the Book."

"Simon, you assume that there was an order. Perhaps this has nothing to do with his job, but instead he is a double?"

"I suppose that he could be one of Towson's men. Good job, by the way."

"Thanks. Do these guys work alone, or could there be a partner somewhere around?"

"DIA is a lot like us; agents can work alone or in tandem. The problem is that the DIA's mission has to do with military intelligence, and this is definitely not strictly military."

"Well, your Admiral is running our mission, which is also decidedly not military."

"Yes, that's true. Let's ask Ramirez." I pulled the jewelry wire from my pocket and used it to fabricate makeshift handcuffs, binding his hands behind him. By now, he is rousing, moaning. I pull him to his feet as his eyes come open, and we march towards the elevator, while Marcia goes ahead to press the call button.

"Chess, you'd better let me go if you don't want a pack of trouble. I am here under orders from the government."

"I am sure, Ramirez, that your orders did not include shooting us. I'd like to know about that."

"My orders are to retrieve the case, by whatever means that are needed. Look, we both work for the same people. I am only doing my job."

The elevator arrives. Inside is an older couple, who stare as we enter with the handcuffed waiter. Both of them press themselves hard into the back wall as Marcia pushes our floor button. As the door opens, I am face to face with a woman in a conservative grey suit, with dark hair and eyes. She stands square in the center of the door as it opens; a slightly haughty expression on her face. But there is nothing haughty about the pistol that is elevated to my nose. She backs up a step to give me room to exit the elevator, and I raise the briefcase to her gun, shoving outward as the agent behinds me lowers his torso and buts me out of the way in his escape from the cab. The woman is pushed off balance, so the shot she fires goes right into the briefcase, but with the metal book inside, the bullet doesn't come out the back. I reach around the briefcase and twist the gun from her grip. She turns to run after her partner as he reaches the stairway on the other side of the corridor, both disappearing out the exit door.

Marcia comes out of the elevator right behind me, and as it closes, we both get a last glimpse of the elderly couple still remaining inside, open mouthed.

The corridor is clear, so we head back to our room. Inside, I re-open the case, to find that the bullet has flattened itself against the cover of the book. A different tray is on the desk; this one with a bottle of wine and some appetizers that Marcia had ordered. The first tray left by the bogus waiter, is gone.

After our wine, we decide to have a rest before this evening's fun and games. I search for the other bullet that the DIA agent fired at me, and find it lodged in the floor near the side wall. I dig it out and comb the carpet fibers over the hole. The bullet is quite deformed, considering its path into the concrete slab under the carpet, but I thought that maybe it would be useful for our lab back home. So I put it in a hotel envelope from the desk drawer, and then slide it next to the sponge rubber protecting the book inside the case.

"Simon, have you been thinking how the DIA got sent after us?"

"The only thing that I can figure out is that the Admiral must have reported up his chain of command, and someone up there likes us."

"The question is not just who, but why. Maybe they don't trust Navy ESCORT to get it back. Or possibly DOD is compromised with a rogue."

"Marcia, if it were a rogue, then I would have been shot instantly by the agent when I let him in. This seemed like a pure retrieval assignment. Dead bodies, particularly those of a family service, would not be appreciated very well back home. No, I would say that someone at DOD or with connections at the top of Defense that could get an order out wanted to bypass our recovery for their own purpose. I'll have to ask Froehlich this evening about that possibility."

"You don't suppose, Simon, that it was Froehlich operating independently behind the scenes, while collaborating with us in the open?"

"Well, that could be true as well. But somehow, I doubt it. Everything that started out as a question regarding Froehlich's character, has resolved itself positively. No, the more I think about it, the source has to be within DOD. If it were the corporate group Froehlich told us about, a private security firm would have been used. If it were from CIA or one of the other agencies, someone would have to expose themselves quite far to get DIA to act where they did not want their own Ops people involved. I would say it was a home-grown DOD effort. That brings up the possibility of the Secretary or any of his Operations Staff, but probably not one of the military services, since they each have their own Special Operations folks like the Navy SEALS. Of course, it could still be someone over at the White House, pulling a favor of the Defense Secretary. But there is one positive part of this – if it is merely an effort to secure the Book, we are less likely to be termination targets."

"Yes, well that gives me a real warm fuzzy. Simon, you were shot at, twice if I remember correctly."

"Well there is that. I do think that we should talk to Froehlich tonight. We've got to trust someone."

Nile TV and MBC are both broadcasting English news, but nothing particularly interesting, so I turn it off and we both lie down for a couple of hours. I put the DIA agent's gun close by, just in case.

# 39 *THURSDAY NIGHT – ALEXANDRIA*

The call to evening prayer had come and gone. The sun was below the horizon but the sky was still pinkish when we awoke, and realize that we have only a few minutes before our dinner appointment. Taking the briefcase, our Passports and the DIA Agent's pistol, we leave the room and head for the downstairs bar.

Froehlich is waiting for us in the hotel Lobby. Before joining him, I go back into the gift shop and purchase another jewelry kit; the last piece of wire lost to the DIA agent. The salesman at the Gift Shop looked at me strangely, but made the sale without questions. Outside, Froehlich has a large car waiting. When we settle in the back, I take the jump seat so that I could face him. I place on the briefcase the other seat. "Dr. Froehlich, would you mind if we skip dinner and went directly to the airport?"

"No, but why the rush? Oh my, you have what you came for, don't you? Is that it?"

"Yes, but we must get to the airport. The Admiral is having us all picked up in two hours, and I would rather wait there than in some quiet restaurant where we would be an easy target."

Froehlich calls to the driver to change directions and to take us to the airport. The driver nods and pulls the car out into traffic. "May I see it?" he asked.

"Yes, go ahead," I answer as I pick the case off the seat and hand it across to him. He opens it and gazes down at the Book. His eyes grow very round as he opens it very carefully. He scans at a couple of the pages. Then he closes the Book and re-closes the case.

"My boy, I can only imagine what is in here. It has a value that is incalculable. How did you find it?"

"When we returned to our room, one of the Keepers was there with it. I suppose they trust me. It's pretty amazing to think that a person of relatively no consequence would be trusted with something as important as this." Froehlich sat back in his seat and let me take the case back, but not without holding on to it for just a moment longer.

"Ordinary people sometimes are given extraordinary responsibilities. This is not unusual in history. I would say that few have lived up to the weight of their burdens. I have no doubt, my boy, that you will do exactly what is needed." Froehlich pontificated.

"Thank you Doctor. I appreciate your vote of confidence. But there is something that I want to show you." I pull out the gun and the DIA I.D. and explain the circumstances of my acquiring it. "Doctor, I sure would like to know how the DIA was put onto this."

"Simon, I have some thoughts on this, but would like to hold off my speculations until we are home and I can check out a couple of things. When is the pickup scheduled?"

"At nine, but I am not sure by what method."

We turned a corner and headed to a more sparsely built section of the city. I leaned across to Froehlich and ask him very quietly "Where did you get the car and driver?"

"Oh, the hotel arranged for it."

"Marcia, Professor; I believe that we are not heading to the airport." There is a security glass between the driver and the back seat. It is open; I could see the driver glancing at us from time to time in the rear view mirror as he drives. "Driver, can you tell us how long until we reach the airport?"

"Only a few minutes, sir; I am taking us around a traffic accident on the direct road."

I thought of my options, and decided to risk a crash, so I reach through the open privacy window and push my pistol into the driver's neck. He stiffens but doesn't say anything. "Stop the car along here," I say.

The driver ignores my request and accelerates, with the gun pressed hard into his neck. I hoped for a light or a traffic jam. But there are no lights, and the traffic is getting sparser. We seemed to be at a stalemate. I guess that so long as he drives fast, I won't risk a shot that would surely get us to crash. So I changed tactics. I reached into my pocket and withdrew the mate to Marcia's glass globe. As we pass through some open land. I pull the gun back and then crack the driver on the head with the globe. The car swerves towards the roadside as the driver falls over sideways against the door. There is a chain link fence surrounding a farm, which we break through without slowing. By the time I was able to push myself through the divider, the car was bumping over deep furrows. I landed upside down in the driver's lap with my hands touching the floor next to the pedals. The driver's head is against the window and he seems to be unconscious or dead. I try to reach up to the shift lever to push it into Neutral, but it wouldn't move so long as his foot remains on the accelerator. The bouncing gets rougher as I grappled for the driver's right foot. I get a piece of his pant cuff and pull the foot off the gas pedal. The speed drops and I fall forward against the pedals. I push the brake with my hand and the car slows to a stop. My feet fly out of the security screen and land against the dashboard.

The car is still in gear, so as soon as I let go the break, it starts moving again. I extricate myself from under the wheel and am finally able to shove the gearshift to neutral. The car stops; the engine ticking in the heat. I untangle myself from the driver and crawl out the door. When I open it, the driver flopped outside, his head landing in the field. I crawl over him and pull him out fully, until he is lying flat and examine him to see if he is still with us. Then I call back to Marcia and Froehlich. Marcia had been thrown forward against the jump seat and had broken off the interior ceiling light with her forehead, but says she is OK. Froehlich answered that he too was all right, having been thrown forward into the jump seat. I pull open the back door and Marcia rolls out, with Froehlich crawling out after her. Marcia's head is bleeding a little, but the skull does not appear to be fractured. Froehlich looked shaken, but not injured.

The driver moans, indicating that he is coming around. I make another set of improvised handcuffs, twisting the wire ends together, and then twist the dangling end of the wire around his belt. By then, the driver was conscious, protesting his treatment in all apparent innocence. I take out my ceremonial dagger, and stick the point into his throat. Then I ask him where he was planning to taking us. He spouts a long diatribe in Arabic in reply. "Dr. Froehlich, do you know any Arabic?"

"No, I am sorry" he answered.

"No matter; Marcia, see if there is a map in the glove compartment." She went back into the front and searched around, but there wasn't any map.

"There's no map, Simon, but there is a GPS navigation system. Maybe he put in a destination. She turned on the key and fired up the system. The text was in Arabic, but she fussed with it for a little while and then announces that we are less than a mile from the destination previously plugged in, which was definitely not the airport. I ask her if she could find the airport and put in a new route. She asks me to wait and goes back to her ministrations with the GPS, occasionally punctuated by a few choice curses that I haven't heard since being aboard ship.

The driver meanwhile, gets to his feet but I keep the blade pointed toward him, so he doesn't run. I could see that he is trying to work on the binding wire.

Marcia finally speaks up to say that she found the airport by scanning, but so far is not able to set up a route. I asked Froehlich to get back in the car, and get in myself. I leave the driver where he stood. The moment the car door is closed, he takes off across the field. I figured that we had about 15 minutes before he alerts somebody, so I drive back across the field towards the road. A farmer's family comes out of the house at the far end the field and shouts at us while the farmer points a shotgun towards us, letting fly a couple of blasts. But we are well out of range. I try to stay as close as I can to our original tracks. As we near the hole in the fence, another blast from the shotgun behind sends pellets after us, and I turn my head, to see that the farmer is now on a tractor in hot pursuit, shaking his fist as he lines up another shot. Fortunately we are still too far.

When we reach the road, I glanced over to where Marcia is still trying to set up a route, and ask her to show me the map again. She brings up the display and I can see the airport is to the southwest, but only a short diversion off line from the driver's destination point, which blinks like a bloody star on the map. We have to risk it, I think to myself as I launch us down the road toward the star.

Marcia adjusts the zoom on the map so I can see the local streets, but it is too small a display to also see the airport. Nevertheless, I point us in the general direction and accelerate as much as I dare. Froehlich, meantime, is bouncing along in the back, holding on to an overhead strap with one hand, and the briefcase with the other. After a while, we come to a wide canal, but do not see a bridge across it. I could see on the GPS that the airport is on the other side. I turn us down the canal on a dirt road which runs like a track for mules to pull canal barges. We pass under one bridge, but there is no access ramp, so we keep going. Just a few yards further, a smaller bridge crosses the canal and connects to the parallel track on the other side. We lurch onto the little bridge and scrape the sides of our car as we carefully negotiate what looks more like a pedestrian walkway.

I stop when we get to the other side to give Marcia a chance to find a direct route to the terminal. But before we could start up again, two cars race across the auto bridge and turn down the track to pin us against the side of the smaller bridge. One comes alongside, one drives around the front, and a third, crossing the pedestrian bridge comes in behind touching bumpers to ours. With the canal now on our right, there is no escape. Several men get out of the cars and motion to us with pistols to do likewise. We don't have much choice, so we get out of the car and stand next to the canal. They direct us to their cars. One opens the back door of our car and pulls out the briefcase, opens it for a moment and then puts into the front seat. We all start in convoy heading up to the road towards the airport, leaving our car on the pedestrian bridge.

After about three minutes of driving, we pull up to a back gate at the airport. The driver of the car in front goes to his trunk and comes out with bolt cutters, which he uses to cut the chain on the gate and we drive in, parking at a disused building beyond the end of the main runway. The cars stop, but no one got out. Then I hear the buzzing clattering of a helicopter. 'No rescue this time' I think. The machine descends to a concrete pad out beyond the building, then the rotors tilted towards us and it taxies to the apron. When it stops, the engine is switched off and the rotors slow. The door opens, and I am not surprised at all to see Towson step down. What surprises me is that Lauren comes out behind him. They both walk over to us. Towson has a grim look on his face instead of his usual placid indifference.

Marcia and I get out of two of the cars, while Froehlich comes out of the third. The driver of my car walks over to Towson, holding up the briefcase, which Towson ignores while he stared at Froehlich. "What brings you here, Johann?" he asked.

"Why Ernst, I have not seen you in some time. I am very interested to see that you are not deceased as of yet." I realized suddenly what the switch really was.

"Lauren, you certainly took me on a merry spin."

"I'm sorry, Simon. But this is my father, after all."

Zilbern-Towson looks at me as he says "I see you have brought the case. Is it inside?"

"Yes. But it will do you no good." I comment.

"Of course it will. I have searched for it for 65 years. Now I have it, finally. Max, kill them," he said the last to his driver as he takes the case and starts back to the helicopter."

I called out to Zilbern "If you are interested, I will tell you why it is of no value to you, and all your efforts are for naught."

Zilbern stopped and looked back at me. "All right, tell me. Your final departure can wait another few minutes."

407

"I have been thinking about this since we were given the case in the hotel. It was just too easy. There we were, nobodies from nowhere, yet these people gave us their greatest and most precious possession, with no reservations. They just walked away. Not a likely situation, don't you agree?" He thought for a moment and then waved for me to continue.

"All along through this minefield of a puzzle, I have wondered about their dealings with me. First, the key was planted on me without my knowing, and all the nonsense about its disappearing and re-appearing just when I apparently lost interest. Then there is the armor which appeared unbidden at John Crawford's office. Of course, then there was the cryptic clue at the Temple in Greece and the childish joke of graffiti in the dirt at Troy. Finally the curator comes into my room at the hotel with his throwaway gift of the greatest of all books, the product of centuries. Were these really clues to test my fidelity? I think not. If they indeed had kept this treasure hidden for so many years, why suddenly are they leading me by the nose right to it? You too have been coaxed along this path to the so called eternal Book. What is its significance? Put it all together, Mr. Cryptologist and see what you get?"

Zilbern walks back to me. Then he looked into my eyes and then at the case. He puts the case on the car fender and opens it. The book lays there, in all its golden glory. He looks at it, turning the pages and thinking. Finally he looks back to me "It is a fake."

"Of course it is: just another deception, like all the others. Take a clue from my Trojan Puzzle Horse. Open it up and the opposite will be found. You expect a friend and get an enemy; you expect a fortune and you get nothing – even less than nothing, because you have exposed yourself in the process. 'What was the point?' I asked myself. I can't believe that these AFAR descendants had any intention of giving us the Book. They recognized that a major enemy was assembling its forces to search out and take their precious history, so a blind, a diversion, an illusion was set up. Dr. Zilbern, you, I Marcia, all of us: we were set up to draw you out into the open. Frankly, I doubt if there really is a book. But even if there is, this certainly isn't it. Perhaps the metal of the pages is valuable. Even perhaps some of the information may be useful, but it is by no means the Holy Grail. Take it or leave it. It doesn't much matter. But just go before you are caught for the evil that you have already done. Now that you are exposed, you will be caught, make no mistake about it. Why don't you just take your helicopter and your daughter, and go."

"You make a good case, but I spent too many years to drop it now. I shall take this Book anyway. It may be useful to me after all. The story alone will bring millions, and as you say, the metal may be quite rare. Perhaps I will write a book myself. Let's go, Lauren. Max, kill them, but not here. Take them somewhere where their bodies will not be found."

"Dr. Zilbern, there are a few minor things that I really wish to know. I realize that it won't matter, but perhaps you will humor me. After all, I will be dead in a little while so it will cost you nothing."

"What is it that you want?"

"First, did you have my first wife, Jean killed?"

"No I did not. It was the Americans who did that. I wanted to capture her because I believed that she was part of the Keeper brotherhood, and I wanted to interrogate her. But a wet team from the U.S. government got to her first. I believe that forces within the U.S. Government that were also onto the Book, captured, tortured and then assassinated her. I learned that the bomb which took her life was chosen as a way of concealing the effects of their torture on her body."

"And what about the couple that took our cruise. What did you do with them?

"My people thought that the couple was the two of you. I had given instructions that the information about the book be obtained from you both. When we realized that you had switched identities, they were disposed of; down in the crater of the new volcano forming in Santorini Harbor. They were nothing: nobodies.

What about the people at the Poseidon Temple?"

"I had nothing to do with that. I knew that the book was not there since it would not have made any sense. Their comings and goings at the Poseidon temple were too public. The book would have been far too exposed there. Whoever killed them had no idea where to find the book."

"I have only one more question. Who is the man you met at your boat in Vallejo?"

"He is someone that has been extremely valuable to me in my search."

"From your conversation with him, I understand that he is actually directing your activities."

"Absolutely not! He has his own agenda, but it certainly is not mine. He is in it for the money."

"Dr. Zilbern, this Book has been your obsession. Why? If you aren't in it for the money, then why?"

"You, as an American, cannot understand. You have always lived in a country that has been victorious in battle, which has dictated to many countries how governments should act, how economies should be built and how politics should be administered. In the process, your country has grown rich, your people prosperous, your companies powerful, and your military the envy of the world. You project this power over weaker nations and peoples with abandon, and do it under a banner which reads "Freedom," and "Democracy." You have never lived in a defeated country, one that has been ruthlessly divided and ruled without respect. I come from just such a country. My homeland struggled for 40 years to get back on its feet after being destroyed by you and your people. My only goal is to bring this back to my people and use it to rebuild the great promise that we once had, to regain our honor, and to take our rightful place as rulers in the world. I will see to it that you and your kind are defeated before it is my turn to die. My daughter, Lauren, shares this belief. She is our future. Her mother was denied the medicine which would have saved her life by your government's hand. It is for this that I have served *my* country for all these years." Zilbern kept the briefcase in his hand as he started for the helicopter.

"Father, stop; this is wrong" Lauren said, looking horrified at her father's words. "You can't do this. Don't kill these people. They are my friends. They helped me. Germany isn't your home anymore."

"Lauren, get on the plane. We have to go."

"Father, please. I helped you because I thought that you were protecting us, that you had been wronged greatly and were righting this wrong. But it has nothing to do with us. The wrong never happened. There was nothing that needed putting right. This is entirely about you and your thirst for power and recognition. Please."

"Lauren, you just don't understand. Froehlich and his kind; they all are out to destroy me, just like they did to my homeland and to your mother. He betrayed us. I trusted him and he betrayed me. He is the Devil incarnate. Don't you see that?"

"I see maybe now. You killed all those people: Towson, that kind Edith, Hudson, and that man John Crawford and his daughter. What did she ever do to you? And now more; and you call them nobodies?"

"Lauren, just get on the plane. How could you understand? You never lived with the bombs that killed your family. Sure, the Americans took me in. But see how they treated me. 'Stay in your laboratory. Work for us. We will take care of you'; meantime, my beautiful Charlotte got sick. 'Keep

410

working. You are valuable to us. Your work is important. We will take care of her.' and she got weaker and needed medicine and a specialist. Lauren, they let her die because they didn't care about anything but what I could do for them. And Froehlich: my friend, my advocate, He is the worst of the lot: tells me he is my friend and then stabs us in the back. Lauren, he stole from us your birthright. I now have regained it. I am only sorry I never killed him sooner. Now; get aboard and we shall go home together."

"But he shared the company with me."

"Don't believe anything that snake says. Get on board right now!"

"No father. No. You go. But leave the case. It is not yours. You can't take it." She grabbed at the case, but Ernst was very strong. He climbed into the helicopter, dragging the case and Lauren with it. With both feet inside, he yells at the pilot to take off. Lauren is still hanging onto the case. The machine starts to lift off, with Lauren clinging to the case and Ernst trying to hang onto the case with one hand, while fumbling with his seatbelt with the other. Lauren's weight drags at the case and starts pulling Ernst out of the seat. The helicopter tilts towards the two bodies hanging out the door. Ernst lunges forward to grab at the back of the pilot's seat but misses the seat, catching the pilot around the neck. Lauren's weight pulls Ernst almost completely out of the machine as he clutches tighter on the pilot's neck to stop from falling out.

"Father, let go" Lauren screams as she is lifted higher, hanging onto the case with both hands.

"Never! Never!" Her father grits his teeth and hangs onto the case with one hand, while desperately clutching the pilot's neck in the other. The machine is about 15 feet above the ground and starts to tilt backwards as the pilot grabs the collective to stop being pulled out, while he also clutches at Ernst's hand choking him. As the machine tilts upward, Lauren's body rises with it; her legs flying towards the tail. Ernst is dragged even further back, and the pilot finally lets go of the Collective and adds his left hand to the right; scratching and pulling at Ernst's hand which has closed off his breath. The machine starts to slide backwards towards the ground, and the tail rotor gets closer to impact. Lauren finally break's Ernst's grip and falls to the ground, clutching the case, while just over her head and a little behind, the copter slides the remaining distance, the rotor catching the concrete. Instantly the blades on the tail rotor shear off and fly like shrapnel everywhere. One large piece flies towards the open door of the machine and just misses catching Ernst in the back as it crashes through the front windshield. The helicopter is no longer able to fly and the main rotor torques the fuselage up in a circle to slam onto the

411

unyielding concrete. The rotor blades strike the ground and shatter apart, pieces folding and spinning across the apron and runway. The fuel lines burst and the disintegrating engine flashes the raw fuel into a huge ball of flame, followed by a black cloud that mushrooms above the wreckage.

Lauren is lying on the ground with her hands still outstretched to the case, which is just past her reach.

When the machine started to crash, it distracts the gunmen so Marcia throws herself at her driver, pulling out her knife and plunging it into his chest as I showed her. I do the same to the nearest gun. The other man from Marcia's car had his gun already pointed at her and pulled the trigger. There was a small puff, and she falls to the concrete. I explode at the fellow, kicking the gun from his hand and then smashing him again and again in this face, breaking his nose and driving it into his brain. I fly at a second man, delivering a roundhouse kick to the side of his head as the third man lines up a shot at me with his gun, but then Froehlich tackles him. They both go down onto the concrete. I started running for the helicopter before I realize that it was all over there. I reversed direction toward Marcia. Another shot rings out and the impact of the bullet into my chest drives me down to the ground. There is no pain at first, but then it hits like an express train and I cry out as I fall. I tried to get to my feet, but cannot. The waves of pain come with blurring eyes and rubber limbs, but I could only see as far as Marcia's body, lying quietly on the rough concrete. I started to drag myself, but my legs aren't working. I use my arms. Each pull brings a new rush of pain, but I have to get to her. She was lying partly across the body of the man she had stabbed. A hole between her shoulders dribbles blood on the ground.

"Marcia" I struggled with the words. "Marcia" I call again. Then I collapse on her. I could hear somewhere in the distance my name being called.

.

412

# 40 *ONE WEEK LATER - WASHINGTON*

The meeting in the secure Situation Room under the White House had just started. In the seat usually reserved for the President, sits the National Security Advisor. Seated around him are the Director of Central Intelligence (CIA), The Director of the National Security Agency (NSA), The Director of the Defense Intelligence Agency (DIA), the Secretary of Homeland Security (DHS), The Secretary of Defense (DOD), the Secretary of State, and the White House Chief of Staff (COS). In the seat usually occupied by the Chairman of the Joint Chiefs of Staff sits Vice Admiral Robert Foster Lewis, Director of the Navy's ESCORT Division of the Office of Naval Intelligence. As a special guest of the National Security Advisor, Dr. Johann Froehlich also sits in on the meeting.

The Advisor was speaking. "Dr. Froehlich, you have studied this Book. Please brief us on its contents?"

"Yes sir. As you all know, it is an archeological anomaly. The language that it is written in is coded, but with the key provided by the Smithsonian Institution, we should be able to complete the translation of its contents.

"From what we have been able to decipher so far, the contents of the book are remarkable and startling. The genetic information alone may prove to provide cures for AIDS, diabetes, cancer, and virtually all auto-immune diseases. With regard to energy generation, it seems to suggest methods and a formula for inexpensively utilizing seawater to produce inexhaustible hydrogen fuel. In farming, there are clues to increasing the yield of rice, for example, by 100 times through genetic mutation and dry-land farms. Gentlemen, this book and the information contained within it may revolutionize many sciences today and provide solutions to major food supply, water distribution, and health management challenges which affect political and social stabilization and human survival."

The Secretary of Defense reacted immediately to Froehlich's words. "World peace and prosperity are very admirable goals, Dr. Froehlich, but this is foolishly idealistic. Our country needs to remain at the top of the economic heap. We cannot allow this to get into the hands of our enemies.

Our entire military advantage would be compromised if cheap plentiful food, fuel and water were made available to everyone."

Everyone around the table nodded. Then the White House Chief of Staff spoke up "Gentlemen, this Book may be political and economic dynamite. Our world-power status is founded on the continuing profitability of our businesses and their productivity. If disease was eliminated, our pharmaceutical industry, health services and insurance industries would become hollow shells overnight. Our energy companies, and particularly our oil companies, would fail along with our auto makers. Our political survival is dependent on the economy. I can assure you that The President will be very interested in any recommendations that you make; provided that you keep these principles paramount in your deliberations."

"For now," responded Froehlich, seeing the turn of conversation and concern, "I believe we should do nothing beyond continuing to maintain an absolute lid on the Book, as well as ensuring the continuing security at its location. The translation is far from complete. I suggest that we continue the work. Once the full nature of information is revealed, we will be in a better position to make a final decision."

The DCI leaned over to the NSA Director and whispered to him; whereupon he nodded and then spoke "It is particularly important that the code of the Book be secured even more than the Book itself. I suggest that the book should be moved to our facilities, and we should be tasked to complete the decoding. It is our mission, after all. Both the DCI and I would be far more comfortable if it is physically under our control. It potentially could compromise our missions."

The White House Security Advisor responded "I agree. This book is far too dangerous to allow it fall into foreign hands. I recommend that it be relocated to NSA or Langley it until the translations are completed."

Admiral Lewis looked around the room "Gentlemen outside of this room, there are very few others that know about this book. As long as it remains in place under tight control, there is little likelihood that word will indeed get out. If it is transferred to Langley or Ft. Meade, many more people will become aware of the work, and it will not remain contained."

The Defense Secretary asked "I agree that it should remain under the Navy's control. But I also suggest that any private individuals who know about it should be detained and held incommunicado until we make our decision?"

"Mr. Secretary" The Admiral responded "While you do have that option under The Patriot Act, I think that would be an over-reaction to your concerns. I will assume full responsibility for keeping these few individuals quiet. You can count on it."

The White House Chief of Staff broke in. "The President has every confidence in you, Admiral Lewis. I agree. Also, gentlemen, this is not a cause for a turf war. The President expects total cooperation among all the agencies represented at this table."

The Defense Secretary started to speak, but then glances around the table to see that the others agreed with the COS, so he kept quiet.

Dr. Froehlich picked up the book, which was lying in the center of the table and said "This shall be returned to the lab and the translation will continue. No one here must speak of it outside of this room. Any leaks could be disastrous for all of us. As he said these last words, he glanced pointedly at the political appointees in the room."

The COS echoed Dr. Froehlich. "If there is a single hint of a leak, we will know precisely where it came from, and you can be assured that The President will not be amused."

Froehlich added one final comment. "I suggest that the recordings which are made of proceedings in this room be destroyed immediately, and any notes, even those in your appointment books as to the fact that this meeting took place, should be destroyed as well."

The meeting broke up, and each of the attendees left the table. Froehlich picked up the slightly battered briefcase with a hole on one face. He opened it and put the book inside. Then he closed the case and left the room.

# 41 *TWO DAYS LATER – JACKSON HOLE, WYOMING*

The Snake River Grille occupies the second floor of a wood frame building just off the main square in the small town of Jackson, Wyoming. On the first floor below, a large shop offers animal hides and clothing made with wild animal products from around the world. In front of the stair leading to the restaurant, an erect grizzly stands guard while tourists send their kids into its arms for photographs. Around the corner is the downtown plaza of Jackson, marked with elk antler arches at the four corners, collected by Boy Scouts in the National Elk Preserve just north of town. During summers and winters alike, visitors on their way to or from Yellowstone or Grand Teton National Parks break their travels to amble along the wooden sidewalks and dream of western life two centuries ago.

The Grille is very popular with locals, but few know of a special back room that is rented for private dining meetings. When the dining room is full, usually every night of the week, no one notices people disappearing past the bathrooms and through an 'employees only' door set in a corridor recess. It has a separate entrance from the kitchen as well, so that tables can be set, meals served and cleared without anyone aware but the kitchen staff.

Tonight, the room is full, with sixteen men and two women. Many of those in attendance know each other, for they meet informally three or four times a year, each time in different location chosen for discretion and isolation as well as venues with good food. Tonight's menu is typical. Idaho Trout, Scottish Salmon, Rack of Lamb and NY Strips are available; each prepared precisely to the diner's specifications. The wine list is tastefully assembled, and includes many fine wines from the west coast. Desserts too, attract the appetite with Bourbon Crème Brulee, deep dish Cheesecake and Rhubarb Pie.

Part of the ritual is to defer business until after dinner; yet this group was all business. Included are the CEOs of three oil companies, three national utilities, two automakers, four pharmaceuticals, two chemical companies and three insurance conglomerates. Financial institutions are not represented tonight, nor any technology company present this evening although two usually attended from each sector. For tonight, they were not

417

invited. There was one representative of the government also attending. He had, in fact, asked for the meeting.

Coffee and brandy were served with dessert. Meetings during prior years usually were blue with cigar smoke, but these days many had curtailed this practice for their health and in deference to the elevation of several women to management positions and representation at this assembly.

The government man rose as the group quieted down. He touched his glass gently with his spoon, bringing remaining conversations to a standstill.

"Gentlemen, and ladies; I have information which will be of great concern to you. I have learned of some researches currently underway in Washington, which can bring ruin to each of your organizations." He waited until he had their undivided attention.

"This past week, there was a meeting in the White House, where a significant discovery was discussed. It concerns a document which was discovered in Egypt. Although this document is quite ancient, it contains remarkable scientific discoveries which would impact the operations of each organization represented here tonight. The advances disclosed by this treatise include energy, health management, basic science, power generation and distribution, molecular biology, and many other physical sciences."

One of the older men, a reactionary skeptic spoke up "What evidence do you have that any of this is real? Or is this another bullshit plot for the government to control our businesses?"

"I can assure you," the speaker replied, and "that the information has been validated by several important scientists."

"So what; there's all kinds of new crap around."

"You need to pay attention. This material isn't just new, it is revolutionary. If it became common knowledge, it would rock your corporations, because you all depend on control over developments in each of your areas of business."

The CEO of one of the pharmaceuticals spoke. "How do we get access to this information?"

"I will refer to this document as the Book. It was written in a complex code that took the research team quite some time to break. Right now, only a portion of the Book has been translated. The code itself appears to be unbreakable by the NSA. The Book itself..."

He was interrupted by an insurance CEO who was accustomed to speaking in superlatives. "So are you saying is that not only is the Book revolutionary, but the code it was written in is unsurpassed?"

"Yes, that is also true. The code is far advanced from current technologies used by the NSA."

"That means that if we could get it, we would be able to communicate without fear of government eavesdroppers." Everyone around the table looked at one another as their imaginations ran with the possibilities.

The government speaker again tapped his glass. "Yes, but to get back to the Book. It is currently in a secure lab, under control of the Navy. The translation is being managed by an archeologist from the Smithsonian."

One of the others interrupted again "How in the hell did it surface?"

"We aren't exactly sure. We did discover that a small group of private individuals had a long history of close control over this material, but for some reason, they chose to disclose it to our government."

"How could this research have gone on without our knowing about it?"

"This is not research that I am talking about, but ancient discoveries that have been lost for centuries; stored in the library at Alexandria. According to the recovery team, the material was hidden for centuries, but no one has any idea why it came to us at this time."

One of the Auto makers spoke "You didn't answer the question about getting it for ourselves!"

"It is possible. Within one month, the Book will be fully translated, and if it is as comprehensive as I believe, the government will determine how it is to be disseminated." At this comment, everyone in the room groaned. One of the women spoke into the mumbling: a clear contralto voice pierced through the mutters.

"I believe that we should retain a security company to gain control over the Book, and any research papers associated with it. The projection of events based upon government control cannot be tolerated. I will pledge 1 million dollars towards this effort, and I expect each of you to pledge the same. I would imagine that 18 million should be a sufficient budget for this mission. I propose that we authorize our chairman, who brought this to our attention, to make whatever arrangements are necessary to accomplish this goal. This Book must be delivered to us soon, and without anyone else knowing our involvement. Does everyone agree?"

The old conservative looked over to the speaker and said "Well I guess girls once in a while can think with their brains instead of their…"

"Now let's leave it at that" interrupted the chairman. "One million each; are we agreed?" One by one, all nodded. "Good. I will take care of the arrangements. It is always a pleasure to deal with people that can make up their minds. I want to warn each of you that independent action by anyone in this room will not be tolerated." He stared at each of the people around the table. These were people who were quite immune to intimidation, unlike many who the government man encountered in his normal day.

With business concluded, the group members returned to lighter issues: upcoming football and speculation on the fall election. Eventually, people excused themselves from the dinner meeting and left the restaurant.

A few miles north of Jackson, the airport manager, who had seen an influx of a dozen large corporate jets in the afternoon, noted their departure. But even this was not unusual due to the numbers of wealthy individuals who maintained homes in Jackson Hole.

# PART THREE - THE SEIGE

# 42 *TWO WEEKS LATER – LAUREL, MARYLAND*

I was dozing in the garden when she comes out and kisses me on the head, as she drops into a chair alongside me. She brought out two glasses of iced tea.

"My digging stick arrived this morning." I still had some pain when I swallowed, but I know that eventually it would fade. Marcia too, had some pain along with a big scar, where they had repaired a lung along with some major bleeders. But she looked fit and was back to her stationary bike and treadmill every day. I took turns with her on the bike and started running again, principally around our neighborhood. We don't see John much as he is still sequestered at the Navy laboratory, working on the Book. But the few times we visited him there, he was very excited about not only the Book, but the healing of his relationship with his former wife, Karen.

"Are you ready to begin digging again?" she asks.

"I'm not sure. How about you?  What do you think, a cryptologist and a hit man: good team?"

"The best, but I think it would be more accurate to say a detective and a hit girl" She is still bothered by the death of the man she knifed.

The telephone rings. Froehlich is on the line "Hello Simon. I wonder if you would mind coming down to your old office this afternoon. The Admiral and I would like to talk over a couple of things with you; say about 3?"

"OK, Doctor," I couldn't get away from calling him anything else, any more than I could Admiral Lewis, although I am pretty finished with the Navy." I will be down. Do you want Marcia to come too, or not?"

"No, let's leave her at home today. It won't take very long."

I go back out to tell her, and then dress. It is already 2:15 when I finally get into the car and drive to the city. 'Well, at least it can't be about the Book" I say to myself. 'That episode is over, thank God.'

After our confrontation in Alexandria, and with the second and final death of Zilbern, the Admiral's team arrived and cleaned up the mess at the airport. Lauren, Marcia and I were flown out to a local hospital where temporary surgery was done to stabilize us before shipping us first to Landstuhl, Germany for surgery on Marcia's lung and on my lesser wounds, and then to Bethesda for recuperation. Lauren just had a few bumps and bruises, so she was released from the Alexandria hospital, and last I heard was back in New Mexico. The Book was taken by the Navy team to their secret lab, where John was put on it. Johann Froehlich visited us on occasion, and we grew quite fond of him through our long talks. Occasionally, he would bring up the subject of the Book, but I deflected his discussion. Neither of us wants to be drawn in again. He told us that Lauren had finally contacted him and he was hoping to visit with her in the upcoming weeks.

So this afternoon, as I drive through the city with the air conditioning on high, I have very little to be concerned about. At Ft. Myer, I enter through the main gate and drive around to the office. In the reception room, Gina has been replaced by a marine. Although he is in civilian clothes, he sits with a brush haircut, erect in a heavily starched shirt – he couldn't be anything but. He must have been alerted, because as soon as I arrive, he buzzes me in to the Admiral's office.

Both the Admiral and Froehlich rise when I come into the room and offer their hands. The Admiral then offers me some coffee: a first; and directs me to his sofa: another first.

"My boy" says Froehlich. "I am afraid that we have a small problem that we need your help with."

I smell a rat. He continues, "We are concerned that the Secretary of Defense has developed paranoia about the Book. We are afraid that he may put you and Marcia in jeopardy."

"What do you mean?"

"Simon" continued the Admiral, "Secretary Hunnsecker is convinced that the Book is dangerous and anyone who knows about it is potentially a threat to national security. We believe that he is trying to get approval to take both of you and anyone else who is in the information loop and detain you somewhere out of communication for an indefinite timeframe. By himself, Hunnsecker is just another paranoid schizophrenic in a responsible government position. But he is gradually getting the ear of the White House Chief of Staff. That's what makes him particularly dangerous."

"Well, that puts a damper on my summer plans." I could tell as they looked at one another that my days with this project were about to resume.

"I think that we would both prefer it if you both could disappear for several months. The problem is, if the Secretary gets authorization, he will bring along the rest of the Intelligence community with him, and it will be very difficult for you both to hide. So rather than running, we suggest an offensive. We would like you to assume security responsibility at the lab where Crawford is doing his translation work. Bring Marcia with you. It this position, you will have official status regarding the work again, so Hunnsecker will not have a leg to stand on. We will make Marcia the liaison between the Book research and the NSA code weenies; so both of you will have an official 'need to know' status and it will deflect any potential threat from DOD."

"Simon," Froehlich added, "I know that neither of you want to be involved again, but it really is for your own protection. Until final disposition is made, the 'spy under every bed' kooks will have a loud voice. As more information comes out, it will get worse, of that I am sure. So please consider taking our suggestion. We have another assignment for you for which your job as Chief of Security will give you good cover. We still don't have any idea who is 'Mr. X'."

"What about Hunnsecker? He fits the description of a highly placed government power broker with the freedom and resources to act independently?"

The Admiral picked up this idea. "I doubt that he is you man. True, he is well placed. But he isn't the brightest bulb in the chandelier, if you know what I mean. But while you are keeping an eye on him, don't stop there."

I agree to talk it over with Marcia tonight, and promise to get back to them later. As I am leaving, the Admiral makes one final warning "Don't let it go past tonight. I am certain that Hunnsecker is doing his worst to stir the pot. The last thing that we want is to have to fight a Presidential Order in addition to SecDef."

I leave in a blue funk: not so much for the impact on Marcia and me, but for the overall atmosphere where government options are now available to take citizens prisoner and detain them indefinitely, without any legal recourse.

When I get home, Marcia is already arranging a salad from the greens that she grows in her conservatory. Fresh tomatoes counterpoint the color and texture. What a supreme pleasure it is to eat a tomato that actually tastes like one, after years of commercial vegetables. Tonight, dinner is very simple; at least simple for her: an onion soup with cheese flowing over the sides of the crock covering a baguette slice and a broth made of four different onion varieties, coupled with the salad and the rest of the baguette. She is still off wine, so we drink fresh ice tea with key limes from the conservatory, and a fruit tart she just happened to throw together for dessert.

I choose not to bring up the subject with dinner, but as we are cleaning up the kitchen, I tell her of my conversation with our two self-appointed guardians. I can see that Marcia is extremely disappointed at having to leave our home again, but I don't think that she is very surprised. She has spent too many years in the governmental corral to not understand the breed of horse that thrives there.

"You had better tell them we are ready to leave whenever they can come for us" she says. "You know; I met Hunnsecker once. He came out to the office for a tour. All he seemed to want is to let people know how important he was. To him, we were merely another group of government groupies that he could impress. What a pompous ass. But he is persistent, I will say that. Well, make your call. I'll pack."

"I asked them if they thought Hunnsecker was Towson's missing partner, but they thought it would take more intelligence than Hunnsecker possessed. You've met him; what do you think?"

"It's hard to tell from one encounter, but I would agree with them. I will say though, that the SecDef is extremely aggressive in preventing breaches of national security. In that, I would say that he was a patriot. In my experience with his personality type; however, I would also add that he might be rigid in his outlook, and take even minor slights as major affronts. He also could be persuaded to see enemies where they might not really exist, and as such, could be manipulated. Such a person would have to be managed with finesse, however. Direct confrontation with such a paranoid personality should be avoided at all costs."

"Thanks, love. I will keep a weather eye out for any hint of action from him. I need to call the Admiral and tell him."

"Simon. Come up when you are done with the telephone. I have something to show you upstairs, before we have to go."

She leaves me downstairs and goes up to our bedroom. I call and reach the Admiral, tell him of our decision, and listen while he tells me that he will send transportation for us later this evening.

Up the stairs I find a rather incredible sight. Marcia is busily storing clothes in two bags, but is doing it completely naked. Lately, she has been somewhat embarrassed at the scar that she has, healing down the center of

426

her rib cage, but tonight, it doesn't seem matter at all to her. I stand in the doorway while she is packing and strip down to my socks. Then I leap into the room and grab her from behind. As we fall onto the piled clothes, she makes no move to clear the decks, but rolls me over and says "I'm glad you didn't leave your shoes on. They leave stains on the duvet," which is the last intelligible remarks I hear for at least 20 minutes before we move apart, breathing deeply in the cool room.

It is time to go. Our bags are packed and waiting by the hall. The doorbell rings and we both reluctantly get up. Outside, there are two vehicles: a limousine and the omnipresent black SUV. A Navy chief is waiting as we lock the door and come down the steps. For the first time, I feel like maybe this will be the last that we see our home. It is not a pleasant thought.

# 43 *SATURDAY – US NAVAL RESEARCH LABORATORIES – POTOMAC RIVER - WASHINGTON*

The buildings which house the U.S. Naval Research Laboratories are set in a beautiful oasis alongside the Potomac River. The Lab has many two and three story white marble faced government-issue edifices, around a huge oval drive. Behind one of the original buildings at the short end of the oval, a long dock projects into the river. When the tide goes out, mud flats emerge along the dock except at the far end, which has been dredged. Many small special function laboratories are sprinkled around the campus, and the entire complex is surrounded by a sturdy security fence, gates, and roving guards. The facility was originally opened in 1923 at the urging of Thomas Edison. Its history is both long and illustrious. Milestones have included the proposal of the original nuclear-powered submarine, secure computer neural networks, and molecular biology advances, earning the researchers a Nobel Prize. But due primarily to the ultra secret nature of the work done here, most of the public is unaware even that it exists. Adjacent to the facility, there is a very large waste water treatment facility for the city of Washington, which more than occasionally sends plumes of foul-smelling gas over the lab buildings. There is even an exit off I-395 but it is not marked and visitors are discouraged.

When Marcia and I reach the lab, all the floodlights are on. Sensors and cameras abound. Out on the river, occasional cruise boats pass by on evening dinner cruises. In the near distance, flights rise and land at Reagan National Airport, and across the river, floodlit buildings highlight our nation's neoclassic capitol.

Our credentials, recently re-issued by ESCORT, get us through the gate and we are taken by a Navy Shore Patrol jeep to one of the smaller laboratory buildings. There the security is exceedingly tight. One at a time, we are directed through a full height clear lexan revolving security door. Our belongings are sent separately through a scanner. The door is the only way in and out.

Even though it is late, the central lab is lit and I see John at his customary place peering through his binocular microscope at a page of the Book, which lies on the table. The scope is connected to a large monitor, on which we can see the tiny diagrams expanded on the screen. As we enter the room, John looks up from his work and a huge smile breaks out on his face. "Marcia, Simon, oh my goodness, it's so good to see you both. What time is it?"

"It about 9, John; didn't you have dinner?" Marcia waggles a finger at him.

"No, I have been working here almost every night. I have a cot in the corner and they won't let me out of the compound, so all my meals are brought in."

"Well, that pattern ends right now. We are your new security team, so let's get you cleaned up and find somewhere else to hang out. You are officially permitted now to leave the area, so long as we escort you. What have you been eating, fast food?"

"Mostly pizza, hamburgers and tacos. I am about fast-food saturated."

"How about Chinese?"

"Yuck. That's my Wednesday and Saturday. But anything is OK with me, as long as it is outside."

John stands up and stretches, strips off his lab coat, and although I have to argue with the guards, we are cleared to leave. The Admiral has assigned us a car. When we leave the main gate, an escort SUV follows closely behind, holding four large plainclothes agents. Hogate's on Maine Avenue calls to me. It's big and noisy, has great seafood, and very, very public, just down the street from the Kennedy Center. We arrive to find that most of the evening rush has ended as we check in with the Receptionist. In no time, we are escorted to a table along the water, overlooking the marina, where large houseboats dominate. I order a bottle of Pinot Grigio to start us off, while John debates choices with the waiter. Even though we ate a light dinner before leaving home, I can't resist the crab cakes: Chesapeake Bay style with a mess of Cole Slaw and hush puppies. Marcia is not as hungry, so she picks a Maine Lobster tail. John, on the other hand, is famished. He starts with she-crab soup and follows with the broiled fisherman's platter, which comes on an oversized plate that barely fits his side of table. To that he adds a separate order of hush puppies for himself, and attacks the cranberry nut bread and cornbread muffins.

Between spoonfuls of the she-crab, he shares with us the progress that he has made. "I am in seventh heaven with this Book. You would not believe how detailed some of the researches are, and how thorough. In history, for example, the gaps in migration patterns that the Book fills show so clearly how very old cultures dealt with climate change, including the last ice age, and how minor changes in temperature and carbon dioxide wrought massive changes in available food and habitats. Do you realize that the Mesopotamian region was once a temperate garden, similar to the Argentinean Pampas? Oh I could go on for days on just one or two pages. So far, the government has left me alone and I brought out a couple of additional researchers from the Smithsonian to help me, but it is slow going. How long, do you think I have, before they come and take it away from me?"

"John, you ask the fundamental question to which we have no answers. We know that the White House is very interested in this, as well as many of the corporations and of course, the military. I would say that at the present time, the tug of war is somewhat under the radar. Each player knows that so long as no other player has an advantage, it will be best if you are left alone to finish your work. The tipping point will come, I suppose, when you complete your researches and the translation. Has there been a photographic record kept of the Book in addition to your notes?"

"Yes. The first thing that we did when the Book arrived was to photograph each page in high resolution, so that it would not be lost if the Book itself went missing again. We also scanned in the text, and our Cray machines have been at it constantly, trying to map the records. One thing that we changed was to move our lab from its clean room to a relatively open environment. The Book is in no danger of deterioration from the effects of heat, light, dust, humidity or pretty much anything else. The diagrams and text are actually etched into the metal, but by what agent we still do not know. The pages are $1/10^{th}$ the thickness of a typical 24 lb. paper-stock, yet the etching is extraordinarily clear on both sides of each page, only a few microns deep. We do have to be careful with page turning, however. The metal is so fine that several of us have sustained severe cuts from the edges. We still have a difficult time disrupting the metal sufficiently for destructive assay. The rings that I sent you, and I see you both still have them on, were attached to the inside of the armor with something akin to solder, so it was not difficult to separate them, but the balance of the metal seems to be made from a single crystalline lattice which has no fracture zone in any direction. We sent the breastplate over to the metallurgy lab, and the folks over there have been scratching their heads for several weeks. I wanted to send the helmet to the supercollider out west for particle analysis, but the Admiral and Froehlich, who by the way are responsible to the White House for our work here, would rather that every component remain here at the Navy lab until the White House decides what to do with it."

"John, let me ask you a slightly off-putting question, if you don't mind."

"Sure"

"If anything happened to you, would the translation still go on?"

"Oh my yes. I can't see that I am the only one with knowledge to deal with this translation. There are many others that have both the experience and the knowledge to attack it. Certainly, with my notes as a reference point, the translation itself would be comparatively easy, but time consuming. The language that it is written in, once decoded, is as unique as the code which encrypted the material. So it might take a language expert, for example our old friend Lauren Sylfern, a little time to learn it, but once that is accomplished, the rules for decryption are written down, so it would only mean deciphering the symbols. A lot is written using unique symbolism that appears elsewhere in the Book. It's kind of like reading Arabic or Hebrew, but with symbols that are created along the way to replace previously generated ideas and concepts. For example, we all know the formula $e=mc^2$ but simplistically, what does it mean without the understanding of each of the equation terms? It would make no sense. Now 'e' means 'energy in ergs', but without knowing what an erg is, we have a sense of energy, but not a quantifiable amount without going backwards and defining and erg, and so on. This is a similar type of problem."

"Thanks, John, it is clear as fish chowder. I think that we need to tell you that there are very powerful forces looking to the Book; whether for fortune, power or greed, we don't know. But we know that they are there, and if you are not a 'necessary' component of this acquisition, your safety would be compromised. Our job is to keep you and the artifacts as safe as possible."

"I appreciate your concern, Simon. Look, sure they could take it, but if the 'they' is a single corporation, only a tiny component of the Book would be useful. Same for the government; the areas are so broad, that dozens and dozens of specialties are involved. What do you propose?"

"Frankly, I don't know. I think that we need some advice. For now, it is important to keep you and your team protected, and the lab inviolate."

Marcia added "Simon, as far as strategy is concerned, has Dr. Froehlich given you any hints?"

"Not specifically. I think that I need to talk with him further on that subject. John, except for the nights that you have been staying at the lab, do you have a hotel room?"

"No. As I said, they have been loath to let me out of the lab."

"Well, let's get you a room at the Radisson close by, so that you can get some decent sleep, I am sure we could arrange sufficient personal security for the team."

"Thanks, Simon. Do you think that I could get Karen in to see me?"

"That's my idea behind the hotel. It would be a lot easier to arrange family visits outside the lab than in. I'll work on it."

I arrange for several rooms, all on the top floor. I also ask the hotel to book the rest of the floor for our team, and to relocate other guests to lower floors in the morning. I contact the security team at the lab and have them detail protection coverage at the hotel. Then we head there over John's protests, but inside the lobby, John realizes that he is just too tired to work. John goes directly to his room. As Marcia is unpacking, I call Froehlich. After reassuring him that there is no problem, I ask him if he has some time to talk with me.

"We have identified two general threat sources, one within the government and one from outside. In both cases, there seems to be countervailing interests: Get control of the material within the book for profit, or bury the material so that current profitable technologies and interests can continue uninterrupted. While both have a common control factor, the first group is interested in preservation, so their techniques for acquisition would be more focused on capture than the second group, who would seek destruction of the material and anyone who might be know about it. Of course, like any agenda, there are those who cross boundaries in both directions– bury the book and use small bits over time, versus gain control to anticipate future trends and then have competitive advantage."

"There is another potential threat: in countries primarily dominated by nationalistic fervor, this material would represent a fast-track to international power. So acquisition and control by any one of the dozens of governments that fit this description should also be recognized. I am afraid that your security problem grows exponentially with both the leaking of Book information, as well as an outcome of whatever decisions come from our own political elite."

"So what you're saying is that virtually all the world powers would be after it? Well that makes sense. I guess we'll have to take them as they come."

"Yes, but we need a plan; a goal, otherwise there is no way that you can prepare for a siege. Just think of yourself as a modern Trojan and go from there. Our problem today is not much different than what Priam and Paris had to be dealt with, all those many years ago."

"Dr. Froehlich, I understand the nature of direct threats, and can usually develop defense strategies. I will just have to deal with this also."

"Let me tell you a story, my boy. It has to do with three normal, inadequate men who had the responsibility for a great secret. They had no idea how it could be kept safe from the ravages of war. So they devised a plan, it wasn't a very elaborate plan, but it had a fundamental basis in human behavior. The plan was to accept the ultimate outcome of a siege, and realize that the only defense was to acquiesce. They used a diversion to lull the enemy into believing that the day was won, but ultimately the enemy succumbed to a far more complex conflict. History is full of sacrifice for a larger purpose, and my story is not much different. So think on this and prepare for your siege. It will come soon enough."

"Doctor, you speak in riddles. I need a plan, and I need to help keep everyone around this book safe, as well as the Book itself."

"I will give you another example of what I am speaking about. You, Simon, are a student of Japanese Unarmed Combat, are you not?"

"Yes, I have studied several different traditions and systems."

"Think on this. Your enemy approaches; they are bigger than you, stronger than you, have more weapons at their command, and come at you from all sides. How do you defeat them?"

"I would try to use their very strength as a force against themselves."

"Exactly; that is the only way you can beat a superior force. You must wait for the attack, and then make them come to you so strongly, so that they overpower themselves. Do you understand?"

"Yes, Doctor, I begin to see what you are suggesting. If power is opposed by power, the stronger power wins. If power is opposed by weakness, power will defeat itself. Power feeds on itself and grows overconfident, thus exposing itself to weaknesses; the greater the power, the greater the opportunity. So it is then that a weak force has an advantage."

"Yes, you do understand. Very well, my boy, I shall tell you one further truism. I do not think that I shall survive this siege. But if my life is ended, you will be delivered something that I want very much for you to have. Now I must go back to my mystery story. The dogs are at my gate. I am being watched day and night, so I must act as if nothing is happening. Good night, my boy."

I hang up, and again wondered if this was the last time I would feel relatively free to act on my own. After I put the telephone down, I realize that Doctor Froehlich was not just giving me advice. He was telling me that actions had already started, and that he was a target.

Marcia comes out of the bathroom wrapped in a towel, her red hair dark against the white of the towel. She sees me sitting on the bed and comes over to give me a kiss. I guess she sees that I am having a lot of difficulty dealing with the complexity of our problem. "Marcia, darling, I have to go out tonight. Dr. Froehlich is being watched, and I need to learn who is behind it, and how strong the opposition is. Did you happen to bring a pair of dark sweats in the bag?"

"Yes and your black sneakers. But are you sure that you have to go out now. Can't you get someone else to do this? I am worried for you."

"Well, I would be a liar if I said that you shouldn't worry, but I do promise that I will be careful. I really have to do this myself. All I am going to do is to locate the people watching Froehlich, and follow them to ground. I think that before we decide how we are going to defend ourselves, we need to gather some tactical intelligence. I will be back late tonight. I'll call you from downstairs before I come up, so do not answer the door to anyone. It will be easier tomorrow when our protection detail is fully mobilized and our floor secured. If I get into trouble, I will try to call. Just leave your cell on tonight. Do you know where Froehlich lives?"

"Yes, he left me his address, in case I should ever need it. She digs into her purse. Here it is: 7719 Fairfax Road in Bethesda. He told me it is an older house on a large piece of property with a guest house accessible from the main house by a covered walkway. He actually asked me if we thought we might like to stay there and visit, but I deferred until this book business was completed."

"Terrific. Thanks, love."

I give Marcia a big hug and kiss, dig out my sneaky clothes, and then dress. Marcia has also packed my old watch cap. Then, with another hug while she is drying her hair, I pocket my magnetic hotel card key, ID wallet, and my regular wallet incase I need some money.

I avoid the Reception desk in the lobby and exit using the side entrance. It is too late for roving taxis. I see, however, that the Shuttle Bus has just come in from an airport pickup. I give him twenty bucks and he agrees to drive me over to Reagan just across the GW Parkway. There, I see that all car rental counters are empty save one. She takes pity on me and reopens her computer. Then she gives me directions to the pickup location. Once

435

there, I select my car, an innocuous sedan, check the gas and map, and head to Bethesda.

At this hour, it only takes me about 20 minutes. The temperature is still uncomfortable, keeping most folks indoors. Fairfax St. turns out to be an old planned subdivision, with large homes and graceful trees. The street is only a few blocks long, curving around a central park. Just north of Doctor Froehlich's house, a main east west artery bisects the subdivision, and provides me with a convenient escape route in case I might need one later.

The house is like Marcia described: a brick two story colonial, in an L shape, with a dark brown roof and a long passageway out the side of the "L" leading to a smaller Guest House. The lot is heavily treed. Close to the house on the north side, is a commercial Medical Suites building, which fronts on the adjacent street. In addition to on-street parking, there is a small lot by the Medical building and another in front of an adjacent commercial building, diagonally behind Froehlich's house. I leave the car in the latter lot. There are no occupied cars near his house or in adjacent driveways, but on first glance, anyone who is professional will not be visible to the casual passerby.

Before leaving the car, I cover my hair with my watch cap, but have nothing to darken my skin, so I will just have to be careful of reflections.

The end of the parking lot has a chain link fence, with a narrow hedge planted alongside. I scoot down below the top of the fence and creep along the hedge until I am opposite his house. On this side of the fence there is a swimming pool. The automatic pool cleaner is sweeping the water surface, so there is a humming noise, punctuated by occasional burps from the drain. This should cover any small sounds I might make. Across the fence on Froehlich's property, there is a heavy planting of shrubs, higher than my head, so there may be a chance for me to get into Froehlich's property without being seen. If I stay here, I remain exposed from across the pool. I take hold of the widest hedge bush I see and test it. The boxwood must be very old because it easily supports my weight. Two steps up and over the fence, I land on a deep bed of mulch on the other side. Then I sidle through the shrubs on my belly until I can see the house, and wait.

The night is quite noisy. Cicadas, crickets and an occasional toad make their presence known in the dark, along with persistent tree frogs. No movements catch my attention. Occasionally I can hear a car pass by. A thin Turkish Moon with its narrow crescent breaks the field of stars, but doesn't give out much light, and there are few streetlights. Once and a while, something small runs near or across my body as I lie here, but

436

probably nothing but a mouse or vole. It is difficult to maintain alert attention as the weather is warm and the mulch is soft. I put my senses out to their fullest and try to feel if there is anyone else nearby, but sense no one. My watch tells me that it is now 1:36, and nothing is moving. If there is a watcher team, sooner or later they will have to change shifts.

By 2:21 there is still nothing moving, and I am beginning to get stiff, staying quietly in one position for all this time. But I know that it is important to remain absolutely still, as I could be not the only one extending senses. At 3:04 there seems to be a tiny movement to my left. A lump under a magnolia tree moves ever so slightly, and then the lump disappears. It is something. Then, from near the ground, I see a tiny greenish glow for a moment or two, before it disappears. Night vision scope or goggles come to mind almost immediately. If they are infra-red, I am cooked, because the heat of my body will stand out against the cool background. But if they are only illumination enhancers, it might still be OK. I decide to verify which by taking a small stick and tossing it about 10' closer towards the house. It makes a little snapping sound when it hits the cobblestoned walk behind the house, and instantly, I see the glow again, moving side to side against the base of the tree, before disappearing again. I guess they're enhancement only. The watcher might have come from either the street or the next property, since there were no cars where I parked. In my circle of the block, I remember seeing a high fence on the adjacent house, which looked like a surround for a tennis court, so I would guess he came from along there somewhere. Across Fairfax St. from Froehlich's house, there is a circular drive with parking for another small office building, and I don't remember if there were any cars there or not. I still wait. It is now 3:47. Then the lump moves. I can hear twigs snapping and leaves rustling as he shifts position and then rises to stand. Even though there is little light, the figure appears to be outfitted for night-combat operations. He has night vision goggles on his head, and a camo suit of light and dark patches, but no weapon that I can see, unless it is a folding type and is still on the ground. Then the figure holds his hand up to his face. The little light there is reflects off what looks like a cell phone or radio and I hear a few low mumbles. The figure moves towards me and I remain absolutely still, as part of the terrain. The figure picks up his feet as he steps through the mulch, and passes me by less than three feet, towards the way I came. When he vaults the fence, I rise to follow.

A car is pulled up in the lot, fairly close to where I have my car. Through the fence, I see it is occupied by another darkly dressed figure, who makes his way towards Froehlich's house, while the other one climbs into the front seat. Then the car pulls to the other end of the lot and stops. I take two steps back under a bush while the new watcher climbs over the fence and walks towards the lookout spot near the back walkway. As he settles himself, I slowly creep over the fence and crouch among the hedges again, crawl to the end of the parking lot and look out. The other car is still stopped near the egress to the street. I can see only the driver's side. I walk very slowly across the lot, keeping to where my background is dark and I stop frequently. Most people believe that you move fast at night, you will be missed by someone else not paying full attention, but the opposite is really the case. My instructors back at Enclave used to emphasize over and over: At night, and particularly in a zone of peripheral vision, movement is very quickly perceived. It will stimulate that unconscious genetic sensitivity, which will then stimulate the threat response. So it is very important to keep movements slow and intermittent.

I get to my car without drawing attention. I had forgotten to pull the fuse on my overhead lamp in the rental, but there is nothing I can do about it now. So I chance it and open the door of the car as the lamp flicks on. The click of the lamp sounds like a gunshot to my hyper-aware senses. Once inside the car, I close the door enough to extinguish the light, pulling it closed just enough to engage the first latch. Then I sit in the car, laying my head back on the headrest to reduce my silhouette. It is now nearly 4:00 and the other car is still sitting here. It occurs to me that they might be downloading a bug in the house, resetting it for the next day. A lot of these bugs have a very limited range.

While I am contemplating, the engine in the other car suddenly starts, and the car leaves the lot, turning east. I start the engine and follow slowly, allowing a good distance to build between us. The car turns right on the next corner as I emerge from the lot. It remains on the same street as it winds toward the center of Bethesda, ending at Wisconsin Avenue, where it turns towards Washington, with me behind. The car eventually turns off and joins Observatory Circle, which it takes part way around, and then stops in a building near the Chinese Embassy. I follow into the circle and then just past the entrance to the building, where I park in one of the open spaces facing the Naval Observatory hill.

The driver of the car has gotten out and gone into the building by the time I walk across the street. On the building, there was no logo or other identifying sign, but the outer doors to the lobby are open, and just inside, I could see over to the guard station. Above it was a sign that read Blackthorn International with a logo showing a clenched fist. It must be a private security firm. But why would a firm like this be hired to watch Froehlich?

I realize that I have wrung out all the possible information here, so I walk over to my rental and drive it back through town towards the hotel. Along the way the thought comes to me that maybe it isn't only Froehlich that is being watched, so I check carefully for a tail, but don't detect one. It's one thing to trust your instincts, and another to be stupid. I will just have to pay more attention.

By the time I get back to the hotel, it is almost 5 AM and the sky is lightening. Inside, I call Marcia. From the speed at which she answers, I believe that she was awake. I announce my arrival and go up in the elevator. When I open the door, Marcia greets me with a hug. She is wearing her pajamas, but the bed stand light is on and a book is face down on the bed. I tell her about my night's adventure, and she suggests that she do some research on the firm and see if there is a chance she can find out who their client is. I think that with Marcia's access to the NSA cut off, she may have a chance doing it through my office; or rather I should say our office now. As I go into the bathroom to wash off the night's accumulation of leaf litter and dirt, I can hear her tapping away on her laptop.

I am drying myself when I hear Marcia give a little yelp and curse. As I come out of the bathroom, she is furiously tapping on the computer keys and then holds up a hand to me to not interrupt her. In a minute or two she finally calls out "Gotcha!" and then shuts down the machine.

"What is it?" I ask.

"A sniffer! They found me through the network and stuck a sniffer in my operating system. I don't know how long it has been there, but probably not longer than a day or so. It was a real sophisticated piece of work. I found it through a timing delay in email scanning. The communication protocols for downloading our emails were too long and too many bytes on our sends, which alerted me to data going out as it was coming in. I realized that each time I opened an email; it sent the contents elsewhere. I set up a sensor at my host end, and picked up the headers as they were remailed. I got rid of the software bundle here, but not until I tracked the recipient through a whole sequence of onion nodes. The final host was guess where? Blackthorn International!"

"If they are looking at us as well, it must have to do with the Book. I will bet that John's laptop is similarly infected. You have a much enhanced spyware sensor on your PC. How is it that it didn't pick up the bug?"

"Newer and newer; hackers are constantly inventing new toys for their black arts."

"How much did they get?"

"I imagine that it picked up transient material, but probably nothing buried in encrypted directories. Considering that we don't save any passwords or IDs on this computer, I would say we are fairly secure, until the next time."

"Do you think that you could hack into Blackthorn's system and find out who their client is?"

"I doubt it. These companies pride themselves on security; after all, it is their business. No; I would say that we can try, but I would rather do so from someplace where any backtracking can't be traced to us individually."

"How about launching a hack from ESCORT?"

"NSA would be better, but that's not possible now."

"How about you go over to the office this morning, while I keep John company at the lab? You take our company car."

I thought that it would be a good idea to get an hour or so rest before trying for another long day. So I lie down and set the alarm for 7, while Marcia called our driver set a pickup time.

While I lay here, I wonder about Blackthorn. In order to hire a firm like that, there had to be a lot of money behind the client. Maybe I could figure out a way to follow the money. But later, first I need to shut my eyes for a little while.

# 44 *SUNDAY - WASHINGTON*

At 7, my eyes are full of crystals, my mouth is a camel track, Marcia is gone and the phone is still ringing. It's Froehlich.

"Did you find my watchers?"

"How did you know? And by the way, Good morning."

"Yes of course. I expect that you did some digging last night. What did you come up with?"

"I found a team from Blackthorn International hiding in your bushes."

"Blackthorn! They are a paramilitary organization made up of ex-Special Operations (SPEC-OPS) personnel. They started up soon after you left the Navy. But I have never heard that they took on a contract inside the U.S. Whoever hired them must have put a lot of money on the table."

"Marcia has gone over to ESCORT to see if she can find out where their contract originated, but she doesn't think she can access their system."

"Usually, their assignments have been the protection of diplomatic staff and supplemental assault operations. In the past, I know that they have been hired by State, Defense and the CIA."

"There was only one operative on site, so I assume it was strictly information gathering. I would guess that your house is wired as well. Do you get a regular sweep?"

"While I was on the NSC staff, they came once a week, but since becoming an outside consultant, that service has been suspended. I will ask Robert to restart it."

"Are you at home now?"

"Yes."

"We have to assume that at least your side of this conversation has been compromised, but if you can get sweepers in right away, it might not be too late. Most of these devices record locally so if it is found before they download it, they won't know about last night."

"I will take care of that right now. Simon you bring up an interesting question, which gives me an idea. Why don't you go over to the office and I will meet you there in an hour. On your way, think about what we spoke of in terms of the best defense? I'll see you later."

"Before you go, have your car checked, as well as your cell phone."

He is strange. The best defense is a good offense. Everyone knows that. I'll just have to wait to hear his idea. What I really need to do first is to have breakfast – but I guess the plastic food down in our lobby will pack in calories, if nothing else.

On the way, I look for tails, but none are evident. If they only started recently, it will probably take a couple of days to get fully mobilized. When I get to the office, I find that a small conference room has been set aside for our use. Froehlich hasn't yet arrived. Marcia tells me that she got a line on Blackthorn's client. Checks from an attorney on K Street have been going into Blackthorn's corporate account for about 2 weeks. The first payment was 3 million and the second for 2 additional million. In my world, that sure is going to buy a lot of surveillance. I will bet anything that it includes a fee for an assault operation. If I were responsible for something like this, it would take a few days to do reconnaissance. Then I would have to mock up the target – say another three days – develop a plan and train for at least a week or two. So that means probably four weeks from inception to go. If the target was overseas, it would probably take a little longer with logistics, but for a worldwide organization, maybe not. They would have stockpiles of materiel: weapons, technology, and training areas. Locally, it might be able to be implemented sooner. But no one in a firm like that would want to mount an ad hoc operation; particularly if they wanted to evade recognition.

Just then, Dr. Froehlich comes into the room, trailed by the Admiral. When the door closes, the Admiral begins "Simon, you were right about Dr. Froehlich's car. Our boys found a GPS tracker and a recording device hidden in the driver's seat, with a ring antenna mounted on the windshield. They are on their way to his house right now to sweep and recover anything there. The auto version was wired into the power supply for the seat adjuster. There is no way to tell how long it was embedded, but the model is manufactured under a classified contract issued by the CIA. It has a serial number on it, so I should be able to find out when it was delivered and to whom. If nothing else, it might provide some ammunition if we come up against opposition at the White House."

"Admiral, one option that is also open to us is for it to be re-placed in Dr. Froehlich's car and used to transmit disinformation to the listeners."

"That is a good idea. I will have it done."

Dr Froehlich walked to the head of the table and, adopting a lecturer's tone, spoke to all of us. "Our concern from the beginning of this search for The Book was that it would be taken by someone or some group for their personal profit. The interesting twist on this agenda was brought out in a time of great stress by Ernst Zilbern. He told us that his primary goal was to secure it for Germany, to use the discoveries to elevate their nation to become a world power again. So his actions, while misguided, could be seen as patriotic with regard to Germany. Whether the person who has been called 'Mr. X' has the same agenda, we do not know. Personally, I doubt that. In any case, he is still out there and no doubt has his own goals. When you both found the Book and we brought it back to Washington, the reaction from our government's administration was quite different. The general consensus of the group we met at the White House was that the Book potentially was a great threat to the stability of our country. But at the same time, they were intrigued by the potential contents. The multiplicity of interest leads us to an inescapable conclusion: unless we know precisely what the ultimate aim of those that seek the Book, we cannot construct an appropriate defense. Furthermore, we have to address our own goals in this matter. Simon, what to you perceive that your objective is?"

"Doctor, I would say that it would be to provide for the greatest benefit for the greatest number."

"But who should make that determination?"

"Don't we have a responsibility to the Keepers? After all, they were the ones that selected us. If they wanted the government to have the Book, it would have been arranged that way from the beginning."

"That's true. But now there are a lot more people in the mix. And these people have far more power than we few."

"If all these people are after the Book, why not just give it to them all. The ones that want to use it for their own purposes would not have an advantage over anyone else. Those that would like to see it buried would also be thwarted."

The Admiral jumped in almost before I finished. "Simon, I think you should consider where we are, and who we work for. You are being unrealistic if you think that you can make that kind of decision on your own. If several who were at the White House meeting heard you, I guarantee that you would be buried somewhere and have no further say in anything. So I am assuming that you are speaking hypothetically, aren't you?" His expression made it clear that he was giving me a serious warning.

Marcia looked from Admiral Lewis back to me. "Simon, this is getting really frightening. It seems like there is no right decision, no matter what we do. I wish the Keepers had not given us the damn thing."

Dr. Froehlich gives Marcia a tiny smile which twinkled his eyes slightly. "Don't get anxious, Marcia. You have to take a step back and think about what we have been given."

"Yes, an unsolvable crisis."

"Marcia, you have faced many serious problems at the NSA. How did you deal with them then?"

"Through simplification and analysis; Doctor, you are right about one thing: emotion is not going to solve anything."

"Now you've got it. Let me help you. One of the major problems in our country today is the ongoing political infighting making it very difficult to deal with any really important issues. Another is the strength of our large corporations in terms of economic control over elected officials. A third is the lack of public oversight over the actions of our overblown governmental bureaucracy. The last, and perhaps one of the most important, is the shift in focus from creative product development to daily and monthly bean-counting by our corporate elite. The idea of public good seems to have been supplanted by greed and avarice. Do you agree? What we have been given is not a Book, but an opportunity. Not a huge one, but one nevertheless. Can you put your finger on what this might be?"

"Well, here is a treasure that many people would like to get their hands on, for many different reasons. We can't give it to them, but we can't bury it again either. While all of them are plotting and scheming, we certainly will become aware of who is behind each agenda."

"Yes, that is the first major opportunity that we have: To expose the rot and rust both inside our government and in the private sector. Of course it doesn't mean all of the players will be exposed, but I think we can assume that the major ones will expose themselves. Then what?"

If we foil all of their attempts, expose them in the process, we stand a chance of some housecleaning, don't we?"

I started to see where Dr. Froehlich was heading. "Doctor, you made an invalid assumption: we do not have the ability to foil everyone, do we?"

"Simon, let me go back to the question that I posed to you this morning. What is the very best defense against these multivariate elements?"

"I thought that you had taken leave of your senses. My immediate answer to that question is that the best defense is a good offense. Your suggestion makes no sense. There is no way that we can mount an offensive strong enough to beat all comers."

"Simon, I was very precise in my question. I did not ask you for a 'good' defense, I asked you for the very best defense. Clearly, the best defense is no defense at all. If there is nothing to defend, then there is no reason to lay siege, is there?" He smiled at me and then the Admiral got this epiphany look on his face and started smiling as well.

I am getting quite frustrated with this. "Doctor; let's not play word games. This is very serious. The Book exists. Everyone in the room knows it exists, and from the surveillance Blackthorn has mounted, it is clear that people outside this room and outside the White House security circle also know it exists. Are you thinking that we should destroy the Book?"

"No, my boy; but we can create a disinformation book which has very little value. In effect, the Book that we can create will be exactly what Ernst thought in Alexandria: a fake."

"Doctor, you are saying that we should construct a duplicate Book; and let it be loosely guarded so it is stolen, then let the perpetrators analyze it and find nothing, thus lulling them into giving up the war. Then what? If we do that, the real Book must then be re-hidden and cannot be ever used for its intended purpose. I don't doubt that we can achieve that, but then everyone loses. All the deaths: for nothing? Is that what you are asking?"

"No, Simon. Not for nothing. Think about Marcia's logic. While all these forces are scurrying about in their acquisition mania, they expose themselves. Those who perpetrated the violent acts beyond what Ernst did, can then be caught and prosecuted. Further, by exposing this, who knows? Perhaps a movement will be started to support oversight and deal with some of the other major problems. Look, we can't deal with everything, but we can put a big dent in the works."

"All of you; we can't protect the Book enough to control what is used for good or evil. Further, the wider the knowledge of what is in the Book, the greater the strength of the opposition focused on obtaining it. Sooner or later, our allies will succumb, either by direct or indirect pressure, one by one, until we are left alone, to lose the ultimate war. Perhaps we are just not ready for something like this Book. Maybe it should be returned to the 'Keepers'. But we can't simply make it disappear. It's too late for that. We have to sacrifice something; there are too many planning the siege. What I am suggesting is that we construct our own Trojan horse. Then, when they finally amass a genuine assault, allow them to take it. Once 'they' have it, we can make two assumptions: they will squabble amongst each other for control, defeating some of them in the process, or they will divide the spoils and then discover the futility of their quest, thus eliminating them from the battlefield. Once the larger battle is concluded, we can quietly restore the Book to its Keepers again."

"Doctor," says Marcia "What about the missed opportunities for taking advantage of all these discoveries?"

"Yes, that will be a tragedy. But you know that every great discovery had a negative as well as positive side. Splitting the atom created incredible advances in medicine and power generation while also facilitating the most destructive force we've ever invented. Antibiotics cured hundreds of deadly diseases, but continue to create a host of stronger and deadlier bugs. Even social welfare programs created a foundation of care for the needy, yet also created entitlements that discourages self actualization. I am certainly not arguing against innovation, but I am suggesting that too much, too quickly can be extraordinarily destabilizing and effectively destructive."

"Doctor, my dear friend," says Admiral Lewis. "I have a lot of difficulty with what you are suggesting. I am sworn to uphold the interests of my country, and to take direction from our elected leadership. It is not possible for me to participate in such a disinformation strategy against our government."

"Robert, I understand your position. But consider, if you will, the greater good. There is no question that control over this technology and the Book's discoveries will be wrested from elected government and pass to private interests, who will subvert its intent, and subdue all competition through the advantage this Book creates. These are not national entities, but private international interests that give no loyalty but to themselves; no honor or responsibility except to their personal aggrandizement and profit. You can't want this disaster to occur, nor will your loyalty to our country permit it, can you?"

"No, but you put me in a very difficult position. I will have to judge for myself."

"I have great faith in your judgment, Robert. I know you will come to the right decision."

Just then, my telephone rings. It's John Crawford. "Excuse me, it may be important" I say to the group as I answer. "John, Good morning, what's up?"

"They're making a run on the lab. There is a small military group outside saying that they have orders from the Secretary of the Navy to remove the Book. Right now, they are in our lobby, while the guard is checking on the authenticity of the order. What should I do?"

"Hold on." I turn to the room and repeat what John just told me. The Admiral says "Tell him that the order requires personal authentication, due to its high classification level. Have John tell the guard to not, under any event, open the security gate for anyone without the Secretary being there to authorize it."

I repeat this to John and he says that he will get back to me. Meantime, the Admiral leaves the conference room goes back to his office. In a minute he returns. "I don't believe it. Someone has gotten to SecNav. The order is real. I'll be back."

I get up to go down to the Lab myself and see if I can help on site, but Dr. Froehlich asks me to wait. Then the Admiral is back. "I just spoke to Stevenson at the White House. They had a little meeting early this morning, but the actual order was to get copies of the translated portions, not the Book itself. Either SecNav screwed up or somebody gave him phony information. I'll be back" and he was gone again. This time, it was only about a minute when he walked in, looking like he had been hit from behind. "I'm out of a job today, as of 1800. SecNav fired me. But he really did screw up. Stevenson kicked his butt so he pointed fingers at Hunnsecker and me. He said that Hunnsecker told him to go get the Book, and that I was not carrying out the order generated in my chain of command." The Admiral sat down at the table.

"Just a minute, Robert. Now it is my turn to make a call."

"What are we going to do?" said Marcia. "We seem to have lost without even a fight."

"Let me call John." I said as I opened my telephone and place the call.

"Hi Simon. Well it is still a standoff. The assault group is outside, and the Secretary has been called. If he comes, there will be nothing that I can do."

"John, is the group military?"

"Well, they are wearing camouflaged uniforms, but I don't see any military insignia. On their shoulders is a patch with a simplified fist on it. Do you know what unit that would be?"

"Absolutely, John, it is an outside contractor called Blackthorn. If they are allowed in, just follow the instructions of the Secretary. Don't be a hero. You have the data, don't you?"

"Yes, it is in my PC here at the lab, with copies in the Lab's mainframe data base."

"Do us all a favor. Put the files on a flash drive and stick it somewhere in the lab where it can't be found. Then corrupt the central database copy so even if they download it, it will be useless. But don't try to hide the Book. If they take it, they take it."

"OK Simon, I will do as you ask."

Froehlich comes back into the room, this time with a cell telephone in his hand. He hands it to the Admiral, who looks questioningly at Dr. Froehlich and then takes the phone and identifies himself. In a half second, he bolts upright and stands at attention, while he listens. Then he says 'yes ma'am' several times and then the call ends.

Froehlich breaks the silence. "I called the President. I thought that she would like to know what was going on. For everyone's information, the order given by Hunnsecker has been rescinded, the Secretary of the Navy was just fired and the Admiral is back at the helm."

Marcia and I break out in a cheer. The Admiral, for the first time in his life, looks almost sheepish. "I think that you can call John Crawford again, but it probably won't be necessary. I will bet that in a moment, he will be calling."

True to his word, my telephone rings again. "Simon, what happened? Blackthorn left without the Book. I did do what you asked anyway, so the file in the Lab database is now garbage and the only digital file is on a jump drive in the burn bag here in my lab."

"Take it out before it is toasted and I will explain everything later. If you see any military types come back, whatever you do, call me."

"Right, Simon, I shall. Will you be coming over here or what?"

"I'll let you know later. Be well."

I close the phone and Froehlich says "One small emergency forestalled. But everyone, this is only the first salvo. I think that we can expect a lot

448

more cannonballs. Now Marcia; before we were so rudely interrupted, you were about to suggest something."

"What if we did what Simon suggested, albeit hypothetically: publish the contents of the Book; made it public?"

The Admiral, who had recovered his composure, spoke to Marcia's question. "As I told Simon, it would never be permitted. The moment that anyone tried to make public something that has been classified this high, it would be instant burial. You would just disappear, and public dispersal would be stopped before anything got out. Let's work on a plan; but first, how about lunch?"

Marcia nods. The Admiral then says "I'm buying today, but next time, John, it is on you!" Froehlich laughs as we go out the door. "So where are you buying lunch, Robert?"

"Where else?" and they both say together "The Commissary."

As we go out of the building and into Froehlich's larger car, Marcia says to him "I didn't know that you knew the President. How do you know her?"

"I met her when she was a freshman member of Congress, about 20 years ago. She wouldn't sit still for seniority and had demanded that a sub-committee be created that would investigate Campaign Financing. It was a subject that many Members of Congress talked about on the media, but did little about in chambers. Even though it became a party platform and a personal objective of hers, there was huge resistance to anything substantive. So she dug in her heels and forced the issue. Unfortunately, by the time it got through the Conference Committee, it was so weak to be only a shadow of its former self."

"Anyway, I was speaking to the committee on behalf of some of my friends at software companies, particularly on behalf strong intellectual property rights. She and I fought at the committee hearing, and fought later at dinner, and some might think that we fight still. But I regard her as a very bright light in this city of dim bulbs, and my friend. Oh, and in answer to your next question: this morning, I thought that she should know how her cabinet secretary was usurping the White House's right to determine policy on something as important as this, and that her supporter, the Admiral here, was being railroaded for his good work. She did not appreciate the actions of her Secretary of Defense, or that of the Secretary of the Navy. I think what particularly irked her was that this end run was tried when everyone was away for their weekend."

When we arrived at the Ft. Myer Commissary, near the Main Gate in the eastern part of the compound, it was already fairly crowded, but we found a spot near one of the south windows. After we found a table, I reasserted my original question with a new twist. "I think that one of our principal adversaries just gave himself away this morning."

"How is that?" asked the Admiral.

"At the Lab, who was it that showed up to 'capture' the Book? It was Blackthorn, all decked out in their nice paramilitary uniforms with arm patches."

"That is useful information, but get to the point. The order came from our ex-SecNav."

"No, sir; the person that sent them on this errand was certainly Secretary Hunnsecker. He's the one that was behind the order that came through the SecNav. If he's the one that sent Blackthorn, then he's the one that hired Blackthorn to watch you, Dr. Froehlich, and to tap into Marcia's, John's and my computers."

"Yes, that is a logical conclusion" said Froehlich. "But it can't be him alone. According to Marcia, the first payment to Blackthorn was a total of 5 million through the K St. Attorney. If I understand how these contractors work, that would represent a down payment of probably half, or one third of the full fee. That means we are looking at a payoff in the vicinity of ten to fifteen million. Hunnsecker is not a wealthy man. I would doubt whether he has that kind of money to spend on an operation like this. So he has to have backers."

"But what if he is financed by your corporate advocacy group?"

"Yes, they could certainly come up with that much untraceable funding,"

"The point is, sir, we now have a fairly solid link between Hunnsecker and Blackthorn. That is more than we had last night."

"So you are saying that possibly Hunnsecker is your Mr. X?"

"Yes. I know that yesterday, you thought otherwise, but we now have a little more evidence. He fits the mold: Paranoid, combative, and ruthless. He did, after all, recommend that you detain the three of us. Also, he has access to the NSA to assign agents to come after me, and he has the clout to set up a SPEC-OPS mission which could have been responsible for Jean's death. Lastly, he has access to military channels of communication, so through DISA (Defense Information Systems Agency, the communications arm) he could have tracked us in Troy and Alexandria.

450

He might even have been secretly sponsoring Zilbern until they reached the objective, with the plan of snatching it from him and leaving him to hang in the wind.

"Simon, don't forget the mission in Greece, where all those people were killed at the Temple of Poseidon!" added Marcia. "Zilbern had no reason to lie when he told us he had nothing to do with that. I would say that Zilbern was handled by Hunnsecker, who ran a parallel op until he no longer needed Zilbern."

The Admiral spoke again "It is one thing to challenge a private citizen like Zilbern, but it is a very different matter to accuse the Secretary of Defense of murder and mayhem, particularly with such a tenuous thread as Blackthorn. They do it all the time. We couldn't have gotten as far as we did in Iraq without contractors like Blackthorn working hand in glove with our official military. You can't call out Hunnsecker on such flimsy evidence."

Froehlich added another sobering thought. "Let's consider Hunnsecker for a moment. I cannot believe that this man has the mental wherewithal to manage such a complex operation over so many years. He isn't the sharpest tack, you know. A lot of his effectiveness comes out of aggressiveness and an ability to choose capable subordinates. If Hunnsecker gave the order to the SecNav, I would say that he too is under another's control."

"What about one of the Chiefs?" asks Marcia.

Admiral Lewis responded "They are all very bright. But I think that U.S. Ops and murders outside their chains of command are not their métier. If there was a threat posed to the nation, or maybe even to their individual service arm, I might offer a different answer. But for massive personal gain, I think not. I would also rule out the DCI and the Directors of the other Intelligence agencies, except maybe for the DDO (Deputy Director of Operations at the CIA). He is a rattlesnake, but that's only for this room. John, do you agree?"

"Yes, I think that he would like to be DCI, but that is his prime ambition. And besides; his wife holds the family purse strings. I couldn't see him coming up with the 15 million without embezzling from the agency or stealing from his wife, which is doubtful."

"So who's left?" I ask of no one in particular. "Unless it is a senior Senator or House member; the only ones left are on the White House staff. The Chief is certainly capable and Machiavellian, but he is ultimately loyal to the President, and does not seem to carry a personal agenda outside of his

451

job. So that gets us right back to a non-governmental agency or organization, with direct control over most-probably Secretary Hunnsecker, and access to both military contractors and unlimited cash."

"I agree" says the Admiral, and Froehlich nods his head as well.

Marcia, however; is not convinced. "Throughout our little adventure, the story has been one of hidden motives, disinformation and distraction. If we assume that there is a Mr. X, and I am not agreeing or disagreeing for the moment. Let us say that this person is intelligent and sly, has access and is wealthy. It's probable, therefore, to assume that Hunnsecker could have been set up – he is a perfect patsy: Paranoid Schizophrenic with delusions of grandeur, extremely aggressive and unable to hold his tongue. He would be my perfect choice to implement the recovery and also be the fall guy when things went sour. Let us take this morning. I would call Blackthorn, send them on their mission, call Hunnsecker and say that a threat was on its way to the Naval Labs to steal the Book. Hunnsecker would call the SecNav to order the Book's withdrawal from the Navy Lab for safekeeping. I would then redirect the SecNav's order to Blackthorn. Virtually no one would think anything was amiss until after the retrieval was accomplished. Blackthorn would bring out the Book, and I would have it picked up. For all Blackthorn knew, it was SOP. My fingerprints would never be detected. Not a very complex sleight of hand for me, so how difficult would it be for our Mr. X? As for the murders, it is just a matter of hiring or controlling the right operations group at the right time."

"But this is pure speculation" says the Admiral. "Simon and Marcia, go dig into Hunnsecker. Let's first rule him out. I will call some Israeli friends and see if they have more information than the last time they tried to snow me. And John, go find that NGO and see if you can rekindle your relationship. OK everyone? Simon, go down to the lab and check the tapes to see if you can ID some of the Blackthorn men so we can ask them a few tough questions. Right now all we have is uniforms. That isn't going to cut it. Marcia, heat up your computer!"

"Aye aye, sir" we both say as we drop off our trays and go back to work.

# 45 *SUNDAY AFTERNOON - WASHINGTON*

Right after lunch, I drive over to the Lab. When I get there, NCIS (Naval Criminal Investigative Service) was conducting an investigation of the attempted invasion. I introduced myself to the lead agent, Master Chief Petty Officer Jacob Stretcher. He is a tall, solid man of about 60, about an inch taller than me, with bright eyes and a kindly face. He is wearing a suit, even though it is Sunday. I could tell instantly that he would be a good interrogator. He apparently knows his stuff. I had never met him before, and probably would not again, but if I did, I was convinced that he would still remember every single word I told him. He looked at my ID very carefully, taking it out of the wallet to scan the back as well, and examined my little badge. He made a joke about his badge being bigger, but that was all the information he shared.

He had a team of agents who already interviewed the guards including the front gate Shore Patrol and scoured the area to pick up anything that would tie back to Blackthorn. "So who do you work for again?"

"Master Chief, I am with a small intelligence arm of the Navy called ESCORT."

"I am sorry, but I am not really familiar with your organization. What is it that you do again?"

"We support Special Operations." I answer.

"And who is it that you work for again?"

"Look, Master Chief, this is not a pissing contest. I have a right to be here and want to work together with NCIS but I have a different mission, which is very hard pressed for time. If I can help you catch the bad guys, great. But I really need to know who sent them. Yes, I know that the SecNav's name was on the order, but it's above him. Tell me what you've got so far."

"Please wait one minute, Captain." He reached into his pocket and produced a tiny card reader; similar to the one I saw Dr. Yancy use at Sandia. He pulled my ID card out of its case and ran the edge through it. He must have been satisfied by the information that appeared on the reader's tiny screen, although he gave no clue in his expression. He handed the ID back to me. "We've got 5 intruders, nominally Blackthorn, arriving with orders to retrieve an item from the lab. My Director got a call that it was a put up job, and my team was assigned to get the details of the attempt. Blackthorn denies any participation. The IDs checked at the gate are phonies, but we are reviewing camera data as we speak. No one penetrated the building perimeter. When they received the abort, the 5 took off in a Humvee registered to the Ft. McNair motor pool. All the intruders wore Desert Camouflage BDUs (Battle Dress Uniforms) with helmets. They all carried Colt M4 Carbines: standard issue weapons. We have the orders that were issued by the SecNav, but have not lifted any prints yet."

"Thank you, Master Chief. All I can tell you is that we believe that the orders may have been a test of our defenses. I doubt whether there will be a repeat. I believe that it would help you to know more details about the 'Book' listed in the retrieval order. But I am afraid it is truly a National Security Need-to-Know at this time. Believe me when I tell you a truer description could not be made. I am going into the lab now, but here is my card. If you get any further information about the assault party, give me a call or send me the file details."

"I will, if I can. It will depend on my Director."

"Thanks." I left him standing in the lobby while I went through the security door into the lab. John was in his usual position at the table with the Book open on the table.

I ask John if he can take a few minutes, and to bring his grey cells. We go to a small lounge set next to the bathrooms, with a few vending machines and a microwave. An attempt was made to lighten the atmosphere with bold stripes on the walls, echoed in the paint-spattered look of the floor tiles. But the atmosphere failed to lighten our concerns.

"John, before I get into any whys, I need you to help me with a question. Would it be possible to make a copy of the Book; one that would look like the original, but with changes in the content?"

"I suppose we could come up with something. We have a few technical problems that would have to be solved first. We don't understand enough about the structure of the metal determine how to make more. The engraving itself would be a challenge, due to the metal's hardness. But given enough time and resources, I think that eventually we could solve these problems. The real difficulty, however; would be in determining exactly what we could change without its being immediately discovered, as well as encoding and duplicating the entries so that they would be identical to the real Book. But this too could be solved over time. Why do you ask?"

"John, it seems that the Book, while apparently a fantastic document, represents a great problem to the foundation of our economy and political structure. While its advances may revolutionize so many fields, it also threatens current technology which supports our economic health. By its very existence, it exposes the nastier side of our free market system. Most of us accept that greed and corruption exist, but we like to think that our nation is administered fairly. Yet a prize such as this stimulates actions which demonstrate the depth of control and influence that personal and corporate agendas have over our political and economic systems. If the original Keepers had, as a goal, the preservation of this document for a time when it would no longer be a corruptive influence in the world, the time may not be now, or at least not yet."

"Both Dr. Froehlich and Admiral Lewis believe that it would be best if the real Book was returned to the Keepers. With all the people now in the information loop, we can't simply make the Book disappear. A solution to this is the creation and dissemination of a book that appears to be real, but after examination, is found to be valueless. Even if the government decides to hide the real Book out of reach, they will not be able to protect it for very long. There are just too many competing, powerful and rich interests. So the plan, which is now under consideration, is to create a disinformation document, allow it to be taken, and let it die of its own accord. As Dr. Froehlich put it, 'the best defense is no defense at all.'"

"Simon, what a sorry state of affairs. Here are all these marvelous discoveries which can't be made available to those who really need them. But I too have been increasingly concerned about the potential misuse if the wrong hands get hold of it. Do you think that maybe some of this information could be released?"

"I don't know. Let's work on that idea while we implement the other plan."

"Simon, it is a good idea, but not very intelligent in its execution. If you can possibly imagine how many disciplines would be needed to construct a false but apparently genuine Book, there would be just too many contributors to insure long term secrecy. It wouldn't take more than one or two and the secret would be out. This is not like the time of the Manhattan Project, when the country was at war, and nationalism was a commonly held value."

"Think about what you are proposing: a monumental task consuming thousands of hours by hundreds of individuals in their specialties. The plan's second flaw is you are missing a basic fact. Except for a very few of us, no one has even seen this document, has any idea of its size or complexity, or knows how many different disciplines are contained within it. We shouldn't have to create anything so large to substitute. A few chapters might be enough, and even those would not have to be re-written, merely altered so slightly as to appear genuine, but actually be useless. My thought is that the substitute Book could be formulated as the inventive fancy of an old culture who wrote speculation rather than science."

"John, that is brilliant. What do you think would be the absolute minimum number of people necessary to undertake such a deception?"

"Probably 10 would be enough. But we would have to be very careful as to which sections to alter, since it has to appear as the genuine result of several thousand years of innovation."

"John, if you were searching for revolutionary invention in today's world, what would you be looking for as the most pressing concerns in the world?"

"I would say energy and food. In energy, there are three discoveries described in the Book that can be very important, particularly to today's energy companies: reproducible, effective and efficient fusion processes, which yield excess heat for all types of applications from low volatility nuclear reactions; stable and safe hydrogen fuels derived from seawater which can replace fossil energy sources; Solar sourced electrical production on a large scale with potential wireless transmission. Any of these would revolutionize the energy industries, in terms of production, distribution and usage. The information on these subjects would immediately cut out the hearts of the oil companies, devalue their resources, and shift the balance of power away from the oil-rich countries."

"And food?"

"Grain protein production is the foundation for the world's food supply. Rice, wheat, corn, soy, barley make up the majority with potatoes not far behind. Current yield of crops is the most pressing problem. Take corn, for example. Currently, an average yield per acre in the U.S. is 200 bushels. What if it was increased to 1,000 bushels overnight? How about rice? If average yields of 8,000 lbs per acre were increased to 50,000 lbs, imagine the impact on world hunger. For many years, worldwide agribusiness has been based on control of supply. If supply were suddenly expanded beyond the need, agribusiness would fail. Military leverage also, is often created by providing or withholding food. Such a radical overabundance would create huge upheavals in all of these venues."

"John, do you think that healthcare is another area we should consider? The rapid growth of profit in the pharmaceutical and delivery organizations is also based upon restrictive controls over production and dissemination."

"OK. What about diabetes?"

"What do you mean?"

"Currently, all the billions in research have been going into two areas: the development of new drugs to both support glucose management as well as reduce complications associated with the disease, and the fundamental genome research to determine which genes produce the weaknesses in the body. But what if there were no pill at all, no medicines of any kind, just an in-vivo fetal injection which eliminated the weaknesses and auto immune reactions entirely. Within a generation, diabetes would be totally exterminated. Pharmaceutical companies and all those in that particular food chain would be severely damaged if 250 million people in the world suddenly no longer needed their products and services."

"OK, that's three. Would you be able to take the information in just these three sections, and modify it so that the data leads to blind alleys?"

"Well, not alone, but with a few others, I could do it. But we still can't manufacture new pages of this metal, nor can we etch it like the original."

"Let me worry about that. I will try to get you some help on the metallurgical end. Will you help fabricate this substitute?"

"Simon. I would much rather be working towards getting this Book out in its original form to all those in the world that needed its discoveries. But I understand the larger problems and will help."

"Thanks, John. We'll get past this, never you mind. Let me get out of here and do my part. You lay out a plan for the phony Book. You know; there may be parts of the original that are relatively benign. I am thinking particularly about discoveries that are already well known, but were not when they were included in the Book. Let's include those as well, to give a simulacrum of reality to the final work."

I bid John goodbye and went out through the security gate. Stretcher and his team were still on premises, sifting through camera records and running fingerprints. They had set up in a command trailer in the parking lot, and I stopped in before I left the site.

"Mr. Chess, my Director gave me the word. We have not gotten any hits on the fingerprints or photos yet. The assault team must have used superglue or latex on their hands. All we got is smudges. Do you want to see the pictures from the security cameras?"

"Sure, but can you speed it up? I don't have the day to spend in real-time."

"Yeah, the pictures come from several pole-mounted cameras, which take 3-second interval shots of the gate, oval and building exteriors. Our techs have pieced them together in a streaming video – about 5 minutes. Josh?"

The tech started the video on a 56" monitor mounted on one of the trailer walls. It showed a jerky sequence starting with the Humvee's original gate stop and debarking of the team. Two went in while the rest waited outside the building. All had assault helmets pulled down and kept from looking at the cameras. After a protracted period the two inside the building come out and they all re-enter their Humvee and leave. I could see nothing of any use, but then, these NCIS people are the experts. I ask Stretcher about any facial recognition, but he said that there are a few isolated glimpses which are currently being enhanced back at HQ. He told me I shouldn't hope for much.

Back at the office, I catch Marcia working the other end. She researched Hunnsecker and came up with many contacts in the Industrial complex, but that would be expected in his job. His bank account seemed to be stable, with no great increases or decreases in recent months. His interviews in the media seem to be getting more paranoid as time goes by, but that's a problem for The President. In reviewing his travel during the key periods of assault, both recently and several years ago, there was no unusual pattern, except he did visit Israel about a month before Jean was killed, where he met with the Defense Minister. Nothing else seemed to pop out.

The only recent trip he took was a hiking trip in the Tetons a few weeks back. However; he did not take his family, unlike other trips. One personal aide accompanied him. He paid for the trip personally, reimbursing the government for his plane usage. I asked Marcia if that was usual for him and she checked while I waited.

"Simon, that is the first time in more than a year that he has flown somewhere on his assigned plane and then reimbursed the government. I wonder if that is important."

"You mean it was important to him that the trip be never questioned, so he abandoned normal routine to hide it?"

"Something like that."

"Before we go further down this road, what do you think of John's version of the disinformation plan?"

"Simon, I think that it solves most of the problems, by reducing the chances for exposure."

"Marcia, I have another idea. Can you create a beacon to identify the aggressors?"

"What do you mean?"

"What if as part of this Book, you hid a virus in it. Something where if they input some of the information into a computer, either to record it or to analyze it, it would trigger some kind of a sensor that would broadcast, giving us a track to follow. If we allow the new Book to be stolen, this would be a way of tracing it, much like a GPS beacon in money shipments or an explosive dye pack – you know, something like that."

"So you are thinking about installing our own 'sniffer' in the gift Book, triggered by its usage?"

"Yes, something along those lines."

"It would mean that one of the solution formulas contains a mathematical expression that would open a gateway in their IP network. Yes, I suppose it could be done. But it would have to be really creative, not to be noticed. Do you know who might be a real help in this?"

"Who in addition to Dr. Froehlich?"

"Remember that mathematician, Alattin Akan who worked with Zilbern? He certainly has the background to create a coded pill in the Book. Oh, and also, in the area of biological disinformation, what about your friend Yancy, what's his name, over at Sandia?"

"Oh yes, Tom Yancy. He's the microbiologist with the mutation codex. Sure, he has a very high clearance, and might be the one to work on that section."

"I know that you are going to find this a bit weird, but I think that Lauren Sylfern and Eleanor Frankel would also be of great help. Lauren has a great deal of knowledge of languages, and can help retranslate the new information we put into the Book back into the old language of the genuine article. Eleanor Frankel is a psychologist, and has intimate knowledge of psychological inferences. Remember, the way we need to put things together to convince our thieves of their success, has to be based on their perceptions, which can be structured by Frankel."

"What about crop yield and energy production?"

"The issue of energy and food both require two aspects. The first and most important part is the impact on business. I would say that Dr. Froehlich can be considered a good candidate for that expertise, but maybe we will need an expert in alternative fuels. The technology itself can be covered by our biologist and generally by all of us. That leaves us with seven in the disinformation team: Sylfern, Frankel, Yancy, Akan, Froehlich, Crawford and me. You run the group and keep us protected. There are two issues that still need to be solved. The first is the technology of the document material itself and its etching process. The second is the toughest part: convincing all of these people that they must work together on this project and never discuss it again."

"I wonder if we could get the Keeper's help with the material and etching. I could go back to Alexandria."

"Why don't you talk to Froehlich about it? I have a feeling that he might have a couple of good ideas on that subject."

"Sure. You know, he has always seemed to be right there with exactly what we needed at the time we needed it. It is almost like he was prescient." I find Dr. Froehlich in another room, a telephone in one ear and an open laptop on the table, both of which have his undivided attention. When he sees me enter the room, he is talking to someone about an upcoming meeting, and I quietly eavesdrop as he points to an empty chair.

"But Felix, it is not so long. I would like to be there and learn for myself....Yes; I believe that it can be done....Thursday would be fine...Very well, you pick me up then. Goodbye Felix... yes I will."

As soon as he disconnects, he turns to me. "Well, Simon. That was a good call. I found someone that missed the last meeting of the corporate caucus and pushed my way into the next meeting – this coming Thursday in Chicago. My friend Felix who runs a software company in Silicon Valley wasn't invited to the last meeting. He is at odds with some of the others about being left out, and is going to the next one. Hopefully, I will learn something. So tell me, what have you learned?"

I tell him about my visit to the lab, John's idea about the gift Book, and Marcia's suggestions for contributory candidates. Then I share with him our concern for needing the metal technology, the source for new pages, and the techniques of the etching. I also tell him of our need to get some assistance from the Keepers. After listening to me, he then responds. "My dear boy; you all have created a miracle! What a perfect idea to create this gift Book for our enemies. It will attract them like flies. And the idea of a virus is brilliant. I think that I might be able to help Marcia with that as well, and put some of my company's software to use. Now as to the candidates, you will have the task of convincing them – and that will not be easy. I think that you will find that Lauren will help. She knows all the others and once she gets aboard, she can bring the others. As to the metal, there is a relatively simple solution. After the debacle at the airport, I took it upon myself to contact the curator at the Archeological section of the Alexandria Library. I am sure that he will help, particularly if we offer to return the Book to their safekeeping, and diffuse others' interests in it. I know that he will be very disappointed about our choice to return the original, but I do believe that we will get what we need to create this monumental deception. Just leave that part to me. I think that we can overcome the holes in our knowledge by collaboration. Your next step is to go to Albuquerque and talk with Lauren. It would be far better if you did it in person, rather than by telephone."

Lauren is very surprised to hear from me after all this time, but agrees to see me tomorrow. I share with Marcia Dr. Froehlich's suggestions and his agreement with our overall plan. As it is getting close to the end of the day, Marcia and I decide to go back to our hotel. She calls John to invite him to have dinner with us, but he declines. He tells her that Karen is coming into town for the evening, and Emily is having an overnight with a friend's family.

Gina seems to be back in her old job. She has printed tickets for me for the following morning on a 7:00 flight, and says goodnight as we leave. We head for the hotel and change out of our work clothes to have a quiet dinner; just the two of us for a change. After discussing options, we settle on 1789 Restaurant, near the western edge of Georgetown. Fortunately, we are able to get reservations, provided that we get there early. Marcia digs out a blazer of mine that has been sitting in the suitcase too long and looks like I slept in it. But a few passes with an iron on a dampened towel steams it back to reasonably presentable condition, at least if the restaurant is dark. My slacks still look like they once had a crease, and my loafers aren't terribly dusty, so Marcia tells me if she issues sunglasses to people we pass by, she might allow herself to be seen with me. What can I say about her? She looks gorgeous in a solid green short skirt and a yellow blouse. Like a daffodil.

I decide to leave the rental here and take advantage of our ESCORT ride. I alert the driver as we finish sprucing up. Sunday night, the majority of the traffic is coming back into town, so the ride out to Georgetown is rather quick, even on GW parkway and Key Bridge. The restaurant is located in an old Federalist residence, with a brick exterior and a wood beamed main dining room. The atmosphere is quiet and elegant. With our cafeteria lunch long behind, we eagerly look at and discuss the menu with our attentive waiter.

"Simon, do you think that we have a chance against these folks?"

I glance around at neighboring tables before I answer. "Actually, I do. But it is not going to be without sacrifice. The big question is what is sacrificed? Or more accurately, who will be sacrificed. The Book by itself won't be enough; it will only be a Book. It is the way that it is obtained, that will guarantee it's acceptance as truth. This is an old lesson in tradecraft. The wrapping is the validation of the meat in any disinformation scheme. If an adversary believes in the wrapping, the meat is far more palatable. I just don't know how we will get to that, without losing someone important to us. When the opportunity surfaces, we have to stay alert to take whatever advantage that is offered."

"Simon that is awful and something I really would prefer to avoid considering, but you are probably right. Darling, when this is over, can we go live in San Francisco for a while. Would you mind that very much?"

"Sure. Our house out there is certainly large enough. If we move the office out of the house, there will be plenty of room for us. Besides, I guess it is because I grew up on the water, but I would really miss not being connected to the sea. So San Francisco works for me. Unless you want to find a new place; you know, someplace where it is ours from the start?"

"That doesn't matter to me. I love the sense of time that your house gives me. I know that you have had it for only 3 years, so it doesn't come with long memories. I think that what appeals to me is that as a house, it's endured, has sheltered good people and nasty people, happy and difficult days, but it is always ready to shelter someone. We can care for it, or we can ignore it, but it still does its job. I would like to be its steward for a while. I think that would give me great joy."

"I don't think that I ever heard a house described like that. But it's like everything else about you, it surprises makes me. I don't have those feelings about the house, but if it gives you pleasure, that's good enough for me. Maybe there is something that you would like to do with it to make it more your own? San Francisco is a great place to bring up a family."

"Simon, do you think we can start one? A family, that is?"

"Well, we can, although we're a little older than most when they start."

"That's not a real problem, is it?"

"No, I was just thinking out loud. It would mean a very different life for us. I mean the work and traveling."

"Simon, when you were small did your parents take you on trips and spend time with you?"

"No, dad worked in the maintenance shop keeping the research ships of the Wood Hole Oceanographic Institute afloat, and seemed always to be working. My mom did odd jobs around town to make extra money. During the summers when the town was filled with tourists and folks going to or coming from Martha's Vineyard or Nantucket, she worked in a clothing shop. In the winter, when the tourists left, she did some part time work at the drug store, or in the bank. We didn't really go anywhere, much. Why?"

"Well, I thought that if we had children, if we wanted to go somewhere, we could just pack them up and take them with us. My mother used to take an annual trip to Europe when I was small, and always left me home. Winters meant boarding school for me, but I always hoped that she would one time take me with her on her trip. But she never did. Promise me that if and when we have children, we will never just leave them. I don't want that to be repeated for another generation."

"No, sure we'll always take them."

Dinner was eaten and coffee sipped when Marcia brought up our assignment again. "Tomorrow, are you going to try to visit each of the guys out at the labs after convincing Lauren?"

"Yes. I plan to get Lauren aboard, and then go together to talk to the rest of them. I think that Froehlich is right; they will be far more receptive if it they are asked by a personal friend, rather than officially by the Navy. If Lauren believes in what we are doing, I would give her the primary lead in gathering the rest,"

I was just starting to find the waiter for our check when he placed the dessert cards at our places, which I know Marcia cannot resist. Her eyes lit up at the choices, and selected Baba au Rum while I reluctantly did not resist the strawberry shortcake's pull, although I drew the line at the vanilla ice cream served with it.

With dinner satiating us, I telephoned our driver who had gone for his own dinner up at the Hamburger Hamlet [one of my favorites] and would be back in a few minutes. On the way to the hotel, the driver, a Navy Chief, told me that since he was going up to Bethesda anyway, he stopped by to see if Dr. Froehlich's house was still being watched, which it is. It occurs to me that the driver has more than one job at ESCORT. When I ask him about it, he tells me that he is an ex-SEAL too, having damaged a wing in Afghanistan, so was working for the Admiral he did a few minor Ops once and a while to keep his hand in.

Back at the hotel, we both opt for a shower. I'm not sure who was first, but we both squeeze into the tub-shower and spend a great deal of time doing the soaping. The steam on the shower door had nothing on us as the warm water cascaded over us and soap made us both slithery. I think that we will both wind up prunes, as we dry each other off and fall into bed.

During the night, I think the telephone rang, but both of us were too far gone to hear it.

# 46 *MONDAY – NEW MEXICO and WASHINGTON*

When I walk out of Baggage Claim on a sunny, warm Albuquerque Monday, I am surprised to see Lauren waiting for me. She tells me that she called the previous evening, but there was no answer, so she called again this morning and told Marcia that she would pick me up. The last time I saw her, she was a wreck. The torture that her father put her through during those few weeks before Alexandria had taken a terrible toll on her sense of loyalty. I believe that it was her fundamental sense of right that drove her to tearing the briefcase from her father's hands, but I have to believe also that she must feel an enormous sense of guilt over causing his death. I don't want to criticize her dad, but I need to find a way to tell her that I believe she did what she had to do.

Without her knowing my agenda today, she suggests that we should go back to her home to talk, but instead, I suggest we find a spot for breakfast. There is a diner not far from the airport called K&I which serves outstanding burritos with lots of great coffee. Its home to a lot of the Santa Fe Railroad workers and is watched over by a senior member of the owning family, affectionately called 'Grandma' by everyone. Grandma is ageless, sitting at the cash register when we walk in. She yells out to one of her kids or grandkids to 'git 'em a table' and chuckles when Lauren plants a sideways kiss on her brown cheek as we pass. She's a tough New Mexico bird and not much flusters her at this age. We are taken to a table through several of the rambling rooms all cobbled together. When we sit, coffee is only one second behind us, followed by one of the younger 50-year old kids who takes our order. Lauren suggests that I order a half-Travis, which is a meat, chile and egg-filled burrito nearly a foot long and about 3 inches in diameter, buried beneath about a half-gallon of fresh French Fries. I cannot imagine anyone attempting to eat a full one, but some of the railroad guys…"

Lauren tells me that it is very nice that I came out to see her, and inquires after Marcia and John. But she pointedly doesn't ask about the Book. So I bring up the subject, tell her about the people after it and their retaining of Blackthorn to do their dirty work.

"I believe that my father did many evil things in his pursuit of the Book, but I did not believe that he did everything that he is accused of. I was sure when after his first death, I was besieged by the NSA agents, followed constantly, and then you and I were both attacked in your office. I knew that there had to be others after the same Book. I just could not separate them from my father, nor could I convince my father that if he found the Book, he should turn it over to somebody like John Crawford. I only wish he had listened to me; he might still be alive."

"Lauren, you must not feel guilty about your father's death. He really brought it on himself, and you have nothing to be ashamed about."

"But I did kill him. If I hadn't…"

"Lauren, do you remember when I told you about my wife Jean being killed? Well I felt the same way. 'If I had only' I used to say to myself over and over, but I didn't and she is gone, and there is nothing that I can ever do to change that fact. Neither can you about your own father's death. You have to grieve, but then you must let it go; besides which, we really need your help."

"Thank you, Simon. Don't expect too much from me. What can I do to help?"

"What I tell you may never, ever be repeated."

"I understand."

"Actually you don't yet. But before I say anything, you also have to know that just having the information that I will give you, will put you in jeopardy again."

"Since my father died, I have been in a kind of never-never land, not really feeling alive. Simon, I am not afraid of danger. What I fear most is continuing this state of limbo."

"OK. You know, I really should ask you to sign a Confidentiality Agreement with the government, but let's go on faith for now."

"I already have one on file with the State Department. Remember, I work as a translator for documents as high as Top Secret. So tell me." She waits, and then starts to laugh.

"What is it?"

"Do you remember when we first met; I said you couldn't repeat what I told you? Funny how things are reversed."

"Yes, it is. I only wish what I have to say was funny. It turns out that the Book contains a huge assortment of discoveries that can be both beneficial as well as harmful, depending on how they are used. We are certain that a major attempt will be made to capture it, and then, a world-wide contest of power will ensue to control the information. In Washington, our team is literally under siege by some of the most powerful forces in the country."

"What can I do to help?"

"We have decided to give it to them. The only difference is that it will be not exactly what they expect. We are putting together a very small team of specialized expertise to create an almost-perfect copy of several sections of this volume. The only difference will be that what we give them will turn out to be almost useless because nothing in the way of 'great solutions' will actually work. We believe that this disinformation should be sufficient to lose interest in this venture. Then the original will be returned for perhaps another generation or two."

"That sounds like a monumental task. But why are you asking me?"

"The proposed team includes John, Marcia, Johann Froehlich, Alattin Akan, Tom Yancy, Eleanor Frankel, and you."

"You are proposing bringing in everyone that knew about dad's quest, and worked with him on some aspect of the search?"

"Yes. The sections of the Book we will mock up include biology, medicine, energy, food production and possibly some basic mathematical problems that have never been solved. The issue that we have to face is that our imitation will undergo rigorous scrutiny, so some things need to be true, and some false. The job of persuasion and validity checking will be Eleanor's. You would handle the translation to the original language; Alattin will do the math section, and Yancy the biology. Froehlich knows the kind of people that are on the opposite side, and will also help with the energy issues. I will be responsible for coordinating the total effort as well as running security. Also, I will get the actual material of the new text fabricated, and etched with our material."

Lauren appeared to be shocked by my revelation. She sat open-mouthed for a few moments but then replied, "I have an idea. There must be things in the Book that are genuinely benign, so it might not matter if that information gets into the wrong hands or not. These, added to the sections covering existing science, will make our version much thicker, and give it a greater sense of genuineness." Now I see that she wasn't shocked at all, merely analyzing what I had said. I think that Froehlich was right again. Lauren could adapt very well to this new role.

I answered her. "Of course; see, I told you that you can help. Now, will you help me convince the others?"

"Simon, you don't have to even be here. I know all the people, and will be able to convince them of the importance of their contribution. They are also used to secrets and have high clearances. Why don't you go home and keep an eye on what's happening there and let me do this. Eleanor will participate just because she cares for me. Alattin, I think might for a similar reason, but also because he owes Dad a great deal. Tom Yancy, I don't know that well. But I would imagine that he would love to be in on it just because he was asked. You know, Simon, this could be a partial vindication of my father's life. It would mean a lot to me."

"Go ahead. But you must emphasize two facts with your friends. First, this will be dangerous. If we are found out, the retribution will be swift and final. Second, no one may ever speak of this work again, to each other or to anyone else. This means that the creativity and invention that comes as a result of the team's work has to be concealed forever. All is lost if any hint gets out. And third, each of the members has to withdraw from their current assignments without bringing any suspicion on them and do it in less than 2 days. By Wednesday, the team has to be in Washington, ready to work 24/7 until the work is completed."

"Yes, I understand. Now, let's get you back to the airport. You don't have any time for sightseeing."

"On the way back, may we make one small detour? I really would like to pick up a gift for Marcia. In all the rush, I never got her a real wedding present."

Lauren agrees and suggests that we go to the Indian Pueblo Cultural Center. I trade a couple of barbs with Grandma before I am released with a kiss.

The Center is on 12$^{th}$ street in the flood plain of the Rio Grande. Inside, we go through the lobby and restaurant area to the open dancing plaza, and behind it, a semi-circular one story adobe building which encloses the back of the plaza. In the building, I walk directly to the jewelry section and ask if they have any fetish necklaces. The young Native American who helps me, shows me quite a few Zuni creations, but all are multi-colored or flat enameled versions, and none are what I am looking for. Then, when she sees that I am disappointed, she asks me to wait and goes out through the back of the building towards the parking lot. In a moment she returns, followed by a very old man with long grey hair tied in two braids, which reach his waist. Although he is hatless, I can see the suntan line on his

468

forehead from many years outside in the New Mexico sun. His hands are the color of the earth, and as rough as sandstone as he shakes my hand. The wrinkles in his eyes and cheeks get deeper as he grins at me when the young girl speaks to him in old tongue. From around his neck, under his shirt, he takes off and holds up to me a magnificent greenish blue turquoise necklace, with a large carved sitting bear and perhaps fifty smaller interwoven animals and birds on either side, rising up the string towards the back of the neck. The top of the necklace is of whipped cord, like a rope splice, but pure white to counterpoint the blue-green of the soft stones. There is no clasp.

I take the necklace and hold it close while I look at it. "This is so very beautiful" I say to the girl "Is this man your father?"

"This is my grandfather, who is also a tribal elder. He carved this necklace from our tribe's mine in Turquoise Mountain west of Albuquerque for his wife, but it took him so long that she died before he finished it. Now he wears it in honor of my grandmother."

"I never imagined that something like this ever existed. Do you think that he could make me one like it for my new wife?"

The young girl speaks to her grandfather, and he back to her while I wait. He looks at me, takes the necklace from my hands and puts it around my neck. Then he grasps my shoulders in both hands and holds them while he speaks to his granddaughter. Taking my two hands and turning them upwards, he looks very closely at my palms and fingers while muttering under his breath. He releases my hands to pull a small medicine bag from under his shirt and sprinkles some powder onto my hands. Then he massages it into my skin as he chants again. Finally the old man takes a step back me and says "This is good medicine for new life." and then he shakes my hand again, gives a brief nod of his head like a tiny bow and goes back out the door, leaving me speechless.

"He made you a great gift," the salesgirl says, as she returns behind the counter and searches for a bag.

"But I cannot take this. This was for your grandmother."

"You don't understand. Her spirit is with him and he will soon be with her again. The spirit in the necklace is only alive and its medicine good if it is worn by a person with a bear spirit. He believes that you have this spirit in you, so it is yours."

"I must give you something for it."

469

"Yes, you give me whatever you believe you would like to pay for it, and I will see that the money goes to our tribe. My grandfather no longer needs money."

"I can't thank you enough. Please tell your grandfather that I shall give this to my wife in love."

"He could see that in your heart. That was payment enough for him." Then the young lady accepts money from me and places it in her pocket. She wraps the necklace and gives it to me. Lauren had watched this play and silently leads me back to the car and drives to the airport.

When we arrive, I find that a flight is going in my direction in a couple of hours, so I buy a new Clive Cussler adventure thriller at the newsstand and read while I wait. I absently reach into my pocket to verify that the necklace is still there and that I hadn't been dreaming.

## WASHINGTON

It was near the end of the day when I got back to Reagan. Back at the lab, it feels like a war zone. A squad of marines was encamped at the gate with a Command and Control Van parked in the oval. I have to show my ID three separate times to get through the perimeter, and even then, at the security door, the ID is cross checked against a photo database of authorized personnel. Inside the lab, all is normal, except that John was off to a meeting when I arrive. After looking around at the security arrangements, I go back to the office. When I walk in, Marcia gave a little yelp and jumps to welcome me.

She has been working on tracing telephone calls to and from various important persons in the Government. Before even asking me what had happened in New Mexico, she tells me that she has something really important to show me. The conference room has a built-in projector to which her computer was attached. On the screen were numerous names, with thousands of lines in various colors linking them like a complex spider web. Marcia tells me it is a social network of communications for the past month. The links made very little sense to me, but clearly it means something to her.

"This is a graphic chart of communications between individuals, originating with Secretary Hunnsecker. This is the way it works. If you call or email someone, a white line is drawn to whoever you call, and a time stamp is put on that line. Calls of less than 30 seconds are dropped from the matrix. If the person you call then makes calls to others, those individuals are likewise linked, and so on. Eventually there are many thousands of nodes created. If a node is not reactive to anyone else more than a minimum set in the program, the node disappears, which means that the network is unreinforced. By setting different limits on contact duration, frequency, and interrelated responses, we can gradually create a pattern of contact for individuals, and generally find repeatable sequences. If you call me, for example, and each time you do, I call John and Froehlich, then this pattern can be predicted, and a network relationship can be identified. Let me show you a filtered sequence of contacts that has been repeated many times in the past month."

Marcia taps a few keys on her laptop and I see a web of contacts begin at one node and lead to a second, then a third, and then fly out to a dozen or more others, which then returns back to the second node and then back to the first. This happens numerous times. "Who are these people?"

"The first is Hunnsecker. The second is his attorney, the third is the CEO of American Gas & Oil; the web is a who's who of industry, all CEOs, and the return directions are almost identically reversed."

"I understand that Hunnsecker uses his attorney to call a number of people in a contact loop, who then return his calls. So what?"

"This sequence is repeated every third day for the past month. It is some kind of working group, with a primary contact and a dozen or so members."

"But why would this have anything to do with our mission?"

"It may not, but it started almost immediately after the Book was recovered by us and brought to Washington by Dr. Froehlich. It is a real coincidence, don't you think?"

"Coincidence, yes, but conspiracy, I wouldn't be able to prosecute that viewpoint. I would have to see a transcript of some of these calls."

"Unfortunately, all of them are encrypted and the crypto-system used is changed daily. We aren't getting a lot of cooperation from the NSA on this."

"Speaking of Froehlich, where is he?"

"He went off our radar this afternoon. He said something about a meeting, and that he wouldn't be back until Wednesday. By the way, how did New Mexico go?"

I relate my talk with Lauren, then call the Admiral, and ask him to arrange transportation for the New Mexico contingent to the lab Wednesday

471

morning. He quizzes me on progress, but doesn't dwell on the subject for very long. Just before hanging up, he asks me if Marcia and I would please stay in the office for a little while this evening, until he can meet with us.

It is close to 7 when Admiral Lewis comes into the office looking grim. "Sit down, both of you. I have important information." I am so used to standing while he speaks to me, that I don't even recognize when I got up from my seat, but I follow his order and sit beside Marcia.

"There is no easy way to say this. Three and a half years ago, the Israeli government was contacted by our Joint Staff with a request for permission to conduct a black op in Jerusalem. The Mossad was told that a meeting was being planned at the Jerusalem Tower Hotel between several important operatives of Al Qaeda during the renovation of the hotel when there would be relatively few guests. The floor that the meeting was to be held was just above an unoccupied level. Our mission was to set up a listening post there. The Mossad offered to do it for us, but we said we would give them copies of anything that we obtained, so they agreed. A Special Forces A-Team was ordered to set charges in the listening post area. They were informed that a CIA team would be following them there. The explosives were to be placed in case they had to destroy their own equipment on discovery, or to assassinate those at the meeting upstairs. The decision was to be made by the incoming CIA eavesdroppers. While the demolitions team was setting the charges, an interrogation team from the DIA came in and took Jean in her room. She was questioned and tortured by the team. Then they sedated her and left. Afterwards, the best we can gather is that someone who has not been identified detonated the charges. There is no question that someone in our government ordered the capture, torture, interrogation and hit on Jean Chess. The Israelis were surprised that they had not heard of any upcoming Al Qaeda meetings, but thought that our intelligence on that organization might be better than theirs for a change. After the hit, the Israelis were asked officially by the CIA and the SecDef to investigate, and a report was sent back to the DCI and SecDef. I have seen that report. It says, in effect 'person or persons unknown' were responsible, and was sanitized for any information gleaned from the interrogation. I am not going to tolerate this. It's one thing to take out enemies of the state, and another assassinating innocent people."

I started to say something, but he stopped me "Wait, there's more. The Israelis rarely trust our intelligence compared to theirs, which has some historical justification, so before the hit; they searched out any of their sources to see if they could verify if such a meeting was to take place. The information about the meeting was manufactured. So with a distrustful eye, they assigned two agents as room service waiters for the floor above, both of whom were killed in the blast, but not before they transmitted some pictures to Mossad Headquarters. They are sending me a copy of these pictures by courier, so we should get them by tomorrow. Frankly, I am surprised that the pictures weren't used for some judicious extortion before this came up, but they were waiting for an appropriate opportunity. Simon, I am really sorry about this, and am remiss at not following it up thoroughly at the time. But it was the job of other people directly involved, so I made a fallacious assumption."

"Admiral, I just knew that it was going to be something like this. I never believed that it was Zilbern. Will you show me the pictures when you get them?"

"Yes, you have a right to see them, whatever they show. But now I have a distasteful job. I have to find out who over at our sister agency is responsible for this. For the DIA to act in concert with an Airborne Ranger Demolitions Team, it had to come from SecDef or someone close to him. He's my boss, which makes it even more abhorrent. I will promise you one thing, Simon. I will not let this rest. I don't give a whit where this goes and who thought they could get away with not only the hit, but the story to cover it."

I thank the Admiral for his commitment; both Marcia and I leave the office for the night. On our drive home, Marcia says "I believe, Simon, that you now can see the futility of your taking any responsibility for what happened to Jean. Neither of us could have done anything. At best, we might even have been blown up with her."

"You are right about giving up the guilt; but not about letting go of retribution. I will find out who gave that order, and see him in hell, if I have to send him there myself."

"As you should; after all, you loved her, and probably still do, and why not? I don't resent it one bit." I smiled back at her as she drives, and realize again that I am extraordinarily lucky to have found two such women in my lifetime.

When we get back to Laurel, the house is musty from being shut up, but soon air conditioning is cooling and the flowers are grateful for some extra water. The rest of the evening after a light dinner, we spend in mundane activities: paying bills, sorting junk mail, and answering personal emails. By 11, we are finished for the night and go upstairs to bed. Both of us are tired and grateful to be able to lie again in our comfortable room.

At 2:30 in the morning, the soft purring of a car engine followed by a car door closing wakes me. I nudge Marcia and grab my Glock from my end table drawer. As I reach the front door, there is a shadow against one of the glazed panels, silhouetted in the moonlight followed by a soft tapping and a voice which whispers through the door "Don't turn on a light. Please." Dr. Froehlich practically falls into my arms as I pull the door open."

"Are you all right?"

"No, my friend, I have been shot" he says as he limps into the room, holding his right thigh.

"Marcia, come down," I call, while I lead him into the kitchen. His clothes are torn and soaking wet. His face is very pale, and he is in obvious pain. Marcia gives a little cry when she sees who it is. We both help Froehlich into the downstairs bathroom, where Marcia produces a pair of scissors, tape, gauze and some triple antibiotic. She cuts off his pants above the hole and cleans the wound. It looks like the bullet plowed a shallow groove in his thigh, which does not appear to be deep. Marcia packs it with gauze and antibiotic, tapes it in place, and we help him to the living room. Marcia goes to make us some tea, while Froehlich catches his breath.

"What happened?"

"It was the Blackthorn men. They were waiting for me when I got home. I just got out of the car when two of them came out from the bushes and tried to grab me. I hit one of them with my briefcase and started to run, but then the other shot me. I don't know why they didn't chase me. I ran to my neighbor's yard and hid under his roses. Eventually, the men drove off in their van, so I got to my car and came here. I have no idea why they came after me and then gave up without pressing their advantage."

"Maybe they were just trying to frighten you or send you a message that they could get to you any time they wanted. It's an old tactic to keep someone off balance."

"Well it worked. I am quite disoriented. Would you mind very much if I imposed on your hospitality and spent the night here?"

"Of course," Marcia said as she returned with tea and cookies. "You may stay here as long as you like. We have plenty of room, and would be very pleased if you accepted."

"You are so very kind," he said as he started to shake. It was very difficult for him to even hold the tea without spilling it. Eventually, his composure returned and he asked for a small dram of brandy. When Marcia brought it, he put half into the remaining tea and the rest he drained down. Then he smiled and said "I must also tell you what I have been up to since yesterday. It is quite interesting."

"Yesterday, after I spoke to my corporate contact, I invited myself into a meeting which is to be held Thursday, as I mentioned to you. But this morning something happened which accelerated the meeting to late this afternoon at the Metropolitan Club on H Street. The three people who I met included my software friend, the man who is Hunnsecker's attorney, and a gentleman who runs one of the largest oil companies in the world. It seems that a purse had been created to retain Blackthorn, but less than half of the sum raised was actually paid. The rest disappeared. The Blackthorn people are very angry at being 'stiffed' as the oilman described it. They have threatened to pull out entirely unless they get the rest of their money. My friend and his software buddies were tapped as a resource for the remainder, while an investigation is made to find out what had become of the missing funds. Both my friend and I pledged additional cash for operation, but my friend wanted to know more about the potential payoff. The oilman said that he could not tell us, except to say that it would return many fold within a few weeks. I asked him if Blackthorn has made any progress so far. He told me that they were training at one of their encampments in Montana and would be prepared to go into action within two weeks. He also told me that the assault would be made against a government installation, but that their group had political support at the very highest levels so there would be no backlash."

"Any names mentioned?"

"None but the intimation was made that the White House knew about the transfer of technology, which is what he called it, from the public to the private sector, and supported it. I asked if the 'highest levels' meant the President, but was refused a direct answer.

"I imagine that Blackthorn followed up and wanted to let you know that they were serious people, which accounts for the incident tonight. My only question is why they chose you, since you have not been involved in their activities until today. But perhaps your meeting today was monitored. I wouldn't be a bit surprised if others had their feathers similarly ruffled."

"Tomorrow, I will make a few calls and see if you are right. But for tonight, would you mind very much if I was shown to my room. I am absolutely exhausted and have a little pain."

"Doctor," says Marcia "I will bet that it is more than just a little." She takes him upstairs and shows him into the guest bedroom.

The good news is that Blackthorn is not yet ready for a full scale assault.

# 47 *WEDNESDAY – WASHINGTON*

At breakfast, Froehlich tells me that he had John Crawford send off two of the other rings from inside the armor to friends at the Ames Laboratories. The NASA scientists were able to complete a destructive analysis of the metal, and believe that they could produce small quantities of it for our Book. They were very excited about the material, since it has some real applications in non-ablative surfaces for the Space Shuttle as well as other high-energy programs. He said that the amounts that we need for the new Book might be produced in one week. Froehlich arranged with a friend in Congress for special black funding undertake this task, without revealing the ultimate source for the new material.

Froehlich said this morning, that 5 of the other corporate plotters were similarly harassed by Blackthorn, but that the money was transmitted early this morning to them so probably further threats have been deferred. He also said that the investigation would be a subject of the coming meeting in Chicago, so he had to wait until then to learn more.

Marcia asks if she can help with planning. I go through the concepts of the disinformation, incorporating the suggestions made by Froehlich, Crawford and Sylfern, as well as hers. She agrees with all the premises, but takes issue with the implementation.

"We can't make it too easy for them. If they come to the lab and try to take the Book, and we don't put the full power of our defenses into action, they will smell a rat. Likewise, if we take the Book out of the lab, unless it is for a legitimate purpose, they will come to the conclusion that we are baiting them, with the same negative result. Simon, let me suggest a wild idea. We know that Froehlich has a longstanding personal relationship with Madam President. Suppose Froehlich was asked by the President to bring the Book to the White House, wouldn't it be likely that somewhere in transit, an ambush would be mounted?"

"That would probably be correct, but it would mean that Froehlich would be attacked and killed in the process. That would not be an option that I would choose."

"What if the Book was sent over by the Navy?"

"Whoever was assigned to protection would undoubtedly be killed in a firefight. We have to come up with a lower-risk alternative."

"Well, keep working on it. Maybe you'll come up with something."

I go back to my scribbling, and before long, the telephone rings. It is Lauren.

"Simon, all of the team is now here with me on the plane on our way east."

"Lauren, that is fantastic. Is everyone on board?"

"Eleanor doesn't think that she can be of particular help, but she wants to support me. Alattin is extremely excited about the prospect of seeing the actual Book. Tom Yancy is convinced that the whole idea of the Book's history is phony, so he wants to see for himself. I have done a refresher into the ancient Mideast languages, so I am ready to dive into it. Will you be able to meet us this afternoon? We should be in the lab by 2. Oh, and on the security issue, each of the team got permission to be away from their labs for a two week period – either for conferences, vacation or recuperation. I don't believe there have been any leaks."

The security office tells me when I call that IDs have already been issued and would be waiting for them upon arrival, as well as protection for each scientist.

It seemed that whatever plan I consider, some defender or courier has to be sacrificed. There had to be a good plan out there somewhere. When Dr. Froehlich comes downstairs to inquire about my progress, I share my dilemma with him. He tells me that he may have some ideas, but would defer until returning from Chicago. The three of us get in the ESCORT car for the drive to the lab. Marcia has brought some ham and brie filled croissants to eat in the car, along with a bowl of crudités with a curried ranch dressing. That woman doesn't stop. I would bet that if we found ourselves stranded on a remote Pacific island, she would still be able to whip up a Poisson Cru with coconut milk and baked breadfruit for an offhand snack at the beach.

We get to the lab around 1:30 and meet John. Before greetings are completed, Marcia whips out a fourth croissant for him, as well. Between bites, John tells us of his work. He has been able to put together a mockup of the facsimile. It is fairly big already. In it, he tells us, are hundreds of important discoveries that have already been documented since the Book was first written, as well as a number of new concepts that would be useful, but not strategically important. For example, there is a method for rapid reforestation of clear-cut sites, fish farm feeds that encourage rapid growth without harmful inorganics, and thin film polymers that have applications for space telescopes. He also included some designs for dirt resistant fabrics, and nanotechnology for medical robots, to name a few. It is unbelievable how these ancients could know about such science. NASA is hard at work on generating the metal pages, and all they need is to come up with an etching process to write on them.

The security team is already expecting the scientists. They have been training for defense, but they are not sure that they can repel all boarders. I let them know that we will have backup available from Navy HQ should it become necessary, and advise them to set some liaison meetings to collaborate on strategies.

By the time I am finished, the scientists have already arrived and are in the lab. I go there, prepared to give a speech. My experience with high flying talent is that they rarely play well together, and need constant ego stroking. I just hope that this assemblage will be different, but I doubt it. When I come in, all of them are elbow to elbow around the table where John is showing them the Book. Every now and then, one would ask a question or make a comment, but for the most part, they appeared to be overwhelmed by what was before them. All but Yancy; He stood back from the others with a sour expression on his face. Every now and then, he would make a derisive comment about whatever subject John was expounding on. I wonder what his problem is and why he volunteered to participate. I will have to watch him.

Eleanor is the most open of all of them. She 'oohs' and 'aahs' at some of the discoveries, and looks like a child on Christmas morning. I could see that Lauren has a few tears in her eyes. I guess that she is thinking about her father and his missed opportunities. Alattin is a little reserved, but nothing like Yancy. A stray thought comes to me as I look at his face. He looks like this was not something new for him. How strange?

I let the conversation continue for a while longer and then call everyone to come out of the crowded lab to a conference room to talk about our plan.

Nine of us arrange ourselves around the table, including Dr. Froehlich and myself. I move to the head and scan each face.

"Thank you for coming together on such short notice. I hope that you took the opportunity on the plane to evaluate one other, since we have little time to build a cohesive working team. Each of you has some knowledge of the document that brings us together. Perhaps I should reiterate the danger that we all share from this moment on. We have learned that there are many in government, private industry and in foreign countries that will exert great efforts to acquire this old Book. These forces are not, by their very nature, evil. But the power that is anticipated to come from control over this information will undoubtedly generate extraordinary action. In the last few months, at least 35 people have been killed so far in the pursuit of this Book, and many others have been suborned. Could we all become targets if we undertake this work? The answer is that we already are. Now let's get to what we are here to accomplish."

"We have the goal of creating a simulacrum of this work, which will appear genuine under intense scrutiny, yet where the discoveries ultimately turn out to be fallacious, at least the important ones. You might call our goal the construction of a modern Trojan Horse, which will be seen as a gift of the Gods, yet will ultimately lead to destruction of the aggressors. Back in Troy, it destroyed the victims of aggression as well, so we'll change the original story a bit. I personally would prefer to share these invention treasures with everyone, but events have shown that for all the good that can come of this material, there is a far greater likelihood of harm."

"So I ask you, each of you on your own, to commit to our purpose. It will not be easy, nor will it be particularly satisfying to anyone who aspires to creativity and discovery. But it is necessary. If you do not agree, please say so, and all that we ask is that you never mention this meeting or the subject ever again. But if you do agree, please let us each say so and we can get started."

Dr. Johann Froehlich: "Yes"

Marcia Chess: "Yes"

Lauren Sylfern: "Yes. I will do what I am able, both for me and for my misguided father."

Thomas Yancy: "Yes, but up to a point. I do not like the idea of putting false science out into the public domain, and I do not like the idea that this Book has garnered such reverence without exhaustive evaluation and peer review. But I will cooperate."

Eleanor Frankel: "I believe that the men and women who would use this for personal greed would stop at nothing to achieve their ends. If we can stick it to them, so much the better. Yes, I'm in."

Alattin Akan: "I believe that ultimately, man will be ready for this information, but apparently not yet. So we must do whatever we are able to preserve it for the future."

John Crawford: "No matter how I feel personally about the discovery and the contents of this great archeological find, I would sooner destroy it. I am committed to this."

And me: "I wish I had the faith that you have, Alattin, but I do not. But I will work towards this end with all my strength, until it is done."

With that completed, I feel that a weight has been lifted from my shoulders, yet at the same time, the responsibility for the group worries me, and I hope that I am up to it.

"We need to analyze the fields to see where we will make changes, and then create the substitution pages. Lauren, you will make the actual translation with John's help. I will take on the process for engraving the new pages, along with obtaining the new metal material. Please let me know how many new pages we will need by tomorrow morning." We all agree to meet each day formally, to review progress, but since much of the work will be done by individuals, each person should be available for ad-hoc consultation and support. I then adjourn the meeting. Alattin asked to stay behind with Marcia and me. I ask Tom Yancy to meet with me later.

The rest go back to the lab and start picking apart the fields. Alattin looks expectantly at both of us and opens the conversation. "Simon, I am glad to have a chance to speak with you both. I wanted to tell you that a few months ago, when you first approached me, I was concerned. But not for the reasons you may think of. I have always admired Lauren from the time when Ernst brought me home for dinner. I secretly harbored hopes that she and I could get to know one another better. When her father disappeared, my hopes grew and I tried to build a relationship with her. But something was always in the way. Later, of course, I became jealous of your relationship with her. I saw that Lauren had pinned so many hopes on your investigation, and was enamored by your sense of responsibility, I thought that she fell for you and I was despondent at the implications for me. Then when you left her and went to Europe, she dissolved into a funk, but even in that she held back from me. She was so angry when you married Marcia, it killed any hope I had for reciprocation. It wasn't until her father died that she responded to my concern and started to relate to me as a man, rather than only a colleague of her fathers. Since then, I regained a little hope. I don't believe that she knows, but I have fallen in love with her. I wanted to let you both know, because I will do my best to not let it interfere with our work here. But if you see a lovesick puppy around, at least you know the whys and wherefores."

Marcia jumps in. "Did you ever tell her?"

"Oh no, I cannot not. You know, I come from a country that still believes in arranged marriages. And she has no father for my family to ask."

"Why don't you tell Dr. Froehlich, or Eleanor, or maybe better, tell both of them together? I know that they both have a great fondness for her, and will want her to be happy. Do not, whatever you do, let this opportunity go by. Tell her, or tell those that care about her. Get it out into the open, and I will bet that you will be pleasantly surprised."

"Alattin, we have something special that needs your help. We want to hide in the text of the new Book, a sniffer program that will give us a better clue as to who ultimately winds up with our version. I would rather not add this burden to any of the other scientists at this time, but if you can think of a way that in one of the modifications, we can insert a bit of special code that will create an aperture for us to their network, we can go after the real backers, not just the greedy lackeys. Marcia can help you with this, so will you work with her?"

"Of course; count on it."

Now I have to tackle Tom Yancy. I find him out by the vending machines rattling a few coins in his hands while he considers the alternatives. I think that the best way to do this is to be forthright.

"Tom, let's go for a walk."

We go out into the steaming heat. Even though both of us are dressed lightly, in a matter of a minute, the perspiration begins to run down our backs. In the oval, trees give us a little protection from the direct sun, but the air that we inhale feels like it just left a blast furnace.

"Tom, I need to know. What's your problem?"

"This whole project is a disaster. You have no right to keep these discoveries hidden. Don't you realize how important this material is? You have been handed solutions to problems that we all have been struggling with, and yet because of a few greedy people, you are going to bury them again."

"Tom, do you have any idea the chaos that all of these discoveries would make?"

"Every day, Simon, we discover something, somewhere. But all that the people who employ us watch for is the effect on them, the cost-benefit to them, and the potential advantage that new knowledge gives to their competition. Simon, I am sick of it. Here is maybe something great. You want to substitute science that is flawed, doomed to failure, and impotent. And you want me to help you."

"Tom, we need you to help, because you are the best. If you do your job with the skill that you can bring to it, no one will ever know that you made a contribution to humanity. But you will know. Your colleagues in there will also know. And what will you have done? You will have given us a breather, time to mature a little more. Tom, which do you think is stronger, the rational thinking mind, or the irrational emotional one?"

"I think that if we open the doors to new ideas, we can trust people to rise to them."

"Tom, I wish we could be so trusting of mankind. The real truth is that there is an enemy out there, ready to kill us to control what we have. We have to stop them. Do you understand that?"

"Well, if you put it that way, I do, but we just can't let this opportunity pass us by."

"Tom, I agree with you that how we act right now is very important, but we don't have the luxury of being idealists."

"Simon, you are not a researcher. You deal by taking action. I work in my lab and think very small – molecular as a matter of fact. All I want to do is to be left alone to do my research."

"Tom, I need you to do more than just that. You have to help. Or if not, then go home and leave it for someone else."

"Oh no, I don't want to be left out. No, I wouldn't want that. OK I will help you, but I still think it is wrong."

"Thanks. But don't rely only on my opinion. Talk to the others when you can, about your doubts. This isn't a one-way street."

"Sure. Just don't expect a lot from me."

"All you can do is your best. That will be just fine."

We walk back to the lab and Tom goes in to work with the others. I am not sure we made the right decision with him, but will have to live with it. I just hope that he doesn't try to go off on his own with stars in his eyes. There's no time to change now. I wonder if this is going to be an example of herding cats. I hope not.

On the way back to my room, my telephone rings. It is the Admiral. "Simon, I don't think there is much doubt that Hunnsecker or someone over at DOD has a hand in what happened to Jean. I got the pictures from

Israel today, and we are able to identify three DIA agents going into Jean's room to interrogate her. I am sorry, but what the Mossad told me is true. We have to look on this side of the pond for the culprits behind her murder. As to the bombing itself, we don't have any pictures of the bombers, but we do of the charges themselves, and they are definitely U.S. Military standard SPEC-OPS focused demolition charges. I needed to tell you, and am so sorry that you suffered so long without knowing."

"Thank you, sir. I appreciate your consideration."

On my way in, I wonder how such a small group of us have taken on such a monumental objective, and are trying to accomplish it virtually without oversight. I sincerely hope we have made the right decision.

# 48 *THURDAY – US NAVAL LAB and NASA AMES/MOFFETT NAS*

With our hotel option voided after the assault attempt, I have arranged trailers to be brought into a corral just outside the lab, fitted out as hotel rooms. I think that if the team stays here, we will have far less security problems. Also, by staying together 24/7, problem-solving and consultations will be facilitated. There is a little grumbling amongst the newbies, but they settle in quickly. This morning, I decide to go out to NASA Ames to see how the work is coming on the pages. The Admiral had arranged an F/A 18E to be put at my disposal, so I strapped in for the brief 2-1/2 hr supersonic flight from Pawtuxet River.

In California, we land right at Moffett Field, in Mountain View. I am driven to the lab while the pilot refuels. The Information Officer is not very happy to see me. Usually, project personnel visit only with advance warning and he organizes a nickel tour, but today, I could care less. We walk across the street to the lab building off Front Street, where he brings me into the Metallurgy Research Center. There I am introduced to the lead scientist, Jacob Weismann, whose team has completed the analysis of the metal ring from the armor. He shows me the small pool of liquid metal that he is now trying to replicate. "It's slow going," he says.

"Do you think that you will be finished in a week?"

"Well, the material will have the same composition, but I can't promise that it will behave exactly the same."

"What could be different, if it made of the exact same components?"

"It is the lattice structure is the problem. You see, the original isn't really metal at all, but an organic crystal. The fibers which bind together are different from the original in that our thin film is rigid, while the original is quite flexible. I am sorry, but I can't promise results like the original."

"What if I got you some help?"

"Well, yes of course. If you could send someone here who was familiar with how the structure was physically created, I would be in a better position to deliver the sheets as was requested."

"May I see one of the sheets that you were able to produce?"

"Yes. Come look here" He opens a drawer and brings out a small sheet of the metal. It is dull, without the sheen of the original, and is extremely stiff, even though it has about the same thickness. If it could be shaped, it would make a great knife blade, the edges are so sharp.

"This won't work. I will get you help."

"Thank you."

"By the way, Dr. Weismann, do you happen to know Dr. Johann Froehlich or Dr. Ernst Zilbern?"

"Oh yes. I worked with both of them back in the War. The three of us worked in Peenemunde together on the V2 rocket."

"Dr. Froehlich is working on this project. Dr. Zilbern, unfortunately, died recently. But his daughter Lauren is also with the project."

"I had great respect for them, but particularly for Froehlich. You know that I was brought to the German rocket lab as a prisoner, while my family remained in a concentration camp. They did not survive. Dr. Froehlich was very kind to me, even though I am a Jew. Zilbern was not, but it's wrong to speak ill of the dead, so I shall not. But his daughter, you say, is working on the project? Is she also a scientist?"

"No sir, she is a linguist whose skills are also needed for our work. If you like, I shall give Dr. Froehlich your regards. Perhaps he may contact you when this work is over?"

"Yes, but I would much rather meet Ernst's daughter. Old men tend to dwell too much on the past for me. It is the young that don't think they will ever die, so they are always looking towards the future. I like young people. But please, do tell Johann that I remember his kindness. Thank you for yours."

On the way from Pax River to the compound, I get the feeling of being followed again. Back at the lab it is dinnertime and all are sitting together around the conference table with their trays. Lauren and Alattin are speaking very quietly together, but the rest are engaged in an argument of some kind. I take a place next to Marcia after picking up a nondescript box labeled with my name.

Each says that they are making progress in analyzing the formulas which lead to the purported solutions. Alattin joins in to say that his mathematical proofs so far prove out. Yancy says he is far from being able to commit. Lauren adds that the language John has deduced is remarkably complex, given its age. She also wonders why the writers of the Book chose to maintain the antiquated styles and syntax when far more modern versions were continuing to be developed as the text was supplemented over the generations. But she believes that she can reconstruct passages in the original without too much of a problem. Eleanor jumps in with a thought that applications alone may not do the trick. She thinks that some kind of overriding preamble needs to be created which will lead the power brokers to validate their own perceptions of the personalities that created the Book. Everyone agrees with this idea, and she promises to construct the personality paragraphs. Froehlich sticks a pin into the collective balloon by proposing that the next day at this same time, each should come up with details of disinformation in his or her area. Yancy objects on the grounds of being forced to create in the dark. Lauren smoothes him over and suggests that perhaps he could use someone else to work with, in the microbiology area. He objects to her inference, and loudly reaffirms his own competence, offering to produce something worthwhile the day after tomorrow. John enters the discussion with a suggestion that no change need be very large, nor very creative, just a tiny departure would be enough to give the impression that the material may not be all it that it is anticipated to be. Yancy cools down and becomes absorbed in his own thoughts.

Alattin asks Lauren if he can walk her to her trailer. She nods and they leave together. Eleanor watches them as they leave. Then she turns back to us still sitting and says to no one in particular "He's a nice boy."

Marcia gives me a little nudge under the table and asks Dr. Froehlich whether he has been able to find more out about Blackthorn. He says that the additional funds have been transmitted to Blackthorn. Of the original 18 million raised, 5 million is still missing. It seems like someone got greedy. He then says that his friend will not tell him who the intermediary with Blackthorn is, but that we would probably find out on Friday. I ask Froehlich if he would like me to go with him to the meeting in Chicago, but he says no. He thinks that at this type of meeting, only principals would be allowed and he is not exactly an insider yet.

Froehlich then switches to the subject of the virus. He tells us that if a translator processes the Book by putting the text into a network, he and Alattin can install isolated segments which can join themselves together inside the network. The resulting worm will contain coherent instructions to will follow the information packets wherever the network sends them, and to replicate itself along with the transmitted data. He believes that Modern anti-virus software will not detect the code supplements because the elements themselves will make no pattern, until the program begins to transmit data to us. In order to prevent detection, Alattin and Marcia have devised an approach that will add an authorized user to any new net, and retain the packets at that user level until we decide to activate the retrieval. Once its identification task is completed, the code will then self-destruct. The only problem that we see is that network users will probably not be the principals. But we will be closer than we are right now.

"Do you think that whoever studies the Book will assume we have prepared some kind of booby-trap?"

"A lot will depend on the provenance. If their acquisition is too easy, the odor will be noxious, no matter what Eleanor creates within the actual document."

"Yes, I agree. I still have not, however; come up with a method of delivery which would convince them that they have overcome our best efforts, yet also which does not risk the life of anyone on our team." I leave Dr. Froehlich and take a walk to think.

Outside, the river calls to me as it oily flows towards the sea. I walk out on the pier that sticks into the Potomac past the mud flats. At the end of the pier, a couple of workers from one of the other labs are fishing. Across the river, I can see the planes taking off and landing at Reagan, and up the river the lights on the government buildings are coming on. Both fishermen ignore me as they concentrate on their lines. I inquire about bait and the catch. Both tell me they are looking for striped bass, which feed just before and just after the tide turns. This section of water still is slightly brackish and bait fish are carried down, so the guys have thrown their lines just at the drop-off between the mud flats and the free flowing deep of the river. So far, neither has been successful, but they are hopeful. I stand for a while and watch them.

The two of them seem to be focused; pulling their lines in when the current takes them downriver and then casting upriver again. Both appear quite fit, despite their baggy clothes and have the somewhat hardened appearance of serving military. With a good-sized tackle box on the pier, their duffle seems a little outsized. I would classify them more as security than scientists or lab rats. Casually, I inquire where they are stationed. One tells me he works over in propulsion systems, but the other says he is a guest, and hopes I won't report him. He points to a small outboard tied up under the dock. I could call our security detail, but then thought I might take care of it myself. Taking a couple of steps backwards, I ask them for IDs. The 'guest' slides open the zipper on the duffle and reaches inside. In the moonlight, something glints inside the bag, but he pulls out only a wallet, which he hands me. The other one puts his rod carefully against the pier railing and starts to cross behind me in what appears to be a classic sandwich play. Since I am unarmed, the only thing handy is his pole. As he reaches behind his waist, I lean over to look at the Driver's License and grab the pole, just as the man in front launches a roundhouse at my head, which just glances off my shoulder. I pick up the pole by the heavy reel and jam the butt into the stomach of the one behind me. He lets out a loud grunt but must have steel abs, because it doesn't faze him. Meanwhile, the one in front launches a second punch, which catches me squarely in the jaw and I go down. The one behind kicks me in the side and then jumps over my prone body as he runs to the side of the pier and drops into the boat. The second one reaches for the duffle, but I grab the handles and roll on it, swinging it over my body away from him. He abandons it and also drops into the boat, whose motor has been started by the first man. As I push myself up, a muffled roar comes from below the pier and the boat runs out into the current, heading upstream. By the time I am fully on my feet, they are about 100 feet away and going strong against the outgoing tide. I realize that am still holding a wallet in my hand. It makes no sense to call anyone, so I brush off my clothes and head back toward my trailer.

Inside, I see that there is the beginning of a bruise on my cheek where I got hit, but am just glad that it was only a fist and not something sharper. I take everything out the wallet. There isn't a lot, but enough: several credit cards, some personal photos, a couple of miscellaneous receipts and a Virginia Driver's License, all in the name of Harold Evans of Alexandria. When the office answers my call, I give them data. I will give odds that it's more Blackthorn. But this time at least I have a name.

In about 10 minutes, my telephone rings, and I learn that Evans is a former Master Sergeant in Special Forces, having retired 6 months ago. His employer is listed on his credit card application as the Silver Group, in DC and his job title is contractor. His recent charges on his credit card have been primarily restaurants in DC and Bethesda. Tomorrow, I think I will visit Blackthorn and see if I can find out anything further. But for tonight, I will just keep this to myself. I really don't want to distract the group with security worries.

Before going to bed, I realize that I had left all the fishermen's belongings out on the dock. The two fishing rods are still there along with the duffle. Upon opening it, I find the remains of somebody's dinner, some fishing gear, and two weapons – a Sig Sauer and an H&K MP2013 with a collapsible stock and an extra magazine. I have never fired one, but am familiar with its capabilities. With an internal silencer and being manufactured of lightweight compound plastics, chambered in 10mm Caseless, it represented an ideal black ops weapon. In the tackle box I find a flexible fillet knife, a bunch of lures and a box of ammo for the Sig as well as an extra magazine for the machine pistol. I pick up all the gear and head back to the trailer. By then, Marcia returned and is getting ready for bed. When she sees the equipment, she asks me if I was fishing or hunting, so I tell her about the small confrontation, but ask her not to tell anyone else yet. In the bathroom, I see another bruise forming along my lower ribs, but quickly don a PJ shirt to not worry Marcia.

# 49 *FRIDAY - CHICAGO*

The Union League in Chicago is an anomaly. It was set up initially to promote honesty and efficiency in government, yet it draws its members from the elite of corporate and political society, and honesty is not on the membership application. Today, one of the private conference dining facilities has been reserved for a follow-up meeting to the Jackson get-together last month. This time, there are 21 participants, the original 18, plus two CEOs representing the computer industry, and Dr. Froehlich. The men and women who meet today are not happy. Money has been stolen and nothing is forthcoming from the first 15 million. There is no dinner before this meeting. Even the pastel tapestries on the meeting room wall and the soft glowing chandeliers of cut glass do nothing to soothe the mood of the eighth floor room. The men and women here are used to getting answers, and do not tolerate failures.

As at the previous meeting, the government man rises to address the group. "I am pleased to welcome our new associates and Dr. Johann Froehlich. Dr. Froehlich, for those of you that are not acquainted with him, has provided most of the communications security and encryption software that you all use in your businesses. In addition, he is intimately knowledgeable about the item which we are all seeking to obtain. I would like to ask Dr. Froehlich to say a few words about the progress towards that end."

"I don't give a shit about that. What the fuck happened to my money." The speaker is an elder of the group, and by nature a Texas reactionary.

One of the other oilmen replies "Skinny, shut your face and you might get an answer."

"I ain't interested in any damn dry hole." He recomposed himself, but not without periodic muttering.

"Thank you Harvey. Dr. Froehlich, if you please? Tell us how the translation is going."

"Thank you Mr. Hunnsecker. As you all know, the Book is currently in the hands of the U.S. Naval Research Laboratory, where a team of specialists is working with archeological investigators to translate the document. I loosely refer to it as a document, but it is actually a series of metal plates on which are etched the information that we all are interested in. Similar, perhaps to the kind of document that one might find in a Time Capsule, this Book is itself a capsule, but not of time. Instead it is a capsule of science which covers many of the industries that you gentlemen and ladies administer. I myself have seen this Book, and can attest to its incredible value. I would say that the translation will be complete within a couple of weeks, three perhaps at the outside."

"Thank you, Dr Froehlich" says Hunnsecker. "Now let us get to the plan for retrieving it."

"Now wait," the insurance exec broke in." I don't want to know details. All I want to know is when I can expect my copy."

"Well let me give you an overview then. As you all agreed at the last meeting, Blackthorn International was retained, and they have been watching all of the people involved in the translation and the document's security. Initially, 18 Million was pledged for this work, and 10 given to the security firm. The remaining 8 was put into a secure account offshore. 5 million is pledged for Blackthorn when the document was retrieved and two for me as my commission on the first installment. I was informed that that 5 of the original 10 never reached them, and he demanded it be sent immediately or they would withdraw from the mission. Dr. Froehlich and his two associates pledged the replacement, which I had delivered. The firm is currently investigating where the remaining 5 disappeared to."

The billionaire CEO if the largest oil company represented at the table looked up at Hunnsecker's face. "That's not good enough. You had the responsibility, and you did not fulfill it. You will bear the cost of the missing funds, yourself. The additional funds raised by Dr. Froehlich will be reimbursed by you, and placed in the account."

"But I do not know where the money went. Who do you think you are, blaming me for this?"

"It was your responsibility. I repeat. You accepted it, and now you will carry the full weight of this. Do not come crying to this table. We are immune to whining."

"May I suggest something?" Dr. Froehlich interjected.

"Of course," says the Oilman.

"The money is of no consequence. Five or fifty, the important issue here is the goal. Let's not be sidetracked by squabbling and finger-pointing. If the

492

money is gone, then so be it. Who here at this table has not taken advantage of an opportunity for personal gain?"

"We get your point" says the drug czar. "But what is to say that when the document is obtained, that we won't be held up for considerably more than we pledged? After all, who can we really trust anyway?"

The old man interjects "Well shit. I sure as hell didn't take it, and I am damn sure that I'll find out who did. I ain't fleeced twice, you can bet your ass on that, brother."

"Now Skinny; Ease up. It'll all come out, and when it does, you'll be covered."

"Let's get those security assholes in here. What's their name? Blackburn?"

"Blackthorn."

"They could be lyin'. Let's get' em in here and put the screws to them – they work for us, you know..."

The insurance man holds up his hand "I told you I want none of the details. I won't risk my future on a lark like this." He gets up to leave the room.

"Sit down" says the oilman. "No one is risking anything on a lark. I've hired Blackthorn before. In fact, we have several contracts with them over in the A-rab countries. They do good work. Expensive, but at least they don't play catch-up with the towelheads. They shoot first. Nobody that hires them has ever told me that they don't fulfill their contracts in spades."

"Do you think we'll need to pledge more?" asks one of the women.

"No, I would say that if no more funny business happens" he looks sharply over to Hunnsecker, who shakes his head. "What we've raised should be enough to get the document into our hands. Are we done?"

"Not quite" says Froehlich. "Each of you has a stake in this. If the document comes into our hands, we must all agree to work together. It wouldn't do if we jointly decided, for example, to bury it, and one of you goes off on your own. When the document is secured, we will meet and decide together what we are going to do with it, and that will be that. Do you all agree?"

The oilman considers for a moment and then nods to Froehlich. One by one, the rest of the table repeats the gesture. Even the old conservative agrees by saying "The smell in this room is like buzzards at a road kill, and I don't like it none, but I'll go along."

The group files out in twos and threes, leaving Froehlich and the oilman at the table. "I don't trust Hunnsecker to work with us." Froehlich says, looking at the oilman.

"I agree. I think that after this is over, he will have to be retired permanently."

The oilman concluded his comments by saying "Skinny wasn't entirely wrong, you know. Money begets untrustworthy bedfellows." He then leaves the room for his lunch downstairs.

# 50 *FRIDAY AFTERNOON – THE LAB*

The scientists assembled at the appointed hour, with almost everyone suffering from lack of sleep. Just before the meeting, I had received a call from Weismann at Ames. He said that early this morning, the help that he asked for arrived, and he was very thankful. Within an hour, he had put a small batch through the sequential electrical stimulation that was recommended to alter the lattice matrix, and the results appeared to be perfect. A sample of the processed material was on its way to me. Weismann also asked his visitor for suggestions regarding the etching process. They had planned lunch together, but the fellow left abruptly and never showed up for lunch. Dr. Weismann asked me if I could get him back to help with some other ongoing researches. If I had to say, I thought to myself, hat somehow the Keepers were still helping.

Everyone reports progress, and listened expectantly to my report on the metal fabrication and etching. Marcia and Alattin came in together, giving Lauren a couple of barely concealed fits, but she covered it up and joined into the discussion. It appeared that of all the scientists, Yancy was the farthest behind, since he was still trying to analyze the discoveries themselves. I will just have to figure a way of coaxing him along.

I suggest to everyone that we take a few hours off and go have a swim over at Ft. Myer. Lauren says that she would rather not go, and Alattin pleads off as well, as he is in the middle of a crucial phase in his work. But the others are for it, so I make the arrangements. I wait with Marcia for everyone to leave, and then suggest that maybe we can duck out for a quiet meal. She giggles like a schoolgirl at deceiving the group. Just as we come out, we witness Alattin sneaking into Lauren's trailer.

"I guess there has been some progress" Marcia says "but not the kind we can write about in the Book."

"I think that it is good for both of them. Lauren needs somebody, and the way Alattin has been mooning around is pretty evident to everyone. I wonder if Eleanor's reticence about going swimming has anything to do with this"

"Mama Cat is off to the pool, so the kitten can play with her yarn. I am not worried. So where did you have in mind for dinner?"

"Have you ever been to Ville D'Este in Alexandria?"

"No, but if it is Northern Italian, I'm sold."

I call for a reservation. "The question is: do we have anything to wear?"

"Never fear. Just get to our trailer and I will show you."

"If you show me what I expect, we'll never get to dinner."

"We shall be properly attired, soon after becoming naked. I'll race you."

I just hope that the trailer has oiled springs. "OK, no time for sleep" Marcia says into my chest. "Up with you and into the shower. I will lay out your clothes. Dinner waits."

I regroup and go all of 5 steps to the shower. The water is tepid, but it doesn't matter. When I come out, I take a giant step back into our miniscule bedroom. On the bed is a fresh set of underwear, a light blue shirt, grey pants and, God forbid, a red tie. "Do I really have to wear this noose?" I shout to her in the shower.

"I can't hear a thing. Just put on your clothes and I will check you when I come out."

I can hardly remember the last time I tied a knot around my neck on purpose. But I follow her directions to the letter. In a couple of minutes, I hear the hairdryer cork off, and then she comes into the room contorting herself into her bra and panties. With her wild red hair and lacy underwear, I am not certain I want to finish dressing, but she waves me away and pulls out a short bright yellow dress with spaghetti straps and steps into it. A red pendant hanging around her neck offsets the rose color of her skin against the yellow dress. Before I put on my jacket that has magically appeared from the closet, I ask Marcia to take off the pendant, as it is not exactly the right thing for tonight. She looks at me a bit oddly, but does what I ask. From the nightstand, I remove a white folded tissue bundle and hand it to her. She looks quizzically at it and then opens it to find the turquoise bear fetish necklace that the old man had given me in Albuquerque.

"Simon; Oh my God; How beautiful." She lifts it up and looks at all the small birds and animals, intertwined and locked together. Then she slides it over her head.

"Sweetheart, it contains the spirit of the bear. I was told that only one with a bear spirit can wear it. It fits you perfectly."

496

"Thank you, my dearest." She takes the two steps to reach me and we hold each other tightly, crushing the necklace between us. Then she steps into her sandals, and I pick up my blazer.

Thankfully, the car is waiting in the oval just outside the trailer, and I hold the door open for Marcia, giving her a little pat on the butt as she bends over to get in the car. I give our driver the address; which is only about 10 minutes away across the bridge in Alexandria.

The restaurant is in an unassuming building at the corner of St. Asaph and Montgomery, in the north end of Old Town Alexandria. Inside, there is an attempt to make it look like the original Villa D'Este at Tivoli outside Rome, but doesn't quite pull that off. The various plaques in the entry attest, however; to the quality of the food and service. As we work our way through our appetizers, Marcia asks me again about our near-term future. "Do you think this will be over in a week or two? I really would love to get on with our lives."

"Don't worry, as soon as we get this off and the Book back to Egypt, we can end this episode. Would you like to travel again?

"Not particularly, although I do want to schedule a visit to China, before it buries itself in smog. John was telling me before we had to move here that there were a number of new artifacts that they got from Taiwan, which the Mainland Chinese were attempting to get returned, so now the Smithsonian is caught between our mutual aid treaty with Taiwan, and our serious business interests on the mainland. He was saying that he really could use some help discovering where and how these items came to his doorstep, and identify who the rightful owners were."

"Do you really want to start another mission so quickly?"

"Well it would be interesting to look into what happened during the revolution there, and how so many treasures were looted by the evacuating Nationalists."

"I'd say that it would be interesting, but perhaps there is something closer to home."

"My love, does it really matter where we are?"

"No, I guess not. Well, I'll think on it."

The car comes for us after dinner, and we head back to the lab, to our little trailer park. Dinner had been three glorious hours away from this place. Before going to bed, I check and see lights on in all the trailers, except for Lauren's and Alattin's. Good for them, I think to myself.

# 51 *SATURDAY - WASHINGTON*

At the Lab, the whole scientific team is hard at work, building their sections.

As each small section is completed, it is reviewed by Dr. Froehlich, and then given to Lauren and John to translate and encode. This morning, I received the sample metal page from Dr. Weismann, complete with the message "Science Rules!" etched on it. To my eye it looks identical to the original. John examined it under his microscope and agreed with my assessment. I email Weisman at Ames, instructing him to manufacture and ship the pages in the exact size of the original book.

Marcia and Alattin finalized the worm for insertion into the scientific sections. The primary control module is carefully worked into a section on fission-fusion modeling. Alattin and Dr. Froehlich have re-analyzed the integrated version, and made several experiments to determine the likelihood of its being caught before the section is entered in a computer file. It seems to appear benign until the other sections are also accessible through the network. The three of them appear quite satisfied.

Eleanor is working on a revised Preamble to the new book, with a new cumulative index covering all the sections that will be included in the document, including those small changes which the team has made.

When Dr. Froehlich finishes his review of the progress, he asks me to join him in his trailer. He appears to have recovered from the Blackthorn attack, although he still favors his left leg. After offering me a cup of coffee, he tells me about the meeting in Chicago the previous day.

"There is no question that Secretary Hunnsecker is deeply involved in gaining control of the Book. But from what I saw at that meeting, he is not the ringleader. Charles Hampton of American Gas and Oil seems to be in the driver's seat. But without concrete evidence, it will be extremely difficult to build a case against him. If we could construct a strategy that would play upon his enormous ego, there may be a chance."

# 52 *MONDAY – THE LAB*

Yancy had finally achieved some measure of success, but he told me this morning that he still had about two more days of work before he would be ready to submit his work to translation and final etching. Eleanor had prepared a codicil to the original preamble to the Book and Lauren was hard at work translating the new material so that it fit into both the style and syntax of the original.

Froehlich and I develop a plan to bring Hunnsecker into the open, while still protecting our own team. Froehlich was not keen about relying on his relationship with the President to overcome Hunnsecker's powerbase. He feels that the Secretary had too many friends among hawks on the Hill, the Military and among powerful corporate PAC funders. Froehlich thinks that I should pay a call on him and rattle his cage. It is a risky move, since he could call Blackthorn to execute a contract on me, or even assign a military SPEC-OPS team; But perhaps if other options grew slim.

Marcia got a tracker bug into Hunnsecker's PC through his ISP server, but doubted that it would survive a daily sweep. She thought that we might try to get ears in his house. She said that the NSA had quite a few bugs that were virtually undetectable unless they were transmitting.  I thought that we should rely on the sniffer in the Book.

By 11 this morning, the Navy delivered a package from Ames, containing about 100 sheets of the Book metal, already cut to the exact size and ready for engraving. Lauren had completed her translation of the Preamble, so John set in motion the etching process and transferred a photographic negative to the metal with something very similar to heart defibrillator coupled to an ion extractor. I am not clear on the exact process, but the result almost magically appeared on the surface of the golden metal. John told me that the organic lattice realigned around the charged negative, leaving a discrete groove in the bookplate. Since the original was hand written, we would take turns writing individual pages, as there were many different handwriting examples among the authors over the centuries. Each discrete contribution would be written on paper, which would then be photographed to create the negative for the etching process. The only one of us who would not participate in the writing was me. My penmanship was atrocious. Lauren coached us on the actual language.

Each of us examines the final result and John declares it to be no different in any perceptible manner from the original. During the afternoon, Lauren received page after page from each of the other scientists, and works on translating any text. Meantime, John assembles original pages which can be included in the new Book, and puts them in chronological order.

By dinnertime, our sheaf of completed pages has grown, but is still far too small. Yancy's is missing at and I find him at his stool, wrapped in an emotional funk. "Simon, I really wish there was some way that we could use this material other than destroying its value. There is so much here that really would revolutionize our approach to disease prevention and treatment. Imagine much stronger genetic material to pass along to our children, and diseases like diabetes and cancer virtually wiped out."

"Tom, it can't go any other way right now. I am only an ex-frogman. I can't anticipate everything that might happen. For now though, we really have no choice. I can't keep making this same argument over and over to you. You just have to trust my judgment, and finish what you started."

"What happens if I decide that I can't accept your judgment and bring some of these discoveries out into the public domain?"

"Tom, let's be clear on this. You will not be allowed. I am not making a threat, but the stakes are just too high and the players too powerful. We all will be watched in the future, and any signs of betrayal of our pledges will be treated with instant retribution. You must understand this as I know it."

"Yes, but it is such a damn shame." With that he goes back to his work. I hope to God that he understands that this is beyond his ability to control. 'What a cruel way treat idealism' I think to myself.

Back at the dinner table, the mood was much improved from Friday. In spite of the exhaustion, I think all of us are buoyed up at the prospect of returning home. I take Eleanor aside and ask her if she can spend a little time with Tom Yancy, to see if she can help him come to terms with his dilemma. She immediately takes her tray to the disposal and goes off to help.

I make my evening call to the Admiral. He answers, as per usual, on the first ring. I wonder if he has a telephone screwed into his ear like a lot of today's teenagers. I fill him in on the progress of the pages, the general attitude, research on Hunnsecker, Tom's depression, and the social progress of Alattin and Lauren. The last is not something I really want to report but it is part of the project and could develop some importance. He asks me about plans for transmittal of the completed Book to the opposition. I let him know the options that we had discussed, and suggested that perhaps I should handle that myself. He is not in favor of the idea, but says it may come down to that if nothing better comes up. Then he broaches a new subject; one that I can tell is personally distasteful to him.

"Simon, you realize that we need to be absolutely sure that none of the participants have the opportunity to disclose anything that would potentially expose the fraud."

"Yes I do, but I can't imagine anyone doing anything to compromise this effort" except, in my mind, Tom Yancy. Knowing the Admiral, I had better voice it all. "Except, possibly Tom Yancy, but I will know more tomorrow after I have had the opportunity to consult with Eleanor, who I sent to talk to Tom earlier this evening."

"Well yes, there's Yancy. But if a group like Blackthorn kidnapped all of you, how many would break?"

"Sir, you know the answer to that. Everyone sooner or later. But for two facts: If we have done our job right, there will be no suspicion to generate such an action; second, everyone will be watched. We both know that. If there is a hint of the disinformation project, the person responsible would have to disappear."

"Yes, but you know how important this is. I need to tell you about a proposal that I received today concerning your team. It has been suggested that everyone in your group be detained incommunicado for an indefinite period so long as any risk whatsoever exists for exposure."

"Admiral, this has been suggested before. In fact, it was the reason you wanted Marcia and I to participate. What is different now?"

"I am not proposing this myself, but there is a group of people over at the White House that has a different view, and those voices are growing louder. I may not be able to overcome them."

"Admiral, I understand your warning, but it would be stupid to have a mass disappearance. The opposition knows of our work in the 'translation'. If we were all to disappear immediately after completing this work, the smell of a rat would be immediately noticeable."

"Yes, of course it would. That is the one ace that I have played. But once the Book is out and the original returned, all can be made to disappear one at a time, in ways that even I couldn't anticipate. The world is a dangerous place, and accidents happen every day. Anyway, I wanted you to know that deceit and betrayal are not only played by bad guys."

"Sir, I can't live my life with one eye over my shoulder and a gun in my belt forever."

"No, son, I know you can't. You also understand that I too am one of the team members who know about the plan. If you and your scientists go, it is because I too have been buried, as well as a few other notables who shall be nameless. No one is immune to this type of paranoia, not even our CINC."

"I can't imagine anyone would take her out."

"Well, it's happened before. But let's not go there just yet. As I said, I just wanted you to know how the wind blows."

"Thank you, sir. Meantime, if you have the chance, send a really big 'well done' to Jacob Weismann and his team at NASA Ames. They really came through for us."

"Yes, I will. Goodnight son. We'll keep watch."

Now I've got a problem that I can't solve alone. I doubt whether I could keep a poker face for very long. When I go into our trailer after the call, Marcia is already in bed, reading. She is quick to notice my face. "Simon, what's happened?"

"I have to talk to you. I had an awful feeling about this idea of constructing a phony Book, and now I am afraid that my worst fears are coming to pass."

"Stop being cryptic and tell me."

"The Admiral told me that the people he reports to are considering detaining our whole team indefinitely, to insure that word of our Trojan horse never gets out. This means all of us, and possibly even the Admiral himself."

"Can they really do that? Well of course they can, but would they?"

"I don't know. I would have thought it was possible, particularly considering the brand of paranoia taking hold among some of our leaders. I think that what scares me most of all is the thought that this scenario would take high priority. If it wasn't a strong possibility, the Admiral would have never mentioned it. The question is: What am I going to do about it?"

"Simon, you have to give this credence."

"I think that we have to tell the group."

"If you do, Simon, you risk their stopping to protect themselves; not that I have any idea of how anyone would go about that."

"I know. I do know. I wish I had a good answer."

"Maybe we should get input from outside."

"Whoever we share information with automatically would be threatened as well. You remember that Dr. Froehlich said something at the very beginning of this program. He said that this work could not be done without a major sacrifice. At the time, I thought he meant that we would be giving up our days and nights in an intense effort to produce this, but now I think that he meant something far more deadly."

"Simon, do you think there is a danger of us being killed to keep the secret?"

"If you had asked me that yesterday, I would have said no, but now I am not so sure."

"I always think more clearly if I lay out the strategy, so let me talk it out." Marcia collected her thoughts and then followed her reasoning chain.

"OK so once the disinformation book is taken and analyzed, we will have a disappointed and angry enemy. The theory of the deception is that they would make use of the benign parts of it, so it wouldn't be a total loss, yet their anger would turn against those amongst them who had promulgated the idea of treasure in the first place. In a sense, it is expected that they would turn upon themselves. Now what we find is that there is an additional enemy already inside our walls, willing to attack us. But the goal of these new attackers is to prevent the secret of the deception getting out. It seems to me that we have to make the treasure poisonous, so that no one will want it. Then everyone wins; both the attackers without and the attackers within. You know, of course what that means?"

"Yes. It means that the real Book has to be disseminated. Its disclosure would so threaten the big corporations and the government alike, that it would be destroyed. So what we are doing is all wrong after all. By creating a worthless phony, we are merely whetting their appetite. But I have a different idea. What if we set the "attackers without" against the "attackers within"? Get them to destroy each other and leave us alone. I am not sure how we would go about doing that, but it follows your logic."

"If our internal foes are within the government, it has to be assumed that they are the ones that gave the information about the Book to the outside corporate group. This siege is not cheap. And no one that has money gives it up without a fight. So suppose the phony Book is perceived as a straw man, designed only to elicit funds from the corporate group. Wouldn't that be grounds for the group turning on their extorters if they get nothing for their economic investments? It would follow that this 'government' group would be those that have the most to lose by exposure of the fraud. That is something we can and should exploit."

"Now we have come back to the original premise. If the fraud is seen to have been perpetrated by those within, the rest would vent their spleens on them. A byproduct of this would be our protection, by removing all our inside enemies from the field. Correct?"

"Yes, that is exactly the point. Now that it is clearer, what do you want to do?"

"No question that we should continue with our plan, but with a twist. The ones who reveal *our* Book to the outside attackers must be those that are most likely to be behind the movement to bury us."

"Yes. So now, Simon, you have an answer to your other question. The one problem that you have had all along with this deception is the sacrifice that Dr. Froehlich spoke of when the project started. You were afraid for whoever took the responsibility of transmitting the Book to the enemy. Froehlich thought that whoever brought the Book out would define its provenance. By their sacrifice, the courier would be seen as holding a valid treasure. Now it should be clear. We must arrange for the Book to be 'left' for the enemy by their trusted government contact. The source is trusted so then the Book is trusted. Then, when the Book is found to be flawed, the source will be blamed for their 'extortion'. You know, you could see this in terms of a boardroom battle, which all of these people are adept at. If you want to get rid of someone, the first thing you do is raise them up. Once they are trusted, you then set them up for failure, and then when they begin to fail, you cut their legs out from under them and regain control. This is a normal corporate as well as governmental bureaucratic tactic. The major difference here is that lives are in the mix, not just some jobs."

"Thanks, my dear. I understand exactly what I have to do."

It is still not so late that I would be concerned about waking Dr. Froehlich. When I knock, he answers the door in his pajamas, but does not look like he was sleeping. I ask him for a few minutes and he invites me in. On the end table next to the bed is a mug of tea. He asks me to sit at his tiny table and brings over his mug.

506

"Dr. Froehlich, I am sorry for the late hour, but we have to make a slight strategy change in getting the Book to our corporate friends. Tonight, the Admiral told me that a small group of government people are coming around to the idea of burying our whole team for an indefinite period to conceal our deception."

"Yes, I realize that the potential for something along these lines was growing."

"Marcia and I have come up with a plan – actually we finally addressed the problem of validating the authenticity of the Book, while protecting the courier."

"When I spoke of sacrifice, I could think of no way around that problem. The group would smell an odiferous rodent if the Book was not protected vigorously and the resistance would undoubtedly result in the loss of life."

"We now believe that the best way for our Book to be couriered, would be to get it into the hands of the government liaison with the corporate group, and let him take it to his friends."

"Excellent idea; but with one additional enhancement; I think that Hunnsecker and his associates should increase their demands for corporate funding, so that the stakes will be higher and the punishment swifter and more final."

"Yes. Will you take care of that?"

"Yes. I will contact him in the morning and put the bug in his bonnet. Then we need to get him to coordinate the 'giving'."

"Doctor, I knew you would understand immediately."

"Simon, don't you think it is about time for you to call me Johann or simply John?"

"Sir, I doubt whether I can. It's not the generational difference; it's more an issue of respect."

"Thank you for that. It is very kind of you."

"Goodnight, Doctor Froehlich."

"Goodnight, my boy."

# 53 *WEDNESDAY – THE LAB*

By 11 this morning, the Book is ready to be assembled. Yesterday, Lauren completed most of the translations of the material submitted by Yancy and Akan, as approved by Crawford and Frankel. The sniffer code devised by Marcia was incorporated, and the original pages which were going to be transferred to the new Book were duplicated by John, with a little help from me. Froehlich had looked over each page and agreed that they would not be detectable as frauds. Although the original Book was bound by a metal strip along one edge, we believed that the copy could be wrapped in a cover of metal and tied, but not bound. Ames had cooperated with a cover of the same metal, which could be taken apart and re-assembled.

Meantime, Froehlich told me that he had gone to a meeting with Secretary Hunnsecker, and suggested obliquely that he and his minions be rewarded far more than they had been. He told me that Hunnsecker's eyes lit up with the prospect of adding to the 5 million he had already appropriated. Froehlich deferred to the corporate group for a final decision, to which Hunnsecker said he would take the subject up with the chairman. Froehlich offered to bring the Book out, but Hunnsecker demanded the right to do it himself.

We all agreed that the transfer would be made this evening. Dr. Froehlich would take the Book home with him, and Hunnsecker would tell the White House that he was going to Froehlich's to review it before a morning viewing by The President, VP and all the Cabinet. While Hunnsecker was visiting with Dr. Froehlich, it is assumed that the Blackthorn people would mount an assault, seize the Book and carry it to Hunnsecker secretly. This way, the Secretary could claim plausible deniability of culpability to his White House associates. Marcia believes that as paranoid as Hunnsecker may be, he is not so stupid to realize that he needs a scapegoat for the theft, conveniently provided by Blackthorn.

Once the play begins, and hopefully enemies start to feed on each other, our team would quietly disband. At least that is the way our plan is laid out. Of course, things don't usually go according to a plan exactly, so I assume the job of watching events unfold at Froehlich's house tonight. If a nudge was needed, I would be there to apply it.

"You know" Froehlich said "It took nine years for the Greeks to come up with a plan to deceive the Trojans. You people have done it in 2 weeks. Congratulations on your supreme effort. I only hope that your deception is as successful as the Greek's." He then gave the Book a final pat and left.

As the hour of 6 arrived, Dr Froehlich bid everyone a warm goodbye, saving Lauren for last. He hugged her and wished her well, like he was sending off his daughter to a new life. I have a twinge of concern, seeing him make it so apparently final. Froehlich put the Book into the battered original briefcase. With the thick cover and the added pages, it fit quite snugly. Then he put it in the trunk of his car and leaves for home. The original book is stored in a safe, and extra pages are sent to Ames for destruction.

The scientists would stay a few additional days in the safety of the lab until any threats to them evaporated. Lauren and Alattin said that they were going out to a restaurant no matter what happened, so that just left Tom, Eleanor and John at the lab as Marcia and I left for home. I am really surprised by Tom Yancy's change in attitude these last couple of days. Eleanor had taken him under her wing, and he responded well to it. In was almost amusing to see the pair of them out walking on the pier – a blonde Adonis with a short dumpy overweight senior as a partner. But you never know by just looking at the outsides of any couple that you might pass along the way, who is strong and who is weak. John has been our rock all through this. He is always cheerful, always helpful, and always positive amid anguish. I hope that we can remain friends for many years to come.

As we sit together in the back of the ESCORT car, I thought back to my first day with my silly puzzle horse. As it turned out, my hidden treasure inside the horse was not the golden key; it is sitting right next to me. How amazing is that! I guess everyone found one another. Tom Yancy found some new emotional strength and Eleanor found a new nephew to mentor. John found his wife Karen again. Johann Froehlich found a new daughter, and Even Ernst Zilbern, I hope, found some peace.

When we get home, Marcia prepares a small meal for us, and then I change into my ninja outfit. I dig out some lampblack for my face and hands this time, because I can't afford to take even the remotest chance of discovery. Marcia looks me over and pronounces me fit for the evening's adventure. She then sends me off with a cheery "Play nice with your friends."

Tonight, I added my Glock and K-bar to my equipment, and also take a lightweight acoustic amplifier, which consists of an infra-red laser which I can point at a window and pick up audio vibrations off the glass, reflecting them back to a small fan-shaped dish connected to an electronic receiver. I also have a fully charged satellite telephone and a second small automatic pistol in my ankle holster. Suitably attired, I drive to Bethesda to camp out at Froehlich's.

When I get to there, it is about 8:30. I put my car in the lot across the street from his house, and locate a position on the north fence where I can see into the living room, yet remain concealed from anyone coming up from the neighbor's house behind me. I unpack my acoustic receptor, unfurl the dish and turn it on. Then I call Froehlich to test the reception and let him know that I have arrived. I can clearly hear the telephone ring in my headphones, and hear him answer. After our brief conversation, I put the phone into one of the vest pockets of my shirt, and settle down to wait

At 8:55, a car driving slowly up Fairfax turns into the driveway. I assume that Hunnsecker has arrived. I see a figure leave the car and go towards the front door, but in the dark, I can't make out any details. In my headphones I hear the doorbell ring and Froehlich's footsteps as he goes to answer the door. At that moment, I remembered that neither Lauren nor Alattin knew of our plan to trap Hunnsecker tonight. I hear Froehlich open the door.

"Lauren, what are you doing here?"

"I have to speak with you. It is very important."

"You have to leave!"

"Doctor Froehlich, this is a matter of life or death to me. Please, won't you let me stay for a minute or two?"

"It is not safe for you here. You must leave right now. But quickly, what's so important?"

"Oh Doctor Froehlich, I don't know what to do. You see, and please don't be angry with me, but Alattin and I...well you see we're in love and Alattin has said he wants to marry me."

"Lauren, that's wonderful. Now please, you have to go. We talk tomorrow."

"Doctor, it won't wait. He can't marry me because his family has no one to ask. And I thought that maybe you could act as my father...would you please?"

"Yes, yes of course, Wonderful. Have them call me, now please go. You can't be here if our guests arrive."

"Oh thank you. I am so grateful. Oh he will be a wonderful husband, Thank you."

At that moment, I hear a crash of breaking glass, and a thump like a small charge going off at the back door. I see a flash of light in the living room, and then more flashes and small thumps. I jump up from my bush and run towards the house. There are some small snapping sounds, a scream, a large boom and then silence. I am only about halfway across the yard as I see a car turn into the driveway. I reach one of the foundation bushes and crouch next to it. The car stops and out steps a figure, who walks slowly up the front steps and rings the bell. When it is answered, he enters, leaving the door open. I remain where I am and listen.

"Did you get it?" asks the new arrival.

"Yeah, but there are some casualties."

"Just give it to me. Make it look like a robbery. Then get out of here."

A figure comes out carrying our briefcase. As he reaches his car, I see him clearly; it's Hunnsecker. He drives off. After the sounds of breaking furniture and glass come from inside, they eventually die off, and all is quiet again.

I slowly make my way around to the back of the home. The door hangs part way off its hinges. Inside, the kitchen is pristine except for the back door. I go around the central island and follow my pointing gun into the main hall. At the far end of the hall, there is a form lying on the floor near the front door. It is not moving. I move slowly along the hall, looking left and right. When I get closer towards the front, I can see that it is Lauren. She has been shot several times and is dead in a still expanding pool of dark blood which covers the marble tiles. In the open doorway to the living room, I find Froehlich dead as well, with his arms over his head, half on the carpet of the living room and half stretched towards Lauren. It must have been a shotgun, because blood and flesh from his body is spattered against the furniture and lamps.

I check on Lauren; then go back through the back door and walk across the street to my car, call the police, and then drive home.

Marcia spends most of the rest of the evening just holding me, as I feel numb by the shock and loss. I finally rouse myself enough to call Alattin and tell him of both murders. Then I call the Admiral. He tells me to come in the following morning. I just hang up and sit in my chair, staring at nothing at all.

# 54 *THURSDAY – WASHINGTON*

I wake up in my bed, really angry. I am going to bring retribution instead of spending more time sitting under a bush while my friends are killed.

Marcia goes with me down to Ft. Myer and we confront the Admiral together. "I want to take Hunnsecker out, and I want to see Blackthorn deballed," I say.

"Simon, I know you are angry, but you have to look at this rationally. Froehlich was a dying man. He knew it and so do you. Lauren's death was an unnecessary tragic consequence of war. You can mourn her later. Right now, you have to focus on the fact that the Book is, or will be soon, in the hands of Hunnsecker's clients. It will probably take a few days for them to analyze it and come to the conclusion that it isn't all Hunnsecker and Froehlich said that it was. What they do about it needs be watched. Do we have a tail and ears on Hunnsecker?"

"Yes, to the tail, but no ears yet; Admiral, can we exact some retribution against Blackthorn? They are acting as outlaw mercenaries here in the U.S... We need to clip their wings. You know, we have a lead into their organization through that wallet I grabbed.

"Do you feel balanced enough to take a run at them? We have the wallet here and you can take copies of his dossier up to their office. Actually, I have a better idea. Let's let the FBI battle on our behalf. I'll call the Director and see if he can help. I would rather not expose you as a principal to the Blackthorn people."

"Admiral, I don't want to sound like Wyatt Earp, but I would like to exert some personal payment for Lauren and for Dr. Froehlich."

"Yes, I suppose that you would. Keep a rein on it for now. I am sure you will get your chance. Remember, the important thing is to get this resolved the way WE want it resolved, not dance to others' tunes."

"I will do my best but I promise you that with or without your support, I will piss on Hunnsecker's grave. But there is one thing that you can do, sir. I don't know who, if anyone was close to Dr. Froehlich. But as his friend, would you manage his funeral, and speak for Lauren at hers?"

"Yes, I plan to do just that." Admiral Lewis answers. "I will arrange it for Saturday morning. Froehlich and Lauren, you know, died in the service of our country, although we can't acknowledge it right now. I will work out something."

I reigned in my emotions for the time being. "So what do we do now?" I ask.

"We have to wait. We have to give them a week at least. Tell the rest of your team to hold tight for a week. By then, it will probably be safe for them to leave the Navy's protection."

## SHORTLY AFTERWARDS – US NAVAL RESEARCH LABORATORIES

The small group that sits together in the conference room is grieving. Eleanor paces around the room, her earth shoes squeaking on the floor. John holds his head in his hands, and Tom rests his on his folded arms. Only Alattin sits upright. I guess he will cry later. But for now, he just sits with his pad and pencils in front of him on the table, waiting. Marcia goes over to him to hug him, and he gives her a small smile. Nobody asks about the Book, or the plan. I wish I could console each of them, but there is nothing that I can say to blunt the pain. It will have to wear away in its own time.

I have to tell them about remaining here for another week, but before I do, Alattin asks me to relate in detail the events of the previous night. As I go through it again, it is almost surreal, as if it is happening in two different time zones at the same moment – I relive it, yet I am removed from it. When I get to the part about the damage to both bodies, I hold off and just say that they were shot, leaving it at that. Everyone reacted to Hunnsecker's identity being revealed. They all start talking about wanting his blood. I tell them that we have to wait, whereupon Tom Yancy stands up and yells "Bullshit. I think that we should go over to Mr. Secretary's house and bring a rope." But then sits down again when he realizes that he can't follow through with vigilante justice. Eleanor takes his hand.

The telephone rings. It is Hunnsecker's minders, who have an audio tape for me. I initiate the speakerphone, and we all listen:

*"Hello" the graveled voice answers.*

*"You know who this is. I have access to the material. But we have to take a big risk to get it. My associates and I want an additional commission for our risk."*

514

*"What were you thinking is a fair value for your few moments of risk?"*

*"We want an additional 10. It shouldn't be hard to get from the group – a mere pittance compared with the value of what I have for you all."*

*"Very well, I will not bother our associates for the additional funding. Meet me this evening, and you shall receive payment. Make it at your house, at 10 tonight. We will make the exchange then. Bring a list of your associates as well. I should like to thank each in person for the great service that you have done for me,"*

Hunnsecker lives in a large home off a curving street in McLean, Virginia. It is not far from CIA Headquarters, and would not be particularly noticed among the other stately homes nearby. The house has a circular drive in front, and I can hear the sounds of a tennis game coming from the back as I come up to the door in my coverall with a Time-Warner logo on it. I had checked earlier on Hunnsecker's cable services provider. Before going into the house, I walk around the outside and find the cable and telephone boxes pinned to the exterior wall. I open my little bag and cut the cable. Then I install an 'F' connector at each end of the separated line. A middle aged athletic woman wearing a tennis dress answers the doorbell. When I tell her that I am here to fix the cable break, she asks me to wait, and goes back into the house. In a minute she is back saying that she did not realize that service was off, but I was welcome to come in, so long as I remove my shoes first. Instead I pull out a pair of plastic booties and she waves me in. Then she shows me where the main TV is in the living room and a second in the kitchen. The third is in the bedroom upstairs, if I have to get at it. Then she tells me that she is watching her daughter play tennis in the back yard. I can find her there if I need her. I pull out a form with the cable carrier's name and logo on it, courtesy of ESCORT, and fill in some of the questions. She watches me for a minute and then disappears into the kitchen. As soon as she goes, I open the TV cabinet and install a tiny pinhole camera in the upper frame of the LCD television. I search the first floor for an office or library and, finding a room that appears to serve both purposes, put a second camera between two hardcover books across the room from the desk. Then I take a third and drill a tiny hole above the door in the front hall closet, pointing to the front door. Inside the closet, high above the door, I mount another tiny camera near the ceiling pointing through the wall. With the cameras in place, I open my laptop and remotely access each of the cameras. Then I put an acoustic pickup device under the kneehole drawer of the desk. I notice that the desk has several telephones, including a red one with a snap ring over the receiver. A second phone is labeled "Pentagon" and a third is a black speakerphone with a bunch of buttons. I return to the hall and put another tiny bug

515

behind the alarm panel near the front door. Then I go back outside and join the two coax connectors I had installed on the cable and return inside the house. I try the TV and it works just fine. I then activate the audio bugs and listen on my laptop speakers. I can hear the TV from there as well.

I pack up my laptop; go out the kitchen door to the back yard and give the Repair Form to Mrs. Hunnsecker to sign, telling her that the TV is now working again, that it was a small break probably due to the wind. I also ask her how her daughter is doing with the game, and she tells me with a laugh that the child is totally uncoordinated, just like her father. I ask her if she would like to see the connector I put in after cutting out the broken part of the cable, but she declines, signs the form and escorts me out the front door.

I figure that these bugs and the cameras are good for a couple of days at best. People at Hunnsecker's pay grade usually get swept by DISA at least once a week, and this visit, duly noted by Mrs. Hunnsecker, will probably alert a sweep tomorrow. The bugs and cameras are store-bought items that anyone can procure, so I am not worried about a trace. I can also turn them on or off remotely, which will delay their being discovered with a signal sensor, although the batteries in the devices are unshielded so can be detected. The transmission signal goes to through a public ISP which we will dump once we have the data. While I was in the house, I had not seen the briefcase anywhere, so assume that he probably has it with him.

Once everything is in place for tonight's meet, I head back home, just in time for the frantic outflow from inside the Beltway. Marcia was going to wait for me at the lab, so instead of heading home, I make like a salmon and swim against the flow southeast through the heart of traffic on this side of the river until I reach the airport, where I can cross and turn down to the lab. Before I arrive, I ask Marcia if she would like me to bring pizza for everyone, and she replies gratefully that it would be a good relief from the commissary or worse. So I detour up to Pennsylvania Avenue and stop at Bertucci's for 4 brick oven pizzas and then stop at an open supermarket for some beer, sodas, coleslaw and some powdered garlic, dried oregano and red pepper. Then it's over to the lab.

When we sit down at dinner, I decide that we all should be in on the money exchange, having contributed so much to it, including our friends' lives. With a run time of 12 hours on the batteries installed in the cameras, and 24 in the bugs, I think that we can safely turn them on while we eat. I plug my VGA port on the laptop to our Plasma Monitor, so that the images can be seen by everyone at the table. After logging onto our Internet link, I type in the unique addresses for each bug and camera. Then, I activate the audio bugs and link them on 2 channels through to the monitor. We now also have sound to go along with the video.

Hunnsecker isn't home yet, or if he is, he is not near any of the cameras. The desk in his office appears the same as it did this afternoon. There must be some activity in the kitchen, because the bug in the hall picks up some muffled voices and the sound of dishes and pots. After a while watching nothing and hearing nothing, we return to our conversations. It is an odd feeling to be seeing and picking up normal activities inside the Hunnsecker home, while we sit here in the lab. People initially are reluctant to speak in normal tones, because the other venue is so visible, but then they get used to it and speak normally.

By 8, we get a little and hope that either of the parties didn't change the location. But then he walks through the front door and waves to his driver, moving in to his office. I trigger my laptop slave drive, so that we will have a permanent record of what transpires. He is carrying two briefcases, one of which we all saw get closed here only a day ago. It is battered on one side where it got dropped from the helicopter in Alexandria and has a bullet hole in its side. From the bookcase camera, we see Hunnsecker shove it into the kneehole of his desk. I am glad that the briefcase isn't a lot larger, or we might have had a 'found bug' problem. But all is well so far. Hunnsecker then goes back out of the office to the front hall and climbs the stairs. In about 15 minutes, Mrs. Hunnsecker comes into the front hall and calls up to her husband to come down for dinner. The answer is muffled, but soon he comes back down the stairs and disappears towards the kitchen. We police our conference room and discard the boxes and debris from dinner, then go off in different directions until close to 10. I leave everything on, since the recording is also being stored on both my local disk as well as through our Navy Intranet port to our Central Records section.

By about 9:45, everyone has re-assembled in the conference room. On our screen, Hunnsecker is sitting at his desk, going through a stack of papers with his personal briefcase open on the desk in front of him. From somewhere in the house, I can hear a TV or audio system, but no one else is in view. Almost exactly at 10, the doorbell rings and Hunnsecker gets up to answer it. Taking his time, I can see. It rings a second time before Hunnsecker pulls open the door and greets his visitor. It is a medium height man in a dark suit, carrying a largish case that looks like the type airline captains carry, with two flaps on the top. He walks towards the camera so we can see him quite clearly. He is about 60, with graying hair and dark eyes. His face is pouched with deep bags under his eyes, but the eyes are sharp under bushy eyebrows. His suit is very well tailored, of dark wool that looks like cashmere from this distance. As they go into his office, I notice that they do not shake hands. Hunnsecker put out his hand, but the visitor ignores it and indicates that Hunnsecker should lead the way. In the office, Hunnsecker goes behind his desk, while the man takes a seat on a sofa to the side of the room, not facing directly at Hunnsecker; forcing Hunnsecker to sit somewhat sideways to face him. Hunnsecker opens the conversation. In the interval, I transmit an image of the other man to my office for facial recognition.

"It took a lot more effort to get the document, and getting through the security protection required every bit of the additional funds that I requested. I am not complaining, but I wanted you to know that I had to put myself in some physical danger, in addition to the risk of discovery."

"Are you negotiating?"

"No, no, I just wanted you to understand. Did you bring the money?"

"Oh yes, I always keep my word." He pushes the large case a few inches towards Hunnsecker, who gets up from the desk, walks across the room, picks it up and then takes it back to the desk. He then opens the case and pulls out a stack of bills, all neatly bound with a paper band. Hunnsecker then asks "10 Million?" and the man nods.

"You promised me a list of associates. Do you have it for me?"

Hunnsecker points to a single sheet of paper he has placed on the corner of the desk. Neither of them gets up to touch it.

Then the man holds out his hand, palm up, Hunnsecker reaches under the desk, pulls out the Book briefcase and carries it over to where the man is sitting. The man drops his hand to the chair. Hunnsecker shrugs and puts it on the floor at his visitor's feet.

Hunnsecker stands for a moment while his visitor stares at him. Then he starts back across the room towards his desk. His gait is somewhat unsteady as he guides himself around the desk until he reaches his chair, then falls heavily into it. His face looks shiny as perspiration breaks out and begins to drip onto his shirt-front. He seems to be having difficulty breathing.

At our end, Marcia's cell rings and she listens for a moment before hanging up. She then announces to the room that Hunnsecker's guest is Charles Selwyn Hampton, Chairman and Chief Executive Officer of American Gas & Oil, the largest oil conglomerate in the world. Their flagship gas stations under the banner "AMGO" can be found in every town and city in the Western World. Scion of an old Main Line family,

Hampton personally is worth \$25.8 billion, but that does not count his family holdings.

In the other room, the play moves on. Hampton rises from his seat and walks over to Hunnsecker. He reaches into Hunnsecker's private briefcase, still on the desk and picks up the folders. As he holds them up one at a time, we can see the bright stripes across their faces: some purple, some red and some yellow: all security classifications. Hunnsecker starts to make a noise of objection, but saliva bubbles are all that come out of his mouth. Hampton looks down at him.

"You have approximately five minutes. You are abysmally stupid to believe that you could get away with fleecing us for 5 million and attempting to extort an additional 10 on top. Just so that you know, it is not the money; it is the arrogance that did you in. It will appear that you suffered a massive stroke, from which you did not recover."

Before he picks up the battered Book briefcase, he strips thin transparent latex gloves from his hands, pulls them inside out, and stuffs the inverted gloves into a zip bag which he takes from his jacket pocket. Then he zips up the bag. Opening the Book briefcase, he looks at the golden Book for a moment, and then tosses the zip bag in and recloses it.

He then walks back to Hunnsecker, who is still sitting in his chair with rivulets of sweat running down his face and froth running out of his mouth. Even in the resolution of the tiny cameras, he looks ashen. Hunnsecker croaks a couple of times and finally gets out the word "How..."

"Why my dear friend, the briefcase with your payoff; it is absorbed through the skin. The drug oxidizes in under an hour. It attacks the Central Nervous System; one of the new toys from our chemical division. Once oxidized, it is undetectable. I think it will have a market in the CIA." Hampton then chuckles as he picks up the Book briefcase and starts to leave the room, but not before he turns back once more to his former associate. "The ten million that I brought you this evening is, of course, yours to keep as it was our bargain. It should be more than adequate compensation to your family for their loss." Hampton quietly walks to the front door and the last we see of him is his fingers, folding a piece of paper around the edge of the door as he closes it.

Back in the room, Hunnsecker takes a few last gasps, his eyes roll up to the ceiling, and he slides out of his chair to the floor beneath his desk.

# 55 *FRIDAY – WASHINGTON*

This morning, Marcia and I are sitting in the kitchen watching the news, which periodically repeats the story about Hunnsecker's death. The local coroner, the story offers, has determined that Secretary Hunnsecker suffered a massive stroke on Thursday night while sitting at his desk at home and succumbed to its effects. Nothing is reported about the money; but, as I said to Marcia, I would bet that over at the FBI, they are tracking down the list of associates that Hampton left on Hunnsecker's desk. Marcia also believes that this morning, his associates will probably be investigated. I suggest to her that Hunnsecker's family would probably never see any of that money.

Before turning in last night, I called Admiral Lewis and updated him on the events of the evening. He told me that he would see if he could get some time with the White House Chief of Staff this morning. He is planning to reveal the tape which nailed Hampton to the wall for Hunnsecker's death and also gave indisputable evidence that it was Hunnsecker behind the Blackthorn killings of Dr. Froehlich and Lauren Sylfern. He told me that he hoped that he would be able to present the evidence to The President, and leave the next steps to her.

As far as the Book was concerned, the Admiral told me that the operation was still running, and that we needed to wait until the Hyenas started fighting over the spoils. Meantime, he was planning to go on with his arrangements for the funeral this morning.

A joint funeral service is scheduled at the U.S. Naval Academy Chapel in Annapolis. Around 10AM we drive the 27 miles to the Naval Academy, and then to the Byzantine white marble chapel with a graceful dome over the transept. There are few guests, mostly our team, plus a couple of other Washington area friends of Dr. Froehlich. The White House is represented by the Chief of Staff and the National Security Advisor. Admiral Lewis gives the short eulogy for Dr, Froehlich, while Alattin talks about his special relationship with Lauren. The two simple coffins are blessed by the chaplain, and then sent to the crematorium. Lauren's ashes will be shipped to Albuquerque, where she would be interred with those of her father.

Froehlich's were sent to Oak Ridge, where his wife is buried near their first home in the United States.

After the services, Marcia and I join the Admiral and the rest of our team at a local Annapolis restaurant, where the Admiral has taken a private room. We eat a quiet lunch together, and share personal stories with the about each of our two departed friends. The Admiral's story concerned the first time that he met John, as he called him, in Oak Ridge a few years after the War. The Admiral, who was then a newly minted Ensign, had been assigned to the interrogation team that had to pass on whether the German Scientists that had come over under the Paperclip contracts should be given permanent resident visas and set on the road to citizenship. The scientist, not many years older than Ensign Lewis, took a liking to the young man and helped him learn enough German so he wouldn't appear foolish in front of other interrogators. Each evening, John gave him private lessons, while at the same time sharing his own experiences under the Nazi regime, beginning with his adoration and leading to his disillusionment and final disgust. Froehlich gave young Lewis a perspective that he never could have obtained from either the interrogations or subsequent visits to Germany; to try to understand how a whole population could come under the spell of such a doctrine that grew more and more totalitarian with each passing month and year. John's kindness was something that Admiral Lewis always loved in his long-time friend.

Alattin spoke about the incredible vitality that Lauren showed as a barely adult 20 year old when he first encountered her. He told us that he fell in love with her then, and never stopped. His only regret, he said, was succumbing to the strait-jacket cultural views on the proprieties in marriage that he clung to foolishly.

At the end of the luncheon, the Admiral told everyone that the team would be gradually dispersed over the next couple of weeks, and everyone would soon be free to return home. Alattin asked the Admiral if he could take joint responsibility with John Crawford for the return of the genuine Book to its ancestral home. I nodded my agreement to that offer. Admiral Lewis then excused himself as he had a pressing appointment. Marcia and I walked out with him and saw him disappear into the back of the White House Limousine along with the COS.

Marcia and I returned to Laurel to wait for news. John left for the lab with Alattin. His first responsibility was to assemble all the records, the huge file of digital images of the Book's pages and every scrap of paper notes and computer files, pack them up and be ready to be picked up by a courier from ESCORT.

When we get home, we suddenly realize that we had nowhere to go and nothing particular to do. Marcia suggested that we start a major clean-up in the garden. We were changing clothes when the doorbell rings. I walk downstairs and looked through the glass. It is a messenger of some sort, so I pulled the door open. Outside stands a youngish man, with a vase full of flowers and a card. In the driveway, a white van is standing, emblazoned with "Rainbow Florists and Decorations". I thank the delivery man and take the flowers inside. "Marcia, somebody send us flowers." I call up the stairs.

"Who sent them?" she calls from the bedroom.

"I'll read the card," I reply, as I open the envelope attached to the vase.

The card is of exceptionally heavy stock, with a deeply embossed Presidential Seal on it. Written on the front, below the seal is a short note which I read to Marcia "*I am very sorry for your loss of two exceptional friends*" it says, but there is no signature.

Marcia comes down the stairs "I guess the Admiral or somebody got word to her about Froehlich and Lauren. But I wonder why we got flowers. It's a very thoughtful gesture. Let me put them in the dining room."

She carries the vase to the dining room and puts it in the middle of the table. But it is too tall, so she takes if off and replaces the original centerpiece, moving the new vase into the front hall. The vase is very heavy cut glass, with a deep marble base in dark green. The flowers are Asian lilies, quite tall with pink and white speckles; the centers of each flower have orange stamens, and the aroma fills the front hall. It strikes me that these flowers are very unusual for a consolatory gift. I pick up the vase again and look at the base. I can see up close that it is not marble, but some solid composition material that has been painted to look like stone. The lower third of the vase is filled with shiny metal balls that hold the flower stems in place under the water. A sudden premonition comes over me and I drop the vase back on the table, while I tear into the kitchen. Grabbing Marcia by the arm, I pull her down the stone stairs into the wine cellar, where I push her to the floor and cover her with my body. She starts squirming under me when a massive explosion rips through the main floor rooms while down here, the bottles in the racks bounce and one of the racks separates from the wall, falling against the back refrigerator. Bottles fall and smash on the stone floor next to us and wine splashes us along with thousands of glass shards. There is a strong smell like fireworks permeating the air.

After a couple of minutes, I raise myself up and help Marcia to her feet. We climb the steps up to the kitchen, to find that the stove and refrigerator are overturned, the sink has split from the wall and water is pouring out of the broken plumbing. Part of the wall between the kitchen and the front hall has disintegrated. Through the gigantic hole, I can see a matching hole through to the outside, where the front door used to be. In the hall, virtually nothing has survived, and there is a new doorway to our living room as well. The ceiling in the hall has come down, along with a small part of the floor above. My shirt back has been penetrated in quite a few spots, but nothing terribly deep. Marcia is wet, covered in red wine and angry, but OK.

I wait while Marcia gets some antibiotic and bandages from our upstairs bathroom. She has had to use the back stairs, since ones in the front hall are kindling. She is ministering to me when sirens round our driveway and a pair of fire trucks skids to a stop. Out boils rain coated firefighters wearing self-contained breathing gear. A chief's car joins the trucks and a white helmeted raincoat steps out of the front seat, directing the men to shut off our gas line, the water, and check for hotspots in the house. Just behind the chief's car, local police join the throng. The last to arrive is an EMT van which cuts across the lawn to find a place close to the house.

Two paramedics examine both of us and suggest strongly that I go the hospital. When I decline, they make me sign a waiver and then depart, tearing another track across the lawn. The police tape off the damaged area and tell us to stay out until after their CSI team has investigated. Finally everyone leaves. I finally locate my cell telephone in the living room debris and call the Admiral. He suggests that we move to a local hotel while he dispatches a security team again. Before hanging up, he tells me that he will speak to the Chief of Staff about our bombing. He also repeats his vow to rattle Blackthorn's cage.

After ESCORT security arrives, we leave, heading for a local Ramada Inn for the night. The bombing makes no sense to me since with the acquisition of the Book and the death of the principal, our potential threat to Hampton would be nil. I mention this to Marcia.

"But what if Hampton isn't the kingpin? Are we loose ends that have to be tied up? Does this mean that the team at the lab is still in jeopardy, regardless of the Book?"

"Love, I agree with you about loose ends. But Blackthorn could have been given termination orders much earlier by Hunnsecker, but could not carry them out since we were out of reach. Maybe they were watching for our return, and took the opportunity to finally fulfill their contract."

"Well, yes that could be the case. But Simon, what if it's true that Hampton works for someone else?"

"Let me see if I understand. Hunnsecker worked for Hampton, or rather used Hampton to extort money in exchange for delivering him the Book. Hampton used his corporate cohorts to fund the exercise. But that would mean Hampton would have to share the Book with all the others, rather than keeping it to himself. Why would he be interested in sharing such a prize? I think that we need to answer that question."

"If it wasn't his plan all along, how would a man with 50 billion dollars be manipulated? It can't be the Book. It has to be something even more important to someone like Hampton. Suppose he knows that the Book is a phony, but it using it to lure a bunch of others into ruining themselves, which would allow him to expand his holdings? Or wait a minute. Maybe he isn't alone in this. Perhaps there is a political presence involved. Suppose, Simon, you are in high Political office. You got there through the efforts of a number of rich and powerful individuals, to whom you now owe a great deal. How would you go about removing that debt? Obviously, you would find ways to create economic or political benefit for them. But suppose you wanted to eliminate the debts in one fell swoop. You can't kill them off; or at least not without exposing yourself. So here comes Charles Selwyn Hampton. Of all your debtors, he is the biggest. You fish him with a story of competitive advantage, gained at the expense of others, using the Book as treasure to pull in the rest of the group. The last thing that you would want is that the Book be real. It has to be a fake, or the group would have nothing to fight and blame one another about. Once the group is duped, and they turn on one another, you prod them along, stimulate their paranoia, and give them access to a firm like Blackthorn, who will do any dirty work for a few shekels. Once they are gone either by death or disgrace, your debts almost totally disappear..."

I finish her sentence "Except for Hampton. So the last to go would have to be him. Once he is gone, the powerful politician would be free of all obligations and can operate to his or her heart's content. You know, this makes all the sense in the world. But where does that leave us?"

"It leaves us with a nice train of logic, but not a shred of evidence. Simon, I doubt if there is any, and even if we were to discover some tenuous thread, who could we tell?"

"I hate to say it, but if we keep after this, I think we will be entirely on our own. If the rot is as high as I believe, I don't think even the Admiral could either protect us, or support us. For the sake of argument, who might be candidates?"

"Politically, it would have to be an elected person rather than appointed, since appointed politicians fundamentally only owe the one that appointed them. Career government personnel, including Cabinet Secretaries do not need or depend upon outside funding for their positions. So that leaves us with The White House with only two candidates, and the most senior members of the House or Senate. No one else fits those criteria. If it were a Senator or Representative, to cross all those industry boundaries it would have to be one of the top four members of each house: Majority and Minority Leaders and Whips. Even these last 8 still rely primarily on their own states for elections, and the funding industries would not cross all those lines."

"So that leaves us the President and the Vice President. From the description and history that Froehlich gave about Madame President, it seems doubtful. But one characteristic of those who reach such levels is their ability to manipulate others. So it would not be beyond the realm of reality to consider either one to be behind this whole endeavor to rid them of debt. I just would find it very hard to believe, and following that thought, if think it unbelievable, then someone like Admiral Lewis would have even a longer stretch of faith. No, my love, I think that we are very much on our own. The last thing I would want to do is to force someone like the Admiral to have to choose between loyalty to us and loyalty to the Commander in Chief."

"Simon, you have neatly boxed us into a corner and isolated ourselves from any potential help. Given that, what do you propose?"

"I say that we should listen carefully to the daily news, watch for any signs that our fears are being realized, and then develop an action plan that takes advantage of the possible threat to Charles Hampton's life to expose the higher-up. I would say that Hampton is powerful enough that if he believed his life were in danger and valued it, like I am sure he does, that we might turn him to be an ally at the critical moment."

"Simon, you are talking about power politics as played by the toughest characters in America, manipulated by the two of us. Is that, or is that not a bit ridiculous? You are more likely to find us consigned to a deep hole somewhere by even hinting at this."

"We have a couple of weeks, until the corporate CEOs get copies of the Book, submit it to evaluation, and come to the realization that someone has taken them to the cleaners. While we are waiting for this to happen, let's do some further research on Hampton, The President and The Vice President, so see if we can find weak places."

"How do you propose to do that without the access of ESCORT, NSA or anyone else?"

"How do most people do this research – Marcia, you are a whiz with the Internet – I know you can do it."

# 56 *THURSDAY - TWO WEEKS LATER – NEW YORK*

The Metropolitan Club in New York is one of its oldest and most prestigious. Located on the corner of Fifth Avenue and 60th Street, the original 1893 building was incorporated in a new East wing, designed by McKim, Mead & White in the Renaissance Revival style popular in 1912. J.P. Morgan and Cornelius Vanderbilt had not been pleased with the men's' clubs that dotted the downtown area near their offices in the financial district. Morgan decided to locate this new home for the financial elite of New York Society uptown across from the Frederick Law Olmstead's Grand Army Plaza entry to 700 acre Central Park. A story circulated at the time portrayed Morgan's impetus as anger at being denied membership in one of the downtown clubs. At Morgan's direction, White oriented the building to 60th Street, and a two-story gated semicircular entry was constructed, to suitably impress those who were not invited to join.

On this night, the rooftop lounge, bar, outdoor terrace and small dining room are closed apparently for some needed maintenance. Actually, they had been quietly reserved by Charles Selwyn Hampton for a private party. In discrete ones and twos, invitees ascended the great curving stairway from the main entry; then continued to a small private elevator, hidden behind a baroque panel within the Butler's pantry serving the main dining room overlooking Fifth Avenue. Upstairs, the dining room was set up in a circle of tables, glistening with sparkling contemporary silver and crystal. 18 places had been set in this space, only opened since 2007. The main passenger and service elevators were locked out tonight, as the somber group gathered.

True to their custom, no business passed among them during the dinner, but most ate mechanically, and ignored the fine counterpoints of cuisine this evening. At the conclusion of the meal, coffee and liquors were served by the elderly waiters whose families had served this elegant club for many years. Then the servants departed, leaving sweet delicacies as they closed and locked the doors.

Hampton called the meeting to order, whereupon immediately a raucous cacophony of angry voices filled the clean lines of this sumptuous room.

Hampton tapped his wineglass with his dessert knife quietly into the discord, until it gradually quieted and, with immediate stress relieved somewhat, all turned to him.

"Ladies and Gentlemen; I offer no apology for the results of your collective analyses, as they undoubtedly match those of my laboratories. But rancor at one another is not an appropriate business response. I have always adopted one simple principle: do not get mad; instead, get even."

"That's fine for you, with a nice 50 billion cushion to fall back on. But for me, I have a board to answer to, and promises have been made" said the insurance executive. Nods and guttural agreement pass around the room.

"Well, for me, I'll say that I am not so very unhappy that some of these 'discoveries' turned out to be phony. I would be out of business if they proved true," offered one of the power company execs.

"And where the fuck was you when they passed out the brains? Speaking of brains, you got your copy ahead of mine. Did you muck with it and then pass the shit on to the rest of u?" asked the old reactionary. "Let me see your copy."

"Don't make an accusation unless you are prepared to back it up," comes the retort. "I always found that the one that protests the loudest is usually the guilty one."

"Don't look at me, you shithead. I'll see you down six feet if you screw with me. "

"And what about this famous code?" echoed a software magnate. "I already invested in a new plan to exploit it, and now I've nothing to exploit but my dinner."

"Gentlemen, Ladies; this is getting us nowhere." Hampton broke in. "Certainly we have been taken advantage of; perhaps by one of us or perhaps by someone outside this room."

"You know I do not make threats, generally," said the family scion CEO of the remaining profitable automaker in the country. "But I will have the head of whoever duped us, regardless of it is. Let's get an outsider to investigate; someone who is not amenable to persuasion."

"Don't try to snow us. There isn't anyone who is immune to pressure," spoke the pharmaceutical head. "I will do my own search. In fact, I already started it and wherever it leads is fine with me."

"We don't seem to be getting anywhere. If everyone is agreed, I think that we should terminate this meeting."

"I'll tell you one thing, Hampton; I am going to piss on some graves before I am done." The old oilman spit on the table, threw himself out of his chair, and stomped to the door. Not bothering to look for the key, he kicked the center of the double doors, broke them open and passed out into the elevator lobby.

The rest broke up into twos and threes and with still angry faces and gestures, left the room. Hampton waited until all were gone. Then he pulled out his cell phone and dialed.

"Mission accomplished" he said. Then he listened for a moment or two and then closed the cell. As he left the room, there was a small smile on his normally placid face.

# 57 *ONE WEEK LATER – SAN FRANCISCO*

*This is MSNBS, with a News Break. This morning, a private plane carrying 5 executives returning from a conference at a secluded retreat near Camp David disappeared off Air Traffic Control's radar. The flight was scheduled to land at Chicago's Midway Airport at 11:17 AM. A search along the route was initiated at 10:45 Eastern Standard Time, by State Police units in Maryland, West Virginia, Pennsylvania and Illinois. The five passengers and three crewmembers were aboard a Grumman Gulfstream IV, owned by American Gas and Oil Company, operated by Fleet Air Taxi Services, a subsidiary of AMGO. The aircraft is presumed to have crashed somewhere in the mountains along the route. Representatives of the company have requested the assistance of the National Transportation Safety Board in the investigation. The identities of the passengers and crew are being withheld pending notification of next-of-kin.*

"Simon, come and look at the news. Hampton's company has lost a plane." I come down from my attic where I had been finally cleaning the lab to join Marcia in the kitchen. We have a small flat panel TV which I mounted on the wall so Marcia could watch House & Garden TV and cooking shows, but this morning, we decided to leave the news on. I can see the crawler at the bottom of the screen, but the letters are too tiny for me to see clearly. The perfectly coiffed talking head was reading her Teleprompter as I turned away to get a refill on coffee, and then join Marcia at the counter.

*We have just learned that wreckage of the downed aircraft has been sighted in a West Virginia mountain valley. Our NSAIR team will be bringing you pictures. Stay tuned.*

"I wonder if Hampton is aboard. I know we were expecting something, but this is pretty bad."

Every couple of minutes, an announcer breaks into the morning news how to repeat the original story. We try a few other programs, but none of the other stations carry any updated information, so we turn the sound down and put back the original station. In about 30 minutes, pictures start being broadcast showing a steep mountainside with irregular pieces of white fuselage and wings. It was too far away to see any details, but it looked like the plane was in a lot of pieces. The news reporter was continuing with the story as we turn up the sound.

*A spokesman for the NTSB refused to comment on the investigation, but your reporter has learned that the plane was considerably below its assigned altitude and the en-route Air Traffic Controller got no warning or call of an emergency prior to its disappearance off his screen. The Public Information Office of American Gas and Oil was not available for comment at this time, but would prepare a statement soon. Stay tuned to MSNBS for the latest updates on this breaking story.*

As we sit, the telephone rings. It is John Crawford, calling to say that he and Karen will be passing through San Francisco tomorrow on their way to Beijing, and wondered if they could see us. Marcia grabs the telephone and tells John that we would not hear of them staying anywhere else for their overnight layover. She also finds out when the flight is arriving, and tells them that we will meet them at the airport.

The morning and early afternoon there is nothing new on TV about the plane crash. Both of us drive out to San Francisco International to pick up the Crawfords from their UAL flight. We still have our Navy Security ID which I show to TSA at the Arrivals ramp, so we are allowed in and Marcia goes in search. When they finally come out, John is buried under luggage.

Back at the house, Marcia ushers them into a now somewhat updated guest room, and then eventually all join me in the kitchen for a needed glass of wine.

Karen is almost an exact opposite from Marcia. Where Marcia is tall, Karen is petite. Her hair is almost platinum blonde and she has very deep blue-violet eyes. The combination of pale skin and deep eyes makes for a very hauntingly attractive picture. She grew up in Maryland, and had met John at the university as undergraduates. They have been together since. Karen is trained as a biologist, but chooses to teach rather than do research. She tends to be quiet and thoughtful, but addresses every problem with a highly analytical mind. She tells us that she and John were invited to Beijing in connection with some artifacts that John is still working on back at his lab. Both of them are looking forward to this trip, after the stresses of the past few months. John echoes and is glad that the whole mess has been put to bed with the Book's return to Alexandria.

Emily seems to have totally recovered from her harrowing kidnapping experience of a few months ago. She is bubbly and curious about everything.

I hold off on saying anything about the crash, so Marcia picks up the hot potato first. "It isn't quite over yet. Unfortunately, Simon and I believe that Hampton is not the top dog in this pack. Did you hear about the plane crash?"

"No," responds John. "We left fairly early this morning, and have not seen any news since last night. What happened?"

"It seems that a private jet owned by Hampton's company crashed in West Virginia. The report said that there were five passengers, but we don't know yet if Hampton is one of them."

"What do you mean about Hampton?" asked Karen.

"Karen, we believe that there was a secret political program to use our work as a means of eliminating obligations from a high elected official to some of his more powerful supporters."

"Yes, I know about the Book. John told me early on after he was confined to the lab. And don't worry, I have told no one else, and don't ever plan to."

I continue, "We think that Hampton was the point man for this plan, and he roped in the rest of the CEOs. After their book was found to contain little of value, the stage was set for removal of the players. I am afraid that we were used in various scenes leading to the final act which is now underway. If we are right, then this plane crash gets rid of 5 prime players."

"Simon that is a frighteningly Machiavellian concept; do you mean to say that the Book itself was never really under any real threat?"

"John, I couldn't say yes or no. I can only say that the opportune moment arrived for someone to take advantage of the Book and circumstances, to impose a super-agenda on all our efforts. You have to wonder why we would be allowed to be in apparent control over something so important. With the huge weight of White House over any activities like we were challenged with, why didn't this might ever get exercised?"

"So what are you thinking about doing?"

"Marcia and I decided to see how it starts to play out and look for an opportunity to get one of the players, maybe even Hampton himself, to betray his boss."

"You know what they say about the boy who smiled at the tiger?" offered Karen.

"I know. But the last thing I want to do is to drag you both into this again."

"It's going to be difficult to get dragged in all the way from China."

Marcia, who had been sitting quietly, turned the TV on again.

*The five executives who lost their lives in the plane crash this morning have been identified. They are Frederick Loesfeld, CEO of Ultrick Pharmaceuticals, Richard Allen Brooke, CEO of American Auto Corporation, Janus Cairns, Chairman of Mega Software Systems, Daryl Murdock, CEO of National Oil, and Stryker Fisher, CEO of United Power. The five executives were at a retreat in the Maryland hills near Camp David. The Flight Operations Manager of Fleet Air Taxi spoke to your reporter earlier:*

The scene cut to an executive, speaking into a microphone with his company logo behind.

*"The aircraft, a Grumman GIV aircraft had 2,650 hours of service, had been inspected within the past three days, and was is perfect operational condition. The pilot, George Crane, was a retired air force colonel with long service in many aircraft platforms. The co-pilot, Frederick Thomas, was also a former U.S. Air Force pilot. Both pilots were re-certified by the FAA within the past three months and both had recently completed rigorous medical examinations by our insurance carrier. The third crewmember, Foster Mendham, was a contractor, not one of our regular stewards. He was on this flight as a replacement for our scheduled attendant, who called in sick early this morning. The NTSB is conducting an investigation of the accident, with our full support and cooperation."*

*"Do you have communications tapes between the plane and your offices?"*

*"I am sorry; all communications have been sealed by the NTSB, pending their investigation. I am prohibited from speaking to you further on that subject."*

*"When do you think there will be information about what caused the accident?"*

*"You will have to consult the NTSB for that information."*

*"Have you been contacted by the FBI about the investigation?"*

*"No, only the NTSB."*

*"What do you think happened aboard the aircraft?"*

*"You will have to wait for the NTSB, as I said. I cannot comment further on something about which I have no information."*

*"These 8 people where the only persons on the flight?"*

*"The manifest was transmitted from our home office in Houston, and is available for the media. All next of kin have been notified by our offices. You should also be aware that even though we are a small company, we have offered grief counseling to relatives, should they desire it."*

*"Thank you"*

*To repeat, the news today was tragic for 5 corporate executives, who died in a fiery crash aboard a Fleet Air Taxi jet this morning. The wreckage is scattered over a wide area in a steep mountain valley in West Virginia. There is no evidence of mechanical difficulties and no emergency communication was received by the FAA Air Traffic Controllers. The pilot and co-pilot's families have not been available for comment. The plane was on its way from a private airfield near Camp David, the Presidential Retreat, to Chicago's Midway Airport. The White House has denied that prior to the flight, meetings were held at Camp David.*

*On another note, scandal erupted in the boardroom of DeKalb Chemicals this morning. The Chairman and CEO, Mark Sanderford, abruptly resigned after it was revealed that he embezzled over 135 million from the company in a phony supplier scam. Mr. Sanderford's attorney, Jason Stockton released a statement stating that Mr. Sanderford is completely innocent and was a victim himself of a move to oust him from the Board of Directors. According to documents provided to this reporter, for the past two years, Mr. Sanderford had a secret agreement with Phillips Petrochemicals, in which both CEOs vouched for each other's purchases. The CEO of Phillips, Cal Worthington also shared the cloud if these allegations prove to be true. The District Attorneys in Wilmington, Delaware and Biloxi, Mississippi have launched investigations.*

*We will bring you the latest, most accurate and reliable news as it becomes known.*

"Oh hell; that's 7 out of 18. I would say the ball is rolling."

"Simon, Hampton was not aboard. . . Are you sure that these others are all part of the conspiracy?"

"They all are on the list that Dr. Froehlich gave me before leaving with the book for the last time."

Emily, who had been sitting quietly during the conversation, suddenly popped up. "I think you should set a trap for the leader, and expose his corruption."

I glanced over to John, who had a small smile pulling at the corners of his mouth. "Emily, you certainly have turned out to be very bright. But this is something you need to keep totally to yourself. It might be dangerous for mom and dad if you ever said anything. "

"I understand. Some people are just too high to be pushed off their pedestals by ordinary people like us."

"Simon, John, Karen;" Marcia responded. "I think Emily expressed a sobering truism. Let's put this aside and enjoy an evening together, please?"

"I'm sorry, love. OK, where would you like to go for dinner? Or would you rather eat here?"

"Simon, let's all go out; how about Masa's?"

"How hungry is everyone?"

"Emily had a protein bar on the plane, but Karen and I missed lunch completely, so we are up for it; Marcia, what about you?"

"Tonight is a special treat to have both of you here. Let's go for it."

I go upstairs and call for a reservation. They can take us at 7, which is good since the Crawfords have to be out early in the morning.

As we drive together to the restaurant, I share some history of this relatively new San Francisco destination. "Masa's is on Nob Hill, right near Union Square. Chef Masataka Kobayashi was lured from *Auberge du Soleil* in Napa Valley by Executive Hotels, to open his own restaurant in the city in 1983. The restaurant was an instant success and Chef Masa was acclaimed as a new generation of French-trained Japanese chefs. Unfortunately, Chef Masa did not enjoy his accolades for very long, as he was found dead in his apartment only a few months later. The mystery of his death was never solved. But the restaurant continued to grow in popularity and to win many awards through the efforts of several top Executive Chefs who led the restaurant through to today. Gregory Short, the current chef, trained under Thomas Keller, the renowned owner of the French Laundry in Napa. The menu is fundamentally French."

When we are seated in the relatively small dining room, Marcia makes a suggestion "Although there are many wonderful individual items on the menu, I would suggest that for a first-time experience, you try either the six or nine course tasting Prix Fixe dinners, combined with the recommended wine pairing selections."

John and Karen both decide that 9 courses would be just too much rich food to precede their long trip west, so both select the 6 course version, which we both join. Emily opted for a macaroni and cheese plate, fluttering her not inconsiderable eyelashes at the waiter as she reinforced her request. "Where do they learn it? I mused as the waiter agrees, revealing he has turned to putty in Emily's hands.

Tonight, our slightly more complex dinner starts with Dungeness Crab Cakes on baby greens with a miso-mustard sauce and some watermelon radish, followed by a fillet of Alaskan Cod with a curry sauce and some vegetables. Following these fish courses comes medallions of aged beef with fingerling potatoes and mushrooms with a bordelaise sauce and baby leeks. To cleanse the palate, a sorbet of apples with huckleberry sauce and a calvados gelee is offered, followed by a Chocolate-Blackberry Glacé which combined a flourless chocolate cake with an orange-vanilla sherbet and a chocolate shortbread cookie, which was accompanied by cofee and some truffles. Emily rejoined the crowd with dessert and a large glass of milk.

We all managed not to groan too loudly after the meal, and were mutually glad that we had not chosen the 9 course version. Accompanying each course was an appropriate wine, so by the end of dinner, we are quite relaxed as well as being well filled.

When we return home, Karen excuses herself and heads up to bed, taking the somewhat reluctant Emily with her, while John asks me if we can chat for a moment.

"Simon, I hesitated to bring up anything during that wonderful dinner, but exactly what do you think you both might do about this political angle to our Book business?"

"John, I don't think that we have a choice. I, for one, do not want to just let it drop. It irks me no end that whoever was behind the behind can get away with the murders of our friends as well as all the others. But it isn't only murder, it's the undermining of some basic principles of government that we specifically are charged to protect against."

"Simon, I admire your sense of justice. But realistically, you don't think that you can singlehandedly, rectify practices that are considered normal in most parts of the world, and also have existed for as long as society itself has existed."

"No I am not so naïve as to think that I can tilt at windmills and win. But I do think that I can use what has happened already to prod along those who might be able to at least clean up at least one cesspool."

"You are talking about Hampton?"

"Yes; I think that I should pay a call on Mr. Charles Selwyn Hampton and try to turn him. You know what they say about axe men. They are brought into an organization to wield the axe, but inevitably are the last to be axed themselves. I think that Hampton should be getting a bit rattled right now, and probably realizes at least subconsciously that his turn is coming. I could play on that and get him to roll over on whoever he is reporting to."

"Simon, I am really worried for you. If you take this on, you are fighting against some very strong powers, and you will be truly alone. I don't mean to say that the three of us won't support you, but we will be powerless to help you."

"I understand. But it is something I have to do."

Marcia looked at me and then said softly "Simon, I understand that you are carrying around the burden of Jean's death as well, and that you have to deal with the source directly. I just don't want to lose you in the process."

"Sweetheart, I would be foolish not to recognize the risk, but it has to be tried."

# 58 *THREE DAYS LATER – IRVING, TX*

After the three Crawfords left for Beijing, I call Hampton's office and make an appointment. I am initially rebuffed by an administrative assistant, until I mention that the subject of the meeting is the Book. I am told that I would have ten minutes, and not to be late.

My appointment is for 4:00 PM today, so I take a UAL flight to Dallas-Fort Worth where AMGO's headquarters in Irving is quite close to the airport. It is close to 4 when my taxi gets to a sprawling campus where Hampton's office shares the fourth floor of one wing with Board facilities and his personal support staff. Even other senior executives of this $400 billion company are not located on this floor, but the one immediately below, connected by a central stair and private elevator. The complex, set in a 300 acre park amid rolling lawns, woods and lakes is an idyllic setting for worldwide energy management.

I emerge from security, having been duly scrutinized, photographed and frisked, fitted with an appropriate visitor's badge, and met by an armed escort. The guard inserts a card key and presses his index finger on a scanner in the elevator before the doors close and we are silently lifted into the sanctuary of Hampton's domain. A tailored and coiffed middle aged secretary greets me at the elevator doors and escorts me to an anteroom, where Italian glove leather couches gently support my body and ice water is placed on a small table next to me. In about 5 minutes, the inner door opens and Hampton himself stands in the threshold with an open hand to welcome me.

He precedes me into his office; an L-shaped room with a lounge area set against the glazed backdrop of the central Texas countryside. Motioning me to one of the two matching lounge chairs, he sits across a low contemporary glass coffee table with a map of the world etched on its surface and small scintillating stars representing AMGO operations around the globe. They must be illuminated from within the table itself, since I can detect no light source. The effect, however, is not gaudy, but very quietly suggestive of their vast network of influence.

Hampton begins the conversation. "Mr. Chess; prior to this meeting, we have not met, but I have heard your name on several occasions, with reference to good intelligence work on behalf of our country and the Navy. You must give my warm regards to my longtime friend, Admiral Lewis. I understand that he is about to receive his fourth star. Please congratulate him when the announcement is made. I will be sorry to lose him as director of ESCORT, as he assumes his new position. But we are all very grateful for his long service."

"Why thank you, Mr. Hampton. I am certain that he will appreciate your good wishes. You must be aware, however; that I am only peripherally connected with his department, having recently retired myself from active duty."

"Yes, I understand that. But let's not digress. What exactly are you here to see me about?"

"First of all, what I have to say is for your eyes and ears only. You will understand that when I start telling you exactly why I am here. I know that many people in your position routinely record and tape visitors' conversations; however, I assure you that you will not want this conversation recorded. I would suggest, for your own protection, that you shut down any recording or imaging."

"Don't be ridiculous, young man. I am not interested in anything that you have to say, but out of friendship with Admiral Lewis, I granted this brief interview. So get on with it."

"Very well. I just wanted to give you the opportunity in advance."

"Continue or leave."

"Mr. Hampton, approximately four weeks ago, you killed Defense Secretary Hunnsecker with poison, administered by skin contact through his palms. This was done during a visit which you made to his home, when you delivered $10 million as supplemental fees in connection with his securing of the Book for you. Do not attempt to deny this, as we have it on digital videotape made during the incident."

Hampton turned slightly pale at the accusation, but kept his poker face intact. He started to bluster, but I cut him off.

"We have no wish to bring this evidence before the District Attorney in Virginia, nor the U.S. Attorney General. I am telling you this so you will understand that the information which I will be giving you comes from a reliable source."

542

"I think, Mr. Chess that you had better leave. Whatever extortion that you may propose does not interest me. I warn you that if you even hint a word of what you have just said, you and your family will greatly regret it. I refer specifically to your very attractive new wife."

"Mr. Hampton, I do not have a goal of extorting nor exposing you for the murderer that you are. Instead, I am here to warn you of plans to terminate you with prejudice, not by my hand, but by another."

"Chess, I live with threats every day. They are part of any major CEO's life. My budget for personal security is many times your annual salary, so don't think that you can frighten me with a death threat."

"Mr. Hampton, let me tell you a short story. There is, in Washington, a powerful politician who got a lot of support and funding for his election to high office from you and your friends. The time came when this person decided that the price for this support was just too high, so he put together a plan to remove his debts from the playing field. He could not simply eliminate the people he owed, so he devised an elaborate plan involving a historical treasure and the illusion of great discoveries to create dissent among those whom he owed, and exacerbated this dissent by playing on their mutual greed and fear. His plan was to cause them to feed on one another, destroying each other until there were only a few left, perhaps only one. Then he would sever the last cord and free himself of all past obligations. Do you follow the story so far?"

"Go on. It is an interesting story."

"Last week, the story turned deadly. A plane crashed, scandals broke, and several people fearfully removed themselves from the field. Does this ring a bell?"

"Yes, we lost a plane with several of our friends, but there was no plot, no assassination; just an accident."

"If you check with the NTSB, you will find an anomaly. The steward that was on that flight went missing. His body has not been found. I would suggest that further investigations will reveal that he was, in fact, an employee of Blackthorn, your mercenary contractor. I would hazard a guess that he initiated a malfunction and parachuted from the stricken aircraft. I think that it is particularly interesting that, given this suggested scenario, there has been no involvement by the FBI. That alone should alert you to manipulations behind the scene."

"I am sure that someone will respond to your conspiracy theories, but I am not one of them. But do go on. You fascinate me with your imagination."

"Mr. Hampton, you are caught in the middle. Your friends are turned against you because of the Book's lack of value. You are caught by evidence that could put you in jail for life. Your boss, I am sure, still assures you of his support. So you still believe that ultimately, even if the world crashes around you, political pressure combined with your money will get you out of this jam. But I can tell you as clearly as you see me here, that such will not be the case. Once all the rest of your gang are dead or emasculated, you will be the last threat. While you may think that this will bring you great ON, as the Japanese say. In reality, it will destroy you. Your only salvation is to expose the corruption and make a deal for your own hide."

"Are you finished?"

"Almost; I wanted to share this with you, because I am naïve. I believe in our country's principles and with all your successes under our flag, I cannot imagine that you would not believe that as well."

"Mr. Chess, I admire your lofty ideals, but I think that if you were totally honest, you would have to admit that you have some other driving emotions as well."

"What do you mean?"

"Your first wife's murder; I know that you are still looking for those that ordered it, and those that carried it out."

"You know what happened?"

"Yes, of course. I have researched you, Chess. I discovered this thorn in your side. If you like, I can tell you precisely who and how."

"I am listening."

"The idea of this shadowy group called the 'Keepers' has been around for a long time. It originally surfaced in communiqués from Sophie Schliemann to her son, which brought the Sureté eventually into the search. They didn't get anywhere. It re-surfaced at the OSS/CIA when Standahl Xyso brought the armor and key out of Greece, hoping to use it to buy his emigration to the United States. This brought Ernst Zilbern and Johann Froehlich into the act. Ernst stole the armor and sent it to Germany from Cyprus, hoping that assay would yield the metal that they needed for the V4 intercontinental missiles they were designing to attack the U.S. Unfortunately, the war was too far gone, and the armor wound up in the hands of the Soviets. It was out of his reach for many years. When the armor was recovered from the Lublyanka, Jean Chess was notified, and consequently was identified as a Keeper link to the NSA. This alerted the

White House National Security Advisor. An official inquiry could not be mounted by the government, so I was approached, since we have such far flung resources. We watched your wife. When she was exiled for her position on Iraq, we followed her through her disenfranchisement and eventual physical banishment to Israel. We were hoping that she would lead us to the rest of the Keepers and to the Book itself. Unfortunately, Hunnsecker, who was by then Secretary of Defense, lost patience and arranged for her seizure and death. Our only link died with her. Zilbern tried to pick up the pieces in Europe, and contacted his old friend Froehlich for help, but it was refused. Zilbern's only remaining thread was the key. His fanaticism drove him to contrive the murder of Xyso and faking his own death. He thought that by going underground, he would be free to finish his quest. Unfortunately for him, the armor turned up at the Smithsonian, and the key wound up in your possession. I assume that these Keepers took those actions to expose Zilbern and us."

"You, of course know the rest of the story. But what you don't know is that through your own search, we watched you. We believe that Zilbern had the Greek Keepers murdered in the Poseidon Temple. I can assure you that we had nothing to do with that. When you put all the pieces together and found the Book in Alexandria, we were very pleased and looked forward to Hunnsecker bringing it out to us. Mr. Chess, it ended with him. His greed sealed his own fate. I have no regrets on that score. As for the Book, it was a gamble, and we lost. That is the end of it, as far as I am concerned. I have risked far more on other wildcat ventures. There was no one pulling Hunnsecker's strings aside from our little group and his own avarice. There is no one pulling my strings, either. Your wife's death was ultimately the act of a depraved psychopath who was determined to ascend the economic ladder through the power that the Book would bring. I am afraid that you are wrong in your assumption that this goes further than us. As for the plane crash, I can't say if members of my fraternity don't act on their suspicions or revenge. But that is among us. Go home, Mr. Chess. If you leave this now, we will consider it ended. Your wife's murderer has been punished, and you can be at ease."

"I appreciate your revealing to me the missing parts to this story, and confirming my suspicions concerning Hunnsecker. If I cannot convince you of any deeper motivations, so be it. Thank you for your time and trust. I am finally finished with this. Your part in Hunnsecker's execution is sealed."

For the first time this afternoon, Hampton allowed a small smile cross his face. After studying it for a moment, I added "but of course you knew this already. My revealing the existence of this evidence came at no surprise to

545

you. I would venture to guess that if anyone looked for the files, they would have been either lost, or corrupted."

"I cannot imagine that any records exist of something that never happened."

"Of course; well, goodbye Mr. Hampton. I do not think that we shall meet again."

"Goodbye Mr. Chess. I wish you and your lovely bride well. Also please extend my good wishes to Drs. Crawford. It is always a pleasure to see good healthy relationships among the next generation."

The door to his office opened, and my escort reappeared. When I turned back to Hampton, he was buried in a thick file at his desk.

# 59 *ONE MONTH LATER – SAN FRANCISCO*

It is fall, and the rains were due any day. I sit in the garden this morning watching the fountain play against the stones and the bamboo canes in our tiny garden clink against each other as the wind ruffled the leaves. I think that my mouse finally departed for a better diet elsewhere, for I had not seen him in days. Back in the kitchen, Marcia was humming a tune while she makes iced tea for us. In the downstairs office, Stephanie was in and on the telephone, cajoling clients to finally pay their bills.

Gone, I think permanently, were Colin Lessant and the Navy, although the Admiral called to say that several of the corporate bosses had retired after the plane crash. Blackthorn was charged by the FBI for undertaking mercenary contracts within the U.S., but since there were no positive identifications of the team that killed Froehlich and Lauren or the bombers of our home, there was not much to base a good prosecution on. In our case, the delivery truck had been stolen, and was found abandoned near the reservoir. The flowers themselves were purchased at the local Laurel florist by a woman, and she paid cash. The plane crash which took the life of five CEOs was classified as a terrorist act and investigations transferred to Homeland Security. AMGO's air steward was never located or identified.

The contractor we had hired in Laurel is almost finished with the reconstruction of the house after the bombing. During these weeks, Marcia prowled the art districts for lighter and brighter paintings for her new home here. She had thrown out my heavy leather furniture in the living room and was gradually transforming the house. The only room I kept to myself was my attic garret, although I wonder lately if I ever will take the dust cover off my telescope. But the lab and the armory are still up there. After all, we did have a business.

Chess Restorations is Marcia's play on words. We certainly do not restore Chess Sets, nor did we do any art restoration, unless you consider the return of stolen art to their rightful owners. Marcia threw herself into building a database of missing and pilfered art, and each day; the web she created draws in more information for our files. John, Karen and Emily visited us after returning from China and gave us all a delightful visit. John says that if he ever gets tired of his work at the Smithsonian, he will come join us and add his talents to our collaboration.

I have not heard anything from any of the other members of our Book Team, and hope that Alattin, particularly, has found some peace. The last I heard, he had returned to the Los Alamos laboratory, and was busy on a new project.

While I sit here contemplating, the telephone rings inside the house and Stephanie answers it and then comes out into the garden. "Simon, Mr. Hampton's office is on the telephone. They would like you to come to Texas for a meeting tomorrow evening. What shall I tell them?"

"Tell them I'll come. Would you please ask what it's about?"

When she returns, she says "it concerns the subject of your last visit. He asks if you could be there by 8:00 tomorrow night."

Marcia looks up from her weeding, and says "Simon, I am really surprised. I thought that all this was over and done. What could he possibly want with you now?"

"I have no idea. But I should go. Maybe we were right and something's happened to change his mind."

"There is no point speculating. But I must tell you, I do not have a very good feeling about this. You still carry your ID and FAA carry permit, don't you?"

"Marcia, do you really think I need to go armed?"

"This came out of the blue. I can't think that it would be something good. Do us both a favor and bring your Glock."

# 60 *THE NEXT DAY – IRVING, TX*

"Skinny, there's only the two of us here; how about dropping the act."

"I've done this for so long, Chuck; it ain't much of an act anymore."

"You know, folks look at your shitkickers and jeans, and never see through to your Ph.D. in Geology or your three books on petro technology."

"You've discovered my secret. It keeps them off balance, and thinking that they got some rube to deal with, I git 'em all the time."

"How long have we been friends?"

"I guess mor'n 50 years. We sure done some great deals. This last one was a real pisser and ain't done us no good. But we gotta pony up if we want to keep the political hacks on our side. It takes mor'n cash these days. Hey; what say we head up to 'laska and git us in some fishin'. I'm plum wore out screwin' around meetin's with them Washington slimeballs. I need some clean air and sippin' whiskey to kill the bad taste."

"Tonight will probably be the last for a while. Next election is about 2 years away, so we should get the word tonight on the slush fund. Between you and me, I figure it'll take 1 bil. to get it done – so we're probably in for a 100 mil. stake between the two of us. What do you say, 50-50?"

"Sheet, that's a whopper. All right; I'll take that action, but I ain't gonna deal with 'em direct. I'll git you the cash and you manage the bank. How much do you think we can lay off on depletion?"

"I guess about a quarter. But you'll have to wait a couple of years."

"No shit. Well, the new leases should pay us back. 'Least we won't have to compete for them."

Both Hampton and Corman were sitting in Hampton's office when the elevator announces their visitor. He is preceded by two security men, who scan the room before letting their protectee in. Then they retreat into the lobby and close the door.

"Charles, Maurice; I wanted to see both of you because we still have a small problem."

"What's the problem?" asked Hampton.

"Only loose ends: Chess and Crawford. Both of them have a history of worrying at bones until every bit of meat has been dug out."

"Don't worry. Chess is now fully convinced that Hunnsecker was the top man. He believes that he ordered the hit on his first wife as well as the duo in Bethesda. The rest of the carnage he chalks up to Ernst Zilbern. We're completely off his radar."

"I don't like the idea that he could pick it up at any time. I think it's time that he had an unfortunate accident."

"Look; he's out of it. Lewis has now been moved up to fry bigger fish. The records are shredded and Chess has started a new art-recovery detective business. If we open the door again, we run a far bigger risk than if we just leave well enough alone. But I do have an idea. You've got friends everywhere. Why not get him invited into a business project that will jump-start his new business in a big way and totally absorb him in new ventures. If he thinks it is important, you'll never have to worry about him again. There's got to be something that you can point his way."

"Well, sure I can do that. But let's leave it for a minute. I have to start thinking about the upcoming election. Are both of you ready to kick in?"

"We figure that the whole deal will cost $1 Billion. We'll take 10% participation between the two of us. And we'll get friends to take another 10%. We'll do like we did last time – you won't have to report it, and PACs will make the expenditures."

"You've thought it through. OK, thanks. You know that you both can call on me. I always pay my debts. Now I have to be off. The Senate is weighing in on a new stimulus package, so I need to be back in Washington." He shook hands with the two oilmen and departed. As the elevator closes behind him, one of the security team remains in the upstairs lobby.

Hampton and Corman return to their drinks as the security man re-enters Hampton's office holding a gun. The gun spit four silenced rounds – two each for each of the oil leaders. Hampton falls on the carpet in front of his desk. Corman had already seated himself. His drink slipped from his hand and splashed across his torso as the glass bounces on the floor. Head shots finish both of them. Then the assassin retreats behind the door frame and waited.

## 8:00 PM

Sunset had not quite come when I step out of the taxi and walk through the revolving glass doors into the lobby. Security has a visitor's badge waiting for me, so I am admitted directly to the elevator without the scanning I had the last time. As I ride up to the fourth floor, I wondered what Hampton would say. The door opened to the silent lobby. Lights softly illuminated the deep red and blue Persian rugs covering the solid wood parquet floors. Both desks are empty, and no escort is waiting. I walk across the room towards the open entry of Hampton's office. When I reach the doorway, I can see someone sitting in one of the lounge chairs near the window, but then I also spot the body on the carpet. Before I could take a further step into the room, a cold gun barrel touches the back of my neck. I freeze as the figure behind me reaches around into my jacket, removing my Glock. Then I am pushed into the room.

When I turn around, I see a dark business suit and a face with a blank expression, while a gun like mine pointed from the end of an outstretched hand.

"On the floor, face down, hands behind your head. You know the drill." I kneeled down and lay with my face in the carpet. My hands are clamped together with flex cuffs. "Now get up and go sit in the chair" he says, pointing with his gun.

I moved to the other lounge chair. Hampton is on the carpet, but I do not know the other fellow was. It is very clear from the head wounds, that this assailant is a professional. While I sit, he put my gun into his pocket and takes a Magnum from his briefcase. He comes over to the body in the other lounge chair and placed it in a dead hand, inserts an index finger into the trigger guard and fires two shots into the wall next to the open door. The sound of the gun is very loud in this quiet space. He lets the hand drop and the gun clatters to the floor. Then he turns towards me. "You came into the room and pointed your gun at Hampton and Corman. Corman got off three shots before you managed to kill them both."

"Three? But you only fired twice."

"The third one didn't miss."

"Why would I want to kill both of them?" I asked.

"Evidence is in Hampton's files showing he gave the order to Hunnsecker for your wife's assassination. You finally tracked him down and killed him. Corman was just collateral damage. You, after all, were still raging, even after all this time."

He pulls me out of the chair and makes me kneel on the floor. Then he cut between the cuffs and steps back. As he did so, he slips on Hampton's blood which had pooled on the wood floor next to the carpet. It wasn't much of a slip, but enough so his gun hand flies up for balance, and I grab my backup pistol from my ankle holster. Thank God for Marcia's warning. I don't hesitate, but thumb the safety and pulled the trigger three times. The first shot hits him in the shoulder before I got the aim right. But the second and third catch him squarely in the face and he flies over Corman's body and crashes against the window glass.

I spin around waiting for his backup. But no one is there. The only sound I hear is my own breathing. Finally, I stand and bend over the killer's body. I notice, for the first time, a flesh colored ear piece with a hair thin coil of wire leading under the collar of his jacket. I check his wrist and sure enough; a microphone is strapped just under the cuff of his shirt. I feel around in his jacket pocket and find my Glock. Then I search for the Magnum and find it against the base of the windows. Since he is not wearing gloves, I do not want to add to the confusion so I take a pen from Hampton's desk tray and used it to pick up the gun. I return it to a position right next to Corman's hand. I then pick up the gun the agent used to kill the oilmen. When I look closely, I recognized it. It is mine. In fact, it is the one that Lt. Jurgens took from my house all those months ago in San Francisco. How it got here, I will never know. But now I see that the setup was designed perfectly. My gun with eventually my prints on it – after I was dead by the third shot from Corman's Magnum, will have killed both of them, and there would be the package: neat and tidy. A classic locked door murder, with the killer dead as well. All obligations resolved. I reversed the setup and put the Glock that had been used to kill the oilmen next to the agent's body, and returned the unfired version back to my shoulder holster. I also took my ankle pistol which I used to kill the assassin and placed it next to Hampton's body. He obviously used it in self-defense against this rogue agent who had come to kill them both; but not until he was hit himself.

I couldn't get out of this unscathed, since the guard below had a record, but rather than touching anything in the room, I call the elevator, thinking that I would tell the guard so he could telephone the police. When the elevator opens on the ground floor lobby, the security guard had disappeared. I call 911.

In about 15 minutes, the police rush through the front door. I show my Navy ID to both cops and wait while they search for the guard to let them into the elevator. In another moment, a detective comes through the front door as the two cops return with a slightly groggy guard, who had been found locked in an office off the lobby. The detective assigns one of the cops to watch me as he, the guard, and the other uniformed cop go upstairs. They return about 20 minutes later, and the detective accosts me.

"Did you go upstairs since you got here?"

"Yes. But when I saw what had happened, I immediately came down and called the police."

"Well it looks like they killed one another. I suppose they got into some kind of argument. Why are you here, by the way?"

"I had some business with Mr. Hampton. I have a small art recovery business in San Francisco, and got a call to come here for a consult. I have no idea exactly why I was called, as he was dead when I arrived." I give him my new business card.

"What about the Navy ID? You showed it to the officers when they arrived."

"Yes, well I recently retired from the Navy, but until my retirement papers are finalized, I am still on active duty. I worked in their diplomatic support branch."

"OK, well I know where to reach you if I need to. Are you staying here in Dallas?"

"No, I was planning to go back home either later tonight or tomorrow morning."

"If you wait until tomorrow morning, I would appreciate your stopping by the station and giving us a statement. Then you will be free to go."

I use the guard's telephone to call for a taxi. Just as I was about to leave the building, the detective calls me back. "We checked you out and were asked to give you full cooperation. I don't know who you are, and I don't want to know. But before you leave, please give me your visitor's badge." I take it out of my pocket and hand it to him. He then said quietly to me "You were never upstairs, understand?" Then he showed me out to a taxi.

I had the driver take me to DFW airport. From there, I call home, reaching our answering machine.

"Hi, dear. Listen, Hampton is dead. I think that he was killed as the final step in house cleaning, like we thought. An agent of some kind did it. They tried to set me up as the killer. I'll tell you about it when I get home, but I am OK. To your other question, I have absolutely no idea, and probably never will."

## EPILOGUE

When the Alexandria Library was constructed, a meeting room was incorporated within the Children's Discovery Center, under the main play area. It was a round room that resembled the space beneath the Temple of Poseidon and several other locations around the world. Each was built along the same lines, a simple room with a table for 12 persons. It had no art on the walls, no communications with the outside world. There was no special security for the space itself, although meeting times were usually scheduled when the rest of the building was closed and empty.

There were not many around the table tonight. Six of their number had been lost and would eventually be replaced. The leader had just arrived and joined the rest at the table.

One of the young men seated at the table asked, "What of the couple that worked out the plan for returning our book?"

"They are well. They moved back to San Francisco and have begun a new venture, helping to put stolen artworks into the hands of their rightful owners." The last I heard they were considering becoming parents."

One of the others asked "What about the Book?"

The leader said "It is back under our control. It is here, in the Library, where it always has been. I had the metal disguised with a cloth cover, and placed it along with other old books in the stacks, among the 3 million texts already here, which will grow to 8 million over the next few years. It will not be found by accident."

"Do you think that the Chess pair will come looking for it again?"

"No they are well out of it. I think that if situations were different, they would have made excellent candidates for our Keeper Brotherhood. We shall have no concerns from them in the future."

"What of the deception?"

"Since there is no indication from any of our people that there is any interest in our Book, we can assume that the deception was successful. But we must also recognize that now that there is some history, there may come a time when the deception is revealed, and a new search is begun.

The only loss is the Book metal itself, since samples are still at NASA Ames. But this is a very small price."

"What about Crawford and the armor?"

"He helped to bring it here, along with the Book. The discovery was something he will never forget, and he appreciated being part of it."

"Where is the armor now?"

"Where else would one put armor? It is in the Archeology Museum in Athens, along with thousands of other pieces of armor from all over the Mediterranean and Middle East. The golden metal was covered with a thin layer of bronze, so it appears to be another fine example of Hittite armor. We produced something along the lines that Heinrich Schliemann did when he stole it from Troy in the first place, but he used clay to make it into a caricature. We made it into a display piece, but not connected with us or our Book. We had promised Sophie Schliemann that it would be returned when we no longer had need of it."

"I am personally very grateful for that," said the newest member of the clan. "You all know that Sophie Schliemann was my great-grandmother, and had written about the Book to my father back in 1932 while he was serving in the French Army. When he died, I inherited his papers, and learned of your existence, which is what brought me here."

"One of the people who stood out in this last incursion, was John Crawford. I suggest that he be considered for membership in our Brotherhood. Do you think that he would be interested in joining us?" asked another young member, replacing one of those lost in Greece.

"I agree with your assessment of Dr. Crawford. But I do not think that he would be interested. However; I will obliquely broach the subject when next I speak with him."

"What of our former Keeper?"

The ashes of our former Keeper, Johann Froehlich, were interred with those of his wife in Oak Ridge, Tennessee. I personally miss him. He served us and our charges very well over these trying years. By encouraging the creation of the fake Book at great risk, he has given us a long breather, although he paid for it with his life."

"Gina, have you tracked the records amassed during their research that were transferred to the U.S. Navy Escort office?"

The young gamin from Admiral Lewis' office stood up and got herself some coffee. "They have been stored deeply in National Secrets Vaults out in the western desert. I saw to it that the locator codes at the National Archives have been permanently misplaced. I do not think that Admiral Lewis, or any of the present or future government will ever see them again. The photographic files of the book which John Crawford made at the Smithsonian and at the Naval Research Center were destroyed. The phony Book was also retrieved from AMGO's lab and stored with the rest of the 'lost' files."

"As you all know, Keeper Froehlich had asked me to build a relationship with Simon Chess after our sister Jean was assassinated. However; he did not respond to my entreaties. But I have some good news in that Jim Carson has asked me to marry him, and he will be moving out of ESCORT over to NSA with his new promotion. Shall I remain at ESCORT?"

"Gina, that choice is up to you. I would suggest that you move to a job which will allow you to attend our meetings. But it is not critical. I do want to particularly thank you, Gina. I know that this has been a difficult time for all of us. You all have acted with great honor and loyalty and are to be commended."

"One more item on our agenda concerns the Israel Mossad. Our sister there reports that there is a new interest developing among the Palestinians for unearthing ancient Semitic tablets which may undermine the old Jewish Torah. These studies may reveal our AFAR role in the Jewish Exodus from Egypt. We need to assign someone to infiltrate this movement to monitor its progress."

One of the other keepers responded. "I have a cousin at the University of Cairo who will probably be contacted by the Palestinians. I will keep in touch with him and take responsibility for that investigation."

"Thank you. Now, if there is nothing more, let us conclude our meeting, and retire. We shall meet again in 6 months, in Beijing."

The men and women filed out. Alattin Akan, who months ago had started this adventure by placing the key in Chess' pocket and then switched the horse puzzle for the picture frame at the museum, was the last to leave, as was the custom for the new head Keeper.

www.ingramcontent.com/pod-product-compliance
Lightning Source LLC
Chambersburg PA
CBHW051929020726
47501CB00001B/49